The Old Faerie

Lark was moving closer, his wing tips brushing the sides of the shower occasionally, leaving strange jumpy fog etchings behind.

Flem stood his ground, his slim Sylph straight, his glorious wings up, out and taut.

The hot steamy water and the incredible fact of being able to be so honest, so *naked*, so bare with who he was, was blissful. He had never felt more comfortable in his own skin in his entire life. Amazing.

"Turn around," ordered Mr. Lark Spurastic.

Flem's heart pounded.

Finally!

He turned around.

Lark dropped to his knees and bent his head to get at those irascible wing scales right at the base of Flem's wings and went to work, licking the sodden wet scales into place, locking rims together with his own raspy tongue, warm water dripping off of Flem's wings and back onto him, shower spray finding him at unexpected moments when the other moved.

The Old Faerie

The Old Faerie

Whimsey C. Nimble

Nimble Finger Productions

The Old Faerie
A Nimble Finger Productions Book
Penn Valley, California

I dedicate this book to my hard working husband David, for all that you have given to keep us afloat in this obsessive dream of mine. Thank you.

Thank you Gaylin for understanding the importance of not smirking too much whilst reading.

Thank you to Mackenzie and Riley for being such inspiration over the years. I would not have had nearly the understanding of human nature without you.

Chapter 1

———— ✦ ————

But a Sylph who *stayed* male. Unheard of.

THE OLD FAERIE wasn't actually *old,* by Sylph standards - he was only one-hundred and twenty-four. Nonetheless, he *felt* old, he sniffed to himsylph as he pulled at the waist band on his human pants. Growling, he let it snap back into place and then tore off the blasted shirt, throwing it across the room where it landed on his hammock, one sleeve trailing the floor.

Twitching his shoulders, he eyed their thickness, heartily tired of disguising himsylph, but what was he to do? Even in a city as liberal as this one, people would still be shocked. And there you have it, *people* would be shocked. He wasn't a person, for Pan's sake, he was a Sylph, a *faerie,* one who looked acceptable enough (with a few adjustments) to pass for human

Faeries, particularly Sylphs, rarely put on excess weight - how could they, eating things like raspberries, nasturtium leaves, violets and other such things? But, when one led such an *unusual* life, much different from virtually all *other* Sylphs, well, things happened. Maybe his mead habit was a little excessive but all Sylphs have a penchant for mead. It was easy to let it slip out of control, especially under such duress. You see, Flem Green didn't live a regular fae life. He was currently living in a *human city,* San Francoa Ramosa, a long ways from his roots in Thimbleberry Canyon on the north end of Cow Valley where all other Sylphs lived. And no one *here* knew he was a faerie.

Things hadn't always been this bad. Before he'd made that fateful decision, *she'd* been Flumaria and like all her Sylph kin, looked forward to the two different phases that each Sylph was presented with over the years at seemingly random times. When someone realized they were actually coming into a fertile period, a rather rare event, they watched to see who became activated by the pheromones. All Sylphs are born with the ability to change

1

to male and father children, the male aspect only being triggered if they themsylves were at a specific spot in their *own* cycle. Each party had the option to continue or not, but the decision to go ahead had to be consensual. Consequently, the population was kept up but not at a ridiculous rate and each Sylphette usually ended up with a few birthing-tree sisters from the widespread population that comprised Thimbleberry Canyon and Cow Valley. Not to be confused with normal sexual activity, this was different.

But a Sylph who had *stayed* male. Unheard of.

Well, not exactly. There was always *some* aunty from *some* obscure tree whom *some*one would quote at *some* party but hardly anyone paid any attention. At least, Flem reflected, he sure hadn't back when *he* was *she*. Cha, looking back, life was like living in knee-deep monkeyflowers compared to now.

Sylphs are not big to begin with and when someone opts to go through the transformation to male, it's not that big of deal. There are the obvious changes of course, breasts disappear as the chest expands becoming broader, a few inches in height is gained, and, of course, genitals are absorbed and reformed. Arms and legs lengthen, a certain firmness of muscle becomes more evident overall, the voice deepens, but *he* is still recognizable as the *she* of just a moment ago, just transmorphed briefly. As the days roll on the pregnancy lust retreats, the two partners go on about their ways, one back to female with the reversal of changes happening just as easily and seamlessly as the first time, and the other to a birthing tree of her choice. Most Sylphs pick their own mother's tree of course, the one where she hersylph grew up. Sister sylphettes of the same tree were communally raised, with the other mothers being known from then on as Aunty. Everyone agreed they enjoyed the *CHANGE* when it happened but all were quite ready to get back to normal life. Consequently, Sylphs had essentially no experience with extra body weight for any great length of time, a rare four months of pregnancy excluded and easily returned to their timeless sylves. Hence, Flem was continuously unsettled by developing a belly that jiggled. It was the mead. It had to be. But what was he to do? Times were rough and mead was the one friend who was always there.

There was no use ruminating any more. He'd lived as a male for a long time, having only recently moved to the City. Maybe this time things would work out. Tugging on the ties that held his wings down to make sure they were secure, he pulled on a bulky fleece top that neatly covered the extra girth across his slim shoulders, then wrapped his neck with a gauzy scarf, adding more layers to the illusion.

Running his fingers through his shaggy hair, he studied himsylph in the spotty old mirror. His face had lost that clean edge that Sylphs were known for. The stress of living as a male, a human male at that, was beginning to show. It was no use, no matter how he tried there was always an aura of depression that clung to him like the smell of wood smoke in a wool sweater. How to fix his life, he wondered for the umpteenth time. Sighing deeply, he looked around at his messy house and before he could regret it, he dived in and started cleaning, straightening cups and snatching up clothing he tended to fling off. Dishes were washed quickly if not thoroughly and stacked helter skelter. To reward himsylph he brought down the mead, the kind made from Manzanita honey, and poured out a small hen's worth, as the shape of the small glass was a chicken and he had a whole set. Slurping noisily, he savored every last drop and couldn't stop himsylph from pouring out another. Grabbing his backpack from its spot near the door, he knocked back his second hen and headed out.

Chapter 2

The voice carried a hint of amusement and yes, derision.

*P*ausing at the door, Flem listened intently before cautiously pushing aside the boulder that sat in a groove, masking the hidden cave. Slipping through, he stood motionless as he peered through the outer foliage before easing his door shut and stepping through the greenery to his other life.

This particular spot in Sycamore Park was usually less populated than other areas and he could go for long stretches without seeing anyone. It was a large park that even had streets within it. He had to be extra careful on the days maintenance cut the grass or worked on the flower beds, but that didn't happen daily. Weekends were a little more dicey as they brought the lookyloos. He didn't care for tourists. But, he reflected wryly, he supposed *he* could technically be called a tourist, since he was so new to town. Well, he didn't feel like a tourist, he felt like he lived here, mostly because he had just gotten a job! Things were looking up.

Walking to the bus stop he adjusted his persona, blending in, allowing this Sylph trait to carry over to his current life. Humans were rather canny, he had to be on his toes all the time he was outside, in their world. His world too. Sort-of.

Always a bit nervous before the bus pulled up, he twitched and blinked, moving his shoulders in tense little circles, watching a fellow passenger arrive. The two studiously ignored the other as the bus came into sight around the long curve, heading back downtown and away from the beach, where the Park ended.

Within minutes both were ensconced in their seats, Flem near the back and Mr. X somewhere in the middle.

Shifting uncomfortably in his seat, leaning back as far as someone could that had bent-over wings strapped down under his shirt, Flem studied the other from behind, envious of his casual look. What did it take to achieve such confidence? What was he doing wrong?

Deep in his soul suspicions lay dormant, waiting to take root.

He suspected he let himsylph become exasperated too easily, too short a fuse, imagining worst case scenarios and didn't bother with making them positive. Jumpy, he was jumpy. It had been a hard adjustment, this staying male business. But he felt like he was finally taking positive steps for his own betterment. Nonetheless, up to this point it had made him sloppy in his habits, wings ratty, not mended and tended with the TLC they should be receiving. It was hard to preen onesylph alone all the time. It really helped having a friend around, one who understood the need that all Sylphs had of a good going-over and as such, was something all Sylphs did for another, whoever it was, instantaneously and without a second thought.

Flem just let it go. His clothes reflected his poor grooming habits, with small rips and tears going unattended. Why bother? It was easier to drink a little mead, relax, putter, ignore, get by.

Pulling himsylph up, he shook his head at his own moroseness today. He'd been doing pretty good for a while now but he was ready to have some things change in his life. It got depressing that he didn't know what to change, although finding this job certainly seemed like an omen. He determined once again to stop drinking so early in the day.

The driver called the street name and Flem rose to get off, as this was where he made his connection, the one that would eventually drop him off on Magnolia street, right in front of Fletcherman's Nursery, his place of employment.

Bumping against people, the awkward young man kept his eyes on his path until a rude jerk grabbed him back, holding him against his will, as if with an iron fist. Whoever it was held on tight and he instinctively scrunched his face back over his shoulder to see behind him, expecting the worst, his arms flailing uselessly. To his great relief and huge chagrin, a *hook* had inserted itself into a small loop on the back of his pack and held him fast against a pole.

Not wanting to break the great indifference that people often wore like an invisible shield, no one offered to help and Flem was mortified when the bus doors closed and they drove on.

Whimsey C. Nimble

Embarrassment lit every cell in his body and he felt the fire kiss his cheeks and run fingertips over his arms and dance into wing muscles as he struggled against an unseen foe.

Suddenly an arm snaked up over the windows directly across from him, fingers pulled a cord, ringing the bell, and the bus slowed for the next stop.

Making her way to the aisle, a young woman's gaze took in the situation at a glance and without breaking stride, smiled into Flem's eyes as she smoothly reached around him and unhooked the dastardly inanimate object. Smiling, almost laughing, she skipped down the aisle, nimbly dancing down the steps and out the door.

Flem jumped after her, barely getting out of the way of the slamming doors.

She turned to the left, intent upon her business, her lips held tight to lock in the mirth plastering itself to her face, her eyes dancing as she tried to control herself before turning away, giving Flem no time for a response as she quickly took off running, long brown braid bouncing on her back, giggles escaping like balloons left behind.

The Sylph watched her go, belatedly remembered his manners and called "Thank you!" after her but she had disappeared.

His mood was not improving, he thought to himsylph as he waited again for the next bus. Impatiently, he swung his pack around to glare at the offending loop, shaking his head.

Five minutes later the behemoth pulled up, loud noises accompanying it. The faerie didn't like it but as he was now living among humans, he did what he could to adjust.

Settling down once again, the delicate young man looked at his watch and decided he would just have time to grab a cup of tea from that shop he'd seen a few weeks back when he'd been out wandering. It was about two and a half blocks up the street from Fletcherman's. Unfortunately, it was in a different direction than where this bus was headed, but he would hurry.

A few minutes later his stop arrived and he dashed out the door, grateful to finally be OFF the blasted contraption. Checking his watch again, eyes lowered, he blundered on, anxious to get to work but anxious for the tea also, anxious, anxious, and kept rehearsing what he was going to say, paying no attention to the world around him, intent on his mission. He found the store and without looking up and taking note of his surroundings, grabbed the door knob to rush in. It didn't budge. Jiggling the handle in a frenzy, anxious to get his drink and get to work, Flem was caught unawares when it burst open but before he had a chance to recollect himsylph, a long, black-clad leg followed by its owner thrust itself through, practically in the Sylph's face, as if to run over anyone in the way.

Sputtering, Flem backed up, irritation competing with bewilderment.

"Sorry, I'm not open yet. This is not Herb's anymore, in case you missed that detail." The voice carried a hint of amusement and yes, derision.

Flem's eyes traveled from the toe of the beautiful black boot that was just peeking out from beneath the black pant leg and on up over the crisp black linen shirt tucked into those pants, and of course, a beautiful black belt. Swallowing, he looked up into penetrating green eyes, ones that held a veiled gleam at being met with such obtuseness.

Feeling like a fool for the second time today and it wasn't even nine o'clock in the morning yet, Flem's hazel eyes widened in embarrassment, as he now took another step back, blinking and mumbling, starting to twitch, swallowing repeatedly.

The other person didn't move but stayed in the doorway, and finally Flem looked up again to find the stranger staring at him.

"What unusual eyes you have," remarked the new owner, " are you from San Francoa Ramosa originally?"

The Sylph was caught off guard once again but finally started to recover as a surge of annoyance strengthened his backbone. It had been a hard morning and he hadn't even made it to work yet. Enough was enough. Who did this guy think he was? For Pan's sake, *he* was the victim here, he didn't have to answer any questions. As his indignation grew, no tea, no tea *shop*, the hook incident, all took on greater importance, growing out of proportion, and Flem leapt into action, finding an unsuitable object to vent his frustrations on. Shoulders heaved and if he had still been back in the Canyon, where *she* grew up, toes would have lifted off the ground and wings would have been up, taut, and quivering sharply.

Instead, he flung his backpack to the ground and little sparks almost seemed to fly from his eyes in his inappropriate anger.

"What business is it of yours where I come from? Who are you, anyway, to question me?" the faerie belligerently threw at the other. "Where are YOU from?"

7

Whimsey C. Nimble

A look of disbelief pulled his opponent's expression into a frozen mask but that didn't last long and instead, with a bark of laughter that was belied by his steely eyes, he shot back, "What is WRONG with you? It was merely an innocent question. Why don't you get off MY stoop and out of *my* way? And don't bother stopping by the next time you're in the neighborhood!"

Eyes snapping, Flem whirled around, reaching unsteadily for his pack, missed, grabbed it, and spun off on his heel back the way he'd come. A car door slammed loudly behind him, a motor roared to life and then sped by angrily, the driver making a rude gesture towards him as he flew by.

The Sylph stalked down the street, feeling worse by the minute as guilt and emotional reaction threatened to overwhelm him. He fought for sylph-control, his hands clenching and unclenching into fists.

Tears welled in his eyes but somehow he managed to make it to work, stumbled in the back door, sniffed deeply, wiped his eyes, and started over.

Chapter 3

⸙

Controlling himsylph instantly, Flem flushed,
mortified he'd let himsylph get so out of control.

GATHERING HIS WITS at the same time he gathered his gloves, the trembling faerie concentrated on the erasable board where daily duties for each of the employees were laid out.

He really liked this job and continuously felt fortunate that it had fallen into his lap, even if it was in a human environment. He was still very new, this being only his fourth day. His hope was to save enough money and move out from underneath that rock. He'd much rather live in a tree but there was fat chance of that happening any time soon. It was the low rent district for him, and his current cave was okay but now that he'd spent most of the winter there, he didn't want a repeat. He needed someplace dry *all* the time, not just when it wasn't raining.

"Are you memorizing that board, Mr. Green, or are you ready to assemble some baskets with me?"

The dry tone came from behind him and he whirled to find Iris Fletcherman. A widow in her mid-fifties, Iris Fletcherman made it a point to always look good. She oozed vitality and appeared to thrive running a large nursery on her own. Things had changed since her husband, Brodiaea, (Brody) had died. The business had grown.

Half glasses perched on the end of her long, patrician nose, she regarded him with a twinkle in her penetrating blue eyes but the question was a serious one.

"Good morning! No, I, um, I'm ready," he stammered, wondering if he would ever get used to living and working in such close proximity to humans.

"Okay, follow me."

Whimsey C. Nimble

Flem quickly smiled and nodded, suppressing the remaining shudders from his trying morning, quelling any residual doubts, putting his best foot forward and exuding confidence. It was hard but he *was* a Sylph and aside from overwhelming curiosity, their second most predominate trait was charm. It was good to get back in practice. Hurrying to keep up, the Sylph strained to hear what his boss was saying.

"Are you familiar with hanging baskets, Mr. Green? When we talked, you said you'd worked with plants for years."

"No, no hanging baskets but I believe I'm fairly well acquainted with most flowers." (One of his favorite foods, actually.)

Wending through the main building, they went out the back door and Iris kept on going, straight to the nearest greenhouse, the one used predominantly for planting and prep work, explaining as she walked, "The Department of Parks and Recreation for the City has an annual theme of Bridge Beautification and for several years now, it directly involves us. They have a standing order of thirty-six hanging baskets, to be delivered towards the end of May. I've known Santolina, the head of the department, for years. We get together every year about this time and go over the order. I had lunch with him yesterday." She paused imperceptibly, a slight rose blooming in her cheeks, and swallowed a smile, both of which Flem caught, before she went on. "He's gotten permission to hang thirty-four more, bless his soul, for the City Center and some other locations around town." Smiling, she looked at Flem but he could see it wasn't him she was smiling at, but her friend Santolina who was giving her the business.

Bringing her attention back, she laughed at the surprised expression on her newest employee's face.

"Yes, seventy baskets! No doubt you'll be an expert by the time we're done with this order! C'mon, let's get started. We're going to make two at the same time, I'll show you what to do as we go. You'll work with me the next couple of hours then I'll probably send someone back later in the day. I figure two weeks and we'll have them ready to grow. I say grow because we keep them here for a while and baby them until they're filled out and ready to hang." Hands on her hips, she stopped talking and indicated the table-like bench in front of them, the one that ran the length of the structure. "Here's our main working area, where we do most of our potting and replanted. You'll become quite familiar with this spot within the next two weeks."

Flem nodded.

The owner of the business continued, "Here in this big barrel is our soil mixture. We make it ourselves and also sell it. When we're potting we don't actually fill from this humongous container, I have Buddleia, who comes in every evening for a few hours, do all my heaviest jobs." Here she sidled a glance askance at the slight Sylph beside her, hmm.

Reading her thoughts clearly, Flem jumped in to reassure her that she had made the right choice.

"I'm quite strong Mrs. Fletcherman, even if I don't look it. Tell me more! What baskets are we to use? This sounds like fun!" He deflected her train of thought and she glanced again at him but this time she grinned. It was hard not to respond to Sylph charm.

"C'mon down here," she said as she moved to the other side of the large barrel, to where a post stuck up out of a hole in the counter.

Flem could see a metal arm that at the moment was laying flush down along the length of the post from where it was attached near the top. Iris reached over and snapped the arm up and into place, a big S hook dangling and swaying from the heavy chain on the end.

"This was my idea," she said with a little self deprecatory smile. "We make all our hanging baskets right here." She went on to explain, "See this button here?" pointing to where it was embedded in the front of the counter.

Flem nodded.

"Watch."

The button was pushed and the post noiselessly slid up another three feet. Before Flem could ask, Iris continued, "Some baskets we do are three feet long and this way we can control where they're hanging so that they're always at the right level for whomever is working on them. You know, YOU!" and *she* winked at him.

Flem couldn't believe it. Another bold human.

"Oh, don't be such a worry-wart, Mr. Green. All my employees will tell you this is a pretty cool place to work. I'm not your usual boss. I don't believe in formality, I believe in having fun with life. And by the way, the thirty-six baskets we're embarking on are all going to be the three-foot ones. The others he ordered, for around town, they're not so big. For them, we'll be able to lower it to right here in front of us." She pushed the button again and the post slid back down to a normal height, where she then easily snapped the arm back down before pushing the button one last time, causing the post to disappear down into the counter. She reached over and pulled a sliding door out, covering up the hole, thus giving them a solid place to work. The counter gently sloped down to a drain positioned right next to the hole and directly below where the S hook would hang.

"Let's walk down to that wall there with all the shelves and we'll pick up a couple of baskets to use," Iris suggested.

Reaching in and pulling two out, she said, "These are tapered, see? And they're three feet long. These others," and she gestured to the second half of the wall, "are the kind we use most of the time, they're not nearly as big, and their bottoms are rounded. Those are what we'll be using for the other thirty four. But these tapered ones are the ones I use over the bridges. They're big, they're heavy-duty, and they'll hold a lot. And believe me, by the time this puppy is planted, it'll be heavy. But that's okay, they have a solid framework from which to hang. Okay, let's get started. I love getting this big order but I'm always glad to see the last one done, too."

Returning to the counter, Iris motioned Flem to raise the pedestals and hang the baskets up. As he did so, she pointed towards an oversized, balloon-type bag that hung from the ceiling, off to their left, and towards the back. "Here is what we're using to line each basket."

Flem squinted, trying to see what it was, it appeared to be some kind of dried plant, then realized it was moss. The bag's opened end hung suspended upside down and was effectively sealed by some kind of elasticized collar that was designed to only let out so much content at one time.

Continuing on, Iris cautioned: "I require everyone to wear gloves and a mask whenever they're working with this moss. There's a little bug called Sporothrix Schenckii that can live in sphagnum moss and cause problems with our skin. It's easy enough to avoid by taking precautions."

Flem nodded, his eyes crinkling in appreciation. "Was this your idea too?" he asked.

Grinning modestly, she nodded but all she said was, "Let me show you the soil we'll be using," lifting up part of the counter nearby to show the faerie another hidden hole filled with good dark dirt.

Unable to resist, the Sylph thrust a hand in, letting the cool medium trickle back through his open fingers. A rich, fecund smell filled his nostrils.

"Don't worry about running out of soil, as I was saying, Buddleia, we just call him Bud, comes in every day at six and refills all our containers. We have quite a stockpile. Come with me and before we start, I'll show you our 'dirt' pile in the back that Bud works continuously. I'm kind of a fanatic about our potting soil and we've been making our own for years now. Brody wasn't that crazy about the idea at first but after I did it anyway and people really liked it, he finally understood. Potting soil should always be light, organic, and drain well, really well. I start with the finest, darkest, hardwood bark mulch I can find, and let it sit for a year. I like to spread it flat so that when it rains it really gets soaked all the way through. As it decomposes, it gets finer and darker. We have three piles going so we've always got some that's ready. This fine decomposed bark is what makes up the bulk of the ingredients for my potting soil. That, and some coarse silica sand, not too much. My third ingredient is compost, and to that end we have several bins going here plus some of my employees bring in their compost from home and I even have one employee who collects it from all her kids' houses! Now, that's dedication! And I love it! I like to think of us as a family here. C'mon, let's go back and get to work," she said and headed towards the work station. Reaching into her smock pocket as they walked, she pulled out a piece of paper. "Here's a list of what we'll be using right off the bat. I'm really looking forward to do-ing some that are a bit more exotic than the first thirty-six. Most of the ones for the Bridge project are our big petunias, with some ivy, alyssum, maybe a little lobelia thrown in, but maybe not, lobelia is so picky, although if I make sure it only gets morning sun, hmmm." Barely taking a breath, she hurried right on, "I think a little moneywort near the bottom. I'm planning on using those large petunias, they're hybrids called grandiflora and wait 'til you see them!" she exclaimed. "They get huge, with the flowers sometimes measur-ing five inches across! And they cascade down!" she cooed.

The faerie grinned, feeling better by the minute. Her enthusiasm was infectious and it was heart warming to be around a human who loved flowers as much as the Sylph did.

"Do you have a color scheme??" he asked, sure that she did. "When do we start?" Gleefully, he clasped his hands together, wishing his wings weren't tied down. He felt like leaping into the air and doing a loop t' loop, but that was a previous lifetime ago and had no place here. A shudder of pure frustration rolled over him, catching him by surprise, making his teeth chat-ter, while his eyes rolled back in his head, just momentarily.

Iris stopped everything and looked at him in alarm.

"Are you alright Mr. Green?" she asked, consternation pulling her features into a fierce scowl.

Controlling himsylph instantly, Flem flushed, mortified he'd let himsylph get so out of control.

"Ah, er, yeah! I'm fine, it's ah, yeah, I'm okay, go on, what were you saying, the colors?" He feebly tried to get her attention off of him and back on track.

Dubiously, she eyed him. "Would you like drink of water? Is it a touch of epilepsy? No need to be embarrassed. Is there anything I can do to help?" she asked sympathetically.

Before he could compose a reply, someone calling "Mother, where are you?" could be heard outside. "Are you out back? Lily said she saw you go through, where are you? Yoo hoo."

Iris took her skeptical eyes from her faerie friend and immediately forgot his troubles in her delight at her daughter's unexpected visit.

"Back here!" she yelled.

Flem flinched as she let loose again, "We're in number one, Mayapple. Come this way!"

The far door opened and to Flem's horror, there stood the young woman from this morning's catastrophe.

Chapter 4

———— ❧ ————

I didn't know you liked sweet ants too!

MAYAPPLE STEPPED THROUGH but as she recognized *who* was standing with her mother, her eyes widened and she hesitated for a moment. Schooling her face to a proper blankness, she hitched her braid over her shoulder and galloped down the aisle.

"Good grief, slow down!" reprimanded Iris as Mayapple hugged her, slinging her pack to the floor. Giving her mom her full attention she avoided looking at the poor geek from this morning. Unfortunately, she knew it was one of those things that would stick in her consciousness to pop up from time to time and give her fits of hilarity. How was she going to face him? She had a tendency to get overwhelmed when she found something that was actually funny. And that poor sap getting hung up on a hook was one of the richest, right up there with pinning her cousin to a clothesline back when she was a kid and he was a toddler. She wondered if there was something wrong with her, that she had such an off sense of humor.

Her mother was talking, introducing her, WHAT WAS HIS NAME? Her eyes bugged out but she got them back to normal before she turned around and ground her teeth together to keep from giving in to the nervous urge of over reacting.

Her brown eyes met his hazel ones and to her relief, and his, nothing happened. In fact, as she shook his long-fingered, delicate hand and looked at him, she realized he was staring at her with what could only be termed, stark terror.

Her heart opened and compassion flooded her senses, replacing everything else. Looking him square in the eye, she politely asked, "Is your name a nickname, Mr. Green?"

Eyes blinked rapidly and a twitch ran through his still clasped hand. He quickly let go, as if her hand burned.

Taking a deep breath he relaxed minutely although still seemed to be having trouble with his blinking and he could not get his mouth to open. His shoulders rippled as he tried to ease the tension, and he licked dry lips, trying to think of an answer.

Mother and daughter looked on a moment too long before Iris jumped in, giving the poor man a break by getting on with business.

"Mayapple, what are you doing here??" she said, turning to her daughter. " It's a bit out of the way from your usual haunts. You must *want* something. What is it?" Spoken like a mother, she waited expectantly to hear what scheme her daughter had going now.

Pouting prettily with pursed lips and beetled brow, Mayapple crossed her arms, shifted her weight to one leg and reached out with the other foot, tapping her toes in mock impatience, scolding her mother: "Mother! What a suspicious mind you have. Can't I just come by to say hi? I love you, I miss you. Did I tell you how good you look today? Have you lost weight?" and she smiled beguilingly, fluttering her lashes.

Iris Fletcherman snorted. "What *do* you want?"

Flem Green stood there, un-noticed, watching in bemusement. Humans. He had been so embarrassed when he saw her again he had gone into a sort of mortifying shock, but, well, he *like*d these two. The realization helped ease him a bit more but he still hoped fervently they would ignore him for as long as possible. He should have known someone would be bound to ask, Flem wasn't a common name. But he wasn't about to mention Flumaria Greenwood, his other existence of too-many years ago. He just wanted to do his job, better himsylph, and get out from that hole under a rock.

Sighing, he looked around while waiting, loving the color of life from inside a greenhouse, it was just magical, reminding him of some trees he'd had the fortune to be invited into, a long time ago.

"Thanks mom," filtered in to his ears and brought his attention back to the present, where Iris and her daughter both stood, looking at him expectantly.

Iris spoke. "Flem, I was going to work with you today but Mayapple here has been around the business as long as I have and she'd going to take over for me. She knows what I want. Running a little low on cash, she finds it convenient to see if mom will hire her and of course, mom will."

Mayapple stood there with her hands in her back pockets, rocking back and forth heel to toe, grinning at the faerie-in-disguise, but now it was because she was happy to have gotten what she wanted. She raised her eyebrows towards him and was obviously so pleased with herself Flem couldn't help but smile back.

"Okay kids, oops, sorry, you're not kids, go to work. Flem, Mayapple is in charge. Mayapple come get me when you are done with the first ones," and she clapped her hands together as if to rid them of old business and left.

Before Flem had a chance to collect himsylph the young woman stuck out her hand and said, "Look, let's just start over, forget about this morning, okay?"

A moment's consternation was stirred up at the mere mention of this morning's disaster, but he soon mastered it, returned her handshake, and smiled his gratitude into her eyes.

"Boy, you've got pretty eyes, Mr. Green. Ready to build some baskets with me?"

Flem nodded quickly, aghast that she'd mentioned his eyes, always a touchy point. A Sylph's eyes only turned hazel for the *CHANGE*, and always went back to their solid color at the end. At least, that's what he'd been taught, and seen, on occasion. Most of the time a Sylph in the male stage was not seen by any except the partner. It was rare but he'd seen hazel eyes once before, a long time ago when WilloB had only been home a few hours from her first change. It was just one of so many things he himsylph had to live with and while he'd gotten used to it, it still bothered him to have attention drawn to it. Or any part of him, really. He liked to be as low-key as possible, invisible to others.

"Put your gloves on, we don't want Mr. Skankii to get us now, do we? I'm sure you got the talk along with the tour, right?" She grinned, one coconspirator to another. "We didn't wear these when my dad ran the place, but mom did some research when I kept getting these wretched rashes, usually right after I'd helped her make the baskets. So now we're more careful."

"What we're going to do first is soak some moss, and while it's soaking, you and I will go collect the plants. Put this on first," she said, handing him a small breathing mask. "Now, take this and hold it just so," and she shoved a pail to sit just under the giant, upside-down bag of dried sphagnum moss, "and I'll guide this monster."

Whimsey C. Nimble

Flem quickly held it in place for her as she pulled the contraption down as far and as close as it would go, manipulating the long neck into the pail, then flipping a small lever to unlock the sphincter that held it closed. Working her fingers behind the metal collar, she spread it out until it let loose its load, quickly filling Flem's bucket before throttling it shut again.

"Okay, now fill it with water, at least half-way and squash the moss as tight as you can get it. There's the faucet."

She waited til he got done and then said, "Good. Now come back and we'll put more in, the idea being to pack both these pails solid with condensed moss, really wet, because this is our 'glue.' It's what keeps all the flowers and dirt in the container, and holds them in even after hanging outside over a windy bridge for several weeks! This is the most important step, in my opinion." She nodded approvingly as his pail filled. "Good. Perfect. Okay, let's do the other one. Of course, we can always do more, but it's nice if we don't have to. At least for the baskets we're working on currently."

Soon both pails were filled and after setting them down out of the way, Flem waited expectantly as Mayapple pushed the bag back away from the counter, stripping his wet gloves and horrible mask off as he did so. Only humans would think of this. He couldn't decide if it was a good idea or a bad idea.

"C'mon," ordered his new boss, " we'll go get a couple of carts from out back on which to load everything."

Heading out the way she'd just come in, Mayapple led Flem along just like he knew where he was going. Heading down a path that bordered in front of all three greenhouses to their right, the back of the main building was along to their left. She turned right past the third greenhouse and kept going. Flem wondered where those wagons were kept, the next block over?

"Careful," cautioned the girl as she took the faerie around a pile of river rock, skirted some weeds and continued merrily on towards the back of the property finally pulling up short in a small square yard with several garden carts parked on it, willy nilly.

"Here, grab one, I'll take this other one, oops, don't get tangled," she instructed, unhooking a long handle from another's upside down wheels.

Righting the two carts, Flem helped her set them properly on the path, saying as he did so, "Is that another greenhouse over there?" pointing towards the back corner where a dilapidated old structure could be seen behind tall weeds and unused overgrown arbors. "Can we look inside?" curiosity overriding good sense.

Mayapple stopped, dropping her wagon handle with a clatter and replied, "Sure, c'mon, we'll take a minute, but not too long, mom is expecting at least two baskets today."

The old glass building had seen better days. Feeling the spark of adventure, they crept around back, pushing aside a jungle of overgrown fennel as they did so, the fragrant licorice smell suddenly filling the air with the disturbance. Flem's eyes crinkled at the unexpected delight, bumping into his partner as she helped the door along with a nudge from her foot before it finally swung in.

They didn't go far.

What a mess. Old cracked pots lay scattered everywhere, shelving was laying on the ground or hung forlornly from its original position, rotten rubber hoses hung like dead snakes, all cast in a pale melancholy green gloom from the preponderance of old algae that coated virtually every pane of glass, every plank of wood, every stepping stone set in the ground. It was beautiful, in an underwater sort of way. It reminded Flem of Flumaria days, when green was the norm, not city traffic and belching busses.

Sighing, he turned and followed Mayapple back outside, waiting as she scraped the door closed again, and they left.

Turning his thoughts back to present time, he docilely grabbed a cart handle and followed Mayapple up the path. "What are we getting? I never did find out what her color scheme was. What is it?"

Ahead of him, Mayapple laughed. "Rainbow!" she shouted back over her shoulder. "She's got three bridges and each side of each bridge is a different color. Let me see," she mumbled as she searched for the list. "Aha! Here it is," she exclaimed as she drew out the now crumpled slip from her pant's pocket.

Pausing a moment in their trek back, she straightened out the list and then proceeded with it held up in her left hand for her to read as she kept walking, pulling the wagon behind.

"Ooh, we're starting with scarlet, won't that be pretty? Did my mom gush on about," and she inserted in a high sing-song voice, "Grandiflora?" batting her eyes, slightly crossing them in a mocking imitation of a *grande dame*.

Flem laughed at Mayapple's irreverence, nodding, feeling slightly guilty, as if he was making fun of Iris Fletcherman, whom he liked.

Whimsey C. Nimble

"Oh don't worry Flem. Can I call you Flem? I love my mother, and, I love flowers as much as she does, but she just gets so, well, excited by them sometimes, ya know? I mean, it's great for business," and with that, she flung open the door to greenhouse number two, pulling her cart in behind her, swearing a little as it bounced over the ridge in the doorway.

Flem lifted his over, barely able to tear his gaze from the sea of green spread out before them.

Mayapple was talking as she walked away and he hurried to catch up.

Pointing to the end of each row, she explained, "Here's where they are, see? It's all very simple. She's got all the colors laid out in her master plan, but you have to read carefully and go exactly by her specs. As you will notice, you can't tell the colors yet on most of them. She is an absolute stickler when she plants and woe be it to anyone who isn't as careful as she is about labeling everything. She even has each person initial everything they do, see here on the I.D. card? So, if it *says* 'Scarlet Grandiflora,' it had better *bloom* Scarlet Grandiflora, as we use a lot of these just as they are about to bloom. Hence, the initials. Everyone is super careful, because she actually fired someone once after twelve baskets had to be redone! Thank God it wasn't me, she'd probably have disowned me. Anyway, these are the ones we want. Let's fill the top two levels of our carts with them. I don't remember how many one of the large baskets holds but I do know it was more that I expected last year. Be sure and get only solid Scarlet Grandiflora, it will read SSGF underneath the full label."

The faerie complied, being extra careful, something he was working on in other parts of his life too. Well, he was thinking frequently about it, it was almost the same thing.

Remembering this morning's tea shop incident, he realized he'd been anything but careful when he blundered into that, that human. Cha. Because he knew it was really himsylph that had gotten out of control, he quickly turned his attention elsewhere rather than his own shame at behaving so foolishly. With any luck, he'd never see that awful guy again. He certainly wasn't about to deliberately go there. Just thinking about it and how he'd act-ed made his face burn with humiliation and he suddenly ached for a soothing hen full of mead. Too bad he hadn't brought any with him. Hmm, something to think about for tomorrow.

"Flem!"

His head jerked up. He'd been daydreaming at work!

"Sorry, but I've said three times that's enough! You've not left any room for the alyssum or ivy and I think we need to get a few moneywort." Mayapple cast him a rather annoyed, puzzled look, shaking her head, privately wondering if she'd been right from the first moment and he really *was* a geek.

Trying to erase his glaring lack of attention, the Sylph chattered nervously, jumping into the conversation. "Alyssum? I love the smell of alyssum. Where does it go? I thought the baskets were just going to be one color? How does it fit in? Do you use it all over or just in one spot? And ivy you say? That ought to be interesting. Are you using it just at the bottom? I love lobelia and lysimachia, you know, moneywort. I would think it would be really pretty to do a basket of that and maybe some vinca, but it'd have to be hung in a morning spot, no afternoon sun, what do you think? Unless it was filtered, then it would be okay, so long as it wasn't scorching. What do you think?" He paused and took a breath, daring a look at his partner.

She just stood there, her head cocked to one side, her eyes wide and speculating, a hint of glee held back, looking at him.

There was an awkward silence, Flem definitely getting greener as his always jumpy sylphesteem plummeted to his knees and his mouth went dry. He could feel his wings getting limp, which was normally a good thing out in public, but right now it felt like they were drooping heavily and he just wilted, right in front of Mayapple, whose expression changed to one of amazement.

Poor guy, thought Mayapple, what is up with him? Never have I met anybody like him, that's for sure. What she said was, "I like your morning basket idea! I don't think mom's ever done one. I'll mention it to her; I bet she'll want you to make it, after all these 'Bridgers' are done."

Like a limp plant absorbing life sustaining water, Flem straightened. His shoulders broadened, his chin came up and a genuine smile graced his lips, his eyes crinkling in pleasure. "Thank you," he said. "Now, about that alyssum?"

An air of confidence and attraction emanated from the Sylph and Mayapple saw him in a completely different light, one that was *attractive*. She looked on in bemusement at her own reaction. He could be charming, couldn't he? Hmm. Maybe she'd better reassess.

"The alyssum, this way," she nodded as she spoke, then took up her handle and with a grunt, as it was much heavier, started down the aisle.

Whimsey C. Nimble

Turning right and then left again, Mayapple led them to the first of many of the soon-to-be white fragrant plants, one often used in borders and barrels.

Pulling up the marker, she checked the label, raising her eyes to count rows and compare it to what she read, then nodded in self agreement.

"You know these come in purple too, right? Mom doesn't keep the two anywhere close to each other because they like to mix their colors. Now, let's fill the second tier with the alyssum, we won't use nearly as many as the petunias. We'll put the ivy and some, what did you call it? Lysasomething? The moneywort? We'll put them on the bottom of the cart, since we don't need very many."

"Lysimachia," responded Flem.

"How come you know the name?" enquired the young woman idly. "Not many people do. I mean, I bet most of the other employees don't even know the full names."

Flem stopped and looked at her for a second, his brain working overtime. He loved plants. He used to pore over catalogs found in dumpsters, often behind nurseries such as this one. One time he had even found a beautiful out-of-date master gardening book, now one of his prize possessions. He couldn't tell her that.

"Ah, just a hobby." If she only knew his extensive taste for plants. He literally drooled over some of the pictures in the booklets he'd collected.

With barely an acknowledgement, the girl said "Oh." Moving on, she continued, "Let's go get the ivy. Mom likes to use ivy, she says it lends the baskets *dignity*. Who knows, but she likes it, and we do it *her* way, she's the boss." Mayapple slid Flem a slightly assertive look, making sure he knew she was the boss's daughter.

He nodded in peaceful agreement.

"When the baskets come back here in late fall, we pull them all apart and we can still use the ivy for other plantings. We recycle everything, as I said about her composting?" Here Mayapple raised her eyebrows at Flem in merriment and they both grinned at the thought of people actually bringing garbage with them to work.

Feeling companionable, they reached the ivy, grabbed three containers, walked a little ways, grabbed a few more pots of moneywort, then left the greenhouse from the front door. Within minutes they were back in number one, standing in front of the planting bench, heavily laden wagons neatly parked side by side.

"I see you've got the baskets hung, ready to go. Good. Let's put some gloves on," and she reached into a nearby cubby to snatch a handful of gloves, separating two to toss to her partner and took two for herself.

"Would you bring over those pails of moss, and set one down by each of us, to the outside?" she requested.

As Flem set the pails down, she continued, "Reach in and grab as big a handful as you can and wring it out but not completely." She demonstrated her words with her own actions. "Now," she continued, "we're going to place it down in this tip and bring it up the sides a little, like this," her hands packing, pushing, and building as she spoke, until the rather pointed end of the basket was solid with dripping matter, little green curlicues hugging the exterior, resisting any smoothing as they were set into place.

"Now that the tip is filled in, we're going to keep building our wall around the inside edge here, see? I'm leaving this space here in the middle for dirt but we still need a wall, which will be the liner of our baskets." A flat surface had emerged across the top of the so-call point, which Mayapple then rimmed with her wet moss, thus leaving a perfect hollow to be filled with dirt.

Flem nodded, a feeling of gratefulness for this job washing through him as he followed her instructions.

"Did she show you our potting medium?" questioned the girl, flipping up the lid in the counter between them to reveal the choice soil.

Not waiting for an answer she caught up a small scoop tucked on a shelf of its own just above the dirt and below the door, saying, "There's another one laying over there, go ahead and use it."

"We put our first layer of dirt right here," and proceeded to dump her scoopful and then several more on top of the moss, tamping it down with her fingertips, most of it encased by the scrunched up moss around the edge.

When Flem completed his, she nodded in approval.

"Now, get that little hose right back there, pull it down to your basket, like so." Gently she pulled and a miniature hose unwound from its wheel.

"My mother thinks of everything. She had Bud – did you meet him yet?" she interrupted herself.

Flem shook his head.

Whimsey C. Nimble

"Anyway, she had Bud put these little nozzles on this tubing just for this reason." Deftly she guided it to her basket, pulling the small trigger and thoroughly soaking the soil in its bed of moss.

"See, the thing with ivy is that for it to take like we need, the soil must be premoistened, the plant roots have to be moist, and the leaves can't be wilted at all."

Dirty water started to trickle from the bottom of her basket, running neatly down into her drain.

"All our waste water is recycled to a small water tank at the back of the lot."

Flem wasn't paying any attention, he had been too struck by the recollection of that broken down old greenhouse when she mentioned the back of the lot, his inner eye picturing it when it used to be full of life. He hadn't seen anything around it at the time. He would make it a point to look though.

"She's got lots of filters and stuff, I'm not sure how it works, but anyway, we reuse all our runoff, which is great for our water bill."

Flem listened in amazement. She seemed so self confident, how did one get so self-assured, he wondered. It made him very sylphconscious about all his perceived short comings.

Mayapple was talking again. Cha, she would be right at home at any Sylph party! Sylphs talked, whether it be babble, the state of the world, or what project they had going on. And when they drank mead, well, it just intensified. Even HE used to talk a lot back then, when someone would listen. Oh dear, that got him thinking about Sylph parties and how he missed them. Not that he'd ever been to that many. But still. He never went to parties anymore. He had no friends, knew no one personally, he was definitely not going to any parties in the near future. His feelings plummeted, diving into poor me.

"Flem! I said LOOK! Geez, come back, wherever you are," and Mayapple showed him a glass someone had left behind that was now thick with ants, but just around the rim. Whatever had been in it had left a sticky residue. The edge was a living mass of crawling blackness.

"Mother's got a strict rule about leaving dishes…" but her voice trailed off as whatever she was going to say died on her lips as the faerie grabbed it from her hand, his eyes still a bit unfocused as he tried to yank himsylph back to human work world, and before her very eyes swiped it with his tongue,

24

which actually sounded a bit raspy, how odd. How odd that I'm thinking about his raspy tongue being odd, she thought to herself, watching him lick the last one off quickly.

"I didn't know you liked sweet ants too!" he exclaimed.

Chapter 5

———— ❧ ————

I think we had too much tequila, that's how it started.

$\mathcal{F}$UNNY HOW A mouthful of ants, a delicacy to some Sylphs, eaten at the wrong time could slap a Sylph out of Sylph-party-la-la-land and jerk him right back to human job. Oh land of Pan, what had he done?

It was too late now. "Heh heh," escaped and he hoped he didn't have any ants crawling through his teeth. Flat out hysteria was starting to build. His wings would have liked to thrash blindly but luckily he had them secure. However, he could feel neurons firing from tip to base and jumping erratically from cell to cell.

Unable to ignore his enormous faux pas any longer, he raised his eyes, figuring to at least gauge her reaction before he lit out at a run, never to return.

A hand was clapped over her mouth so hard he could see her fingernails becoming pale.

The eyes above the hand were huge.

The other arm was stiff with that hand braced against the counter, the only thing apparently keeping her motionless.

Possibly from throwing up, thought Flem.

It was true, her stomach had heaved but it was the least of her troubles. And she was losing the battle. Sounds were now being blown from between her fingers, sounds like mud pots boiling over, a soft 'pop,' then a long SSSSSS squirmed through her fingers, escaping. The wave built and she gave up trying to control herself, instead throwing her head back as she danced from leg to leg, hands clasped at her throat as she now made gagging noises. "Eew, eew, eew! You ate them! Eew! I can't believe it. I haven't seen anybody eat bugs since that night we all went to Chinatown and had dinner at that Cantonese place. Oh. My. God. I think we had too much tequila, that's how it started. Oh, let me tell you what *I* ate, yes, *I* ate. We started with appetizers of water beetles, they marinate them in soy sauce and ginger, and then, THEN, you just pop the legs, wings, and heads off and toss 'em back. Mmmmm mmm mmm. Next, we had stir-fried silkworm pupae, sautéed with garlic, onion, ginger, and rice wine. And did you know silkworm pupae is supposed to be good for rheumatism?" she asked rhetorically. "Still not going to eat them again though, un ugh, no sireee."

Forgetting his own woe as he listened to her, Flem realized he could get away with this horrible mistake if he could just dredge up enough bravado. Where would he find it?

Pretending he was not the stupidest Sylph on the face of this Earth, but a sophisticated human male, he put on a cloak of superiority. Thank the Gods she'd told him *she'd* eaten bugs, otherwise he's never have known what to do.

Registering a slightly disgusted disdain, he said rather primly, "Oh, I would *never* eat something like *that*." Grimacing, his chin came down as he made a shooing motion with his hands towards her, a sourness to his features. "Sorry, my grandmother was from the south and we always had sweet ants when we'd visit her." Which was in fact, sort of true. No need to mention the wild party and the mead, and how the sweet ant eating had started in the first place. Cha, he *really* needed to start paying attention!

Becoming very business-like to try and get past this, Flem threw his whole attention back to packing soil into his moss, working it into place, ending with pulling his own hose over and soaking not only his basket but part of himsylph also.

Mayapple kept giggling, trying to be serious but no matter how many deep breaths she took, or how firm her resolve, she could not bring herself under control, her eyes rolling over him way too often in blatant speculation. Pressing her lips together, she reached to the cart and started removing ivy, alyssum, and some moneywort.

Grinning, she continued her instructions. "Loosen the ivy like this," and she carefully squeezed the small container while rapping it in various places with her scoop, fingers splayed wide over the plant itself as she upended it into her hand.

The Sylph copied her, the look in his eyes not quite matching the quirk he bravely wore on his lips. He was desperate to brazen this out and put it behind him but try as he might, he couldn't keep the fear from his gaze, no matter how jovially he played along.

Mayapple demonstrated in between breathy gasps of stifled laughter, as she laid the plant on its side, gently arranging the vine so that it barely stuck out head first between the narrow bars of the basket, its moist root pack laying fully flush upon the premoistened soil. The beautiful green mossy edge could barely be seen. Taking up a moneywort she laid it down next before resuming with the ivy, filling in the gaps between with wet soil, adding the dripping moss in the right spots as she went. Compressing her lips to keep her loud mouth from shooting around, she carefully spread a little more dirt on top, leveling it off. Eyeing Flem, who was almost keeping up with her, she built her next layer adding about three inches of soil, keeping within the green rim. Brushing her hands together to rid them of clinging dirt, she reached for the hose and wet it all down, being alert to not making mud.

Giving him a friendly smile, one that made her mouth twitch as she worked, she deftly slipped an alyssum into place, explaining as she did so: "The plan is to have something trailing down from what will be a virtual hanging garden of red. Or orange. Or blue. You get the picture. The main body will fill their eye with gorgeous color, and these will add the finishing touch down at the bottom. Of course, we'll be using the white alyssum here and there throughout to help add fullness and body, but the stars will be the petunias themselves."

Wiping her hands on her shirt tail she stepped over to watch him as he finished, reaching up to monitor how tight he had gotten his edging with a soft pinch. Nodding, she returning to her own work. Try as she might to banish it, the image of Flem slurping down ants kept popping into her mind unbidden and hysteria loomed, making her eyes water but she rode the wave to the end. Biting her lip to keep it locked down, she determinedly pressed on. "Now here we are going to add our first red petunia," she said, easily removing the plant after double checking the identification, lining it up on its side next to the alyssum. Working quickly she soon filled in a circle, one alyssum for every two petunias, heads barely outside the cage, dirt between and packed moss holding it all in, leaving a nice ring of soon-to-be flower heads buttoned up neatly.

Flem nodded in agreement and approval, sliding his gaze quickly across hers, not wanting contact. He could *feel* the tension she was under and knew it was her reaction to him. Of course. Cha. He couldn't seem to be normal no matter what.

Mustering his courage, he pulled himsylph together, *pretending* he was a likeable, charming, human male. Who had just eaten ants but that it was *not* unnatural. After all, she confessed to eating, what was it, *beetles*, and oh Pan, silkworm pupae. Oh gag.

He could do this. He could.

Thrusting his old insecurities aside he smiled warmly at his boss as he too finished his row of petunia-alyssum.

Something in his eyes triggered Mayapple to once again see him in a new light, to realize his eating habit were *his* business. Who cared?

Her emotions softened, naturally diffusing the hysterical edge. Appreciation pulled her in and she found herself saying "Nice job! Have you made baskets before?"

Shaking his head, he smiled demurely; eyes downcast, he reached for more moss, intent upon building a new reality here.

A new camaraderie was subtly formed and by lunch time, the first baskets were complete.

"I'll go get mom. Go ahead and wash up. After she okays these, we'll probably go to lunch and then continue this afternoon. Our goal is four a day, that should bring us to her quota just inside of two weeks, like she wanted."

"Here," she said, "Help me transfer these to that cart over there, see it? The one with the tall rack. Yes, right here, thank you," she acknowledged as he rolled it up to the edge of the work counter.

Extending a heavy bar from the top of the cart, she brought it into line, sliding it right where the basket hook hung from the S hook, so the basket now hung from two sturdy pieces. She then smoothly pulled back the arm from the post in the counter, leaving the heavy planter swaying, barely an inch from its original location, but now mobile, still attached to the same S hook. Flem looked on in appreciation.

Grunting, she eased the cart with the swinging basket over to Flem's side and once again effortlessly manipulated the heavy object to the mobile wagon.

"Cha! You made that look so easy, those must weigh a ton!" Flem exclaimed.

Whimsey C. Nimble

"Not quite. I think they weigh in between forty and fifty pounds, more or less. They are pretty heavy, considering the basket itself and all that wet dirt. Which is why we don't have to do another thing but pull the wagon over here, against the wall, and Buddleia will take it from here. We leave all our heavy work for him, did mom tell you that?" she asked.

"Yeah. This guy, Bud, is he huge?" asked Flem nervously.

"No! Not really. It's just that he's strong, and well, you'll see. You'll like him. He has broad shoulders just like you. And his arms are so long and lean, oh my God. He's a dancer too, I've heard. You can tell because he moves really gracefully." Mayapple said this without the least self consciousness, and Flem thought hmm, somebody's got a crush...

Mayapple giggled like a little girl. "I think he must work out somewhere, because his body is superb, all tan with golden hair sprinkled down his arms."

Her eyes were half closed and Flem could see she was obviously half infatuated with this *Bud*, whomever he was. I mean, muscles weren't everything. Cha. A sharp wit counted for an awful lot back in Thimbleberry Canyon. He had never really thought about knowing someone who was, well, *big*. Sylphs weren't big. Not *big*. Flying and climbing and swimming kept everyone in shape. Sylphs didn't change that much over their many year lifetime, and while he himsylph was taller than he had been when he was she, it was strictly because of being stuck in limbo, whatever caused the 'switch' to stay *on*. There was of course the matter of his expanding waistband. But that didn't count. He suspected, no, he *knew* that was from his fondness for that elixir of the Gods and Goddesses, mead. Just thinking about it made his mouth water. Too bad he hadn't brought any with him for lunch, realizing that that was not a good idea, but not discounting it either. Tsk. Bringing his attention back on track, he asked, " Was this," tilting his head towards the slightly swaying hanging gardens, "your mother's idea too? The transfer arm?"

"Of course," she replied with a grin. "She likes to think she thinks of everything, but as her daughter, I of course, take exception to that. *I* am the one with good ideas!" she laughed. "Anyway, I'll go get her. Be right back," and she bounced out the door, calling hello to another employee loudly as she ducked into the back of the main building.

A few minutes later, Iris was testing the density of the soil, the liner, and eyeing the overall appearance. Issuing admonitions to please wear their aprons next time, that the two of them looked like they had been making mud pies, she gave her approval and then dismissed them for their lunch break.

Mayapple simply said "See you in half an hour," and took off, leaving Flem to his own resources. Grabbing his pack, he headed for the grass beneath the large catalpa out back and sat down, flicking ants *away* this time. What a morning he'd had. It sure felt good to get a breather, he reflected, as he pulled out several small bags of various food stuffs he'd brought along, wishing he had something to drink other than the water fountain inside but glad at the same time that he didn't. He needed to make a firm commitment to not drinking during the day. And to not have any before he left for work every morning. Well, one thing at a time.

All too soon it was time to get back to work and before he knew it, two more baskets had been assembled and it was just about six. He felt pretty good about the day, mishaps notwithstanding.

"Are you working tomorrow, Flem?" enquired Mayapple.

Nodding his head, he helped her clean up, asking if she would be back tomorrow also, and she replied she would.

"We can leave the wagons right here, Bud will take them down to number three and hang them up when he gets here. He comes in at six, you should get a chance to meet him tonight. Hey, I'm going down to number three myself right now, so if I'm not here when Buddleia comes in, send him my way, okay? I want to make sure there's a space cleared for the fabulous baskets we made today! Great working with you Flem. I look forward to 'Sunset Orange' tomorrow – the next piece of her rainbow. This ought to be interesting, she said she wants to make sure we get pictures at the peak of the season to use for advertising, that sounds like a fun job. Well, see you," and she headed for the back at a half run.

Flem finally caught up with her train of thought but by that time she was at the back door, slipping through and he barely got out a quick wave and a "Bye!" before she was gone.

Looking at the clock it was only ten to six and he wondered what he could do for ten minutes. Everything was clean and put away, Mayapple was pretty quick and thorough; he liked her and looked forward to working with her tomorrow. Imagine that, he was actually looking forward to coming back to work tomorrow!

Whimsey C. Nimble

The door suddenly opened, scattering Flem's musings and his first thought was, oh, this can't be Bud. He had pictured someone more garden-like, straw hat and gloves. There was no straw hat but there was a pair of fancy red gloves hanging from his rear pocket. His skin glistened, a golden brown, with broad shoulders and a scarf around his neck. Hmm, he liked that scarf.

Flem couldn't help but stare, couldn't believe his eyes that THIS was Buddleia.

"Bud?" he asked.

The golden one nodded.

Flem creakily went on, "Hi, I'm Flem Green, we haven't met before, I'm new here. You don't look that, well, big." This last was said and immediately Flem could have bitten his tongue, couldn't believe that he'd said what he'd been thinking.

Bud smiled, hanging up a light jacket on the hook provided inside the doorway. He moved over to greet the faerie, a look of tentativeness in his eye, as he too sized up the newest employee in return, and said, "Am I suppose to be big?" but laughed as he said it, not taking it any further and stuck out his hand to say hello.

Flem shook, surprised that it was long, like his. A very firm but no bone-crusher handshake like so many human males felt they must make. Thank Pan. It was hard to make friends but especially for someone of a faerie's sensibilities. He may have always been a little weirder than most, but he was still a Sylph, even if he was a male right now. He still cherished the thought that some day, somehow, magic would happen, and he would change back. He knew there had to be a way, he just hadn't found it yet.

"Hey, I'm Buddleia, call me Bud. You like it here?" he asked with great friendliness.

Flem nodded quickly.

Bud continued, "Yeah, it *is* a good place to work. Iris is great."

Flem wondered how great and what he meant by that.

Bud laughed, he could see what the other was thinking and explained, "Hey, the only thing between me and the boss is dirt, and I mean the organic kind," he grinned.

"Plus," Buddleia continued, "she's really flexible with my schedule when I've got a gig. She just lets me off."

"A gig. Whatever do you mean?" asked Flem.

"Oh, I'm a dancer," replied the other modestly.

Flem's eyes grew wide as he said "Dancing? What kind of dancing?"

Bud said, "Oh, a little of this, a little of that," without really telling Flem anything.

Admiration leaped through the faerie. He now understood a little more about why both Mayapple and her mother seemed to get so happy when they mentioned Bud who moved the heavy things. He got it. He could see he liked working here a whole lot more than even a moment ago, and he'd really liked it a moment ago. Maybe he wouldn't need to bring a little mead to work after all. He could save it 'til he got home.

"Oh before I forget, Mayapple said to send you down to her, she's in number three," blurted the Sylph.

Bud arched his back and moved his shoulders around in little circles, and Flem knew exactly how he felt, it was something he did frequently him-sylph. Averting his eyes quickly, he awkwardly scanned the erasable board, as if it would tell him something new. And by golly, it did. A poster was attached at the bottom of it, advertising some event in some park this weekend. He squinted and hunched a little closer, feeling good that he could avoid contact legitimately with Bud, oh my God, he was so gorgeous, so together, so perfect, it embarrassed Flem to just be in his presence, when the man himself spoke.

"I put that poster there. There's an artisan fair this weekend, it's being held in the Lonicera Grove over at Sycamore Park. Do you know where that is?"

Sycamore Park! Well, as a matter of fact, he did. He *lived* in Sycamore Park. Casually, he said, "Oh yeah, I've been there a few times, but I don't remember that particular grove. Is it easy to find?"

"Oh yeah. Which way you coming from?"

Flem started, gulping, shoulders held rigidly. "Oh, East! No, more South. Probably."

Bud cocked his head, smiling quizzically, his brows pulled together as he tried to decipher this man.

Ignoring the strange response, he went on. "You know the Bridge, right?" referring to a well known landmark that had become synonymous with this City.

Flem laughed, and it sounded so false in his own ears, "Oh, of course!"

"Well, part of the Park is right beneath it, on this side. Ever been there?"

"No, but I'm sure I can find it! I'm pretty new here, but I know the Park. And I can certainly find the Bridge! I see it all the time." Oh no, he thought, WHY had he said that? What if Bud picked up on how close he lived!

But Buddleia merely said, "The fair starts at ten Saturday morning and goes 'til around six Saturday night, and the same for the next day. Where you from, anyway?" This was tacked on so easily but still it was wrenching for the Sylph.

"I'm, ah, from a place about three hours from here, a little town. How about you?" Quickly he lobbed the ball back into Bud's court, trying to act as normal as possible but so uncomfortable. He had come up with this today and it was sort of true, finally thinking ahead for once and trying to prepare his way around a regular job, with real people, in a city of humans.

Bud replied smoothly, "Oh, I've been here for years," and neatly evaded answering the direct question. "Well, I better get to work. Hope to see you this weekend! I've got a booth there. In addition to working for Iris," he smiled as if working for Iris was fun, "I do a bit of jewelry making. I don't do that many events but I try to make good use of the nice weather and from here on I've got a few fairs lined up for over the coming summer."

Flem lost his nervousness at this astonishing piece of news.

"And you DANCE too?"

"Dancing is my passion. Everything else is to just keep me going. And Iris is really sweet, if you know what I mean."

Flem didn't but he had an inkling. What was it with these people? Everybody seemed to like one another and liked working around each other, how interesting. How refreshing. He relaxed and was able to say, just as if he was anybody at all and him and Bud were just two coworkers talking at work, "I'll try and get there this weekend. Thanks! Do you work tomorrow?"

"Yes, but I don't come in until eight tomorrow night and then only for a couple of hours. Well, I better go find Mayapple, where did you say she was?"

"Out back, number three she said." Flem still stared in awe. He was embarrassed to do so but couldn't stop himsylph.

Glancing over at the newly planted baskets Bud gave an appreciative whistle with a quick nod to Flem and carefully backed the heavy cart away from the wall, maneuvering it out the door and went to find Mayapple.

Flem stared after him for several minutes, star struck, and then jumped into motion, propelled by something, friendship? He didn't know.

Dashing out the backdoor he threw a look down the lane just in time to see Bud disappear through the last greenhouse's entry.

He was about to pull his head back when Mayapple stuck *her* head out and yelled, "Gee, I hope you don't get hung up on your way to work tomorrow!" laughter peeling out, shiny bubbles of merriment floating off into the air before she quickly ducked out of sight.

A wave of disbelief boxed his ears but he decided to let it go. What else was he to do? He didn't like it, but since he was a likeable, capable, sophisticated human, he must put on a show.

Turning to go back inside, her voice rang out again in his ears: "Hey, don't worry, I'll try to catch the same bus tomorrow!"

Whipping around, there was no sign of her. However, he could easily *hear* her.

"Bye, see you tomorrow," and she popped out to grin infectiously at him. "Oh c'mon, don't get *antsy* over it!" going into great gales of laughter, unable to control herself now that the day was essentially over.

Flem scowled but couldn't really be mad, she was having such a good time. At his expense. Oh well, nothing new there. In some ways it was just like being back in the canyon, but at least here he knew she really did like him, he could tell from today's workday. He knew if he didn't blow it, that he really might have a chance of becoming friends with her, if he could just get her toned down a little.

But Pan, she was so loud. Did the whole world have to know his business? "Shhhhhhhhhhh!"

Wiping her eyes, she bubbled to a stop, that crazed inner core finally having let off enough steam for her to slow down, and to realize she was making him uncomfortable. Her heart melted and a little bit of common sense reasserted itself, and then she felt bad for her outrageous behavior at his expense.

"I'm sorry Flem," she apologized. "Really. I'll see you tomorrow, I'm looking forward to it. I hope you have a nice night. Just ignore me. I'm a brat, ask my mother. No respect." And then she did the most unbelievable thing. She skipped up the path and came right to him, he thought she was going by but she threw her arms around him and gave him a big squeeze.

Whimsey C. Nimble

"I'm sorry," she said again as she stepped back after the spontaneous hug. "I'm actually glad it was me this morning, and that I could help. That must have been a wretched experience. Hey, let's eat lunch together tomorrow, okay? We'll talk. It'll be fun. I better get back, Bud's waiting for me. Hey, now you know Bud, huh?" she asked with an overly suggestive manner and she grinned, trying to be lewd.

Flem grinned back at her, he couldn't believe it, this was *him* having a conversation with a typical human! Well, maybe not a *typical* human, more an atypical one it seemed, but still, it made him feel so normal. He actually felt good. And he didn't care anymore about those awful incidents of the morning. They were behind him. Tomorrow was another day.

Chapter 6

———— ❧ ————

The Sylph sat the sack down beside
him, savoring the moment.

S MILING TO HIMSYLPH Flem adjusted his scarf, pulling it out from under
his pack, a frequent occurrence as he always used his pack and a scarf,
never venturing forth without either. He patiently waited for the bus, thinking about dinner and that first glass of mead, almost drooling.

A line was forming as the city transit could be seen off in the distance
and in no time at all the faerie was climbing aboard number twenty-eight
along with everyone else.

Tomorrow was Friday and he had almost worked a full week in a human
establishment. This was a first for him and he felt pretty proud of himsylph.
Going home held more of an appeal now that he had some place else to go
during the day. He still couldn't believe his luck. A nursery. He actually felt
like he might fit in there. Never would he have thought to be in this position,
working with humans but he really liked Iris and Mayapple. And Bud. Just
thinking about him evoked a deep sigh from the Sylph.

Resting his head against the smudged window pane, he gave himsylph
over to fantasizing about that perfect man. He was so perfect he could be
Sylph laughed Flem to himsylph, his own inside joke.

How did one ever get there, he wondered, seeing again that calm, serene
manner that Bud emanated.

He certainly seemed to be on Mayapple's good side thought the faerie,
sensing the easy camaraderie between the two. Mayapple was lucky to have
such a network; he remember when *he* used to have one too. Well, in actuality there had been problems, he acknowledged grimly to himsylph. Even
then he never had quite the same style as others, although for the life of him

he couldn't figure out why. He wanted friends but couldn't keep from being so, well, needy. There, he'd said it. Usually he didn't acknowledge it, even to himsylph but life was looking fairly rosy at the moment and he was able to be a little more honest within because of it. He wondered how long before he'd be able to move up and out of his current house. It didn't appear as if it would be anytime in the foreseeable future. Oh well.

Changing busses with no fanfare and surprisingly little downtime, he was almost home when he caught sight of one of the thrift stores in his neighborhood and impulsively decided to get off and walk the remaining few blocks, cruising the store first.

Sylph culture was so different from human. There were no stores back in Thimbleberry Canyon, everyone usually made their own tunics, easily gathered foodstuffs as most of it grew nearby, and traded with others who had cultivated specialties, contact often being made through one of their highly renown parties. There were of course gathering places and he remembered fondly the establishment called Windfall Café, owned by Pootsy Koons. Cha, that place always sold the best mead! Golden amber color but never cloying. Those were the days, he thought fondly, ignoring the fact that he had never been happy.

Lost in fancy he wandered, letting his eyes drift unconsciously over the ocean of used goods, riding the contours as he rode his own reminiscence. Emerging out of the fog, his eyes latched onto something before his mind understood what he was seeing. A half hidden hummock of hammock came into view, buried beneath miscellaneous debris and he instinctively reached out for it but as luck would have it, another hand reached to uncover the treasure at the exact same time. The other was a mite faster and Flem gasped as his find was snatched from before his very eyes. How rude!

"Sorry, I saw it first, I'm sure you don't mind," came a sort of familiar voice, and the Sylph's heart plummeted to his toes. No, please no.

Green eyes assaulted him as their owner took control once again.

"Oh YOU. Well, isn't this a coincidence twice in one day?"

Childishly Flem said the first thing that came to mind. "I saw it first."

Peevishly, the man in black retorted, "Maybe. Maybe not. But I got there first, now didn't I?"

Flem's eyes snapped at the intentional insult. Wing musculature tightened and he found himsylph automatically rearranging his scarf to maximum concealment, nervousness warring with anger, buying a little time.

Deliberately, the hammock holder turned his back and shook out the length of finely woven material, inspecting it nonchalantly for holes and frayed edges.

Flem's mouth dropped open as he took in the enormity of the insult. If he had been back in the canyon, this gesture was the supreme insult. He had never experienced it before but it threw him right back to his worst times, undermining completely any personal confidence gains he'd made in the past week.

Had he been singled out for specific torture by a vengeful God? A rueful smile twitched one corner of his mouth as he made the humorless observation. *Sylphs* understood 'God' to be a benevolent, nurturing energy, more feminine than male – that aspect being a *human* interpretation.

Making a choice he knew he might well regret, he pushed past this unconscious human being with a rude shove, merely attaining a brief unbalancing of his foe.

"Oh, excuse me!" he viciously spat in too little retaliation for how he felt, head held high.

"Pansy!" was hurled after him, sharp as a knife point.

Sweeping past his adversary, Flem swept his scarf regally around his neck, ruffling his hair back between his fingers, determined to maintain his outward composure even if he felt like a cherimoya inside.

Haughtily ignoring the wretched human, Flem moved deeper into the shop, heart racing, Sylph adrenalin pumping through his fae veins, making it impossible to think clearly as his counterpoint moved to the cashier with his purchase. Blinking rapidly, the Sylph could feel his wings heaving, straining against their binding.

Almost choking from the stress, he managed to get to the door through focused determination. By Pan, he was not going to quiver and give in. He would get through this.

Head down, he plowed on, as if through a snowstorm when in fact it was a warm sunny day in early spring, and there certainly was no snow within two hundred miles.

Whimsey C. Nimble

It was so irritating that his emotions got the better of him at the worst times. He could have all the resolve in the world but give him an unexpected nasty surprise and there went his composure. How did one keep their cool through all, he wondered. What would Bud do?

Bud would probably let it all go, he reflected. Why did he take things so personally? He didn't need a new hammock. He merely needed to sit and mend the old one for Pan's sake. Feeling more in tune by the moment, he understood that that indeed was the answer, to make the best of his situation, to not let someone else's bad manners dictate how he should act.

A feeling of acceptance stole over him and a new awareness of himsylph being okay just the way he was, was born.

With a sigh of relief and glistening eyes, the faerie let his feet carry him away.

Straightening his backbone, he walked resolutely on, towards the Park, anxious to get home.

It was in the last block that he suddenly remembered another shop. It was up around the corner, what was it called? Oh yes, *Blossom's Attic*. He'd only been there once before.

Iris hadn't paid him yet, but payday was on Fridays she'd said, and he would get paid tomorrow. In time for the weekend, and THIS weekend he had somewhere to go! He wondered what this fair that Bud worked at was like. He couldn't imagine.

Turning at the corner of Spruce and Pine, he headed south and could just make out the red neon glow from the sign above the door.

Bracing himsylph for the slight human interaction that was inevitable, he let himsylph in, shutting the door carefully behind him.

A young human woman with spiky black braids and a full tangerine mouth was hunched over the glass counter talking to some customers about an item in the case below, but when she heard the door she looked up, made eye contact, smiled and nodded before going back to what she was doing.

With relief, Flem cast his eyes about to see which way he wanted to go first.

Incense drifted through the air and the two other customers drifted with it.

Flem felt good. The stolen hammock incident was old news. Pfft. Who cared?

A lazy smile appeared and the Sylph realized he really had let the dumb incident go, and that he had given it too much energy and let it get the better of him. He still didn't care for that *man* but that was okay too. This was the beginning of a new time, he determined. From now on he would be that whom he portrayed—the likable, charming, sophisticated human male.

It was five minutes later, after he had consciously let go of the other *incident*, and internalized how much he really did like his old hammock, what would he do with two anyway, that he found it. Or rather, *it* jumped out at him.

Little bird feet prickles of excitement skittered up and down his arms, raising the hair in their knowingness, moving on to run lickety split to his wing base, shooting to the tops bringing life electric to his Sylph self. Oh, he needed to fly *so* bad.

How much was it, that was the question.

In the background he heard the store door open and close and then the young woman, "Blossom" was on her name tag, came up behind him commenting on his new found booty.

"Boy, that's a find, isn't it? It just came in this morning. You're the third person to look at it today. We take lay-a-way, you know. Where are you going to hang it?" She spoke as if it was already his, a done deal.

Where was he going to hang it, he thought momentarily but it was of no consequence, this was his, no matter what it cost. Finding his voice, he asked "How much is it?"

"Thirty-five," she said as she turned over the tag to reveal the price. "It's a beauty, isn't it? I'll tell you what, I'll give it to you for twenty-five. Here, let's hold it out, I'll take this end," she said, shaking the deep red hammock out. The material was tightly woven of some kind of very small natural rope and silky to the touch. Flem couldn't believe his fortune. *Thank you*, he thought in gratitude, closing his eyes briefly in reverence.

"Wow, look at that, there's a pattern of some kind. I didn't notice that earlier. Oh look, it's birds!" Blossom exclaimed in delight as she interpreted what the black splotches were here and there.

They both studied the hammock, admiring the exquisite handiwork.

Looking up, Flem's smiling gaze caught the young woman's and he said "I'll take it. Oh," he continued, "Can you hold it for me 'til tomorrow? I get paid on Fridays."

Whimsey C. Nimble

"Sure," she replied, "What's your name? I'll put a note on it with SOLD." She grinned and he grinned back at her, happy dealers.

They walked up front, she still carrying his precious find.

After watching her stow it in a bag beneath the cash register and tape his name to it with a sold sticker, he left, feeling euphoric for the first time in a very long time.

Turning the corner back onto Spruce street, he headed west, whistling, towards Sycamore Park, which was only a block away, on Poplar.

Once inside the Park he briskly kept to the sidewalk, an air of detachment about him, just another pedestrian in the famous Park.

Fifteen minutes later he approached his hedge, scanning for camouflaged visitors who were unintentionally blending in with the surrounding eucalyptus.

Quickening his step, he double checked all around again, eyes rolling like they were greased. One side-step and he was through, the sidewalk now devoid of people.

Breathing a sigh of relief, he relaxed. He was home.

Dropping his pack with a thud, he put both hands to the rock, boulder really, and gave it a shove. A groove had been carved in by the original designer and it glided aside. Flem climbed through and carefully shut the door behind him.

The scarf got hung up and the shirt came off before he'd taken three steps into the room. Reaching under one arm he tried not to hurry so much in his angst to let his cramped wings out before he furled again - Sylphs always furled indoors, it was just good manners, drilled into them at their birthing tree.

Slowly he untied the silk from its various places and within minutes stood in all his glory in the middle of his own living room which doubled as a kitchen and bedroom, his (OLD) hammock off to one side.

He really couldn't move much with his wings at full attention and his well-earned henfull was calling his name. Arching his back, he straightened his spine 'til every sinew was tight, pulling his glorious outstretched wings to their limits, uneven filaments snagging near the base. A fierce longing pierced him as it hadn't for a long time, a *need* to be with his own kind, where preening was automatic and wing bases were always licked into place by another, no matter who you were.

Giving his new resolution a try, he let the frustration go, snapping his wings a couple of times to get the kinks out before bringing them back to the loose furl that allowed for free movement when inside.

Slipping off the rest of the human clothing, he pulled out his favorite tunic, the kind all Sylphs wore back at home. Stepping into it, he pulled the soft material into place around his wings to fasten it. This was something he would never wear out in public, *they* would think it was a dress.

Padding contently to a cupboard, he unhurriedly took down a small bag and an empty glass, grabbing the mead bottle with one finger around its neck before shuffling to his hammock.

Grinning, he held his dinner aloft as he positioned his rear and plopped down, pushing his legs out stiffly into the webbing, avoiding the numerous small holes where it had started to unwind. Sitting thusly, the hammock opened sideways rather than lengthwise as it did to accommodate him when he slept.

The Sylph sat the sack down beside him, savoring the moment.

Filling his hen to the tip of her beak, he inhaled the beloved aroma, and then let the first sip coat the inside of his mouth before swallowing.

Oh, he had earned this, what a day, he mused, nursing his drink, and then another, nibbling his violets, searching for the sunflower seeds that always fell to the bottom of the bag.

Feeling more content than he had in years, once again his old friend mead put him to sleep, spilling a bit on his tunic, the hammock, and the floor as he let himsylph topple over, crushing flower petals beneath him, his precious elixir ebbing onto the floor from where he's set it.

Soon heavy Sylph snores, the product of too much to drink, emitted heavily throughout his darkened house, safely hidden away under a rock, in Sycamore Park.

Chapter 7

— ❧ —

No time to go there now, he flung the sweater
on, not realizing it was inside out.

*H*E COULD HEAR it in his sleep. What *was* it? It was so annoying, he
thought, rolling over to his other side, wishing it would *stop*.

Consciousness seeped in, work, Friday, mead, oh Pan, WORK!

Opening gummy eyes he realized his arm was littered with candied violet pieces stuck to it and that there was a dark stain across his tunic. Oh cha.
When would he learn? He had justified it this time because it had been such
an eventful day.

Swinging his feet around and onto the floor, he dropped his head into his
hands, running his fingers through his hair, picking out bits of food, eew.

His wings were a mess, furled but crumpled, drooping dismally.

He wondered if he could get out of work.

Oh Pan, the noise outside droned on and on, louder than ever.

They must be moving the grass again. It irritated him. He disliked the
maintenance people, wishing wholeheartedly they would go away, but of
course since *he* lived in *their* world they didn't.

Oh, he was a mess.

His head hurt.

It was dark.

Work!

Forcing himsylph upright, he stumbled to move a root here, a rock there,
letting light creep in surreptitiously, hating the world. Reaching towards the
cupboard he managed to grab his tea but the wily cupboard door bounced back,
hitting him in the cheek. Swearing savagely he banged it shut again, barely

ducking out of the way, wanting to rip it from its hinges. Growling, he stepped away, a cup dangling from his index finger.

The buzz of the mower kept approaching and retreating and finally it dawned on him that it quite possibly was later than he thought, since Park Maintenance was already working.

Oh Cha.

Setting everything aside he grabbed his pack and started rummaging for the old watch he'd found that still kept accurate time.

He had *five minutes* to get washed, dressed, eat, and make a lunch. Closing his eyes in despair, he inhaled deeply, trying to remember what it was he'd felt so good about yesterday. None of it seemed particularly relevant today. The last thing he felt like was a likeable human male. BAH.

Stiffening his resolve, he gathered the needed impetus and flew into action, zipped his pack shut and threw it near the door. Grabbing the bag of candied violet leaves he shook it to see if there were any left and it rattled slightly so he figured that was lunch, tossing it to join his pack. Dashing across the room he stripped off his stained tunic, snagged the dreaded pants and hurriedly pulled them on with a grimace.

Furling tightly, he knelt and stuck his head in a bucket of water, splashing his face, arms, and the floor.

Wiping off, he looked around for the shirt and spied it inside out at the bottom of the hammock where he'd apparently slept on it. Oh well, who cared. It didn't show the wrinkles anyway. Except when he looked at it, there was mead on it. Cha!

Glancing wildly around, starting to panic now that he'd gotten the ball rolling, he remembered the brown sweater, found it on a hook and started to yank it on, bending a wing in half. Wings! He hadn't tied his wings down. Off came the sweater. Quickly he snatched up the ties from the floor and did the distasteful deed, wondering madly *how* it was again he came to be here, TYING HIS WINGS DOWN, for Pan's sake!

No time to go there now, he flung the sweater on, not realizing it was inside out.

Stress had him wrapped around its little finger by this time and he no longer had a brain. Running for the door, he stepped on the bag of leftovers that was to be his lunch, flattening it completely. Kicking it viciously aside, he snatched up his pack, spied the empty mead bottle, but wait! It wasn't empty! Hurray!

Throwing his head back, he drained every drop, tossing the bottle onto the floor where it rolled under the hammock, listened for two seconds and placed his hands on the rock when voices could be heard.

The crazed Sylph froze in place, a raw fear clutching at his entrails, that of discovery.

Holding his breath, he listened intently. He could still hear them but they were fading.

Slowly he pushed the boulder back an inch and listened. Irritation at this wasted time frissoned up his back but he clamped down on it, listening.

Cha, he could still hear them, but he did not want to be late!

Throwing caution to the wind, he let the rock glide back, slipped through and hunched down right in front of it, every fiber straining to detect any sound.

It seemed they were across the lawn and he knew he should just be able to slip through the bush that surrounded his rock like a donut but it was so scary.

Gritting his teeth, his body tense, he slowly straightened, peering through the impossible mesh to listen and quickly side-stepped through his greenery illusion, emerging into the hemmed in space that surrounded his bush and rock.

Trying to act nonchalant, he flicked his hair back and reached for his scarf automatically but his hands came away empty. No scarf! Panic assailed him like an unexpected squall on the open ocean.

Gulping convulsively, blinking out of control, he held his breath for a moment before he gasped and sucked in air, blindly looking around.

No one was in sight. He crashed back through, running, running, and in only seconds had a precious scarf once more in place around his too big shoulders.

Starting to shake, he took a deep breath, calmed himsylph, and stepped through the green hedge of normalcy again.

Keeping the big tree between him and the maintenance crew of two he stealthily drifted around the corner and out onto the sidewalk, making a bee-line towards the street. Not a moment too soon either, as the bus lumbered into sight.

Within minutes he was obscure in a window seat near the back. He'd made it. Now that he could relax, his pulse slowed and his mind stopped frittering around like water drops on a hot skillet. It was payday. And he had a new hammock to pick up tonight. That was something to look forward to, too bad he felt so lousy.

Hugging his pack to his chest he sat rather sideways on the seat as if ready to spring forward at any moment.

Impatient now that he was on his way, he dashed off at his first stop, merely to be first in line for this next bus, and when it showed up, he swung into the seat directly behind the driver, it having just been vacated.

The driver's eyes couldn't leave this new passenger and he stared into the long smoky mirror, studying him. The bus seemed to know where to go by itself, human hands barely guiding the large and agile steering wheel.

It was all moot to Flem, wrapped up in his own world as he was.

Adjusting his scarf, the urge to run a hand down behind him and scratch right between his wing blades was almost overwhelming. He couldn't and it made him twitch all the more, rubbing the back of one hand under his nose. Pan, he was a mess today. If only he hadn't finished the mead. Why couldn't he get himsylph under control? Cha, now he had no mead after work and it was Friday. Unfortunately he had celebrated *last* night. Ugh.

The bus slowed for Magnolia street and Flem rose, moving to stand in position beside the driver, waiting for the doors to open.

The vehicle stopped, the driver's eyes scanning the back of the poor bum who was getting off. Beside the deformity he was trying to hide with that ratty old scarf, he looked like he'd been on a bender. His sweater was inside out, the tag sticking out awkwardly in the back, his hair sure hadn't been washed recently and, (here the driver leaned towards him under the pretense of checking his ticket machine) sniffed. Yes, he thought he could detect an odor, but it was more a sweet aroma, much to his surprise.

The back of the Sylph's neck prickled under such close personal scrutiny directed directly at him and he shuddered, running a hand around the base of his neck to ease the gooseflesh as he bounded down the three steps and out the open door.

Out of sight out of mind, and the bus moved on, the driver once more the stoic behind the wheel, impervious to the world.

Whimsey C. Nimble

Fletcherman's loomed and the fae young man quickened his step, dreading the long day to get through. He wondered if he was late, as he hightailed it towards their driveway.

Thrusting through his fog, Mayapple's voice rang out sharp and clear, "Hi Flem! Do you think we're late? Hurry up, we'll go in at the same time. Want to have lunch together later? I think it's orange *Grande Flora* today, that ought to be fun, now that we've got the system down, hey?" and she actually paused for breath.

Oh thank Pan, thought the faerie.

Pasting on his happy face earlier than he'd planned, he sniffed sharply, fluttering his eyelashes as he smiled brightly at the young human woman, whom he liked.

"I don't know if we're late. Probably not, I caught the same bus as usual and I came right here."

"What IS that in your hair?" she exclaimed, picking him over as they walked up the driveway side by side.

"Yuck. And look at this, you've got your sweater on wrong side out! Geez. Kind of in a hurry this morning, were you?" she snorted and laughed. "Been there, done that. God, you're a *mess*, aren't you?" she asked rhetorically, a twinkle in her eye.

Giving him a playful shove, she said, "Go on to the men's room, I'll check you in. We don't want mother dearest seeing you like this, now do we? Mrs. Fletcherman may be a cool boss but she's down on people having too much fun on a work night, if you know what I mean."

Flem wanted to kiss her, he was so grateful, tears forming in his eyes with emotion.

"Don't be silly," she admonished, waving him away. "Go!" and she briskly walked on, calling hello to someone on her way to the board and today's listed duties, sharp heels making crisp clicks on the hard tile floor.

Ducking into the clean well-lit bathroom, the faerie in disguise gave himsylph the once over, grimacing at what he saw. Mayapple was right, he looked terrible, and look at his sweater! Oh great Pan, he had ridden on two busses to get here. How embarrassing. Mayapple's calm acceptance broke the dark bubble he'd been wearing and hopeful sunshine poured in. It was *Friday*. It was *payday*. His hammock awaited. Weekend plans.

Sylph respect shot up and it was a new 'man' who exited the men's room ten minutes later. Sleek. Suave. Sophisticated. Frowsy old scarf tossed regally around his neck, hanging perfectly down his back.

Mayapple watched from a distance, her eyebrows twitching in mirth at this manifestation, admiration for the quick change artist coming into play. She felt a pang of pity about the strange lumpiness one could detect beneath the scarf and around his shoulders. She was hoping to one day gain his confidence and perhaps he would tell her more about himself. She'd never met anyone like him and was fascinated by his reactions to things. Sometimes it was like he was from another planet or even species.

"Hey look, Bud's left us a note," she waved the paper towards him, urging him to hurry up, hurry up.

Grateful for her presence, the faerie, who looked much brighter she thought, smiled and said, "Well, what's it say?" now understanding Mayapple's delight in Bud and sharing the sentiment quite freely.

"He's reminding us of the fair this weekend at Sycamore Park. Do you know where that is? Hey, where do you live, anyway?"

Before he could think of an answer, she went on: "He says he won't see us tonight he'll be in late, but to be sure and look him up this weekend, and to bring lots of friends with money!" She laughed over this last piece and then returned her eyes to Flem.

"Oh, I live near the Park, where do you live? Roommates? Pets?" smiling brightly, hoping to deflect specifics.

She blithely replied, "Oh, I live downtown, and yeah I've got a roommate. Are you planning on going to that fair?"

"Yes, as a matter of fact, I am. Are you?" he returned.

"Well, yes I am, since Bud's going to be there. Oh, hi mom!" Mayapple greeted as Iris came up to them.

"Hi honey. Good morning Flem, how are you on this beautiful morning?" the owner asked, sending the Sylph into orbit instantly with fear she knew about last night but before anybody said anything more, Mayapple interrupted with "So, we're starting on the 'Orange Glow' today, hmm?"

Iris nodded, her question to the faerie being more rhetorical anyway. "Bud moved your baskets from yesterday down to number three, they're nice and tight, good job."

"Yeah, I was still here when he moved them. Thanks. Hey, did you see the flyer he brought in? Are you going to that fair, mom? I think me and Flem are going, aren't we?" She turned and gave her partner a questioning look.

"Yes," smiled Flem back at her, wondering how this had become *the plan* and wondering if this was what he wanted but it was too late now. I guess it *is* the plan, he decided. He would work with it, after all Mayapple had now stepped in twice today to help him, and counting the hook calamity, he certainly owed her for her great support as a friend. It was the least he could do.

"Yes," he repeated again, more firmly. "And I know where we can meet." "Well, you two need to figure that out later, okay?" said the boss, a bit of an edge lacing her voice.

"Yes sir, mommee!" responded her daughter with a snapping salute. "C'mon Flem, we've just been ordered to get to work!" Grabbing his arm, she linked hers through it, pulling him away briskly, effecting a stiff military march, talking low into his ear—"Best to get out of sight immediately I've found, or she's likely to come up with more work and we already have our work cut out for us, now don't we?" She tucked a stray curl behind her ear as they strode along and let go of his arm. (Which he was happy about but felt strangely bereft without, as fleeting as it had been; it had been years since someone had touched him so warmly.) Back in the canyon everyone engaged in free preening, there was no social hierarchy; if someone's wing scales were rough and sticking out, especially right there over the base where it was impossible to reach on one's own, why, it was rude *not* to lick them into place for them. Cha, everybody knew that, it was taught as soon as a Sylphette started to sprout her wings!

Following Mayapple out back, Flem was arrested by the sight of several new plants that were in the process of being watered. Much struck by their unusualness, he stopped in mid-stride, calling out to Mayapple, "I'll be right there!" and stood motionless, watching a woman remove straw and whatnot from around each one. She straightened, saw she had an audience and stuck out a hand, introducing herself. "Hi. I'm Ginger, I don't believe we've actually met, though I've seen you around. This is your first week, isn't it?"

Flem nodded, shaking her hand, wishing her grip wasn't so darn hard. What was it with these humans, that they had to crush a poor Sylph's hand when they greeted you?

Mayapple doubled back, materializing right beside him to listen in on the conversation.

"Hey Ginger, I see you've met Flem?"

A brief look of astonishment lit the woman's features, but she squelched it immediately as she smiled at him and nodded.

Continuing on with her task, she said, "Watch it," as she pulled a hose along with her, wetting the whole tier down.

"What *are* those?" questioned the Sylph. "I've never seen anything like it."

"Those funny looking plants are Liatris. You might know the common name, Gayfeather?"

"No."

Enjoying her expertise, Ginger expounded: "These little guys can reach six foot tall, believe it or not. And, guess what, they each have the potential for their flower plume to reach over a foot long. There was even one recorded at fifteen inches! Pretty cool, huh? Foot long flowers! They're perennials and they're native from someplace back east. Iris just told me all about them, that's why I happen to be such a wealth of knowledge," she laughed.

Mayapple was tugging at Flem's sleeve but he had to ask, "What color are they?"

"Just one. Rosy purple. Which means you need to plan where they go in your garden so they don't end up clashing with their neighbors. They're great in perennial borders and they're pretty hardy but they do like the sun."

"C'm-*ON* Flem. You can see your precious Gayfeather later. We need to get started!"

Flem wheeled around, catching Mayapple by surprise as he took her hand, leading *her* away.

"Thanks!" he called to Ginger, who stood watching for a second before turning back and continuing on with her job.

"Boy, you're quite the talker once we get you going, aren't you?" teased Mayapple.

Look who's talking, thought the faerie, Miss Babble Bling herself, and he laughed out loud.

"What? What's so funny?" demanded his coworker.

"Oh nothing," he said nonchalantly. Changing the subject, he inquired, "Same routine as yesterday?"

"Yep."

"Oh, don't be silly Mayapple," admonished Flem. "I was just thinking I'm not the only one who likes to talk, hm?" and he raised an eyebrow at her.

Both burst into laughter at the same time and the fae young man gloried in the interchange. It was almost like they were friends.

After that the morning went quickly and by noon two more baskets were ready, waiting for Bud.

"What are you doing for lunch today?" asked the young woman, wiping her hands off on her pants.

Oh Cha, thought the Sylph, lunch. He flashed on the crushed bag at home.

"Tsk tsk tsk," mocked the girl. "How DO you get along without me? Come along my friend, unless you have other plans? No? I just happen to have an extra cheese sandwich. Let's go sit under the catalpa and talk."

At the stricken look upon his face, she almost laughed. "What? You don't like cheese? It's Havarti. And I have an extra apple. C'mon," she wheedled.

Feeling trapped, the last thing he wanted to do was talk, she'd probably *grill* him, for Pan's sake, about his past, oh, what was he to do?

"Mayapple!" came the sharp command from behind them both, causing them to jump and spin around.

"Mother! God, don't DO that!"

"Sorry, I just wanted to catch you before you went to lunch. Did you bring something to eat today?" She eyeballed them, including Flem in her query.

"Well, yeah mom, don't I always? You only drilled it into me since I was five. Geez."

Flem laughed, causing Iris to cast him a sharp look but she immediately softened as she continued, "Here, I'm buying today," she said, thrusting a handful of money towards her daughter. "I heard there's a new bakery just up the street, you know, where that tea shop was we liked? Herb's was the name."

Her daughter was looking dispiritedly into a paper sack and shaking her head.

"Oh *what*, for goodness sake?"

"Why didn't you tell me this last night, mom? I wouldn't have brought lunch today. Crap."

"Oh for goodness sake, never mind then."

"No, no, I'll put it in the 'fridge, that's okay. What the heck. Flem, don't bring your lunch on Monday and you can eat old cheese sandwiches and wrinkled apples with me, okay?" Her sense of humor caught up with her as she snatched the money her mother held out. "Misery loves company, so we have a date on Monday, okay?" she grinned but now the foolish faerie looked frozen again. What was *wrong* with this guy?

"Flem?"

Chapter 8

Here she comes! Can you act normal?

$\mathcal{A}$s FLEM LISTENED to this exchange, it dawned on him just where Iris was requesting Mayapple to go.

Unreasonable panic assailed him as that awful incident was relived, one he had thought was completely behind him, never to be brought to life again, but *no*, apparently it was just the opposite, I mean, if The Fletchermans were already going to do business there, it was, in fact, *inescapable*. Oh no!

"Flem!"

Turning his head, he tried to focus on Mayapple, but he was having a hard time breathing and his wings, oh Pan, his wings were strapped down, was he absolutely mad? It was not a rhetorical question, he was seriously wondering about his sanity.

Both boss and daughter were now looking at him, and that only made it worse.

He couldn't control it, Pan knows he tried.

Blinking, blinking, blinking, his shoulders heaved and his back arched.

Summoning will he hadn't known he possessed, he tightened. And then he tightened some more. A growing wave gathered energy, escaping his rule, his body having a mind of its own. Like a one-armed bandit finally giving up its jackpot, all numbers lining up, aligning, his pent-up system revolted but could not find freedom, appendages were tied down and so, instead, a giant spasm wracked his entire frame from the tips of his toes to the top of his head, ending with his eyes rolling back in his head momentarily but then snapping open to stare right at Mayapple.

He was beyond horror. This had to be the end of the world, surely. The end of *his* world, anyway.

No one moved.

Then Mayapple again flabbergasted him. Stepping forward she ran her hands up and down his arms from shoulder to wrist several times, rubbing life and assurance and love into them, ending by taking one of his hands between hers, which she kept chafing, as if she was trying to warm him up. It was most peculiar. But it worked.

Iris abruptly said, "I'll get you a glass of water. Mayapple, make him sit down. I think it's a touch of epilepsy. See if he's got any pills with him. Oh, and keep his tongue from between his teeth." She hurried off to get the water.

Mayapple still held onto Flem but she stared at her mother's retreating back in bemusement, before turning back to her charge.

Hard put to keep hysterical consternation at bay, she nonetheless snorted with disdain, saying, "Epilepsy? I don't think so. No, I don't think so. I don't understand and maybe someday you'll enlighten me, but you're not epileptic, are you?"

Flem didn't know what that was but was fairly sure he wasn't.

Shaking his head, his eyes met hers, worrying his bottom lip with his teeth.

"Here she comes! Can you act normal?" Mayapple spoke in a hurried whisper.

Flem nodded quickly and calmly smiled at Mrs. Fletcherman, thanking her for the glass of water, so wishing it were a hen-full.

"I don't have any pills I take Mrs. Fletcherman, although I do have some, ah, something at home that, ah, calms my nerves when these, ah, times come over me. It's a genetic thing. I don't believe I have epilepsy," he added, looking at Mayapple as if she knew.

"About lunch, mom?"

Prodded back to daily life, Iris looked at her watch, said "Oh shit. Oops! Pardon my French! Looks like those cheese sandwiches are going to get eaten after all. You kids still have two more baskets to go, so, if Mr. Green here is up to it, I'd suggest you eat and get those flowers hung. I'll tell you what. Get those baskets done, with my approval of course, and you can both leave early. It is after all, Friday, and payday. Your checks are in your timecard slots." Iris paused, running a hand through her short, stylish hair. "Oh Mayapple?" She raised a well shaped eyebrow, holding out her hand, rubbing her thumb and fingers together in that classic time-honored way of all peoples to indicate expected payment.

"Rats!" tossed off her daughter, "I was hoping for a raise already. Here," she joked, tossing the folded bills to her mom.

Flem breathed a sigh of relief that disaster had loomed and he still lived to tell about it.

Iris hesitated, saying they'd just do lunch sometime next week then and after a prolonged assessment of the Sylph, with a direct look at Mayapple, which he worried about, she seemed to make up her mind and left.

Mayapple could tell she'd just gotten orders to report in, (alone) before she left so they could confer about Flem. She would, but she wasn't about to disclose all she suspected to her mom. At least, not yet.

Carefully smiling her easiest, warmest smile she looked at Flem who now appeared to be ready to do anything she asked.

Good. It was a place to start.

"C'mon, it's lunch time and you're eating with me," she told him. "We're going out back to the catalpa."

The faerie nodded docilely. It felt so good to let someone else make the decisions. For some reason, Mayapple seemed to like him. He knew he could be likeable but it always surprised him when it actually happened.

What a day, he thought to himsylph as he rubbed his eyes with his knuckles, leaving a black smear from a previously hidden little piece of dirt.

He was wrung out. No breakfast, waking up late, too much mead, and now this; how much would Iris Fletcherman put up with? So far Mayapple had saved his skin, always stepping in when he was about to go under in his own little whirlpool of disaster, and he was grateful.

He felt the impulse to tell her who he was.

It was an odd feeling, he had never told anyone about himsylph. They all KNEW back in the canyon, at least he supposed they did, but that was now years ago. He'd lived with his secret a long time. Perhaps it was time to trust again.

Feeling more relieved the more he thought about it, he could hardly wait to tell her. Cha! Wouldn't *she* be surprised! He had never come out to *anyone*.

His heart started to beat a little faster and if his wings had been up, where they belonged, they would have been pulsing in time instead of throbbing under his shirt. Oh *when* would he ever be free again?

"Yes, I'm coming!" he called in response to Mayapple, who was hustling right along, heading out back it appeared, as he followed her down between numbers two and three greenhouses.

"Where are you going, do you know?" he demanded rhetorically, stomping through high weeds.

"Right here. Come sit down," she again ordered, plopping down upon a flat, lichen covered rock barely protruding from the ground at the base of the old catalpa tree behind the decrepit old greenhouse. Legs stuck out in front of her, she leaned back, gazing up into the mass of giant, heart-shaped leaves, watching the dangling seed pods sway in the breeze.

"I've always loved this tree. There's just something so comforting about it. 'Course, it makes a mess with all these old pods littering the ground," and here she kicked a few with her toe, "and mom always complains about it, but heck, it's been here as long as I have," she trailed off.

Looking at the fae young man beside her, she let her eyes drop back down to the bag in her lap, telling herself not to be too pushy, he would tell her what was going on with him all in good time. She just had to be patient.

Flem was studiously ignoring her, making a big show of nonchalance, casually leaning against the tree, but he obviously couldn't get comfortable with that lumpy back of his, squirming and fidgeting every thirty seconds.

Trying to work up his nerve and not knowing where to start, he said nothing, Questions hounded Mayapple, Flem was a big mystery, an enigma in her world and she was just itching to get answers.

Pulling out two sandwiches, she handed one to her friend followed by a small red apple.

Taking a deep breath, he blurted "Mayapple, I'm a—" at the same exact moment she started with, "You said you knew where we could meet tomorrow?" and they both laughed.

Before he could recover, she jumped in and asked, "What were you saying? Does it have to do with your deformity? It's hard not to miss it Flem. Were you born like this? It must be so hard," and she looked so sympathetic that the faerie couldn't quite find it within himsylph to disabuse her.

Their eyes locked and Flem was quiet, trying to figure out what to do, what to say.

She dropped her eyes first, taking a bite of sandwich. "I'm sorry," she mumbled, "It's none of my business."

"No, no, it's not that, it's, well, it's hard to talk about," admitted the Sylph.

"Okay, let's not then. It's fine, don't worry about it. Let's decide where we're going to meet tomorrow and what time."

Just like that he was let off the hook.

Being somewhat of a coward he took it, but he *did* say "I will tell you about it, but just not today, okay?"

Mayapple whipped around, holding him with her eyes.

"You will? Really? We'll actually *talk*?"

Her manner was so intense Flem felt almost like some poor rodent caught in a predator's snare, but he merely nodded, pulling back a few inches, and then held up his sandwich, saying, "Thank you."

Her eyes twinkled once again as she grinned at him.

"I DO like you! I feel sure we're going to be *good* friends."

The faerie choked, and Mayapple handed him her bottle of water, pounding him on the back, still grinning.

Once he caught his breath, they didn't say much, just continued to eat in companionable silence, Mayapple's eyes occasionally flickering over Flem when she thought he wouldn't notice, but of course he did because he was doing the same thing to her.

Finishing the last bite of his free lunch he went and stood next to the dilapidated greenhouse not too far away, peering in through a broken window.

Birds swooped near the roof, freely at home within the human structure, a partial nest visible in amongst the cables still attached in the ceiling crevice.

Longingly, Flem looked all around, imagining it alive again, windows fixed and cranked open here and there, plants bursting with life everywhere.

"Hey, let's go," called Mayapple, "Quit lolly-gagging, we've got two more baskets to make *and* we haven't figured out where we're meeting tomorrow. You still want to go, right?"

Real food and a real friend went a long way to restoring balance in the faerie. He felt positively expansive.

"There's a little café on Poplar street a couple of blocks from the Park. It's on the left hand side going west. It's called Canterbury's. Do you know it? It's got outside tables and great bagels."

"Oh yes, I *do* know it. I've actually been there but it's been ages ago. So, maybe ten-ish?" she suggested.

"Sounds good," he replied. It was the wrong direction for him, he would be back tracking but it was easier than having her get too close. One thing at a time. He still planned on actually telling her, but this way he could come up with a plan.

They worked hard the rest of the afternoon, Mayapple doing most of the talking, chattering on endlessly. She didn't seem to require much of a response from him, although she couldn't keep the speculative gleam from her eye as she occasionally glanced over. It was just as well to Flem that he didn't need to respond, the day was catching up with him and now that his belly was full, he was starting to get downright sleepy. Cha, he was so glad it was Friday!

Five thirty rolled around and both baskets were in the final stages. Glancing at the clock, Mayapple whistled at how early they were finishing up, torn between telling her mother they were done and not telling her how early they'd finished, there was always the possibility Iris would request one more task.

"Okay, let's get these ready for Buddleia to move and then wipe up here. It's always nice to come back to a clean work area the next morning. Or Monday morning, as the case may be. Then we'll take the scenic route back and I'll show you some of my favorite areas, we'll still get to leave early and mom won't put us to work because we're done *too* early."

Flem laughed at her slyness, wholeheartedly agreeing with her. It was a delicious feeling—a job, a friend, Friday, payday, and weekend plans! He couldn't believe it was *his* life.

"So, where do you bank at?" asked Mayapple as they wandered around, trying to look as if they were on a very important mission versus, well, wandering.

"Bank?" said Flem blankly.

"You know, where you put money in so you can take money out and pay bills, eat, pay rent, stuff like that." She laughed, one hand gently fondling the arm of a small shrubby plant as they passed by.

"What *is* that?" exclaimed the faire, easily diverting her as the air was promptly filled with the most wondrous odor, rather lemony.

"Oh, you're not familiar with pelargoniums? Flem, you are in for such a treat! "Come here," she ordered, turning down a small aisle that had recently been watered. Racks rose up in tiers, water plopping sporadically on both sides of them, the greenery effectively cutting them off from view to all but one who was standing at one end or the other of the aisle.

"These are my absolute favorites. Look," she commanded, pulling him along, pointing to one particular pot. "Smell," she said, gently fingering a substantial woodsy leaf. "What does that remind you of?"

Flem obliged, inhaling the delightful fragrance, trying to place the smell. "I'm not sure. Some kind of flower?" he said,

Baffled, he reached for the tag but Mayapple was quicker and pulled his hand back, saying, "Wait! Try this one, see if you can identify it." There was a definite gleam in her eye.

Smiling at her endearing silliness, the Sylph played along, leaning in to inhale deeply. "Ooh, that is wonderful. C'mon, what is it?" he cajoled. "It's still kind of citrusy but not like the other one."

"Nope. Wait. All will be revealed," she droned with a deep mysterious tone, her eyes laughing.

He couldn't help it, he started laughing too, her manner infectious.

"Okay, now this, eyes closed, please sir. No peeking. This is the last one."

Obediently, the faerie bent over while Mayapple softly stroked a small branch she held under his nose.

"Oh great Pan girl, what are they? That one is fabulous. They all are. Wow. Do we get a discount?"

"As I said, they belong to the pelargonium family—that's geranium. These are all different varieties of scented geranium, and I have one of each at home. That first one was rose, then we went to lemon, and that last one was peppermint. They also come in lime and apple! Aren't they cool! I make sachets with their leaves to put in with my clothes and I'm thinking of making some jellies just for the fun of it. Also, when I have someone over and we have tea, I put out scented fingerbowls," she finished once again in her *grande dame* la-la imitation, eyes fluttering, mouth pinched tightly in a small rosebud.

Flem's eyes bugged out when he heard all this. She was a wealth of interesting ideas. He greatly admired her at this point.

"Well, it's almost six, let's go check out. It's Friday, yippie skippie! C'mon!" she ordered again, waving him to hurry up as she stepped by him to lead the way.

Threading their way through the various areas, it was no time at all before they were standing between the card slot and the duty board.

Iris was waiting for them.

"Everything cleaned up back there?" she asked.

Both nodded their heads vigorously.

"I know it is, I was just back there. Where have you two been? Oh never mind. Your baskets look good, good job. Mayapple, could I see you in my office a minute? Oh Flem, do you want to cash your check here? Just tell Ginger, she's on the cash register, that I said it was okay." With that, she leaned over and plucked an envelope from the time card slot and handed it to him.

A thrill of pride such as he had never known coursed through his veins.

"Thank you Mrs. Fletcherman. Um, I just wanted to say, well, how much I like this job, and, ah, how much I, ah, appreciate the fact that you've hired me. Thank you." He smiled shyly at her before looking down at his toes, not sure what to do. This woman had seen him at his worst and he really wanted her to know he was happy here and would try his best to be a good employee.

Sylph charm leaked out, there was nothing to prevent it; after all, Sylphs *are* charming, even ones down on their luck and who had the misfortune to stay male.

"Oh Flem," gushed the owner of the nursery, "You are so welcome! We're happy to have you here, aren't we Mayapple?"

Impulsively, Iris Fletcherman gave him a hug, being careful of his lumpy shoulder area, hoping she wasn't hurting him in any way.

Flem was frozen with mortification, his eyes wide with shock, as he awkwardly hugged her back.

Letting him go quickly, Iris wished him a great weekend, telling him he needn't sign out, she would sign him out herself at six, and winked at him once again!

"Mom, you're giving the poor guy a complex, geez, c'mon. It's Friday and I've got places to go and people to see. What do you want?"

"Remind me not to hire any more relatives. God, you're bossy. Let's step into my office for a minute, if you think you can spare the time, missy?"

Mayapple snorted and laughed, then took off first, calling over her shoulder, "See you tomorrow, Flem!"

Whimsey C. Nimble

Iris turned, saying "Good night Mr. Green. Thanks for a good week. Hey, don't take me too seriously, okay? I won't eat you, ya know."

Smiling, Flem nodded and grabbed his pack from the hook by the door before heading up front to cash his check.

It promised to be a good night.

Chapter 9

Mr. Lasciviousness narrowed his piggy eyes and licked
his lips as he eyed the attractive morsel before him.

SLINGING HIS PACK over his shoulder, Flem sailed through the front
door of Fletcherman's Nursery actually whistling through his teeth, a
nameless, tuneless, almost irritating sound. Life was good. Even the normal
underlying anxiety that never stayed dormant for very long was nowhere in
sight. He was a new Sylph, albeit a tired one, it had been a long week and
a rough couple of days but it had sure turned out okay in the long run. He
vowed never to drink too much mead again.

Oh Cha! He was OUT of mead! Not that it mattered. Well, it did. He
still wanted his one-a-day henfull. Now what was he going to do? Wait. It
seemed he'd seen a liquor store just down the street—he could always catch
number twenty-eight anywhere down Magnolia street, he'd just walk a bit
and pick up a bottle or two, since he had, yes he did, money in his pocket.

It was odd, he realized, here he was almost obsessing over having a bottle
of mead at home as he always did and yet, he actually had *no desire* for it at this
very moment. In fact, he hardly given it a thought all day while working with
Mayapple. Grimacing, all the other times he really could have used a henfull
also flashed through his mind. Cha. Thinking about it made him worry what
Iris thought of him. He wondered what epilepsy was and was glad he didn't
have it. He would ask Mayapple, he decided.

Mayapple. He didn't have epilepsy *and* he wasn't deformed. A laugh
broke through unbidden. Quickly he looked around to see if anyone noticed.
No one was near.

Ah yes, mead. His steps kept time with his thoughts as he strode along.

He didn't need a drink but he needed to know he had a nice full bottle in the cupboard. Tsk. One step at a time, he told himsylph.

Ah, there was the liquor store and he could see a bus stop right out front. That made him smile. His first of two purchases, he had a hammock to go.

Opening the door, the bell jangled right above the frame and right below a big round convex mirror showing the distorted aisles with all their myriad of bottles. It also showed the God's eye view of two wavy customers studying those shelves.

Flem smiled politely at the obese man in the slightly dirty white sweat-shirt and asked, "Where's your mead?"

Moving his toothpick from one side of his mouth to the other, the small brown beady eyes of the human studied the slight Sylph in front of him be-fore deciding to be helpful.

Flem's skin started to crawl and his wings shuddered in place, but it didn't show. Yet.

An obsequious smile pulled the clerk's features in the right direction but it was merely a screen.

Removing the toothpick delicately between two fingers, he pointed it towards a back corner, saying "Back there. Right hand side. I don't know why there's a run on that donkey piss all of sudden." It ended rather like a mutter, his glassy-eyed stare returning to the open magazine laying in front of him.

Flem frowned and moved away, left with the feeling of a greasy cloud over his previously sunshiny mood.

Determined to be quick about it, he kept his gaze on the products lining the wall, working his way towards the back, hoping he was going in the right direction.

He was just past the red wines and coming to specialty items when he realized there was another customer right where he wanted to be. The man already had two bottles in his arms and was reading the label of a third. His back was slightly turned to the approaching faerie.

Pulling his energy in 'til he felt like an invisible shadow, the Sylph care-fully stepped behind the man, trying surreptitiously to glance at the shelf as he went by and see what it was, oh Cha, and of course it was the mead.

Balancing from one foot to the other he peered over the man's shoulder, trying to see what was there.

"Tche! Who is *dancing* behind me?" the well dressed man clad only in black said with irritation, looking up from his bottle.

Flem froze in place, pinned by green eyes. He couldn't move. All thought completely left his mind. If someone were to touch him, he would surely have shattered into four thousand pieces of broken brittle faerie.

Snorting with disbelief, the man shook his head at too many coincidences. Luckily, this time his mouth sort of quirked into a half smile.

With a gallant mocking bow, he stepped aside, waving the other into his spot, right before the mead section. "Please! I was just leaving."

Flem jerkily moved forward, shards of Sylph adrenalin shooting painfully through his veins.

"So, you're a mead drinker too, huh?" It was said in a neutral tone, one might even call it conversationally.

Flem nodded, his eyes wide as he stared at his nemesis.

"Oh look, let's forget it. We all have bad days. What do you say?" and Mr. Green Eyes transferred the third bottle to join the other two in the crook of his left arm, and extended his right hand.

Flem was having a hard time getting past stark fear, but realized he must attempt it.

Letting out a held breath with a little too much force, he licked his lips before taking the hand that was held out.

A brief clasp while each noted the other's grip was firm but not a bone crusher. What a pleasant surprise.

Eyes never leaving the other, Flem looked like he was facing a hungry lion, green gaze boring into hazel.

Breaking the contact first, the man in black transferred a bottle back to his right hand, nodded goodbye and looked up the aisle towards the fat man, who was now picking his nose.

Turning back he said, "Hey. Sorry for, well, you know. See you around."

He left quickly, only once turning to throw a stare at the Sylph-in-disguise back at the mead section before pocketing his change, gathering his purchases and leaving.

Alone in the anonymity of a public place, Flem shakily stared straight ahead, seeing nothing. Slowly his world came back together and his eyes flicked from bottle to bottle, a new awareness taking up residence, changing things again. Trying it on bit by bit, the new reality showed promise. *He* did not have an enemy, as he'd previously perceived. It seemed Green Eyes was willing to start over. How novel. How refreshing. Hmmph. In his mind's eye Flem suddenly saw the man's armful and they were *all* mead. *That* certainly spoke well of him!

Regaining his composure, he got back to the delightful decision of figuring out which mead to buy.

Mayapple sat on her mom's desk, swinging her legs as they talked about Iris's newest employee.

"Mom! It's NOT epilepsy. He's got some kind of medical condition and I'll bet it has to do with that deformity he thinks he's hiding. But he's so cute! I'm hoping he'll tell me about it sometime."

Iris studied her daughter for a moment. "You're not considering him for boyfriend material, are you? He can be very charming, but really Mayapple. He is not whom I want as a son-in-law. What if he passes those, those, fits, or whatever they are on to your kids?"

"Oh my God, I can't believe you said that! You are so prejudiced. No, I wasn't planning on him as a boyfriend but now I just might. God, why can't you be more open minded mom?" An angry scowl pulled her eyebrows to one straight line across her forehead and she swung her feet extra hard, banging her mother's desk with a resounding THUNK.

"Oh stop! You are acting like such a child. He's a fine young man, but honey, you saw those fits or whatever they were, didn't you? What if he was waiting on a customer and that happened?"

"OH MY GOD, you are so close minded!"

"Would you PLEASE stop saying 'oh my God' and I am *not* close minded."

Mayapple jumped down. "So what if he was waiting on a customer? They probably wouldn't be nearly as narrow minded as you and would probably just want to *help* him."

"Oh for God's sake Mayapple, must you distort everything I say? Nobody said I didn't want to help him. What is the matter with you?"

"Oh, now there's something the matter with *me* too, huh? I'm going," she spat out, dark clouds scudding across her face. "Thanks for starting my weekend so *great*."

"No, don't go away mad. C'mon now. Stay here a minute. Let's talk." Iris softened her voice and silently put a restraining hand on her daughter's arm.

Mayapple frowned, not quite willing to give up her hurt feelings or her righteousness so quickly.

Her mother looked at her with love and hopefulness, waiting, fried nerves overlaid with patience through long practice.

A small smile escaped as Mayapple relinquished her angry stance and said, "Sorry. I know you don't mean him any ill will. He is kind of strange, isn't he? I mean, I like him, but well, he is different. You're not going to fire him, are you? He IS a good worker mom, and he does know his plants, at least, a lot of them. He didn't know about scented geraniums until today though."

"Oh, so *that's* where you were hiding. I wondered where you went."

"We weren't hiding! Well, okay, maybe we did hide just a little bit, but hey, he needs to be familiar with ALL departments, right?" she smiled.

"Go on, get out of here. No, of course I'm not going to fire him because he's got physical, or something, problems. I'm not the ogre you sometimes try and make me out to be."

"Oh, I know. Hey, you never said, are you going to that artist's fair this weekend? Bud's got a booth there, isn't that cool? I've never seen his stuff, have you?"

Iris shook her head negatively in response, then said, "Yeah, I might go," but there was an odd little smile on her mouth and her eyes half closed when she said it. Mayapple wondered what the heck that was all about but didn't comment on it. Instead she hugged her mom on her way out, reiterating, "Check's in the time card slot?"

"Yes honey."

Flem took his purchase to the counter, abhorring having to actually do business with Mr. Lasciviousness Sweat Hog who was working the register but there seemed to be no other recourse if he wanted to take home mead, and he did.

The clerk narrowed his piggy eyes and licked his lips as he eyed the attractive morsel before him. Staring a little too long, he made sure his hand touched Flem's when he handed him his receipt, his eyes sending the message that he was all his, if Flem was so inclined.

Whimsey C. Nimble

Flem looked down and realized this, this, Oh Pan, he was so the opposite of everything Flem was, oh EW EWW ICK ICK ICK, had audaciously given him a slip of paper with his number on it!

Jerking inside with overwhelming reaction, Flem opened wide frantic eyes and looked right at him, spouting, "NO! No, not me! Gotta go," and snatched up his precious cargo, running to the door, stumbling, trying to get out but finally the door closed behind him and oh great Pan, number twenty-eight was just pulling up to the curb! He couldn't believe his luck and within minutes he was safely slouched in the back of the bus, pulling away, away, hurray! The relief was almost palatable.

The horror of the encounter still rode with him but hilarity was seeping in and suddenly he couldn't wait to tell Mayapple about it. But not about Mr. Green Eyes. Not yet.

Settling back at a more comfortable angle, he let the monotony of the wheels lull him to calmness. He started to feel better with every passing minute thinking about his second stop. He still didn't know what he was going to do with two hammocks, but that made no difference, this was a had-to-have.

He transferred and finally his stop was nearing. The paper bag that he carried in his hands seemed to grow heavier and the top was damp where he'd been clutching it. Feeling exhausted by this time he wished he didn't live so far from his job.

Standing up too soon, he whacked his shoulder on the side of the slowing bus, and his poor bent-over wing went numb. He cursed silently, wincing, suddenly beyond ready to be over this whole charade and be normal once again, whatever that meant.

Sighing deeply as if it were the old days and oh woe is me times, he suddenly realized what he was doing, *not* seeing the bigger picture, and snapped out of it. The truth was, he was really satisfied with life as it was right now. Yes, things were definitely still stressful and unknown, but not unmanageable. It was best to focus on what was *right* with his life.

The bus slowed and before long Flem was clambering down and out the back door of the temporarily motionless but still breathing bus. Looking up the street he saw two young human males about to enter the same thrift shop he was going to, Blossom's Attic. One wore a long black trench coat of sorts with no sleeves in it that flapped open as he walked. Knee high black boots with big silver studs of some kind flashed even from where Flem stood as the mohawked man held the door open for his friend. His friend glanced down the street just before he disappeared inside and the faerie caught a glimpse of lots of silver, seemingly embedded in and around his face.

Involuntarily Flem cringed and ran his free hand around the back of his neck, pulling his sweater up a little before fluffing out his scarf as he determinedly walked on.

Catching the door with a bit of a bang, he stepped smartly through not surprised to see Blossom engaged in conversation with the two young men.

She looked up at him and smiled, excusing herself from her admirers as she rummaged on a hidden shelf for his hammock.

Saying something quietly to her two friends, they immediately drifted off to cruise while she conducted business.

"You're back!" she stated unnecessarily. "Here you go. Have you decided where to hang it yet? It's a great deal, like I said, I almost kept it myself. You live around here?" Finally she stopped, and for once the Sylph had the presence of mind to simply smile and say, "Yes I do, near the park." (Ha! IN the park!) "How 'bout you? This is a great store by the way. Is it yours?"

"Yes." She smiled with pride saying, "Thank you. I'm glad you like it."

Flem took the now fully paid-for treasure and tucked it beneath an arm, looking up to catch Blossom's smoldering look.

Blinking, he quickly looked down. This human woman was staring big eyes into his, *flirting*, sending him mating signals, for Pan's sake. For the second time today, a *human* thought *he* was attractive. Albeit the liquor store clerk almost didn't qualify as human, but still.

He smiled back, feeling out of his depth.

A sylphconscious little laugh bloomed into ongoing giggles which trailed behind him as he eased away from the counter, still unable to stop smiling back at her.

Amusement lit her eyes and they crinkled at the corners as she pointed out that he should be careful, there was a large mirror behind him.

"Oops! Oops!" he blathered, finally turning around and heading out, a quick last glance at his admirer.

She waved, calling "Come back again. Soon!"

"Oh yeah!" he agreed, bobbing his head like it was on springs before making his escape. Oh, he thought, I really have to work on my social interactions. Maybe Mayapple can help.

Whimsey C. Nimble

Ah Mayapple. He wondered how to tell her, and when. He had promised he would. Perhaps tomorrow.

Half an hour later he was home, his new prize stored in a corner 'til he decided what to do with it, and his one henfull sitting untasted until the exact moment he was ready, a golden reward for doing everything a good Sylph should.

Sitting on a small stool, he carefully untied the dratted wing bindings, feeling impatience drag like sharp claws along his nerves, wondering if he really *could* explode, as he felt.

But he didn't. His attention starved wings sprang up but were rubbing noisily behind him and he started licking and pulling, at least what he could reach. He couldn't believe he'd let it go for so long, that's what happened when you had no friends. (Or sylphrespect, he thought unwillingly.) Or even Sylph acquaintances. You couldn't reach your own wing base, for Pan's sake, so why bother with the rest of it? Well, that was changing right now and he proceeded to preen what he could, first one wing and then the other, focusing on each little part until they were rippling in place, a bit rough yet right there at the base of the wingulacture but much better than before.

Slowly, methodically, the old faerie who wasn't so old by Sylph standards, who had no friends, who was used to drinking too much mead but not tonight, who lived under a rock, but not forever, lovingly took care of himsylph, a bright weekend ahead of him to look forward to.

Chapter 10

Because I want to show you something that
I can't let anybody else see, that's why.

Drifting up Poplar street and past Sycamore Park and on, the soft fog promised to not stick around all morning as sunshine could be seen occasionally filtering through.

Flem stepped up his pace, wishing it would hurry up and burn off, he was cold.

A hooded sweatshirt had been layered over a stretchy long sleeved shirt and with his scarf made a rather high mound behind his head.

Nonetheless, the bite in the air put a rosy flush in his cheeks and his eyes were bright with anticipation.

Nearing Canterbury's, he kept watch for Mayapple but no one was outside, probably due to the mist.

Pausing a moment before the door, he peered through the glass and there she was, standing in line, second from the last. A wave of pleasure washed over him and he suddenly couldn't wait to talk to her. He was so lucky to have a human friend!

Opening the door was like stepping next to a lavender patch on a warm day, the hum of conversation a loud buzz.

Flem took his place as last just as Mayapple turned around to scan for him, a big smile breaking out on her face to see him right there. She quickly shooed the person between them ahead of her and moved back to stand with the faerie.

"You're looking pretty chipper this morning, must have gotten a good night's sleep, hmmmm?" she asked with a questioning look.

The Sylph just grinned.

Mayapple turned back to study the menu board and Flem followed suit.

Fifteen minutes later they were on their way to the Park, each sipping a hot drink to keep the chill at bay.

Tasting his first ever latte, Flem swiped the foam off of his upper lip with his tongue, asking "What is this again?" before taking another sip. He couldn't believe how delicious it was and resolved to drink more every chance he got in the future.

Mayapple repeated "Chai Soy Latte" then asked, "Do you usually drink caffeine, Flem?"

"What's that? I thought this was Chai something, not a caffeine." He looked at her, still sipping, wincing as he took another hot swallow, already addicted.

"God Flem, slow down! I thought you drank tea, don't you? What kind do you usually drink?" She took a swallow from her own cup, blowing onto the top, trying to cool it off.

"Oh, I don't know. What's available I guess. I like mint. I like chamomile, I like rose hips. Why?"

Biting her top lip, she gazed at him from under beetled brow, obviously thinking something.

"What?" He exclaimed impatiently before going on with "Oh, this is *so* good." Sip. "I'm so glad you told me to put extra cinnamon in it. And that sprinkle of fresh nutmeg, wow." He gulped, he sipped, he drank. "Hey, let's pick up the pace, I want to see what this fair is all about. Do you suppose we'll see Bud there?" Sip. "Of course we will, where do you suppose he'll be? Do you know what he sells? Have you been to Lonicera Grove before?" Gulp. "C'mon, let's GO."

He started walking faster and faster, his companion skipping to catch up, setting her legs in motion with his.

"Caffeine is something that is IN different things, mostly beverages, although none of the herbs you mentioned have it. Haven't you ever had black tea before? How can you not know about caffeine? Flem?" She stopped him for a second, latching onto his arm to halt his building maniacal pace. If he strode any faster she'd bet he'd be flying down the street.

Wiping off his mouth with his sleeve, his eyeballs were practically spinning in his head. Cha, this was *better* than mead!

"C'mon, you're too slow, can't you walk any faster?" and he took off again, urging her to hurry up, hurry up, over his shoulder.

She gave up and kept pace with him until they were making good time, the park easily able to be seen in the distance, the haze of mist thinning in the sky above it.

As they got closer, Mayapple felt a hysterical urge to laugh. It was obvious that Flem had not had caffeine before. How strange that he didn't even know what it was, she thought, where'd he been living, under a rock somewhere?

"Hey, wait up," she gasped as he leaped over the curb ready to practically run, it seemed.

"Oh, I wish I could *FLY*," he said with great frustration and then realized what he'd just *said*, out in public, to a *human*.

Mayapple never batted an eye, merely replying in a dry tone, with a touch of asperity, "You ARE flying. If you went any faster, you'd have to grow wings." Shaking her head in mock despair, she continued with, "Do YOU know where Lonicera Grove is?"

Flem had oddly come to a complete standstill, head hanging down. Straightening, he turned, giving her an enigmatic smile. "Yes, I'd have to grow wings to fly, wouldn't I? What a thought."

Taking a sip from her almost empty cup, she frowned at him. Sniffing, she kept looking at him long enough to be rude, but then, he looked right back at her, so I guess it wasn't rude.

"So, what's up with you?" she finally asked, staring into his eyes. "Can I ask you that? You did say you'd tell me what was going on." Giving him a last look, she broke eye contact to walk over and deposit her cup in a recycling container, stuffing her hands in the pockets of her long over-sweater as she returned.

Flem kept staring at her, his mind racing from his delicious drink, but Pan he was on overload now, whooooooeeeeee. It *turned* on you! His mouth went dry, and even though he now knew what caffeine was, he didn't have anything else to drink and he certainly couldn't take her *home* where he could get some water, so, he took another drink. It was still good although now that he was near the bottom, it was getting a bit cloying; oh, for some water.

Could he tell somebody? Could he tell Mayapple? Ah yes, Mayapple. He *could* tell her. She *was* his friend. How to start?

Whimsey C. Nimble

As if reading his mind, she said rather sympathetically, "Start at the beginning. Were you born like this?" She nodded at his shoulders, very seriously.

A wild laugh erupted out of Flem's mouth and he could contain himsylph no longer as the caffeine careened through his bloodstream. His shoulders heaved and then settled down to a fast throb, not quite disguised by his sweatshirt and scarf.

He didn't know what to do but could only think of one thing and it was the last thing he wanted to do. He desperately needed to let his wings OUT, he never should have drank that caffeine! Oh great Pan in the moon, just how was he to know caffeine would have such an effect? His wings felt absolutely trapped in claustrophobia.

There was a wild look in his eye as he suddenly grabbed Mayapple's hands and stared into her face. "Can you really and truly *not* tell *any*body, *ever*, forever? I mean, not anybody, forever. Or 'til I say it's okay. Can you? Don't say yes unless you mean it." He glared to prove he was serious.

"Yes," she stated instantaneously and emphatically. "Absolutely. You can trust me," not even beginning to have one iota whatsoever of the shock she about to go through and which she would remember for the rest of her life.

Flem had not felt so intensely for years, (wince,) since he had turned male. He was taking a big step, one that would change his life.

"Do you have some time to spare?" he asked rather hoarsely.

"Sure, we don't have any schedule. We can take all day if we want."

"Then let's not go to the fair just yet, let's go this way instead." Taking a big breath, he quickly asked the fateful question, "Do you want to see where I live?"

"Yeah, sure. *Why?*" she replied with a totally confused look on her face.

"Because I want to show you something I can't let anybody else see, that's why."

Now Mayapple was getting nervous. What had she gotten into? She forgot all the moments this past week when she'd been so sympathetic and curious.

"Er, you must live close to here, huh?"

"This way," Flem gestured and instead of turning right inside the park entrance he turned left. "Do you mind walking a ways yet?" He looked around and then remarked "The fog hasn't lifted yet, now's the best time. Come on, follow me."

Loving the adventure and intrigued by the mystery, still Mayapple was a tad bit wary. Nonetheless, she affirmed her consent ending with, "But why are we still in the park? Is it a shortcut?"

"No, it's not a shortcut," Flem answered curtly.

Mayapple didn't say anything, curiosity building with every passing second.

Striding along, she tried to keep quiet, to just wait and see but it was well nigh impossible.

"Oh My God. Where is it? What is it? *Why* isn't this a shortcut?" burst out of her.

Flem looked at her with an unreadable expression for a moment but didn't say a word as they hurried along.

Muscles in his cheek moved as he found himsylph grinding his teeth with the emotion that threatened to become overwhelming.

He couldn't believe he was doing this.

Trying to breathe deeply, he sucked in air too quickly, and soon felt lightheaded, veering off the sidewalk to drop onto a big log set back a little ways, a big Camilla bush on each end.

Leaning over, his head almost fell into his hands, and he ran his fingers through his curly hair, rubbing his eyes with his palms.

Positioned thusly, his abnormal body structure really stuck out even more, practically thrusting itsylph under Mayapple's nose.

He didn't look up, just groaned.

Mayapple stared. This didn't seem good. Just then a breeze made the leaves rustle while also playing with the Sylph's scarf, blowing it off his hunched shoulders.

He twitched and before her very eyes a ripple started in the middle of his back and followed an actual pattern. She couldn't tell what it was but it was almost like something was *alive* under there, traveling from point A to point B.

What?

Cocking her head, she willed it to happen again but just then Flem raised his head and looked at her. "Sit down," he ordered.

She sat.

Whimsey C. Nimble

"I'm not a human male like you think I am. I'm a *Sylph*, of the *faerie* race. Those are my *WINGS* under there! Oh Pan, my *wing*," he said in an anguished voice before continuing, "which I have tied down so that I can look like a human male, you see, but I'm *not* a HUMAN MALE, I'm a SYLPH. A Sylph. Oh my Pan, I'm saying it, it's been so long. I AM A SYLPH!"

Mayapple gaped.

"That's about it. Now you know. Don't tell your mom, okay? You promised, remember? Do you still want to go to the fair with me? In fact, do you still want to be friends? I guess I don't have to go home, I'm probably okay with the wings right now. Mayapple?" He looked up.

Mayapple gaped.

Unable to move, she could hardly comprehend the enormity of what he'd just told her. It just couldn't be true. But it had to be true. Nobody could make this up.

Trying to unravel her confusion, she asked "So, where we going? Do you live right near here?" as if he hadn't just told her she was with a real, live, *FAERIE*. OH. MY. GOD.

With a pained but resigned look, he studied her for a moment. What the heck, he was already in deep at this point. "I live IN the park, Mayapple, IN the park. About a fifteen minute walk from here. Do you really want to go there right now? Or should we go to the fair first?"

Was that even a choice?

"Oh Flem, PLEASE can we go there now? I would so love to see where you've been living. How can you live in the park, I don't understand."

Sighing deeply, the faerie reflected he didn't actually feel that bad. Caffeine was still dancing through him but there was such a great relief in *finally* sharing his secret with someone who was a friend, that it kept him buoyant. The extreme edge was tempered by his confession. Suddenly, he felt great.

With an exasperated look at her but a smile twitching his lips, he merely said "C'mon. I can only show you. Can you be stealthy? I mean invisible, okay?"

They took off, wings on their heels. (sort-of) And, on one's back.

Mayapple was crazed but kept it under strict control, a jail with no key.

After fifteen minutes of brisk walking, past several very public displays with lots of cars parked around them, Flem cut to the right again, onto another cross street and turned left down it for about two blocks before turning down yet another seemingly inconsequential street that was a connection to another not-so-main thoroughfare, all within the park, out near the western edge which was the more secluded area. Mayapple had grown up in the City and she did vaguely remember being back here before but it had been a long time ago. And she thought *she* knew the park. Ha.

They walked down the deserted sidewalk that bordered the lush green grounds, surrounded by giant trees, vines and flowers on all sides.

Flem stopped, motioning with his finger at his lips to be quiet, and looked around.

One minute he was there and the next he had sidestepped neatly through a hedge and was gone.

Mayapple peered furtively around and almost panicked when she saw two people crossing the street down about a half a block away but they kept on going and didn't even glance her way.

No one in sight and Flem's demanding whisper to "Come on!" moved her silently through the greenery after her partner.

He grinned at her. She looked around and they were in a hidden circle enclosed by the hedge.

He lived *here*? She didn't even see a sleeping bag. Eew. He was a *homeless* man? Well, faerie. Whatever.

Beckoning her closer, he again cautioned her to be aware and motioned her to bend over so no one would see the top of her hair inadvertently. He touched something and a boulder slid aside and she gasped out loud, her eyes wide.

"Watch your step," he advised as she gingerly picked her way down into the cave.

He followed, closing his door behind them.

Chapter 11

We *lick* them. That's what I meant by we have spit.

FLEM TURNED AROUND, seeing his home through Mayapple's eyes. It wasn't a pretty sight.

Suddenly extremely nervous, he didn't know what to do and started to hyperventilate.

Mayapple spun around after taking stock of the place through the dimness and her eyes landed on her faerie friend.

"Flem! God, relax. It's okay, it's *me*, Mayapple. Sit down for crying out loud, get those wings undone *now*! How awful to have wings and not be able to use them! I'm so sorry. (As if it were her fault.)

Flem just looked at her, unable to believe his ears.

"Really?" he squeaked.

"God yes," she answered.

"But, but, what about the fair?"

"Oh, don't worry, we'll get there. It doesn't end 'til *six*. And I bet it's only around eleven right now."

He did a quick calculation and said, "We've got *seven* hours?"

"RightO" she encouraged, nodding her head, looking hopeful. "Seven hours, Flem, seven. Go ahead, let your wings out, tell me about your, ah, *home* here. Relax. I intend to be your friend, okay? I promise to always help you, whatever it is you need."

Flem stood in shock, his psyche reeling from such fantastic fortune. And the kicker was, it was *real*. It was like the universe had responded to him, *her*, the real essence of who he was. It was unbelievable, hard to take in, but yet it felt deserved, this fortune, for after all wasn't he at heart a loving person? He *was*, he thought, and I always have been! I DO deserve this, by Pan I *do*.

"Really?" he asked rhetorically by this time. "REALLY?"

"Yep," she replied, "*really*. Let your wings out."

"Okay!" he shouted, throwing all caution to the wind, trusting in the goodness, the love that was unfolding.

Oh it felt so *good*, he thought as he yanked off his scarf, the confining sweatshirt, the too tight brown stretchy shirt. A frenzy overtook him and Mayapple leaped up to help him with the bindings, untying one side while he undid the other, and before her very astonished eyes, *wings*, yes, WINGS came out and snapped into place, forcing her to take a step back, her eyes wide, her mouth a little round circle of awe.

The Sylph stood although she could see he was still in the throes of unsurity, but it didn't stop him from rippling and flexing, waving his wings, OHMYGOD, his WINGS, and Mayapple almost swooned. "Oh *Flem*."

Filaments of happiness pulled him erect and he stood, caught up in the moment, the pure joy of unfettered freedom and *approval*, for just *him* as he was right now, a male Sylph with wings in all his glory. The caffeine lent him an air, he stood a little straighter, he could feel the controlled energy running up his spine, out, *out* to his very wing tips, oh my, he was proud of who he was, proud but humble in the sincerity of the moment. He'd *never* felt this good, this honest, this real.

What a splendid friend this human Mayapple Fletcherman was.

He fell to his knees in front of her, grabbing her hand and kissing it.

"Oh for God's sake, stop that! Get up! Flem! Get up," Mayapple shook him off, slapping at his adoration, his capitulation, as if it were every day she had a faerie's undying gratitude.

A sense of the absurd overcame her and she started to laugh as the hilarity of the situation picked at her, poking her with the unbelievableness of what was happening, right here, right now.

Taking charge, she doggedly ignored the overwhelming emotional reaction racing through her and clung to a bit of objectivity, rode it, making it her only reality, even though her eyes watered with the effort.

"Well!" she uttered with finality, as if that settled all.

Hysteria kept peeking around the corner as she looked at this *man* and his WINGS, so she turned her back and said in a squeaky voice, "How long have you lived here? This is, ah, charming."

Flem got a hold of himsylph, what was he doing? starting to be sylphconscious, wondering if he was showing off.

"Do you sleep here?" asked Mayapple, fingering his old hammock.

Too late, Flem saw the empty mead bottle resting in the corner beneath it. How embarrassing.

Mayapple ignored it but there was no way it could have escaped her attention.

Flem started to blink convulsively but consciously willed himsylph to relax. "Yes, I do," he sighed but then the sight of his recent purchase jolted him and he rushed to retrieve his new hammock, exclaiming, "Oh Mayapple, guess what I bought!" Sylphconsciousness fled in the face of camaraderie and his newly preened wings furled smoothly, only catching at the rough spots left at the inaccessible base. He was so happy he had taken the time to groom himsylph the night before.

"Here," he bossed Mayapple, "Take this end and we'll stretch it out so you can see."

"Ooh, very nice. Where are you going to hang it though?" she asked, looking around the rather dark and dingy cave that he called home, wondering how he came to be here.

"I don't know, I just knew I had to have it."

Mayapple sniffed and handed her corner back to him, unable to not stare, although she was doing her utmost to be casual, as if it was just an everyday occurrence to be standing in an underground cave in Sycamore Park, with a, what did he say? A Sylph? Whom she worked with. Ho hum.

"Boy, I'm glad you're not deformed and you don't have epilepsy!" she suddenly whooped, and they both laughed but the roller coaster of emotion they'd been riding wouldn't let them off so easily and the relief only added fuel to their frenzy until tears were rolling down their cheeks. Finally, Mayapple got a hold of herself and collapsed onto a small wooden stool, dabbing her eyes with the edge of her knotty alpaca sweater.

Flem lay sprawled in his bed, arms and legs spread-eagle hanging over the edges, wings furled tightly into long firm tubes beneath him, soft hiccupping sounds still erupting randomly.

"Does it hurt to wear them tied down all day?" the girl asked, feeling close enough by this time to be able to ask such a question.

"No, they're really flexible," he said as he sat up.

"Could I, can I, *touch* one?" she asked.

Giggling, he maneuvered himsylph over the edge, standing and unfurling like a jib in a slight wind and presented his back to her, an open invitation

"Oh Flem, they're beautiful," she breathed reverently, tracing the pulsing musculature curve with one finger, marveling at how *strong* they looked.

"Hmmph, would you look at that," she mused to herself, " it looks like, scales?" her voice ended in a question.

"They are scales, sort-of. See how they snap together?" he asked before continuing on, "I know it looks like one continuous sheet of skin, but it's not." With a deep sigh, he remarked, "It's one of the things I miss most about back home, no one to help preen."

Mayapple cocked her head sideways, studying her friend's back. She had so *many* questions but didn't want to overtax their fragile union. Instead, she replied, "Help preen? Whatever do you mean?"

"See between my wing scapulature?"

"Oh, you mean your shoulder blades?"

"Yeah, I guess so. See how those areas look sort of prickly? They're scales that need to be locked down, so your wings will glide as they rub against each other. All Sylphs have the same problem so everybody helps each other."

"Well I'll help. What do I do?" offered Mayapple without a second thought.

Flem was thunderstruck. Never in a million years had it occurred to him that someone else, a *human*, for Pan's sake, would offer to help.

Suddenly he was embarrassed to be so vulnerable before her eyes and he shrugged, mumbling, "No, no that's okay, don't worry about it," but Mayapple retorted, "Don't be silly! Of course I'll help. Hey, you're going to owe me a big favor some day, don't think you're getting off scot free!" Running her hands back over her hair, she ordered, "Hold on just a minute, I want to put my hair back," and worked a little band around her mass of thick hair, pulling it into a tail. She then pushed up her sleeves, rubbed her hands together and stated: "I'm ready." This was an opportunity she was going to fully immerse herself in. Image, *preening a faerie*. Life did not get better than this.

Flem wasn't so sure. Another Sylph would automatically fall to their knees and with a 'hold-on,' proceed to lick those nasty hard-to-reach wing scales right into place, smoothing down snags, biting the thicker rim of each scale, locking them together. Sylphs were very sociable for the most part, and it was a frequent occurrence when one moved about in public. Even he had been taken care of, albeit not as often as he would have preferred.

"What's the matter?" asked Mayapple after Flem hadn't moved or said anything for several long seconds.

He couldn't answer, it stuck in his throat, and he worried his bottom lip, wings starting to droop.

"Okay, tell me. Tell me how you-all preen and then let's see if we can't figure out what *I* can do. Geez, you've got to loosen up and learn to speak up for yourself, Flem. Trust me with you feelings, tell me what's going on, okay?" She was busily pushing her thumbs around his scapula from which both wings emerged. They *did* feel rough, she realized, leaning in for a closer look.

"Don't you have more light?" she complained.

"Er, yeah, just a minute." He hopped around the room, wings furling automatically as soon as he left the open space in the middle where they had been standing, removing a rock here, adjusting a root there and sure enough, daylight filtered in.

"Let's move over here," she said as he unfurled, backing into place and pulled him by the arm to a thin patch of light.

Working more by feel than by sight, she let her fingers see for her as she interpreted the bristle covering the knobs and part way up each wing.

Doing her best, she tried to 'snap' them together where there seemed to be two areas that felt like they should go together but wouldn't. Sometimes it worked, sometimes it didn't.

Her tongue stuck out the side of her mouth as she gave it her full attention.

"Do you have any water Flem? Perhaps if I dip my fingers in it, they'll glide easier."

"Of course!" he replied. "We have spit!"

"WHAT? You don't have any water here, you only have *spit*?" cried Mayapple, her fingers stopped cold by this amazing fact.

"No! No! I have water." He dashed off and returned immediately with a cup of water for her.

"So Flem how exactly do you preen one another? Or can't you tell me? Is it too personal? If you can't, that's okay. I understand."

It worked. Like a trout after an emergent caddisfly, he rose and took the bait. Mayapple smiled to herself.

"We *lick* them. That's what I meant by we have spit," he laughed.

"Ah," said Mayapple knowingly, like it all made sense. "I see."

An image of Flem licking ants off of the glass and the sound she'd heard flashed through her mind.

"Mr. Green?" she asked in a sweet innocent tone, "Can I see your tongue?"

Turning around to stare at her, he hesitated but then thrust his rough, cat-like tongue out at her, trying not to laugh, as did she.

"Ah yes," she repeated, and this time it DID make sense. Rough wet tongues would be just the tool needed to slap these irascible wing scales into place.

"Okay, turn around again," she ordered, dipping her fingers into the cup.

It worked. Deft nimble fingers started at the very bottom, and, dipping frequently, worked their way up to first one wing knob and then the other, clicking and snapping sharp edges together until all felt smooth. It didn't take very long, considering how long it had been.

Her fingers were now kneading and rubbing circles up his main wing cartilage and she marveled at how warm and alive they were under her hands.

Wingtips sagged as the faerie let himsylph be tended, loved and appreciated.

No one had touched him like this for years and tears came to his eyes, it felt so good, so natural.

He didn't say anything more and neither did she, both giving themselves up to the moment.

Working his back over and falling into the rhythm of it, Mayapple's eyes roamed around the dark cave landing to rest on the empty bottle under the hammock.

"I like mead too," she said, breaking the silence. "What's your favorite kind?"

For once he was too relaxed to freak out at the mere mention of his drinking problem and then he realized she didn't know he had a problem.

He doubled his intention to never drink too much again, to tuck that unsavory piece of who he *used* to be back into a little box and pretend it didn't exist.

The urbane, sophisticated male Sylph smoothly replied, "I like Manzanita, what about you?" feeling so proud. Determined to be that person he was pretending to be.

"Manzanita mead?" asked Mayapple, working his left wing with both hands, rubbing the fine, living skin-like appendage with soft, penetrating fingers, marveling, marveling, marveling.

"Where do you get it?" she asked, doing her utmost to draw this moment out for as long as possible, unable to really believe where she was and what she was doing. Deformity, *no*, she chuckled to herself. Flem was not at all whom she had thought he was. This was much more intriguing!

By this time the fae faerie Sylph was putty in her hands. Wherever she lead, he would follow. Long live Queen Mayapple! he giggled to himsylph. He would never be the same.

She was just starting up the other side when he was overcome with gratitude and turned around, stepping out of her warm, comforting grip.

Wrapping his arms around her neck, he pulled her close to him in a warm hug and said with great sincerity, "I'm so glad we're sisters."

"Oh, are we *sisters*, Flem?" Mayapple asked dryly, mouth twitching.

"Yes, we are," he replied. "Oh!" A hand came up and covered his mouth, "Oh!" he said again. "I'm sorry, I haven't done that in years!"

"Done what?"

"Thought of mysylph as Flumaria—that was my name before I, uh, well, went through the *change*, and, uh, became male, and well, here I am. That was my name, Flumaria Greenwood back when I was female and still lived in the canyon."

Back when I was FEMALE? thought Mayapple, hearing it reverberate in her ears, wondering if she'd missed that part back there at the log but she swallowed and calmly backed up, turning him around by his shoulders to face the other way again and started smoothing him back down.

"Which canyon would that be?" she asked faintly.

With a sigh for fond remembrances and things lost, the distracted Sylph replied, "Thimbleberry. Oh, that feels so good. Thank you so much."

So many questions, where to start, thought the human giving the faerie a back rub. Well, wing rub.

"How old were you when you, ah, became a male?" carefully phrased Mayapple, amazed her tongue could even say things like that.

Bending a little to accommodate her helping hands, he said, "Well, this has been the only time *I've* gone through the *change*, I've known others who've gone male a few times. I'm not very old, I'm only a hundred and twenty-four."

"Oh. Really. Only a hundred and twenty-four. How old do Sylphs *get?*" Mayapple asked, her mind boggling.

"Oh, let's see, who was the oldest I knew of…I guess it would be Rose Moschata. I never met her but then, I didn't have quite the social circle others did." (Ha, what social circle, he asked himsylph, remembering how lonely he'd been. How inept.) "She was three-hundred something –"

Recalling his senses, he forced himsylph to not take advantage of this very accommodating woman and reluctantly moved away, furling as he did so. A moment later he closed his eyes in sheer bliss.

"You have no idea what you just did," he said softly, looking at her with his big hazel eyes.

"You asked me how long I've been male? It's been six years. Usually it lasts at the very most, two weeks. I've lived here in San Francoa Ramosa about six months. I've moved a *lot*. It was too hard to stay in either canyon," he paused reflectively.

"*Either* canyon?"

"Uh, Cow Valley is several miles down and instead of running north/south, runs east/west, at the mouth of Thimbleberry.

Grappling with the complicated drama of it all, Mayapple decided to act like this was just as normal as having a mother who ran a large nursery in the City. She liked Flem. Who cared about all that other stuff? Not that she wasn't sympathetic of course. Sympathetic and completely fascinated. But also overloaded. It was like standing on the edge of a cosmos she hadn't known existed till today. Taking a deep breath, she deliberately let it all be and decided to carry on, at least for now. Getting antsy, she started looking around and Flem said, "Wanna go?"

Smiling at each other, she automatically helped him tie those precious wings back into place, unfolding the back of his shirt when it stayed tucked under itself.

Carefully, the rock was pushed momentarily aside and they slipped through, Flem letting it glide back into place, Mayapple blinking at how much brighter it was out here.

Feeling like a naughty child with a most important secret, Mayapple hunched over, following her faerie friend back through the bushes to life outside.

Chapter 12

A low vibrating voice, no, not a voice, what *was* that noise?

A BRISK WALK, ONE that warmed them both up as the sun made a full appearance, banishing the fog and taking outright control, brought them to the entrance of the Fair where a big white banner was strung between two eucalyptus trees, announcing 'LONICERA GROVE 23ʀᴅ ARTISAN & CRAFT FAIR APRIL 16 & 17, 2012.' Stylized honeysuckle decorated the edges.

"Have you ever been to a Fair before?" asked Mayapple looking at Flem.

"No. We had gatherings back in the canyon. But it was more about socializing, everybody talking, you know Sylphs have to be the chattiest of the lot, and then add a little mead and start bartering...well, more like a party." (For *some*, he added silently with his habitual inner whine.)

"Sounds like fun!" she laughed, her mind staggering with the idea of *more faeries*.

Soon they were under the banner, white tent tops spread out before them like mushrooms after a spring rain.

"Yum, something smells good," remarked Mayapple. "I think the food booths are at the back and hey, there's a mead booth too, I believe. At least there was last year. I wonder if there's going to be music? Oh, look at those!" and she was off, darting into a canvas doorway where gauzy, multi-colored skirts drifted with the air currents.

Flem didn't want to look at skirts so he meandered a few more steps, keeping an eye out for his friend's return.

He was so relaxed, he realized, that it felt like a magic day. Warm salt air, soft sunshine, money in his pocket, a *friend* to share it all with. Time seemed suspended.

The next booth sold nothing but soap and he dallied, inhaling the various scents, liking the peppermint the best but the lemon was also a real draw.

"Hey!" called Mayapple from his doorway as she waved to let him know she was back. Pantomiming, she pointed her way to the next booth and waved again, this time goodbye as she moved on.

Feeling rich as a king, Flem bought two bars of soap, one as a gift for Mayapple.

Waiting outside the booth that sold all kinds of leather purses and custom shoes, Flem watched as Mayapple tried on a pair of supple brown sandals. Walking in, he said "I thought it was a couch you were saving for, not shoes."

Mayapple looked over at him but with a rather glazed look in her eye. "Why would I want more furniture when I could get these instead?" Snapping out of it, she put the shoes back, grabbed his arm and steered him outside. "You're right, I need to look at everything first, don't I, and then decide. But look!" She pointed to his hand which held a small paper sack. "You're a fine one to talk, Mr. Green, you're spending money!"

"Ah, but I spent under ten dollars, not a hundred and fifty. And besides, one of these is for you," he finished with a shy smile, digging into the bag and pulling out both bars. "Here, which one do you want?"

"Ooh, look what you did. Oh Flem, how sweet. Thank you!" she said, looking them both over before handing the peppermint one back after one last deep appreciative sniff.

Linking her arm in his again, they moved on.

"Yes," she said, referring to their previous conversation, " I could go though a lot of money here," pulling him to another display where some enterprising artist displayed funny sayings that had been stamped into pieces of bone.

Walking on, she said "Where do you think Bud's booth is? I hope we don't miss him. Oh, look at those vests, Flem!" and away she went, leaving him alone.

"Flem, is that you? Are you here with Mayapple?" The questioning voice came from behind him and was none other that his boss, Iris Fletcherman.

Turning, he smiled into her eyes, then nodded to where Mayapple could be seen, trying on bodices with lots of lacings up the front, some obviously cut a lot lower than others. She looked up and saw them all watching her, modeling the vest for their approval, wondering who that man was with her mother. *He* explained that unknown thing she'd noticed the other day, it was like her mom had had a secret, and here he was, secret revealed.

Moments later, no purchase in hand, (I'm just looking, Flem!) she stood with the other three, eyeing the newcomer with frank interest.

Gesturing with her right hand since her left was clasped firmly by her companion, Iris made the introductions: "Mayapple, Flem, this is Santolina. Santolina, my daughter Mayapple and our friend, Flem, who works with us." She looked slightly flushed.

Santolina inclined his head to each with respect, dark brown eyes making direct contact with each as he said, in a slight accent, "I would shake your hands but I would then have to let go of this lovely lady's hand and I can't do that, I've been wanting to hold it for a long time," and he brought her hand up to his lips, where he placed a kiss upon it, turning to stare into Iris's eyes.

Mayapple couldn't believe her mother went along with such phony showmanship but much to her daughter's amazement, she seemed to eat it right up, giggling and blushing.

Doing a quick reassessment, Mayapple revised her first flippant impression of the short, dark, handsome man.

"Santolina is the head of the Parks and Rec Department for the City. He's the one you have to please with those baskets, kids! Oh, don't worry, they're *fine*. You're doing a good job," she reassured, squeezing Santolina's hand and giving him a warm look.

"Well, have a good time. We're off. No doubt we'll run into you again. Bye," Iris dismissed them as the couple sauntered away, heads together, laughing privately in their own world.

Flem didn't think twice about it, but Mayapple stared at their departing backs, noticing they were almost the same height, Santolina being just a few inches taller than her mother's five foot five. They made an attractive couple, trim and healthy looking but rather than the thinness of twenty-something, there was a look of maturity and solidness. His dark brown skin and rather tightly curled hair complemented nicely Iris's silver short stylish hair and tanned arms.

Mayapple turned back and looked at Flem with a speculative gleam in her eye.

"I take it this is new? She mentioned him when she first told me about the Bridge Project. You know, he's giving her business from the City - extra baskets. Did she tell you that?" Flem enquired.

"No kidding. Hmmm. Good for her." But Flem could tell she wasn't so sure about this new development. "Let's go."

Strolling past the last booth as the end of the row, they came to the food area.

"Let's get something to eat, I'm hungry, aren't you Flem? Gee, I wonder if they have any ANTS!" and she scampered about six foot away and stood laughing at him.

Shaking his head, he merely raised his eyebrows at her and said, "Perhaps we'll find, what was it? Oh yeah, 'stir-fried silkworm pupae,' that was it, yumm. Suppose they got a booth for *that* here? Shall we look?"

Giving him a droll look, Mayapple turned her back on him, making a show of reading all the food booth signs. There were plenty of picnic tables scattered about also.

Coming up beside her, he joined her in her perusal. It was then that the mead booth down at the far corner in amongst a stand of cedar caught his attention. His eyes widened but he resolved not to do anything foolish.

Mayapple was pointing and talking. "How about that one? Lots of salad and warm bread. So much of this other stuff is so greasy. I don't know why people think they can't cook without a gallon of oil," she complained. "They just don't want to bother to do it right."

Since the Sylph didn't often eat a lot of cooked foods, he ignored most of what she said and they went after greens.

The sun was high and seagulls drifted up near where a few puffy clouds rode, pigeons spiraled higher and higher in the lazy noontime, and once a stately heron flew over.

Gathering their used dishes, Mayapple carefully sorted every piece into its respective recycling can before returning to her friend.

Satiated, they moved along, down the next magical aisle.

"All of this is handmade, huh?" queried the Sylph.

"Yeah, most of it. Ooh, I want to go in there," she said, turning sharply. "Do you want to come with me?" she asked, dragging him in her wake.

"No, I don't. I'll be close by."

"Okay, see you in a bit." She hurried off, distracted by the call of velveteen.

Whimsey C. Nimble

Flem stood undecided, looking around, sniffing the slight wind, listening to happy human chatter rise and fall around him. It was like a different world, one sufficient unto itself, at least for the day. There appeared to be an unconscious common agreement whereby people suspended all their daily dramas and stories and joined in the spirit and fun of the fair.

A low vibrating voice, no, not a voice, what *was* that noise? There was rhythm inherent but it made fingers dance up his spine, into his wing base, down his long arms, pulling, insisting, inviting, demanding him to investigate.

There were two of them interwoven, and they played off of each other, below the noise level of the fair, subtly weaving into everybody's speech. Nobody cared because they fit so well in and around and under the words that they became part of all conversations, and as such, it was assumed they belonged there.

Having no choice in the matter, Flem followed the summons, finally entering a mysterious canvas cavern where he found the source of such intrigue.

Two midnight-colored men sat across the room from one another, the taller of the two, with the longer hair, on Flem's left and the older, more grizzled fellow with a headband, to his right. Each had a long, narrow, wooden-looking tube in front of his lips, with the opposite end resting on the floor, way out past their feet.

A conversation was ensuing between the two instruments that first asked then demanded but before there was true resolution, the two were off on a wild journey, skipping and frolicking, laughing at all those not fortunate to be privy to their fun.

Flem stood transfixed, his ears widening and pointing imperceptibly as the moment encapsulated him. People started piling up behind him and he glanced up once to assess the crowd but it didn't matter and like a rubber band his attention snapped back to the musicians. He folded his arms and stuck his hands into his armpits, preparing to settle in.

A hand painted sign on the back wall came into focus and Flem read it avidly:

Didgeridoo, Family business
Kakadu Region, Northern Territory, Australia
Didgeridoos made from Eucalyptus, sometimes Bamboo

Other Names: Yirdaki, Yidaki, (from Yolngu people)
If Didgeridoo from Arnhemland, will have wax mouth piece called a
'sugarbag,' made with black beeswax from wild bees
Lengths vary up to ten feet with four feet being most common
Free instruction book with purchase
Health benefits! Happier marriages, less snoring!

Eyebrows drew together briefly as the faerie contemplated that last sentence but was soon entranced again as he listened, wondering how they managed to never break for breath.

Apparently someone else besides him wanted to know the same thing for he overheard a whispered conversation behind him.

"It's called what?"

"Circular breathing. I guess it's a technique where they expel air from their mouths using their tongue and cheeks while breathing in through their nose at the same time. Supposedly this strengthens the upper airway muscles, which theoretically anyway, reduces snoring. That's what the old guy told me anyway."

Flem nodded to himsylph, thinking yes, that could make sense.

Oblivious to time, the faire lost himsylph in the travels and play between the two Aboriginal men, eyes wandering, drinking in their appearance, so different from his own.

If the mood created by these masters of manipulation hadn't been so thick about his ears, the normally sensitive Sylph would have felt the prickles of focus he was getting from someone intently watching *him*.

Standing in the doorway behind a crowd of didgeridooers, the man's gaze never left the back of Flem's head, staring at the higher-than-normal, and lumpy at that, shoulders, picturing so clearly the tell-tale *hazel* eyes.

Adjusting his thick black sweatshirt, he pulled out a black bandana and with a quick flick of his wrist, rolled it up and wrapped it around his neck, tying it loosely. Holding the stiff collar of the sweatshirt up, he tucked the scarf inside, pulling the ends down to little points. Adjusting his jeans, he yanked the pull-over down, all the while listening to these fabulous musicians and keeping watch of Flem, who was finally rubbing the back of his neck with unconscious acknowledgement.

After several minutes, Lark Spurastic moved on.

Chapter 13

———— ✖ ————

Oh that's right, it wasn't *hair* that needed
to be let down, it was *WINGS*!

$\mathcal{L}$ONG BROWN HAIR blew across Mayapple's face as she leaned in over a
jewelry case at Buddleia's booth. Impatiently, she unstuck a few strands
caught in her mouth, and then shifted her pack to the ground so she could
pull her hair back once again.

Bud's booth was like a cone flower but one with only five petals. Each
side consisted of a large shelf or petal that could be closed up to the main
body by way of little chains that pulled them up or lowered them down like
a drawbridge. The middle of this flower was a one person cabin where Bud
sat on a rolling stool and took money, replaced inventory and in between,
worked on a piece of jewelry.

He and Mayapple were talking about Flem and his absence. Mayapple
was not happy about Flem's disappearance. There was a tad bit of guilt accompanying this and try as she might she could not eradicate it. She *had*
rather gone off by herself when she had seen those velveteen pants. Still,
it had seemed like a perfectly normal expectation to suppose he wouldn't
go too far. Starting nearby, she had searched, picking up speed as she went
further and further from where they'd last seen each other until somewhere
down the line she'd finally run into Buddleia's booth and here she'd stopped,
glad to have a legitimate place to just hang out. Surely he would turn up,
sooner or later.

Losing herself in the beauty of Bud's work, Mayapple held up a pendant
shaped like a triangle. Beautiful green swirls and waves made up the stone
that Bud had set in a bezel of sterling silver.

Holding it up to her breast bone, she studied it in the hanging mirror placed conveniently near by. "I love malachite, it's one of my favorites. This is beautiful."

Bud smiled and said, "Thank you. Did you know that malachite is good for developing balance in relationship? It's also reputed to absorb negative energies and to help open your heart chakra to unconditional love."

Mayapple looked at him in surprise and then down at the piece in her hand. Reverently she laid it back down, picking up a beautiful dark blue stone that had two matching smaller pieces with it, a set.

"That's lapis lazuli, said to aid in comprehension, assisting one to say the right thing at the right time. It's best worn right above the heart. Also, traditionally, it was only reserved for royalty," Bud explained with a little laugh. Going on, he picked up another piece, this one a small round ball of pink and continued, "This is rose quartz, associated with unconditional love in all matters, self love, love of others, whatever."

Mayapple fingered a bracelet that was composed of small squarish black stones that each had a pattern within it that resembled snowflakes. "What's this?"

"That is snowflake obsidian," he replied, "and it's good for the recognition of old patterns within ourselves and helping us to change them."

Mayapple shook her head at him in awe, astonished at his in-depth knowledge.

Moving on, she gasped when she saw a tiny, light-pink and green obelisk capped with gold. "What is *this*?" she asked.

"*That* is watermelon tourmaline. It's easy to see how it got its name, isn't it? Yeah, it's a beauty, one of my favorites actually and associated with inner peace, tranquility, elevation of mood. It's suppose to help one, ah, experience the moment is how it's put."

Coming to another display, she realized it was lit from beneath and immediately saw why. The stones within looked to be alive, various colors flashing as if they were electrified. "Opals," she breathed.

Nodding his head, he said, "Yeah, from Australia. Good for letting go of anger and managing existing traits."

Regretfully turning away, she backtracked to once again pick up the first piece she'd touched, the malachite.

"That would look good on you, it goes well with your dark hair."

Mayapple raised her eyes and said only one work: " Salesman."

Bud laughed. "Hey, I have to make a living, you know. And just for you, Mayapple Fletcherman, everything's twenty five percent off."

"Really?"

"Yes."

"I thought you had to make a living?" she teased.

"I do! Tell your mother she needs to give me a raise!"

At that, they both laughed.

As the two men set their instruments against a rack designed just for that and prepared to take a break, the invisible spell broke, freeing the faerie to think again.

Music immediately filled the air but this time it was a recording and consequently not nearly as charismatic as the live performance.

Blinking, Flem wondered how long he'd been in there and where Mayapple was. Oh Cha. Mayapple. He had completely forgotten her.

Hurrying out with the crowd, he paused in the doorway, gently stroking a didgeridoo, one decorated with a brilliant design depicted with only dots. Idly he turned over the price tag. One hundred and forty-five dollars. Not this time, he thought wistfully.

Stepping outside he tried to gather his wits and figure out what to do next. He winced as he wondered again where Mayapple had gone. He knew her well enough by this time to expect a bit of attitude that he'd gone off my himsylph. Frowning, he mentally saw her hurrying off to that pants place. Hmm. Come to think of it, *she* hadn't made a plan before *she* took off. Smiling, he filed that fact away in case he needed it later, if there was a 'Mayapple attack'.

Cruising, he looked up to see that self-same booth, the one with velvet that had pulled her in and this time decided to check it out.

Soft heavy pants hung in a row, beckoning to be touched. Velvets, velours, velveteen patterns assaulted him from every side and he let his fingers caress them, bringing a pant-leg up to rub on his face, running his cheek over it, delighting in the sensuousness of the rich fabric.

"Can I help you?" She materialized through the sea of clothing, herself dressed in soft flowing attire, a shawl of elaborate design with a rose woven in, in small pile, draped around her back and down over her upper arms.

Two braids the color of red clay that Flem remembered from the canyon were wound around her head, forming a coronet up at the top.

Her feet were encased in unusual shoes, soft rounded green leather toes peeking out below full pant-legs, no heels to speak of, instead all was one flowing line that followed the shape of her foot, rising with the delicate arch.

"No. Thank you. Not right now. These are so beautiful. How much are the pants?"

A thin smile that didn't reach her eyes formed on her face as she lifted the tag on the nearest one and read "Eighty-Five," then glanced at him as if to say, too expensive for you, buddy boy.

The old insecurities from life came screaming back into place and Flem stumbled back a step, feeling incompetent, clumsy, and inferior.

"Oh," he said brilliantly, and made for the door, deciding to make a concerted effort to find Mayapple. No more being waylaid.

Determinedly he struck off, barely noticing what was being offered to the right or to his left.

Striding along, he kept his eyes roaming, watching for a familiar figure, not thinking about anything, just searching, his mind on idle.

Casting ahead, his gaze snagged and he found it hard to tear his eyes away, studying someone who was standing back in the shadow of a recessed shop front, someone oblivious to the world as he fingered his way through a rack of clothing.

With a shock, the Sylph in disguise recognized the man in black, who hadn't seen *him* yet and wouldn't, Flem decided.

But the urge to spy on him was irresistible and the faire ducked into the closest tent with lots of crowded aisles and hanging long dresses, never taking his eyes off this *person* whom he kept running into. It was so odd.

Hidden behind a row of soft cotton, the faerie peeped out over the top, trying to look casual but remain hidden.

He certainly looked *good*. Per usual, thought Flem with a tinge of envy.

The man across the street moved deeper into the shop, circling with a round clothing rack, which not surprisingly, held mostly dark attire. Flem squinted, trying to see what they were and realized the ones on this side anyway were dresses, short dresses, deep forest greens, midnight blues, lush browns and of course, black.

As he watched, the man turned around to a long mirror and held up a little black dress in front of him.

Flem's eyebrows about flew off his face, his mouth dropped open and his eyes acted like they couldn't believe it.

Maybe this guy isn't the same one I keep running into, he thought dubiously.

Stealthily, Flem parted hanging clothes and stepped through, quickly shielded his face and darted across the thoroughfare, slipping into the same shop his quarry was in, dashing to the opposite side of the establishment behind a big pole and two more racks of clothing.

Crouching down, he kept out of sight but watching really carefully to see the man's face.

It was indeed the almost-friendly, mead drinking, hostile new-shop own-er. Flem watched furtively as the guy actually went up to the counter, bought a little black dress, and left.

Slowly rising, Flem let him go. He was not a stalker, merely a spy, he giggled to himsylph. For some reason, because the guy hadn't seen him, he felt a boost, like somehow, it made him superior in some way.

What nonsense, he thought, setting out once again to track Mayapple down. There was a definite lilt in his walk though, and a sylphsatisfied smile on his lips as he took off. He knew a secret.

"There you are!" shouted Mayapple as Flem walked right up to her. "God, I *looked* for you. Where *were* you?"

"Well, after you left to go to that pants place, which I don't like by the way, I got caught by some unbelievable music. Oh Mayapple, you must come back with me later, okay? Please?"

"Sure, what was it?"

"They were from, Australia?" he started, a question in his voice and Mayapple jumped in immediately.

"Oh, I bet it was the didgeridoo place wasn't it? So you liked it, huh? Yeah, they're pretty sweet. Are you going to buy one?"

Flem scoffed. "I don't know. Do you think your mom will give me a raise yet? I've been there a whole week."

Bud erupted into laughter behind them. "Exactly!"

"Oh you two. Just because I'm the boss's daughter doesn't mean you should suck up to *me*. Trust me, I have no influence with that woman in matters like these. Heck, she barely pays me."

She turned back to the jewelry display, perusing the glittering fields.

Flem followed suit. "Do you make all this?" he asked in awe.

Bud studied him kindly as his hands wrapped silver wire around a piece of turquoise. "Yep. Gotta keep busy in the evenings. I might get into trouble otherwise." He grinned.

Head bent over another area, Mayapple spoke without looking up. "Oh, you mean after work, dancing and who knows what all you're doing? Where *do* you get your energy?" she asked, half rhetorically.

Bud took her literally. "I eat really healthy and I'm careful with my time. I drink lots of herb teas, I take supplements, I meditate. I don't drink too much or party all the time. Consequently, I'm healthy, and I get lots of exercise. I make a *little*, ahem, money at Fletcherman's Nursery, you might know it? And here's my creative outlet. It works for me." Bud paused, and then added, "It hasn't always been like this, of course. I had to orchestrate my life, work at it. But, if you know what you want and keep whittling away at it, well, it all comes together. You just have to focus."

Mayapple didn't look up but shook her head as if it were hard to believe there was somebody as together as Bud purported to be.

"Well," she finally sighed, "Come on Flem, let's do the rest of the show. Did you still want to make our way back to that didgeridoo place?"

"Yeah, let's go. Nice stuff, Bud, very impressive. What do you..." but before he could finish that thought Bud interrupted him by calling to someone whose head was turned in the other direction as he walked by, someone dressed in black, with a small package under one arm.

"Hey Lark, I didn't think you were going to be here today. The boss let you have the day off?" He asked this last question in jest as his friend Lark Spurastic was the owner of his own business. New owner that is. "Come and meet my friends," continued Bud.

By this time Flem had concluded the inevitable but nonetheless, sauntered quickly to stand behind Mayapple, tugging on her, whispering urgently, "Let's go, let's go."

Giving him an odd look, Mayapple straightened up, holding her hair with one hand as she adjusted her pack.

Whimsey C. Nimble

Buddleia was making introductions and Mayapple looked at Flem with a quelling frown.

"Hi," she said to the attractive newcomer, a green eyed man. "You look familiar."

Bud spoke up. "Mr. Spurastic here took over Herb's old place, remember Mayapple where we got those chai soy lattes that time?"

A spurt of jealousy shot through the faerie. *Bud* had had lattes with Mayapple too? He had thought he was special, but perhaps not, said his old insecuresylph.

"And this is Flem, we all work together at Fletcherman's. Oh, by the way, Mayapple's last name is Fletcherman, so be careful what you say," Bud joked.

"Ah, we meet again. Flem, is it?" Smiling benignly at the Sylph, the strange man reached out to Flem after giving Mayapple's hand a firm shake.

Reluctantly, Flem met his eyes, his heart in his throat and once again took the proffered hand in a quick clasp.

"'H-lo," he said as briefly as he could, his lips pulled back into a facsimile of a smile, risking only an extremely abbreviated glance.

Immediately, he willed himsylph invisible, hunching backwards into the ethers, silently begging Mayapple for help.

Mayapple by this time had sensed something was wrong but had no idea what. It was beginning to seem like Flem was always in some kind of jam, but it seemed to her it was almost always of his own making... He needed to relax and let his hair down.

Oh, that's right, it wasn't *hair* that needed to be let down, it was *WINGS*! She had forgotten, he was a FAERIE! He was just Flem to her, a most intriguing friend.

True to form, she immediately nodded goodbye to Lark, turned and smiled at Bud, saying they'd be back, they needed to walk awhile.

Buddleia looked up in mild surprise at her abruptness but merely inclined his head and said "DO come back. Are you going to be here tomorrow too?"

"I don't know. But I'll be back before six. That's when it closes, right?" she asked.

Bud nodded.

Lark merely observed, hands clasped behind his back.

After Flem and Mayapple left Bud cocked an eye at his friend in a silent question.

Meeting his eyes, Lard read the question and nodded thoughtfully.

Chapter 14

I guess it's your lucky day.

$\mathcal{I}$T WAS FOUR hours later and Mayapple and Flem sat slumped on a green metal bench bolted to some concrete back a ways from the main traffic area.

"I can't afford that didgeridoo, Mayapple, really, not yet. Can you afford all *those*?" he nodded towards her many packages.

Smiling ruefully, she answered, "Looks like I'll be working for mom a bit longer than I originally planned. Ah well," she sighed. "Someday I'll get that new couch and rug."

Both sat quietly for a moment, watching people go by, lost in their own thoughts, content to just sit for a while since they'd been going strong all day.

"Hey, I've got a good idea," Mayapple said as she turned to Flem with a speculative look in her eye. "Let's go back and say goodbye to Bud and then go have just one glass of mead before I catch the bus. I need to get going, I've got *plans* this evening," she said.

Flem was tired. It had been a fun but exhausting day. His whole life had changed and for the better, he thought. A glass of mead sounded extremely inviting. He still had a few dollars in his pocket, surely one glass would be permissible. He had not bought the didgeridoo, as much as he had wanted to.

"Okay," he agreed, his body manner starting to come alive again at the thought of sharing his favorite drink with Mayapple.

Winding around they eventually spotted Buddleia's booth in the distance. Flem looked avidly to see if he could spot that man, Lark Spurastic, but to his great relief he was nowhere in sight.

The thought of mead loomed and he walked a little faster. Mayapple kept up with him, anxious to see a specific piece of jewelry again and to talk to Bud and ask him to hold it until tomorrow.

As they neared the booth, little yellow twinkly lights suddenly bloomed in big sweeping loops around the edges of each 'petal,' and the middle, cone-shaped cabin lit up in dark purple making the whole thing look like a glowing magical flower.

Mayapple and Flem were temporarily stopped in their tracks with de-lighted surprise but after a quick appreciative glance at the other, hurried on.

Bud was just leaning out to adjust a light strand as the two of them came striding up and once again Flem was aware of how attractive Bud was. His smile was warm and genuine. He seemed to really like people. But it was also obvious that he cared about himself, he moved with an inner grace that radiated out no matter what task he was working on, be it mixing soil, or making jewelry. Flem wondered if it was being involved in dance that caused it. He also wondered if Bud ever had a bad day. He couldn't imagine it. To him, Bud looked like the epitome of the perfect human male. It was probably a good bet that *he* had never gotten caught on a hook and had to be saved...

Mayapple was intently looking over another tray and started talking to Bud. Flem went and stood with his back to them, hands in back pockets, looking off in the direction he knew the mead booth to lay. A wave of impa-tience snuck up on him, the thought of that one glass of mead calling him. He wished Mayapple would quit talking and hurry up. After all, she was the one that had *plans* tonight and had to hurry off.

Now she was laughing, carrying on and Bud seemed to launch in to some story.

Cha!

"Hey Mayapple, yoo hoo," he rudely broke in and she glared at him.

"Are you going to be long?" called Flem, his burgeoning bad mood seep-ing into his voice.

"No. Just give me a minute, would you?"

Flem stood, getting more cranky by the minute, impatient to sit down and relax but how could he if she wouldn't come, and besides, now he was starting to get irritated with her, the way she kept delaying their time together and laughing with Bud. *She* was the one who had to leave soon! How was he even going to enjoy the mead if they had to hurry through it?

He couldn't stop himsylph. "Mayapple!" he broke in again, only sharper this time.

"Flem, stop! I'm hurrying but geez, just hold on a minute!"

Impulsively he bit out, "Hey, I'm going down to the mead booth, I'll meet you there, okay?"

She scowled at him. "Can't you wait? Oh, never mind. Go. I'll be along in five minutes." She tried to smile but it didn't work awfully well.

Flem half grimaced back at her and took off, a little stiff because of the emotion that kept popping up like little sharp devils all over his body.

Muttering to himsylph, he slipped into the alcohol booth, waiting in line behind three others and finally it was his turn to order.

A large white sign proclaimed a choice of three: Cranberry Bog, Apple Blush and something called Egret's Beak.

Eyes bright, he slapped three dollars down on the counter and licked his lips, trying to decide. He'd never had any of these before as Manzanita mead was the one he always bought, something that had been common back in the canyon.

Shoulders and neck twitched as he ran a finger along beneath his nose a couple of times, trying to decide.

The smiling bartender never wavered, keeping her emotions off her face.

"Alright, Cranberry!" he finally proclaimed.

Feeling delighted with himsylph, he looked around for a place to sit, then headed for a small table way back in the corner, half hidden by a giant magnolia tree.

Bringing the small glass to his lips, his tongue transported him to a sundrenched bog, a siren from a sea of cranberries and he reveled in the full red taste of a new mead.

His thoughts drifted as he savored the delectable taste, unable to halt the constant sipping. The alcohol seeped into his veins and he slowed down, the long day catching up with him. Unfortunately, the glass was empty way too soon. Hmm, he thought, perhaps I should have a glass of water with it. He wondered when Mayapple was going to show up, but his former petulance had evaporated. Lazily, he contemplated the idea of buying another, warning bells without a clapper trying to get his attention, which were completely ignored when he heard Mayapple's voice talking to the bartender and by the time she was halfway across the courtyard coming towards him, he was halfway across the courtyard meeting her. She held two glasses in her hands rather awkwardly since she had an assortment of bags hanging off of her.

"Here," she said, thrusting a too-full glass at him. "Sorry I took so long. Did you have one already? What did you have? This is that Apple Blush. What do you suppose Egret's Beak is, for God sake's. Are you okay?" She finally finished rather breathlessly before adding, "You're so quiet."

The Sylph just looked rather agog at her, amazed she'd said all that in practically one breath.

Not concerned with an answer, she settled herself, packages dropping to the small table and down on the ground. Finally stilled, she took a deep sip from the miniature goblet and said appreciatively, "*Mmm*, this is good."

Through half closed eyes, Flem nodded and took a sip, relishing another new mead. He was a fortunate faerie. Ah mead, the elixir of the Gods. And the Goddesses.

"We had a pretty good day, didn't we?" Mayapple slanted her eyes at him, looking at him with great fondness.

Leaning closer she said softly, "Thank you Flem for sharing your incredible secret with me."

He impassively looked at her for a moment before blinking very deliberately once in acknowledgment, his eyes never leaving hers. He raised his glass in salute to her and she returned the favor. A bond was forged.

Sitting companionably, they chit-chatted about the day, Mayapple taking great delight in pawing through her purchases to pull out a pair of long dark velvet leggings. "Look at these!" she commanded and Flem obediently oohed and ahhed, wishing he could wear them too. But so far not many human males wore velvet tights out in public that he could see.

"Oh no, is that really the time?" groaned Mayapple draining her glass and setting it down with a thump as she caught sight of a clock up on the side of the mead booth.

"I've got to go! I told my friend I'd be home by six and it's ten to six right now." Alarm spread over her features as she started gathering her stuff together rapidly.

"Are those from the same shop you went into when we first got lost?" Flem asked artlessly.

Whimsey C. Nimble

Mayapple shook her head vigorously before bursting out with "Oooh, that lady! Did you go in there? I didn't like her although I sure liked her stuff. But, ha ha, I found another vendor that sold *these* so I bought them from Soft Touch instead of her. That first one had some kind of attitude problem."

Flem answered, "Yeah, I came back and went looking for you. Sorry I didn't wait, Mayapple," he finished contritely, blinking a little with guilt. "I just, oh, those didgeridoos! Oh Pan, they were *so* incredible." He sighed. "Someday I'd sure like one. Do you suppose I could ever learn to play like that?"

Mayapple smiled a gentle smile and covered his hand with hers where it lay on the table and with tears in her eyes, said, "Oh Flem, I just love you. Let's always be friends, okay?"

Taken aback by such naked emotion he could only nod, eyes glittering suspiciously as he then put his other hand on top of hers.

As one, they let go and came around the table to hug, Mayapple getting in a surreptitious wing rub with her thumbs as they did so.

Releasing him abruptly, she sniffed, rubbing her eyes with her sweater tail and immediately picked up every bag in sight, standing straight and tall for a moment.

"Hey, are you, do you want to come back tomorrow? Should we just meet here or maybe at Bud's or what?" She spoke quickly, in a hurry now to go, looking around.

"Sure," Flem said, not sure of the plan, "tomorrow, yeah. I'll see you here somewhere. What time do you think you'll be here?"

"I don't know. Not too early, I'm going out tonight. Speaking of which, I'm late! We'll find each other. See you tomorrow!" And she was gone, beelining through the courtyard where they sat, disappearing into the thinning crowd.

There was just a glimmer left in the bottom of his glass and Flem sat nursing it, rolling the goblet back and forth between his hands, legs now stretched out below the entire table.

He felt good. Damned good. What a day. Surely this was a day to celebrate if ever there was.

How much money did he have left, he wondered, pulling out a bigger wad than he'd hoped for.

Feeling content with two meads under his (human) belt, he contemplated what to do. He sure wanted to try Egret's Beak. But three meads... when he had firmly resolved to limit himsylph to one. He felt two was permissible because of the special circumstances of today, but he decided he would forgo that third drink, no matter how much he wanted to try it.

It was at that point that fate (the devil?) stepped in. An old white-haired guy walked right up to him with a half full bottle of Egret's Beak and filled his empty glass before he even knew what was happening. Astonished, his eyes flew to the man's face, who grinned and poured another into a glass he'd brought with him and set that down too!

"Here ya go, young fella, we're closing and I hate to see good liquor go down the drain. Nah, keep your money, it's on the house," shaking his head at Flem's feeble attempt to figure out what to do as he fumbled with the pile of bills in front of him.

The man nodded and grinned as if he was doing the faerie a great favor, saying, "I guess it's your lucky day. 'Scuse me, I gotta go clean up." Turning, he started picking up loose trash and helping the other two volunteers who were anxious to get out and go home. Within minutes the mead booth's rolling window was slammed shut, lights were off, and the faerie sat with the other few patrons, enjoying the twilight under the trees.

Flem liked mead too much to feel anything but exhilaration at his extreme good fortune, although those clapperless warning bells were bouncing like crazy in his head again. What could go wrong? Tomorrow was Sunday, he didn't have to go to work. He was *in* the park, so he didn't have far to go home. The old man was right, this *was* his lucky day.

Bringing the brimming beverage to his nose, he inhaled deeply before starting in on his forbidden nectar, glee bounding at such impromptu treasure.

A few people sat quietly but it was obviously the end of the fair, and most were drifting off.

The Sylph couldn't contain himsylph and drank a little more quickly than propriety called for, not being able to slow down. It was heavenly, light but full bodied, a beautiful translucent color, a perfect delight to the taste buds. By far the favorite of the three. And, he still had one more to go, right in front of him!

It was too much mead. He knew that. But it was *free*. Surely that made up for silly rules *he'd* made up. Who cared? Only him. He could change the rules, for Pan's sake, after all, he was the one making them. Then again, maybe he shouldn't drink this last one, maybe he could take it home with him. Oh, that was a good one, what was he going to do, carry the glass home with him? Chuckling at the absurdity of that, he replayed the old white-haired guy giving it to him, *giving* it to him!

Soon he was slumped over the table, his forehead held up by one hand, the other raising the free drink over and over to his lips, where he now slurped it in.

The sun had changed and he felt the evening coming on as day prepared to vacate.

Cha, where was everybody, he wondered, looking around, coming back to his surroundings.

There was no one left in the courtyard. A few people were talking amongst all the vendors but most of them were working to close their booths up for the night at the same time.

He needed to get home. Cha. Good thing he lived here, but it wasn't as comforting as it had been previously. He was really tired now. Tendrils of fog started to creep in, like wolves drawn by a forbidden campfire.

He looked down; a full half glass remained but somehow it just wasn't as appealing as it had been earlier. A burp erupted as he gazed blearily at the glass. By Pan, he *would* take it with him, he decided. No sense wasting good mead. Good FREE mead. Ha!

Adjusting his scarf so most of it trailed down his back and only one little piece wrapped around his neck, he stood up and unsteadily set off, his pack hanging at a funny angle on his back, the small FREE glass gripped tightly from above with one hand, lumpy shoulders at different elevations.

No one paid any attention to him.

Unsteadily he made his way to the entrance of the courtyard and then stood for several long moments, trying to get his bearings, to place the archway where he and Mayapple had come in.

Slowly his gaze understood that if he followed the people who were walking, they would no doubt lead him right along.

A half smile on his face, he stumbled along, an unsteady shadow following a group of five.

None of it looked familiar but he figured it was because he was tired, so tired. His hammock seemed like an unreachable but highly desirable beacon in his mind. He just wanted to be home.

Looking up, he realized his group was no longer there. Panic came up from his stomach and clenched at his lungs, freezing his tongue next. Wildly he looked around, realizing Sycamore Park was behind him and the group he followed must have simply come out another exit.

Whirling around, he marched back into the park and set off at a brisk meander.

He realized it had not been a good idea to whirl around like that as the contents of his stomach still hadn't caught up and he was decidedly not feeling well, in fact, he felt rather green.

Things seemed familiar now, but he couldn't quite place where, exactly, he was. He kept walking.

It was getting darker and the park was rapidly losing the joyful crowds it had held all day.

Ah, that little side street looked right, but after ten minutes Flem knew he was lost. It was getting rather dark. He'd had way too much to drink. And he was so tired.

A lone car drove slowly by, a visitor enjoying the twilight drive that could go on for hours through the maze of streets inside the park, if they so desired.

Cha.

He sat down on a small green hill dotted with a spotty carpet of pink and white little flowers and shed all the baggage he carried, except for his half-full glass of mead.

Pan, he was in a mess this time. He took a drink of mead, giving in to the hopelessness of the situation. He was *not* going to get home tonight. He could hardly bear the thought and took another drink.

Another lone car drove very slowly by, the same car as before, actually, but the sodden, drunken faerie didn't notice.

The car backed up.

Flem blearily scowled, taking another drink.

The window rolled down smoothly on the side nearest Flem and a voice floated out. "Flem, is that you? Are you alright?"

What was *he* doing here?

"Pwwwwhgh. I'm fine. Don-need *your* help," and he fell right over, glass spilling sideways to lay and bleed free mead into mother earth.

Chapter 15

Here. Eat. Don't worry, most of the time I'm a nice guy.

THE FAERIE LAY immobile, his consciousness waking up, trying to take stock of life and yesterday and last night…

His gummy eyes didn't want to open because it didn't feel like his hammock that he was laying in. There *was* a sway but it wasn't a hammock sway, it was more like a bobbing, yes, a definite slosh.

Braving it, he peered out from between slits and nothing looked right.

Oh Pan, *where was he?*

He heard birds, seagulls, outside and one sounded extremely close as it went on and on with its raucous demanding call.

Daring to look around he half sat up, leaning back on his elbows, his mind cloudy and boggled by the furnishings.

He was in a bed, but to his delight a hammock hung nearby. That made him feel immensely better, surely things couldn't be all bad if the person who lived here had a hammock. A window was open and he could hear ocean noises coming through it. Seals barked in the distance.

Utterly confused he saw his pack and an empty glass laying on a chair across the room. The empty glass, ooooh yes, it was all coming back, too much mead, AGAIN, oh Pan. Would he *ever* be able to control himsylph?

But he still didn't know how he got *here*, or even where *here* was.

A truck chugged up a nearby hill and he heard the rest of the land noises overlapping the water ones.

Reaching behind him to straighten out a lump his hand found his scarf wadded up and he automatically straightened it to wrap around his neck. What a night. His poor wings screamed to be let out, incensed to be tied down overnight. He was sure he looked as bad as he felt too.

He had to get home.

Groaning, he ran his hands through his hair, managing to make it stick out in various places.

His mouth was thicker than a swamp at the end of dry season.

Cha.

Trying to straighten himsylph, his eye caught on a bit of fabric sticking out from a closet door.

It was black.

It looked like it could be from a short tunic, in fact. Or a human woman's dress. He couldn't really see exactly how long it was but it certainly wasn't a shirt. And it didn't reach to the floor. It was something short.

With a sinking feeling, Flem had a very strong feeling of just *whose* piece of black clothing that was.

Eyes darted nervously around the room, backtracking with a sudden jerk to a lump in the corner and Flem realized with a start it was the hammock – the one that rude man had stolen from him. His heart warmed at the remembrance that he had then gone on to find a better one. Ha. Small comfort though, now, waking up in *his* room.

A soft knock was heard on the door and Flem was able to gurgle "Yeah!" just before the door opened.

Lark lounged in the doorway, crossing his arms as he leaned against the doorjamb. "How are you feeling?" he asked with no glimmer of sarcasm to be heard.

Like a wary cornered animal, the Sylph watched the human but too hung over to even raise any adrenalin.

"I'm okay," he finally said. "How'd I get here? Where are we, anyway?" He looked around, still not quite believing he wasn't home, under his rock. A little twitch wanted to erupt on one scapula and he knew that a tic would jump out under his left eye if he gave it any encouragement whatsoever. Carefully, he gathered what little aplomb he could summon, affecting poise in a dastardly situation.

"On my houseboat. We're in the Marina, the one on the south side of the city. Here," here he said, coming into the room and opening another closet door, pulling a big plush towel down from the shelf and giving it to his guest. "Shower's in there," he nodded to an open doorway through which a glass enclosed shower stall could be seen beneath a large skylight. In the skylight itself hung a giant Boston fern, small hemp ropes going from it and up and over a small pulley located in the peak of the window and then down to a double hook on the wooden door frame.

His host's eyes traveled up to the plant peak along with Flem's and looked right back at him when Flem involuntarily looked back at him with awe, which he tried not to show.

Lark just smiled at him disarmingly, further astounding his new faerie friend with this proclamation, "Go ahead and get cleaned up, then follow this hall," he tilted his head, "and go to the right before you get to the very end – that's the kitchen and that's where I'll be. We'll eat. Then I'll give you a lift home, how's that sound?" Curious but warm eyes asked the question of Flem.

What a dilemma. How could he possibly refuse? The guy practically saved him. Cha, the guy *did* save him. But he couldn't show him where he lived.

"Sure, that'd be great," he agree, buying time to think of a solution.

The door shut.

The Sylph sagged, he couldn't help it. When would he learn not to *drink* too much? Cha. What a mess. What was he going to do?

Take a shower, apparently. He looked at it appreciatively, wondering if he dared untie his wings, and knowing he dared not to, as this was an opportunity not to be missed. Sylphs didn't normally have much body odor but the male hormone that kicked on for Flumaria's *CHANGE*, had also turned up her sweat glands. Just one more irritating result that he dealt with because he had to. But a real shower and not out of a bucket or leaning over, licking his own wing scales, now *that* was enticing.

It never occurred to him to lock the door and he started fiddling with the faucets until he had them figured out. Quickly shedding his raunchy clothing, he untied his wings. They sprang up into a flapping furl, one that had a life of its own as the urge to straighten was almost overwhelming.

Opening the transparent door, he walked in. It was BIG, bigger than he'd expected. Big enough for him to be *completely* himsylph. He looked around in disbelief at the luxuriousness. His wings were coming to full attention, with plenty of room on each side. Slowly, he swirled under the hard pelting spray, noting another shower head in the far wall, his back arching with the glory of the warm rain. There was nothing he wanted more out of life at this moment than this incredible shower. Not even Penlei or WilloB back in the canyon had showers this elaborate.

Soft pearly soap filled his hand and the redolent scent of sweet peas rolled over him, the fern above him bringing an undeniably green stately presence.

Filling his lungs with hot steam, Flem let the water kiss his very soul, caressing every Sylph cell.

The cloudiness retreated. Confidence made an appearance on a far horizon as every moment washed more of his negativity down the drain. His blood woke up.

Wings stretched to their fullest, singing freedom, and he loved them like they were meant to be loved. It had been so long since he'd indulged in such gloriousness. Oh, to live like this all the time, he thought.

An image of crashing waves suddenly showed up in his mind and Flem decided he would go to the beach, and that he would have Lark drop him off at that little coffee shop first.

Pumping more soft soap into his hand, the Sylph continuously caressed his body over and over, every bare spot getting the once over many times until it seemed like a ritual, a holy ritual.

Lost in thought, he soaped and cleaned and rinsed non-stop and never even noticed when the door opened just enough to let some eyes glue themselves to the steamy enclosure that kept being streaked by something from inside, brushing across them.

Wings, big, beautiful, almost transparent wings.

The faerie was oblivious.

Lark had seen enough and went to make a phone call.

Twenty minutes later, Flem pushed himsylph out from under the water and turned it off.

Dripping heavily, the sodden Sylph started toweling off, looking around. It was a good size bathroom and pretty light since two walls were translucent glass.

Three shelves lined the wall to his left, which was one big mirror. Myriads of baskets stood at different angles on each of the shelves, several with items hanging out haphazardly.

Whimsey C. Nimble

Glancing towards the door, wondering if it was locked, (too late now, buddy boy!) he lay the towel on the seat and padded down to appease his curiosity, wings at half-sail behind him, tips drooping. He wanted to use a dryer on them and was happy to see his host had three. One was hung up and he could see two sticking up out of a fairly deep basket. Unable to contain his nosiness, he put out a hand to touch some colored strips that crawled over the edge of their container. Pulling one, several more came with it; made of various colors, they were soft and flexible, skinny and gel filled. Each was about a foot long and durable. Putting them back he moved on to another basket, worrying he was taking too much time but couldn't hurry. This one was also a deep basket and to his delight scarves of every shape, color, and texture filled it. Impulsively he thrust his hand in and squeezed all he could, feeling sly, as if it was some great retribution he was enacting by stealthily fondling another man's scarves...

Moving back towards the sink, he was trying to decide what to do next when a switch with the word 'dryer' above it caught his eye. Of course he had to flip it. A heat lamp in the ceiling came on and from around it warm air rushed down to engulf him. Immediately he backed up to get the full brunt of the effect. In no time at all his wings were dry.

Turning the switch off, he eyeballed the cabinet in front of him and with a quick peek over his shoulder opened it to look inside. A vast array, a predominance of sore muscle creams and ointments lined the shelves and what was that, he wondered, picking up a little double case. Opening one side, he discovered a small green dish-like thing. The color was familiar, where had he seen that color, he puzzled, and then realized it was the color of Lark's eyes. *These* were his green eyes? He wondered what color they really were.

Deciding it would be a good thing not to dally any longer, he quickly finished drying himsylph off and then proceeded to clean up the bathroom, hanging the towel up, retrieving his inside-out clothing and his wing ties.

Another basket held combs and the Sylph chose a big blue-toothed one to run speedily through his own damp curls before furling and then pulling his wings over to tie firmly in place.

Wrinkling his nose, he donned yesterday's clothes, shades of heavy hangover seeming to invade him simultaneously. Feeling his true nature come out he longed for clean clothing.

Straightening his bed, he adjusted his scarf around his neck hoping his disguise was not apparent. It occurred to him he must be in the master bedroom which meant Lark had given him his room. He wasn't even going to think about that now, he would tuck it away for some evening when he had nothing else to do.

Gathering up his pack and the, ah, dirty glass, he unzipped the top and thrust the dang thing into the hole, no visible reminder of just *why* he was here, anyway.

Hand on knob, he paused and took a deep breath, a faerie reborn, before opening it quickly and stepping through, something he dreaded whole heartedly. He did not want to be reminded of his sad lack of control last night and every moment more that he stayed here screamed it at him. He wondered what Lark would say.

Making his way down the hallway, he glimpsed two more bedrooms, another bath and here he was at the kitchen.

Laying aside some recipe cards, his green-eyed host smiled warmly and innocently at him as if Flem were actually a good friend invited to spend the weekend, rather than the intruder he felt himsylph to be.

"Tea?" Lark asked brightly.

"Oh yes, tea. Thank you," replied the faerie.

"Sit," invited Lark, waving him to a place at his table as he rose to turn off the simmering kettle.

Awkwardly, Flem slid onto a chair, his demeanor eroding rapidly to his old social-misfit persona, feeling so terribly inferior, a feeling he'd thought he'd overcome recently. Where was the new suave Sylph he'd been cultivating?

"So, how's it going?" Lark asked inanely.

Flem just nodded his head, ignoring the banality of the remark, trying to smile. "Great place. It's beautiful." He glanced around to show the other what he meant, feeling more like a dolt by the minute.

Lark held his eyes and Flem had a fleeting moment of panic and thought oh no, here it comes! flinching in preparation.

"Where do you live?" is what his adversary really said, as he handed him a cup of mint tea with two rosebuds floating in it.

The faerie looked up in surprise, as he'd been drinking mint tea with rosebuds on and off for years, "Thanks!" he said, giving his host a quizzical look.

Green Eyes merely smiled, sipping his own hot tea slowly from where he held it with both hands.

Setting his cup down, he stood and turned to the counter behind him, transferring delectable items to a large platter on the table at which Flem sat.

"I'm a baker," he stated. "Have you found a new coffee shop, by the way?" His eyes twinkled as he poked a bit of soft fun at Flem.

Smiling into his mug against his will, Flem couldn't look up and shook his head to the negative. It *was* funny. At least, some day it would be. Right now it felt more like embarrassment, hysterical humiliation that made him want to dive into the cup and disappear.

"Here. Eat. Don't worry, most of the time I'm a nice guy." His host kept putting out more small bowls and containers filled with small savories.

The faerie looked on in astonishment at the array of finger foods present, experiencing a strange sort of déjà vu as if he was transported to a Sylph gathering back in the canyon.

Lark slid into place, hovering over the selection, dipping into the hazel nuts and sultans, throwing them into his mouth before moving on to the fresh raspberries. Green pumpkin seeds were next.

"Help yourself. Here." He handed a plate to his guest filled with freshly made sweet rolls. "I made these this morning."

Even with last night's indulgence permeating his pores, his mouth still watered. Reaching out, the faerie pulled off a soft fragrant piece of heaven that Lark held out and placed it on the plate his host had set in front of him. Taking a bite, he closed his eyes in appreciation, and then opened them as he recognized a familiar flavor. It was so incongruous, he couldn't believe it. "What is that you've sprinkled on top?" he asked disbelieving.

"Oh! Candied violet leaves, one of my favorite things. Do you like them too? It's a specialty item, I can't get them from my regular supplier but luckily I have another source." He smiled blandly.

The juices were flowing now and Flem filled his plate, taking another of the proffered sweet rolls, a new food to him, licking his lips. He hoped he wasn't overdoing it, and that it wouldn't make him sick later, after all that mead.

As he joined Lark in the simple ritual of eating together, drinking mint rosebud tea and eating candied violet leaves, for Pan's sake, the Sylph relaxed.

This guy really knew how to live. And the mint tea appeared to be soothing his system.

"I'm sorry," he blurted, "I'm sorry for being such a ninny hammer at the shop the other day. *Your* shop. I'm, well, I'm new here, San Francoa, and I'm, um, getting better everyday, but, well, sometimes my life is a little more, ah, *stressful* than I'd like it to be." Flem finally smiled sincerely for the first time and then said, "*Thank you.* You've been really nice to me."

The baker in black stopped chewing, swallowed, and gave Flem his undivided attention. "You're welcome." His eyes bore into the Sylph's for a moment and Flem got the feeling there was something else the man wanted to say but instead he looked away, offering his guest another dish, this time of dried cherries.

Flem stared, sensing a mystery but his logical mind pushed it away and he spoke up with "Hey, can you drop me at Canterbury's? It's a-"

"I know Canterbury's. I'll be supplying them with kolaches and apple bread," broke in Lark with a smile. "What, you don't like what I have to offer, so you're going to a *real* restaurant?" he continued grinning mischievously.

"No! No, that's not –" but before he could finish his denial, Lark held up a hand, saying,

"Hey, don't worry about it, I was just kidding. I'll drop you wherever you want, even *home*." Here he shot the faerie a sideways question before adding, "I have to run by the bakery anyway."

Thirty minutes later Flem watched as Lark's car disappeared down the street. Waiting a extra couple of minutes, the Sylph loitered on the sidewalk in front of Canterbury's, pretending to read headlines through the dim glass in a newspaper stand. After a couple of minutes he headed west, lost in thought.

Chapter 16

⚜

The fair was over, the weekend done.

𝒜FTER SUCH A memorable twenty-four hours, the faerie had been left in rather a daze. It wasn't until late that same afternoon after he woke up from a nap far down on the beach that he finally remembered he had told Mayapple he would meet her again at the fair. A gut wrenching feeling of remorse swept over him.

Magnificent long breakers crashed off to his left, the sky above ablaze with the fire of the setting sun.

The fair was over, the weekend done.

Monday lurked uncomfortably close, like a hungry relative. Dread took up residence in the pit of his stomach, shoving over the last dregs of hangover queasiness to sit side by side.

He knew he was in for it for standing her up. Cha. Just one more weight to bear. It was hard to see the positive side of this as his tumultuous emotions seemed to drive his wits with little regard for rationality. He also knew that drinking too much the night before was having an effect on his ability to see things in a positive light but it didn't make him feel any better. It seemed emotions just wouldn't follow directions. What would it take to get his life under control, one that was on more of an even-keel, he wondered. He was tired of always messing things up. For what seemed to be the millionth time, he resolved to get it together.

Chapter 17

Meow?

WALKING BRISKLY UP to Fletcherman's Nursery, Flem slipped in the front door. He didn't think his nervousness showed. Inside, his heart was fluttering, gearing him up for panic, run! Gulping a deep breath he strode on, smiling at Ginger who was behind the check out counter as he went by but not slowing down. His mind kept reminding himsylph that all was in good shape in his world, and it actually was but he abhorred confrontation, he got too out of control sometimes and was embarrassed later. So he avoided it like the sticky nits and didn't go there. He really liked Mayapple but he also knew she had an unexpected, explosive, opinionated side and it was this that he knew he would have to get through in order to just get back to being friends. At least, that's what he had built up in his head as his nerves got the better of him. Oh why had he drank all that mead Saturday night? He really needed to work on his sylphcontrol. If he hadn't of been so greedy he wouldn't be in the mess he was in now.

But there was a little unacknowledged dim spot that waited to shine: Lark. Lark terrified him, intimidated him with his new benevolence and offer of friendship? That was really a big part of the catalyst fueling his over-the-edge dread that was galloping around in his head as he headed for the time clock. And Mayapple!

A low groan escaped on a deeply expelled sigh.

The Sylph blinked hard, running his fingers through his hair as he came to a halt in the employee area.

"Good morning Flem. Did you and Mayapple have a good time? Did you go both days? We did." A pretty blush brightened Iris Fletcherman's eyes as she smiled at him referring to their encounter on Saturday at the fair.

117

Whimsey C. Nimble

Her casual friendliness immediately distilled some of the faerie's angst before sharpening his ears at what he heard next: "Mayapple won't be in today, she called me this morning." No further explanation followed. As this piece of unexpected but gratefully accepted piece of news sank in, Flem's dark mood lifted and he felt better, his guilt temporarily banished.

Iris continued, "I don't have another person to spare so anything you can do to speed up the process with the baskets would sure be appreciated. I need to stay on schedule with that delivery if at all possible. I would help you but I've got an appointment across the Bridge (referring to the biggest one, the one not too far from the northern edge of Sycamore Park and not the three over the river) and I'll be out until later today. Do you think you'll be okay alone?" she asked hopefully.

From blackest despair to cloud hopping, Flem rode the wave, convinced *this* was the real him and despair would never darken his mood again. Confidence and assurance swelled his chest as he assured her he was the man for the job.

At his immediate avowal, she then said, "Good. I was counting on you to say that. What are you working on?"

Taken aback at having to think quick he nonetheless was the faerie for the job and hastily outlined what he was going to do, Sylph adrenalin spiking in apprehension.

Nodding approval as she listened, Iris smiled and said, "Looks like I have nothing to worry about. Okay, I'll see you later," and tuned to have a few words with the other employees before she left for the day.

Flem wondered where she was going but soon forgot her as he started planning his day, happy to be on his own and nobody to tell him what to do, watch over his shoulder, tease him, or, even talk to him. His mood dampened a little as he remembered Mayapple, *Mayapple* his friend, not just someone who was going to yell at him. He wondered how come she wasn't coming in and if she was sick. Catching a glimpse of his boss in the distance, he saw her pause near Lily on the way out the door and impulsively, ran up and stood beside her, waiting.

She finished and looked at him expectantly.

"Is Mayapple okay?" he blurted.

"She said she's sick," announced Iris dryly.

Flem stood awkwardly for another moment and then fled, saying "Okay, thanks. Have a good day."

Iris stared at his retreating back a moment then turned back to her cashier and said goodbye.

Slowing to muse, he walked back to the planting shed, thinking of the prospect of putting baskets together by himsylph. Going over Iris's words, the phrase 'anything you can do to speed up the process would sure be appreciated' rang out and he gave pause to that thought, rolling it around to see how it fit.

The first thing he did was go to Mayapple's personal drawer and blatantly rifle through her tea collection she kept stashed here at work. His herb teas had their special niche but after that chai latte, wow, he wanted to see if Mayapple had any with, what did she call it, caffeine? A quick perusal and he guessed that something called The Morning Glories black tea would do the trick. It did not say caffeine free on it as so many of the others did.

Ten minutes later Flem's blood was urging him to move and he set the cup down regretfully, heading off to get a wagon to fill with supplies.

Making the journey around the outskirts of the three greenhouses, he came to the wagon yard, deciding impulsively to take two. It would be awkward but he figured it would save time in the long run as he was resolved to get two done by lunch, and that meant top speed if he was actually to make twice the normal amount.

Glancing over, his eye caught on an out of place movement in the tall grass near the dilapidated old green house. His eyes sharpened as they zeroed in and his curiosity shot up. There was something *in* the grass. Stealthily, he crept closer, never taking his eyes off the location.

Creeping up slowly, he peered intently to see a small black and white kitten seriously trying to catch a small blue butterfly that kept landing in different spots around him, ignoring the thrust of small but sharp and deadly paws.

Flem watched, fascinated. Pet birds were common to many of the Sylph race but never caged, what with living in the woods and such, but never a cat. He had never been this close to one before, although he had seen strays in the Park.

Work forgotten, he stood with his hands behind his back, captivated. Bending over, he put a hesitant finger on the creature's head, reveling in the downy softness.

Whimsey C. Nimble

Immediately tiny eyes looked up at him, pushing against his finger instinctively, then changed its mind, hissed like it was ferocious and ran off down the path towards the old structure, disappearing inside.

Unable to resist, Flem followed, trying to figure out where it went.

Looking around, his eyes fell on the two carts but he barely gave them a second thought, caffeine pushing him on. He wanted to see where that itty bitty cat went. Did he live here, he wondered. Besides, snicker snicker, the boss was gone! And no Mayapple. He'd never have a better chance.

"Hi kitty cat, where are you?" he sang in a silly Sylph singsong voice, wondering at this new side of himsylph but he couldn't stop.

Stepping high through dry grass he aimed for a broken window and after removing some threatening splinters, hauled himsylph up and over, landing inside. The remnants of a former life greeted him and he wondered how come the Fletchermans had never cleaned it up. The other three greenhouses were modern, solid, and organized. This place was a mess.

Hands on hips he looked around, his head jerking at a blur that came into sight for a moment between piles of rubbish. Stepping carefully he started picking up old brittle planters, tossing them to one spot as he maneuvered to the last sighting. Picking up a cracked crate, he almost dropped it again at the sight that befell his eyes – momma cat lay nursing her six babies that were just a few weeks old but looking like little miniature cats, including the rogue who'd been outside exploring. Twenty four pussy paws pulled and pushed as they kneaded her soft tummy.

At the unexpected sight of the faerie, momma jerked away as if to flee, with milky kitten mouths popping loose, protests forming but the Sylph started talking to her softly and she flopped back down, purring, looking up at him with limpid trusting eyes, as if to say, isn't this glorious? Aren't I wonderful?

His heart was stolen.

What a fabulous discovery, he felt like The Great Protector, instantly resolving to do all he could for them.

Rummaging in his pockets he came up with bits of dried cheese and lint, easing them down in front of the working mother, who gratefully sniffed them and then noisily ate the tidbits of cheese, purring as if it were the most delicious food she'd ever had.

Finishing their meal at about the same time as their parent five kittens snuggled in, curling to go to sleep. Kitten number six however proceeded to give himself a bath, eyeing Flem with a doubtful look every now and then.

Flem never moved, enchanted with this pocket of life before him.

Braving it, he reached down and his long fingers easily wrapped around the little black and white body and he brought it up close to his chest, where the raspy tongue cleaned a spot on his fingers briefly before curling into a ball and closing its eyes.

"Flem?" a voice was heard far away. It came again, interspersed with a low murmur, as if two people were talking. "Flem, are you back here somewhere?" came faintly before the same voice went on, "C'mon. I know where the annuals are, I'll show you but I'll need to keep an eye on the front register."

Cha! What was he doing? He was at *work*.

Nonetheless, it didn't change the fact he had a baby sleeping cat in his hands. Carefully he set the smidgeon of felinity back down, nestling it in with the others, assuring momma he would be back as she raised a sleepy look at him.

Moving slowly he deliberately placed the crate back into position, giving them shelter from any prying eyes, backing away.

Minutes later he was lurking to see if anyone else was about, and since the coast was clear, loped back to his discarded garden carts. Grabbing the handles, he got back on track, composing himsylph as if no time had lapsed.

Soon he was deep among lysimachia, alyssum, and petunias, flying in fact, grunting as he tried to hurry, pulling two heavily laden carts back to the potting area.

He realized belatedly that he should have soaked the moss before he took off. Well, no matter. He'd do it now. Filling the two big pails, he got to work, donning a face mask and a pair of gloves. Minutes later he had the two containers full to the brim of water packed moss which he carefully set nearby.

It occurred to him he could go back and check on the cats as soon as he had two baskets made and take his lunch break back there. This incentive added more fire to his determination to get the normal amount of baskets done so that Iris Fletcherman wouldn't fall behind in her schedule.

Brimming with goodwill and a righteous attitude, the faire found depths of focus he never knew he had, working intensely, nimble fingers packing and soaking and placing roots just so.

Whimsey C. Nimble

Three and a half hours later he was a mess, his work area was filthy and the floor downright muddy but there was pride in his soul as he swiped his arm over his forehead, looking at where two completed baskets now hung.

It was time for his well deserved lunch break, just as soon as he cleaned up.

Things were neat and tidy in no time. Gathering his pack, he passed Lily who was putting out various watering cans on a shelf.

She shyly looked at him, called "Hi Flem!" really quickly and side stepped to the other side of the barrier, no longer in sight.

"Hi Lily," called the Sylph back. Smiling to himsylph, the pleasant realization dawned on him the Lily had just acted as if she *liked* him. His chest filled with oxygen and happiness bubbles. Smiling even more, he resolved, and this time *he meant it*, to not drink too much any more. He could have *one*.

The sun shone brightly in the salty marine air with a few clouds far overhead. Cats! Pan, it was just so exciting he thought. Who knew! His heart picked up as he neared the old greenhouse and he eased himsylph over the edge of the broken sill and padded softly towards his family of cats.

Quietly but firmly he lifted the old crate, holding it aloft to look inside.

His eyes widened, his mouth forming a moue and he looked wildly around. No cats.

"Helloooo?" he called softly, ignoring the threat of disappointed tears that embarrassingly were forming over his eyes when a "Meow?" came from the ethers.

Swallowing, Flem carefully replaced the box he held.

Eyes searched every dirty nook and cobwebby corner.

"Erough?" came again and the fae Sylph's ears traced the sound to a corner in the back.

Picking his way around he soon knelt by the new nest where momma had moved her family.

Digging into his pack, his hurried fingers unearthed all the tidbits that comprised his lunch and offered the queen her choice if she so desired. The little ones were quite taken with their visitor and all six came to visit with his person, much to his astonishment.

Kittens climbed on him, their own faerie mountain. They had no respect for scarves or wings under pressure and pranced assertively around his head and over his 'deformity.' He giggled to himsylph, never before experiencing such heady adoration. He was putty in their paws.

"Meow?" came the question and momma wanted to know if this was all he had? She was *hungry*, she couldn't eat flowers, seeds and nuts. "Me-ow?" she asked again, plaintively.

Flem didn't know what to do. He wondered what cats ate. Birds came suspiciously to mind and he banished the image immediately. He would go to the store right now and ask. Unfortunately, the only store he was aware of in the neighborhood was right next to where Herb's used to be…

Cha.

He didn't have time to dither so he looked her intently in the eye and promised, "I'll be back. But it might not be 'til dinner time, so hang in there." A tentative touch to her ears soon found her whole head being stroked as she danced around his questing fingers, arching her back as if to say, please, feel free, pet me as much as you like.

Finally withdrawing his hand through sheer will power, he stood up, promised again he'd be back and scurried out the way he'd come in.

Striding back through the grounds, Flem gave in and sprinted down the driveway, resolving to be calm, cool, no matter who he ran into and to stop and think before he blundered into anything. Perhaps this is a sign of maturity, he thought solemnly to himsylph as he glided and hurried and almost ran around the other sidewalk patrons. He felt great. He had a project, a purpose, a mission, a reason to live!

"Oh Cha Flemmy, now you're being overly dramatic. Reason to live?" he chattered to himsylph to keep his nerves at bay.

Nonetheless, his life had taken on more meaning and it lead directly back to the, *his*, cat family.

And, he reflected, he had lots of good things happening right now. Again he resolved to NOT drink too much. He was turning over a new leaf.

Slowing, he looked up at the Blackberry Bakery next door first and then walked resolutely into the small neighborhood market right next to it.

Chapter 18

---❈---

The Sylph's head jerked like a mutinous
puppeteer's revenge.

*J*UST AS THE door closed behind him, it opened again rapidly and Lark
Spurastic took a step, reached in and poked Flem's shoulder. "Hey!"
was all he said.

Flem's head swiveled around, his Sylph adrenalin spiked and he wondered if he would ever get over his shyness around strangers.

"I've got to get back, I'm there all alone but come by after you're done
here, why don't you? I've got raspberry tarts, you can have one. I know you
like raspberries," he smiled enticingly at the tall fae young man with the
nervous hazel eyes.

Flem stared but soon his sylphconfidence rose to meet the occasion and
it felt good to say yes. He nodded his acceptance.

That little dim awareness of Lark Spurastic was beginning to grow
brighter. And he sure was a snappy dresser!

Flem turned back and quickly perused shelves 'til he found pet food and
bought two cans of Simply Super Sardines.

Retracing his steps he pushed himsylph to hurry and carefully opened
the door of the Blackberry Bakery, squashing the trepidation that seized him
like sharp-toed talons.

Lark smiled and raised his eyebrows at him for a moment from where
he was talking with a customer, wiping his hands on the white half-apron he
wore over his black pants.

The smell of fresh baking permeated the air, fat calories floating free.
Flem's mouth watered.

Clutching the two cans of cat food, his eyes roamed the interior. Breads were lined up, each with a little placard in front of it: Whole Wheat with Walnuts, Poppy Seed, Sunflower Seed, Sweet Apricot Pecan, Sesame Crunch Crust, Rosemary Sourdough. A big twisted flat loaf held filling of some kind and Flem leaned over to read, 'Apple Bread.' Raisins could be seen dotting the ocean of cooked fruit and Flem thought he smelled a hint of nutmeg. Mr. Spurastic sure was talented. On the opposite wall tarts and kolaches lined up, and Flem looked longingly at them. He hadn't had a kolache since a rare visit to Aunt Milla's back when he was a mere Sylphette, at least a hundred years ago. He recognized what he thought was lemon and raspberry and of course, the famous blackberry. But a dark shiny brown filling looked unfamiliar. He made a note to ask Lark about it. Apparently the neighborhood appreciated a baker in their midst as there were plenty of empty baskets with nothing left but crumbs.

In point of fact another customer came in and Flem waited.

An apologetic eyebrow twitch came his way and he smiled back but really, he had to get back to work.

What seemed like a march of a thousand little ants suddenly ran around his belly, making his skin prickle.

He was beginning to realize he'd had no lunch and that tea of Mayapple's was beginning to wear really thin, making him rather jumpy and irritable. He resolved to *not* get out of control. He just needed to eat a little something.

CHA, when *was* he going to be done *talking*? Flem's nerves flared up and he gritted his back teeth, trying to take his mind off waiting, for Lark, in his bakery.

A poster on this side of the front counter suddenly caught his eye, his impatience arrested and deflated temporarily. He had to read it about three times before the words started to make sense. 'Revelry With Cybele' it said in bright blue iridescent letters, 'Special Guest Stars, the Corybants!' Evidently it was some kind of event, music or perhaps a play, Flem couldn't figure it out. Silhouettes of wild gyrating dancers leaped and sprang, shouting energy from all over the page. It gave a date about two weeks hence.

The last customer left and Lark followed her, whipping over the 'back in 5 minutes' sign and locking the door behind him.

"I just wanted to say hello. Here,' he reached to the nearby shelf and brought out two tarts, a raspberry and a blackberry, wrapped them in white crinkly paper, then slid them into a smooth and shiny pink paper bag, which he handed to Flem after folding over the top in a crisp crease.

Flem's nervous irritation turned instead towards empty headed giddiness.

"Hey, c'mon back here for a minute," Lark invited, taking off his apron and hanging it up.

Following him hesitantly, Flem watched Lark open a square stainless steel refrigerator and pull out some dainty sandwiches along with a pitcher of iced herbal tea and set them on the counter of a high wooden island.

Grabbing a couple of glasses, Lark poured and handed one to his guest. "Here, eat. I bet you haven't eaten today, have you? I always make a few sandwiches early on so I can grab a quick bite when I have the chance."

The sense of déjà vu was overwhelming, and he was drooling again. This was the second time in two days this man had fed him. It was so good and so unusual it made him very wary. It also humbled and touched him and as he looked up and opened his mouth to express gratitude he saw that Lark's head was bent down and instead, *he* started talking.

With a jolt, it occurred to the faerie that this man, this snappy dresser who drove a car and owned a bakery, who had seen *him* at his worst, was a bit shy himself. It floored him.

A strange sense of power ran through his veins, but it was a power of himsylph, the confidence that he was really, just another living soul and everyone should treat each other like this.

Now that he reflected on it, *this* was really Sylph style, at least when one was still a Sylph, which I am, he thought, just not female at the moment. It was plain kindness and acceptance. Like Mayapple. He wondered if all young human females were like her. He just loved her, he realized. She was a sister.

"...so, Flem?"

The Sylph's head jerked like a mutinous puppeteer's revenge. Oh Pan! He had to curb this habit of daydreaming!

Work screamed at him.

"What?" he reacted sharply, "I've got to go," he added breathlessly, wishing he'd paid more attention since he'd only gotten to swallow two bites worth.

"Okay, okay you can tell me later, I'll stop by. What time do you get off?" asked Lark, green eyes intent, rising from his stool.

"Tell you later?" echoed the faire, momentarily nonplussed. "What are you talking about?"

Shaking his head with amusement, it appeared Lark just figured Flem was being funny and nodded at the cat food in his hand, questioning "You've got a cat, huh? I've never had one, I'm used to birds."

Flem stared but then momma cat flashed through his mind and he forgot all else. He looked distractedly around, a wild panic showing its face for a mere nanosecond. Lark took the hint and quickly escorted his guest to the door, saying, "So, can I come by when you get off work?"

"Sure!" Flem responded a little too brightly, not very happy by this prospect, although he should be, he knew.

"Well?"

"Well what?" the faerie was reaching for the doorknob and it was obvious he was starting to get crazed, so Lark quickly said, "Well, what *time* do you get off?"

A flash of suppressed irritation rolled up the faerie's back and he could feel it on the backs of his legs. How was he going to feed his cat family if Lark was there?

Lark watched impassively at the visible tightening occurring over the man's frame.

"Is there a problem?" he finally asked.

"No! I get off at six." Who are you, he asked himsylph as he agreed to go into unknown territory.

"Good. Think about going to Revelry with me a week from Friday, okay? I went last year and it was great! Okay, see you later, enjoy your tarts."

Flem wasn't really hearing him, befuddled as he was with his perceived lateness, the cats, *Lark*, and a full fledged spasm was lurking dangerously close. He also knew drinking caffeine and not eating was something he should not do again. Eating those two bites of miniature sandwiches was just not enough and his insides were jumpy, tying themsylves in knots. Finally he was out the door and racing back to work.

Sliding in, he realized he was five minutes late and who should be waiting there for him but Mayapple.

"*There* you are. Where have you been, you look kind of guilty. What's the matter, are you late? Don't worry, I'll fix it. Why do you have cat food in your hands? Is there a cat here? Oh my God, *where?*" she exclaimed all in one breath, not missing a thing, as usual.

Flem groaned. How had his life gotten so complicated? But really, he was enjoying it, he knew; his life had never been so full.

Not letting her barrage affect him he turned the tables and fired back, "Where were *you* this morning? You don't look very sick to me."

"Oh, I didn't feel good, honest," but she put on such an innocent face, Flem was suspect.

"Ooh, and where were YOU yesterday? Weren't we suppose to *meet* on Sunday, Mr. Green, or did I misunderstand? Man, I looked everywhere for you! I did not go to your *house*, however." This last was said defiantly but also to let him know his secret was safe with her, even though she was really mad.

"Well," he said, drooping ever so slightly, "it's a long story. I'm so sorry! Don't be mad. I'll tell you about it sometime, just not now, okay?" he appealed with a hopeful look in his eye.

Mayapple was quiet, her fingers brushing back and forth along her lips as she looked at him, thinking.

Finally she softened, linked her arm in his and said, "Cat food?"

Before answering, he asked, "Are you staying to work, or are you merely here to harass me?"

"I'm here to work AND to harass you. Hey, I saw you got two done by yourself this morning, how'd you do that, Speedy?"

"Oh. Heh heh. I drank some tea. I think it must have had caffeine in it. I hope that was okay?"

"Yeah sure. You know Flem, caffeine might not be such a good idea-"

But Flem broke in with, "I know. *Not* a good idea. Well, good at first, but-"

"Yessss," she finished for him and they both laughed.

"Cat food?" she prompted.

"Wait 'til you see!" gushed the faerie, suddenly thrilled to have someone to share the news with. "C'mon," and he took off, Mayapple in tow.

Minutes later the faerie and the human knelt by the nest and watched as the mother cat greedily gulped down a can of cat food that Flem had dumped on an old piece of plastic. Kittens abounded, two trying to eat like their parent but who kept sneezing and shaking their heads at this strange new substance, three who were up a plank playing with one another and one, a rogue, who came to investigate the visitors.

Purring like a miniature tug boat, the black and white ball of fluff stopped and batted at Flem's toes until it was just worn out and sat down directly on top of his foot.

"Looks like we know which one belongs to you," crowed Mayapple. "What are you going to name him?"

Flem hadn't got past the enormity of the whole cat family yet to be able to think of one just for him. In a way, they were *all* his. Carefully he dislodged the bump on his shoe, setting it gently back with its mother, grinning uninhibitedly into his companion's face.

Mayapple's teeth gleamed as she laughed with him in delight.

"C'mon Speedo, why don't you show me just how fast you can go this afternoon?"

Leaving a satiated momma cat, they picked their way back to the potting area, a comfortable silence between them.

Getting in the groove, Flem set to with a vengeance, determined to shine as a productive employee, quietly assuming that the more he accomplished, the better the odds were of there being no problem with cats on the premises.

Six o'clock rolled around bringing Bud in. Nodding politely to Flem, he tactfully said nothing about his obvious absence at the fair yesterday and was immediately snared into conversation with Mayapple, who pumped him with questions regarding his jewelry business.

A prickle of jealously snaked through the Sylph's blood but Bud was such a likable guy that Flem relaxed, especially after Mayapple caught his eye and gave him a quick conspiratorial wink before turning back to Bud.

"Um, I'll see you tomorrow, Mayapple, Bud," the faerie put forth hesitantly. "Will you be here in the morning?" he asked of the girl, mostly to just get a rise out of her.

Making eyes at him, she drolly replied, "Yes."

Grinning, he slung his pack over his shoulder, adjusted his scarf, and headed out back.

"Hey, wrong way!" jokingly called Bud, as he went on about his business of moving the two completed baskets out of the way, leaving the ones just made right where they hung.

"Oh, well, yeah, I ah, need to check on something," he stammered and stumbled, not sure if it was okay to tell everybody about his find. Not really wanting to.

"Meow," was Mayapple's only contribution.

He flashed his eyes at her and escaped with no thought what-so-ever of Lark saying he'd be by when Flem got off work.

Hurrying, he practically hopped from rock to rock on his way to the old greenhouse. Mead was also something else he gave absolutely no thought to. He was too busy living.

Chapter 19

—✦—

"Oh, you boys." This was accompanied with a
warm look and it suddenly came to Flem that
Iris Fletcherman had been drinking.

SLIDING THROUGH THE window, he hurried towards the back and around
the corner, his eyes searching and was rewarded with glimpses of moving fur in a couple of places.

Dusting his hands off, he starting calling hello, hello, as he walked towards them. Momma cat immediately came to greet him, twining herself
around his legs, youngsters tumbling behind.

Flem's heart soared. Who knew.

Pushing aside some debris, he sat, opened his pack and pulled out the
other can, dumping it where the other one had been and this time all the kittens leaped on it along with their mother, again with much sneezing, spitting,
and head shaking.

Looking around, the faerie had a strong urge to clean up the place. Pan,
there was nothing waiting for him at home. He could stay as late as he wanted, he'd just catch a later bus. Standing up he started organizing bit by bit
just around him, keeping an eye on the whirling cat energy that seemed to
surround the family.

Methodically he concentrated on only the broken pots, taking them by
the armful and dumping them out a back window, shaking each one out first
and starting a mound of old dirt just outside the stuck back door.

In no time at all there were no more pots in the immediate vicinity.

Feeling a sense of quiet sylphsatisfaction, he barely paid any attention
to a tinkle of Mayapple's laughter as it floated out somewhere down by number one but then faded. Sleepy cats spilled around his feet and momma sat

washing her chest and anytime a kitten got close, she washed its face and ears thoroughly too.

Moving back to sit down, the faerie leaned back on his elbows, sharing the afterglow of dinner and made himsylph right at home, one of them.

Momma cat got up and with a questioning "Mrr?" which must have been rhetorical as she did not wait for an answer, instead climbed onto his lap and proceeded to try and clean her own face by licking a paw and then scrubbing it over her eyes and ears. Bath time was apparently very important.

Flem flashed on his own wings and how rarely they got the attention they deserved but quickly shoved the guilty thought aside and went on thinking fondly of Mayapple. She was such a boon to his heart. He wondered what he could do for her to show his appreciation.

Meanwhile momma cat settled in, assuming the Sylph was her bed for the night. The rumble coming from her chest vibrated all the way to Flem's bones, his wings absorbing the joy and contentment she radiated.

Kittens tucked themselves around and between his legs, obviously preparing to spend the night.

Youngsters asleep, momma cat couldn't quite finish her washing, trying valiantly to get as close as possible beneath her own chin.

Bending over it was with pure instinct that the faerie's raspy tongue came out and started cleaning where poor momma's tongue just wouldn't reach.

Arching into it, the cat stilled, holding herself in place, purring louder and louder 'til his whole head buzzed with the reverberation.

Closing his eyes, his hands simultaneously came around her and he started kneading softly, running scratching fingers up and down her spine, licking her upper chest for her.

So fully engrossed in this act of love, Flem never saw Lark, Mayapple, or Bud standing outside looking in, watching, not saying a word, each wondering how the others were going to react.

As of one mind, all respectfully backed up as quietly as possible, retracing their steps with much deliberation. As they neared number two, Bud broke the awkward silence by cracking, "Likes cats, huh?"

Ducking inside, all three let loose with muffled hilarity.

"Okay, not a word you two!" hiccupped Mayapple, looking out for Flem's best interest as usual. "You did not see that."

"Do you think he'll get hair balls?" gasped Lark, and the three of them fell to pieces once again, tears in their eyes from laughing at the absurdity.

After everyone had settled down, Bud asked, "Did you see who's in town?" and while he was ostensibly talking to both Mayapple and Lark it was really Lark he was asking.

"Yes! Revelry! A week from Friday. I told Flem about it this morning when he came by at noon, to buy cat food, I guess," replied Lark as they all giggled and snickered at the words 'cat food.' "I don't think he heard me though, he seemed awfully distracted," he finished.

"Are you talking about Revelry with Cybele? I've never been, what's it like?" interjected Mayapple, looking from one to the other. They seemed like old friends.

"Ooh, we should all go! C'mon Lark, let's show Mayapple and Flem how to do Revelry right," urged Bud.

It wasn't quite what Lark had planned but was nonetheless a very scintillating idea. Biting his lower lip, he slowly nodded, looking first at Bud, then at Mayapple. "Okay, it's a date. Mayapple?"

"You bet! I'll talk to Flem."

It was early evening but it felt much later, thought Flem. It was probably because he'd had so little to eat today and all the excitement. Reluctance to move hampered his efforts to get up but he really needed to get going, home was still two bus rides away and the sun was definitely low in the sky.

Carefully extricating himsylph, the babies kept sleeping but momma cat gave him the eye. Feeling responsible, Flem assured her he'd be back again. That meant more food, he realized. Hmm. A sense of just how expensive this could be manifested for the first time. Nonetheless, he decided he would make it work and the firmness of his conviction surprised even him.

Gliding out the greenhouse window, feeling like an intruder, the faerie wondered who was around. The place was pretty quiet. Just then Bud came out of the main building, crossed the little path and disappeared into number one without ever looking up.

Flem stated walking again, feeling guilty just through habit. Hoping to just slide unseen out into the night, he'd almost made it when Bud called out to him from where he stood in the doorway of the greenhouse, watching the Sylph's back disappear down the driveway.

Stopping abruptly, Flem sighed. Was he never going to get home? Turning, he smiled shyly at Bud.

"Hi!" greeted Bud and seemed to be smiling just a little too much, thought Flem. Why?

"Hey," responded Flem back. "I'm out of here, see you, have a good night," hoping against hope that he would be able to just keep walking but it was not to be.

Bud was feeling chatty and kept throwing out words, like lassos around fence posts. "Do you like pizza? I just ordered one and it should be here any minute. Have you eaten?"

What was it with these people and food, wondered the faerie, starved for pizza but not entirely sure what it was. He'd seen signs advertising it but had never eaten it. Sylphs didn't eat pizza. Did they? Again, the lure of human food enticed him.

"Come in and sit down—you're off work. You don't have to get home right away, I'll bet. Stay and have pizza with me." This was said as they casually moved into the greenhouse.

Unable to resist, Flem gave in, curiosity and hunger winning over what he perceived as reasonable.

"I've got to keep working 'til the pizza arrives, then I'll take my break, okay?" Bud remarked rhetorically as he picked up a shovel and started filling the dirt bins in front of which Mayapple and Flem spent most of their day.

Flem gratefully sank onto a nearby stool, idly watching the fluid movements of his co-worker as he wondered what to say.

Before he had a chance, Bud asked "So, did you have a good time at the fair?" as if it wasn't the most loaded question in the world.

Smiling blandly even though a wave of heat flushed over him, Flem nodded rather quickly, immediately wondering just how much Bud knew.

Suddenly uncomfortable, the impulse to jump up was eliminated by the appearance of the pizza delivery person. Flem stared, trying not to.

A half smile that was pretty much a perennial expression easily highlighted the gap between his two front teeth, while on his head was a little red paper hat in the shape of a boat. His eyes were rather vacant and Flem wondered what his world was like.

Bud leaped to get his money, striding over to relieve the man of his flat hot box.

Darting a look at Flem the man immediately came back to Bud and the money being handed him, watching it being put in his hand.

Flem realized finally that the man was simply slow witted and tore his eyes away, fixing them only on Bud, trying to take a cue from his sophisticated neutral manner, as if he didn't see a thing out of the ordinary.

The man carefully removed a wallet from his back pocket, his mouth hanging open as he put the money away, turning at last to stare at Flem with large dark eyes that gave away nothing.

"Ah, thanks!" offered Flem, compelled to say *something.*

Bud immediately echoed it, walking forcefully toward the door, Mr. Pizza being swept along in his path.

Sucking on his bottom lip, the man in the too-short red pants paused in the doorway, turned back to the Sylph who was staring rudely and met his eyes without saying a word, just staring back before slipping out.

Bud hurried back, chuckling. "Whoa. He was, ah, colorful, wasn't he? That was a great uniform, especially with that hat. Maybe we should talk to Iris about doing something like that here, what do you think?"

Flem looked at Bud with disbelief and Bud choked with laughter, pushing the box towards him as he opened the top. "Here, have some," he offered, still snorting.

Gingerly, Flem lifted a string-drippin' piece out of the box as Bud dug in from the other side.

Flem's expression gave him away as they started eating and Bud laughed good naturedly, asking, "You haven't had pizza before, have you?"

Flem shook his head, shyness building.

Bud smiled and didn't say anything more, just kept eating.

Finally Flem realized all these stressful things that had been building up all day and were hounding him silently weren't really a bad as they had seemed earlier.

Relaxing, the faerie reached for another piece of warm food and was overcome with a wave of gratefulness to his co-worker for inviting him to this pizza and companionship. He had to learn to trust more, he thought, and not worry so much about everything.

"Thank you," he said, " Thank you, this was just what I needed." Shaking his head, he confessed, "Mayapple wasn't here this morning and I was here alone so I decided to have some tea of Mayapple's, the kind with caffeine in it, and well, it wore off a long time ago and I haven't had much to eat all day, and—"

"Oh, I know about caffeine," said Bud holding up his hand to prove he had experience. "I don't drink too much caffeine these days, mostly just green tea now and then- and even that's a lot sometimes." He added, "I used to be a coffee drinker, but not anymore."

Seeing Flem's blank expression, he explained, "Coffee. It has about twice the amount of caffeine that say, black tea has, and about three to four times the caffeine that green tea has. 'Course, it all depends on lots of other factors too, how long it's brewed, the conditions under which the coffee beans (which are actually seeds) were picked, and the same thing for the tea leaves." He started to say more but Flem looked so overwhelmed and lost by this information that he simply finished up with, "I drank coffee all the time when I first moved here, but that was a long time ago. Things change." He smiled enigmatically.

"Oh, you're not from here?" said Flem, surprised.

"No, let's just say I didn't fit in at home," replied Buddleia as he stood and stretched his arms up and over his head. "Hey, I've got to get back to work, but you're welcome to stay and talk if you want. I only work 'til nine, we could go and get a drink. I know a place not too far from here."

Flem flashed him an astonished look. Bud was so *perfect*, and here he was, offering a friendship gesture to *him*. He almost gasped in disbelief but instead went with trusting the universe that all was well and good, opening himsylph to change. Throwing caution to the wind, he decided he would get home when he got there. Not believing his own ears, he said, "Okay!" a little too emphatically and grinned sheepishly.

Bud nodded in approval, inviting Flem to go with him to 'play in the dirt,' as he worded it, referring to making potting soil.

The next hour passed quickly as the Sylph tagged along, Bud explaining his duties and what Iris expected of him, as they went along.

It was almost nine and Bud was just about done dumping moss into the large hanging bag, Flem holding it steady for him when Iris's voice was heard calling Bud's name.

She suddenly appeared in the doorway, smiling, relaxed, rather mussed and flushed.

"Flem! Hi! Good idea, you helping Bud. Wait. Wait. You don't work this late. How come you're still here?"

Bud overrode Flem's look of dismay with, "Hey Iris. You're sure looking pretty tonight. What are you doing here so late? Don't worry about Flem, we just got to talking and he's waiting for me. We're going around the corner to Oleander's for a quick drink. Want to come with us?"

"Oh, you boys." This was accompanied with a warm look and it suddenly came to Flem that Iris Fletcherman had been drinking. It floored him but he immediately relaxed his guard and smiled at her, exuding charm and batting his eyelashes a little more than necessary.

Bud folded his lips together, repressing a laugh as he watch Flem flirt with the owner.

"I just stopped by to pick up some papers that I forgot here this morning before we left."

Flem suddenly remembered she'd been going over the Bridge somewhere with Santolina. He hadn't given her another thought all day. Was she just getting back now, at nine o'clock at night? Looks like they stopped for dinner, Flem thought privately.

"Did you have a good day, Mrs. Fletcherman?" asked Flem in his best voice.

"Oh, call me Iris, Mr. Green." Iris giggled at the hilarity of calling him Mr. Green.

"Well, I better go," she said, waving some papers in her right hand. "Santolina's waiting in the parking lot for me." She hiccupped and rolled her eyes at the two of them who by now were standing there, grinning at their boss.

"Don't drink too much at Oleander's," she admonished. "You have to work tomorrow, and we don't want any slackers, now do we?" again laughing at her own humor as she herself tipsily made her way back up front, calling "G'night!" to Lily, who was counting money and closing down the cash register for the day.

Turning back to the giant moss dispenser, Bud gave it a final pat and shake, then closed off the cap and jumped down.

"Grab your stuff, I'm done here," advised Bud as he stuck a broad-billed cap on his head and headed for the panel of switches.

With several clicks, he turned off various systems, while activating one dripper line for the evening and motioned Flem out before him, pulling the door closed behind them.

Behind them, Lily was turning off lights and readying each room for the night. She stuck her head out the door as they walked near and said, "I'll lock up, Bud, I'm not done here yet."

"Okay! Bye. C'mon Flem." He smiled and did a quick wave at her as they headed out.

Chapter 20

Smiling guilelessly, he looked Flem right in the eye,
shrugged and said, "What does it matter, I age well."

"*I*T'S JUST AROUND the corner. I think you'll like it, it's pretty low key," chatted Bud as they walked along, a bit of chill permeating the air, sending a few pre-fog tendrils up the backs of their necks.

Flem's wings shuttered momentarily and he repressed any acknowledgement of it whatsoever, but his companion sensed it even if he didn't let on.

Most shops were closed and as they walked uphill around the corner, the tinkle of music and people talking filtered through, getting louder with their approach until there they were, Bud motioning Flem through the open door first.

As Flem looked around he realized he was in one of those delightful establishments that always appeared so inviting with its myriad of couches and hanging ferns, people milling and sipping drinks. Usually it was just him looking longingly in as he walked by.

"Flem? What do you want? It's on me. Beer? Wine? Mead? Tea? I wouldn't advise any caffeine but that's up to you."

Flem laughed along with him.

"What are you having?" he ventured, watching Bud greet people here and there while waiting for his answer.

"I like mead. They got one here called Autumn Glory that I really like. I keep trying to duplicate it but so far no luck. There must be some elusive ingredient in it that I just haven't figured out yet. Do you like mead?"

This was all said so artlessly and casual that Flem instantly assumed Bud didn't know a thing about his escapade Saturday night and Lark's house and totally missed the import of what Bud had just revealed. He wondered how good of friends they were and if Lark would tell him all about it.

A shadow passed over his face.

Was this a test, wondered the suspicious Sylph.

He looked at Bud who smiled and waited for him to make up his mind.

The bartender stood while Bud imperiously held up a finger, imploring the good man to be patient for just one more minute.

The man rolled his eyes at the ceiling, shook his head and headed down the bar to take another order.

Flem gulped.

This *was a* test, he decided, but it was one he knew how to pass. Strengthening his will, he decided to have one drink and then, go see the kitties just for a minute before finally heading home.

"Yes, I like mead. I'll have a mead," smiled the Sylph, hoping Bud wasn't going to ask him a dozen questions like everybody else was wont to do.

Before long they each had a small glass in their hand and they mutually agreed to head towards the one empty spot, a far wall where two deep armchairs sat empty, a low table between them, a candle flickering invitingly. Two empty bottles and a crumpled napkin remained from its last occupants. A waiter materialized, grabbed the debris, swiped the table, acknowledged Bud with a big smile, and left.

Bud sank into his seat, a happy smile on his face, and said, "I don't stay long but I like to grab a mead sometimes before I head home, after work."

Flem smiled.

"How do you like San Francoa Ramosa?"

"Oh, it's okay I guess. It's better now that I have a job. How long have you lived here?" returned the faerie, trying to deflect interest from himsylph.

Taking a sip, Bud replied, "A long time. Years."

Flem's was surprised which he tried to cover up but couldn't stand it and blurted "You only look like you're in your twenties. How old were you when you got here?" He knew he was being nosy and he was a bit embarrassed but Sylphs and curiosity were part and parcel.

His companion took a sip, savoring the liquor and twitched a little in his own chair.

Smiling guilelessly, he looked Flem right in the eye, shrugged and said, "What does it matter? I age well."

Flem nodded. After all, so did he.

After fifteen minutes of weather and work talk, most of their mead gone, Bud carefully worked in, "You know, this City has many secrets. I guess we all have our own. But I'm sure of one thing—I've made some good friends here over the years I've been here and secrets get easier when they're shared." He was looking past the faerie as he said this, as if he were only thinking aloud.

Flem didn't quite know what to say, it made him nervous talking about secrets. His chest got warm, his heart beat a little harder, and it was a little uncomfortable. Was Bud alluding to anything, he worried. Cha.

Momma cat flashed into his mind and he immediately drained his glass, licking his lips to savor every last drop. He was working up the courage to move on, hopefully without Bud, when an older man with a little devilish beard and salt and pepper hair that hung to his shoulders came directly to their table and commanded Bud's attention, barely acknowledging the Sylph.

Which was okay with him, he wanted to leave unnoticed but at the same time felt the man to be rather rude. He could see that Bud was fidgeting and was about to make the introductions but he was faster and eased up, motioning the man to take his seat, as he cut off anything Bud was about to interject, with, " I've got to go. Thanks for the drink. Oh, and dinner! See you tomorrow at work. Bye," and was through the crowd and out the door before Bud's new guest was even completely settled.

Ah, it felt good to be striding along in the cold but fresh air. Tucking his arms in, he covered the distance downhill back to the nursery in no time at all but it was with great dismay that he suddenly came up against great, barred, closed *gates* across Fletcherman's driveway. What?

How come he'd never seen these before, he wondered, aghast at this impediment to seeing his cats. Where the Pan had these come from? He realized too late that obviously there was always someone here before he arrived in the mornings, and he left before they closed. Duh.

Stepping back he saw where the gates rested during the day when the place was open, sliding back behind a low wall that flanked each side of the broad driveway, which in turn was hidden by espaliered thick vines, and brush.

Frustration washed over him in waves. If his *wings* weren't in hiding, he could have easily flown over but no, here he was, locked out. Grr.

He no longer cared about getting home at a decent hour, he'd get home when he got there.

It was now ten o'clock at night and the fog was condensing to coat whatever it could find, heavy, wet, muffled.

Pan, what was he suppose to do? He decided to walk the perimeter to see if there was a way in.

High walls or other buildings presented an indifferent too-high shoulder every step of the way.

After twenty minutes he was standing in the adjoining alley but no closer to getting in. Dejected, he was ready to give up and go home when a muffled "Mew?" filtered in to his ears.

"Meow?" he drawled in an excited whisper.

At that, a plaintive insistent voice spilled out into the night, telling Flem he was lost, lost, lost, and things were bad, bad, bad, and he needed some help right now AND he was hungry. He wanted his mother. Now.

Heart racing with the need to be on the inside, Flem started whispering furiously to the misplaced kitten, who kept up his demands throughout it all. "I'm coming!"

There was a woozy open-sided garage with various barrels and an old car in it along with other misshapen whatnot just ahead of him, and an idea started to form. He would climb up and go over, somehow.

Trying to be as quiet as possible, he was soon up on the creaky, unstable roof, scrambling to get over the fence but he was still too low. A dismal street light shone mutely through the fog from the far end of the alley. Flem paid no attention to it. After pacing back and forth a couple of times on top of the roof, he finally had had enough and sat down abruptly, flinging his pack to one side with a sound from deep in his throat.

"Meow?" did not help his nerves at all.

Past caring, he stripped off his human shirt, yanked the scarf next then viciously tore into his pants pocket, whipped out a little knife, cut those wretched wing bindings and shoved the blade home, practically all in one motion.

Wings that should have gone up slowly instead burst into place, tight, taut, proud, and sore. Ah well, tomorrow would take care of itself. Grinning in spite of it all, he rippled his wing scapulature, hands on hips, the world be damned.

Unable to resist, he jumped off the roof and flew down the alley, exhilaration filling every cell. Pan, he hadn't flown in months!

Months. A wave of horror washed over him at that thought, and he wondered just how he should fix that. The reason he hadn't flown was because he didn't have a place to let his wings out. Nothing had changed there and it brought his attention back to the present with a jerk.

Focusing his attention on the old garage, he swooped back to the roof to land with a jolt before striding over and bunching up the shirt, scarf and bindings into one hand, grabbed his pack to sling over a shoulder, feeling it bump into his right wing blade. It would be okay for the moment.

Without wasting any more time, he was up and over. The second his feet touched the ground, his wings furled and thanks to Mayapple's preening a while back, weren't nearly as rough as they had been, but he was due for another real soon.

"Meow?" he called, immediately scanning the wall with the garage behind it for a wayward cat.

A black and white movement rustled just before it skittered up a low tree branch and out onto a long thin branch, dark shadows hiding details.

"C'mon kitty, let's take you home." Flem easily scooped the troublemaker out of the tree and held him close to his chest as he turned but being a wild cat with no manners, the rescued feline wriggled free and made a dash for Flem's back, digging in tiny sharp nails as he went, making the faerie dance with pained surprise. Moments later he was wedged in the hollow between the Sylph's wingulacture. After shrugging and twitching and trying to get him out of there, Flem gave up, feeling like a hostage and wondering how come he'd been so *worried*...

Quietly he made his way to the greenhouse and up and over the sill to see that mamma cat was done nursing and all the other kids, except for the one between his wing blades, were sleeping. And he knew *he* wasn't sleeping because he could feel a miniature earthquake on his back, with an occasional little lick being thrown in, perhaps as a lick of gratitude? He had to laugh.

Whimsey C. Nimble

Bending down he ran his fingers over momma's silky head, and her rumble of contentment radiated out, loud and throaty. Soon he had slid down beside her, digging in a little nest of his own, wishing he had a hammock to lay in. Now that he thought about it, he *did* have an extra hammock, didn't he? Hmm. This would bear thinking more about, he thought, as he snuggled in, draping an arm over her back, fingers barely touching but offering a world of love.

It wasn't long before his furry stow-a-way crawled out to snuggle with momma but by the commanding little snap of *meow* that he threw at Flem as he exited, the faerie got a pretty good idea that he'd be back and that he, Flem, was merely to do as the cat wished. Flem marveled at such command in one so minute.

Soon all were asleep as pale foggy moonlight filtered through old green glass, casting magic fingers onto old forgotten worlds.

Lark and Bud were in Lark's car. After working late at the bakery finishing up the cleaning and prepping for early in the morning, Lark had finally turned the light off.

He was tired but curiosity was nibbling him around the fringes and he decided to just take a quick peek at Oleander's to see if Bud was there before he headed home.

Bud was, and just getting ready to leave when Lark stepped through the door.

"I'll buy. You want another Glory?" asked the man in floury black.

"You want to give me a ride home?" returned Bud.

"No problem," replied Mr. Spurastic.

Sitting back down, the two men who had been friends for years began to compare notes. Each had a tale concerning the newest member of their acquaintance, Flem Green.

It ended with much mirth regarding the cats and for some reason they were both struck with the same thought at the same time—Flem wasn't going home without visiting those cats one more time since they were just around the corner.

Quickly settling their tab, Lark threw a tip on the table and they headed out.

It didn't take long, in fact their timing was perfect.

Flem never even turned his head in their direction.

They watched from the end of the alley, first spotting his profile as he walked stoop-shouldered down the alley away from them. They watched as he scaled the low saggy garage. They watched as he transformed to his real Sylph, gave a test flight in the opposite direction and then disappearing over the edge.

All perfectly visible to anyone who happened to be looking, albeit it was murky and indistinct through the pale fog but nonetheless, easily discernable to the occupants of Lark's car in the street at the entrance to the alley.

It was a sobering sight, especially since he was taking chances now.

"We have to do something soon," Bud remarked. "I tried to tonight but I think I made him nervous."

"Yeah, I know," replied Lark. "Soon."

Chapter 21

***

Out too late, not enough sleep, and too much to drink.

$\mathscr{A}$WAKENING SLOWLY, FLEM's breath quickened, soon turning into a faint pant of apprehension. Pan. He was still at Fletcherman's and it was light out. He'd never gone home and probably couldn't now, before work. Cha.

He wondered what time it was and sat slowly up, kittens making their way over him, drawn by a hot mamma with some warm milk and a loving touch.

A faint church bell sounded off in the distance and the faerie held his breath as he counted six bongs.

He abruptly decided he *did* have time to zip home and grab some stuff for the day, maybe a clean shirt. He had three hours.

Standing up, he brushed himsylph off, momma cat catching his eye with "Meoooow?" in a very sweet polite voice and Flem realized he had no more cat food. Another stop in his short time. He'd just have to hurry more.

Stretching, he quickly bound up his wings and threw on the icky clothes, reassuring momma cat of his plan.

She seemed to agree with it but gave him an imploring look that was meant to impress him with the urgency of her hunger and his responsibility.

He assured her about his continued presence in their lives and she blinked as if she'd known it all along, but still, she needed breakfast.

Slipping over the edge of the sill, he looked up quickly once at the far door and resolved to take a look at it the next time he got back here, although he *did* like entering through the window, it lent an added little piece of adventure. He felt directed, a new clarity in his life, not one focused on 'poor me.' And, he'd only had one drink the night before, and it had been perfect. He was actually quite proud of himsylph and determined to stay on the path of true joy.

Now, how to get out of Fletcherman's so early in the morning? Adrenalin spiked as he realized he was going to brazenly strip off the clothes he'd just put back on and *fly* back over the wall to the alley! Feeling exceedingly nervous but exhilarated at the same time, he scanned a quick perimeter check from where he was standing and then listened intently for a minute or so, and everything was good. Grinning at his bravery, he headed for the wall, pulling the icky-anyway shirt off and untying his wings, only this time they came up deliberately, unfurling with a slower happiness.

Stepping back, he gazed for the most likely spot and realized he could scale the tree and actually look down the alley to see if anyone was about. No one was.

He was up, wings whirring for a moment then over in no time, landing just this side of the old garage. Quickly he resumed his human disguise and walked out of the alley, looking in the direction his bus came from. Good fortune was surely smiling on him this morning as there was actually a bus to be seen coming towards him in the distance.

In just a matter of minutes elation filled him and he smiled warmly at the driver who smiled and nodded back. The day was off to a good start. It was true that the circumstances in his life were a bit extreme right now, but it was a *good* extreme, he thought. Finally!

His first stop came none-too-soon and he waited impatiently for the second bus. It came every twenty three minutes and even though he only waited seven, it still seemed to take forever before he actually got home, ducking in his own door, closing the rock behind him.

Rather giddy over everything, his feet leaped up and did a little happy dance as he crossed the room to get a new shirt and scarf. And money. He had to buy more cat food. The only accessible coin he had was what he had stashed away to buy more mead. But he had bought mead. And what he had should last him since he was on a strict henfull a day.

Smiling, he dug into the small basket, gleaning out every bashful coin.

A thought came to him.

He could stay there, at work, again tonight. He told himsylph it was a bad idea, fraught with numerous possibilities of *why* it was a bad idea, but he DID have a spare hammock.

That's why he'd bought it, he thought delightedly, it was to stash at the Fletcherman's old greenhouse, the one that currently housed his cats, heh heh, and this way, he would always have a nook to sleep in, if so inclined…

Whimsey C. Nimble

Oh, he was so smart.

He wondered if he should stash anything else there too, and he realized that of course he should—tea, a cup, a spare set of clothes, some wing ties. Looking around this hole under the ground behind a rock that he called home, he realized that he really wasn't that attached to it. It had been a real find when he accidentally discovered it one night when he'd had too much to drink way back when, but really, he could do better, he thought, with something very akin to sylphconscious confidence. He was moving up in the world.

Food. Going through his cupboard, he nimbly folded each of six little bags into as small a parcel as he could manage, thrusting them into various pockets about his fae person.

Tea was next along with his cup and these he stuffed into his pack. Another change of clothes, a human toothbrush which he really liked, a few more wing ties, (Ah, but he had plans for possible flight tests in and around the nursery, if he happened to stay there, and who would see at two in the morning?) but STILL he would need more wing ties, unfortunately.

The cupboard across the way stood open and Flem's eyes fell on it as he realized with a jolt that he had never even thought about taking his mead. Unbelievable.

Should he take it?

He wavered. No, he decided, as old times crept in and his mouth watered for a henfull even though it was only a little after seven in the morning. He was sorely tempted for a minute but common sense finally prevailed, and he shut the open door with a small bang, proving to himsylph that he meant it.

Throwing a glance around, he was out the door, his pack awkward with the bulky hidden hammock, and waiting for the bus and its return trip all in under fifteen minutes. He was good, he was.

By the time he got back, the gates were no longer in sight and Flem cautiously slipped in, as stealthily as he could. A noise told him someone was in the main building and he practically ran by, slipping between numbers one and two greenhouses before pausing breathlessly to look around.

All was quiet.

Quickly he darted to the back, climbed in the open window and then remembered he FORGOT to buy cat food! Oh Cha, it would have to wait until noon now.

"Sorry," the sad Sylph said as he stashed all his sundries into nooks and crannies around the cat's nest. Pulling a bag open, he shook a little green into his hand, letting the cat smell it. She nosed at it, looking up at him with a questioning eye, is this IT? I can't eat *this*. "It's my catmint tea, if you like." She felt of it with her paw, pushing it around, smelling it, and finally taking a nibble. Her purr started as she tried to gracefully pick out what was edible from the chaff, and he felt a stab of responsibility go right through him. He determined that buying cat food was at the top of his list as soon as lunch time rolled around.

The busying sounds of pre-opening pricked his ears and he turned right around and stumbled back the way he'd came, wondering what time it was.

Mayapple hailed him from where she was coming up the driveway. "Hey Flem! You're here early. Here, I brought you something," and she held up a bag of cat food.

Flem's heart flipped and he grabbed her and kissed her, then hugged her again.

"Wow, you're welcome!" she laughed, digging into her own bag while they walked towards the check in area. As they got there she handed four cans to the faerie.

Mayapple.

Mayapple had brought him a bag of cat food *and* four cans. He couldn't believe it. Speechless, he looked at her, his eyes glimmering with liquid emotion.

Slapping him on the shoulder, she implored him to "Oh *stop*," and motioned him to go feed his cats.

"I'll sign you in, go—hurry up and then come back and meet me in number one, okay?" she directed.

Biting his lip, Flem took off, excited by the idea of feeding his cats and soon had an open can and some dry food set down before a most grateful momma cat.

Tidying up quickly before he left, he couldn't help himsylph and looked around, wondering about a good spot where he could unobtrusively hang his hammock. There was a little office space with bamboo walls and as his eyes fell on it he was drawn over, peeking in, seeing it as it could be. Grabbing the bulky, rolled-up hammock he pushed it into a corner and pulled some old brittle fronds in front of it, hiding it from sight. Taking a fast look back at the eating cat and her seemingly perfect kittens, he turned and hurried away, back to number one, arriving there just a few minutes before Iris Fletcherman walked in.

Flem and Mayapple exchanged quick glances.

"I see you made it to work on time, Mr. Green," commented Iris with a knowing look. "Myself, I don't feel so good," she admitted with a smile.

Mayapple looked with furrowed brow between Flem and her mother, wondering if something else was going on here that she didn't know about.

From the sort of sickly half smile that Flem gave her, she decided she was right.

"What are you talking about, Mother?" she demanded.

"Oh, we stopped by last night and I'd had some wine with dinner, that's all." She took a breath and continued, "Buddleia nicely invited me to go with him and Mr. Green here to Oleander's, wasn't it?" Her voice ended on a questioning inflective and she looked to Flem for confirmation at the name and he quickly nodded, smiling at Mayapple and mouthing the words "I'll tell you later" to her before turning back to the boss.

Feeling put out as she wasn't in on the secret and why was Flem here *last night*, anyway, Mayapple gave Flem a look that he knew meant she could easily drain every last secret he'd ever held from him if she so chose. He acquiesced to the inevitable.

In the meantime, Iris started in with some questions on where they were and what they were using and Mayapple gave it about thirty seconds before she rudely interrupted with a blanket "*Mom!*" Mayapple's intent was to get her mother out of here as fast as possible so they could get to work, and talk.

Iris darted a surprised look at her daughter and Mayapple jumped in before she said another word with, "Mom, we *know* what we're doing! It's okay, you don't have to tell us again. All right?"

Iris was annoyed at the freshness of Mayapple's tone but realized it probably *was* her and not these two who was acting odd. She should not have had four glasses of wine last night, she thought. Not enough sleep, out too late, and too much to drink. She smiled fondly at the memory and Mayapple frowned at her.

Abruptly she mumbled, "Sorry. Carry on," nodded her head at both and turned right around and headed back towards the main building without another word.

Mayapple watched her go, a look of bemusement upon her face before turning back to her partner who still had his eyes on her mother's retreating back.

Flem had a pretty good idea of what was going on, although he'd bet his nights of drinking too much and waking up with a hangover hadn't been nearly as much fun as Iris's had been, she'd had a friend there and dinner was probably included.

With an inner smile, he turned to find Mayapple staring at him.

"Oleander's?"

Briefly he filled her in on his sojourn with Bud to the bar around the corner, refraining from saying anything about cats or spending the night…

As they talked, they were both doing the dance of work, Flem prepping the moss as Mayapple impatiently waited for him so they could go collect their needed ingredients. Soon they would be ready for the blues and purples and when the purples were finished in a few days, the Bridge Baskets would be done. But Iris had that other big order for the Rec Department and the faerie wondered if Mayapple and he would be working on that too. He thought longingly of making a basket with just black-eyed susan vines, but figured he'd been here way too short a time to even ask so instead he started paying attention to what Mayapple was talking about.

"Have you ever heard of Revelry With Cybele, Flem? Lark said he mentioned it to you. Well, Bud and Lark and I were talking and they want all four of us to go together! What do you think?" Her eyes flashed with excitement.

The poster he'd seen flashed through his head and he asked, "What is it?"

"I'm not sure," she replied, her hands busy loading plants onto the cart as they talked. "It's a show of some kind. Last year was the first one and I didn't go but I sure wished I had. It got rave reviews and was sold out. Everybody was talking about it."

"Yeah sure, I'll go. You're going too, right?" he asked rather nervously, suddenly sure he absolutely would *not* go without her. In such a short amount of time, she had somehow become indispensable in his life. How had that happened?

She stopped momentarily and looked at him. "Of course I'm going! Good God, what a question." She snorted in disbelief at his obtuseness, then resumed her loading, saying, "Ready?" as she started forward, back to the planting counter.

Whimsey C. Nimble

The day passed quickly and Flem was surprised when six o'clock rolled around and Mayapple was gone in a twinkle. That was a first. He planned on sneaking back to the cats in an hour or two, *before* the gates closed at nine...

Feeling luxurious with his time, it was so novel to not have to hurry and catch the bus, he was surprised when Bud whizzed in on his bike, obviously in a hurry and it suddenly struck the faerie that he wasn't the only one to experience life's little bumps, so to speak. It was only five after, he knew there would be no repercussions but still it made him feel much more Bud's equal, him being late. Flem laughed at himsylph for such foolishness, whistling tunelessly between his teeth as he tuned the corner of the driveway and headed down the block in the opposite direction from his usual bus stop.

The sun would be much lower in an hour or so and he figured that when the time was right, he'd make for Fletcherman's. Meanwhile, he could explore. And he didn't have to buy cat food!

As he ambled down the street his curiosity was ignited by an arresting scene: a small window set behind some grill work at just about toe level, with a small neon sign rippling in rainbow colors advertising something. A neat concrete spiral set of stairs led right down to a door.

Feeling himsylph pulled in like an iron filing to a magnet, the Sylph streamed down the stairs, bursting with curiosity over such a Sylph-like charming place.

Finally he was close enough to read the sign:

RAINBOW MERKIVA
INTUITIVE & CARD READER

His hand was on the doorknob and he was in before he could think about it.

Chapter 22

Or perhaps there are no questions in your life?

WHISPERY CHANTING MUSIC filled the air and incense tantalized his nostrils. Candles flickered around the interior, interspersed with small lights of unusual shapes.

Compact overhead lighting shone down in seemingly random patterns but the faerie noticed the resultant spots illuminated specific areas which beckoned with a come- hither lure.

A woman who was older than Mayapple but younger than Iris sat behind the counter, perched on a tall stool. Her short hair was an instant eye catcher, layered in the colors of the rainbow.

What was it with women and rainbows, wondered Flem.

Large silver loops that dripped silvery delicate chains dangled from her ears and she seemed to have an indeterminate amount of layers of clothing on. And, she sported small, human-made *wings* on her back! Flem grinned in delight, noticing there were more for sale enclosed in plastic bags up the wall behind her.

As she moved her head to greet him, she passed through a small beam of light that illuminated the row of diamond studs rising up her left ear.

"Hello, welcome," she offered warmly. "Feel free to look around." She waved an arm in invitation.

"Oh. Okay. Thanks," and he quickly stepped past her towards a display built into the back wall, where a myriad of tiny bottles beckoned.

"The first one in each row is a tester, so help yourself." She smiled and looked down at the oversized cards she held, shuffling them in an absent-mindedly way.

Whimsey C. Nimble

He loved scents and immersed himsylph into scrutinizing what she offered. Never had he been around such an extensive collection. Deliberately, the faire indulged his senses, breathing deeply, feeling himsylph drifting, inhaling the essence of one in particular, a mixture of almond, amber and midnight rose one more time before turning away. Moving about the store, he came upon a rack of lavish clothing, bright extreme designs with bells and such on many. They were beautiful but one didn't see these fashions much in the everyday world.

The rainbow lady's voice interrupted his thoughts.

"Would you like a card reading?" she queried.

Flem hesitated but curiosity won out. "Sure. What's that?" he said, looking up.

"This is a deck of animal cards, each one represents a specific type of energy. When we lay them out in certain positions, they give us a message about what's going on in our lives on the subtle planes." She smiled into his eyes as she said this, before continuing, "Or perhaps there are no questions in your life?" She let this dangle with a speculative look.

"Ha!" burst out of Flem and he said "Oh yeah, everything is real clear in my life…" thinking of life at home under a rock in Sycamore Park. Thinking of his newly acquired cat family. Thinking of his friendship with Mayapple and all that that entailed. Of Lark, and the strange relationship they seemed to be forming. Of friendly and talented Bud. Of his boss Iris and her budding romance.

"What will it tell me?" he asked intently. "How will I know what it means, or if it means anything?"

She smiled a little to herself and said, "Shuffle the cards until you feel they're mixed enough then I'll tell you how to lay them out."

He nodded and awkwardly mixed the cards until she directed him to lay them all face down in a specific pattern. She then tapped one and told him to turn it over.

A bristly Wild Boar's head stared back, one with little piggy eyes and two curved tusks that grew upon each side of the long snout.

Looking at Flem, she woman widened her eyes and made a noncommittal sound deep in her throat.

"This position represents the Past. Whether it's something specific, like maybe someone getting in your face for something, or perhaps a set of circumstances you've experienced, only *you* can know. What it means is that you've had to confront some*thing* or some*one* to get to where you are today. It's about learning to confront your challenges in a warrior way, but with the *inner* warrior, not fighting it, do you see? Ideally, it represents confrontation without fear."

Oh, Flem saw. His whole life after the *change* had been one big confrontation. It was only lately that he'd found some relief from the constant angst he'd lived with for so many years. It *did* have to do with less fear, he realized. For the first time since back when he was female, he was busy living. And while the same old problems were the same old problems, they didn't seem so overwhelming as they had previously.

"Go on," he urged.

With a single nod, she pointed to the second one.

He turned it over to stare at a Lynx.

"Hmm, interesting," she muttered, almost under her breath. "This is the Present card," she continued, "what's going on right now in your life. This cat represents secrets, so I would say there must be things going on in your life that are quite unresolved and you don't have answers to some big issues, which, of course, are the 'secrets' this refers to."

Flem couldn't believe his ears. "Oh yeah, you could say that -" he spoke with a quiet voice that belied the great quiver he felt inside, hiding his own great secret.

Biting her bottom lip, the lady with the multi-colored hair looked at him intensely before tapping the third and saying "Future."

By this time he was hooked and with great care, flipped the third in the row over, revealing a beautiful white swan.

"Ahhh," breathed the woman, "perfect."

Flem waited.

"I see this as grace. It tells me that whatever secrets you carry, you will eventually find your answers and it won't be because someone gave them to you, but rather, through your own inner growth, that it will be you who finds the solutions to life's questions - by surrendering to the grace of the rhythm of the universe, a journey not unlike an ugly duckling that grows into the beautiful swan."

The faerie was dumbfounded. It was like she was pointing him in the right direction, giving him an encouraging pat on the back, and really, it was *him* that was already going that way! Oh, he felt much better about his life! It was okay to be happy. Things were changing, nothing new there, but this time was different. Things were changing for the better and it gave him a deeper confidence than he'd ever had in his life. Not only were circumstances improving but he was the one instigating and maintaining the thread; well, and Mayapple. He smiled. Whatever would he do without Mayapple? Mistily blinking, he nodded for her to go on.

She pointed to a bottom card. "This is about a set of lessons you've recently completed."

Flem turned it over to reveal a great black cat, a panther, peering out through some jungle leaves, watching all who came into his line of vision.

"Hmmph…I would say you've just taken some kind of big step, perhaps you've moved? Or gotten a new job? Something that required you to step into the unknown in order to further your life, anyway."

The faire by this time was in thrall of the magic that was springing up around him, intangible and subtle, but there was no denying it. Magic was touching him, just like the old Sylph days of long ago. And what was magic anyway, but just a change of consciousness?

A lump of gratitude started forming in his throat and he swallowed, trying to get back under control. He hadn't known what a 'reading' was before today but he saw the truth of the cards.

"Go on," he urged, smiling at her entreatingly. "Please, do go on."

"Alright, next we'll go here," she tapped a card in the top row.

The faerie smiled at the sight of a stately turkey head, wondering how exactly a *turkey* fit into the overall picture.

"Oh! Lucky you. This position reflects something that's happening right now in your life. It's the 'current' energy, so what I take that to mean is – you are going to get a gift of some kind. It may be big, it may be small, or it may be intangible, like a beautiful sunset, but turkey is the give-a-way card, and, because of the position it's in—*current* energy—I would hazard to say you'll be given something today."

"I already have!" exclaimed the delighted Sylph, thinking of all the cat food Mayapple had given him and realizing he was also being gifted *this*, this powerful, unexpected session by this very intriguing person.

Eyeing him with favor, the woman told him, "We have two positions left. The bottom right signifies our challenges, most of the time meaning our own weak spots that we carry within, but again, it could be literal, an obstacle in our way, depending on the card. Either way, it represents something working *against* us." She went on to say, "This top one," and she touched the very top left hand corner, "is what's working *for* you. So. You decide; what's next—what's working for you, or, what's working against you?"

"Let's end on a good note," he joked, and turned over the bottom right, leaving what was working *for* him, last.

A rabbit timidly looked out at him and with a sinking feeling in his belly, he thought to himsylph that he just couldn't imagine rabbit bringing him any good news. "Okay, what is it?" he asked trepidatiously.

Smiling in a reassuring way, she started with, "First of all, all these traits are really our *own* traits manifesting in our lives, and so, you could say that *fear*, which rabbit represents, in this position, is more of a universal admonishment. Of course fear is working against you, it's working against all of us! It's our own blind side to what we're doing that works against ourselves. We all have them, they're our weak spots, the lessons we have the hardest time overcoming."

Laying her hand over his momentarily, she continued, "Rabbit represents fear, the fear that someone feels when in a panic over something in the moment or, it can be, a habitual way of living, someone who worries all the time, talks about it and predicts it. Guess what? They'll call the response to that kind of energy right to them, thus fulfilling their own doom and gloom prophecy. It's so much better to *choose* to stay positive and look for meaningful resolutions. Pretend someone really wise is advising you, and let that someone be you. THAT'S what it means when it says fear is working against you. The more we let go of our fears and embrace whatever is happening in our lives in a more optimistic manner, the more we make oneness with it. The more we make oneness with it, the more we start to see that that elusive goal of happiness (also known as 'fulfilled desires') is not a place, but a path. A path highlighted by the universe, the Great Spirit, Source, whatever you want to call it and it's about recognizing we are each responsible for what we project out. We draw to ourselves what we put out. The more we call our many responses to various things by its correct name, acknowledging *fear* in its many disguises, the more effective we can be at purposefully emanating love, trust and gratitude instead. By demonstrating active love, we are encouraging wholeness and reflecting back to our Divine Source the brightest light we are capable of. I believe it's our *duty* to be as happy as possible because only in that way do we bring joy and love to our creator's heart. The only way to be truly happy is by taking that next step, whatever that may be. And to remember that growth is usually not accomplished overnight. Sometimes, most times, one must build what they want in their life, one step at a time, through conscious intent. Patience pays off."

Instead of the painful reminder of all his foibles, Flem found instead he was inspired by this sudden impassioned speech. Cha. It even fit his life and those he'd known back when he was she and lived in Thimbleberry Canyon. NOW he was starting to realize it was his own attitude and not just rotten luck working against him. If he had relaxed a little, perhaps he would have felt what he felt here, especially at Fletcherman's. It had been so long since he'd felt such support and love, and now here was this confirmation, that it was okay to be happy, to feel joy

They didn't say anything for a moment and finally Flem reached over and flipped up the last card. A large blue butterfly floated into his vision and he looked up hopefully into her face.

"Wow. Looks like you're going through some transitions and it all looks good. But it appears things have been and will continue to really change in your life. Is that true? Do you have a lot going on?" she asked, rather squinting at him for confirmation.

"Um, yes. Yes I do. A lot. But it's okay. It's good. This has been so fascinating," but before he could say more she interrupted him with, "The butterfly. The butterfly is the change a person goes through as they grow through some inner journey until they metamorphize into a fuller, deeper person, wiser for the experience. Whatever you've got going on, I would suggest you pay attention and make sure you keep your integrity about you all the time, since it appears you are in touch with a joyous, growing path. Just remember that no matter how complicated it gets, and how confusing at times it seems, that if you bear with it and do your best in whatever situation you find yourself, that eventually it will all take a step up and you will automatically arrive at a new vista, a new you, one with a bigger and more expansive, more *confiden*t understanding."

"As this right here points out," she leaned over and tapped the rabbit, "fear must be overcome and most of the time that just means *relaxing* and sending out love as the replacement."

She dipped her head momentarily and then said, "Congratulations on your hard work. Keep it up." She smiled and put out her hands in front of her in a prayerful pose saying "Namaste," inclining her head as she did so.

Instinctively, he copied her gesture, returning her bow of respect, wondering what it meant.

As if reading his question, she highlighted, "The Divine in my soul greets the Divine in yours," inclining her head in a respectful tilt.

Wishing desperately that he had some money with him, it suddenly occurred to him that he did have, he had his mead money that had been for cat food. Patting his pocket, he joyfully realized it was still in there and he could buy a bottle of scented oil.

"That was amazing. Thank you for such insight. It was so... so, *true*. I will definitely be back and you can be sure I'll bring my friends here," he said, thinking of Mayapple. "I remembered I had some money with me, so I'm going to get a bottle of," but he stopped when he saw a poster advertising 'Revelry With Cybele,' the same poster in fact that hung at Lark's. His heels came to a halt and he stared. TICKETS AVAILABLE HERE was posted right next to it.

"Oh, do you know Revelry?" the shopkeeper said sharply but there was a note of suppressed excitement hidden in her voice.

"No. Well, yes, that is, my friends (Oh Panwookiewoo, he'd just said my *friends*, and it was true. He had friends to refer to for the first time in his life since he'd been a Sylphette and still in the birthing tree!)

His wings surged against their binding and his faerie blood surged hot through his veins.

He grinned at the rainbow lady with the wings, magnanimous in the moment, and repeated, "My friends and I are going. There's four of us, Lark, Bud, Mayapple and mysylph. My name is Flem Green, I work around the corner at Fletcherman's Nursery. I believe my friends," he grinned like a slap-happy silly Sylph, "have been to the event last year. I have not gone yet. We are all going next Friday night, I believe." And he grinned some more.

Smiling prettily, the woman returned his nicety with, "My name is the same as on the shingle out front, Rainbow Merkiva," and stuck out her hand for a shake. She giggled and said "Look for me at Revelry. You can't miss my part. Bring your friends backstage after the show to say hello, if you want."

Chapter 23

"Can't be long, he's as jumpy as apple
blossoms in a stiff breeze," replied Lark.

*H*ARDLY ABLE TO contain his glee at this electrifying invitation, his
eyes got bigger and brighter and he felt a tightening run up behind
his ears, all the way to the tips where it jumped off and became an irrepressible shudder.

This had to be the most satisfying, gratifying, glorious moment of his
entire life and pride flushed through him, starting with the back of his legs
and heating the rest of his body 'til it felt like his eyelids tingled.

His wings surged and he forced himsylph to breathe deep.

Rainbow's smile never wavered but her eyes widened imperceptibly as
she took in the overall affect on the young man in front of her.

Feeling like he'd been given a precious gift, the faerie could hardly make
polite conversation and he knew he had to take himsylph strictly in hand and
pretend he was the suave, urban, human male, once again.

Squelching his hot and unruly blood, he inclined his head respectfully
and was able to say "Thank you. I'll take you up on that. Well, I best be going. Oh! Here," and he dug into his pocket for his money, handing her one
bottle of oil.

Suddenly shy, he looked down momentarily but was driven by the burgeoning gratitude within his heart, his eyes flying to hers. "Thank you," he
said emphatically but a comical look upon his face, as if to ask, really, she was
inviting *him* back stage?

Smiling intently directly into his hazel eyes, Rainbow Merkiva just said,
"See you there."

The faerie grinned in sheer unadulterated delight and hurried out the door, pausing for a quick grateful look back at her before he shut the door and climbed the stone steps, his innersylph bouncing like water on a hot griddle. His hands shook as he straightened his scarf and his wing's pulse beat time with every breath he took, causing him to not only feel its throb but hearing it in his ears also.

He walked quickly, elation lashing at his heels as he tried to figure out what to do next, his rational mind on vacation, it seemed.

The thought crossed his mind that he should probably eat something but he didn't want to take the time. What he *really* wanted to do was *fly*, that's what he really wanted to do, he thought, rather savagely to himsylph. Instantly, irritation hooked on to jubilation, an unwanted hitchhiker that snatched the reins.

With a sharp stop, he abruptly did an about face and started walking briskly back towards Fletcherman's Nursery.

He suddenly knew with crystal clarity *exactly* what he was going to do.

He was going to hightail it back to the greenhouse, and, have a good fly, in the wee hours of the morning behind the 'closed' doors of Fletcherman's. With his cats, ahh.

A sudden poignant longing came over him and he wondered at the fact that he hadn't had that longing for a henfull in a long time. Several hours, anyway.

Could he test himsylph? Was he strong enough to deliberately hold himsylph to one?

He felt pretty sure he could although his track record stunk.

It occurred to him he had left all his mead in Sycamore Park. Buy more? Change plans, go home? He stopped for a moment, fingers drumming his lips as he fell into deep contemplation at his two options.

Perhaps he should just forget the whole idea and go back to plan A, cats and night flying. And just like that, he let it go—falling back in life itsylph, the joy of friends and adventure and cats.

Walking along, he looked up and a noodle sign caught his attention. The impromptu urge came over him and he veered up to the front counter where he quickly started reading the large overhead menu before his courage fled.

Whimsey C. Nimble

Fingering the four remaining dollars in his pocket, he was able to order a small container of Spicy Basil Garlic Noodles To Go without too much ado and was soon off again, supper swinging from his slim Sylph fingers.

The Nursery gates came into view and he stepped into the shadows, cautious now. While he really liked Bud, he did not want a repeat of last night, he wanted to creep unseen and hide out, quietly, and not make a peep 'til all were long gone and everything was locked up tight.

There were no cars in the parking lot, and Flem could see Lily through the window behind the cash register, it appeared she was closing up and doing the day's paperwork. The place had the eminent desolate look of one that was about to become empty, letting the night take over.

A light breeze blew by, rustling some trash and Flem shivered, the cat family an ever brighter beacon.

He wondered what to do, try and sneak in or wait 'til they left and fly over the wall again.

At that moment the lights went off in the main building and Lily came out the front door, turning to lock it behind her. "See you tomorrow, Bud!" rang out.

Bud's disembodied voice floated back, "'Night Lily. Have a good one."

She strode down the driveway pulling her hair out from underneath her jacket collar as she did and stepped right by the flattened ivy shadow that breathed.

If he hesitated he would lose the moment, and, hoping Bud wasn't promptly behind, the faerie practically ran inside the gates and blundered as quietly as he could along the outside wall through Iris's landscaping that had a bit of the feel of underbrush to it. He hoped he wasn't making too much noise or irretrievably bending branches. About half way to the back he stopped and peered out, trying to catch sight of Buddleia.

There was no noise but then a flicker of movement and he saw Bud off in the distance, coming out of number one. The metal thump of doors closing was heard, the light was vanquished, and the gates creaked into place with a final clunk.

Holding his breath, Flem waited, listening, every cell alive with adventure. After a long ten minutes of no movement, no more lights, he relaxed. It appeared he was alone.

To be on the safe side, he waited another five minutes, impatience being fed by hunger and Sylph adrenalin.

Catching a breath he then daringly darted right into the open, bag swinging crazily as he lurched along, cutting across the back lot, taking the shortest route to his destination, practically throwing himsylph through the open window, barely avoiding spilling his dinner but catching it in time, admonishing himsylph to slow down, relax, it was all good.

At his appearance momma cat trotted out to greet him, eyes blinking in love, a great purr rumbling beneath his fingers as she implored him to pet her, feed her, scratch her.

Kittens ran in excited little bursts, attacking and jumping freely. Flem's pulse raced along with them and a wave of love at such unexpected fortune assailed him.

Reverently, he kept moving, letting his vision adjust to the dim interior. It would be so much easier if there were an uncluttered path, but of course there wasn't.

Setting the container down carefully, he shrugged out of his pack, unwinding the scarf and dropping them together.

Looking around, his plan came together: eat, then clean, yes clean, find a spot to hang his hammock, (such a thrill of satisfaction this whole hammock thing was, he thought) wait a bit, and then, *FLY!*

Rubbing his hands together in anticipation he sat down with his back against an old cupboard and brought his knees up in front of him, pulling his noodley supper right between his feet.

Instantly he was the center of attention and realized his mistake immediately, snapped the lid quickly back into place, and stood up.

"Okay, okay sorry! I'm new at this," he smiled and apologized as he unearthed a can of Savory Sea Feast, thinking about a cute little dish he should find somewhere for momma's food, a new treasure hunt to look forward to.

Watching as she gobbled down the offering, he frowned as once again a vision of all six kittens being her size and *all* of them eating as much as *she* did. He wondered how many cans *that* would take and if it would be twice a day too. Hmm.

Satisfied they were busy, Flem flopped back down and commenced making short work of his human food and was happy once more for Mayapple's ease with which she led him into unknown territory. Before going to Bud's Art Fair last Saturday he would never have felt so comfortable talking to shop owners and ordering dinner and having his *cards* read. Ooh, that was fun, he thought.

Tipping the virtually empty container up to capture every last bit, he therefore didn't see the little rogue break off from his family and come pussy footing purposefully towards him.

As he brought his hand back down, a small furry head with a wet nose bumped it and a tiny "Meow?" was voiced.

His long fingers encircled the smidgeon of cat and a raspy tongue furiously licked the faerie's fingers, specifically the ones he'd gotten noodle juice on.

Laughing, the Sylph sat and scratched behind the ears, then pinched the little backbone gently from neck to tail.

Petting absently, the faerie looked around and was about to set the little feline aside when it ducked from his grasp and skittered up the front of his shirt, leaving miniscule nail holes all the way through to his sensitive fae hide.

Wiggling, he brushed along his host's chin, nosing his way in, heading for the back country.

Flem tried to grab him but he eluded capture as if he'd been born for it, making his way to a certain hollow, snug between the two large wing scapula and then proceeded to brace himself, pulling Flem's shirt with him to fill in the gaps.

Flem felt rather flummoxed but it was completely offset by the kitten's casual attitude of ownership.

Never had anyone just assumed they were blatantly welcome just because they loved him and Flem wouldn't have dislodged his border under any circumstances. If that little cat assumed Flem loved him, well, by Pan, he'd do his best to live up to the reputation.

Acutely aware of the extra lump on his back, he rose slowly, wiggling the wing blade on each side of the fur ball.

Again the longing for a taste of mead came over him and he couldn't decide if that was a good thing or a bad thing that he didn't have any here. It felt more like a bad thing but he put it aside quickly and went back to figuring out what to do next. There wasn't much light, just the ambient, overall diffused light that was everywhere, part of city life, Flem knew by now. He thought of his cave in The Park, and how it was always dark, ha! Good for sleeping though.

The moon would be up later, he would wait for that.

In the meantime he looked around with renewed curiosity, wondering where he might actually hang his hammock.

Whistling tunelessly in little snatches interspersed with grins, he picked up junk and hauled it out back handful by handful.

Most of the glass in the panels that surrounded him was intact to some degree but there were a lot of gaps. Back in the corner was where he'd stashed his hammock and he decided to investigate further, setting aside the junk he carried to go look once again behind the bamboo. He found a partial wall that seemed solid enough to hang his hammock on, and it was a private corner, shielded at least from the front. From the back, however, it was completely exposed to the back yard through old greenhouse glass which revealed a small tangled path outside and the high impassable fence.

Smiling to himsylph, he puttered and fixed and cleaned and threw away, just like he was making himsylph right at home, and he knew it but he couldn't stop himsylph, he was having too much fun.

Bud and Lark were on the top floor at the *S* Club, putting the finishing touches on their appearance before leaving.

With a nod, Lark inquired, "Ready?"

"Yes, let's go. Oh, wait a minute, here." Reaching behind his friend's head, Bud adjusted the black silk scarf.

"Okay," he said and reached down and picked up a small compact bag with his special clothes in it and they headed out the foyer and down the two flights of stairs until they were on the street, the black quilted faux-leather doors with the dark pink embroidered *S* shutting firmly behind them.

"You want to come over for a drink?" invited Lark fumbling in his pocket for his car keys.

"Well," hedged Bud, thinking of his bike and the long ride home from Lark's house after dark.

Whimsey C. Nimble

"I'll give you a ride home afterwards too! Cha, you bike people. I can't understand your aversion to owning a car. I'm surprised you even have a license."

"Hey, what Mrs. Fletcherman wants, Mrs. Fletcherman gets. I get along just fine riding in the great outdoors, thank you. I can always take a bus or a taxi if I have to. This city has enough vehicles, why should I add to it? Although…I must say, at times it IS a trifle inconvenient."

Lark threw back his head and laughed at his friend's admission.

"Finally!" he ejaculated. "You admit there might be something to it." He slapped his friend playfully on the arm and said, "Bring your bike around to the back. I picked up a bike rack not too long ago just for occasions such as this."

Bus was flattered and looked appreciatively at Lark and said, by way of thanks, "You know, you don't look so bad for such an old guy."

Lark practically choked on his own spit with surprise before a short bark of laugher erupted.

Bud took the opportunity to unlock his bicycle and roll it around to the back of the low black car, laughing with Lark as he did so.

Together they lifted the bike and after throwing a covert glance around, Lark retorted, "*Me?* I do believe you're the senior here, grandpa." He grunted as they nudged the bike into place and snapped the bar down, locking it securely.

Bud waited as his long-time friend unlocked the doors and then slid down onto the soft padded seat. He did admire this acquisition of Lark's and never failed to be mildly surprised by it, it was quite a step. No one had ever dreamed something like this back home. And while they had discovered common roots when it came to where they had both grown up, they hadn't known each other at that time.

It was only here, in San Francoa Ramosa, that they had met and become friends, old friends, now. With a lot in common.

"I may be older, buddy boy," said Bud, "but let's face it, you've had more time to get used to this whole crazy business. You've been here how long, ninety-four, ninety-five years, right?"

"Yeah, I came directly here after that old, what was her name? Oh yeah, Zinnia, do you remember her? Well anyway, it was right after it happened, or *didn't* happen, ha ha, and she found me, looked *me* up, and suggested moving -"

A knowing look passed between them as Lark expertly guided them through the streets, back to the marina on the south side.

"Well, you were pretty lucky then, I'd say. Pan, I had to knock around for years before making my way here. And I *do* remember Zinnia, she lived north of the junction, didn't she, *in* Cow valley and not up the canyon?"

Lark nodded without taking his eyes off the road, slowing to turn into the marina.

"What do you think we should do about Flem?" asked Lark, guiding the car into its usual parking spot before switching the engine off and turning to face Bud.

"I think we should let him acclimate a while longer, get used to city life. How long do you think he's lived here, has he said?" Bud responded.

"Can't be long, he's as jumpy as apple blossoms in a stiff breeze," Lark replied. "I think Mayapple is good for him though. She seems to calm him down. Well, we'll see how they do at Revelry, that ought to be a good indicator, for all of us."

Both young men got out of the car, Lark locked it and then Bud followed him through the front door of the houseboat.

Chapter 24

The kitten braced his feet a bit more securely,
his electric sea-green eyes open wide.

S EVERAL HOURS LATER it seemed to Flem that only he and a smattering
few were still awake. Occasionally a distant bus in low gear could be
heard climbing a hill, an everyday sound but now one that served to emphasize the lonely hour. A siren wailed and Flem was reminded quite clearly of
how close he still lived to that other world, the uncertain one that had been
his reality too, not so long ago.

He was so fortunate to have found Fletcherman's.

Musing, he walked over to the window he used as a door and looked out.
The moon was high and round and the urge, the *need* to fly filled his soul,
obliterating all other senses.

Turning away from the old greenish wooden frame, he carefully retraced
his steps back to momma cat, who was deeply sleeping with five snug babies
tucked around her.

How to dislodge with the least disturbance his passenger, forever tied
to Flem's heart now, that was the next and last order of business. He
leaned over 'til his nose was almost touching the ground and shimmied
and shook, urging the kitten to drop out, easily, a quick *plop t*o the ground
but that little feline never moved except to brace his tiny legs to keep from
falling out.

Flem laughed but it had a rather strained sound and he was distracted by
the invisible pull to become air born.

His shoulders twitched with irritation before he could help it but it didn't
faze his guest.

Next, he knelt down and leaned back, sticking both arms out in an effort to create an even deeper hollow between his scapula, rocking from side to side, sort of a swaying Sylph dance which did no good at all.

He decided to proceed with his plan anyway. Perhaps with his shirt off and his wings up, his little furry tick would understand and kindly run home.

Nervously he went to the window and peered out, double checking that there really wasn't anyone around, and of course there wasn't, it was, after all, three o'clock in the morning. It was one thing to be caught here with the cats, quite another to be found with wings.

The lure was irresistible, stronger with every moment now that the plan was made, the goal at hand, the opportunity presented.

Peeling off his shirt, it balked and caught at the log (leg) jam in the middle of his back.

A deep sigh of frustration was expelled as he tugged and rolled and gave small impatient jerks that eventually freed his shirt but *not* his stow-a-way.

He was getting close to overload, he could feel it building and with a rather crazed look in his eye, he yanked those damned bindings OFF and his wings swooshed up into giant, loose furls and it was all he could do to keep them under control and not jump into formation but he did it, ever mindful of his tenacious friend.

By this time he had worked up a right case of crossness at this hindrance to this new and daring great plan and was feeling rather snappish at his darling companion.

What to do? His back molars grated against each other as he clenched his jaw.

Moonlight lay like a well mannered guest, gently ignoring the deep shadows which lay cheek by jowl alongside, enticing with a deceptive innocence, all propelling him towards his unorthodox door.

Taking a deep breath of clean night air, he could no longer control himsylph and escaped over the sill, his furled appendages bending as they went through but luckily not catching on the rough wood. I have to learn to slow down, he thought distractedly to himsylph but did not change his speed.

Kitten cat burrowed deeper, if that was possible, and Flem felt tiny cool feet shift to accommodate this bumpy, naked-wing ride.

Whimsey C. Nimble

The second he was free of the grasp of the beleaguered old building, his wings sought their rightful place, unfurling to dance proudly with a slight tremor behind their owner.

It was such a deeply gratifying moment, this restoration of who he really was, that he could do nothing but stand in one spot, reveling in this planned *choice* of what he was about to do. But it was better than just ripping away and taking off from the alley like the night before. He shuddered to think of the risk and while he had no regrets about what he was planning to do, still, he would be *cautious*. It was foolish to act on such impulse as last night and he resolved to take better care of himsylph from now on. No more dangerous chances.

Mead flashed through his mind and all the times he'd gotten so out of control and the chances he'd ignored that inherently went along with that.

He resolved to keep that bottle at his Sycamore Park place. He didn't need complications, he decided, and was pleased at such wisdom in himsylph.

This was a bit risky, he knew that. He hadn't counted on a passenger and it baffled him as what to do, but he was compelled to carry on, regardless.

Ready to take that leap, he nonetheless stood in place and shook like a wet dog, determined to once again dislodge his guest, but no dice.

Oh well, he had his chance, thought Flem and finally ignored him. With a great vibration he rose into the moon filled air.

The kitten braced his feet a bit more securely, his electric sea-green eyes open wide.

Flem's heart jumped and his pulse jerked as a tree branch suddenly loomed but he instantly recovered. Slowly and deliberately he hung in place for a moment, working his wings up to speed, toes pointed skyward as the wing power he exuded pulled his calf muscles taut, flexing his feet. Putting his hands on his hips, he gazed about, almost giddy with old remembrances of loop t' loops high in the sky above Thimbleberry Canyon, back in his younger days.

Feeling like he was regaining a crucial piece of himsylph, he looked straight up above him and then proceeded to fly in a slow, ever widening spiral up, up, until he was high enough to see roof tops and power lines, street lights and moving vehicles. It was all neatly laid out, but so much more obvious from above, like little landscape pieces set in place. He wasn't sure what to do next, he'd only gotten as far as *must fly*, and here he was. The kitten was forgotten in the wonder of the moment and he decided he would make it a short flight but by Pan he was going to get in a good couple of minutes before he returned to solid ground and with that he shot straight up, high in the sky and did two huge circles, like a giant living Ferris wheel before he remembered that snippet of brash personality still riding his back, high in the air with him, far from the hard ground. Caution slipped into his soul and he lowered himsylph carefully back down, the slight breeze that accompanied his wings creating a ripple in the grass on the ground.

With a piercing ache, his eyes swam and superimposed over his vision was the platform he'd used for taking off and landing, the one he'd built himsylph (hersylph) down at the end of the thick branch, back in the oak tree in the canyon that he *used* to call home.

Quickly he squelched the old familiar home sickness as he'd learned how to do over the years and stepped forth on solid ground, wings furling, his joy tempered but thinking about next time and where he would go. His confidence soared with this easy success and the rest of his life was too precious to not plan scrupulously. He would not overdo it, like he'd been so wont to do with his mead drinking... But that was behind him he resolved once again, and this time he *really* meant it, even though he always meant it. But this time he was proving it, as there wasn't even any mead here.

Hmm. Did he want to bring it here? Was he strong enough to have it in such close proximity? He thought about it for a moment then decided there was no hurry, if he wanted a drink, he would just go back to that hole under a rock in the Park.

Padding barefoot, wings furled, he changed into soft human pants and then went and sat by momma cat, petting her with long sweeping movements, thinking of that warm spot on his back riding with him, and realized it was fate. That kitty belonged with him. Smiling to himsylph, he wondered what he would do about his passenger when it was time for work but decided that was a problem he would fix when he came to it. Meanwhile, he gave one last scratch to momma's chin and got up to go see about hanging his hammock.

He needed to get some sleep but it wasn't looking too promising, even though he still had five hours or so 'til he had to be at work. His blood was still moving. So, he found the perfect spot for the hammock, and out of sight, too. He reached up and tugged as hard as he could on the small metal hook imbedded in the top of the old four by four but it didn't budge and neither did the post.

Stepping through weeds in the dim light he nearly tripped over an old broken and rusted pair of trimming shears half buried in the ground and stopped to pry them up out of his way in the thinning moonlight. Carefully he tossed them near the back door to be disposed of tomorrow.

Looking towards the bamboo wall, he saw just what he wanted—another post and it had a stout nail rearing up from it at a jagged angle but it just might work.

Quickly he went and uncovered his fabulous treasure, hugging it to him-sylph as he carried it back to the corner.

Holding his breath, he performed the ritual of hanging his hammock and as it slipped into place, Flem felt a rippling up his arms and around his shoulder blades, running with a centipede's feet to tickle every nerve ending he had in his body, his wings fluffing in their furl, tiny feather-like scales standing straight up right next to each other at the base.

This was new; he'd had many runaway frustrations that had leapt about his body but this, this wasn't that. This was more like a knowing energy playing havoc with him, a breath being blown over his body, dancing up his skin, ruffling his feathers, so-to-speak.

Just when he thought it was over, a spark rolled down his right arm and hopped from fingernail to fingernail and back again.

Slowly the Sylph straightened up, trying to make sense of this, wondering what was going on. He looked at his right hand to see if he could see anything when he felt his little finger spring and a mere spec of bright golden light appeared about two inches from his head, up in the air.

A faint remembrance tickled his mind and a ghostly image of *someone* from back in Thimbleberry came flickering through, talking about an energy being that had followed them around for a while. He strained to remember as his eyes never left the pulsating consciousness. Pieces of information came bleeding through, something about an energy highway that they traveled, congregating at intersections with occasionally one getting pulled off, attracted to the light of someone's mushrooming energy, and POP, they showed up. Surprise!

Impulsively, Flem suddenly spurted, "What the Pan are you, anyway?"

To his surprise, the light turned a brilliant glowing emerald green and he started hearing a word repeatedly, "ZING ZING ZING" and then higher and faster: "ZING ZING ZING." There was a slight burr that underscored it so it was more like a vibration than a word.

By this time the freeloader on Flem's back was sitting up, braced with his back legs and sure enough, a tiny answering rumble picked up the thread of conversation and the dot 'flew' in a deliberate arc to hover over the faerie's back for a minute but then abruptly rose straight up and then out a window with a large gaping hole in it.

Flem all but ran to look out the back door and sure enough, a bright pinprick of light was wedged in a knot hole in the old pine fence behind the greenhouse.

As the Sylph watched, its glow never moved but simply faded from sight.

Shaking his head as if to clear it, he glanced around, his gaze falling on his hammock. Smiling, he moved from the door and continued with his inroads of cleaning until finally he gave up and went to bed, his little furry partner right along with him.°

Chapter 25

———— ❦ ————

That Mayapple. How did she always know
what was going on with him?

ᖴOOTSTEPS CRUNCHED FAINTLY and Flem waited for them to disappear but they didn't. In fact, they got louder and when he suddenly couldn't hear them on the path, he panicked, blanching a pale sickly green at being found out.

Heart in mouth he edged back to the furthest corner behind the bamboo, clutching his hands together in fear. What if they saw him! Oh, why had he stayed here?

A scuffle was heard and then a soft voice calling "Kitty? Kitty, kitty, kitty?"

Mayapple! Giddy with relief, Flem flung his hands down, grabbed his shirt from a nearby hook and called softly, "Mayapple?"

There was dead silence for a second, but only a second, and then Mayapple came crashing the rest of the way in the window door.

"Flem?" Disbelief was in her voice, "Flem, is that you? What the heck are you doing here so early? I came to see your cats. Where are you?" She stood not too far from the window door and looked around for him, not seeing him but seeing traces of him, little paths of organization everywhere. Hmmm.

Finally the faerie stepped from behind the partition, having taken the precious time to bind his wings and throw on a shirt. Momma and kids traipsed behind, most interested in this new arrival.

"Oooh, look!" gushed Mayapple in a sappy baby voice, thrusting a couple more cans at him as she rushed by. "Hi kitty! C'mere, c'mon kitty kitty," and immediately sat down on an old upside down crate just this side of

Flem's bamboo bedroom wall. Momma purred and rumbled, brushing back and forth against her legs, kittens batting at various pieces of clothing that dropped from the girl.

Flem swallowed and pulled himsylph together, thinking fast. Mayapple had *not* realized he'd stayed here and she hadn't seen his hammock. He'd rather keep it that way.

"What are you doing here so early too? Come to feed the cats?" he asked with a smile, adjusting his shirt around the foolish one still in the middle of his back.

Mayapple didn't answer immediately but kept playing and talking to the cat family who had no trouble at all reciprocating the attention.

She smiled up at him, love bubbling from her eyes.

"You know, we'll have to find a home for these guys, so start thinking of whom you could ask. I wonder if Bud and Lark could be persuaded? We won't tell mom just yet—our secret—but eventually I will and maybe she'll take one too. *I* want one, Blakeana needs a friend, and *you've* got to have that one that liked you so much, where is he anyway? He's not here, is he?" She started looking around, and not seeing him, looked back at Flem with concern and nosiness in her eyes.

The faerie just stood there, dumb.

"Flem? What's the matter? Where is he, do you know? Why are you acting so weird?"

Deciding to brazen it out, he clenched his jaws and rather squinted at her, saying in a forced jolly sort-of-way, "I don't know."

Mayapple stared as his shirt moved by itself, just briefly, and then an evil glint entered her eyes as she asked very sweetly if he needed to be preened? they had time.

Flem couldn't help it, he burst out laughing. "How *do* you do that?" he asked. "Am I *that* transparent?"

"I'm just a good guesser, that's all. Ah ha!" she exclaimed as she found and petted a soft bump under his shirt, between his shoulder blades.

"Were you serious about that preening?" he asked, shy but hopeful.

"Sure. Take your shirt off. Mom's coming in a little late today but we still need to be back over there by nine."

"Oh, absolutely," agreed the faerie as he gulped at what they were doing but bared his back to her, wings, rogue and all.

Whimsey C. Nimble

Making calming conversation, Mayapple marveled at his hitchhiker who stared at her intently.

"What time did you get here?" she asked guilelessly, wetting her fingertips with saliva since there was no glass of water nearby that she could see.

Flem was artfully casual, even as lulled as he was by her human touch. How could someone else's fingers feel so good?

"Oh, I was here early," he replied innocuously, which was true. "I wanted to see the cats," which again, was true.

"Flem!" Mayapple suddenly barked, pinching one knobby scapula. "Did you *stay here* last night?"

"No!" He managed to sound aghast that she would even think that.

"It's all right, I won't tell," Mayapple continued smoothing down and locking together ruffled rough edges, looking into the staring kitten's eyes at the same time. It was almost like he didn't quite approve of her. She stared, he stared, and finally she gave up, turning the Sylph around to face her once again.

"C'mon bucko, we need to get to work. What's happening with your buddy here, is he part of the package?"

Flem was by this time putty in her hands and was agreeable to pretty much anything she said. Dreamily, he replied, "I don't know how to get him unstuck. Can you take him down from there?"

"Okay," Mayapple replied breezily, reaching for the furball but as soon as her fingers came close, he hissed and spat and tried to take a swipe at her.

She laughed in astonishment, backing away

"Yeah, right! Here, I'll try again." Unable to resist her sweet singsong voice, the kitten snuggled right back in but the moment the girl once again tried to touch him, he turned and bit her. Not hard, just an attention-getter. Didn't even break the skin. Nonetheless, she jerked her hand away and watched him warily, mistrust replacing adoration instantly.

"Well. Hmmph. I will do my best to distract my mother, Flem, but I make no promises. It looks like he's going with you. Here, I'll help you put your ties on, let me see."

Flem's heart sank at this news, but unfortunately it didn't surprise him after the ride they'd taken last night.

That Mayapple. How did she always know what was going on with him? It was good, for the most part, but rather unnerving as he wasn't entirely sure he wanted her to know everything about him. He resolved privately to be extra careful around her, although it would probably do no good, she was like Sylph radar, that girl. He had never had a friend like her. The fact of the matter was, he'd never had a *friend* before, merely neighborly acquaintances. He smiled wryly to himsylph that in all this time, it would be now, under these *strange* circumstances, that he would finally make some friends. Unable to help it, his mind brought up Bud and Lark, dwelling on Lark. Why did he get the feeling there was something else going on?

"F-l-e-m, you-hoo, come back," sang Mayapple, standing there looking rather cross, eyes narrowed as she studied him.

Snapping to attention, he straightened right up, wondering where his scarf was, and how to get it without Miss Nosy dogging his steps to his contraband hammock.

Mayapple eyeballed him, shaking her head, smiling. "I'm going before it gets any later. Why don't you take a minute to get your scarf and whatever else you need, and meet me at number one, I'll sign you in. And don't lollygag! We're almost through with the Bridgers-"

Orders flew so easily from her mouth, Flem marveled at it but there was no offensiveness to it as there had been in the past when certain Sylphs back home had thought to boss him (her) around. It seemed a lifetime ago.

Swinging her legs over the sill, the young woman groaned as her loose hair caught on a wicked splinter and she was stopped in mid motion 'til it was extricated by deft fingers and then with a "Bye!" she was gone.

Moments later momma cat was rumbling amidst a new dish of dry food, the faerie's scarf was around his neck, and his rider was emitting a tiny, almost imperceptible purr, a live presence on his back.

Clambering through the window door, he reared back and looked at the ugly splinter Mayapple's hair had snagged on and resolved to smooth it out the first chance he got.

He was almost to number one, lost in his own pre-work musings, remembering Zing from last night when Mayapple's sharp greeting snapped him awake: "Hey chop chop, let's go!" and she snapped her fingers twice to show him how fast. Grinning broadly, she had her work cup in her other hand and raised it daintily to take a sip, her eyes dancing with humor. "Shall I make you a cup too, dearie?"

Whimsey C. Nimble

Shaking his head in resignation, Flem stuck his hands in his pockets as he caught up with her. "No," he laughed, "No caffeine for a while. Let's just get to it."

Three hours later, Mayapple sighed and after clapping her hands to get rid of the excess dirt, leaned back and started rubbing the small of her back to ease the kinks. "Okay, we're almost done, partner. We'll finish the blues and then on to the purples this afternoon and tomorrow, and then we get to be creative! Thirty four baskets, and they won't be as big as these, that'll be nice. Mom has a list but I bet she'll take any special requests we make seriously and consider it."

Flem now stood up and stretched also, wandering over to the open door to stand outside with Mayapple.

"So, you have any ideas?" she asked, taking a five minute break, craning her neck and doing some squats.

Before he could answer, tiny claws dug in as his passenger readjusted and then settled back down. The faerie's eyes and eyebrows flew up in surprise, and his mouth opened in protest as his backbone straightened.

He looked at Mayapple in dismay that he'd so quickly given himsylph away. Good thing Iris wasn't here!

She turned him around and patted things into apparent orderliness before she said, "Tsk. My mother is going to notice things like that you know. You better learn to adjust," but by now her sense of the absurd was climbing up her neck and she started to laugh.

Flem thought OH NO, not again, flashing on her before they met and she'd unhooked him. Embarrassment burned in a little hot prickle all its own.

Her hand went over her mouth in a futile attempt to control the escaping steam but it came from the inside and even though she kept sniffling, he could see it was a losing battle.

Giving up, Mayapple's cheeks tightened in mirth and a loud "WHO!" came bursting out before multiplying into lots of little whos, building and then cascading as she turned away and bent over in uncontrollable laughter.

For the first thirty seconds he felt rather mortified but as the moments ticked by, after-all, it was nothing he'd actually done, it was all innocent, all natural, he began to build a rather pissed-off, yes, pissed off feeling.

PFFT. Who cared what *she* thought anyway? Feeling offended he lifted his chin and made to move by her when she came to her senses.

Throwing her arms around him, she gasped, "I'm sorry! Really. You just have to understand how hard it is for plain little ole' human *me* to be friends with *a faerie*! Flem, I'm honored to call you my friend, but I don't know anyone else who has wings, for goodness sake, or a kitten on his back. Don't be mad. I just get overcome with hysteria occasionally. We all have our faults, don't we?"

Appeased back to benevolence, he agreed with her and folded his offended senses back where they belonged.

Giving him a big heartfelt hug, Mayapple took a moment to ease her thumbs down his strained muscles, laughing in delight as a sudden bounce came from inside the Sylph's shirt as his stow-a-way batted at her traveling fingers.

"Hey!" yelped Flem. "Stop, both of you."

"You're right, let's get to work!" exclaimed Mayapple, stepping back and releasing him.

Chapter 26

───── ❧ ─────

Even as she watched, he had a minor fit or whatever it was.

*I*ʀɪѕ Fʟᴇᴛᴄʜᴇʀᴍᴀɴ'ѕ ᴍɪɴᴅ flitted between the enigmatic Flem Green, and her boyfriend, Santolina. A master gardener with a heart of gold, he was a wonderful addition to her life. And as such, she was feeling more and more expansive all the time, her heart growing as she relaxed more in her quest to lead a successful life. She glowed as she reflected on the fact that, by God, she'd *earned* this - she was due to have everything fall into place, and play a little. She'd certainly worked hard to get where she was now. Smiling, she let her mind drift again back to her newest and strangest employee.

Glancing in the rear view mirror, she was distracted by her makeup, and looked critically at her shapely eyebrows, wishing she'd taken the time this morning to darken them.

An image of Santolina sitting on the edge of his bed as she went off to the shower came unbidden into her mind briefly and her eyes softened but then her thoughts of Flem came crowding back and she concentrated on him and his odd mannerisms. Something was off here, but she couldn't quite figure out what. Briefly she considered talking it over with her daughter but scenes from their last conference halted her and she shelved that idea, at least temporarily.

Epilepsy, that was the closest she could come, but she knew that wasn't the answer.

Perhaps she'd discuss her concerns with Santolina, maybe think of a way to get the two together. Her analytical self took over and she wondered if she was plotting.

Well, how else would things get done if she didn't *think*, for crying out loud. She exhaled sharply, exasperated with all those 'authority' voices in her head, the critical chorus, made up of only God knew who.

Turning in the driveway of Fletcherman's, she did a quick over-see all around to assure herself all was right in her own little world, when her eyes fell upon Flem and her daughter, standing outside of number one. Turning the car off she studied the pair covertly, hidden by the fringe of some trees and her windshield.

He just looked lumpy for some reason. She wondered again if he was deformed like Mayapple had mentioned.

Even as she watched, he had a minor fit or whatever it was.

Spying for all she was worth, the boss watched unblinkingly as her daughter went into action.

Mystified, Iris watched, as, instead of the alarming scenario she expected, the young man slumped and beneath Mayapple's twirling fingers, spinning around to face away from her. She then proceeded to bat at his back until he held up his hand in protest and then, they both *laughed*.

Voices were heard and then Lily was coming towards her, a customer in tow.

Regaining her professional demeanor, Iris Fletcherman instantly slapped a business smile on her face and got out of the car, grabbing her purse and papers as she did so.

"Oh good, you're here! Iris, this is Mr. Kohlrabi, he has a question about the potting soil he's been using and I told him *you* were the one he must talk to!"

Immediately, the knowledgeable owner of Fletcherman's Nursery went to work and Flem was forgotten for the time being.

Chapter 27

***

"Sit down!" she ordered. "Is it that darn
muscle spasm again, Flem?"

"*L*AST *WEEK*? THIS happened last week, and here it is almost the end of
the following week, and Oh My God. I can't believe you *forgot* to tell
me we're invited *backstage* at Revelry?" By this time Mayapple had given up
all pretense of working and stood, looking rather outlandish with her hair in
a sloppy, straggly pony-tail, big black wet smudge on her work smock, yellow, elbow-length rubber gloves on that were covered with dirt. Mr.Skankii
wouldn't get her.

She was holding the bucket in place as Flem worked the controls on the
large bag of moss hanging between them.

Since she stopped, he had to stop too, so no work was getting done.

Flem's heart was in his throat for a moment at her wild intense reaction
and he wondered briefly if there was ever any physical danger from her as
when she got like this, it always looked like she was about to attack.

He prepared himsylph to run, which he knew was a silly reaction but
nonetheless his body tensed.

To his immense relief, she threw herself right back into work, urging
him to go faster, as her whole demeanor became jerkily animated.

"Oh, what am I going to *wear*?" she wailed, turning ferocious eyes upon
him, as if this was his problem.

"Oh My God! Have you told Bud and Lark yet?"

"No, I, um, I forgot, like I said. Guess I just had other things going on,
you know? And hey, I believe someone just mentioned not too long ago that
'we all have our faults,' right?" He smiled at her with a sweet look, relishing
handing her words back to her.

Ignoring his righteousness, she rolled her eyes at his answer, acknowledging his point.

"Whatever," she grinned in defeat, immediately reverting back to excitement over this piece of very thrilling news.

Her enthusiasm was catching and Flem started to get nervous over the whole event. What with cats, hammock, the old greenhouse and an illicit fly, the great event that had seemed so far away was now, in fact, just around the corner.

And he hadn't actually *forgotten* completely, he just never remembered at the right time. Plus, there for a while, he'd contemplated not saying anything and surprising them but taut nerves overran him like little birds at a newly filled feeder and he was wound up. It was hard to control himsylph, well, his mouth anyway. Working with Mayapple was like working with an old friend and he talked more with her than he'd ever talked in his life. Mind you, not a hard feat as Sylphs are *known* for their love of their own voice but he had not had that many occasions to where he *could* talk non-stop. Grinning, he thought to himsylph that he felt more like *her*sylph *now*, when *she* was *he*, and was hiding out, in a human city, as one of their males. "Ha!" burst out of him.

Mayapple gave him a skeptical look but went back to soaking the moss and then walked back to her planting station, perusing the selection of candidates for the second order from the Parks & Rec.

"So what are *you* going to wear, Flem?" she asked, hanging up a round bottom empty basket frame and then adjusting it the right height for her to easily work on. "Got anything snappy?"

At his stricken look, she asked, "You haven't figured out what you're going to wear, have you? Hey, let's go back to your place after work and you can show me, wait, you *are* staying there still, aren't you?" Her gaze bored into him and compelled him to tell the truth. At least, that's what she intended.

"Yes, of course! Well, quite lot. I was just there, really."

"Yeah, you sly Sylph, you're probably lying through your teeth to me and I'll bet you probably checked in there over the weekend but that's probably about it. Right?"

The faerie blanched at her astute guess. He was also really glad she liked him because she was way too familiar with him by this time to not be friends. He vowed to stay on her good side and realized he didn't have much to worry about, she might laugh a lot at the wrong times but her heart was gold and she loved him. As he did her.

He smiled at her and she stopped and smiled back.

"I like you Mayapple, you're my best friend and I'm so glad. Listen," he said, deciding to take a plunge, one he had *not* anticipated but one he wanted to take at some point and now seemed as good a time as any.

"Listen I need to tell you something, something personal. Okay?" His heart jumped up a beat.

Mayapple, struck by his sincerity, turned completely towards him and nodded. "Go ahead. What is it?"

Oh Cha. The moment was here.

"I drink too much," he blurted, mortified that he'd actually said the words out loud. It made it real.

Eyeing him, listening, waiting, Mayapple finally said, "When? I've never seen it."

Sniffing awkwardly, he spastically recounted the events of last Saturday night. He also threw in a couple of other times just for good measure, wondering if by omission he was not guilty of all those extra henfulls he'd had at home…

Feeling rather cleansed but horrified at his own confession, Flem wondered if he'd been foolish foolish foolish to open his big faire mouth and now look what he'd done. Left himsylph wide open.

Mayapple was looking at him very seriously.

"Do you have a bottle here?"

"No! No, no, it's at my Sycamore Park place."

"Have you ever had a drink here at work?"

"No! Well, I did go with Bud to Oleander's a few nights back," he said, thinking of that night and his escapade later.

"But that was after work, right?"

"Yes."

"How many did you have?"

"Just one."

"Are you trying to quit?"

"Well…" his face screwed up at the idea of never tasting mead again and he slowly said, "My plan is to just have one."

"Can you do that?" she asked crisply.

"I think so. But sometimes I'm not very good at it. So I, um, I was wondering, well, if you'd help me?" This last was said in a big rush as it took every ounce of Sylph to say that.

"Oh Flem. Of course. And YOU can be in charge of ME, okay?" This last was said with a flippant shake of the head and Flem appreciated her lighthearted way of responding, wondering if perhaps this was a bad idea…

"I'm glad you told me, that took a lot of courage. Hey," she said, changing the subject, "I've got a brilliant idea. I know a great place, let's go shopping! I'll help you find something *hot* for this crazy thing we're going to, and you can help me, okay? What are you doing after work?"

Sparks were igniting in her eyes of excitement and seeing them, he decided to play *her* for a moment.

"Have you eaten today?" he asked in apparent concern.

"I did eat. I had a sandwich at lunch, thank you for asking." She brushed the back of her yellow gloves over her forehead trying to brush the hair out of her eyes and left a streak of dirt across her skin.

Flem looked down and smiled to himsylph deciding he'd wait a while to tell her, and just laugh instead every time he looked at her for the rest of the day. It felt kind of mean but was irresistible.

"SO?" asked Mayapple, getting impatient and rubbed her nose with a gloved finger, once again leaving a trace of black to distract the eye. "C'mon, we better keep working," and she slung some moss around the bottom rungs of the metal basket, letting it drip onto the counter.

"Sure," affirmed Flem, scratching his knee just before he too swung into action, studying the conglomeration of baby plants they had assembled between them.

"So-ah, how's your 'friend' doing, still got a hitch-hiker, Flem? I've been meaning to ask. Either you've gotten better at hiding him or he's not back there."

"Oh, he's still there, trust me. I think I'm getting almost equal time with his mother. Lucky me. See?" He turned his back to her, and after really looking around, pulled his shoulders and back, wide and taut, so that the bump between two lumps could plainly be seen.

Mayapple giggled but turned her attention back to her basket, trying to decide what she wanted. Her mom had given them plenty of lee-way when it came to choice so long as they picked from her list. Mayapple shook her head as she read, hearing her mother's voice in her head:

"Gypsophilia Paniculata, use Bristol Fairy variety.
Viola - any variety, pansy, violets, or violas.
Ipomoea - morning glory. Read tags, and be sure to get complimentary colors!
Hedara – Ivy. Use Helix/English Ivy.
Lobelia, don't use for baskets that get full sun.
Alyssum - don't use with lobelia unless Ms. Lobelia gets more shade and the alyssum gets lots of sun.
Fuchsia – any.
Lysimachia, A.K.A. - moneywort, creeping Jenny.
Strawberries.
Saxifraga-use stolonifera variety (strawberry geranium).
Chlorophytum comosum - spider plant.
Thunbergia - use Alata-black- eyed Susan vine, or grandiflora- sky flower.
Miniature rose

And there was an admonition to please use their heads and not combine strange bedfellows off the list such as miniature rose with something like pansies. The pansies would overtake it and hide it but something light and airy would work with the rose, for instance, gypsophilia otherwise known as baby's breath, or perhaps alyssum around the edges. In fact, alyssum worked well with almost everybody, although she preferred the Thunbergia to be solitaire. The note ending with her saying she was trusting Mayapple's good taste to be in charge and to watch out for what Flem put together.

Mayapple was rather aghast at her mother for this last line and felt it was insensitive, what if he saw the note?

She had carefully cut off the bottom edge and just kept the body of it. From that list, she and the faerie had assembled just about every plant mentioned and brought it all back on the cart which now sat between them, bulging with new life.

"Do we know the light situation for the thirty-four spots, are any in complete shade? Or did they just give us a blanket order for thirty-four more, just not quite as big?"

"Ooh, good point Flem! Let's see if the note mentions it," and she pulled it out of her smock pocket, but it fell and Flem reached down and picked it up.

"May I?" he asked, taking for granted that he could of course, and Mayapple was immensely gratified she'd edited it.

Iris chose that moment to pop through the door, talking already. "Oh good, you've started. What did you come up with, what's your plan?" She stopped finally as she took in who was holding her instructions, and was remembering what she'd written...

Mayapple glared at her, flashing eye signals that really, told Iris Fletcherman nothing. Iris knew it was about that last sentence but for the life of her couldn't decipher Mayapple's camouflaged contortions.

Ah, children.

Deliberately, she turned her attentions to Flem, hoping for the best.

To cover her ill-considered remark, she inanely asked, rather too loudly, "Well, what do you think Flem? See anything on there you have a special fondness for?" and grinned hopefully, all sweet bluff.

The Sylph didn't look up right away, unknowingly making Iris sweat a little but then raised his eyes to her and smiled.

"Oh, I love your list," he gushed and handed it back to Mayapple before bending his knees to pick out some barely opened purple and yellow violas.

"Back home we call these Johnny-jump-ups," he said, his hands already reaching for some alyssum to go with it.

"Oh, where do you hail from, Mr. Green?" Iris easily picked up the conversational thread he left dangling.

Unfortunately he realized his mistake too late and then wouldn't you know it, two seconds after his heart started beating erratically, little puss head stretched and dug in his darling little sharp claws, all of which managed to make the faerie stand up ramrod straight, like there was steel in his backbone.

A tiny "Ah!" escaped his lips and his head jerked a little to one side, wings silently straining.

Whimsey C. Nimble

Oh cha, now what was he going to do? Mayapple watched in amazement but her mouth was twitching, her eyes wide as she intuited exactly what was going on.

"Sit down!" she ordered. "Is it that darn muscle spasm again, Flem?"

Quickly she turned to her mother, who was looking astonished and rather frightened.

"Mom! It's okay - he told me about these muscle spasms he gets every now and then. That's what we saw before, remember?" she improvised, feeling rather proud of herself for such quick thinking and it was good, too. "Flem, are you taking those magnesium pills we talked about?"

Realizing he once again had a way out, he latched onto her lead and faltering, took a chance and blurted, "No. I forgot them," his eyes intense with panic, not sure what it was she wanted him to say.

"You look better. Has the spasm passed?" she asked solicitously. "I'm glad you told me about these Flem, we were so worried about you, weren't we mother? I meant to tell you, sorry." She looked innocently at her parent.

Flem bounced up, ready to prove he was not in any way hindered by this annoyance and Iris nodded to him as if to give her blessing but was in fact much puzzled.

"Where were we?" she blinked. "Ah yes, I see you're going with alyssum and violas. Very good."

She turned to her daughter, whose innocence was proclaimed through every cell in her body, but nonetheless Iris wasn't completely fooled, *something* had just happened but she didn't know what. She would figure it out though, given enough time.

"I think I'll do a fuchsia. Oh that reminds me, do we have any special lighting we need to work with? Are we working with only shade anywhere? I mean, you've got lobelia and violets on the list mom."

Effectively detoured, Iris Fletcherman brightened during this conversation as it returned her thoughts to Santolina. Distractedly, she smiled, looking off in the distance before returning her attention back to sunny or shady locations.

"That's a good question Mayapple," she exclaimed delightedly. "I'll go call the Parks and Rec department right now and find out."

She turned to rush off but Mayapple interjected with, "It was actually Flem's question, mom."

Still smiling, Iris wrinkled her nose and sort of bunched her shoulders at him, as if he was the sweetest baby she'd ever seen, and her eyes slanted as she proclaimed jovially, "Good observation, Mr. Green. Very astute. I'll get back to you." With a "Bye," she turned and fled.

Unable to control themselves, the two partners went into hysterics as soon as the boss disappeared through the far door.

Chapter 28

———— ❧ ————

The Silk Tassel was one door down, its windows
full of lacey mannequins made up of wicker
half-people done in various spring colors.

SMALLER BASKETS WENT much faster Flem thought happily, at work on his second one for the afternoon. Mayapple had just finished hers and was eyeballing their choices again.

"How far is this place where we're going shopping? What's the name of it?" questioned Flem as he carefully maneuvered his finished basket to the waiting cart where two others hung.

"It's a short bus ride from here, not far. It's called the Silk Tassel, and it's run by a woman named Garriya. She used to work here, back when dad was still around. Her shop is really cool. It's got new, used, and consignment all mixed together, plus she's got a little space in the back with books and a table where you can hang out and have a cup of tea. We'll go as soon as we're off work, okay? Then we can both get home fairly early, ahem...wherever *that* might be..." She gave him a look.

"What are you making next?" he asked, ignoring her, hands on hips, and then continued with, "I love black-eyed susan vines. I knew someone back in the canyon by the name of Pootsy Koons, she owns Windfall Café, and she had two, one on each side of the front door to the Café. I've loved them ever since, so that's what I'm going to work on."

"I think I'll actually do the same," Mayapple concurred. "They're so pretty when incandescent."

"Incandescent! What the Pan is incandescent?"

"Oh you know - blooming," she replied with a mischievous twinkle in her eye. "C'mon, let's get these done and get out of here. I'm hoping the boss will let us go early if we explain our important mission to her: shopping!"

By five-thirty they were just about finished and by five-forty-five the place was cleaned up.

Mayapple called the shots: " You stay here. Or, better yet, go look after your cat family, do whatever you need to do, and meet back here in fifteen minutes, okay? See if kiddo there, in Scapula Hollow, will take a powder." She eyeballed his back waiting for him to comprehend what she was saying.

"Got it," he replied seriously, but broke into a big grin immediately, viewing her with great admiration.

"See you a few minutes. I'm off to placate Mrs. Fletcherman and get us out of here early. Wish me luck." She moved off with a determined look in her eye.

Flem watched her go, wondering if it was always a good thing to trust Mayapple's ideas. What if Iris said no and came back here and no one was here? AND the place was already cleaned up?... It didn't bear thinking about so he put on his best 'on-a-mission' face and sidled out and down the path. He would trust in the great Goddess, Mayapple Fletcherman.

Momma cat was glad to see him and loudly purred her greeting but telling him nicely that it was dinner time by continuously tapping him with one paw on his back when he sat down next to her for a minute. To his utter relief and amazement, the little ruffian flew into action and within ten seconds his back was blessedly free. He jumped up before his itchy passenger changed his mind again and quickly set about assuaging the poor starving cat's dilemma.

Mere minutes later he was assiduously sweeping the clean floor back in number one, nervous, but just as his worry started to escalate, Mayapple herself flew through the door and shouted, "Let's go!"

Grabbing his pack and rewinding his scarf, he followed her out and soon they were forced to idleness as they waited for a bus.

"Did your friend come too? Let's see, turn around." She gave his shoulder a slight shove so she could peruse his back, pretending to adjust his scarf but really feeling his lumpy back for additions.

"Ah, you lost him. Were you able to dislodge him or did he finally leave on his own?".

Whimsey C. Nimble

"He actually just jumped off when we got near momma and cha, I tell you, I HURRIED before he changed his mind again! I do believe he's worse than Velcro."

Both starting laughing at the same time and the girl noticed the approach of their ride. "Okay, straighten up, there's the bus," she ordered and Flem noticed once again, it didn't rankle him when she bossed him around. That was pretty amazing.

Twenty minutes later they stepped down onto Beech street, Flem following Mayapple around a corner to a little place on Solandra Lane past a coffee shop with the name of Cup of Gold.

The Silk Tassel was one door down, its windows full of lacey mannequins made up of wicker half-people done in various spring colors.

To a green Sylph, recently of Thimbleberry Canyon, (all right, it'd been a few years, but still-) it looked like another world, one he would never have dared breech before now. When his feet inexplicably stopped before he could get through the door, Mayapple simply reached back, caught his sleeve and yanked him in, tucking her arm through his.

"Relax" she whispered, "I've got this.

"*Mayapple?* It is! Hey girl! Come in, come in. Are you here to shop or can we sit and talk a few minutes in the back? Who's your good looking friend? Hi, I'm Garriya, call me Gary."

Flem seized the proffered hand, taking her in. Her color scheme reminded him of canyon days and he heartily approved of the dark green V neck top over those dark grey wooly looking pants but it was her scarf he really drooled over. A diaphanous yellowish- green affair with a pattern of long pale catkins, or tassels, interspersed with clusters of hanging globular maroon fruit floated around her neck.

Letting go, he remarked, "Nice scarf."

Gary smiled gracefully, dipping her head in acknowledgement and pulled her attention back to her friend but not before giving the faerie a direct stare that made him gulp as he realized she was sending some kind of personal signal. He sighed. These crazy humans, did they think of nothing else? Cha! It was those same impulses that got him where he was now, he was not about to go there again for a long time.

Lark flittered through his mind but he resolutely pushed that idea away, daunted by the very fact that it had occurred to him at all...

The two women moved towards the back, chatting as they went.

Flem ambled to a row of clothing along the back wall, fingering the black pants, admiring bits of silver or gold sewn on as tasteful highlights.

After several minutes, Mayapple reappeared beside him, holding a flashy black shirt shot through with red and gold thread. Holding it up to him she said, "Boy, this would go great with a pair of those pants. Did you see the scarves over there?" She pointed to where a veritable waterfall of color and textures spilled over a long wooden arm.

"Here." She thrust the shirt at him and said, "Why don't you find your size in there," she pointed, "and try this on with them? There's the dressing room, over there. Call me when you're ready, so I can come see." Softening the order, she smiled into his eyes and asked, "Okay? If you want to, that is."

Since Flem had no clue about actually shopping for clothes, he agreed readily, thanking his lucky stars once again that he had such a sophisticated friend, and he nodded, heading out.

Five minutes later he was tucking the soft shirt tail in, wishing he had a different scarf when a hand magically appeared over the dressing room door and Mayapple's voice rang through, " I imagine you'll want one of these too, won't you?" a handful of luxurious scarves dangling from her fingers.

"Ah, thank you. I'll be done in a second."

"Sure, take your time. I want to try something on, so I'll meet you in front of the long mirrors, you'll see them, they're across the room."

Minutes later Flem the rock star stepped out of the small cubicle, feeling, well, *HOT.*

He tried to be casual about it but it leaked out with every breath he took. He was looking good.

Mayapple wasn't out yet, so he stopped momentarily 'til he spotted the trio of big wooden mirrors that stood like mammas at a dance chaperoning their daughters, bunched together, reflecting all their thoughts about the world.

He sauntered over, his blood singing with such fine apparel and good fortune. Pan, he *was* hot, he thought, wishing his proud wings weren't tied down, feeling his strength surge through his body with Sylph adrenalin, making his shoulders quiver. He had to calm down, he thought with an edge of panic. His shoulders really were trembling, he could see them clearly in the mirror and here came Gary.

Whimsey C. Nimble

"Wow, those fit you really, really well, ahh, Flem, is it? You look fabulous." Her tongue moistened her lips and sunshine poured forth from her eyes, bathing him.

Mayapple, thought Flem with distress and like magic, the other dressing room door flew open and Mayapple the gardener turned siren stepped out.

A long wolf whistle came from the shop owner's lips and Flem just stared.

Mayapple had taken the time to brush out her hair and it hung past her shoulders, curls slowly forming. If given the chance by being shorn shorter, it would surely spring with glee. For now, it helped give the young woman a vibrating image and electricity seemed to crackle around her as she walked across the pale green carpet. The dress she wore fit her like a second skin and the Sylph had a hard time figuring out where one ended and the other started. Small, well-behaved feathers, fine and refined covered her and as his eye traveled up he saw hidden in plain sight a beautiful necklace of russet points, separated by black dots on a background of grey. But as his eye absorbed it, it came to him it was *not* a necklace but part of the dress. And then he saw the subtle enhancements and for a moment it seemed like a sleek and sexy bird was approaching.

Her legs were encased in sheerest black, and slim boots accentuated her calves.

As she came to stand beside him and check herself out in front of the mirrors, she suddenly thrust out a leg, and demanded "Look!"

In the right light, more tiny russet feathers could be seen in a continuous pattern down the outside of each thigh.

Flem was forcibly struck with a strong resemblance to a Sylph's natural coloring. All Sylphs had a pattern that ran up the outside of each leg and down each arm, usually ending in the hairline and at the ankle. Each design was different, just like each Sylph. The pattern itsylph was barely discernable except in just the right light.

Flem's eyes practically bulged at Mayapple and he couldn't say a word.

"Woo-hoo! I guess that means you approve. And look!" She produced a small feathered hat done in dark green, rust, and black that she pinned off to the side, up high on her head.

Finally the faerie found his speech and stuttered, "But, but, the *birds*..."

Before Mayapple could say a word, Gary spoke up. "Oh, don't worry. They're not real. I make sure nothing I sell comes from the animal kingdom."

Flem's estimation of her went up and he chanced a sweet smile at her which caused her to make suggestive eyes at him. Hurriedly, he cast his gaze back to Mayapple but she was staring out the window.

"Flem look. There's Bud and Lark."

"What?" He quickly turned around to stare out the window and sure enough, there they were, coming out of a building not too far away. The door settled into place behind them, a big *S* easily seen.

They walked in profile down the street and it struck both Flem and Mayapple that there was something peculiar about them, but neither mentioned it, and neither could figure out what it was.

"Friends of yours?" inquired Garriya, neutrally, her gaze including both of them.

"Yes, Bud works at the Nursery, I guess he got hired after you left," replied the feathery Diva, turning back to the present.

With a thoughtful expression Flem turned back too, a niggling awareness trying to worm its way in, but he shut the door in its face, he needed to pay attention to *now*.

Just then the phone rang and Gary took herself off to answer it.

"Well, what do you think? I've got to have this. All of it. How 'bout you? You look *great*, Flem," Mayapple finished, stars in her eyes.

Unable to do anything but nod in agreement, Flem's head bobbed like a cork in a squall.

Chapter 29

Nose, shoulders, elbows, shoulders.

*L*ADEN DOWN WITH packages, the two friends finally made it out the door, Flem feeling like a mouse who had outmaneuvered a cat.

"See? Shopping is fun, isn't it?" chattered Mayapple, "although I was beginning to wonder if Garriya was ever going to let you go!"

Flem just looked at her with big knowing eyes that spoke volumes about his opinion but all he said was "Great shop," as he lifted his bag slightly for emphasis.

Laughing, Mayapple went on talking but when she looked up Flem was not paying any attention to her but was staring at a windowed restaurant on the other side of the street, a few doors down.

"Hey look, they didn't get far. Isn't that Bud and Lark?" he asked, never removing his gaze.

Brushing her hair back, Mayapple stared. "Yep. C'mon, let's go crash their party," and took off, assuming the faerie would keep up, and he did.

Minutes later the Sylph was standing awkwardly at Mayapple's elbow, trying his best to appear as a sylphassured, confident human male, when in truth he was feeling very shy and wanted nothing more than to go home, be alone and regroup.

But it was not to be. Bud was grabbing an empty chair from behind him and Lark had hopped up and snagged another, so Flem surrendered to the moment, making himsylph comfortable.

Bud commented on how beautiful all the bridge baskets were and the next thing you knew he and Mayapple were off and running about the different combination possibilities, with Bud expressing a great longing to make one also.

Lark sat quietly, his eyes flickering over Flem's averted face frequently, wondering how to put him at ease and what to say when Flem surprised him by suddenly turning to him and asking with frank curiosity, "What are you guys doing in this neighborhood? We saw you coming out of that building over there," his thumb made a little jab up the block. "What's that door got an *S* on it for?"

Lark nodded in appreciation of Flem's forthright curiosity and breezily replied, "Oh, it's a club we go to sometimes, it's got a workout room upstairs. Do you like to workout?"

"Yes," Flem replied thinking of the workout he used to get a long time ago, working the ropes at the gymnasium down in Cow Valley, and now, when he exercised his wings on his wee morning flights, not that there'd been that many, it hardly counted as exercise.

A waitress manifested between them and Lark stared shortly into Flem's eyes before he said, "What are you having? I'm buying." Then looking around at the three and signaled to the young woman to give him the check.

Mayapple's remembrance of Flem's confession jolted her and she looked at him with panic in her eyes, saying in a trembley voice, "Flem? They have really good lemonade here-"

"I think I'll have a mead, thank you. Just one, I need to get home." Silent darts traveled like little invisible birds straight to Mayapple's eyes, messages bound to each carrier's leg which she had no problem unraveling.

"Okay. One. Then we'll go." A relieved smile pulled her lips up at his hidden message.

"So Flem," Bud started, "Mayapple tells me you each just got done planting Thunbergia. What is that?"

Lark gladly took the opportunity to openly watch the Sylph's face, his gaze soft as he wondered about his story. *Everybody* had a story, especially if they'd arrived in San Francoa Ramosa from someplace else, and most everyone did. Natives were rare, a different breed.

Flem was talking about what he had just planted: "I was happy to see Mrs. Fletcherman had them on her list. I used to know a place, a little café back home, that had two baskets, one on each side of the entry. I always wanted to do the same thing and here it was, presented to me."

Their drinks arrived, interrupting him and Mayapple was beguiled once again by the innocent charm of her fae friend.

Whimsey C. Nimble

Meanwhile, Lark and Bud had frozen in place, their eyes locked on one another until Lark snapped to and whipped out a wallet, a hard glance at the waitress who was just straightening up and digging through a small notepad on her tray.

Time released and instantly they were back to their old sylves.

Mayapple held out her glass and pronounced, "Here's to Revelry! Can't wait."

Four glasses ca-chinked, everyone took a sip and relaxed back, Lark keeping the ball going with, "What are you guys doing in the neighborhood?"

Before they could answer though, Bud threw back the rest of his drink and stood up, unwrinkling his pant knees, saying, "I've got to go, I've got to get to work. Mayapple. Flem. No, don't get up Lark. I've got my wheels."

Within a minute he was guiding a handsome bike past the window, swinging a leg over and pushing off.

Now Mayapple stood, making a 'stay' motion with her hand, explaining "I'm off to the Ladies Room. I'll be right back and then we'll go, okay Flem?"

"Oh yeah. Sure. Good idea." He watched her go, acutely aware of Lark beside him.

They both watched her weave a crooked path through the crowded room and finally cast a speculative glance at the other.

Lark grinned with good humor and repeated his earlier question. "So, what brings you to this side of town?"

Flem looked at Mr. Green Eyes and involuntarily thought once again how attractive he was. Such broad shoulders.

"Shopping!" the faerie declared a little too breathlessly, nerves pushing his mouth towards babble. "Have you ever been to the Silk Tassel? Ooh, beautiful stuff. Wait 'til you see what Mayapple's going to wear. She looks, or she will," he babbled, "when she's dressed. You know, in-"

But Lark shushed him by putting a finger to his lips to stop the chatter, letting the tip trail along one cheekbone just briefly before removing his hand.

Looking deeply into Flem's hazel eyes he said, "Someday we'll trade secrets. Let me know when you're ready."

Stepping out of the restroom at that moment, Mayapple paused to get her bearings and a vision caught hold of her. Flem and Lark were clearly silhouetted in the distance against the front window and Mayapple stared.

What was she seeing, she wondered. Something. Something was different. What was it? What were they talking about, their heads so close together.

A figure ran by the window, appearing only briefly and a second later, another did the same, looking back over his shoulder and both Flem and Lark leaned towards the view, heads in twin profiles as they attempted to see what the commotion was all about.

Nose, shoulders, elbows, shoulders. Eyes narrowed as the young woman's analytical skills leaped into action.

Lark's *shoulders*. They looked just like Flem's. What?

And then it hit her. Lark was built an awful lot like Flem.

No, it couldn't be. And yet, there was a deep feeling, a knowingness that she couldn't ignore. She could see it. Not literally, of course. But no, that wasn't true, now that she saw their essences, she could see it in their framework. Literally.

And it sure looked like Lark had designs on her friend.

Flem didn't seem to be objecting though, now did he?

Hmmph. Fingers came up and pressed against her mouth as she voyeured shamelessly, wondering what she was seeing.

Flem turned back and fell into those compelling green eyes, shuddering at the audacity of this intense man. He was hopelessly enamored.

Something about him was so easy, so *Sylph*. And to think he apparently liked *him*, Flem, was almost overwhelming. But not quite. He didn't move but savored the feel of that finger on his cheek.

Mayapple stood witness to magic and knew that somehow, things had changed. She wondered if Flem would tell her and how long it would take.

A piece of conversation floated through her mind and she could hear Lark saying something about Revelry and Flem and it occurred to her that Lark might have asked Flem out and Flem didn't know it. The pieces slid together easily in her mind.

Lark leaned back, folding his hands in front of him, studying Flem.

Flem grew hot, uncomfortable beneath this close scrutiny.

Mayapple hurried through the crowd, back to their table, talking as she got closer.

"Ready Flem? Nice to see you Lark. Thanks for the drink."

Flem hastily stood back and collected himsylph, adjusting his scarf.

Whimsey C. Nimble

His eyes kept straying to Lark's, unable to unstick himsylph from the tangible energy that seemed to envelope the two of them.

Lark didn't help at all, smiling serenely with a veiled message being sent to Flem. "See you soon!" he called and twiddled his fingers a couple of times as the two friends made it out the door.

Flem almost ran into the door frame from not looking where he was going and did in fact bump it with a shoulder, as he stumbled after Mayapple.

Mayapple was quiet. After five minutes of walking and letting his senses settle back down, he finally noticed, Mayapple was quiet.

Walking rather determinedly, Flem kept right up with her, doing his best to ooze Sylph charm.

She kept walking but now she slanted a sideways glance at him, slowing down and walking with measured pace, trying to act normal but she didn't know how, now that she saw things differently. Feelings were feelings and it was hard to hide things that affected her. She remembered almost laughing at Flem when they'd first met and she'd unhooked him, and how flustered he must have felt. A feeling of remorse swept over her, even as she laughed now at the memory.

"Flem!" This was said as she came to a screeching halt and astonished him by taking both hands in hers. His eyes opened wide as he prepared himsylph for what was coming, a shock of some kind no doubt. Mayapple was never quiet so he figured she'd taken the last five minutes to build up and now was going to blow.

"Flem!" she said again and it started to dawn on him she'd seen Lark's fingers lingering.

"Everything okay?" she asked, as recognition emerged slowly in his eyes and understanding once again ran between them.

A very slow smile came from the inside out and Flem said, "Yeah. Things are okay. They are. Are *you* okay?"

A deep feeling of warmth suffused the girl also and she loved this Flem, *her* friend, a *faerie*, very much and pulled him into a tight hug, right there on the street.

"Oh Flemmy, be careful. You're my best friend and I love you."

Flem's eyes filled with hot tears.

"And you're my best friend, Mayapple. I don't know how I have lived this long without you, but please always be a part of my life, okay?"

"Absolutely." She paused and then went on, "He's definitely an attractive man, isn't he?"

"He is that," agreed the Sylph.

Mayapple looked at him sharply, wondering if he knew, and wondering if it was true, or was she losing her mind? Still she was fairly certain of what she'd seen.

Chapter 30

———— ❧ ————

Just before he closed his eyes, he winked at the
faerie and promised, "I never saw ya."

*A*s THEY STEPPED down in front of the Nursery, Mayapple said, "See you tomorrow. I'm going around the corner to wait for my other bus. What are you doing, Flem?" she tacked on carelessly.

He looked at her blankly but she smiled knowingly and said "Meow," shaking her head. "Be careful. I mean it. See you tomorrow," and she turned and walked away.

Minutes later with only a little stealth needed, the faerie was ensconced in his hammock, and so far, no one was tagging him.

The Sylph relaxed, glad the day was over. His eyes closed and as he sat there thinking about the day, he fell asleep.

It was the gloaming hour, just getting dark when the clang of the gates floated into his dream and he woke up, slowly looking around to realize where he was.

The entire cat family was asleep and he let sleeping cats lay, moving as quietly as he Sylphly could, silently padding away.

A soft glow beckoned his eye abruptly and he picked his way to the back door giving it a kick with his toe as he lifted the whole frame, or tried to. It swung out, squeaking in protest and he stepped past, his gaze caught by the bright spot illuminating a swirly hole in the fence.

As if in greeting, it darted out and soon Flem's ears were buzzing.

Zing apparently liked the night time and after resounding around the Sylph's head several times, drifted up the nearby tree and proceeded to hover in its tall, narrow crotch.

A frown of betwixtment overtook the Sylph and he rubbed his brow in confusion before arriving at a 'sure, why not?' point. There was a dim memory of one of his old neighbors, WilloB perhaps, whom he seemed to remember had had a HotSpot follow her. But of course since he couldn't actually call her an old *friend*, he didn't actually know the whole story. Sylphs in general didn't need an invitation, if word got out that the party was at so and so's house, anyone could go. But Flumaria had been such a sylph-proclaimed misfit, peering from behind small windows in her tree, watching more than doing, that if she did dredge up enough nerve to go it was always awkward. It didn't take too long for the word to be passed and a buzz created.

How she had longed to understand what it was about her that was different from the others although when the change was offered and both parties agreed, she'd thought that everything would be different from then on. Ha. It was different all right. It got *worse*. She stayed male. It didn't get more misfit than that.

Pulling himsylph together, he walked back to the sleeping cat family, watching and musing. The temptation to fly was very strong. But it was early yet, only a little after nine. He hadn't been home in two days and he started thinking about a scarf he'd left there and maybe some other things. He decided a trip to Sycamore Park was needed. He wasn't sure if he'd be back here tonight but flying was in his blood once again so *somewhere* he was going to fly tonight. His confidence had been growing lately and he hoped he wasn't being foolhardy, careless with joy. But he'd regained an important piece of sylphconfidence recently and believed he was more aware now-a-days compared to Canyon Days. He even felt better, constant exercise and no mead. Well, *less* mead. New clothes. And, the mystery of *Lark*.

By this time he had caught the second bus and was almost home. It felt different now, coming to the Park. Not quite so desperate.

He hopped off easily at his stop, more appreciative now that he'd been gone.

Sycamore Park was quiet, it being past ten o'clock at night and everyone was out on the main roads and not strolling in the woods.

As he got closer, he glanced over his shoulder to survey every nook and cranny before disappearing through the greenery, popping out inside his donut of camouflage shrubbery.

Whimsey C. Nimble

Carefully, he bent over and rolled his rock out of the way, stepping through quickly before turning and sealing the entrance.

Soon, soft illumination created a working glow.

It was so much easier to see this hole in the ground with a more positive attitude now that he had alternatives.

Well, one anyway. He grinned.

Rummaging through his piles, he spied not only the scarf he wanted but decided to take two more and another pair of pants. Within an hour he had accumulated enough stuff to fill his pack, having pulled more tea, another cup, a small blanket, several old gardening magazines, and a small book.

He still had a lot of stuff here but none of it did he want to take tonight. He was just taking necessities.

He paused for a moment and tried to be rational, where was this going? But he couldn't intellectualize it, not now. He had to follow his feelings of joy and how *right* it felt there, in the back of Fletcherman's Nursery.

Smiling to himsylph, he thought about how far he'd come in just a couple of weeks. He was on his way to becoming a new Sylph!

A wild surge of hot fae joy coursed through him and his wings let him know he'd forgotten about them. That's what came from pretending to be human, for Pan's sake, for the better part of each day anymore. He really wanted to let them out, let them vibrate at their own high speed but since he had decided to wait 'til he got back to his new digs, there was no sense in giving in now.

Looking around, he went to douse the first light when a novel thought flitted across his brain waves. It was late, getting later. There was nobody *in* the park. Perhaps he *would* take a quick fly, right now, right here. He'd be careful, he promised himsylph, getting irretrievably giddy at the daring of it all.

A part of him was screaming in the background, 'Bad idea! Bad idea! You've been taking too many chances as it is, lately. Go get on the bus. It's not too late!'

He ignored it.

His blood quickened and a surge started that was like a low voltage shock running along his muscles. A deep breath did nothing to dampen it.

Extinguishing all but one little light, he tossed his pack to the floor near his hammock. As he turned back to dash out, the mead cupboard stilled his eye.

He hadn't even thought about taking it but suddenly it seemed like a good idea. Maybe he would have one now! He started to move towards it as it was such an appealing idea and then remembered: he'd already had his one, earlier tonight with the gang. And Lark.

Shutting the door on his stash, he decided he *would* take it with him when he left but he would not have a drink right now. He felt very righteous.

Where to unfurl, that was the question.

He stepped outside like a shadow, intent on being invisible.

Catching the small boulder, he eased it back into place, straightening to let out a breath and looked cautiously around.

Nothing stirred and he stepped through his protective green wall of shrubbery and into the other world.

He could hear the muffled traffic and see the lights in the distance but each was quite far away. Nobody came to the Park at night, and he was, in fact, hidden in plain sight. He couldn't help it and started grinning, vastly amused by his own Sylph. It felt good.

Casually, he walked along, heart racing with what he was about to do, impulsively heading into heavy shadows as he strode deeper amongst the rhododendrons, Camilla bushes, oleanders, and the ever present eucalyptus – those stately Gods of benevolence and airy health. There was enough ambient light to let him explore further a field than he normally ventured and he soon came upon exactly what he was looking for – a large open area beringed with a woodsy copse. It was perfect, he could fly unencumbered and not have to go too high to really get some exercise but with enough easily accessible areas that he could quickly get out of sight, if need be.

After one last look around he sniffed once to brace himsylph, adrenalin igniting every cell. Off came the wing ties.

The moon appeared from where it had been silently watching behind some high clouds and he gave in to the sheer exuberance of the moment.

A flick of the eyes around the dim perimeter of his flying field, the barest acknowledgement of his human surroundings, and he took off at a run, his steps climbing a small knoll which he used to catapult himsylph into the air, turning his leap into a smooth swan dive, an over exaggerated Sylph summersault of sorts.

Glee climbed with him as he rocketed up, a high pitched hum emanating from his vocal chords in his unbridled happiness.

Whimsey C. Nimble

As he rose above the tree tops, the whole city could be seen oozing out on all sides of him like a sea of lights.

Hardly able to control his actions, he was taken aback when a pulsating point of intense energy buzzed him, circling closer and closer, a white hot little dot, that rang in his ears – Zing! Zing! Zing!

Laughing like a mad Sylph he darted towards his stalker but it was no use and they circled one another like sugar-crazed hummingbirds, except one was merely a HotSpot and the other, a full grown Sylph, bigger than the Sylphs back in the canyon, because he was a male.

Around and around they went, up, down, zigzag, every geometric shape they could think of, first one chasing the other and then reversing until with a "ZingZingZing!" Flem's playmate took off at stellar speed and winked out.

The crazy fae got hold of himsylph and looked around. The moon was high and had traveled far. If he was going back tonight, he'd better simmer down.

Not bothering to keep careful surveillance, he swooped in to a big branched eucalyptus, standing on a thick branch near the top, furling for a moment and peering down to the ground. It was almost like old times when he really was a creature of the air, not a hidden 'human male,' a creature of the ground.

Hanging on to the trunk with one arm he contemplated his life as objectively as he could, the endorphins being released from his central nervous system and pituitary due to all the exercise of *flying* definitely boosting his view.

He was happy, actually happy he realized, under such adverse conditions. Oh sweet Pan, it was funny.

Wings popped out and he jumped off his perch into thin air, softly fluttering to let himsylph down.

His feet touched the ground, his wings furled and as he dug into a pocket for the dratted ties his eyes caught a flicker of movement.

A grubby unshaven man of indeterminate age sat on the ground ten feet away, watching every move.

A sleeping bag was crumpled around and behind him, and several odd pieces of clothing were stretched out on nearby bushes is if they'd been put there to dry. Other personal items were lined up neatly in a row off to one side.

Flem noted all this without taking his eyes off the human.

No one spoke.

Flem swallowed, trying to ease his burgeoning panic.

"Well for goodness sake, don't stare at me like that. I ain't the one with wings. You must be one of them there airy faeries I heard about."

This was delivered so matter-of-factly, that Flem nodded.

"Oh, don't worry, your secret's safe with me. Who'm I gonna tell? The gang at St. Loopy's soup kitchen? Hee hee! Yep, they'll believe me all right. They'll say 'Yeah, Weed, have another drink!' Hee hee. So I guess I will! Want one?"

Flem couldn't help it. He relaxed. He actually laughed.

"No, no, huh-ugh, thanks anyway." He held his hand up, shaking it, negating any such thought at all, both to this Mr. Weed, and to reinforce himsylph against any temptation. After all, a free drink was a free drink.

Deciding it was no use in pretending to be anything but what and who he was, he shrugged his shoulders in a nonchalant way, still sort of grinning and continued tying his wings down, glancing dubiously at his companion of thirty seconds.

Weed was enjoying the show, his eyes never once leaving this intruder who had wandered into his life. Licking his lips he raised a half empty bottle of amber liquid and took a healthy swig.

A bright hard gleam shone from the backs of his eye. He couldn't wait to tell Maizey in the morning.

He took another drink. "Here's to you. Say, need some help with that one?" he impulsively asked as Flem fumbled with the upper tie on his left shoulder. Quickly screwing the cap back on to his bottle he rolled it away on the ground and stood, pulling his pants up with both hands. A second later his putrid breath was coming in heavily near the faerie's ear and before Flem could stop him, Weed was leaning in to take over the tie job.

Holding the flinch in, the Sylph steeled himsylph and turned his face away, clenching his jaw.

"There! Nice and tidy." The helpful human stepped back, stumbling over a rock, hands waving wildly for a moment but didn't fall.

"I've got to get home," stated Flem. "Um, thanks for your help." He looked about, trying to reorient himsylph.

"Oh, where do you live?" quickly interjected the man as if there were a chance in hell he'd ever hear that answer.

"Nowhere! Well, that is, nowhere near here!" Flem smiled, a foreign faerie grimace that lied with every muscle, feeling himsylph revert back to canyon days and not sure how to just *be*. And wanting to be away.

Seeing the Sylph grow so uncomfortable, the human shut down and let his heart out. "Don't worry, I'm not your enemy. I'm just pleased to meet you. Go ahead."

Turning his back, he deliberately picked his way back to his sleeping bag and sat down heavily, keeping his eyes averted as he made a show of opening his bottle.

The faerie was touched and buttoning his shirt, he strode over, sticking out a hand to shake as the humans were so fond of doing.

"My name is Flumaria Greenwood, Flem Green now-a-days. Nice to meet you." He smiled.

Weed's eyes crinkled at the corners and he immediately clasped the gesture of respect.

They nodded at each other, a tacit agreement unspoken between them.

Flem adjusted his shirt and pulled a wadded up scarf from one of its pockets, wrapping it around his throat. He looked quite the sophisticated human although he didn't realize it.

Weed was smiling approvingly as he took one more sip, a 'nightcap,' he explained, and then proceeded to lay down and snuggle back into his skimpy bed. Just before he closed his eyes, he winked at the faerie and promised, "I never saw ya."

Chapter 31

By God, *something* just fluttered and
then bounced out of sight again.

$\mathcal{F}$LEM WAS UP early the next morning. It was amazing how good he felt
considering how little sleep he'd gotten the night before. It must have
been the exercise.

The city was just waking up, bright cheerful sounds in the background,
birds calling, a fresh breeze, two people talking on some street nearby. Flem
figured one must be a truck driver and the other a shop owner, considering
how loud their voices were.

Sitting in the back on the broken stoop, he gingerly leaned against the
old grey wooden door frame, sipping his lemon mint tea, watching the fog
tendrils reach insubstantial fingers through the air.

Ruefully, he remembered his encounter of the night before. No harm
done, but still, it was his own darn fault. Cha. He hadn't *looked* first, for Pan's
sake. Shaking his head he resolved to be more careful. Not everybody was
so accepting.

A small furry feline was once again entrenched into the hollow of his
wingulacture.

Setting his cup aside, the Sylph stood up and stretched then went to do
some more cleaning. He found if he kept doing one little area at a time, it
added up.

Once again a cautioning voice spoke up, a brakeman who jumped up and
down on a runaway train, venting frustration at the driver's total disregard
for someone else's property. He was nuts to hang his heart here.

Coldly he stomped the little bugger out, a tinder to be doused. He preferred to go with his passion, his joy, and not by the rules. He'd tried to play

by the rules back at Thimbleberry and it just hadn't worked. Mostly 'cause he just couldn't figure them out...

Here, he did know the rules, and was actually learning how to play by them, but that didn't mean he wasn't also learning that he could play by his *own* rules too, which centered around his feelings. (Well, that and stealth...)

Here were people, yes humans, who just seemed to accept him. He closed his eyes for probably about the hundredth time and sent a wave of gratitude out to the Universe for his luck at getting a job at Fletcherman's Nursery. His karma must be pretty good after all.

Digging some rotted frames out from they were stuck in the damp matted ground he dumped them out back alongside the cracked pots he'd stacked over the last few days.

He'd decided to make only, what he deemed, unnoticeable, changes to the main body of the old structure for the time being, that way it still looked relatively the same to a casual passerbyer. But behind the bamboo wall he'd made great headway, what windows there were, were as clean as he could get them although green still stained many a corner. He'd consolidated all his possessions to one solid cupboard that was in remarkably good shape and sat in the opposite corner from his hammock.

The fennel plant at the corner of the building out back was so big it almost blocked the path that ran between the rear of the greenhouse and the fence. He loved the smell of it and would often stick a hand out through the non-existent window pane and pull some feathery fronds through his fingers, just to get the aroma to release.

His gaze swept onto his new hammock and he doubled it up onto one hook to be less obvious.

Everything was looking quite homey. He figured he had a couple of hours before the first person showed up, which was usually Iris, but not always. Sometimes it was Lily. There was still another hour after that before he and Mayapple were due.

Unable to resist, he started eyeballing the neglected ceiling of the whole greenhouse, mentally pulling down that old watering systems that hung in tatters.

With a gleam upwards, he walked to the side and yanked on one of several dangling rubber hoses which hung like a tangle of headless snakes, and it gave way unexpectedly. He jumped back but not quite fast enough and a small rain of old debris sifted over him, causing his pulse to startle like a frightened horse. Cha. He hadn't actually meant to brings things down, to *change* anything, even if it was old and decrepit.

He felt like such an intruder all of a sudden and got very sylphconscious. Broken pots were one thing, but pulling things down was quite another.

Brushing himsylph off, a new idea seized him and he was terrified and exhilarated at the forwardness of it. Dare he do this? Since he had such a case of nerves already, maybe he'd just get out, go for a walk, peek in at Lark's Blackberry Bakery. He had plenty of time. And then he could hurry to work, right in time with Mayapple. It was brilliant! He'd be sure to arrive back early so he could stake out her arrival and get the timing just right.

Grinning, he looked up and saw which piece should come down next, and it wouldn't be hard either, he just had to unfasten it from the far end.

Perhaps tonight. He'd wait 'til everyone was gone and it was late, then fly up to that perch where he could undo the junction of that mess.

Feeling better with a plan in place he finished his ablutions, but leaving his shirt and ties off 'til he got over the wall. Running his fingers through his hair, he shook his head and wished for a mirror.

Opening his cupboard, he took out a small woven pouch where he kept his money and removed a twenty.

Picking up his scarf, he wound it securely around one hand and slipped out the old window-door before it got any later.

He wondered what time the bakery opened. No doubt early.

A bit breathlessly he looked around the backyard here, behind the greenhouses and main building. Not a soul in sight.

Taking a deep breath he stood about ten feet in front of his stolen home and let his wings unfurl.

Minute snags near the base caught briefly and he wondered when he could get Mayapple to help again. Probably anytime he wanted, he grinned to himsylph, sticking his tongue in his cheek at such luxury in his life.

Meanwhile, he whirred to take the chill out, revving his engines for takeoff.

Ascending straight up, he barely attained nine feet, just enough to see over the back wall and up and down the alley.

Whimsey C. Nimble

The coast was clear. Within seconds he was up, over and out, his wings furled and restrained, and he was jauntily on his way to go see Lark.

Unbeknownst to Flem, Santolina had dropped Iris at work that morning and she had slipped through the gates and hadn't raised the rolling door but merely let herself in with her key. It was early because Santolina had had an early appointment and Iris had opted to just come to work instead of going all the way home to get her own car.

Santolina was long gone and Iris Fletcherman sat in her dim office going over paperwork that she'd been putting off for too long, a to-go container of fresh coffee at hand.

Reaching for the cup on the desk in front of her, a sudden out-of-place movement out back between the greenhouses caught her attention.

Poised in motion, she narrowed her eyes and studied the action.

What the hell was it? She half rose from her seat as she leaned closer to the window, her curiosity enflamed.

By God, *something* just fluttered and then bounced out of sight again.

She took off at a dead run, throwing herself into silent pursuit, Chocolate Carmel Latte left wobbling precariously on her desk.

Hardly daring to breathe, she ran though number one 'til, close to the back, she ducked down and waddled as fast as she could, coming up right below the back window. Easing up, she brought her gaze to just above the sill, keeping to one side in line with some hanging crystals Mayapple had hung there several years ago. Cobwebs helped her mission.

Some*thing* or some*one* was still hanging in the air, for Pete's sake and her disbelieving gaze took it in.

It *had* to be Flem, her newest employee, but it didn't look like him but yet it did. The hair was the same, the legs looked right.

What the hell?

He had *wings?*

His epileptic fits replayed through her mind and she realized, they *weren't* epileptic fits.

For God's sake, he was a *faerie*. She'd heard about them of course, but she'd never knowingly met one before. And what was he doing here, at this hour, anyway? Bossily concerns crowded in and she straightened up to watch unabashedly as he flew right over the back fence and disappeared.

Without a moment's hesitation she ran lickety-split back the way she'd come, straight to the small curtained window facing the front street in the main building. She was hoping against hope that's where he was heading.

Breathlessly, she took up her watch and sure enough, she didn't have long to wait.

Flem himsylph, the big *faerie*, came strolling out of the alley and turned left, right past her concealed nose. Not a wing in sight.

Outrage at his deception fried her sense of justice at being deceived.

Well!

Guilt over her voyeurism of course took no part. Ah, the self righteous state, so blameless.

He adjusted his scarf as he looked furtively around and her sense of wonder swam up from the depths, displacing the shock, her sense of awe dissipating all other emotions.

Now that she really looked at those shoulders, it was so obvious he didn't just have brawn across that slim chest. Of course.

Letting the curtain fall back in place, she tapped her front teeth with one finger, thinking.

Turning, she decided to go investigate.

Feeling emboldened at his daring, the fae young man who was really one hundred and twenty-four and not a man, headed on, his adrenalin picking up speed the closer he got.

His mouth went dry but he forced himsylph to stay with the plan. He knew by now, for Pan's sake, that if you didn't force yoursylph to go beyond your normal routine at least occasionally, things didn't change. That's how ruts happened. He still didn't like it in some ways when you got right down to it, but again, *his* rules were coming into play also. He was starting to get it, this *life* thing. Someday – SOMEDAY- he'd go home again and by Pan, he bet they'd be surprised by the new *him*.

Approaching from down the street, he watched the front of the store and saw the door to the Blackberry Bakery opening and closing with surprising regularity, as the pre-work crowd sallied forth to stock up on Lark's delectable goodies.

Walking up to the door, he almost lost his nerve but pushed on, resolve and determination stiffening his backbone. Until Mayapple had practically fallen in his lap as a friend, he'd never know how to be 'normal,' to just be himsylph around others.

Another customer came in right behind Flem and the faerie stepped awkwardly back, out of her way, as it was quite obvious she was in a hurry.

Two more came in right behind her and Flem stepped back even further, into sweetroll territory.

Another person tried to come in at that moment but stopped as she saw how crowded it was but then hunger and good sense came to her rescue and she eased in, slowly shutting the door behind her.

Flem relaxed, no one was paying any attention to him at all. Hungrily he studied the tender looking pastries in front of him, seeing little signs stuck here and there - Raspberry, Blueberry, Apple-Walnut, Lemon Cream Cheese, and he was almost overcome with a sweet lust. His tongue came out and wet a corner of his mouth and he found himsylph licking his lips in anticipation.

Raising his head he looked towards the cash register and a jolt of energy ran right into his solar plexus taking his breath away.

Lark was watching *him*, green eyes never faltering and over the heads of a shop full of customers he held Flem's gaze and deliberately licked his lips too in response, a mirror image to Flem's unconscious movement.

Flem gulped, not sure if he was reading what seemed to be a predatory action, correctly. Maybe Lark was just mocking him because he had just licked his lips but he didn't think so. Lark was sending him mating signals, that's what was going on.

Caught like a moth to a light, Flem threw caution to the wind and ran his raspy tongue quickly over just his top lip and a spark danced from his eye and over to the man in black who was paying no attention to the customer in front of him.

Before he could catch himsylph the faerie in the bay window surrounded by temptation wrinkled his nose, his *nose*, at the man up front and then blinked coyly with a sweet little come-hither grin before getting a hold of himsylph and looking down.

Oh Great Pan! Never had he imagined *himsylph* doing anything like that! Blood roared through his ears at what he'd just done. Unable to not look, he sought Lark, wondering if he'd just made a complete fool of himsylph.

The suave owner of the business was busy ringing in sales and Flem drew in a deep breath, inhaling the moment.

Whipping around, he fumbled with the tissue paper and carefully extracted six rolls, filling a little bag completely.

He was bringing them back to work he decided. A gift.

Folding the top over he went and stood in line, which was five deep, twenty dollars burning hotly in his pocket.

Moments later, eeeek! he was staring in to Lark's intense gaze, blindly holding the twenty dollars out with numb fingers, surprised on some remote level he was living through this.

"Oh for goodness sake, put your money away. Enjoy – tell Iris hello. Is Mayapple working today too?" grinned the object of his affections.

Just then the door closed again, squeezing another shopper in and two people were trying to get Lark's attention. A timer went off in the back room, the phone rang and the lady right behind Flem let out a big breathy sigh, as if she'd been there for too long.

Flem thought fast - he still had at least a spare hour.

"Anything I can do to help out here?" he queried. "I can't run the cash register but anything else? I've got a little time if you need me."

Lark's eyes opened wide in appreciation and he snapped out, "Yes! Go to the back to the biggest oven and check my rolls, please! If they're nicely browned, take them out and set them on the racks – you'll see 'em. If not, re-set the timer for three minutes, okay?"

Nodding briskly, Flem came around the end of the corner, looking up as Lark continued, "Be sure to wash your hands first." After a bare pause he continued, "Thank you," but it was drawn out with a special look and a sexy voice before he turned abruptly back to next customer.

Chapter 32

⸺ ❧ ⸺

Mayapple lifted out a raspberry-filled piece of heaven, her
mouth watering so, she could hardly say "Thank you."

FEELING VERY SYLPHIMPORTANT, Flem the faerie helper tossed his bag
of temptation onto a nearby counter and snatched up two heavy hot
pads next to a gleaming large oven and threw open the door.

Waves of hot air assailed him and he wondered if his eyelashes were
singed as he was sure he felt them curl.

Blinking rapidly, he peered into the cave-like depths of the oven and saw
a myriad of miniature twinkling brown loaves, row after row, glistening with
micro bubbles of love.

Quickly he shut the door again and looked around. Wire racks were
waiting about three steps away.

Scanning the oven controls he flipped two to 'off, ' hoping that's what
was suppose to happen. Working steadily, he transferred all the rolls to the
tiered rack.

That was that.

Sticking his head back through, he asked his boss if there was anything
else and Lark held up a hand to shush him, as he was in the middle of a
transaction.

"Oops," muttered Flem, abashed. "Sorry," he said, even lower.

Breathing in through his delicate Sylph nostrils, he told himsylph it was
not the end of the world to have blundered like that but before he could go
any further with *that* line of thought, Lark was calling his name.

With saucer like eyes he approached the great god Lark and Lark said,
"Boo! Flem, it's okay. Thanks for checking on them. Were they done?"

At Flem's nod, Lark went on, "Can you do a couple more things while you're here?"

A smile broke through and delight shone in the fae young man's eyes. He was really loving this and so admired this man in black.

"Yes, of course," and he grinned enchantingly.

Lark smiled into his eyes and Flem felt a frisson of electricity zip down his back bone.

"Hellooo?" came a singsong voice disrupting the energy thread held between them and Lark quickly turned back with a big smile and oozed charm to the next customer, but interjecting directions to Flem as he did so -

"Will you fill the sides for me Flem? If the basket is really low, I have replacement in the back, on the left. Just read the signs and be sure to refill with the same. Can you do that? Do you have time? That'll be six forty-eight, thank you," he directed at the customer as she held out a ten dollar bill, as if he hadn't missed a beat.

"Sure," replied Flem quickly and cruised the perimeter really quickly to get some idea of what went where.

Minutes later he was easily refilling all the luscious pastries and breads and even managed to refill the low glass shelving in front of Lark. Unobtrusively of course.

As he returned for the last time he asked, "Anything else?" his heart beating with pride at this easy accomplishment.

The line was three deep but Lark said "Excuse me for a moment," to the next in line and turned to Flem with a look of gratitude.

Reaching out to the other, he gave his friend's shoulder a quick soft pinch, and Flem melted, putty in his hands, trying hard not to show it, trying to behave as if this was just another common occurrence in his life.

"Don't forget your bag. Where is it?" Lark asked.

Flem grinned sheepishly and ducked around the corner to retrieve it.

"Thanks Flem. You really saved the day! Can't wait 'til Revelry," and with that, turned around and continued conducting business but kept one eye on Flem too as he made his way to the door.

As the Sylph pulled it open, trying to not get flustered *now*, his eyes flew back up front for one more look and there was Lark, talking as he made change but his radar was working and he was innocently licking his lips as he raised his eyes to Flem's and then looked back at his customer, smiling a little more than necessary.

Unable to contain himsylph, Flem laughed out loud, suddenly not flustered at all but very happy.

And, he had free sweetrolls to boot!

Scurrying back to Fletcherman's, he practically skipped, his wings full and heavy with the need to let go but he consciously relaxed them, easing taut muscles back to limpness then contracting them into as neat a package as he could summon.

He was getting the hang of this.

Uncontrollable giddiness overtook him and he grinned happily at every person he passed, looking them in the eye whenever possible. Most smiled back, sharing the secret with him as they passed one another. One looked through him as if he were transparent and it felt like the old days for a brief second but then another smile was shared and Flem understood that universal bond of simple appreciation for the love of life.

He passed a tall green metal pole with a white clock face in it and saw that he had a good thirty minutes to make it to work.

Hustling along he was soon in sight of the Nursery. Giggling a little at his unexpected morning, the thought of Lark caused a rather warm blustery sensation in his chest and he had to stop because he lost his breath, his heart doing a strange little flutter.

As he stood down the block from work, he studied just where he could intercept Mayapple when a bus pulled up in front and Mayapple herself stepped onto the pavement.

Well, cha! No time for planning *now*. Her hurried to catch her before she strode away and she jumped when he touched her arm.

"Flem! Where'd you come from? Did you just get here too? I didn't see you on the bus... What's that, ooh, did you go to the Bakery, Flem? Oh yum. C'mon, let's go see your cats," and she smiled happily, glad to see him. "How's those irascible *wings* (she whispered the words) of yours doing? Need a quick fix?" She gleamed at him shyly.

Flem looked at her askance as they cut through the main building, heading out back, not paying any attention except to each other, which is why they both stopped cold when Iris Fletcherman materialized like a ghost right beside them framed in an open doorway.

"Good morning, Mayapple; Flem. Aren't you going the wrong way? Time cards are back that direction." She pointed to the area they'd just passed.

"Oh, hi mom," greeted her daughter coolly.

"Good morning, Mrs. Fletcherman," gulped the faerie, feeling guilty guilty guilty.

Iris cast him a speculative look that lingered a bit too long as she searched his face.

He wondered what the Pan was going on and if he was imagining it.

Abruptly, Iris smiled brightly at him and said, "I'm short an employee today, so Flem, how'd you like to learn something new?"

Taken aback by this totally unexpected turn of events what could he do but express the greatest joy ever at such a wondrous proposition, while inside he was screaming: Oh cha! No! Not now, not today. I like my life set up just the way it is, don't change it *now*.

Heedless to his dilemma, Iris went on, "I've got a delivery truck arriving anytime now from The Green Thumb. I'm going to show you how to check it in so when it gets here, you'll be ready to go, okay? Mayapple, I need you on the cash register. I hate to take time off from the Parks and Rec's baskets but it can't be helped."

An involuntary grin came up at the mere mention of the Parks and Rec and Mayapple thought, 'Oh my God, mom has it really bad,' before nodding blandly to her parent. "Sure. No problem," her detached manner hiding her daughterly astonishment.

"Oh, it's not nine yet, is it, and here I am assuming you're both ready for work. Sorry! Were you kids on you way somewhere special?" So ingeniously this was said and Mayapple replied just as casual.

"Nah, just out back for a minute. It can wait. I'll see you at noon, okay Flem? Oh!" she ended with a note of surprise as she remembered his cache of goodies, her eyes betraying her as they flew to the white bakery bag in his hand.

Recovering himsylph with aplomb, the faerie responded, holding the bag aloft, saying, "Oh, I thought we'd wait for lunch time, what do you think?"

Her mouth opened and closed and she swallowed, not wanting to actually *ask* and he finally took pity on her and drawled, "Oh, don't be foolish, of course we'll have them now. Here," and he rushed over to hold the bag for her, opening it with the other hand.

219

Whimsey C. Nimble

Drooling, Mayapple lifted out a raspberry-filled piece of heaven, her mouth watering so, she could hardly say "Thank you."

"Mrs. Fletcherman?" His best and most sincere, award winning smile was shone full upon Iris, as he innocently offered his gift.

He sure didn't act like someone with something to hide thought Iris, charmed in spite of herself once again by this fetching faerie, her recent findings and their perceived implications rendered moot by this sweet creature.

Sighing, she reached in and took out the first one on top, a blackberry tart, its tender crust practically crumbling in her hand.

"Oh Mr. Green, these look so luscious." Another deep sigh, "I can resist anything but temptation," she muttered just before taking a huge bite, a look of ecstasy on her face at such decadence.

Chewing, she held up an arm and checked the time, motioning them to go and saying to be back by nine, she was going back to her office, she'd see them in twenty minutes, walking off with one hand cupped below the other to be sure and catch any precious falling morsels.

"Does your mother *know* about me?" questioned Flem the minute she was gone.

"Nope. I don't think so. How could she? Well, if she does, it's not because *I* told her. I wouldn't. I hope you don't think I did."

"No, no. She just looked at me funny there for a minute, that's all."

"Hmmph," grunted the girl, deciding right then to feel her mom out, see how much she did know. She would plan it and not just blunder into conversation with her.

By this time their two treats were devoured and wiping their hands on their pants, they crawled through the window door without even a thought.

"Here kitty kitty," Flem was calling as he headed towards the back.

Mayapple stood nearby, looking around and wondered about the bamboo wall and what might possible be behind it. She hoped Flem hadn't moved in completely, she was worried about what her mom would say but decided she would stick up for her friend no matter what.

A light bulb went off in her mind as an idea formed for the first time and a trickle of excitement pooled in out-of-the-way places to steep for a while until she could work out the details.

Flem was rolling up the cat food bag and stowed it and an empty can in with like trash. Looking up, he enquired, "Ready?"

"No, no, I'm not ready, I haven't even gotten to pet them!"

"Well, hel*lo*, why are you standing there gawking around then? We've got stuff to do today, you heard your mom."

"Oh my God, I can't believe you're bossing *me* around! What IS this world coming to?" She bent to stroke mamma as she ate and the cat arched with her stroke, from neck to tail but did not remove her head from the food dish.

Little kittens abounded, pretending to be fascinated with this food but it was a thin veneer and they were really ready to play. Except for sticktight of course. He was latched onto mamma, laying upside down under her, all four feet kneading her belly.

"Let's go," Mayapple capitulated as they both laughed at cat antics.

They were five minutes early and Iris was waiting for them.

Mayapple frowned at her mother who frowned back, mostly on principle. She then smiled sweetly and said, "Okay, you've got the front this morning honey. Go get the change drawer from my desk. Bye!"

Mayapple scowled a little more at being so summarily dismissed but she *was* the employee, after all.

Grudgingly she smiled back and Iris gave her a knowing grin and Mayapple knew then a chat was coming soon.

Chapter 33

I think he's too old for you Lily. He's kind of
strange, really. I think he's got problems.

"THIS HERE IS my order sheet, it's alphabetical. After they unload you'll both verify the order at the same time. One of them will read the identification sticker on the plant, the other will find it on their invoice while you'll find it on ours. Be sure any bundles include the amount it says I've ordered, it'll be right there next to the box. At the end, I circle any empty spots in red, that way it makes it easy to see if any are missing. Here's where he'll pull in," she waved to their wide double doors, "and you can stack everything over there," she pointed.

"Once the order is verified, I'll expect the computer updated. Let me show you." She turned to the computer and it sprang to life already at the appropriate page. "Here, see this? Just move it so, and copy your info from the page." She shook the paper for emphasis. "That way we can see at a glance what's in stock right from the computer, as the cash register automatically deducts something when it's rung up."

"And here, this tells us the date it came in, so be sure to fill that in too, okay? And this button shows if we've paid the invoice, a red 'flag' the bookkeeper checks, but you don't have to worry about that one at all. This here will 'save' the whole shebang, okay? Don't forget to hit that button as the last thing you do! Very important!"

Flem concentrated as he nodded. It actually looked pretty simple.

She continued, "When you're all done, take your completed invoice and file it over here." A tall flat file holder with a tag above it that said 'Accounts Payable' stood empty, next to the computer.

"Moneywort, our accountant, comes in every Monday and pulls 'em and pays 'em. Then she files them here," she pointed to the second drawer down in a large, old fashioned filing cabinet, "alphabetically, where they're kept for a year. I'm happy to say all our accounts are paid on time now-a-days, unlike when I first took over, when Brodiaea died." She spoke candidly for a moment and it surprised the Sylph although she was the one who drank too much, stayed out too late with her boyfriend and winked at him occasionally, so why was he surprised again? He should stop trying to figure Iris Fletcherman out and drop all ideas of who he thought she was.

"You see Mr. Green, things weren't always so rosy as they now seem, but through some good ideas and a little hutzpah, I've managed to turn this place around! Things are *good* now. Well," she amended, "they were always *good*, we're just more, ah, *prosperous* now."

She paused and then finished with, "Well, come find me when you're done. I may put you someplace else this afternoon. Any questions?"

Flem was thinking how easy it suddenly seemed; first this morning with Lark at his business and now here, at the Nursery. This sneaking suspicion started to dawn on him and he wondered at the novel idea that *perhaps* life was much easier than he'd made it and *perhaps* it was him who had always made things so hard...

Oh cha. Was it really that simple?

"Sure, no problem. It looks easy enough," he replied, giving Mrs. Fletcherman a confident grin.

Iris tilted her head at him, a direct look with what seemed to be a silent question.

A quizzical look came into his eyes as he tried to fathom what was going on.

A loud truck engine was heard pulling into the driveway and Iris smoothly transitioned with it.

"Perfect timing. C'mon, I'll introduce you to the Campion brothers. You won't believe they're brothers, but they are. Acaulis is short and rather, *stout*, shall we say, and he's got tight curly reddish hair and his brother Schafta is tall and rather wiry, and what hair he has is more like tufts upon his head. I think he's the older of the two because his hair, which probably used to be red, is now a soft rosy purple."

Whimsey C. Nimble

Flem made a funny face at her as if finding this interesting but strange and followed her off to greet the truck, which was backing into place.

Schafta was driving and Acaulis (the short egg-shaped one) jumped down and trotted to the back, 'spotting' his brother, guiding the vehicle into place then holding up a clenched fist to signal him to stop, he was there.

Curly eyebrows matched the springy mat of hair that carpeted his head and Iris introduced them just as Schafta came up to be included too.

Chit chat was made for about a minute and then they got right down to work. These boys had a system.

Iris watched for a moment then looked at Flem and said, "I'm leaving. Find me if you have a problem." She waited 'til she got his nod of acceptance, and then turned and said "Bye! Nice to see you again, boys. Give my regards to your dad, Moss, okay?"

The brothers waved at her and nodded, immediately returning to business.

Flem stood by, check-in paper clutched rather awkwardly but Schafta and Acaulis took him right in hand.

"Come with me," offered Schafta and they stepped over to where Acaulis was waiting.

"We have duplicates of Iris's order and theoretically, yours should match exactly. It doesn't always work like that though for some unfathomable reason." The brothers shook their heads glumly at each other regarding misfortunes they had known and Acaulis took over where Schafta left off.

"Here, let's get started and we'll see soon enough how well we all match."

Acaulis rolled up the back of the truck and dropped the tail gate. Boxes, flats of plants, statues, hoses and more could be seen crowded neatly.

Flem saw at a glance that there was some kind of color system going on, as pink, yellow, red, and white ribbons were attached, one each, to everything for quick identification.

Working together the brothers quickly removed all inventory with pink flags, and then systematically started verifying, one brother doing the reading off, the other answering with an affirmative, pausing to cast a questioning look at Flem.

He nodded as he quickly caught on and kept up, finding it easy to understand, proud of himsylph.

It didn't take long before all was recorded and the Sylph was feeling better by the minute, especially glad that all inventory sheets matched.

At that point he received his copy of the invoice, and The Green Thumb team, Acaulis and Schafta, Moss Campion's boys, made haste, long tall Schafta folding himself behind the wheel and dumpy Acaulis clamboring into the passenger's side. A shifting of gears and they were off.

Half an hour later, the computer was updated, invoice put away and the faerie went to find Mrs. Fletcherman which took some doing until he finally traced her down to her office. The door was open and as he approached he realized he could see Iris's profile against the window, illuminated at the far end. She was on the phone and her back was to him. He coughed but she apparently didn't hear him.

He just stood there, waiting.

He cleared his throat again but she obviously was intent on her phone call.

His eyes roamed past her and he saw the top of the old greenhouse and the trees around it, framed perfectly right behind the row of the newer greenhouses, one, two, and three. Instantly he realized she, Iris, could easily SEE him flying IF she happen to be here at night, which he couldn't imagine any reason she would be. But still.

Oh cha.

Iris was turning around but hadn't seen him yet, although his eyes easily fell on her and he watched as she smiled and her lips said I love you before she hung up, looked up, and instantly motioned him in with two fingers, a unreadable professional look upon her face.

Again, she gave him an immense mini stare before asking him about the recent delivery and he wondered if he was imagining things, they went by so fast.

She was quiet so he quickly recapped the delivery, ending with "...and I stapled their sheet with ours and left it in the tray for Moneywort."

Iris nodded. "Why don't you go to lunch, and afterwards you and Mayapple can refill some of the perennial display, out in the pergola. Say, one o'clock?"

Flem agree and turned to go, Iris already picking up a catalogue from her stack of mail. His eyes slid over the back window and his belly tightened at this possible peep hole.

He thought, with a little sylphgrimace, that it was rather late now to start being so careful. Unfortunately, rational thought was now overriding passion and his old nemesis *worry* started to creep in.

Rather unsettled, the Sylph made his way to the front where Mayapple was checking out a customer.

Waiting respectfully 'til the customer left, Flem then said "Hi" to Mayapple, a soft smile at the mere sight of her lighting up his features. It was good to have a friend, someone to trust.

"Hey Flem, I hear we're restocking the perennials this afternoon. Lily should be in any minute and I can go to lunch and then meet you at one out back, okay? I've got errands to run, I wish she'd hurry up and get here, so I can go."

Flem nodded and merely said, "Okay, see you at one. Oh, there's Lily now. Hi Lily!" he called.

Mayapple was a bit surprised to see Flem actually taking the initiative but the way Lily giggled and greeted him made her think twice. She looked from one to the other, a bit disconcerted by the feeling of possessiveness that washed through her.

Flem the fool never noticed, he was too busy charming the cashier just before he came back to his senses and took his leave, parting with "See you at one, Mayapple," before blithely turning away and heading towards his cat house.

Mayapple stared after him, watching him saunter and listening to a tuneless whistle while he did so.

Lily was all smiles, as she stowed sweater and purse below the cash register, turning to Mayapple and saying "He's pretty cute, isn't he? How old do you think he is? Twenty-eight, twenty-nine?"

"I think he's too old for you Lily. And he's kind of strange, really. I think he has problems." Mayapple was utterly amazed when she heard herself say these bald untruths right to Lily's face, and such gall, behind Flem the faerie's back. Her friend. *Her* friend.

"Really?" asked Lily in an unbelieving voice. "He seems so nice..." She let her words trail off.

Feeling triumphant, Mayapple quickly excused herself and practically ran out the door in her guilt.

Until this moment, Flem had merely been her friend, whom she loved dearly.

Resigning herself to her evil ways she gave a rather wicked little laugh as she went about her business, wondering if *she* had a crush on Flem too.

First Lark, now Lily. Apparently she wasn't the only one who appreciated Sylph charm. A feeling of possessiveness coursed through her which she diligently tried to rationalize away but it left its imprint, of course.

Thirty minutes later the two of them were knee deep in daisies so-to-speak, Flem listening as Mayapple kept up a steady stream of chatter, never missing a beat as she reached down into the extra large carton that contained fifty small peat pots and handed him various herbs, two at a thyme. He marveled that she could keep on track and cover so many subjects but she kept coming back to the fast approaching Revelry with Cybele as her main interest.

Mayapple was excited but she also had an ulterior motive: she wanted to see if she could get Flem to talk about Lark. Curiosity was eating her alive.

A twinge that it wasn't her that fit so well with him tweaked her for a moment but she let it pass on by. It wasn't meant to be.

And strangely enough she wasn't actually jealous of Lark. Or repelled. She actually thought they'd be cute together. And Flem was a fast learner, he'd soon pick up Lark's sophisticated ways.

"Yoo hoo!" Iris's greeting brought them both up silent, turning to watch her approach.

She seemed rather breathless. "Listen, something's come up and I've got to go out. Finish up here, then start working on that new delivery. If you've got time, water everything outside, okay? If you get that done, well, then go work on your baskets. I'll see you tomorrow." She sounded very brisk but Mayapple was immediately suspicious. Was her mom skipping out, going to play hooky? Mayapple's irreverent mind sang out, or, ' going to play nooky?' and she started to laugh, a sound through her nose, at first. Giggles, very uncorrect, unfunny, horrible giggles ran out her mouth in little triplets until she sucked them back in and swallowed. Pulling it together she hardened her guise back to Proper Daughter and with thin pressed lips, said, "Okay. Have a good time. We'll take care of it here. Where are you off to, may I ask?" So innocently. But no one was fooled.

"Oh, there's a question about the Bridge Project from the Parks Department and Santolina needs me to go with him to the Records building downtown and while we're there, we're going to take a look at where the baskets will be going." She smiled sweetly but Mayapple easily read between the lines – she was taking the afternoon off to stroll around the river with the bridges with her sweetie. For *business* reasons. They would both get paid for this meeting and probably lunch too. Geeez.

Mayapple grudgingly smiled and said, "You're a good example, mom. I hope I can follow in your footsteps someday."

Iris grinned at this, took a step forward and pinched her little girl's cheek. "Of course you will sweetheart. After all, you're *my* daughter!"

Both laughed at Iris's undauntable confidence, easily understanding what was really going on.

"Bye!" Iris fluttered her fingers and sailed for the door, eager to see her man.

Chapter 34

"Mr. Stinkweed, Mr. Stinkweed, *calm down!*"

THREE HOURS LATER the display was long filled, the inventory put away and everything watered. "Crap, we still have an hour to go. I don't feel like starting another basket, do you? What should we do?" Mayapple slouched a little, her hands in her back pockets, her knees wet from the soaking they'd just given everything. "I'd like to see the kitties, we could check on them," she added.

"Let's go see Lily first" countered Flem.

Mayapple scowled and said "Go ahead. I'm going to go out back," and she scowled even more.

Flem unconsciously frowned right back at her and said "Go ahead!" then turned and headed up front.

Growling, Mayapple stomped off, chiding herself as she went. How ridiculous to be jealous. Flem deserved all the friends he could get. Everybody did.

By this time she was sliding through the window door and cats were coming towards her, meowing and running towards this person in their midst. Ten minutes of devoted adoration later and she was free to go. Everyone got an extra scratch and a tidbit of treat; thus distracted, she was able to walk cleanly away but not before making a side trip towards the bamboo wall.

Nice and tidy and very homey. Junk piled outside. Windows, (what there were of them) cleaned. Paths. Nice cupboard. His new hammock carefully folded onto one hook. All was as she expected, no surprises. She just hoped her friend Flem the faerie wasn't going to get kicked out by the property owner... She'd have to intervene before that happened. How many other people could say they had a faerie living in their back yard?

Whimsey C. Nimble

Making her way back to find Flem, she caught sight of him standing quietly behind Lily's shoulder, observing as she made change for a lady, smiling and nodding to himsylph.

Her heart warmed towards the two of them and she straightened out her unruly emotions, letting her heart be her guide, realizing there was no reason to ever be jealous, there was simply love to be shared.

As she approached, another customer, a man with a long rake in one hand and a bucket of artichoke plant in the other also approached.

After you, he indicated.

"No, no I work here," she smiled.

"Lucky them," he commented, giving her a warm look.

Mayapple, queen of live talk, the consistent commentator, the Mayapple magpie of childhood, had nothing to say and only blushed in response.

None of this was lost on Flem who was still sort-of talking to Lily about the functions of the cash register.

"Can I check you out?" blurted Mayapple before she realized how it would sound.

"Absolutely. Anytime. I'd be happy to return the favor too," was the immediate response, a grin lighting his eyes at his jest.

"I mean Lily. Lily can help you," she blundered on, red faced.

"Oh, I don't need *her* help checking you out, I'll bet you don't need help checking *me* out, do you?" The gall, the outrageous comments he was making sent Mayapple into a tailspin.

Unfortunately, she started to laugh and Flem knew what was coming. To save face, he spoke loudly in Lily's ear, making her jump: "Lily, can you show me again how to ring a sale up?" while throwing daggers at Mayapple to get a hold of herself.

A gasp from her was covered as he bumped into her pretty hard and managed to get in a pinch at the same time.

A wheeze was heard as she struggled with her maniacal hilarity.

The rake now stood uncertainly, artichoke drooping perilously low reflecting a question where before irrepressible charm had shone.

Lily was a bit discombobulated and just stood there.

Flem slipped into action, easily duplicating the motions she had been demonstrating to him only moments before.

The soul of Mayapple returned. Self confidence and an ability to act as if all was normal, everything fine, rose to the surface, saving her.

"Our artichokes are really healthy this year. You know, it's best to have several, as not all of them bloom." She smiled into the handsome customer's eyes.

"Can you show me where they are again? I'm afraid I don't remember. Maybe I should get two or three more. You're right. Can I set these here 'til we get back? Providing you're free, of course." A dazzling smile aimed only at the young woman in front of him.

Without a backward glance the two set off and now it was Flem's turn to feel rather put out, watching his best girl walk away with a handsome stranger. A *human* stranger.

Cha.

Lily tugged on his sleeve and he looked down into her flushed face, liking her freckles and admiring how well the little green points on her sweater complimented her coloring. A choker of yellow beads added its own resonant flair.

"Come on, I'll show you how I look up inventory in the computer without making a sale, people are always calling and asking if we've got such and such and how much it is."

Feeling rather bereft, the Sylph let this pretty young human distract him with work and soon he felt like a business man. Ah, business Sylph. It all seemed so easy.

He couldn't wait to tell Lark.

What?!

Well, Lark had a cash register too - it would be a good topic to discuss – how similar they were.

Smiling, he listened attentively to every word Lily said, filing it all away for later.

Mayapple came back chattering away, carrying two more artichokes as did the man behind her. Old friends now, thought Flem rather sarcastically to himsylph.

She rang him up and he finally left, Mayapple walking him to the car and ordering Flem to lend a hand if he would in carrying the rake and last plant.

"Please," she added but hardly looked at him, just kept bending the poor guy's ear.

Whimsey C. Nimble

Flem was not happy. He tried to give her a little kick to snap her out of it but she merely sidestepped him, shooting *him* a look.

Sulkily he followed her to the man's shiny new pick-up truck and thumped his two items into the back.

"Here," he grumbled.

Mayapple mouthed "What is WRONG with you?" quickly behind her new boyfriend's back and Flem stuck out his tongue at her and rolled his eyes.

Mayapple laughed and mouthed the word "Go!" to him, immediately turning back to handsome and smoothly continuing with, "Dinner would be great. Here's my address. I'll see you at seven."

He nodded and hopped into the cab, grinning.

She turned and hurried to catch up with the sulky Sylph.

"Flem!" but before she could go any further, Lily was at the door holding the phone out to her.

"Here! You talk to him. Some customer who's hopping mad about *some*thing."

With great trepidation, Mayapple gingerly held out her hand for the mess, wondering how bad it could be. Assuming her sternest voice, she said, "Hi. The owner's not here, I'm her daughter Mayapple, perhaps I can help you? What seems to be the problem?" her other hand at her throat as she assumed the persona of authority.

"I see," she repeated at intervals.

A pause as she bit her bottom lip and then, "My mother is an honest businesswoman, Mr. Stinkweed. I really find it hard to believe she would deliberately charge you for something you didn't get. Mr. Stinkweed, Mr. Stinkweed, *calm down!* Give me your phone number and I'll see what I can find out." She grabbed the pencil Lily held out and felt a rush of gratitude towards Flem as he used two hands to secure a piece of paper for her to write on.

"Got it," she affirmed. "I'll look into it and call you back personally. No one is trying to 'pull one over on you,' honest. Goodbye. I'm hanging up now Mr. Stinkweed. Goodbye!" She hung up.

Lily and Flem stood by, eyes big with apprehension.

"Yowzers! Just think, if my dear mother hadn't been 'needed,' by the, ahem, Parks and Rec department this afternoon *I* wouldn't have had to take that phone call." A lone wild giggle followed this statement but didn't multiply, to everyone's relief.

"I'm going to go find all the records I can pertaining to this guy. Flem? I think it's a good idea to have Lily show you how to use the cash register." She smiled at him and Lily who smiled shyly back before looking away. Lily was several years younger than Mayapple and was always rather in awe of the boss's daughter.

As the boss's daughter, people naturally sucked up to her but Mayapple never took advantage of it. Rather, she tended to champion causes she favored to her mother and was known for her fair mindedness. And, of course, her disability in the mirth department. "So, are you coming with me or staying here?"

"I'm coming with you. I'd like to see what you're going to do."

He turned to Lily. "Thank you Lily, you've been most informative."

Lily simpered, Mayapple couldn't believe it but simply nodded at her and took off, rolling her eyes to herself. She wondered if Flem found Lily attractive. Many times had she been surprised by men's reactions to a pretty girl, no matter what *dribble* came out of her mouth. Perhaps Sylphs-turned-male weren't any less susceptible than human males. NOT that Lily wasn't smart. She was.

She hurried along and Flem kept up with her, aware something was bubbling beneath the surface but not sure what.

"That Lily, she's sweet, isn't she?" Flem asked innocently before adding, "Kind of young, awfully giggly. Good cashier though. She seems to really know what she's doing. I learned quite a bit." He sounded surprised in spite of himsylph.

Relief poured through Mayapple at this admission and she knew she really had been jealous no matter how she white washed it.

"Yeah, she's giggly, but I like her too," replied Mayapple, opening the door to her mother's office. "C'mon, we only have fifteen minutes 'til it's time to go home, and *I* have a date!"

Flem was dismayed by this declaration but was quickly reassured when his best friend tucked her arm in his and said, "I *do* have a date, Flem. But you know YOU will always be my best friend, don't you?" Her big eyes stared into his, and he nodded, mesmerized by her sincerity.

Whimsey C. Nimble

She gave him a quick hug and then pulled back to say, "As your friend, I just want you to be happy, so- whatever that means…okay?" She had an odd look in her eye that Flem couldn't quite decipher, but he nodded, a trifle confused.

Mayapple gave his thinking process a little nudge with "Those pastries were sure good. That Lark, he's really good at what he does, isn't he?"

Flem remembered the morning and helping Lark and with a rather vacant look, he said, "Yeah…"

Mayapple's elbow dug into his rib cage, and he snapped around to stare at her.

They each waited for the other to say something and finally Mayapple capitulated, saying, "He's pretty cool, huh Flem?"

He got it then. She *knew*. He hardly knew himsylph and yet *she* knew.

"He *is*," Flem finally said out loud going on to regale her with how he had helped out this morning at the Bakery.

Mayapple listened politely to his story.

He finished with "..so you don't think I'm *imagining* things, do you?"

"No, I think he likes you Flem. Why wouldn't he? You're great!" She reached up and pinched his cheek condescendingly but he knew she actually meant it.

"So, let me show you how I'm going to go about finding this guy's records. Stinkweed! Ha. That ought to be an easy name to spot."

He peered over her shoulder and the two of them went to work.

Chapter 35

———— ✠ ————

Unexpectedly, the front door of the house
they were parked in front of flew open and a
man with bushy eyebrows that could be seen
all the way to the curb stood there.

Six o'clock rolled around and Flem decided he didn't need to watch Mayapple backtrack through invoices anymore, he'd learned enough, he was leaving. "How long are you staying? I seem to remember someone with a hot date tonight."

Mayapple stopped what she was doing and looked up. "Oh I'm leaving really soon, I just want to find that blasted invoice that's he's talking about. You go ahead, I'll see you tomorrow."

Flem smiled warmly at his favorite human and gave her the cat blink that said it all, then turned and left.

Mayapple wondered for a moment where he was going and if he'd spend the night but her own plate was pretty full, what with the dratted Stinkweed problem and a date. Why oh why did he have to call on the same afternoon that Dicksonia came in? She paused for a moment to sigh over how incredibly handsome he was, such blue eyes. And those dimples, wow.

Impatiently she yanked out a folder that had been stuck on another right in front of it and there was "Stinkweed," with a note attached. The book-keeper had seen where someone had added up the total wrong, and she had corrected it with a letter and a reimbursement check. It was dated today.

Feeling a gratifying 'Ah-Ha!' Mayapple slammed the file closed and sketched a quick note to her mother requesting her not to move this, that she'd explain in the morning.

Whimsey C. Nimble

Laying the pen down on top of it, she nearly jumped out of her skin when Iris spoke from behind her, "Mayapple, what are you doing in my office?"

"I'm handling a problem for you, mom." She paused imperceptibly and added with a straight face, "I think it's time we started talking about a raise."

Iris waited.

Mayapple sighed and started explaining and by the time she got to the note, her mother was congratulating her and agreeing, she should handle it in the morning. Exactly what Mayapple had known she'd say from the very beginning. Another sigh. It was now six fifteen.

"Mom, I've got a date, I've got to get out of here!"

"It's not with Flem, is it?" her mother asked, sounding skeptical.

"Oh, for Pete's sake, there is nothing wrong with Flem!"

"Just how well do you know him, Mayapple?"

The rather serious tone in her mother's voice caught her ear and she looked sharply at her parent, who was watching her as if in expectation of a real answer.

"Well, I know him pretty well, actually," she declared, a rather challenging look arising in her eye, preparing to do battle if necessary.

"*Really?*" There almost seemed to be a note of mockery in her mother's voice and all of Mayapple's warning signals started going off. Something was up. Could her mother possibly *know?*

Very casually, Iris asked "Been out to your dad's old greenhouse lately?"

Oh holy shit. Mayapple didn't know how to respond.

She wet her lips trying to think how to go about this when Iris started talking and Mayapple followed her mother's pointed finger as she revealed what she'd seen so recently right back there, pointing through her rear window, and went on to describe what she'd spied in the old greenhouse while Flem was out.

Well, the jig was definitely up, time to see what the damages were.

Wondering if she'd ever get home and to her date, Mayapple gave up and admitted she knew Flem was a faerie. Editing out about ninety percent of the story, she polished little nuggets of reality, softening corners, embellishing here, building up there, and Iris wondered about the *real* story, since she was sure she wasn't getting it but had to be satisfied with what she got. Mayapple had a soft spot for the underdog but Iris wasn't convinced quite yet that all was as rosy as her daughter painted.

"Don't say anything to him, mom! Not yet anyway. Give him a chance."

Shaking her head at Mayapple's naivety, Iris nonetheless promised nothing would be said anytime in the immediate future and she would talk to Mayapple before she did anything. "Now, GO. You said you had a date, right? Don't worry" she added, "It'll all work out."

Looking warily at her mother, she decided to believe her, at least temporarily, and hopped up to give her a quick squeeze. "Thanks Mom, I'll see you tomorrow." In a flash, she was gone.

Rummaging on her desk top, Iris found her current book – a sensation novel that made her laugh in its absurdity and stuck it in her briefcase.

Pausing before she did a last minute walk-through, she heard Bud's voice calling goodbye to her daughter. Then, all was quiet. Customers dwindled during the dinner hour but sometimes picked up again around seven. Fletcherman's stayed open 'til nine for the working folk and it paid off. They got business and loyalty others didn't.

Planning on leaving immediately, Iris finished straightening, took what she needed, then turned off the light, pulling the door closed behind her and locking it.

Heading out, she saw Bud before she got very far, just disappearing through the doorway of number three greenhouse.

"Hey Bud?" she called, but was too late. She needed to speak with him about a new ingredient she was thinking about ordering for the compost, and she wanted his opinion before tomorrow.

Swallowing a little surge of annoyance, she hurried down the path. Arriving at number three where all the baskets that had been made so far hung, she stopped just inside to squint around, looking for her elusive employee. "Bud?" she called tentatively.

No answer. She started down an aisle, admiring the burgeoning life from where it hung on each side of her, feeling a sense of pride at how well they looked.

But slowly, something peculiar started to make itself known to her. Some baskets were much fuller than others. She frowned and quickly counted plants but each held the same amount.

Bud appeared by her side, smiling blandly, the perfect helper, his face giving nothing away.

Baffled, she marched on, fingering foliage. "What do you make of it, Bud?" she asked, nonplussed.

Whimsey C. Nimble

Bud had a pretty good idea what was happening but far be it for him to spill the beans. He kept his mouth shut. "Hmmph," was all he said as he sidestepped the real question.

"How many are different?" Iris questioned, counting. "Eighteen," she answered herself, making a tally. "Half."

Bud looked up as a suspicion bloomed in Iris's mind, and she looked at Bud who gave her a blank, non-committal shrug.

"Do we know who made which ones?" The suspicion was trying to take root in her mind but found it hard to land.

"Mmm, I don't think so Mrs. Fletcherman. You'd have to ask them. Or I can."

Cocking an eye at him, she enquired, "Are you sure this isn't from that new fertilizer I ordered? They said it was really suppose to increase the size of the whole plant."

"No ma'am. I haven't used it yet."

"Hmmmph. Thanks Bud. Nonetheless, we're going to be hanging these soon. Give those others a shot of the new Robusta Royal, okay? Let's try to even 'em out. How odd. I'll talk to Mayapple and Flem and see what they did different." She looked thoughtful.

A quirk of his mouth hid the inward humor and he wondered if Iris Fletcherman would ever catch on. This was getting more interesting all the time. Ah, life in the city, definitely more interesting than life back home.

When Flem got to work the next morning, Mayapple dangled keys in front of him and said, "C'mon, the boss requested we deliver this in person," and she patted her breast pocket where a folded paper could be seen. "Remember Stinkweed?"

"Ha! Who could forget!"

"Well, somebody added his bill up wrong and I'm taking him a reimbursement check. Moneywort had put it in today's mail but I caught it before it went out. We are to deliver it in person; good PR, you know?"

"What is this 'PR,' you're talking about?" asked Flem, a little skeptical but not adverse to a ride through the city.

"Oh God, Flem, where've you been living, under a rock someplace? Oh. Wait. Sorry. Well, listen, just to let you know, I'm the one that convinced her Majesty you should go too, for your FYI."

"Mayapple, WHAT are you talking about? What is this 'PR,' and this 'FYI'? Cha."

"Oh God, Flem, get with the program. Geez. Okay, PR is simply public relations, you know, someone from a local business, uh, for instance, Fletcherman's Nursery, I'll bet you've heard of it, and that local business goes out of their way to do something good for the, ahem, public, you know, a customer. Stinkweed, to be specific. Mom said he's been a customer for as long as she can remember and he's kind of a prickly character, and so, we're delivering the check to him personally, see? A personal touch, he doesn't have to wait for the mail to deliver it to him. FYI. For your information. I also had to put up with a bit of sarcasm from my dear mother, something about how heavy that check was, what with two people needing to carry it...but that yes, you could go too, she felt perhaps you needed to get out more." Mayapple was careful not to look at him with that last sentence.

Feeling like he was on an adventure, the faerie followed his friend carefully through the building out to the parking lot where the company van sat - what had been a white vehicle now saturated with giant pink and yellow blooms, the words 'Fletcherman's Nursery' in flowing black script along both sides.

He had never been in a van before and a car, only once. Well, twice. He just didn't remember the ride *to* Lark's house that night.

"Wow, it's so different from the bus. Or a car." He added, flashing on Lark dropping him off that fateful weekend of the fair.

Mayapple laughed out loud and commented, "Oh yeah, like you've been out driving a lot, huh?" but didn't wait for an answer. "Well c'mon, time's a wasting, put your seat belt on," she ordered.

Flem complied, letting her sharp observation flow on past him and instead focused on the *perks* of city life.

Pulling down a laminated screen that was rolled up and affixed to the ceiling, Mayapple quickly verified on the city map where they were going and what route to take before flicking it up and out of the way.

Whimsey C. Nimble

"I could have looked it up," she explained, "but I prefer this old map. We didn't do nearly as many deliveries when dad was alive." A funny little moue harkened on her lips and Flem wasn't sure how to respond.

As usual, Mayapple took up the gap, immediately giving orders and pointing out pieces of the scenery.

"For God's sake Flem, let go of the armrest. Relax!"

Flem felt that last expertly executed maneuver swish over him like a tidal wave of pin pricks, raising the hair on the back of his neck. His shoulder blades involuntarily clenched: it appeared that everyone drove like a maniac.

He was surprised to find that it actually held a faint scandalous appeal.

They wound higher and higher up a hill and foliage got thicker as homes were further and further apart.

Mayapple chattered away as usual, more like she was thinking out loud. "I'm kind of surprised, mom agreeing so readily to the two of us delivering this check. When I told her about the problem, she smiled in a funny way and said maybe he'll show you his garden..."

Mayapple paused. "Why we would want to see his garden, I don't know. Oh well," she chuckled. "At least we're out of there for an hour, that's good!"

Flem nodded but didn't encourage her, instead looked around appreciatively. There were actually patches of what seemed to be wild area – trees and overgrown shrubbery.

Just as the van came to a stop sign, Flem caught sight of a strange shape, almost like a hut but it was way up in a tree back in the woodsy area they were now leaving behind. Flem stared and caught tantalizing glimpses of more, what looked like, structures, strewn throughout the leaves. He squinted as he fought to make sense of what he was seeing but it never clicked in his brain and then it was gone. He turned back around in his seat as Mayapple slowed down, peering at street signs.

"Yesss," she uttered sibilantly under her breath and turned right onto Chokecherry Court, crawling down the meandering little street 'til she saw the house number that matched the address she was holding.

At this time of morning there was ample parking and the long, splashy van slid easily into place and stopped.

"Okay, let's go schmooze," she half ordered, sliding out the door, smiling brightly at her co-worker who also just happened to be a faerie.

Unexpectedly, the front door of the house they were parked in front of flew open and a man with bushy eyebrows that could be seen all the way to the curb stood there.

Mayapple was hallooing and Flem could hear a hard brightness in her voice that wasn't normally there.

She must be nervous, realized the faerie with sudden insight and hurried to stand beside her for moral support. Mayapple's eyes flicked over him but she was already geared up.

The old man in the doorway was looking grumpy and Flem swallowed but Mayapple oozed delight and good will, her hand out pumping Stinkweed's hand enough to do a politician proud.

The old man now went from grumpy to bemused and of course, Mayapple never stopped talking.

Apologizing profusely for the mistake on the part of Fletcherman's Nursery, Mayapple was quick to end it with the reimbursement check that included an extra ten percent from the total of that order, which she was also quick to point out.

Bathrobe flapped to the sides and old grey mules slapped the floor behind him as Stinkweed turned abruptly and "Gotta get my glasses" could be pieced together in his wake.

The delivery people were left to stand awkwardly on the stoop making faces at each other before a grumble from inside ordered them to "Come in, come in. Shut the door. Be just a moment."

Holding Mayapple's envelope in one hand, the old man wearing a worn-out maroon bathrobe over a thin white tee-shirt and baggy, used-to-be-blue pants was fumbling to hook glasses over his large hairy ears and onto his purplish nose.

"Lemme see, lemme see," he kept repeating as he pawed through a table top littered with paper 'til he grabbed the right one and studied it assiduously.

"Mmmmm," he grunted, clearly engaged in verifying what Mayapple had just said, reading, calculating and cogitating.

Finally laying his paper down, he opened Mayapple's offering and again, a "Mmmmm" before he finally gave in with "Yep, yep, always said Fletcherman's was a fair deal. Thank you missy. You too," and his eyes caught on Flem's fair form and were arrested.

Faerie and human went eye to eye and Flem felt a flush flow over him uncomfortably as the man downright stared before finally removing his sticky gaze from him. Cha!

Eyes downcast, Flem backed up and would have bolted except for the fact that Mayapple grabbed his sleeve just as the old grump apologized by way of saying, "You look like my *cousin*," he said in a smarmy voice. "Yeah, sorry, it took me by surprise."

Flem was shocked to think Stinkweed could be related to any Sylph when it dawned on him the human was lying. He was covering up what he was really thinking.

Risking a glance at Mayapple he was gratified at her puzzled look and knew it hadn't set well with her either.

Trying to bring balance back, Mayapple the loyal gabber attempted to sew the rift. "Stinkweed. Hmmph. That's an unusual name, isn't it? Um, mom said something about your garden?" she left it hanging awkwardly, wishing she'd never said a word.

Flem looked at her and Stinkweed chewed his lip but before her face got red, he abruptly came to a decision. "C'mon. I'll show you."

With a skeptical look at each other, but one spilling over with curiosity, both fell in line behind Mr. Bah-Humbug and followed him through the house around the cluttered kitchen table and out another door.

"Watch your step," he grunted over his shoulder but Flem and Mayapple were so busy picking out their way as they trailed behind him, they hardly heard. *Stuff* was piled everywhere, *everywhere*, and both were appalled at his hidden out-of-control obsession. Stacks of newspapers, books, and miscellaneous mail-- advertisements, bills, everything paper, made neat hedges and low walls.

It appeared that at one time the room they were passing through had been a bedroom but now it was filled to the brim with useless crap.

Carefully, both kept their faces straight and their astonishment under a guise of neutrality.

"Follow me down these stairs," Mr. Stinkweed uttered, and Flem stuck his hand out and held the door open for Mayapple after their host opened it.

She risked a wide eyed hot stare at him as she ducked by and he grinned, hopping into place at the end of their funny little parade.

The covered outside back stairs were dark, lit only my morning daylight through dirty glass. Again, their path was a narrow one, their companions on each step no longer paper but pieces of old fans, blades, motors and chains of different sorts littering almost every available space.

Flem started shaking his head and couldn't stop.

Finally they were down and the Fletcherman crew of two pulled up short behind the owner of the house, who had stopped, motionless, with his hand on the door.

"Mmmgh," he gurgled, then cleared his throat. "Just need to say a word here," he gruffly got out. "Before I show you my, my *garden*, I need your word that you won't turn this into a three-ring circus. You're Brodiaea's kid, aren't ya? This ain't no bo-tanical garden for the public, see? Your dad saw it, long time ago. I don't want no pub-licity, he got that and respected it, so, I expect the same from you, girlie. And you too, bub. Got it? I'm only doing this 'cause I like Fletcherman's, always have. Your mom, give her my best regards, would you?" he interrupted himself but then continued on, "Your mother is one fine lady, yes siree. I bet she's the reason you came in person, ain't it?"

He nodded with no surprise at Mayapple's affirmative.

Brought off track by his recollection of what a hot number Iris Fletcherman was, old man Stinkweed stumbled in his thought process, suddenly inspired with a new idea. "Sorry about your dad, kid. Did your mom remarry?" he asked, like the strange blundering, insensitive old man that he was, his motives clearly defined on his sleeve, like old egg yolk.

Mayapple was appalled but rose to the occasion with a quick detour: "Oh, she's got a serious squeeze, I think they're even talking marriage." Better to squash any thoughts in that direction right now. Santolina was a class act, she could see that real clearly all of a sudden.

Flem nodded, lips compressed to a thin line, arms akimbo.

"Oh, too bad," the unkempt, distasteful gentlemen said, "Guess I missed my chance. Well c'mon. Mind what I said! I don't want *NObody* ringing my bell and saying "Oh Mr. Stinkweed, *please!*" this last said in a high mincing falsetto voice.

He glared at the two of them, his caterpillar eyebrows slanting dangerously towards the middle.

"Oh no sir, no sir! You're secret's good with us! Ain't that right, Flem?" and the Sylph wondered at her lapse in speech, but jumped in whole heartedly.

Whimsey C. Nimble

A snort of laughter erupted out of their host but was immediately squelched and Mayapple wondered how much of the sloppy buffoon was really authentic or if it was a joke he'd played so long, that it had now gone native.

With no further ado, the door opened.

Chapter 36

Imagine a tuber, an *eighty-two pound* tuber, six feet around.

"O<small>H MY</small> G<small>OD</small>! *Yuck.* What is that horrible smell?" Mayapple of course, as she drew the neck of her shirt up around her nose and looked around for an obvious source.

Clenching his back teeth, Flem fought the faint nausea that rolled like ungainly fog around his midriff, hoping to Pan it wouldn't creep up and gag him.

Gleefully, the old man turned boyish in his enthusiasm, clasping his hands as he walked backwards for a moment.

Mayapple watched his performance with a critical eye, wishing he didn't look so damn goofy, it made it hard to concentrate on what he was saying.

"Wait 'til you see. Nobody's seen my garden in years. And today, today she blooms!"

Flem and Mayapple exchanged a look. This was getting curiouser and curiouser.

The back yard was open to the sky but just barely. Honeycombed around the inside of the perimeter were giant bubble-like sections, each a green hologram of strange exotic plants. It looked like a garden from another planet, possibly one built by strange bee-like people who lived in the tropics.

"Come, I will share my carrion flower with you!" Stinkweed said with a flourish.

Mayapple's first reaction was he couldn't possibly have said *carrion* flower, could he? Images of dark-red, daisy-like flowers poking up from barely buried bodies came to mind. A fleeting terror went though her, what if he was going to kill them and use them for fertilizer but her heart blotted it out as ludicrous.

Whimsey C. Nimble

Flem first thought was oh, he eats flowers too. Then no, no! Ick! *Carrion* flowers, Cha! What could a carrion flower possibly be? Dead squirrels in the shape of big blossoms was the impossible image, so immature, so sylphettish, that he grimaced.

A frantic look was tossed between the faerie and the girl but curiosity overwhelmed all else and they hurried along, anxious to not miss a thing.

"You're in luck, that's what you are!" Stinkweed crowed. "If you only knew how few people have this opportunity. Ah yes, here we are." He gestured for them to come closer but then stopped almost immediately with an outstretched arm. "Careful! People have been know to pass out from taking too close a whiff!"

There was no need to stop them, they both hung in suspended animation, awe rendering them speechless, motionless, the miracle blanketing their senses.

Bile rose up the back of Flem's throat, the stench was overpowering and he abruptly grasped Mayapple's arm in alarm.

She dropped the neck of her top to say something but when she did so, the nauseating aroma overpowered her too and she gagged as she frantically pulled the cloth back into place. Her eyes slanted to Flem, wide with consternation at their strange predicament.

Steeling his nerve, the faerie drew in a breath through his scarf, reminding himsylph to breathe through his nose, and to relax.

His eyes on the other hand, ate it up.

Mayapple was squeezing his hand so hard it hurt.

Before them was the most outlandish, awesome thing either had ever seen.

It was a flower, a gigantic alien blossom. One circular leaf, from which a gigantic, phallic protuberance sprang, had to be at least ten feet in circumference.

It hung in pleated folds of dark crimson as if draped over the rim of an enormous bowl, a living plant skirt.

Stinkweed let them bask in its unsullified glory for a whole five minutes before he motioned them to one side, assumed his glorified manners and started reciting facts:

"Officially, this is an Amorphophallus Titanium. Unofficially, it's referred to as bunga bangkai, or, corpse flower. They're native of the tropics in

Sumatra, Indonesia. The spadix there - that thing in the middle?" he pointed and both his guests nodded in awe. He continued, "That spadix there, hee hee, is almost eight feet tall!"

He paused then said, "This is the first year it's bloomed. Tomorrow you'd be too late, the spathe will close up."

Mayapple repeated, "Spathe?"

"Yes yes, the skirt there. That's the spathe. Seven years, that's how long I've been hoping this would happen. Seven years. And you two showed up today, of all days. Uncanny timing."

Mayapple looked up at him but he was lost in thought, hands behind his back as he contemplated the amazing phenomena in his own backyard.

"I grew this from a seed, believe it or not. Which eventually gave me a tuber and then a bigger tuber every year until this year. This year, I got lucky!" He hugged himself in joy, and since joy is contagious, Mayapple and Flem were soon grinning uncontrollably also.

"Guess how much that tuber weights," he ordered.

After a moment, Flem spoke up hesitantly. "Forty pounds?"

Mayapple offered, "Fifty?"

"Eighty-two. They can get up to one-hundred and I've seen one that was a little bigger than this one." He nodded and then went on, "I measured around it and it's not quite six feet."

Mayapple and Flem were dazzled. Imagine a tuber, an *eighty-two pound* tuber, six feet around. A *flower* tuber. Unimaginable, but here it was.

Beaming, Mr. Stinkweed motioned for them to follow him and Mayapple caught a glimpse of his watch. A bit of reality seeped in.

"Ah, Mr. Stinkweed, do you know the time? We have to get back to work soon," Mayapple interjected.

"Oh, call me Jimson. I don't show my garden to just anybody, you know. You've got time. Don't worry about it. C'mon," and he brusquely brushed aside her concerns, Flem scowled as he followed behind. He reached out to nudge Mayapple but stopped short at the abrupt change in her posture. Her mouth hung open and one hand came up to shade her eyes, her manner frozen.

Flem spun around, wondering what she was so googley-eyed about and then he too shaded his eyes, trying to make out what they were seeing.

The owner said nothing, just let them look.

Whimsey C. Nimble

Hands once again behind his back, Stinkweed rocked back and forth on his heels, his unsightly robe rippling in time as he squinted with great satisfaction at Rafflesiaceae, another pet but one that lasted longer than a day.

"I don't understand," stated the girl, and Flem was shaking his head back and forth in negative agreement with her.

"I don't get it either, is that the flower, that giant pink thing? Where's it coming from? It just seems to be sitting in midair in that tangle of vines."

Giggles jumped out of the old man's mouth and he grinned around them. His head started to bob in excitement and he rubbed his hands together, his shoulders giving involuntary twitches.

Flem was struck by the sudden image of himsylph as Mrs. Fletcherman must have seen him, twitching, and he laughed, causing both of his companions to shoot him a sharp look.

"Sorry," he mumbled, focusing.

"Rafflesiaceae. This particular one is Rafflesiaceae Arnoldii. I call her Arnold." He smiled. "That's all you'll see is the head there. The rest of its body is *inside* that woody vine you see draped everywhere."

Mayapple's eyes narrowed at his words, and Flem tried to make sense of what he'd just heard.

"*Inside* the vine?" asked Mayapple incredulously.

"That's right. It's technically the world's largest flower, a lily, and it grows endoparasitcally. The host vine there, that's a Tetrastigma, cousin of the grape. If we were in its homeland of Sumatra and Borneo we could walk right by it and not even know that a complete Rafflesiaceae plant lived inside its stem. Of the four million or so seeds produced by one flower, one must be fortunate to lodge in a moist crevice of a host vine, where it germinates and penetrates the host's bark. Over time, a labyrinth of microscopic filaments of cells expand into a fungus-like network of vascular tissue which eventually masses to produce one mammoth blossom which pushes out through its host stem. Come closer, as close as you dare! As you've already noticed, *carrion* flowers have an odor of a stinking corpse..."

Eyes wide, Flem and Mayapple approached cautiously, breathing in little gasps. A three-foot in diameter blossom floated before their eyes sporting five red fleshy lobes, each densely populated with raised white spots.

"Amazing," breathed Flem and Mayapple agreed but work was starting to dance along her nerves and she fidgeted, turning to tug on Flem's arm surreptitiously.

He looked over at her, his brain still seeing the flower phenomena.

"We have to get back to work Flem," she whispered. "Mom said we had about an hour and it's been almost that right now."

Stinkweed overheard and butted in with "Oh, you can't leave yet. Look over here," he cajoled, leading the way down a crooked path.

"This one is closer to home. This is Aristolchia Californica, found right here in California in the coastal range and further up, in the foothills," he stated, pulling them in easily.

"Oh my, look at that, Flem! Why, that's exquisite."

They were beholding a slim, serpentine sprawling vine from which short wiry stems protruded, each ending in a small precise yellow and red Dutchman's Pipe ensemble, a plant with an open orifice that led to a throat and then to a chamber below, so named as the curious blossoms resembled a shape reminiscent of Sherlock Home's pipe.

Lost in wonderland, Flem asked, "And this, this is also a *carrion* flower?" hardly able to believe something so delicate could have a stink to it.

"Yes," replied their host, going on to explain: "See how each flower is held rigidly upright? That design facilitates the emitance of its foul odor. Carrion *gnats* are coaxed in by its fetid promise but then slip down a waxy thorough-fare into the bottom inflated chamber. There, they're incarcerated by dense downward-pointing hairs which prevent them from climbing out and they're fed miniscule rations of nectar for several days. When the anthers are finally ripe with pollen, the jail hairs wilt, the flower tips horizontally, and the pollen-laden insects are free to go and make their way to the next receptive floral trap on another plant."

Put that way, it made the two visitors grin with delight.

"One more and I'll let you get back. I'm sure the boss of Fletcherman's Nursery will understand; after all, it's not like you're not on an educational tour." This was said rather cryptically but nonetheless was true and the two guests each agreed silently.

Following Jimson, Mayapple peered past him to get a glimpse of what looked like a giant oversize egg, the illusion being produced by the mass of yellow flowers inside its own egg-shaped biosphere.

Whimsey C. Nimble

"Hey, I know these!" Flem burst out excitedly.

Mayapple turned to look at him with surprise. "Do tell," she murmured.

"I was up north, out in the woods and I came to a whole patch but I didn't notice any smell," he looked questioningly at their mentor, refraining from mentioning the feast he'd had and blanching at the thought he'd been eating carrion flowers, eew, ick.

"Yes, these too are in the carrion *family*, but I use that word lightly as it's a variety of *unrelated* plant families, this family being a more *spiritual* one of a dominant main characteristic, sort of like a, *stinkweed* trait," clarified the older man.

He turned to Mayapple with a grin and she turned her full charm on him. Impulsively she held out her hands and said, "Thank you so much."

He grasped them in his and rather awkwardly replied, "You're welcome. It was an honor to share my beloveds with you. You ever need anything, you come see me, okay?"

Flem coughed and Mayapple, who by now was rather embarrassed by Stinkweed's change and demeanor from old grump to munificent uncle, quickly let go of his clasp.

Flem smiled for all he was worth, bobbing his head and repeating, "Thank you. Thank you. Thank you," 'til Mayapple poked him in the ribs with her elbow and scowled.

Sniffing to hide his reaction to this darling girl, like mother like daughter he thought, Stinkweed turned quickly back to the shiny arums and finished his tour.

"Good old American Skunk Cabbage. Lysichiton Americanum. This is our variety here, from the Pacific Northwest. Our western variety is much milder that their eastern fetid smelling relatives. These," and he pointed to the patch of flowers where each consisted of an approximately eight-inch-wide, petal-like yellow spathe protectively raising up around a stiff, phallic-like spadix heavily populated at its waving end with a rough cap about two inches long. Big green leaves grew among the patch of flowers, looking much like chard or perhaps romaine lettuce.

"These," he repeated, "only smell skunky and the smell fades with time. These still have a weak odor and my guess is that the ones you saw up north had probably been open a while, or maybe you just weren't close enough." He smiled gently at the faerie and Flem nodded enigmatically. Oh, he'd been close enough all right. If his memory served him properly, he seemed to recall laying amongst them, along with a whole bottle of mead he'd purchased just before coming upon them and if he remembered right, he'd *spent the night there* and there was no more mead the next day. Actually, it hurt to think about it, he was so glad his life had taken a new path! He didn't drink like that anymore. He had a job. And friends.

Coming back to his senses, he looked up to find their host watching him intently and a shiver ran along his clavicle and his wings unaccountably shuddered, as if a breezy chill had run up and down them unexpectedly.

Stinkweed's eyes bore into his own and Flem felt that shiver go straight up to his ears. He averted his eyes almost guiltily, startling Mayapple with "Hey! We better get going," making her jump.

The moment broke and the tour guide faded back to old disheveled man. "Come around this way," he waved his guests to follow him back around the outside of the house, leading them through a long, overgrown tunnel of jasmine to the front yard.

"Ah, there's the delicate fragrance of one of our well loved companions but *nothing* compares to a 'Stinkweed!" laughed Mayapple as they emerged, smiling at the older man.

A dull red crept up the gentleman's stubbly, unshaven neck and kept going 'til his whole countenance was suffused with heat from the blush.

"Alright missy, you better get back to work. You've been belly aching about it for the last half hour. Say hello to your mother for me, and tell her thanks for the refund. She's a lucky woman. And you're a lucky girl! You did say she had a boyfriend, right?" His eyes already knew the answer his mouth asked fruitlessly.

Smiling and nodding, Mayapple started the van. Jimson backed up and moved over to stand in the grass, his eyes flicking to stare into Flem's as he mouthed the word, "Bye," and waved.

Flem raised one hand in response and nodded as Mayapple pulled away from the curb.

Chapter 37

———— ✦ ————

Oh My God, Flem, *look*. Look! These are *yours*. Oh
my God, what did you do differently from me?

*I*T WAS HERE. Flem could hardly believe it, it had seemed to loom in
the future for so long. A strange thrill shot through his body and he
knew that that little burn of electricity skimming his nerves would no doubt
be a full-on case of the jitters as it drew close to the time for them to meet
Lark and go pick up Bud.

He hoped not. His wings would be so hard to control. It was just the
most exciting event in his life, that was all. And it was *fun*. He was having fun.
Him. Flem Green. A.K.A. Flumaria Greenwood. With friends.

Confidence bloomed and he smiled to himsylph like a lovesick faerie but
it was simply joy, growing from his own sylphconfidence.

Unseen, Iris paused some distance away, watching him work and thought
about how much healthier he'd become since she'd first met him only a few
weeks ago. Mayapple steadily worked at her too, singing his praises every
chance she got and while Iris got sick of Mayapple on her soap box, it did not
fall on deaf ears. There was something about him that drew her in.

A sudden picture flashed in her mind and she wondered if it was the connection she'd been looking for. Without a second thought, she acted on it and
cleared her throat to let him know she was approaching.

The faerie's head bounced up when he heard her and the smile everyone
saves for their boss plastered itself across his face.

"Hello there!" he sang out before continuing, as if to head her off,
"Mayapple'll be right back, she just went to go get a few more alyssum. These
smaller baskets go a lot faster than those first ones," referring to the original
Bridge Project. "We've already completed six and should be able to each get

two more done before we leave." He wondered if he was babbling or trying too hard to please.

Iris squinted at him intently but Flem got the feeling she wasn't listening to what he was saying.

"Great! You guys'll be done in no time, then, won't you?" she replied but still, she looked distracted.

Flem nodded his head in agreement but skepticism was confusing him at these mixed signals.

"Uh, is anything wrong, Mrs. Fletcherman?" he asked, feeling his heart creep to his throat with painful fatalism at all the good things in his world that could suddenly topple. Old fears flashed to the surface, too familiar, suffocating feelings of inadequacy choking his breath off blindly. His wings tensed and a sharp pinprick from a tiny cat's claw made it clear he was to control himsylph, there was no room here for hysterics, he had a *passenger* to consider. Always think of the cat, *first*.

Perspective righted itself and he was able to take a big breath and say, "What is it? Do you *need* something? Can I get something for you?"

"Mr. Green."

"Yes?"

"Will you walk with me a moment? Oh, hi Mayapple, Flem and I are going to make a quick trip down to number three, why don't you come too?"

As if there were a choice.

Mayapple looked as confused as Flem felt. Her fae friend shrugged an 'I don't know?' at her as they obediently followed the boss down the path, Mayapple wiping dirt on her jeans, and Flem hitching up his pants.

"What is going on?" whispered Mayapple to Flem. "What'd she say before I got here?"

"She said we were doing great work," Flem replied just before Iris stopped and turned around.

Trying to hold a stern look on her face, she gave in to a small smile which pulled one corner of her mouth, but her eyes held a question. Hand on hips, she just stared at the two of them, before announcing: "I have a mystery on my hands and I need your help," her gaze watching each intently.

Completely baffled by this time, Mayapple took the lead and nodded quickly, saying, "Well, lead on mother. What the heck are you talking about?"

Whimsey C. Nimble

Again Iris looked at her but refrained from saying anything more before she transferred her gaze to the employee with the secret identity, saying innocently to them both as she turned away, "Do you think you'll have any trouble figuring out who made which baskets?"

"Which *baskets*? Why?" immediately piped up Mayapple. "What's the matter, are some falling apart or did they dry out in one spot, or what? Are we in trouble?"

Flem's heart was constricting in anticipation of all *his* work being the guilty party, the ones in shambles, his future *gone*, up in smoke.

He started to choke. Wings kept trying to come undone, held against their will and his back heaved with a startled lump shooting straight down his back, under his shirt, pushing off with mean little sharp toes from one ankle and pfft, was gone in a flash.

Iris actually DID see it, couldn't believe it, and pretended not to.

Flem was mortified, Mayapple aghast and the boss, serene.

Holding the door to number three open, she motioned for them to precede her and Flem felt another surge of panic at the idea of Iris Fletcherman being *right* behind him, when his wings were breathing with a life of their own.

Gulping convulsively Flem tried to control himsylph but to his horror it wasn't working and he was starting to shudder under a full blown attack (*not* epilepsy!) when Mayapple grabbed him by the arm and pulled him up beside her, saying, "Oh My God, Flem, *look*. LOOK! These are *yours*. Oh my God, what did you do differently than me?"

Iris waited. That's exactly what she wanted to know too.

Flem stared. A rather high giggle erupted briefly as the implications, the proof, was right before their very eyes. But how to explain it? How to explain a phenomena that was taken for granted back in Thimbleberry Canyon?

When a Sylph's life was following a true bent, and she was following her innate creativity to do the best she could, a response was elicited from whatever was being worked on. Flem had heard it called *glamour* when the life force in everything responded to the fae love being put out, but Sylph didn't call it that. They just knew. That was an outside description. And until *now*, for Pan's sake, he had never noticed it working for *him*. He certainly hadn't noticed it when he was she. Back then it had seemed more like the *opposite* happened, things rarely worked out the way he wanted, often carrying their own dissonance, always leaving him dissatisfied. He never could quite get the hang of making it all work for him. Always a misfit, proven even further by her inability to return to female after the change. Ha! He was beginning to see it just might have a golden lining, as here before his very eyes was proof. What the Pan was the world coming to?

Mayapple and her mother waited and even Mayapple couldn't help out this time, it was obvious she was as baffled and enchanted as the boss.

As the faerie thought his way through this, he relaxed, sylphsatisfaction vying with a needed explanation.

"I, uh, I don't know," he replied lamely, as innocent and confused as he could muster up, knowing full well what was going on and for the life of him couldn't keep a small Sylph smile off his silly face, he just couldn't.

"Wow," said Mayapple. "Wow. Look at this mom, this is great! I think whatever is going on is certainly in your favor, now isn't that a fact, Mrs. Fletcherman, ahem?" Grinning delightedly, Mayapple inspected each blooming beauty, breathing in the heady aroma of the alyssum on each one she passed and Flem wondered if she wasn't getting dizzy from all those deep breaths.

No matter how he tried he couldn't stop smiling, even though he thought he really should, to be professional.

Mrs. Fletcherman studied him a moment more and normally he would have been quelled completely by such frank appraisal but the appearance of his own latent abilities was such a hopeful sign from his own universe that it couldn't be denied; *he*, not *she*, was in-tune! Happiness with his soul took root and he determined to do his best to keep it there.

He dared a look at Iris right across from him but cha, he kept smiling and a Sylph in full charm mode is irresistible.

She broke into laughter smiling back at him and Mayapple hooted in the background, still inspecting each bigger than normal planter.

Daringly, Flem spoke up. "So, I'm not in trouble then, right?"

"No, no you're not in trouble Mr. Green. You *didn't* add extra fertilizer to each one, did you?" knowing full well he hadn't.

"No. No I didn't. Guess I'm just lucky is all," he tried to pass it off.

"Yeah," she replied dryly, before letting them off the hook with, "Well, get back to work and Flem? Please show Mayapple how to inject all that *love* into her work, like you do with yours, okay?" This was said in a sing-song joking manner meant to release them but Flem realized she had unintentionally hit the nail on the head, and captured the truth of the fae. The more of their heart and soul that went into something, the more *something* responded. Flem had rarely experienced it, as she rarely had invested her whole Sylph into much of anything, although, the old landing platform she'd built so long ago had turned out remarkably well.

Snapping to attention, the faerie realized Iris was not able to take her gaze off of him but as he met her eyes she abruptly smiled and nodded before marching away, a few loose pieces of gravel splaying out from her heels. "Okay, back to work," she called over her shoulder. "Thanks!"

Mayapple's eyebrows knitted together in bemusement as she shook her head at her faerie friend.

"Flem? Do you really not know what is going on, or is that just the story you told the boss?"

Flem turned into a Sylph with a secret who was just bursting to share.

Linking arms, they walked back, heads together as Mayapple listened, her imagination on fire, her gratitude for this wonderful opportunity boundless.

Iris watched, hidden, and wondered about their relationship, wondering if she knew anybody else who, like the mysterious Flem Green, was a closet faerie. She suspected some of the people she knew were, but how to tell if you weren't in that circle?

Six o'clock rolled around and Flem thought he would expire with anticipation, his nerves a wild fire fed by the tinder of Mayapple's own excitement and nonstop speculation on the evening ahead. It completely rattled him.

Mayapple took charge, as usual.

"Flemmy! I have a great idea. Where are your good clothes at, you know, the ones from your girlfriend Garriya's?"

Throwing her a pretend scowl, he drolly replied, "Why, they're at *home*, of course." And smiled.

Fixing him with a semi-reproachful look, she sweetly inquired "*Which* home, Mr. Green?"

"I only have one home, Mayapple," he kidded.

"Oh for Pete's sake, all I want to know is can you come home with me after work and bring your outfit? We'll feed the kitties first, of course. You don't have anything else you need to do, do you?" she cajoled.

Flem's heart flipped flopped at the ordinariness of such a request and he relished everything about it as he replied, "Nope! It's a plan."

Chapter 38

Slowly, methodically, she massaged his shoulders,
dipping down to fondle his wing knobs, but she
stopped and said, "I need water, don't I?

*F*EELING EXTREMELY SYLPHCONSCIOUS, the faerie ducked back out the window in the old greenhouse, right behind Mayapple, his pack swinging awkwardly as he bent over. Clutched in one hand was the thin glossy bag with little handles that contained his purchase from the Silk Tassel. He rather gulped at the idea of changing clothes in someone else's home but it *was* Mayapple, after all. He relaxed but his sinuses were awfully clear, nonetheless, as he headed into unknown territory, and, Revelry with Cybele. The evening had begun. He was on Full Alert, hoping he could stay to one mead, but also knowing it probably wasn't going to happen tonight, giving himsylph permission to just be aware of how much he was drinking.

Shivering with delighted anticipation, Mayapple hugged herself then threw her arms around Flem as they walked out together, squeezing him sideways.

Giggling, Flem fended her off, "Stop, stop" ineffectually coming out of his mouth.

They didn't see Bud standing beneath the open arbor connected to the main building, arms crossed, hands tucked into arm pits, thumbs on the outside straight up and wiggling in amusement. Feet braced apart, he stood in relaxed alertness, ready to spring into action. He wondered when they would see him and was rewarded with Flem's awareness all of a sudden and Mayapple's jerk around, scanning for him. Red leather gloves dangled haphazardly from a rear pocket, a baseball cap hugged his head, and a small dapper scarf was around his neck.

Whimsey C. Nimble

Laughing, he stepped from the shadows as Mayapple bounded over and starting hugging him next.

"Oooh, tonight, tonight, tonight!" she sang as she squeezed him in time with each word.

Laughing helplessly, Bud appealed to Flem for help with the crazy woman but all the faerie could do was giggle and watch.

"Go home! Get ready!" Bud was finally able to gasp out as he extricated Mayapple's arms from around him, a twinkle burning brightly in his eye at her infectious mood.

"Yes! We're going. C'mon Flem, let's go get ready for Revelry, ooh ooh!" and with one more squeeze, she started walking off with Flem right behind her before stopping and turning around. "How late are you working Bud? Aren't we picking you up?"

"I'm only here for a bit. Iris wanted extra soil made for the weekend and I said I'd do it. I won't be here long. Hey - I'll see you guys soon! Lark's picking you up first, right? So, I'll see you in a couple of hours. Can't wait. You'll love it." He turned and strode off towards the various piles he worked and babied for Mrs. Fletcherman's precious potting soil.

Trying to restrain herself, Mayapple gave up and danced down the driveway, yelling "C'mon Flem!" as she skipped to the bus stop, peering down the street, willing the bus to appear *now*.

It did not. It took five minutes.

Flem was mildly embarrassed by Mayapple's exuberance and in his shyness seemed reserved but Mayapple's wake was buoyant enough to keep him afloat all the way to her house.

Jabbering constantly, she needed little interaction from Flem other than an occasional 'Uh-huh' as an agreement and soon they were off at her bus stop, walking through a cute little commercial area, passing a bar and pizza joint, a consignment shop, a small bakery with tables outside, and then a bookstore with the name "Goldenrod's' in bright yellow letters across a dark green awning on the corner.

Mayapple turned right onto Olive street. Not quite half way down the block she turned right again, down a long driveway past a big house on the left, with a wall of greenery on their right which ran all the way to the back fence. Morning glories and bougainvillea cascaded freely and abundantly, a riot of colorful accompaniment.

"Wow," breathed the Sylph, "This is beautiful."

"Yeah, come on in," replied Mayapple, oblivious for once to the splendor of her surroundings.

Following her meekly up two steps of a darling little cottage, the door was unlocked in a flash.

"Have a seat for a minute, I'll be right back," she ordered as a skinny black cat came running out from a doorway who then stopped with a startled stare when he saw a stranger in their midst.

Dropping her stuff on a low couch, Mayapple scooped up the kitty who instantly settled in to greeting his mistress after a long hard day at work.

Snuffling endearments into the cat's fur, Mayapple's muffled voice filtered out, "Hi darling boy, how's my Blakeana, hmm? Did you have a hard day at work darlin', no doubt sleeping all day, weren't you Mr. Puss?"

A revelation washed over the faerie. Everybody had a special relationship with their cat, if they had one. He couldn't imagine not having one, if offered the choice, and wondered about Iris, Bud and Lark. Well, he knew Lark didn't. He hadn't seen one anyway. And what about Lily? Did she own one?

"Does Lily have a cat too? Maybe she'd like a kitten." Flem spoke without thinking and Mayapple gave him the oddest look, while carefully setting Blackie down.

"I don't know Flem, why don't you ask her next week?"

Flem caught himsylph and heard the teensiest little note, just a mere hint of *something* in Mayapple's comeback and wisely changed the subject.

"Did you tell me you had a roommate too?"

"Yes, he's gone most of the time, so I pretty much live alone, except he pays half the rent! It's a great arrangement. He's a professor here at Carissa College and also down at the College of Nymphaea in the Peninsula area, so he splits his time," she volunteered.

Moving into the kitchen, she kept talking, "Are you hungry? We better eat something before we go. Flem!" she switched to high gear once more, where she'd been most of the day. "Oh my God, it's TONIGHT!" she squealed and Flem felt the same way but was still rather shy, being inside Mayapple's house. His wings responded though with a helpless beat of Sylph adrenalin and Mayapple sprang to life.

"I'll lock the door. You go into that room right there and let those poor wings out! Would you like me to, ah, you know, do you want me to, ah?"

"Yes. Yes!" He jumped in at the idea of Mayapple giving him a good preening before they left. Oh, life was sweet tonight.

Kitchen cabinet doors were being opened and banged shut as Mayapple scanned the cupboards for tidbits to feed her faerie friend. Her *faerie friend*. Here! Right now. She hugged herself with glee.

"Can I come out?" called Flem.

Balancing small bowls of carrots, cucumbers, some cherries, and three bags of crackers, Mayapple dashed into the room where Flem stood flexing his shoulders and wings, wings still furled.

Dumping everything onto her dresser with a clatter, she said "Let me see," as she turned and surveyed him. "No, wait 'til I get the house secure."

"Here," she stated, adjusting the blinds at the windows so as to admit light but not eyes.

"I'll be right back, go ahead an unfurl," but she stood transfixed as his filmy appendages started to move as if they were alive, and they were.

With shining big eyes and a look of amazement on her face, Mayapple watched once again as this beautiful Sylph unfolded right before her very eyes, and it was magic. It would always be magic.

"Oh Flem, look at you, you're so *beautiful*. It's such a crime to have to hide your wings, I'm so sorry," she said with utter sincerity, as if she had something to do with it, one hand landing on her hip, the other over her mouth.

Feeling beautiful by her obvious admiration, he struck a pose and pirou-etted slowly for her. This must be how WilloB felt he thought, she was one of the sexiest Sylphs he knew back in the canyon, everybody liked her and she was always winking at somebody. (Rarely him though.)

Tearing herself away, Mayapple quickly ran around her house adjusting all windows for privacy, double checking the lock on both doors, front and back.

Popping back in, her breath caught in her throat at the sight of Flem, her buddy, her co-worker, with nothing on but his long soft pants, wings up and out at full attention behind him, edges fluttering and rippling as current flowed through them, unhindered.

Walking over to him, she turned him around and slid cool fingers onto his neck and he stilled.

Slowly, methodically, she massaged his shoulders, dipping down to fondle his wing knobs but she stopped and said, "I need water, don't I?"

"Oh, that'd be perfect, yes, oh down low at the base, *that's* where I really need it."

Mayapple spun into the adjoining bathroom (such luxury, thought Flem) and was back in a flash with a glass of water, still sloshing, dipped her fingers in and set to work.

Like pop beads made out of living organic material, the small segments easily rejoined at the seams around each scale, coming together like one entity, a pinch of wettened fingers all that was needed. (or a raspy tongue...)

Mayapple concentrated but couldn't keep the joy under control, what with *Flem* and Revelry! She vibrated at a higher pitch and Flem picked up on it immediately, his wings humming, edges flapping like loose lace.

Slowly Mayapple zipped and kneaded, casually working in "Mmmm. That Lark, I'll bet he looks HOT tonight! Have you noticed he only wears black? Funny for a baker, huh. I wonder what Bud will have on?"

Flem tensed momentarily at her mention of Lark, but was soon limp putty once again in her hands. With her deft fingers Mayapple had worked off the excess excitement that had been building all day, the munchies that constituted dinner were gone, and both felt much more grounded and ready for a night out.

"Lark said he would pick us up here around eight-thirty, so we still have plenty of time to get ready. Do you want to take a shower, err, can you? I mean, you know, with your wings, ahh, I don't know. There's my shower. There's the towels. I'll help, if you need me," and unflusterable Mayapple who was always in control, blushed and stammered and felt ridiculous. *She*, who had just given him a good preening.

"Relax," laughed Flem, amused not only by her unexpected shyness but by him telling her to settle down. The shoe was on the other foot for once.

"Yes, thank you, I will; I'll just keep them furled," he explained but what he was remembering was how big Lark's shower was compared to this miniscule one of Mayapple's.

"Is this shower size pretty normal?" he couldn't help asking.

Mayapple narrowed her eyes at him but simply replied, "Yes, more or less. You haven't had many showers, have you Flem?" She looked at him speculatively and he hastened to assure her he was a very clean faerie.

Whimsey C. Nimble

He wondered what she was thinking and guessed it was probably about his old days, back under his rock.

"Are you…?" she almost asked but he beat her to the punch with "Yeah, of course. I'm there a lot," but he looked so innocent when he said it, Mayapple knew he was lying and she squinted her eyes at him 'till he confessed.

"No," he sighed, "I haven't been back in quite a while."

A moment's pause before they both broke out in irreverent giggles, then Mayapple snapped her fingers and pointed to the shower.

"Go. I want one too, and we need to get dressed. Here," she grabbed a big soft towel and tossed it at him. "Call me as soon as you're decent, okay?" She headed off to some imaginary clean up in the kitchen and to feed the cat.

An hour later, Mayapple had yet to emerge from her bedroom and Flem sat in the living room, waiting, practically purring with sylphcontent. He had already looked at everything on the walls and was now just idling along. His wings shuddered slightly but it was in tune with the deep thrum coming from within and he assumed in the crush of the evening no one would notice.

A knock on the door and his heart leaped, Mayapple was suppose to be ready by now and *she* should be opening her door to Lark, not he.

"Hey, that's Lark. Oh my God, is it eight-thirty already? Sorry! Open the door, Flem!" She gave orders just as easily as ever, sight unseen. Mayapple for president.

Flem jumped up and hurriedly opened the door, stumbling a bit in his haste.

Lark, the tall dark Lord of the Bakery, stood there in all his black splendor, his green eyes locked on Flem's hazel ones.

Daring it, he commented "Such beautiful eyes, so unusual." It was all he said but it echoed of the past and they both remembered what had come next. 'Where are you from,' hung between them and Flem realized that was when *he'd* gotten mad.

Smiling disarmingly with a hint of amusement locked away, Lark dispatched the moment by looking Flem up and down, making eyes at him the whole time to let him know that what he saw, looked *good*.

Flem blushed, but he felt proud of himsylph because, by Pan, he *did* look good!

Their eyes caught, or rather, Lark caught Flem's gaze and wouldn't let go, speaking an unspoken language and Flem drifted into possibilities, never having had a real lover other than that intense time of The Change. That was more like his body had been on fire with the need to mate and then it was over. And he had moved away. And here he was. Lark spoke to his soul, his need for understanding, and he didn't know why. Why wasn't it Mayapple to spark this awareness in him? Logically he thought that's what made sense, but no, no it was Lark who mesmerized him.

Mayapple coughed loudly in her room, slammed a drawer shut with a bang and then called out, "Okay, I'm ready. Prepare yourselves."

Flem backed up, and Lark stepped through, all eyes on Mayapple.

Chapter 39

Soft jungle music filled the air, creating a throbbing
awareness of life and its many nuances.

*P*LAYING IT FOR all she was worth, Mayapple stopped just inside the
doorway so she was half hidden, thrusting out one long, stocking-
clad leg wearing shapely over-the-calf black boots before the rest of her appeared, the feather dress hugging her frame like she was born for the sky.

Doing her best to emanate sultry and mysterious, especially since her
two guests were obviously in thrall, she nevertheless couldn't keep it up and
broke into giggles in her nervousness, altering the spell.

Both Lark and Flem stared at her with new appreciation, Lark letting
out a long, low wolf-whistle. Flem closed his open mouth. That Mayapple
was something.

"Shall we go?" she asked, smoothing down her dress, not one feather out
of place, her hands going up to make sure her little side hat pinned up high
was secure, riding saucily on a sea of glossy brown curls.

Turning the tables, she took control and stepped back, giving the two of
them a full appreciative stare. "Ooh my, you two look good enough to eat,"
she exclaimed, winking at Flem when Lark couldn't see.

What she noticed right away was what a handsome couple they made,
Flem standing tall and lithe, his black pants with a hint of gold in the seams
hugging his slim hips, the loose black silk shirt glittering with hints of red
and gold, his wings carefully concealed by the gorgeous scarf he'd picked out
at the Silk Tassel, a flowing elegant *evening* scarf bunched artlessly around
his neck and shoulders. Mayapple bet to herself that he had no idea just *how*
charming and sexy he looked.

From the way green-eyes looked at him, Mayapple realized she was going to have competition this evening for Flem's attention. She let it go. He deserved an admirer and while she would have loved to flaunt a love affair with a faerie in her mother's concern, she actually wasn't attracted to Flem in a romantic way, he reminded her too much of a little brother, if she'd had one. There was a big part of her that sorely regretted that fact but underneath the giggly laughing girl was a wise woman who believed passionately that one must be true to oneself first and foremost. And it was obvious Flem needed to be true to his own nature. She just wished she could figure out how to help him let his wings out. A new image filled her mind and that was of Flem, flying. Oh my God, could her life get any more exciting?

Smiling, she shooed them out the door, leaving a small lamp burning on a side table, some soft music on for Blakeana, and Blakeana himself watching soulfully from where he lay in resignation on the sofa, nails occasionally being splayed, revealing the hidden angst at *mom* leaving.

Lark strode ahead to open the car door, gallantly nodding Flem into the back, showing Mayapple the passenger seat in front before hurrying around and slipping into the driver's set.

With a muffled roar they were off.

Making conversation, Lark asked, "Have either of you been to Bud's place before?" as he expertly shifted gears and they started to climb.

"No," replied Mayapple, which Flem echoed.

"Wait 'til you see it. He lives up in this great area, much more woodsy than down here, it's just off Chokecherry."

Chokecherry had a familiar ring to it but Flem couldn't figure out why 'til Mayapple burst out with, "I thought this looked familiar. Flem, *Chokecherry*, remember? We were just here not too long ago. *Stinkweed* lives on Chokecherry."

Flem peered intently out his window but it was getting dark and hard to see. A glimpse of something mildly familiar flashed by but then he realized with a start they were very near where he had seen that intriguing structure. A prickle of premonition ran across his shoulders and down his spine, making his back tighten.

Slowing down, Lark turned right onto Lobelia Lane, a double-laned path just before Chokecherry Court. Easing the low black car down the narrow road, Lark beeped his horn lightly to signal Bud they were there.

Whimsey C. Nimble

At the end of the long driveway, a shadowy, lofty 'village' could be seen, some kind of rope or something strung between three visible structures, high in the trees.

Two were dark, and the light went out in the third, which was the one closest. The door opened and Buddleia came through. Waving, he turned and trotted down the stairs, bounding over to the car, where Lark popped up.

Smiling at his old friend, Lark teased, "What, no bicycle tonight? You sure? We could meet you there you know."

Bud gave him a droll look as he peered past, into the back seat and said, "Hey, Flem. Ooh, you're looking pretty!" as he climbed in.

Lark rolled his eyes, hiding the twinge he felt at someone else mildly flirting with Flem, and he wasn't even flirting, for Pan's sake. "Just get in, Mr. Gabby," he ordered as Bud settled himself.

Mayapple was staring in disbelief at where Bud lived, finally finding her voice. "Oh my God, I can't *believe* you live here. Bud, you sly dog, you. *When* do we get a tour?" She said it jokingly but it was pretty obvious she really meant it.

"Actually...tonight. I was hoping you-all would come back for an after-show party."

Flem's eyes rounded, his heart picked up speed. *He* was being invited to a party, a *real* party. Oh, the parties he had missed but certainly heard about, back in the canyon. There had been a few of course, but this, this was different. His heart ached with the poignancy of the moment, his eyes filled with overwhelming emotion and he could barely breathe.

Mayapple was squealing, bouncing in her seat.

"Ah, I guess that's a yes from you, hey Mayapple?" dryly remarked Lark watching her, hoping she wasn't doing his expensive vehicle any harm with her shenanigans.

Bud had a grin on his face as Lark backed up, turned in his seat to watch behind them as he maneuvered back out Lobelia Lane.

Crossing his legs, Bud clasped his hands around his knee, and happen to glance at his back-seat companion, as he was also watching Lark's drive backward.

Shocked by the raw emotion on the faerie's face, he quickly diverted his attention but briefly and blindly extended one hand to give a heartfelt squeeze in silent support to Flem's leg.

Flem almost choked, taken unaware. His eyes flew to Bud's and Bud smiled and asked, "Do you think you can make to my party later? I hope so." His eyes spoke volumes of understanding and empathy.

Flem managed to croak out, "Nice place. Up in the trees, huh? Nice touch," thinking it was so, so *Sylph*.

They were at the end of the driveway by this time, and after backing out sedately, and pausing momentarily, Lark shifted and they peeled off as if the devil himself were chasing them.

That shut everybody up for a moment 'til he came to a stop sign and drove the speed limit from then on, causing everyone to laugh, releasing some of that pre-Revelry steam like bleeding a valve on a pressure cooker.

Flem collected himsylph with aplomb, pushing his nervousness away, feeling the kinship between them all and acknowledging he was a part of it.

Sylphesteem grew.

Finding his voice, Flem turned and asked Bud how long he'd lived back there, in the *magic kingdom?*

Mayapple's ears perked up and she tilted her head to catch the response.

"Oh, it's been years in the making, I ah, bought the land a long time ago. It was just a lot and, yeah! It's comfortable! I'm pretty happy there. Hey, you know where you're going, don't you Lark? I thought you would have turned back there."

He successfully diverted the conversation and Lark looked at him in the rear view mirror. "Mmm," he answered, deftly making a series of turns to bring them to a, as yet, still empty parking lot, but one that was filling up fast with a steady stream of cars.

In the distance, large columns were silhouetted against an intense orange sunset.

Lark stopped the car and Flem took a deep breath, his Sylph sinuses clearing in the damp marine air. Was that fog way out there he wondered, as he looked west over the ocean but his attention snapped back immediately as they started to walk, Lark fingering his keys loosely in his pants pocket. Flem realized they were all a little on edge, which once again reassured him, he was not the only sensitive one, they all were.

Lark and Bud lead the way in, with Mayapple clutching excitedly at Flem's arm as they followed behind, the four of them merely a small part of the large influx of people funneling down to the gates.

Whimsey C. Nimble

Soon they were within the breathtaking grounds, giant bare tulip trees in full bloom accenting the Olympian pillars they were walking among, set against the sunlit sky. Small black arrows announced seating that was partially camouflaged, tucked into the sides of an amphitheater. An empty stage drew the eye down to it, the middle hidden by curtains of some kind, pulled into a concealing circle.

Glancing at the admission stubs, Lark lead them down until eye level with the stage, picking his way along a path to an area that was rather private but with an excellent unobstructed view, not too far from the stage.

"Here we are." He sidled sideways, dropping into the last seat and Mayapple would have followed but Bud, upon getting a raised brow plea from Lark, asked her a question and she drew back, waving Flem to go next.

He did, his eyes flickering uncertainly to Lark's, who caught his gaze and smiled guilelessly, holding that gaze a bit too long, making Flem swallow. He was new at this.

Soft jungle music filled the air, creating a throbbing awareness of life and its many nuances. The energy was building, making human and Sylph blood, start to tingle.

Mayapple plopped down next to him and he smiled in relief, suddenly overwhelmingly glad she was there. Lark was *so* attractive and Flem was getting rather faint with nervousness at the other's overt mating signals.

He dived into conversation with her asking her nonsensical questions about her hat and the stage and how about Bud's party, until she grabbed him by the shoulders and shook him for a moment to try and damper that wild look in his eye.

"Flem! We're here." She linked her arm through his and squeezed tight, looking up at him, "And you look *HOT*, buddy!"

His face softened and her grounding brought him back to earth.

Then her eyebrows rose speculatively several times as she made eyes and nodded towards Lark then turned back making 'kissy' faces at the Sylph.

"STOP!" he hissed, it being too close to home and brought back all the nervousness of a minute ago.

Shaking his head he turned away to bump right back into Lark's deep gaze and floundered into etheric quick-sand.

"I like your scarf, Flem. In fact, you look really nice." It was said so sincerely and warmly that Flem forgot his nervousness and before long the two were engrossed in easy small talk.

Mayapple glanced over and saw them animatedly talking and once again noted the similar set of their shoulders.

Bud cleared his throat, watching them also from the other side of Mayapple and she looked over at him, wondering how much he knew about Flem and also her intuitions about Lark.

He looked at her and silently asked her the same question.

Both were loathe to speak first.

Finally, Mayapple squinted at him and softly said, "You know?" taking a chance.

Eyes locked, he nodded and carefully repeated back to her, "*You* know?"

Mayapple wondered if they were both talking about Flem, but nodded, yes, she knew he was fae.

Bud wondered how much she knew. Did she know about Lark? Nah, she couldn't. Lark was good. They both were.

Chapter 40

⸻❧⸻

At first Flem was flabbergasted, embarrassed
by such intimate contact but then it came
to him *what* he had his finger *on*.

S OFT LIGHTS WERE multiplying in the dusk around them, making shadows dance and the crowd was lent an even more mysterious air.

The music got louder, more intense.

A murmur grew audible, a separate entity born for the occasion, as speculation ran rampant. By this time, Flem was open to whatever the evening
brought. Never had he experienced anything remotely like this back in the
canyon. Sylphs drank mead and talked and schmoozed and yes, partied hard
but they did it in someone's tree, not at huge public events.

Some were industrious, some weren't. It was pretty easy to live, food
was abundant and housekeeping simple. It was up to each Sylph to design
her own living quarters usually in a tree but he knew one, Whimsey C.
Nimble, who was reputed to live in a cave behind one of the boulders of
Moonlight Creek, a gentle ravine, one of many that brought water down to
Thimbleberry Canyon. Pootsy Koons had told him that a long time ago,
when he'd stopped in at her place, Windfall Café, for a mead back when he
was a she.

Best to not go there right now he quickly realized, swallowing homesick
feelings in a flash, throwing himsylph back into the moment, the stage dimming in the distance.

Glancing around he saw many, many people all tucked into cozy little
arrangements from the bottom tier to the top, each level staggered with lush
greenery.

Lark's arm rested casually across the back of Flem's chair and Flem had noticed but it seemed *right* to him and he let it be. New boundaries were happening tonight and this attitude of sylphconfidence was shored up each time he looked around by what he saw - Mayapple and Bud, his friends; the mere fact that he was *here*, with them, and *Lark*, Lark who fascinated him like no other. And besides, he had new clothes, hadn't had his one mead yet and, Rainbow Merkiva was here somewhere and *he* was going to find her afterwards. He, and his friends. Ha. Before they went to Bud's *party*.

The music changed tempo, still a jungle beat but with a slower throb and the center stage was plunged into complete darkness, accompanied by drastically reduced lighting in the whole place.

The crowd rustled in anticipation with a few stragglers hurrying to their places.

Slowly the ambient light faded as the music became little more than a vibration felt in the warm dark air, caressing and lulling, a ruse to hypnotize the senses before a different personality was realized to have replaced it, a tribal, insistent calling.

As the scene took shape, the drumming heightened and Flem could easily discern the volcano seen smoldering in the background, its top a dull orange glow. Gradually the faerie's eyes adjusted and he saw figures immobilized around it, as if a slice of time had been flash frozen.

The drumming intensified again, and Flem looked carefully, trying to figure out where it was coming from but he had no time as the addictive beat filled the air louder and louder.

The audience's eyes were glued to the stage and when the music exploded freeing the dancers they jumped collectively.

Flem was no exception and Lark couldn't resist giving him a little squeeze on one side, Mayapple covering the right with a poke in the ribs from her elbow. The faerie had never felt so loved.

Leaping, gyrating wild *women?* were jumping and dancing like monkeys on fire, pretending to drink from overlarge bottles, as they pranced around the orange glowing mountain top, careening and bouncing as if made out of bendable wire and the floor, rubber.

Crazed with passion, one by one they refroze into some outlandish position and there they stayed, the music once again a separate entity, 'til it too backed off and allowed a voice to come through.

Whimsey C. Nimble

"Welcome to Revelry With Cybele!" boomed out a deep and resonant voice that commanded attention. "I give you Cybele and the Corybants!" upon which the dancers came to life once again, as if jolted with electricity, but this time a pattern was seen to emerge as two lines formed, and the low chanting grew, building an entrance for the star of the show, Cybele. The music swelled and crashed, pulled and demanded, and then unexpectedly diminished to a beckoning pitter patter, a soft rain of musical roses being strewn about, drawing out the moment 'til *she* arrived.

Suddenly a primal roar cut through everything and then another, causing Flem's heart to constrict in his chest, chilling his blood, fear globules coalescing where before there had been none. His hand somehow contacted Lark's and they squeezed together, even as Mayapple sat rigid in her seat on the other side gripping his other hand in wide-eyed wonderment, while Bud sat relaxed, his arm casually laid across her seat back.

Ignoring the two between them, an amused look was silently passed as Bud and Lark's eyes briefly met.

Against the intense chanting the pitter-patter rhythm took on a steadier beat, the roar came again, and people, and fae, squirmed in their seats. Bud and Lark were nothing but cool amusement, messieurs Sang and Froid, with neither admitting to the chill that chased itself down their respective spines and people everywhere found themselves with dry mouths, trying to swallow that primal response of fear.

As if out of nowhere, a flaming chariot leaped onto the broad round, revolving stage, powered by a team of five lions, a large majestic alpha male leading four smaller females.

It seemed awfully dangerous to Flem who had never seen a lion before, let along heard their primal roar designed to inspire, and he froze stiff, watching in utter amazement at the scene unfolding not fifty feet away.

The chorus of Corybants faded into the glowing volcano's lush sides, as around the outer edge the chariot flew. None of the beasts looked overtly happy about the show for humans that they were engaged in but Flem noticed they were well trained and didn't fight the harnesses and trusses that bound them all together.

Holding the reins was the most striking woman, unusually tall, her statuesque body well proportioned. She looked like a gladiator with one leg braced in front of her, riding the continuous curve, the gilded short skirt barely showing a ripple. A matching halter top encased her magnificent upper body and a sublime pair of long, elbow length gold gloves graced her fierce grip on the reins.

Her right hand flicked and a responding roar came from the powerful lead cat. The four behind all snarled in synchronistic timing and the vehicle slowed to a crawl, then suddenly disappeared completely as the star of the show was striding around the stage, microphone in hand.

Flem squinted, astonished, trying to figure out how that happened and couldn't. He turned to Mayapple but Mayapple mouthed the word "Door" at him and pointed down low, opposite from where they were sitting. His eyes crinkled and they immediately turned back to Cybele. That Mayapple. He figured she must know everything.

A big spotlight kept track of the star as she continuously moved around the stage, a primitive jungle scene illuminating the mountainous sides of the volcano behind her.

A deep throaty laugh, a slow rumble not unlike a cat's roar came tumbling out and she asked, "Not bad for an entrance, is it?" and the crowd cheered, clapped, whistled, and stomped their approval, making her and everyone else laugh. She went on to reassure the audience about her pet 'kitties,' as she called them, assuring all they were loved and adored as they should be.

Flem could hardly breathe he was having so much fun and time became suspended as they listened to this wild woman talk and sing and tell small anecdotes.

After an hour and a particularly funny song, the lights dimmed to blackness for a minute and when they partially came up again, she was gone.

A slow murmur could be heard, a swish of words leaking out of everyone's mouths in muted voice.

The lights were dim but the environment could still be discerned and Flem's head started to swivel as he looked avidly around. As everyone else was doing.

Several men of various ages made it a point to either dash over to where Bud sat, or call his name for a hello from where they sat. One sent a greeting past Mayapple and Flem to Lark but was received rather distantly by the recipient, so he moved on rather briskly.

In no time at all, the lights started to fade again, but slowly, slowly, giving the restless ones a chance to regain their tier.

Whimsey C. Nimble

Soon, all was once again enveloped in darkness, low chanting becoming louder and louder 'til it held everyone in place.

Gradually, the glowing volcano came back to life, the lava cap a dark orange, trails of smoke seemingly erupting from its top. The land appeared closer, the dense vegetation it depicted, real. Soft lighting crept in and the audience's focus sharpened.

Where was Cybele?

Once again the chanting gave way to a cacophony of a rhythmic tribal beat, crescendoing before falling back to make way for the Goddess.

A pale rose spotlight materialized off to one side and there, sitting in a bower of interwoven greenery sat Cybele, long legs tucked together and off to one side.

If not for her size and that devilish twinkle in her eyes, she almost could have passed for a sweet young maid, delicate lace frills extending into the deep cleavage of her virginal pink dress.

With a look of innocence, she launched into a series of tongue-in-cheek, straight-faced, ribald songs and ballads that soon had the audience gasping and laughing.

Mayapple was shocked but the humor got to her and she didn't even try to control her self, hooting and hollering along with the rest.

Flem didn't know what to think. These humans! Sex, sex, sex, was *everything* about mating all the time? Still, it was rather refreshing to just let everything hang out, say what you will, make fun, and he admired the strong personality manipulating people's sensibilities, up on stage.

Force emanated from her, one she projected, shaping it to what she wanted people to believe and Flem started to understand *he* could do the same thing. It was just a matter of deciding to play a part and carrying through, whether for an hour or a day, such as at work. *He* was in control of *his* future. The unknown entity that hauled him along was, in fact, his own default, his own reaction or non-reaction to events in his life.

She, Cybele, was obviously very in control of her life reflected Flem as her voice faded.

Darkness descended except for the volcano which glowed with a smoldering promise. The side lights flickered but not enough to signal another intermission and people sat, waiting with bated breath, a slight rustle announcing the fact they still lived and breathed.

They didn't have long to wait.

The volcano came to life, smoke pouring from its angry orange mouth, a sound like an Earth rumble being felt more than heard.

Mayapple clutched Flem's hand in excitement, making eyes of 'Oh boy!' at him as the excitement built.

They were not disappointed.

A soft light came into focus as the stage moved with the speed of shadows chasing the evening sun, the drumming picking up and moving past it easily.

Mayapple and Flem strained to make out the scene, Bud and Lark as their bookends leaning in with them.

An elaborate delicate chair sat like a throne, scarlet dipladenia framing the flowing Earth Mother seated within, a Goddess in their midst clothed in a red swirling diaphanous cloud.

Smiling into the audience, she waved a hand and introduced, "My Dactyls."

The spot light grew to include a circle of something surrounding her - short and strangely shaped - people? Yes, possibly men but they looked so odd and the colors of their costumes so muted, even in a spotlight.

Like small shafts of autumn vegetation in soft hues of black, brown, and ruddy pink, they stood at attention surrounding Cybele, shiny bald heads separated from their rather tight costumes by several folds of turtle-neck satin.

The Goddess Mother bestowed a smiling, knowing, lascivious look around her and they began to dance, awkwardly weaving and waving their whole bodies in a swaying motion towards their queen.

The volcano grew brighter, smoke pouring from the top, bigger rumbles felt in every body and the dancers grew frantic in their writhing, circling, moving in closer to their magnet.

As the sphere of dancers tightened around her, Cybele's throne easily shape-shifted to a platform where she now stood, dancing to the crazed beat that filled the blood of every person and Sylph in the place.

The pace increased and the audience watched as from the bottom of each dancer's costume, shooting lights could be seen traveling towards the top, like fireworks on its way up.

The rolls of satin cloth around each dactyl's neck caught the lights and held them, as they raced in circles through the folds.

Whimsey C. Nimble

Of one accord the drumming, the volcano, the dactyls and Cybele reaching the apex of their agitation, with lava shooting out the top and over the edge in all directions, the drumming just as insistent but faltering occasionally, Cybele swirling and twirling and wriggling for all she was worth as her arms swam through the air and the dactyls bending over, ecstasy spent, loosing large white pearls the size of gumballs upon the stage at Cybele's feet.

The room was plunged into darkness.

The audience sat stunned and no sound was made until one person clapped and they roared to life, bringing down the house, if they'd been in one.

The music insinuated itself once again as ambient light helped people return to their own self or Sylph.

Laughter started breaking out as first one and then another found release for the hilarity they'd all just experienced together.

Mayapple was no exception and Flem tried to pull himsylph together because he could hear the crazed bug that she got in her voice, but he was still caught up in the climatic scene they'd just left.

Gasping a little at the enormity of everything, he started downhill with overloaded emotions and his wings actually buzzed momentarily in his consternation. Neither Bud nor Lark actually saw it but both caught the tell-tale clacking sound and cast a knowing look at the other.

Mayapple was now trying to control herself from the hoots and trills she was exhibiting but couldn't. She bent over, a feathery little bird holding her knees, and laughing between them.

Flem's emotions abruptly clanged the other way and his eyes started to water in contagious hilarity, madness really, and he couldn't stand it any longer, giving in to Mayapple's mirth. His wings relaxed.

Bud and Lark sniggered on the ends trying to be cool about it, but it was impossible to repress.

For some reason, many in the audience felt the same way and people were laughing everywhere.

The lights came up and Flem took a deep breath and asked, "Is it over?"

Lark quickly replied, "I'm pretty sure we get Act Three yet, I think that's what it said," referring to the program he was consulting in his hand.

Bud was standing, stretching in the aisle and offered, "After that I need a drink. I'll go get us each a mead, okay? My treat." He looked at each for a confirmation before dashing off, up a hill.

Flem resolved this was it, he wouldn't have another this evening. Ooh, but a party at Bud's? How could he not?

Mayapple was giving him a look, as if she was reading his mind, and leaned over to whisper, "Don't worry, I'll help you," but her eyes saw someone and the next thing Flem knew, she was squeezing his arm, her little purse whamming against his knee as she got up and stepped out to the aisle. Flem watched open mouthed as she threw out "Be right back!" over her shoulder, turning away and yodeling, "Yoo hoo! Dicksonia!" to her hot date of the week before.

Closing his mouth, Flem turned automatically to see what Lark was doing, and Lark was watching *him*.

Pulling on his urbane, sophisticated male act, his sinuses cleared with the exhilaration of it all and he sniffed, smiling at Lark, raising his eyebrows at 'all this.'

Lark returned his smile enigmatically but one finger traced a short path back and forth on Flem's arm.

"Bud's party ought to be fun. He hasn't had a party in *ages*. Wait 'til you see his place, I mean really see it, it's so, so," Sylph is what he thought but "interesting," is what he said, his eyes never betraying his impertinent finger walking.

Flem was nonplussed and didn't know how to reply. Was he suppose to just ignore Lark's wandering hands?

Just then a "Hey!" was interjected by Mayapple, who was obviously wound up, her perky little hat drooping precariously and Flem noted one of the longer feathers was bent. His eyes left it to go back to her face and she looked, well, *mussed*, her lipstick smudged, her lips rather swollen.

Flem narrowed his eyes as she hitched up a bra strap and hic-cupped accidentally.

"Were you drinking? Where'd you go?" Flem mockingly scowled and made a to-do over looking behind her, as if in search of a kidnapper.

She gave him a disgusted look as she came back to her seat but then said on a sigh, "I saw Dicksonia."

Whimsey C. Nimble

Before Flem could reply, Bud materialized with four glasses and handed them around with the tidbit, "You can keep these, they're commemoratives of the occasion."

"To the Muse!" he saluted and the four clinked together. Lark never gave it a thought but Flem was struck with the ancient Sylph toast, and did a double take, watching Bud delicately sip from the miniature engraved goblet.

Lost in strange speculation, he forgot himsylph and took a healthy swig of his favorite drink instead of the socially acceptable sip and got hooked on Mayapple's direct stare, which caused him to catch himsylph before he spat it back into the glass, a bigger no-no than gulping.

Grinning behind her mead, Mayapple nodded graciously and Flem wasn't sure he was happy about her help or not.

The lights dimmed and came back up, signaling people it was *time*, and everyone settled in. Darkness fell.

A stray cough was heard as the stage illuminated softly to reveal three women standing before a microphone, framed by the woodsy scene in the background, where the volcano had last been seen going off but was now a mere distant scenic backdrop.

The Corybants hugged the round inner perimeter and chanted up and down in a fast soft hush.

The spotlight found the three, and a flute coupled with some fast drumming and a lively guitar jumped in and overlaid the soft chorus in the background with a catchy beat that soon had everyone tapping a toe and nodding as they waited.

The women were moving with the music, the two in the back wildly exaggerating every move. The introduction faded and Cybele's voice rang out: " Ladies and gentlemen, I present to you, Women with Wings!"

Flem was all eyes, as were his companions.

As the woman in the middle stepped even closer to the microphone, the other two stepped back and apart, full, over-blown, real-looking wings suddenly popping out on all three.

Flem couldn't believe his incredible fortune, for she was none other than Rainbow Merkiva turned diva! Her wings looked similar to the other two, but something was different. Hers were smaller and they didn't seem to glide as easily as the other two's.

Flem poked Mayapple with an elbow as she had done to him and whispered, "That's my friend."

She turned to him in amazement and said, "*Her?*"

He nodded, almost ready to burst with happiness but managed to stay in his seat.

Behind his back Mayapple whispered to Bud, who looked at Flem with new appreciation. Lark looked over and Bud pantomimed "*That's* Flem's friend!"

All were properly impressed.

The womens' wings were large luminous affairs that sparkled and glimmered and Flem could even see bursts of lights twinkling within.

Suspiciously, they looked very similar to his own. Especially the two in the back. It was most puzzling. These *were* human women. Weren't they?

His brow unconsciously wrinkled. He stole a look at his friends. Mayapple sat rapt, her eyes shining bright with furor, and Flem could see she was hooked. Whatever they were selling, she was buying.

Slanting his eyes, he glanced at Bud who sat with his chin in his hand, elbow propped on one knee, apparently mesmerized, a big silly grin on his face.

As he watched the women, the hair on the back of his neck lifted, sending a sister runner down his back bone, diverting to climb bony wing ridges and up into the nether regions of tied-down wings. His chest tightened in response giving acknowledgment to the shiver, which then ran back again before leaping away, leaving a path of sylphdestruction in its tiny wake. Rainbow Merkiva did not look like a Sylph to him but those other two...

His head jerked around as he felt a physical finger running up and around and down the outline of his camouflaged, and folded over, wings.

It wasn't Mayapple, she had both hands in sight as she sat leaning forward, rather rigid in her enthrallment.

Heart in throat, Flem fell into Lark's green depths, finding it impossible to pull away.

Lark's finger moved ever so slowly, following the hidden road of cartilage in its tortuous confines beneath Flem's fancy shirt. Without breaking eye contact, he took Flem's hand and put one of his fingers onto his own shoulder.

Whimsey C. Nimble

At first Flem was flabbergasted, embarrassed by such intimate contact but with a shock it came to him *what* he had his finger *on*.

It couldn't be. He traced it.

Lark looked deep into his eyes, willing him to accept the truth.

Flem swallowed, his emotions high, his disbelief mirrored on his face as shock.

But that shock started to crumble, to be replaced by unmitigated joy, a joy so sweet it knew no bounds.

Lark was *not* a human male. Lark was a Sylph, disguised as a human male.

And he wanted to be friends with *him*, Flem.

Good thing he was sitting down.

Lark poked him, smiled kindly, and pointed towards the stage, where the show was progressing, keeping his fingers on Flem's back, massaging lightly.

All three women were dancing, taking wild leaps into the air that supposedly required wing power to get them back down

Flem wondered how they kept their wings on and if there were cables hidden somewhere on their bodies to help boost them along.

As the number came to an end, the two women in back 'flew' to a big tree nearby.

Rainbow Merkiva found a fallen log behind her where the still-present Corybants had parted and all became still, the light fading.

Immediately several flashing colored spots danced around the stage, the chorus emitting a remarkable deep buzz to accompany them, building in intensity until only one spotlight roamed by itself, settling on another figure off to one side.

Cybele herself unfolded into the full spotlight, a half-primal song springing from her lips, a lament of some sort.

The chorus agreed, urging her along, almost baiting her. The two "faeries" in the tree and the one on the log all consoling her, adding their tweets, twerts, chirps, and general howls to the uproar.

This went on for quite some time until, dramatically, it all stopped at once, the white spotlight illuminating Cybele as never before.

The chorus couldn't shut up and kept the beat going, challenging the intense soft drumming behind them.

Drawing the moment out, Cybele rose on a small mountain platform that thrust her up, along with her own, giant *wings*!

Flem laughed out loud at the sheer magnificence of her audacity, not really believing his eyes. Oh, to be able to let *his* wings out like they were pretending to do onstage.

His head whipped back to Lark who gave him a noncommittal grin and Flem couldn't tell if there was more going on than he thought, or not.

None of these others were Sylphs, were they? He directed a look of question to Lark who sweetly shook his head as if he had no idea what Flem was asking.

Nah. Couldn't be. They all looked like human women. They were, weren't they?

Cybele finished her number and the spotlight returned to a beaming Rainbow Merkiva and the two 'faeries' in the tree.

Rainbow stood up and walked back towards the audience, her two sisters swooping down to fall in behind, wildness dropping from them like droplets from a dew-laden branch, until there they stood, three lovely ladies sporting beautifully crafted wings, pretending to be faeries, of all things. All the wings looked real but real in an artsy way although the 'veins' in the *wingulacture*, especially near the base, looked remarkably like his very own wings, especially on those two behind Rainbow, thought Flem.

He watched as they all sang another passionate call and response self-claiming jungle song, big wings keeping a vivid beat with every breath taken. Flem had never seen wings that gigantic before, the two in the back each a different color, vivid emerald green and deep glowing purple backing up the singer with her own brilliant sunset burst of oranges, yellow, and reds, oh my.

There were no Sylphs that color. All Sylphs *were* a different color but mostly muted. And each pattern down their legs and arms was different from one to the other, barely discernable except upon closer inspection. *Sylphs* would see it.

With wonder in his eye, Flem turned and looked at Lark.

Biting his lower lip in amazement Flem was jerked back to reality as Mayapple skewered him again in the side with her sharp elbow, laughing hysterically at what was going on but Flem missed it and only smiled.

The final number came to an end and soon all the performers were on stage, drummers being revealed from behind layers of woodsy scene, Corybants and Dactyls (erect once again) intermingling near the center around the edge of the woods, and Cybele herself minus her recent wings, beaming in the spotlight as she thanked the audience and turned and thanked her crew, all of whom bowed and nodded and by chance, Flem caught Rainbow Merkiva's eye.

Her eyebrows lifted in happy remembrance and she winked at him, nodding quickly, causing a cascade of heat to roll up his body and suffuse his cheeks with color.

Several people turned in their seats, nosiness getting the better of them.

A ring of fire burned around the faerie's neck in sylphconsciousness.

Mayapple pinched him just to remind him she was there, taking it all in too.

Bud leaned over and grinned down the row to his coworker.

Lark poked him with one finger and whispered, "You're HOT baby. Hot. Hot. HOT."

Flem laughed, his wings thrusting against bindings to be let out.

"Easy, we're in public," came a soft warning and Flem heeded it, pulling himsylph together urbanely.

Cybele's eyes were quick and she caught an exchange between an audience member and Rainbow Merkiva just before she waved her hand and the jungle lights illuminated the entire area, including the audience, and in a unforeseen finale, led her troops off the stage and wove them in a sinuey dance throughout the entire place. As she headed back toward the stage, the line disintegrated, performers flowing towards the back and the paying crowd straggling towards the exits.

A path opened up seamlessly for Rainbow Merkiva, still dancing to her own beat as her two colorful winged companions trailed behind. Coming to a stop right beside Flem, she greeted him enthusiastically, "Hi Flem! These must be the friends you mentioned. Boy, you've got great taste! Look at you guys."

Mayapple was gurgling in wonderment, and Bud and Lark were standing up straight, all manners and impeccable taste.

Flem nodded, his eyes bright with glee and he majestically introduced his three wonderful friends.

Graciously acknowledging each one, the sunset burst with matching hair tucked her arm in Flem's and said 'C'mon. Let's go backstage."

Chapter 41

—— ❧ ——

Yes. Don't go *diving* into the nectar, try to
keep mysylph under control. Right?

 AYAPPLE GRINNED AT their good fortune as she and Lark and Bud fell into step behind Ms. Merkiva who was leading Flem away, or should we say, astray.

Mayapple felt a small spurt of jealousy at seeing someone else's arm tucked through Flem's, her personal good friend and faerie.

She chided herself for her sylphishness.

Lark felt sort of hollow, watching him be led away by such a bright personality who no doubt would hold just as much sway as his own Sylph.

Ridiculous, he told himsylph, smiling at Bud, and Bud of course knew exactly what was going on in Lark's mind and said, "Ooh, she is a pretty one, isn't she?" rubbing his hands together and making lascivious noises while smacking his lips.

Lark laughed and punched him in the arm.

Bud pranced in front of him and Mayapple was torn between watching Flem in front and Bud and Lark behind her.

They followed the duo and slipped behind a heavy velvet curtain, starting down a long straight hall, surrounded by all the cast members moving freely among them until they got to a big room that had lots of mirrors and dressing tables and lights, where the Corybants were all plopping down here and there, Dactlys starting to filter in also. Rainbow stopped at a long table laid out in a feast of sumptuous finger foods and said "Help yourself, I'll be right back." She walked over to a door marked 'Rainbow Merkiva' right next to one labeled C & C, and disappeared through it.

Whimsey C. Nimble

Flem turned back to his friends who were busily sampling various goodies.

Rainbow showed up a few minutes later with a bottle of champagne under each arm but said, "I can't open this 'til China and Cat get here. Oh, there they are! Hurry up, come and meet Flem and his friends." She waved them over, immediately thrusting a small cloth over one of the bottles, walking the cork up until with a muffled pop! she was ready.

China grabbed a glass off the table and Cat was right behind her with six more.

Lark, Bud, Flem, and Mayapple stood in awe at the three would-be faeries who seemed bigger than life, a club unto themselves. Studying the wings that were still out and wide, Flem realized there were layers upon layers and that that was the reason they looked so big. Obviously, IF they had been Sylphs, they would have furled by now. But that was lame reasoning, and he knew it.

Everyone now held a slender flute of champagne in their hand and Rainbow spoke up with a toast she said she'd heard and decided to adopt as her own: "To the Muse!" She smiled broadly at China and Cat, saluting them in their partnership in the show which they returned and then offered to the four guests.

Bud and Lark's ears rang with the toast and Flem was clearly taken aback upon hearing it again. The three stared hard at Rainbow, their eyes flickering to the other two. China and Cat eyeballed them right back, with interest.

Rainbow leaped in, "Flem, everyone, these two characters are some new friends of mine, Chinaberry and this here is Catalpah, we met at the auditions. And these are?..."

Flem broke in quickly and waved a gallant hand as he first introduced his little feathered friend, Mayapple, who curtsied as if being presented to the queen.

Bud and Lark were standing rapturously tall and straight, giddy underneath, debonair and suave on the outside.

The seven gazed at one another with unabashed curiosity, Flem studying the group opposite with great interest as he sipped his first taste of bubbly, trying to decide if their life-like appendages were authentic or not. Chinaberry and Catalpah were impressive and Flem looked hard to see who they were beneath the glitz. He sipped, his eyes traveling to where their wings connected but it was *inside* the costume.

He took another drink and turned to look at Rainbow Merkiva's wings and she and Mayapple both turned and smiled happily to catch his eye, both talking to him simultaneously, laughing, carrying on again, talking talking talking nonstop and now wrapping him in their words, pulling him to them.

He grinned and Rainbow poured more champagne into his glass before he knew it, topping off Mayapple's also before her own and then setting the empty bottle back on the table, just as Cat opened the second bottle.

The noise level in the whole place went up.

A Corybant with half her makeup gone came over and draped a long bronzed tattooed arm over Rainbow's shoulders, liberally pouring everyone another round from her bottle, except for Lark, who said, "Thanks. No more. I'm driving."

Flem was sucking it all up, his firm resolutions turned to mush. Mayapple was no help, she was guzzling her third glass.

Flem sipped slowly, his mind alive with so much activity, and then an image in one of the mirrors caught his eye.

He couldn't quite believe it and looked around furtively, his gaze sharpening. Human men were emerging as the makeup came off and costumes stripped away.

His jaw dropped as he no longer could conceal his amazement and his eyes flew from one Corybant to the next, watching the tall sculptured women transmorph right before his very eyes, to men. Talk about shades of Sylph. Great Pan, it was mind blowing.

He was finally able to bring his focus back to the two tall, winged women right in front of him, laughing and flirting with Buddleia.

But *Lark* was a Sylph. What about Bud? How did this all work, he wondered.

The purple one, Chinaberry, was telling some story and his two friends were rapt with their attention, Catalpah smiling and jumping in, finishing the other's sentences.

Flem was confused but he didn't really mind since as he was now secure enough to relish the mysteries around him.

Catalpah and Chinaberry were laughing at something so hard they were actually snorting, Bud was turned away, slapping his thigh and Lark was standing there looking smug, obviously the proprietor of some witty comment.

Rainbow tugged on his arm, "Well, did you like our show?" she asked, fishing.

Flem laughed, smiling at her, but before he could comment, Bud was heard to say, "Hey, I'm having a few friends over tonight, after the show. You're all welcome to come!"

Chinaberry and Catalpah thought it was a great idea as did all the others in the entire room, as many voices chimed in "Yeah, we'd love to. You bet! Leave the directions there on the table, and we'll find you! Can we bring out friends? Oh, that's right, our friends are all here!" and a great titter swept the room until everybody was laughing together, many of the voice's owners now making their way to ingratiate themselves with the good looking man having a party.

Taking out a folded invitation from his pocket, Bud held it up for all to see and made the announcement that it would be right here on the table next to the cheese dip and not to lose it.

With that, an impromptu smattering of applause broke out and by this time it was pretty obvious hardly any of the Corybants were women, but all beautiful young men.

The Dactyls on the other hand were indeed short and kind of dumpy bald-headed men, much like they had portrayed. They didn't seem to have dressing tables but more of a locker room area in the far corner. Flem wondered if they'd come to the party too.

Now his curiosity was really whetted. Were *any* of the Dactyls women? What about China and Cat? Women? Or were they too, men? They looked like women, only, more-so. And their wing structure was 'built' amazingly like his own. How did they know to do that? Were they Sylph also? He glanced over at Rainbow and there was a difference. There was no doubt she was a human even though her wings looked amazingly like the other two's. But more, well, *constructed*.

Mayapple pulled him away, still talking, "..so we'll see you soon, right? You got the directions?"

"Oh, we'll be there, won't we boys?" Rainbow answered, taking it upon herself to speak for the whole troupe, China and Cat nodding in the background. Women? Men? Faeries? Dactyls? Corybants? Who was what?

It was all a mystery and Flem sighed in contentment, wondering if there was any more champagne.

Mayapple plucked the empty glass from his hand, shaking her head at how much *she'd* been drinking and knew he'd had the same. And a party to go to. Tsk. What to do.

"Flem," she said very seriously, licking her lips, "I've decided something. Les'see what you think." She hiccupped, then laughed.

" 'Course, I *know* what you'll say!" and she started to laugh at her own brilliance.

Flem shook his head, knowing he'd had too much champagne and wanted to ask Mayapple's advice but apparently, she'd had too much also.

"Tonight!" she announced, "Only tonight, I think we should make an exception to your drinkin' rule." She tried to be stern but couldn't stop smiling which was making it harder.

"Tomorrow, we're back to the one rule, how's that?" she asked.

Instantly Flem's eyes brightened right up and they were already pretty bright.

"Okay!" he agreed. Then he stuck his hand out to touch hers and said sincerely, "Thank you Mayapple, you're my best friend."

"Oh Flemmy."

Overcome with love, they hugged quickly, a tear in each eye, then straightened right up, Mayapple playfully shaking a finger at him and saying, "Now just because we have no rules tonight, doesn't mean there aren't *any* *r*ules, do'ya understand what I mean?"

"Yes. Don't go *diving* into the nectar, try to keep mysylph under control. Right?"

Pinching his cheek in pleasure, Mayapple exclaimed, "You're a quick study! What did I do before you came to work at Fletcherman's?" She rubbed his shoulders surreptitiously and Rainbow Merkiva's lively gaze didn't miss a thing.

She was going to have to get to know this young lady better. There was so much going on here. Obviously, she was good friends with Flem and her previous suspicions bloomed like a red tide in April.

Lark spoke up, "Well, c'mon you two, let's go. I want to see if Bud here can still throw a decent party, he used to have quite the reputation in the *old* days." He clapped a hand on Bud's shoulder being careful not to look at him as Buddleia shot him a sharp look.

Whimsey C. Nimble

Mayapple wondered what passed between them. Secrets were afloat.

She was turning to go, adjusting her purse strap when Rainbow tapped her on the shoulder and with a knowing look, said, "Lynx medicine."

Mayapple regarded her with a completely blank look so she explained: "Lynx medicine means there are secrets afloat. We all have secrets, don't we?" She turned an innocent face to Mayapple with her question, continuing on with, "I read animal medicine cards and I see that one of the energies here tonight is Lynx: secrets. I'll see you at the party."

Mayapple nodded, not sure what to say.

Lark, Bud, and Flem were slowly walking but Flem stopped, imploring Mayapple to catch up.

Linking her arm in his, they strode along behind Bud and Lark, happy to be in the moment.

Chapter 42

———— ❧ ————

"Mead," he observed. "One should be able
to clearly see the dancing flame through
the body of it. That's the standard."

$\mathcal{T}$RAILING BEHIND MAYAPPLE, Bud and Lark as they ascended the outside wooden staircase, the faerie's excitement mounted with every step
leading to Bud's door and he was greatly atwitch with Sylph adrenalin and
alcohol. He was doing his best to appear nonchalant but it was the furtherest
thing from the truth. Every hair on his body, every scale in his wings was
standing up. They stepped in and Bud glided around snapping on lights, setting ambiance as Lark steered a course right to the bar, Mayapple and Flem
drifting along behind him, agog with Bud's abode.

"Help yourself," tossed Bud over his shoulder as he disappeared through
a door but Lark was already reaching for a small crystal goblet, filling it from
a big dispenser set right on the counter at one end.

Flem's eyes widened in recognition. Pootsy Koons had its twin back at
Windfall Café in Thimbleberry Canyon. Hers was also filled with mead.
A sliver of suspicion, like a tiny darting minnow, made an appearance but
glided into the shadows immediately. Flem shook his head, wondering if he
was crazy, startled when Lark settled a heavy rounded glass into his fingers.

Grinning, that suave Sylph in black took a sensuous sip, his tongue coming out seductively to touch the taste on his lips as he looked at the other
faerie.

Bud reappeared, an infectious grin on his lips that wouldn't stop, his
hands once again in his back pockets and Lark laughed and said, "Quite the
ta-do, you sly Syl-, ah, ..fellow."

Whimsey C. Nimble

Bud proceeded with a quick hiss, like perhaps Lark had been going to say something other than fellow.

At least, that's what Flem heard. '*Sylph*' perhaps?

Mayapple was savoring the silken touch of the golden nectar on her tongue, wondering where he got it, he certainly had a lot of it. She reflected that the glass jug that held the mead was at least a five gallon container.

Flem's eyes closed and he held the goblet right under his nose, inhaling deeply.

Lark smiled like it was all his doing and announced, "Bud makes this."

"Really?" breathed Mayapple, taking another reverent sip, letting it roll about on her tongue indolently.

Flem was staring at Buddleia.

Could it be?

"You *make* this?" repeated Flem. "How? Where?" his mind whirling with implications.

Bud deigned not to answer, instead smiling as slamming car doors could be heard below, voices punctuating the pandemonium.

A clatter could be heard progressing up the stairs.

Ah, just like the old days, thought Lark with satisfaction, only with a *twist*. A big twist, he laughed to himsylph, as the door burst open.

Rainbow Merkiva and her entourage spilled into the room.

No wings were in sight but it was obvious they were all flying and without hesitation headed for the corner where Lark was playing bartender.

Flem stood in awe. These *women* were dazzling. Catalpah had traded her wings for a long sparkling green scarf that accentuated her every move and Flem wondered at the breadth of her shoulders. Her hair was shaggy short and set off high cheekbones.

Cha, she looked like a Sylph. But of course that was nuts. Wasn't it?

Chinaberry was even more flamboyant than Catalpah, a purple sequined loose jacket flowing around her black pants, with exotic eyes and a bosom that dropped deep but there didn't seem much cleavage to go with it. She too sported handsome shoulders.

Graceful beringed fingers gestured with every word they spoke, almost like a musical accompaniment, but with no sound.

Both women stood easily as tall as the rest of them, being head and shoulders above Rainbow and Mayapple.

Rainbow dazzled in her after-show finery – a short silver wrap around her shoulders, a chunky red corral necklace around her throat and tight red glistening pants that ended just below her knees, the better to show off her red and silver heels, with a matching red coral bracelet adorning her wrist.

Flem decided when he saw them come through Bud's door that nothing would be able to surprise him anymore. His world had gone Pan crazy.

He wondered if these were 'the boys,' Rainbow had referred to backstage. He looked harder.

What a strange lot these city people were, he reflected.

Apparently Bud had invited the whole city, as people continued to pour in and shortly it was wall to wall bodies.

"C'mon, let's take a stroll," Mayapple said, standing up.

Flem needed no urging, it was like being at a Sylph party, but only him and Lark were Sylphs.

Hmm. He looked around.

He *assumed* only he and Lark were Sylphs. Could there be more? He couldn't get a handle on what these other two, Chinaberry and Catalpah, were. Bud? Who else?

Mayapple tugged, lacing her fingers with his so they wouldn't get separated, threading her way through the crowd, using light fingertip touches with the other hand to part the way.

As he squeezed along behind her, he watched each and every one avidly as he went by, hungry for this close contact, of being somewhere where he was accepted automatically. And at a party. A big party. *In* a tree house, for Pan's sake! It was so Sylph. So cathartic for his long abused soul.

Mayapple stopped and said, "Oh good, a bathroom. Don't go anywhere," and disappeared leaving the faerie on his own.

He rather relished it and gazed back the way they'd come, his eyes landing on Bud, who was actively *still* talking to Rainbow, China, Cat and Lark.

What an attractive man he is, thought Flem. Lark leaned across him momentarily before straightening back up and Flem searched his profile next to Bud's and suddenly, he knew; he could see it. Bud *was* a Sylph.

He looked away and then back again, taking a sip of mead. Now that he saw it, he couldn't imagine he hadn't *always* seen it.

Mayapple opened the door, and said, "Ready? Let's go see what's back here." She took off through a small connecting hallway and came out at some

Whimsey C. Nimble

French doors opening onto a deck, a magical place strewn with hidden lights that wound through the open rafters and on out, over a *foot bridge*, a hanging foot bridge that led to *another* tree house.

Clamping a hand over her mouth in delight, Mayapple practically danced onto it, holding the small goblet aloft to sway in unison with her steps. People of indeterminate ages smiled at her as they shuffled to let them pass.

Several greeted Flem, letting him know they were a Corybant and they'd seen him with Rainbow, commenting on how remarkable she was, and smiling as they also mentioned Cat and China casually.

Much to Flem's surprise two women stopped him also, saying *they* were Corybants and Flem wondered, was nobody what they seemed or was it just that all were androgynous at soul level?

Sidling along, smiling sylphconsciously, everyone grinned back at the tall and charming young man and feathery woman as she led the way.

Looking out over the lighted railing between two people, Flem's breath caught in his throat and he tugged on Mayapple's shoulder to halt her progress.

"Look," he gestured.

It was one thirty in the morning and obviously night time but the trees around them were lit up in various pastel shades. Bud had obviously gone to enormous lengths.

"Wow," breathed Mayapple, "it really is a *faerie* land, isn't it?"

Flem looked at her.

She didn't notice.

He so wanted to tell her about Lark and Bud, but it wasn't *his* to tell.

They moved onto the deck of the next treehouse, wandering straight in through the open door. It looked to be a bedroom and Flem wondered if it was Bud's or a spare. Seven people sat on the bed that was below a skylight and one more was swinging in the hammock that was hung between two enormous tree trunks that pierced the room. Another door was glimpsed and Flem realized it was a large bathroom he was looking at, up *here*, of all places.

The other side of the room was one big window seat set into a bay window, and it too was filled with people.

Mayapple kept going, making her way through the room 'til she reached the exit and out they went.

"Ooh ooh, Flem, look!" she cried, pointing to another swinging bridge leading to another tree house of sorts.

Flem was impressed. Bud was certainly successful. 'Course, he worked at it, it appeared he had very little free time, unless one counted the wee hours of the morning. Like now. Obviously he was well adjusted, look at how many people he knew! Cha, half the City must be here.

The last bridge didn't have nearly as many people and they stopped to gaze about. Neighboring houses could be seen in the distance on three sides through the trees but lower, on the ground.

From where they hung suspended twenty feet in the air between the last two cabins they had a perfect view of, what had quickly become, the parking lot. It was still busy down there, people walking in from where they'd had to park on the street and one car leaving, with someone immediately taking their space, and another nosing around.

A motorcycle came into hearing and then popped into view as it crept up the driveway.

Pulling in between two cars close to the bottom of the stairs, Flem and Mayapple watched as a tall, well-built person got off and hung up her helmet, leaving her leather jacket on, running her hands through her short dark hair, then digging into a compartment for a mirror and a lipstick.

"I wonder who that is?" Mayapple asked rather absently.

Flem stared.

"Mayapple, is that *Cybele*?"

"What? Is it? No. How could, why would, no, is it?" Mayapple questioned as they both followed her ascent up the round-about steps two tree-houses away.

She disappeared. Immediately some sort of cheer went up inside the room she entered, getting louder with many whistles and cat calls.

Flem grinned at Mayapple, "I guess that's our answer!"

They turned to continue but a noise down below drew Mayapple's attention for a moment.

A familiar figure, in fact, two familiar figures were walking from a car towards the main stairs, arms entwined around each other.

"Oh shit," said Mayapple under her breath.

The faerie stopped in his tracks, looking at her.

Whimsey C. Nimble

"Mom. Santolina," she explained tossing her head in their general direction down below.

"Ha ha! Imagine that. You don't think *they* were at Revelry too, do you?" asked Flem as the thought came to him.

"I doubt it." She paused. "Probably Bud mentioned the party to her. Hey, let's go see this last treehouse of his and then we'll head back into the crush, okay?"

Iris listened to the whoopin' and holloring going on upstairs, then saw the big black bike by the first step, noticing that whoever had parked it had been very conscientious and it was nowhere near the sprawling hydrangea at the base of the tree, a big green bush that were just now blushing blue in two places.

The owner of Fletcherman's Nursery approved. It spoke well of Bud and his guests.

The loud sounds coming from upstairs made her shiver with delightful fear and anticipation and she clutched her escort's strong biceps, reassured by warmth and vitality.

Santolina adjusted his belt, straightening his back, making sure his shirt was tucked in.

He would do anything for Iris, even attend some kooky party in the middle of the night in some damn *treehouse*, for God's sake.

He couldn't wait to tell Pisonia about it on Monday. He was a very open minded man, but these artistic types just weren't his cup of tea, the fact of the matter was he just could not comprehend the world they lived in. They actually kind of scared him but it was only for a very brief moment that he let himself acknowledge it before tripping up the stairs dutifully right behind his love. He patted her rear affectionately and she snapped around with a laugh, "Don't *do* that!" climbing higher, anticipating just what kind of party Bud would give. He was so gallant and thoughtful and yet rarely gave much of himsylph away. She knew he didn't do things lightly and it was obvious from everything she'd seen so far, *this* place was no exception. It was delightful.

"Oough!" Santolina grunted as he bumped into the back of her when she came to a abrupt stop at the top landing across from the open noisy door where the party spilled out.

Strange people were draped over every surface and Santolina sort of flinched inside. He had never really been good at any kind of social scene but years in public service with the Parks and Rec had nonetheless given him some polish.

Smiling and nodding, he looked past people's shoulders to the far wall, and didn't make eye contact, just followed his vivacious girlfriend as she worked the room.

Bud saw them coming and raised an arm in greeting, beckoning them to come closer.

"Let's keep going," invited Mayapple as she sidestepped the door and headed on, passing a couple on a bench set against the side of the treehouse under a low hanging bough. The walkway came to an unusual solitary point nearest the woods before continuing on, wrapping around the house.

Walking out onto it, Mayapple remarked, "Hmm. Look at this, his own little observation deck. Pretty sweet."

Flem grunted noncommittally, knowing what he was seeing, a flight pad disguised in plain sight. This confirmed his suspicion.

Suddenly he was anxious to get back and see Lark, and Bud, as fast as possible. Was it really true?

By this time they had come to the back door and could see what Bud used the third treehouse for, it was obviously work space with a large desk along one wall, two deep chairs with a small table and lamp set between twin built-in book shelves along another and a *still* of some kind along with shelves holding various equipment taking up a corner in its own right.

Flem's eyes widened in awe at this further proof of Bud's background.

He was a *mead* maker. Well, Lark had said that, but, *cha*. Flem's admiration grew by leaps and bounds.

"Do you think this is where he makes the mead, Flem?" asked Mayapple.

"Oh yes, that's mead," replied the faerie with sylphassurance, licking his lips. He'd seen another set-up years ago, back in the canyon.

"I don't remember how it works but I know it involves honey," he said squatting down to study the set-up, admiring the giant basket encasing the large glass bottle.

Whimsey C. Nimble

The whole house shook a little as many people crossed the swaying bridge and a few seconds later, Bud and Lark stepped into the room apparently leading the entire retinue of party-goers, Iris and Santolina next in line behind them, with Cybele, Rainbow, Chinaberry, and Catalpah on their heels at the head of the crowd.

Flem straightened up like a naughty child, an unsuspecting surge of old insecure adrenalin making his nervous system a pin cushion for a bright moment.

"Hey Flem. Mayapple. I see you found my work room," Bud smiled impishly, leading his entourage straight to them.

Flem scootched over next to Mayapple and Bud took over, smiling warmly at Flem as was Lark.

Flem's heart bounced into his throat and he smiled back.

Mayapple, who missed nothing, pinched Flem's arm and encouraged, "Go, go talk to him. I'm going to go show mom and Santolina my dress. *Imagine* seeing them here," and off she went.

Lark slipped by Bud, who was talking to Cybele.

Flem's eyes kept going back to Mayapple as he watched Lark approach. She was talking animatedly with her mother, and Santolina wasn't saying much, just kept sort-of smiling and nodding, his eyes rather glazed. Flem suddenly realized he must feel out of place, as he himsylph had, so many times. A surge of compassion rolled over him.

Lark, tall handsome Lark of the green eyes was now right beside him, one hand rubbing his arm up high as together they watched the crowd for a moment.

Santolina's head came around and he nodded in affirmation at something Bud said, then turning as Cybele spoke up.

Cybele towered a good head and shoulders over Santolina and Iris, being in fact, even taller than their host.

Her shoulders were broad but her arms were definitely feminine and soft, a few bangles with a delicate tattoo up one wrist. The black V-neck t-shirt showed her ample bosom to full advantage.

Dark styled hair was accentuated by a subtle deep purple and fuchsia streak along one temple.

A slight blondish woman materialized beside her and Cybele looped an arm around her neck, pulling her in for a quick kiss.

Flem just watched, spellbound by it all.

"So, Flem, do you know about Cybele?" asked Lark quietly.

Flem turned to him with a question in his eyes and shook his head, scowling a little at some implied mystery.

"*She* used to be male, a human male. And *she* changed that." He paused. "Lots of people end up here in the City, and everyone has a background..." He let it hang, willing Flem to understand what a blessing it could be to live in a city where everyone was accepted for who they were. He stared hard at Flem for a moment before Flem's head swiveled around and he understood her body type then. He was fascinated.

Her voice was deep, rich, velvety, with a throaty quality and she laughed easily.

Oh trust Mayapple, she was now talking, chattering apparently, with Cybele and her friend.

Flem saw her hand them a piece of paper and then ask Bud something, who nodded and cleared his throat, pinging his small crystal goblet with a long metal tool.

Slowly it quieted down.

Bud raised his voice and sort of yelled out to the crowd - "It's been requested that I give a brief talk on the art of making mead. Are you sure that's what you want?"

"Pfft!" scoffed Lark, "look at him, he's in his element. Watch."

Sure enough, everyone clamored for the bit of wisdom he could impart and soon all were listening intently.

"Clarity," he said, holding aloft a small golden bottle to the crowd then picking up a lighted candle which he stuck right behind the bottle, showing everyone that the flame was clearly to be seen. Making eye contact all over the room, he infused the moment with the reverence it decreed. Instantly, everyone sobered up and the proper attitude and respect was shone.

"Mead, " he observed. "One should be able to clearly see the dancing flame through the body of it. That's the standard. From earliest times, honey has been regarded as Godstuff, the only naturally occurring sugar in pre-dawn civilization. When it's removed from the beehive, it ferments naturally. Fermented honey, or mead, is generally acknowledged to be the oldest alcoholic beverage known to humanity (and fae, he added silently).

He pick up his glass and held it out. "To The Muse!"

Whimsey C. Nimble

Glasses started clinking, the tinkling making an amusing thunder as it built, arms lifted everywhere.

"Yes, we LOVE it, that's *ob*vious," came a voice from the crowd just outside the bottle-necked entry, "but I thought we were going to learn how you *make* it."

The crowd nodded, sipping and smiling, willing to go along with the show, urging Bud to continue.

"Ah," breathed the handsome trim man in their midst, looking so hot, so in control of his ownsylph, that every person there inwardly drooled over the elusive Buddleia.

"Well, patience is a must." He paused, took a sip.

"And, a *must* is also a mixture of essentially honey and water with a handful of other things that we start in here, the primary fermenter." He used the same long metal tool to tap a large empty crock and eyeballed the crowd. They were nodding, repeating it to themselves as if they knew what they were talking about.

"The finished product can take up to a year. And that's *before* bottling and aging!

"If there are any bubbles *here*," he pointed to a glass jug, "it's still fermenting.

"What you hold in your hands is from my private reserve." He smiled, much like a cat with feathers around his mouth. "I've been a mead maker for quite some time."

"This," he continued as he swept a graceful hand towards an intriguing set-up of hoses and a giant glass bottle sitting in its own nest accompanied by several smaller bottles at different altitudes around it, "is the basic set-up. After the initial whoop-ti-do is all done, which takes about a week-" but another voice in the crowd broke in with "What the heck are you talking about, *whoop-ti-do?*"

Grunts of agreement echoed and Bud acquiesced charmingly with a modest bow of his head.

"Okay, from the beginning. Honey and water are the basics. *Mead* is produced when honey, the primary sugar source, is diluted down to a concentration that will support yeast growth.

"As I said, a *must* is the diluted solution of honey water plus a few other things, including yeast and ingredients to feed the yeast. I alternate between raisins, bee pollen, or, sometimes, crushed bee larvae. "It's good to know bee keepers," he added as an aside, his eyes traveling to a quiet unassuming man buried in the midst of the crowd.

"I add a little something for acid from citrus, I favor lemon peel, but one can also make use of skins, pulps and juice from other fruit. For tannin," he continued, "I like black tea but I know other mead makers," and here his eyes flew to a couple on the far side of the room, "who think it's more fun with the woodsy approach and so utilize leaves, stems, and bark in the brew."

He grinned at the assorted grimaces in the room, his gaze landing on his two friends Lark and Flem right beside him, before with a conspiratorial air he turned back to affirm: "Oh, I can attest to the flavor. It's excellent." He nodded and raised his glass in appreciation to the couple who were now getting speculative looks from all around them.

He went on, "As I was saying, when the yeast is *pitched* into our soup and covered lightly, the fun begins. That first fermentation takes place here," he tapped the big empty open ceramic crock. "This is our primary fermenter, remember?"

Everyone nodded, a few muttering *must* under their breath, as virtually everyone's eyes traveled to the empty crock.

"The whoop-ti-do starts almost immediately as the yeast gobbles up the sugars, giving off alcohol as a by-product with great masses of froth and foam building. The foam lasts about a week, and I skim it daily. The liquid is siphoned off, or *racked*, into the 'secondary fermenter.'"

All eyes fastened onto a massive glass bottle, otherwise known as a carboy where it rested in its unique basket of heavily woven bamboo. Empty smaller jugs sat below it on another shelf. A long tube curled on the wall behind them, next to a tea strainer that hung near a small notebook on a chain.

At that moment the strange bubbler-like thing stuck through the rubber stopper in the neck of the carboy glubbed and swallowed, and everyone tittered, indulging the innocent passing of gas.

Grinning like a proud papa, Buddleia explained: "The fermenting brew continues to give off carbon dioxide but in greatly diminished amounts, which are the bubbles you will see rising to the surface.

"I fill the airlock here half full of water," he pointed, "which allows the brew to burp but not inhale; carbon dioxide escapes but no oxygen gets in.

Whimsey C. Nimble

"Once a month I carefully rack the mead off the sediment, and try it of course. But other than that, I leave it alone. Depending on whether the mead maker wants to help it along or not, it can take a year before it's perfect.

"Sometimes it doesn't work. Something's just off. But luckily those haven't happened too often, I've been fortunate."

Lark threw a careless arm around Flem and pulled him close as he whispered, "Yeah, he calls it fortunate, I call it anal, he's so obsessed with cleanliness and sterilization and measurements. I've even said to him, "Hey, you do know there are cultures that still make mead in goat skins and gourds, don't you? But he ignores me. And considering I've never tasted a bad batch from all his experiments, well, I guess he's on to something.

"See that notebook hanging back there? He keeps notes on *everything*."

Lark paused, his arm dangling loosely around Flem's neck and Flem couldn't help himsylph, he was grinning like a fool.

Bud paused a moment, throwing a narrowed glance at the two of them, the picture of innocence, before concluding, "Mead made from a stronger honey tends to improve with age, and that not-quite-right batch you bottled will oft times evolve into a gem in ten years. You just keep tasting.

"I tend to like the lighter meads mysylph, those made with flowers, technically a variation called a metheglin, which is any mead made with herbs and spices. Rose petals have their very own class – Rhodomel."

The crowd was fascinated.

Lark moved so that his breath was warm and moist against Flem's ear.

Flem's heart was pounding with the implications. This was all new territory for him, one not driven by Sylph hormones, well, not the kind involved in the blind lust of the *change*.

This was different. This felt more real. He didn't know the end scripted for this. He wasn't sure what to do and looked up to find Mayapple's eyes upon them and with a sly nod of encouragement she urged him on.

"Let's drop Mayapple off first on the way home, what do you say? And then we'll see where you want to be dropped off for the night, hmmm?" breathed Lark into Flem's ear, one hand hidden, working Flem's neck and upper wingulacture.

Chapter 43

───────※───────

Lark's heart and nerve were thick about
his ears as he looked at Flem.

*I*T WAS FOUR in the morning with only a few stragglers immersed in
some far flung passionate conversation, as if all the world's problems
were about to be solved.

Mayapple and Rainbow Merkiva were two such people and Flem watched
from where he slouched against the door jamb.

Mayapple was finding the older woman fascinating and a wealth of information but from the first moment they'd started talking she had felt there
was something else, something Rainbow was holding back. Mayapple wondered how much she knew, and glanced suspiciously at her two wild looking
friends, Cat and China.

Sipping her mead, Rainbow continued on with what she was saying, laying a hand on Mayapple's leg as she bent forward and asked innocuously,
"You're pretty good friends with Flem, aren't you?" She leaned back and
looked at the girl speculatively over the rim of her goblet, but her eyes were
asking something else, something Mayapple couldn't decipher.

The young woman smiled and nodded her head of course.

Rainbow didn't say anything more for a minute, just looked at her new
friend while biting her lower lip.

Mayapple wanted badly to pop this mysterious invisible element, and just
like the natural dehiscence of a perfectly ripe capsule of a prickly poppy, finally burst with impatience, "*What?* What *is* it with you? Is there something
you'd like to tell me? Something *I* should tell you? What? I keep getting the
feeling I'm missing something here."

Whimsey C. Nimble

Still the woman did nothing but sniff as if trying to come to a decision, and finally she did. Her smiled was neutral but her eyes narrowed and her gaze pierced Mayapple's before she deliberately turned and gave the group in the other room a pointed look before returning her gaze to her friend. Slowly an inkling trickled into Mayapple's psyche, her eyes widening in disbelief. She stared back at the woman.

As one, their two sets of eyes traveled to where Lark, Flem, Bud, China and Cat stood gathered in the kitchen, then back at each other, Mayapple's expression one of avid speculation, Rainbow's one of satisfaction, her eyebrows raised in confirmation.

"No..." breathed Mayapple.

Rainbow nodded. "Yes, I believe so..."

Involuntarily, Mayapple's eyes sought Flem and Rainbow's eyes went right with her.

When they both looked at him, Flem knew they were talking about him and he pushed off from the post and strolled over.

"What are you guys talking about?" he inquired, smiling sweetly at Mayapple, pinning her to the spot.

Mayapple rose to the occasion, smiled impishly back and toasted him with her remaining drink.

"We were just conferring on how nice it was to have good friends, Flem, like you. And Lark. And Bud, of course. And, ah, Chinaberry and Catalpah," whereupon all three looked over to where Chinaberry sat on the kitchen counter with Cat right beside her, head cocked to one side, listening to Bud while Lark stood silently, his weight on one leg as he waited for him to finish.

The party had dissipated, leaving this last little ragtag remnant of the seven of them, the atmosphere clean and light from extended good humor, everyone homogenized for the moment.

"Well, I need to get going. China, Cat, am I giving you a ride home?" Rainbow spoke from where she was sitting and hopped down and walked towards the small party.

Everyone was exchanging information and Mayapple thought she detected a little something more between Bud and Catalpah but she couldn't be sure.

Wandering out to the landing, Bud gaily waved goodbye to the trio, adding, "Yeah, I'll see you soon," before car doors slammed and they disappeared into the night. Well, morning by this time.

"Hey, c'mon, I'll give you two a ride home too. Mayapple? Flem?" Lark offered.

Unobtrusively, Bud caught Lark's eye and gave him a silent look.

Lark merely raised his eyebrows but couldn't keep a small closed grin from twitching his mouth momentarily.

With a great benevolent look Bud waved them all on their way, shushing Mayapple's feeble comments about helping him clean up.

"Go," he commanded. "I'll see you Monday at work. Go get some sleep, that's what I'm going to do." He looked meaningfully at Lark.

Lark was practically petting Flem and Flem's senses were a jumble of sensory overload, compounded by too much alcohol.

Mayapple was tired and missed most of the byplay, ready to go home by this time, her little hat dripping dispiritedly, held by one hair pin. A few feathers were ruffled and torn in various places around her dress.

She looked a bit bedraggled.

Once again Bud stood in the open doorway and watched distractedly as Lark herded the other two towards his car.

Laughing at Lark's obviousness, he went back inside, shutting the door behind.

Trying not to hurry, Lark gallantly cleared the way for Mayapple to exit his car, doing his utmost to seem casual.

Finally, she was gone and on her own steps, unlocking her door and slipped inside, a finger twirl to say 'bye over her shoulder.

Lark's heart and nerve were thick about his ears as he looked at Flem. He wanted him, Sylph to Sylph. Something about Flem really sparked his delicate sensibilities and he was filled with an insatiable urge to see him in all his glory, wings spread wide. He wondered who was doing his wing-base preening for him, he would bet it was Mayapple the way she dominated everything about him.

"Where you going?" asked his passenger, bringing him back to the delightful present. "Not the Park..." he started to say but Lark just looked at him with smoldering eyes and Flem's voice petered out.

They made their way to the marina, the fog getting thicker in that pre-dawn mist the closer they got to the water.

Whimsey C. Nimble

"Do you think this is a good idea?" ventured Flem nervously, licking suddenly dry lips, trying to swallow with the enormity of what he was doing. He was beginning to wonder if this really *was* his life, it sure didn't resemble any previous existence he remembered.

"Wouldn't you like to see my wings, Flem? I know I'd like to see yours," Lark said huskily. He paused, then continued in a softer voice, "How long has it been since you *changed*? I remember my own coming out, it was so hard. It wasn't 'til I landed here, in San Fran and did just what you're doing - became a 'human' male, to fit in, that I found out it wasn't so bad. And it got easier. There's a lot to show you and a lot of help available. I've been here ninety-three years. I came here about a year after my change, so I've had time to adjust. Bud's been here, oh let's see, I think about seventy-two, seventy-three years. He and I met after he'd been here a few months. And no, this isn't how I welcome all newcomers to the City, in case you're wondering." His hand had crept up to Flem's neck and he rubbed the tense muscles coming up the back of it.

"So, what do you say, want to come in and let those glorious wings we all keep hidden, out? Me and you. Maybe a hot shower to ease those aches and pains?"

Oh my goodness.

How could he resist?

"Yes," he admitted. "Yes, it sounds glorious," and he threw caution to the wind, embracing the joy life had to offer.

Chapter 44

By this time the glassed-in shower was as
foggy as a heavy English spring.

TREMBLING, FLEM SHED his sleek black pants, nervously unbuttoning his black shirt, letting both drop unnoticed on the bathroom floor.

Stepping over them he headed for the shower door, the air getting steamier by the moment.

His wings were still tied down but he felt no embarrassment at all as he could see Lark, *another* male Sylph, through the thickening atmosphere and he had one wing out, struggling with a knot that held the other.

Without a second thought, Flem hurried over to help, hot water pounding them from two directions.

As his long Sylph fingers dug in to the colored strip holding Lark's appendage captive, he recognized the colorful soft, gel-filled ties from his last visit when he'd snooped through the baskets on the shelf. Hmmmph. Now it all made sense. As did all the dryers. If he hadn't been so flummoxed at the time, he would have been more suspicious.

Finally, the knot was gone and up sprang the other half of an exquisite pair of golden tan and dusty green *wings*.

Oh Pan.

Lark's own fingers were rabidly digging at Flem's bondage, his breath coming fast as he found it hard to control himsylph.

"Cha! Who tied these so tight?" he complained rhetorically, but Flem answered regardless.

"Mayapple, of course."

"I figured that. You two are pretty good friends, huh?" He slanted a look at Flem before continuing. "I haven't had a human girl friend since Lantana left, years ago." He sighed unconsciously as the last knot came loose from Flem's left wing, stepping to one side to allow its full ascent.

Wiping the dripping water from his face, he twirled Flem around so he could get to the other side.

"You must try my ties, they're much easier on the shoulders and wings than these. I buy them at the *S* Club."

Flem was thunderstruck. "The *S* Club! Great Pan, what IS that?"

"Oh Flem," Lark started to explain but interrupted himsylph with an aside question to Flem again, saying, "Say, does anybody ever call you Flim-Flem?" he joked, returning immediately to his subject, the *S* Club, in the same breath.

Flem laughed at Lark's quip and once again replied to a rhetorical statement.

"No, no Flim-Flems. My real name or rather, my old name is Flumaria. Flumaria Greenwood. It just got shortened by itself after, well, afterwards."

By this time the glassed-in shower was as foggy as a heavy English spring.

Smiling into each other's eyes for a moment, Flem realized with a shock that he was looking into beautiful *hazel* eyes, just like his.

Lark read his expression, "They're over there, in their container."

"So," Flem started, "your eyes stayed hazel too then, huh? You mentioned the *S* Club. Are there more of us? Does everyone have hazel eyes?" he asked. "What about Bud, and Chinaberry and Catalpah?" thinking back to that dynamic duo's emerald and amethyst eye colors.

Lark stared for a moment, although why he was surprised he didn't know. "I'm relatively sure they're both Sylph. Like you, I just met them tonight for the first time, but I'd say it was a pretty safe bet. Right?" he was asking for confirmation and Flem was flattered.

"Yeah, I thought so."

Lark was moving closer, his wing tips brushing the sides of the shower occasionally, leaving strange jumpy fog etchings behind.

Flem stood his ground, his slim Sylph straight, his glorious wings up, out and taut.

The hot steamy water and the incredible fact of being able to be so honest, so *naked*, so bare with who he was, was blissful. He had never felt more comfortable in his own skin in his entire life. Amazing.

"Turn around," ordered Mr. Lark Spurastic.

Flem's heart pounded.

Finally!

He turned around.

Lark dropped to his knees and bent his head to get at those irascible wing scales right at the base of Flem's wings and went to work, licking the sodden wet scales into place, locking rims together with his own raspy tongue, warm water dripping off Flem's wings and back onto him, shower spray finding him at unexpected moments when the other moved.

Flem couldn't speak. First Mayapple helping preen him and now Lark. This was more preenings in the last month than he'd had in years. Back at the Canyon, oh Pan, he'd been such a misfit *before* the *change*, that he'd never gotten enough. Oh, other Sylphs would volunteer if nearby, but it seemed like most went out of their way not to get too close.

Pootsy Koons would preen him when he made it to Windfall Café and occasionally if Whimsey Nimble were around, as her and Pootsy were quite good friends, she would preen him also.

But it was a rare occurrence.

With a last lick, and a small bite to really click an unruly rim back into place, Lark stood, his hands rubbing the hollow between Flem's wingulacture and then gliding out, pushing against the silky soft but firm living sea of scales that comprised a Sylph's wings.

"My turn," said Flem huskily, his blood tingling from the contact.

Slowly the taller of the two turned and presented himsylph to the other, groaning in satisfaction as he felt the rough tongue upon his private, unreachable spots.

"Usually I go to the *S* Club when I can't take it anymore."

"Yes, yes tell me – about the *S* Club," ejaculated Flem, aflame with curiosity, his movements quick as he licked those damn scales in hot little motions, the minute popping sounds they made as they clicked into place bringing him immense satisfaction.

"Ooh yes, right there," encouraged Lark, wriggling around 'til Flem reached up and grabbed a wrist to hold him steady.

"The Club is just a, oooh yes, " he interrupted himsylph and then surprised Flem by spinning around and pulling Flem to his feet.

"The *S* Club," he said, running his fingertips out to the end of Flem's right wing as he laid his other hand along his neck, "The *S* Club is where we'll, you and I and probably Buddleia will be going. Soon, in fact," but he didn't get any further because a high rolling breaker came in right then causing the whole houseboat and everything in it to glide up and over a tall hill and then slide back down again over the other side, another following on its heels.

"Brace yoursylph, it must be a freighter coming in to the other side of the harbor."

Holding on to Lark, Flem stumbled with the strange swaying floor and soon the two faeries were clasp together, their hands no longer on each other's wings.

The fog etchings once again started to appear on the steamy glass as flexible wings constantly brushed up against it unknowingly, uncaringly.

Before long the glass itself was a mess, almost swiped clean in places by the frenzied slapping of wet wings as Flem Green, A.K.A. Flumaria Greenwood, and Lark Spurastic got to know one another in a very *Sylph*-conscience way.

Chapter 45

Well, what do you think caused it, the seafood?
Or all that, ah, *chocolate* we had for dessert?

*I*T WAS EARLY on a Monday morning and Flem lay in his contraband corner, one arm and a leg slung over the top edge of the hammock, his thoughts ajumble. His sleep had been restless. Life kept getting better but there was an uneasiness he couldn't pin down. He felt sly and sylphish, like he'd clandestinely imported something of great value that had no business being here, and so, must remain hidden. Much like him. It was a dilemma and he alternated constantly between outright fear of discovery and the energy that constantly pulled him in, a sweet thrill that basically overrode, what he thought of as, his good sense. There was just something about this place, Fletcherman's Nursery, that got in his blood, invisible glue that thrived here.

He hadn't seen Mayapple since Saturday night, or rather Sunday morning, when they'd dropped her off

Before.

He wondered if she'd be able to tell just by looking at him... He hoped not but had a sneaking suspicion it would be written all over his face no matter how he tried to hide it. A nervous excitement skipped briefly through his veins and he realized he was a little jumpy this morning. He hoped it wasn't some kind of premonition.

Mayapple was okay, he knew that but Iris made him a bit leery. She was the boss and while she was a cool boss, she still lived in a different reality than his. She was always very cordial but Flem bet she didn't knowingly have any faerie friends and wondered what she thought about Bud.

The sky was turning pink and he figured he still had time to catch a bit more sleep before he stealthily slipped out and to a little café down the street.

Whimsey C. Nimble

He had taken to waiting there before hurrying back just in time to show up at work. He didn't know if it fooled Mayapple but he felt like everybody else bought it. He was very casual, a game he played with himsylph.

He had just drifted off when an animal landed feet first all around his head and he winced as he opened his eyes to a kitten's belly. "Cha!"

A muscle twitched in one wing spasmodically for just a second, an irritating, unreachable twinge at how close those toenails had come. Obviously it was time to feed the cat. Oh silly him to think he'd get a few more minutes of quiet time.

An hour later he was set, the place as neat and tidy as he could get it for the time being. There was still a long ways to go but his sphere of influence was quite discernible amidst the littered ground that made up the largest portion of the greenhouse. Always tempted to do more, the thought of being discovered tempered his cleaning impulses.

Hooking the hammock over onto itself to get it on one hook and out of the way, Flem stopped in mid-motion to gaze at his cat family. The babies were definitely bigger and he wondered how long mama cat would let them nurse.

Mayapple had mentioned one time about *who* would want a kitten and he wondered how to proceed with that.

The black and white rogue fur-ball pulled back, milk running down his chin unheeded and watched Flem with an intensity that rather unnerved him.

When he started disengaging himself from the rest of the kittens, Flem knew if he didn't make it out the window door fast, he would have a passenger once again. It was one thing to let his feline friend ride around here, at home (*home?*) and quite another to take him to work.

Mrs. Fletcherman had already caught him unaware at awkward moments and he had decided to not give her any more opportunities, if possible.

No, kitten cat stayed here.

By this time he was almost to his window door, money in pocket, backpack on back, hair combed, wings camouflaged, scarf in place but when he ducked his head a cannonball fired from across the way, and as he completed pulling his leg through and onto the ground he was almost bowled over by the momentum.

The kitten was a little bigger but nonetheless didn't have much trouble burrowing under the knapsack to try and get into his hollow. Unfortunately there was no way in and a piteous yowl went up as he butted his head against Flem's from the back, batting at the scarf that blocked access

"*What* are you doing?" demanded the faerie, "Let go!" He batted ineffectually with both hands.

Luckily he knew he still had time enough before nine o'clock and ducked back around the corner, attempting to extricate his scarf from sharp paws which proceeded to hinder him at every step of the way.

Ten minutes later, thoroughly exasperated, a big snag hanging from his favorite scarf, he had won and was on his way to the Dancing Lady café to get his tea. The bus stopped right in front of it, so it was a good cover.

No longer dapper, his mood was a bit frayed around the edges as he pulled open the door to the café, bound wings twitching under his shirt. This new routine of his was suppose to be comforting but today something was off, although he tried to deny it.

Pushing on regardless, he tried to recapture those other times that were perfect but it didn't quite work.

The line was longer than he'd anticipated and he stood at the back, jiggling nervously wondering if he should forget the whole thing and just loiter around out front til he saw her bus pull up. He decided to wait it out, feeling more pressured by the moment but kept his place in line.

Finally it was his turn and after waiting for an interminable time the hot cup of chai was in his hand and he was on his way.

Unfortunately for him the door slipped as three new customers came in, banging into his elbow, sending hot tea bursting out the top, carrying the lid that hadn't been placed on tightly enough, with it.

Most of the contents sloshed harmlessly to the sidewalk but not completely. First it dribbled and drabbled down his front, catching part of his scarf of course, and making sure to soak all the way through to his shirt where it would be sure to be noticed, and some near his waist, on his pants. Right down the front of him, in fact, and now there was barely any tea left that he'd just paid for and had yet to taste. At least it hadn't hit the snag, he noted sarcastically, wondering why *Mondays* seem to be more prone to chaos such as this.

Whimsey C. Nimble

Regretfully, he did not have time to change. Surely the day would get better.

Stopping momentarily, he took a sip of his still-hot remaining tea. It was remarkably good and he regretted having only a few swallows left.

Feeling somewhat mollified, he hurried on, trying to make the best of it, keeping an eye out for Mayapple's arrival.

Standing at the bottom of the Nursery's driveway, Flem stopped and finished his pitiful amount of yummy tea, squashing the cup, pulling himsylph together to face this coming week and what it entailed by simply stepping through that door yonder. Straightening his backbone he resolutely strode up the blacktop as if he'd just gotten off the bus himsylph.

The place was oddly quiet. Slipping in the front door, he saw no one. It was unlocked, so *someone* must be here but none of the overhead lights were on and he frowned as he tentatively called out, "Lily? Mrs. Fletcherman? Hello? Anybody?" It was rather late to be so dark.

Taking matters into his own hands, he briskly turned on all the lights, moving from one area to the next, glad Lily and Mayapple had shown him where they were.

Just then a door could be heard opening and he turned to see Lily emerge from the restroom.

"Hi Lily. Boy, it sure is quiet isn't it? Where is everybody? What's the matter, are you okay?" he asked with concern when he saw her face.

"Oh, yeah. I guess so. I don't feel so good, that's all. I'll be okay. Where is everybody, anyway?" She groaned and sat down heavily on a nearby stool.

"I'm going to go sign in and then I'll be back," he announced, starting to feel rather heavy as the day was certainly shaping up oddly.

As he got to the employee area in the back, he noticed a note tacked up at the time card post. Apparently they'd been short handed over the weekend and hadn't been able to load a special order of oversized heavy pots for a customer when she showed up, and she had not been happy. She would be back today. Oh Pan.

Great. Well, perhaps with Mayapple's help, but Iris Fletcherman stepped through the door just then and proceeded to push the button to raise the big metal door where the trucks unloaded deliveries.

That did not bode well. Something was causing Flem's stomach to sour. He suspected it was precognition because sure enough, Iris spoke up.

"Good morning Flem. I hope you had a good weekend and got lots of sleep last night and that you're healthy."

Flem cocked an eyebrow at her, not wanting her to finish but she went on: "Mayapple's not coming in. Bud's not coming in. Lily's sick, and I need to send her home. Bah! Mondays. Look's like it's me and you. Do you remember how to check in an order? I've got a truck coming sometime today and I need to watch the cash register."

Taking a deep breath, Flem nodded quickly.

He watched as Iris stopped what she was doing and started scratching her forearm with a franticness before yanking down her sleeve and heading toward the front.

He started to turn away but did a double take when he saw her stop again and slip off a shoe, rubbing her instep vigorously on her other leg. She then threw a hand over her shoulder and tried to reach the middle of her back with her stretching fingers but it wasn't enough and with a frustrated jerk, took off again towards the front, where Lily was standing dumpily, coughing into a tissue.

"Call me first thing in the morning and let me know how you are, okay Lily?"

The young woman was feebly protesting but it didn't have the heat it took and left without much persuasion.

As Flem watched blatantly, Iris started fidgeting, rubbing her neck and collar bones, then up behind her ears, yanking a sleeve up to scratch an arm again and then attacking the other, as if she had no control.

A customer came in but Flem saw immediately it was no customer but Santolina and he stood near Iris, questioning her about something but she kept shaking her head, no.

The short dark man in the official Parks and Rec jacket obviously didn't like what he was hearing because he leaned in across the slight barrier of the front desk and tapped the counter, and then, jerked his thumb back in Flem's direction.

Flem decided the mystery had to stop, and clutching his courage in hand he hurried up to the front before he could stop himsylph, asking "What's wrong, Mrs. Fletcherman, is everything okay? Is there anything I can do to help?"

"Flem, didn't Lily show you how to use the cash register last week? Good. Do you think you could handle it here alone? I'll call Ginger to see if she can come in, but I think she's out of town.

"Santolina has convinced me I need to see a doctor, I can't stop itching, everywhere, and I guess he's right.

"When the truck comes in, don't worry about checking it on the computer, just verify it, you'll find the order sheet on my desk. Here's the spare key to my office. Don't lose it!

"If you need to ring somebody up while the truck is here, excuse yourself from the delivery for a few minutes, and do it.

"I hate to do this to you, but obviously, something's going on and I need to get it fixed so I can get back here!"

She cast a glance at the man waiting for her and with an irritated purr asked, "Well, which do you think caused it, the seafood? Or all that, ah, *chocolate* we had for dessert?" She managed a rather stilted, innocent look at her lover, while starting in on another frenzy of scratching.

It made Santolina give a little snort in veiled amusement but he didn't say a word, just looked at her.

Vexed at the whole situation, Iris was trying hard to still be a good sport but it was wearing thin with all the drama going on and her own skin playing traitor to her.

Flem hovered earnestly nearby.

You could see she did *not* want to leave only Flem, the faerie-in-disguise she'd just discovered working for her all by himsylph but her intuition said he would do well and to trust. Did she have a choice?

Twitching herself, Flem kept his face bland at her little spasms but couldn't help a bit of satisfaction at her dilemma, what with her twitching instead of him. His heart still went out to her though.

"Don't you worry, I will be right here until you come back or call me. Bud's not coming in, you say?"

Iris by this time was resigned but it didn't take the itching away and she tried so hard not to break down but a big crocodile tear slid from first one eye and then the other.

Flem and Santolina jumped to attention, Flem wringing his hands in consternation, assuring her over and over that he could handle it and to just go with Santolina to the doctor, please.

Santolina kept patting her arm and urging her to come, come, let's go.

She did. They left.

Monday morning at the Blackberry Bakery wasn't going so well either. Lark had arrived at his usual time, four in the morning, to start the baking for the day and things had progressed nicely. It wasn't until he was really awake and into the second batch of so many things, that he noticed the small worms in the scoop of flour he was holding in his right hand…

Panic set in slowly at first, as his rational mind blotted out what he'd unfortunately *known* the moment he saw the little evil weevils.

He was going to have to throw out all the lemon rolls, poppy seed rolls, and cherry tarts he'd JUST MADE! It ALL had whole wheat flour in it. Most also had unbleached white and it was with a fatal air that he scooped up some white and spread it out on the counter surface to check for bugs there too.

One was all it took.

Trying not to cry himsylph, Lark swallowed back the lump that was forming in his throat and resolutely wrote out a note on a white bag with a big black marker, 'Closed 'til further notice due to an emergency'.

Chapter 46

⸺ ❧ ⸺

"Hello!" he shouted into the phone on the sixth ring.

So much for professionalism he thought a bit too late.

THE FAE YOUNG man in charge of the entire Nursery would probably have gotten nervous if he'd had time to think about it but the phone rang immediately and he answered, "Good morning, Fletcherman's Nursery. This is Flem Green. How can I help you?" as if it was what he did every day. He had always wanted to answer a phone and now that he had, he found it very satisfying and waited to see what happened next.

"Hello, can I speak to the manager, Flem?"

Flem paused, wondering who this was that seemed to know his name. "Well, the manager's out at the moment, can I help you?"

The woman's voice launched into a series of rapid questions, most of which Flem replied to with a 'no,' until finally the last question was about did he want to increase their sales and do his best for the business so of course he said yes. The next thing he knew a salesperson named Lilium Superbum was coming to meet him at four o'clock this afternoon and show him her botanical selections.

Feeling a bit dazed, Flem hung up just as a customer strolled through the door, pointed at the dark sign and said with some friendly advice: "You better turn that on!" and kept going towards the back.

"Yeah, thanks!" he called to her as she disappeared around the corner, and nimbly hopped over to the long pull string and turned the red neon 'OPEN' sign on.

His ears suddenly picked up the faint rumble of a large vehicle lumbering into their driveway.

The phone rang again and like it was second nature, he answered the summons very professionally although he wondered how long it would take this time, as he was sure that was the delivery Mrs. Fletcherman had spoken of. What a hectic morning and it had hardly begun.

Slightly stressed, he listened to the speaker, "Is Mayapple there?"

"No," he replied with half a mind, "she called in," and then wondered why.

"Is she at home?" persisted a young female voice.

"I don't know. Probably." Irritation spurred by stress leaked into his voice and he had a sudden insight as to *why* Iris Fletcherman wasn't always in a good mood and *why* she sometimes seemed so preoccupied.

"Well, do you have her number?"

Cha! "No! No, I don't. Is this business related? Is there something I can help you with?" his anxiety about the incoming truck turning him waspish.

Much to his relief, the caller seemed rather taken aback and hurriedly assured him she was a friend of Mayapple's and she'd lost her number; she would try another friend, thank you and goodbye. Click.

With relief Flem set the phone down and was heading for the delivery door when he was hailed by a matron who had just come in and was standing by the front counter.

"Yoo hoo, yoo hoo, I've come for my pots. I was here yesterday but no one could help me." Jokingly she added, "They're pretty good size, I hope you've got big help today!"

Flem's heart lurched at that statement and he saw trouble coming but he wouldn't go there yet.

It was obvious the Green Thumb truck was backing into the bay with the rolling door and Flem held up an appeasing finger to the waiting customer.

"I'll be right there! We're pretty short handed today, I'm the only one here." With that said, he briskly walked over to where he could see the brake lights of the truck brighten and then go out.

Just after Flem caught egg-shaped Acaulais's profile on the driver's side, his brother Schafta jumped down from the other, a sheaf of papers clutched in one hand.

"'Morning." He nodded at Flem in recognition but both he and Flem were caught by the woman at the cash register.

Whimsey C. Nimble

"Yoo hoo again. Are you going to be long? Maybe you could call somebody else? Where is everybody, is Iris here yet?"

Flem groaned and started to say something but the skinny, almost bald-headed man interrupted him.

"Short handed a bit here this morning, are you? Go ahead and take care of her. We'll unload and then we'll all go over the list together."

Relief washed over Flem at this easy solution. "Thank you! I'll be right back," he replied gratefully, his eyes noticing that Acaulais was already opening the back and lowering the tail gate, to reveal a jungle-like cavern with a small fork lift in the middle.

Turning, he hurried back to his waiting customer.

Oblivious still to Flem's dilemma, she asked again, "Where is everybody?"

The faerie's jaw clenched for just a moment before he pleasantly replied, "Ah, well, Mrs. Fletcherman had to step out a while unexpectedly; Lily, our cashier is sick. She came in but Iris sent her home before, well, before she stepped out. And Mayapple I guess, is sick. But not to worry, I'm sure I can help. Now, you said something about an order that came in?"

"Oh dear, oh dear. You're here alone you say? Pardon me, but you don't look big enough," she said worriedly, wringing her hands. "They're pots, BIG pots and I need them and I want them to be loaded into the back of my truck. I have two men coming over at three to unload them for me. I *so* wanted them today, but I expect I'll have to come back *again*, won't I?" A rather whiny peevishness had crept into her voice. "What's your name? You must be new." She said this as if this were a *fault* of Flem's and by this time he had run the gamut of emotions with her reasoning, from nervousness at having to deal with her beyond ringing up a sale, (thank you Lily) to her forgone conclusion *he* couldn't help her.

Rather incensed, he brusquely said, "Let me see if I can find anything here on your order, Mrs.?" He let it dangle to get her attention, and it did.

She huffed back at him "*Ms.* Bulbosa. Calypso Bulbosa. I ordered two big pots, Mr.?" She too knew how to dangle.

"Green. Flem Green. Glad to meet you," he added, and sort of smiled, remembering *he* alone represented Fletcherman's Nursery at the moment and the customer was always right.

Mollified, the rather stout woman dug into her oversized shoulder bag and produced a set of papers, which she handed to Flem.

He studied them a moment and then did a quick perusal behind the front counter and around the cash register when he spied a green notebook that had the words 'Special Orders' printed on it.

Opening it up, he turned to the last notation and sure enough there was a note and the price. His eyes opened in astonishment at the price tag for just one. Six hundred and ninety five dollars! Holy Panola! And the other two were both four hundred and ninety dollars apiece! These must be some pots but as he started to head towards the area in the back where stuff was stored, the phone rang again.

Smiling a quick what-can-I-do? look at Ms. Bulbosa, he snatched it up.

"Hello. Fletcherman's." He didn't elaborate, hoping the caller would get the message and leave him alone but no, she had a question.

"Hi. I was wondering if you could help me. I've got some cherry and apricot trees that get lots of blooms but that have never produced any fruit. Do you have any idea why?"

Flem thought back to an article he'd read in one of those old gardening magazines he used to read and said, "You said cherry and apricot specifically?"

She affirmed yes.

"Sometimes certain varieties won't bear fruit unless they're pollinated with a different variety. Do you only have one of each?"

"No," she exclaimed. "I have four, two cherry of the same variety and two apricot, again the same variety. Huh. Imagine that."

Flem added for good measure, "You're okay with apples, pears, peaches and plums. They're all self-fertile. We have several varieties of cherry and apricot trees out back. You're welcome to come in and look." He really hoped that was enough and interjected, "Look, I'm really busy-" and would have said more but his satisfied caller interrupted with "No problem! I'll be in this week. Thank you! What'd you say your name was?"

"Flem," he said shortly.

"Thanks again Flem. See you later," and she mercifully hung up.

Luckily it hadn't taken very long and Calypso Bulbosa waited patiently.

Flem glanced over and the Campion boys were still unloading.

Whimsey C. Nimble

He was still good to go. Not quite satisfaction, more like abated frustration lurked in his chest, driving him on to do the best he could for Iris.

"Okay, c'mon. Let's go find your pots. Big, are they?" He thought to himsylph that they'd have to be pretty Pan special to be six hundred dollars. The mere thought made him quail being here alone to handle this.

Heels clicking, she followed him back to the outside arbor bordering the parking lot and to the corner where things sat waiting for processing.

Ms. Bulbosa spotted them immediately. "That's them right there, see the crates? Aren't they *beautiful*? I'm going to have to come back, aren't I? I can't imagine how *you'd* get them loaded by yourself, not a chance," she finished negatively, and Flem's heart plummeted as he realized she had the right of it. There was really no way he could even begin to carry one, let alone lift it into her vehicle.

Suddenly an image flashed across his mind. An idea took shape, if only he could get both parties to comply.

Mustering all his Sylph charm, he turned a full wattage smile onto this difficult customer.

Walking up to the taller urn, he reverently touched the blue porcelain through the narrow wooden slats.

"My, these are incredible. What do you plan to put in them? You must have a spectacular garden already, if these are going in it," he praised.

Visibly preening, Calypso Bulbosa grinned, distracted for the moment.

"Oh, I'm making some changes around the pond in the back yard. I'm going to add a Buddha and some bamboo. The big pot will sit in front of the bamboo and these two," pointing to the two smaller vase-like pots, "are going on either side of the big one. I'm not sure yet what's going in them, but they're so majestic and alive, don't you think?"

Flem nodded, but couldn't really see that much of the enameled urns to say. He was happy to see the heavy duty crates were still around each one.

"Will you excuse me a minute? I need to check on those delivery guys. I'll be right back, it won't take moment." He looked at her beseechingly.

Giving him a small rueful smile, she nodded once, and off he took like he had wings on his feet.

They were still organizing but Flem figured they'd be done pretty soon and waiting for him.

"Hi boys," he greeted. Jumping right to it, he enquired if there was anyway they could help him by using the forklift and setting some items into the back of a customer's truck?

They didn't mind at all, providing the customer didn't mind waiting 'til everything they'd come to deliver was checked in.

Flem was grinning at how it was all coming together and promised to return as soon as possible. He took off again to impart the good news to Ms. Calypso Bulbosa.

Happy to hear she was getting what she wanted, she smiled graciously at his request and said sure, she could wait a bit longer.

"Ill be looking around. Come find me when you're ready," she told him.

Patting himsylph on the back at his own ingenuity, the faerie helper was soon checking off Iris's order as Schafta checked his while Acaulis moved from plant to plant in verification.

They finished and Flem ran an eye down his list, checking for anything that had been ordered and not delivered. Two different spots came up empty, as it did on the Green Thumb's sheets, and no, they didn't know what had happened to those items.

Regretfully, the total had already been calculated and included the missing two orders.

Shaking his head Acaulis reached into his front pocket for a big red grease pencil and marked a note across Fletcherman's invoice subtracting the two items for them, then handing it to Flem, casting an accusing look at his own brother who squinted back at him with a baleful look at the implied accusation.

Sensing a breakdown of temper, Flem hastily stepped in with, "Boy, you guys are always so efficient, Mrs. Fletcherman has remarked several times how much she likes working with you. Especially now, doing this huge favor for her while she's ah, indisposed."

Iris Fletcherman was laid up, this was news to the Campion boys, both tucking it away to speculate on later with their father, Moss.

Schafta spoke up, "Well, let's get the Mighty Midget out." Barely were the words spoken before Acaulis brought the forklift engine to life and carefully maneuvered it, ready to follow Flem.

By this time Ms. Bulbosa was standing and waiting, ready to take the lead. Gratefully, all three let her do it and in no time at all the precious pots were standing in the back of her large pick-up truck, snuggled up close to the rear window.

Not sure what to do next, Flem wondered if they shouldn't be secured better when Schafta and Acaulais finished the job for him, using all the extra rope and bungee cords Calypso had had the foresight to bring along and even returning to their own vehicle to add one of their own before they were satisfied.

"How'rya planning on getting them off there, ma'am, if I may be so bold as to ask," inquired Acaulis rather gruffly, her concerns becoming his briefly.

"Oh, I have two very large men coming by at three this afternoon. They'll be able to handle it," she replied.

Taking charge again, Ms. Bulbosa looked both Acaulais and Schafta in the eye, and bosom heaving, thanked them prettily and asked if they had a card? she was always needing some kind of help from a big strong man and perhaps they could do more business in the future?

Falling all over themselves to each give her a card, Flem laughed silently at the lessons he was getting today. So far, not too painful.

The phone rang.

The Green Thumb crew took it as the signal that it was time to take off, their good deed of the day complete. Waving Flem on, the Might Midget chugged back to the loading dock.

"Thanks!" called Flem

Schafta waved a hand in acknowledgment but they were headed out.

The phone persisted.

"Go! I'll follow," ordered Calypso. "When you're done, let's go back outside and you can help me with a few more things I found while I was waiting." She smiled and the implication of her spending more money filtered through to Flem.

His blood raced with satisfaction at his success.

"Hello!" he shouted into the receiver on the sixth ring. So much for professionalism he thought a bit too late.

"Flem! What's the matter? Is everything okay down there??" Mrs. Fletcherman asked in a panic.

Oh, of course.

Hot embarrassment flooded his cheeks at being caught and he stuttered and stammered but Calypso got his attention, giving him the nod and thumbs up, good-job look.

Élan flowed back through him and he enunciated quite clearly: "Things are *great*, Mrs. Fletcherman, you have nothing to worry about! How are *you*?" He looked at Calypso and she was nodded her head in encouragement.

Stifling a grin, he listened attentively to his boss wail that she would not be in the rest of the day, possibly not for several days. Did he think he could possibly hold down the fort for her tomorrow too? She was not happy about Mayapple being one of the ones not there also, but moved on to bemoan her predicament: hives, with the main suspect being the shellfish from the evening before. Or, maybe it was the chocolate. She did not mention the quantity involved and the things they had done with it. That was between her, Santolina, and the dermatologist.

"Do you know about baking soda?" her best employee asked, remembering an incident Whimsey Nimble had told him about once.

"Baking soda?" repeated Iris blankly. "*What* are you talking about, Flem?"

"Uh," losing his nerve he blurted out, "Take a bath with baking soda in it. I've heard it helps the itching. We're pretty busy, I should go," he added.

"Baking soda? I'll tell Santolina, maybe we can pick some up after they release me." She paused. "Things are really under control? You doing okay?" she asked in a small beaten voice that sounded like she was trying not to cry.

"Your delivery is checked in, and Ms. Calypso Bulbosa's pots are in the back of her truck, tied securely, and she even now waits for me to get off the phone as she has a couple more things she wants to buy," he replied crisply, a great sense of well being and confidence permeating his Sylph cells.

"Oh! Oh! Oh, I should let you go! Good job Flem, I feel better already! Hey, " she said with a touch of the old optimism, "Why you're at it, call Mayapple, when you get the time of course, and see what's going on with her, would you? I can't believe that girl called in on a Monday."

"Will do," he answered with a salute in his voice, wondering when he would find the time, but the day wasn't over yet.

"Okay, thanks Flem. Call me tonight if you have any problems, otherwise I'll talk to you in the morning. Bye!" She hung up.

Whimsey C. Nimble

By now Calypso and Flem felt more like co-conspirators, comrades on a mission, and Flem dived into his role, gracefully accepting his status as hero-who-saved-the-day. The magic was upon him and he followed Calypso out back and around the corner to where Fletcherman's own demonstration pond was gurgling away.

Smiling happily at her own wonderful self, Ms. Bulbosa pointed to a good sized statue of a Nymphaea plant where two long-toed jacana birds stood poised in mid-step on its big showy leaf near the deep notch where the leaf stalk was attached.

"That beautiful lotus. I must have it in with the cat tails I've got planned. And I need to get some pompous grass. I didn't see any here. Do you have some? Or can you at least order it?" She went on, "And I want some of those to go with it," she said a bit rapturously, switching to point at several floating water lilies in the pond.

Flem's eyes had turned in to dollar signs at her comments. Mrs. Fletcherman was not going to believe this.

He hesitated but then spoke up in a very mild voice.

"Ah, technically those two aren't exactly the same," he corrected, stammering a little in his nerve. "That statue there? It's actually a Nympheaceae, a water lily, not to be confused with nelumba, the lotus flower. Most people get them confused." Pointing to the casting, he continued, "See how the large leaf stalk of the water lily is *to one side*, with that deep notch? Whereas a *lotus's* stalk attaches from the *center* of the leaf. Also, you see this?" He pointed to a display of dried flowers but specifically to an obvious hunk of matter, perforated with holes. "This is the dried fruit of the nelumba plant, the lotus; the water lilies doesn't have them."

He smiled.

Calypso looked at him in amazement, temporarily speechless, but then laughed and said "Whatever! I like 'em all! I know I'm a bit excessive. But who's going to spend my dead husband's money if I don't?" She twinkled and added, "Besides, aren't you happy I'm spending it here?"

Oh my yes.

Chapter 47

—✠—

"Boy, you're busier that a one-legged man in a butt-kicken' contest, aren't ya?" cackled Calypso.

FLEM SUDDENLY REALIZED he had another big item to get into his customer's truck and Calypso Bulbosa had wondered how long it would take him to come to that.

She already had a plan but Flem surprised her with, "This was just put out recently and I'm pretty sure the crate is out back. Mrs. Fletcherman usually saves 'em for the customers to use. I'll go get it, nail it up, and I'm pretty sure I can get it on the dolly and maybe you can give me a hand here and there?" he asked sweetly, sure of himsylph.

Calypso was smiling, nodding. This guy was better than she expected. And he was cute too, although awfully young. She wondered if he liked older women.

It didn't take long, the wooden crate was indeed out back, and between the two of them it went pretty quickly. Flem bungeed it onto the hand truck and with Ms. Bulbosa standing in the pickup bed, they managed to upload, maneuver and slide it 'til it was snug against her other purchases, where he quickly secured it as Acaulais and Schafta had taught him, unintentionally.

He jumped down from the tail gate in time with the shrill demand of the phone.

"Cha!" he blurted out in frustration, shaking his head.

"Boy, you're busier than a one-legged man in a butt-kicken' contest, aren't ya?" cackled Calypso. "Go catch that. I'll be here."

Flem ran, dashed just inside to the employee area and caught the offending instrument in the middle of the fifth ring.

"Hello," he gasped, "Fletcherman's." He was an old hand by this time.

Whimsey C. Nimble

"Hi, I was wondering if you had any Black-Eyed Susan *vines*, not just the seeds, but any actual plants?" said a serious enquirer.

A flush of faint pleasure washed over the Sylph at this evidence of a kindred spirit.

"Ooh," he gushed, "I just *adore* Black-Eyed Susan vines! 'Thunbergia Alatin,'" he pronounced in stentorian tones. "I do believe I saw some small pots back in our growing area, where the boss starts so much of our stock." He swept a hand as if she could see him. "Actually, I'm hoping to do a hanging basket with *only* Thunbergia, but we've been too busy."

Before he could say more, the voice on the phone jumped in excitedly, "Oh, I'll take one! That's a great idea! How much do you think you'll charge for it? Can I give you my name and number and will you call me when it's done? Oooh, this is so cool!"

Flem was scrabbling for paper and pen and found them just in time as she rattled off "Carlotta Viburnum" and her number.

He scratched it down immediately and wrote 'B.E.S. *vine*, call when BASKET is ready. Talk to I.F. asap,' and the date, and stuck it in the Special Orders notebook, making a note mentally to remember it.

They hung up and Flem raced back to find Calypso again, but she wasn't where he'd left her. Voices drifted to him just then and they seemed to be coming from the front, near the cash register.

Oh great Pan, he'd forgotten he was suppose to lock the cash register every time he stepped away from it! Then, chagrined, he remembered they'd never unlocked it. Lily had gone home, Iris had left with Santolina and no one had given it a thought.

Calypso Bulbosa was standing in front of the counter, chatting to another customer who was waiting to be rung up. He hadn't even realized she'd come in.

Flem hastened his step, pulling out a small key from deep in his pocket and quickly proceeded to bring the register to life.

Minutes later the transaction was complete and the woman left.

"And there's nobody coming in to help? Well you've got your work cut out for you, don't you sweet pea?" Calypso laughed. "My water lilies? Oh. Are they water lilies or Lotus? Either way, do you think you could have time to dredge some up for me? I put the pond in last year but I didn't get any at that time, just a couple of cat tails."

Gearing up, Flem locked his register back up and slapped the key into his pocket. Ten minutes later, Ms. Bulbosa had her wallet out and a large box of five individually- bagged water lilies at her feet.

Flem rang up the total sale, trying to keep his wits about him but it was hard. This one sale alone came to just under three thousand dollars. He didn't know if that was normal or not, but it seemed like a lot to him.

Smiling in satisfaction, Calypso tucked the receipt into her bag, ready to go, finally.

Looking up, she invited warmly, "If you're ever in my neighborhood, I'd love to show you my pond." She paused, then said "I could always use a professional's opinion," and handed him a card with her name and address on it.

Flem got the distinct impression she was offering more than a look at her pond and it made him acutely uncomfortable. He couldn't believe this was happening again. Cha!

Pulling on a strong, suave demeanor, one he hoped was a little distant, he retreated behind the social mask and ignored any undertones what-so-ever that this woman, Calypso Bulbosa, gave off.

Gracefully, he took the card and nodded that he would certainly keep her offer in mind.

She held his eyes a little too long and then grinned in good natured defeat and left.

He was standing outside the counter, his eyes still on the door where his last customer had left, a rather perplexed look on his face, one hand absently rubbing his shoulder where wing muscles ached, when a voice behind him asked, "Excuse me. Do you work here?"

The faerie jumped, a bright smile plastered on his face. "Yes! Ready?"

"Actually, I just need some advice on my hydrangeas. Do you know anything about them?"

"Well, yes I do. A little bit anyway," he answered hesitantly.

"I have two hydrangea bushes in my yard and they both had perfect blooms the first year, three years ago, but ever since they've not bloomed! Why?"

"Well, from what I remember reading about them, they require at least a half a day's worth of sun, so it might be their location. Or, if you pruned them- you might have loped off too much?" He looked at her to see if she recognized either one.

Whimsey C. Nimble

She shook her head.

"How'd they look each spring, did they get damaged over the winter? Too cold a spot, maybe?"

By this time two more customers had materialized nearby, listening attentively, waiting for answers.

"Is your soil rich and does it drain well? They're big water drinkers, and they don't like to be directly in the sun all day but you can get away with it here in our coastal area. If it's not any of these reasons, you could try root pruning. Take a shovel or a flat-backed spade and make a deep cut in a circle around your plants at the *weep* line."

"And that is...?" a woman said from near the glove display. Everyone's head bobbed in agreement with her question.

"It's also called the 'drip line'" he clarified. "It's the furtherest point to which a plant or a tree's branches hang over. Rain water tends to drip from this point. It's a common reference among gardeners for feeding and watering, or whatever. So, you've got your circle out on the ground; now take a gallon container and fill it nine-tenths full with warm water, then a big glug of apple juice, roughly ten percent, mix it and pour it into that opening, all around your hydrangeas. It should draw the roots out to it, and hopefully, boost flower production."

"Hmmph!" came from different people as they absorbed this information and then another spoke up. "Do you have any advice for making my begonias and gladiolas last longer when they're blooming?"

"Well, yes I do. Mrs. Fletcherman told me just the other day that if you pinch off the withered flowers on the begonia, it'll extend the flowering period, and for the glads, just make sure you remove the bottom blooms and it'll help the blooms on top to open," Flem replied, distracted instead of overwhelmed by being the center of attention accidentally.

One of the customers spoke up admiringly, "Gee, you know a lot about plants. Are you going to be giving any classes in the future?"

"Ha ha. Me?" grinned the Sylph, amused at the concept.

The other women spoke up and agree, "Yes, you. I'll sign up."

"Here, I've got a paper right here. Who's got a pen?" said another, tearing a sheet from her notebook.

Within minutes, Flem was handed a list with three names and numbers on it, and someone had the foresight to write in big letters below them: 'Your first three students!' and a smiley face.

He held it a moment but then one of the ladies snatched it back and asked, "What's your name?"

"Ah, Flem," he replied and she scratched off 'Your' and wrote in 'F L E M 'S' in place of it before shoving it back at him with the admonition, "Don't lose this!"

Laughing, he took it and folded it, not sure where to put it when he spied the 'Special Orders' book and quickly stuck it inside the cover.

Two of the women drifted away and the other was ready to check out. The receipt was barely in her hand when the damn phone rang again and Flem rolled his eyes at this strange hectic stressful day he was having.

He took a moment to smile and thank the customer, which she appreciated, reinforcing her good opinion of him and his charming manners, and then she left.

"Hello!" he said rather forcefully, "Fletcherman's Nursery!" *Now what*, he added silently to himsylph, impatient with the whole day all of a sudden, nerves snapping in little bursts like split ends.

Someone croaked on the other end and Flem said *"Mayapple?"*

She croaked again, "I'm sick, I sound worse than I am though. Guess I shouldn't have drank that tequila last night with Dicksonia."

"Mayapple." Flem was actually rather shocked at how bad she sounded.

As Flem stood there, a customer could be seen approaching and he sighed, resigning himsylph to where ever this wave was taking him, he obviously had no choice but to buck up and pay attention.

"Um, Mayapple, I've got to go. I've been really busy here all alone," but before he finished his sentence she jumped in with a splash.

"All alone? What do'ya mean, all alone?" she sounded nasally and sick but nosy as ever.

So Flem told her about Lily and Bud, and oh yeah, your mom's got hives.

"What? Why didn't you tell me that right away?" she accused very unfairly and Flem actually pulled back from the phone and looked at it, wondering if she looked as crazy as she sounded.

"I gotta go Mayapple. I'm *busy*. Do you think you'll be in tomorrow?" Great Pan, I'm beginning to sound like Iris, thought Flem in astonishment.

"I think so. I gotta call my mom, so bye." She paused and then added, "Hang in there. Call me if you have a question."

"Oh Mayapple. Thanks; hope you feel better. Bye-oops, hello! Gotta go, Mayapple, I'm busy."

Chapter 48

———— ✤ ————

"Can you get in by eight?" she asked again,
just like she hadn't seen his quarters and
knew he was her back yard squatter.

AND SO THE day went until Flem looked up and it was close to three o'clock in the afternoon. He was so surprised that he missed the cradle to the phone as he, by now automatically, blindly reached to hang it up, sending it clattering embarrassingly to the floor. Heat surged through his system flooding his cheeks prettily.

A customer was waiting to be rung up, of course.

Making small talk, she inadvertently said the wrong thing, "Boy, quiet in here, isn't it?"

Flem's eyes widened at how little *she* knew about it, here he was barely able to catch his breath.

Words tumbled from his mouth, his shoulders heaving in his haste to correct. "Oh, oh everyone's *sick.* Or *something.* I'm here. *I'm* busy. Well, I mean I've *been* busy-" but the ring of the phone tried to blot them out.

Rolling his eyes in exasperation at this customer's seeming obtuseness, Flem dumped her change rather heavily into her hand.

Damn that phone. He wondered about just leaving it off the hook for a while and as much as the idea appealed to him, he knew he didn't dare. It wasn't *his* nursery, it was merely his *job* and he didn't want to lose it.

Beating a hasty retreat, the customer pocketed her money, giving him a rather suspicious, quizzical look as she left.

Not able to swallow the sigh, Flem answered with a groan as he dispiritedly said, "Fletcherman's."

"By any chance do you carry horehound? My regular supplier ran out some time ago and so I thought I'd just grow some myself."

Flem's spirits rose as he laughed at a special memory tucked away regarding the bitter tasting herb and the patches he'd known back in the canyon. He hadn't seen any since.

Regretfully, he replied, "No, not that I know of. The only time I've seen it has been out in the country, back in a canyon I know, along a road. It seems to like a sunny, rather disturbed area."

"Oh! Out in the country you say? Do you think you could find it again? I would *love* to see it growing. Do you know more about herbs and where they grow in the wild? You know, what's edible and what's good for various ailments?"

"Well," he laughed sylphdeprecatingly, "actually I DO," thinking of most Sylphs' diets, which consisted of everything in the forests, meadows, and along the banks of streams and rivers.

"Do you think you would be interested in leading a group, if I put one together, ah, what's your name?"

"Flem. Flem Green," he answered, becoming rather befuddled.

"Hmm. Interesting name. Well, would you think about it? I'll leave my number. I know probably five or six people, maybe more, who'd all pay for a field trip with a chatty knowledgeable guide. Think about it."

By now, Flem was braced with pencil in hand ready to take dictation and after he wrote down 'Stevia' and her number, it too went in the Special Orders book.

"Sorry!" he threw out to another now-waiting customer.

Someone else got in line behind the first and about that time a third showed up who needed help carrying a something.

Heaving a rather dramatic sigh, Flem pasted an 'I-can-do-it' look on his face and clenched his back teeth just slightly. Nodding to the three women, he quickly rang up the first two and was soon at the disposal of the third.

In no time at all they were on their way back, Flem, the tall strong Sylph in men's clothing, carrying a big fat round pot and his companion swinging a black container with a beautiful little mimosa tree in it.

Ten minutes later he was transporting her pot once again but out the door to her car.

Whimsey C. Nimble

Walking back in, the manager of the day caught his breath and listened for the phone to ring but it did not.

He wondered if he would get to eat today and what Lark was doing.

A wild idea burst in his brain and without another thought, he acted on it, putting any doubts in the far corner of his mind to possibly regret later.

He first took the phone off the hook.

Fumbling, he then hastily scrawled a note before one more person set foot through the door.

The wild hair was now galloping in his veins, it was late in the afternoon, and the only thing he'd eaten was tea. And not much of that! This morning seemed a million years away.

Dashing through the nursery he hurriedly locked the back door then turned and ran up front and out the main entrance, closing with a slam, locked it from the outside, hurriedly taping his note to the glass, 'Back in 5 minutes.'

As he swirled around his eyes fell on the open metal rolling door and whooooieee! Was he glad they did! A Sylph on a daring mission, he did not let it deter him even a moment and forcing himsylph to calm down, he reopened the locked door in front of him, stepped through and ran to the open bay, finger out and jabbing the button that commenced the creaking and groaning, rattling and screeching lumbering metal door on its journey. Oh Pan, he hoped he wasn't overstepping his limits and wouldn't get in trouble for *closing* the store during business hours!

With a quick scan he reassured himsylph all would be well, even though the gates at the end of the driveway were still wide open…and took off. Surely anyone that came by would see his note and kindly wait.

He was going to surprise Lark at the bakery and couldn't wait to tell him what was happening. He figured he could be gone ten minutes without feeling too guilty. Maybe he should have called Iris but by that time no doubt a customer would have come in, he assuaged his conscience.

Bounding up to the door, he was met with unpleasant shades of déjà vu as he tried to open the door and it wouldn't budge.

CHA!

Exhaling like a frustrated bull, he backed up to really look, which, he realized, was exactly what he hadn't done that fateful first time either, until too late. Had he learned *nothing?*

Oh no. The big black letters said impossible things. *Closed*! *Why*? Oh no.

He pounded on the door, shading his eyes to peer in but it was dark, no movement.

Pan. All his pent up energy sank and he was left wavering on the doorstep, momentarily stymied, 'til he remember, WORK!

One last sharp rap on the glass which did no good, nor his heartfelt murmurings of *Lark*.

Gearing up he realized he could still buy a quick salad at the store down the street and take it back to work with him, which he did.

Adrenalin nipped at his heels and it was with a sigh of relief that he arrived back at work with nothing looking any different.

The note was snatched down, the doors flung open and he hurried out and about, planning on doing a quick perusal of the grounds before returning to his station at the cash register once again.

Throwing a quick glance down the path out back that went right by all three greenhouses, he was pulled up short by a dark stain marring the landscape.

Troubled, his brows beetled together and one wing twitched deeply right on the hollow where they came together, irritation skipping across to the other, this day turning into something from the unknown.

Was that *water*, he wondered, why was everything so wet back here, including the path, which never got wet...

Groaning, the faerie slouched into himsylph as he sought an answer, looking for the culprit, cutting over through the outdoor plants, off the path, to the edge of the main building.

He easily found a big valve with faucets set above it. Hoping for an easy solution, he tried each faucet but they were indeed in the off position, yet the ground was wet beneath his feet. It didn't make sense.

About this time a thousand little bugs jumped up and down, curling their tiny miniscule toes around his backbone and yanked.

Frustration at the whole blasted day overtook him and his wings surged against their bindings, making his shoulders bulge with a life of their own.

CHA!

Scanning the seepage he traced it to one spot that seemed closer to the building than the rest.

Whimsey C. Nimble

Hoping there wasn't a line of customers a mile long inside, he looked around until he spied what he wanted – a shovel leaning against the doorjamb of the greenhouse across the way.

Darting over, he was quickly back, tool in hand. Working on instinct he carefully started lifting spadefulls of wet dirt out of the ground, making a neat little mound to one side until he heard a dull thunk, which was what he had been waiting for. Using just the tip of his shovel, he gently removed the soil from around the buried water pipe, thereby exposing a spot that was darker and wetter than anything around it.

Rolling his sleeves up out of the way, he fell to his knees, flinging the shovel to one side, the knees of his pants going down into the slop.

Using his fingertips he pushed a big buried rock out of the way where it lay right against the exposed four inch pipe, water leaking from a long horizontal crack.

Great.

Was there no end to this day?

"Hello? Anybody here?" sang a voice from the back door of the main building.

"Yes! I'm here, I'll be right there. I've a bit of a problem here," his voice trailed into a mutter.

Not really knowing what to do, he quickly started opening and closing some nearby faucets, water gushing for a moment each time but that did no good that he could see.

Wishing he was somewhere else he plowed on, turning the next thing that might do some good, the big valve. He wound it tight, keeping an eye on the leaking water to see if it slowed at all, but it didn't seem to. Again, he opened faucets but this time no water came out.

So, now he knew the valve controlled the faucets.

Sitting back on his haunches, he rubbed a dirty hand over his forehead in frustration, leaving a tail of dirt. As he sighed his eyes followed the line of the buildings and fell upon another set of faucets. Hope blossomed when he saw a pipe that looked suspiciously like the cracked one coming out on this side of the stand before angling down into the ground, and it looked to be coming this way. Dare he hope?

Holding his breath, he dashed towards it, bending over to zero in and close the biggest valve there.

Nothing happened.

Quickly he ran back to the other spot and before his very eyes, the leak stopped! Hurray! He'd done it. But of course, he hadn't really fixed anything, now had he? He'd merely turned the water off so that it stopped leaking. And they needed water.

His head started to hurt and his knees were wet and cold as he stood up, wiping his dirty hands on his dirty pants. Oh well. Shaking his head, he rose, turning a nearby spigot to rinse off his filthy fingers but of course, no water came out and he shook his head at his own stupidity, briefly running his fingers through his hair before he caught himsylph. Starting back up front, he called out an apology to the still waiting customer as he brought the register back to life, trying to be delicate with dirty fingers.

The woman waiting didn't say a word, looking anywhere but at his misshapen shoulders, the smudge around one eye, the damp hands, the saggy baggy wet knees in his pants, and hair that stood up in spikes in places. Keeping her eyes glued to her purchase, she got out fast, a muffled snort swallowed at the door.

Flem hated to hang the phone up but he did.

Taking a deep breath, he decided to grab a quick bite before he tackled the looming immediate problem and was able to finish most of his greens before a car door slammed in the parking lot and Flem heard a strange noise, a rattle and a bang along with a few choice words, approaching.

A vague recollection suddenly grew bigger, blooming into full memory of *someone*, what was her name? – showing up here at four o'clock. Cha. Not now, great Pan. He did not want to give time to a salesperson, he had no authority. Oh, if only he'd not agreed with her. What *was* her name?

Lilium Superbum's small cart came in first and Flem slid off his stool and hurried over to see who if she needed help but she merely waved him aside.

Lowering the handles slowly, she braced them with a kickstand and held out her hand to Flem, just as the phone rang. Again.

"Excuse me, the phone has not quit ringing all day, and I'm here alone!" His eyes fairly snapped as he bit these out in aggravation, using this as a convenient cover to hide his dismay over the new situation. He was determined not to show how intimidated he was. Unfortunately, he had to crane his neck to look up at her, which didn't help matters at all. She was at least six foot tall.

Whimsey C. Nimble

He dashed away, almost tripping on the rug and the bright and bold salesperson followed at her leisure.

Dressed in a pale orange silk shirt tucked into darker orange denim pants, she complemented this ensemble with a puffy yellow scarf dotted with splotches of brown around her neck, which in turn matched her wide brown belt and matching brown boots. But the most amazing, arresting thing about her were her eyes. Her irises were yellow but flecked with deep brown spots.

Happily *this* phone call was a wrong number and Flem hung up smiling but it drooped a little at the sight before him.

"Er, um, what exactly do you sell again, ma'am? I've had a pretty busy day, and, ah," stumbled Flem.

"Lilies! Beautiful, gorgeous, lilies! You don't think with a name like I've got, I'd sell anything else, do you?" but it wasn't a question, it was a declaration.

She stopped and handed him her card, a work of art composed of overlays of bright yellow and orange lilies with the name *Lilium Superbum* superimposed across the front in big gold letters.

Not sure what to do, Flem headed for a corner that was a little more spacious and roomy where he could keep an eye on the cash register, but where they wouldn't be right in the way.

Seeing opportunity where it existed, Lilium Superbum started assembling something as Flem stood by, watching.

He could already see the bottom of a large triangle on the floor, in front of the nursery's gloves section but far enough away that people could easily get around.

She stopped piling individually boxed sets of bulbs for a moment and instead grabbed a good-sized cut-out made out of colorful cardboard, of herself, and was busily putting it together to stand freely, pointing at her display. She smiled hugely at Flem and for a moment there she looked so *happy*, Flem was half afraid she was going to reach out and pinch his cheek or kiss him.

"Ah," he began, "Listen, I don't have the authority to buy anything, Ms. Ah, Superbum? I'm not the manager, she's sick," but sputtered to a halt when a shaking finger waved itself rather too close to his face in time with a staccatoed "Ah! Ah! Ah!" rising in pitch with each sharp syllable.

"*Flem*, right?" affirmed the flower lady about his name, rather condescendingly, he privately thought.

"Have I mentioned money?" she asked in disbelief with all the sauciness of someone in the right profession and a big personality to go with it.

Flem was looking more like a simmering thundercloud by the moment, feeling embarrassed by this lack of experience.

Lilium smiled sweetly as she continued building her display, talking the entire time, focusing and pulling the Sylph's attention to her product, weaving an atmosphere of wonder with her tale:

"Originally, the only lilies available were the ones found in the wilds, in North America, Europe, and parts of Asia, but back around nineteen twenty-five, lily growers got together and embarked upon a significant breeding program," she explained.

Flem was interested despite himsylph and the saleswoman smiled inwardly at her prowess as she continued, "New hybrids came about, resulting in varieties that were healthier, hardier, and easier to grow. Not only that, but with new colors, new forms and that could be grown in large quantities. What that means to you, Mr. Green, is that your boss has access to a fabulous deal, right here, and doesn't have to do a thing but ring up the sales. Don't you think she'd like that?"

Flem had no idea if Mrs. Fletcherman would like this or not but it was an artful display, so he nodded his agreement hesitantly.

"Now, what's different about my lilies, Flem, is this: I have access to the widest variety you could ever want, I specialize in unusual, especially colorful specimens. And here," she handed him a brochure, "are complete instructions and problem solving plus background on all my selections. Now listen closely Flem, your boss is going to *love* this! No money is required for thirty days. And then, she only owes for what's sold. I'll come in once a month and restock and she can pay me at that time. What could be simpler? There is no risk involved, the display is built for her and hey, like I said, she's got nothing to do but ring up sales!"

It did seem like a good idea, her arguments unassailable, but still he felt like there had to be a catch, wondering if he'd get into trouble for this new product. It felt like he was way overstepping his boundaries but the moment had taken over and he was helpless in its wave. And besides, his rebellious side said, *he* wasn't suppose to be here, alone, anyway! It would *have* to be okay.

He noticed he still felt rather guilty though, and wished he could be more blasé. That was the problem, his newly won sylphconfidence hadn't penetrated his very core yet. Perhaps in time…

Lilium knew when to be quiet and let the customer think, hopefully her own words reverberating in his cute little skull. Patting a box back into place, it was soon flush with the wall of the pyramid she'd constructed.

She finally decided to help him along, away from any second thoughts he might be having. "Lilies have really only three basic requirements, Flem. They like their roots to be cool and shady, they need *year round* moisture because they never stop growing completely, and, they must have well-drained loose soil, preferably deep."

The Sylph was nodding his head and the saleslady took it as a good sign, continuing on with her lesson.

"Lilies, as you probably know," she cocked any eyebrow at the Fletcherman's representative standing in front of her, "should be planted as soon as possible after you get them or stick them in a cool place temporarily. In climates such as you have here in the City along the coast where it gets foggy you can actually plant them in open sunny places, so long as they're protected from strong winds. Now, up in the foothills areas where it's so much warmer and drier, you really want filtered or light shade."

Flem's eyes were beginning to glaze but now it was from the abundance, the saturation of color and glory spilling through his imagination from the towering display this tall wild woman had built. *Nobody* had yellow and brown eyes for Pan's sake. What was with her?

He turned to ask but she pinned him silent, her gaze like a boring beetle and his opened mouth, shut.

"Yes," he said involuntarily, wondering who he was, as she smiled and stared at him, encouraging him with little head nods.

"And we (*'we?'*) don't pay anything now?" he heard his voice and marveled.

"That's right. Your boss will love this," she assured him. "I'll be back this way in a month to restock and to collect a big fat check from all that have sold. They *will* sell, they always do."

She shoved an order form into his hand, pointing to two columns side by side and said, "Here's the retail price the customer pays. This number is how much *I* collect off of every one sold, and the difference is how much Fletcherman's is putting in their pocket for doing nothing but giving up a two foot square of floor space! Man, could it get any easier?" She smiled. "Just mark each sale of the day on a new order form and there you have your record for that day.

"You're doing the right thing, Flem. You're boss is going to love this. If you have any problems or questions, call me. My number is on the card and also right here," pointing to the back of the form, just as the phone started again.

She gave him one last order: "Be sure to hang this form," she joggled it for emphasis, "right next to the cash register."

Flem looked at her beseechingly, the shrill sound breaking the spell and she nodded, as if to give permission.

He flew to the front counter, catching it on the third peal, involuntarily looking at the clock. Almost five. Normally, he would be counting the minutes 'til six when he got off, but not tonight.

"Hello. Fletcherman's," he said dispiritedly, and waited, feeling rather fatalistic by now.

Listening, he watched Lilium Superbum creak past him and let herself out, waving as she went.

"Flem? Are you okay?" came Iris Fletcherman's voice.

"Mrs. Fletcherman! Yes! Everything's *great*. Yes sir, ma'am. Oh, ha ha! No problems here!" He wondered if she could tell he was a little nervous talking to her. Cha.

"Flem, are you okay to stay after six? We CAN close early if you need to..."

"Oh, no problem! I can stay," he hurried to assure her and would have said more but she kept talking.

"So, when you DO close, be sure to turn the sign off, okay? It's the one hanging over by the front door, below the window on the left. And be sure to *lock everything*! So, how's the day going, were you busy? Did you have any problems?"

He started to explain the riotous day he'd had but he prefaced it with "Oh, everything went fine, Iris, but," when she cut in, not really paying attention.

"Listen Flem, do you think you can open for me too, in the morning? I can't imagine I'm going to feel good enough to show off my rashy body. I'll try to get a hold of *somebody* to make sure you have some help. Is that okay with you?" she ordered in a questioning voice. "Can you get in by eight?" she asked again, just like she hadn't seen his quarters and knew he was her back yard squatter.

The faerie's sylphconfidence shot through the roof, gratitude for time to get a handle on things, a picture of the broken water line taking over his mind.

Warmth flooded his cheeks with affection for this woman and he said, "Absolutely, Mrs. Fletcherman, and thank you for trusting me. I have had an interesting day and I look forward to sharing it with you when the time is right."

Flem could hear the smile in her voice as she replied, "Well, you have an honest face, Flem, so never hesitate to, ah, confide in me, If you ever, ah, need any, oh I don't know, advice?" She hemmed and hawed with this strange idea, and Flem wondered what the Pan she knew. She must know something about him. Where he was staying?

Blind fear and panic assailed him like a wet and heavy blanket, blotting out his own sweet Sylph and common sense.

He dropped the phone.

Picking it up speedily, horrified, he spoke, "Sorry!" into the mouthpiece immediately, following it with, "No worries Mrs. Fletcherman, I'll be happy to open at eight for you. But right now I've got to go, I've got a customer waiting," his eyes roaming the empty store as he said it.

"Oh! Okay. Thanks Flem, I know I can count on you." She hung up.

Ah, Flem breathed a sigh of relief to be off the phone with her, but his heart was still beating a little fast with the next thought. Iris *knew* something. Cha.

Chapter 49

***

Wait! What? Are you telling me you just drove to
the Canyon, *Thimbleberry* Canyon, today, *today?*

THREE MORE CUSTOMERS came and went after Lilium Superbum's visit
and it was thirty minutes before he gave in to the dither over what to
do about the water system being down. He wanted to run back there, work
on the leak somehow but vacillation between closing and not closing was
keeping him immobile. Feeling like he should keep the store open, he did not
want to leave the front wide open, while he, the only employee, was nowhere
in sight. He twitched in angst, his wings tensing and untensing as he agitated
behind the front counter, caught in indecision.

He thought back to his spilled tea this morning with regret and sighed.
Well, enough dilly-dallying, shilly-shallying. Taking charge, he walked over
to lock up the cash register, then closed the metal rolling door, and taped a
sign to the front door that said 'OUT BACK, YELL IF YOU NEED ME.'

Satisfied, he hurried to take another look at the situation, intent on coming up with some kind of plan.

Arriving at the muddy exposed spot he stopped, feeling rather depressed
and daunted but he pushed those rude feelings aside and played captain, letting the whole unknown structure seep into his consciousness, trying to become one with it and sure enough, the bigger picture easily popped into view,
the answer obvious.

He wondered if there was a tool shed somewhere for the Nursery's personal use. There must be. A little scouting about, an official sanctioned nosiness indulged, brought him to the afore mentioned little building, and he
picked out a big hand saw, a tape measure and a hunk of pipe that looked to
be the right size.

Hurrying back, he knelt down happily in the damp soil measuring across the span of the cracked pipe. He then measured the pipe he brought with him and was gratified to find they were the same.

His plan was to make a cut on each side of the leak but it finally occurred to him he had no way to hold them together once he replaced the piece.

What a bird brain he was.

A feeling of blocked energy settled over him, frustration hampering his ability to breathe.

Cha!

He sat back and the image of hot tea flitted across his mind and he decided to take a break, close the store completely for a few minutes and go get a hot drink to bring back. Perhaps it would give him a fresh perspective.

Quickly he locked up, tugging the open sign off and pulling on the blue neon closed one beside it.

He'd sure come a long way since yesterday! Feeling pretty good to finally have his own time even if it was just temporary, his spirits lifted. He straightened his clothes and tucked his scarf snuggly around his neck, curling his hands into the side pockets of his jacket, and set out at a jaunty pace.

The closer he got to The Dancing Lady, the more his hunger grew. His mind was absorbed with pictures of muffins and salads and blueberries and he was starting to drool when he passed a hardware store and it yanked him in.

"Hi! Can I help you?" a nice young man asked from behind the front counter which held a big round bowl of goldfish.

Flem found himsylph describing his water problem.

Hands behind his back, the gentleman listened sympathetically, quietly letting this quirky young man tell his story.

Flem was flummoxed but to his joyful ears the man replied, "That's pretty simple, actually. How big did you say that pipe was? Four inch? That's rather standard. Come with me and I'll show you our plumbing section. Oh, I can see where you'd think you might have to cut it but believe me, there's something much simpler."

Flem followed happily, soft heel squeaks shushing on the linoleum.

Leading him right to the spot, the helpful clerk handed him a large round band of metal with a rubberized interior.

"This is a repair clamp. If the crack's not too long, this is a great 'band-daid.' They come in different sizes." He demonstrated by nimbly picking them out from their various hooks, hanging them on his arm, a gift of varying widths of silver to show the customer. "I would recommend this one," he smiled and held out a wide pipe 'bandaid.'

Flem smiled and then it got bigger. He met the clerk's eyes, "*Yes.* Thank you!" "Do I need some kind of glue?"

"Nope. Say, where you from, is this your water line or do you run a business around here?"

Flem's heart had constricted at what he first thought was a personal question but soon went to a different gallop at his *own* standing. He *was* running a business around here, albeit, it was not what, he peered at the clerk's name tag, Mr. Alloplectus, meant.

"Long story. The short answer is yes, I'm working for Fletcherman's Nursery." He stopped, hoping it would suffice.

It did.

"Oh, Fletcherman's! Hey, they got an account here. Want me to put this on it? You seem like a nice fellow, I can't imagine making up a leaky pipe story and I know Mayapple and her mother, Iris. How is Mayapple, have you met her? She's Iris's daughter. We went to school together. Is she still as pretty as ever? I always did have a crush on her all through school but I'm not her type."

Flem stepped back and looked rather amused at this sudden confidence he'd done nothing to earn. Other than work at the right place.

He thought fondly of Mayapple, and now her secret admirer.

Sticking out his hand, he introduced himsylph, "Hi. Name's Flem. Flem Green."

It was grabbed immediately and the clerk, Mr. Alloplectus, responded, "Larry. Short for Nummularia, from my mom's side, but I've been Larry since I was a just a minnow. Nice to meet you."

In no time at all, Flem was out the door and a few steps later, there was the tea shop.

It was late and there was no line, for which he was thankful as he was now starved.

One lone person was working the shop, constantly moving, giving Flem a opportunity to peruse the deli case for something edible.

His eyes lit up at a tray of cream cheese and pineapple-filled nasturtium blossoms and he flashed on the one he'd had at Pootsy Koons in Windfall

Whimsey C. Nimble

Café in Thimbleberry Canyon. If he ever went back, he'd be sure to bring her some.

The woman behind the case was beginning to massage the spot between her eyes so he quickly gave his order: six filled nasturtiums, please.

Then he spied the bean salad and lo and behold, there were nasturtiums in there too! What luck.

He quickly added on a pint of bean salad. Day-old baked goods caught his eye next and a giant lemon-poppy seed muffin joined the line up, to be topped off with a large chai soy latte. He felt like he was having a little party all by himsylph, and it felt wonderful.

He'd not only survived the day, he'd come out on top. Now, to just get that leak fixed before Mrs. Fletcherman came in tomorrow, and then he remembered, she wasn't! He was almost giddy with power.

Paying for his booty, his eyes fell on the business license hanging on the wall and read the words 'Oncidium Varicosum doing business as, The Dancing Lady, licensed for food and beverage.'

A dancing woman was seen on the counter person's small nametag but Flem took a guess and asked, "This your place?"

Looking up tiredly, she pushed a lock of dirty-blond hair out of her face and gave him a rueful smile. "Yeah. Sorry. I'm not at my best right now, everybody called in sick today, and I've been here alone since six a.m."

The slight Sylph snorted in astonishment and empathy before he finally swallowed and managed to squeak out, "Ah, me too!" in a high squeaky voice.

Rubbing her aching back, she asked, "What did you say? 'Me too?'"

His eyes snapped at her and he nodded, clearing his throat, feeling very important. "I work at Fletcherman's Nursery, do you know it?"

"Yeah, cool place. I keep meaning to go in there, but seems like I'm always working, you know? So you worked all alone all day too, huh? Man, what a day, I'll tell ya." She shook her head.

Wanting to leave but enjoying himsylph every step of the way, Flem practiced his flirting skills, bringing out old Sylph charm.

Arranging his purchases for transport, he smiled up at Onci, feeling kinship with 'another' shop owner, as his mind laughed at what a *fake* he was. He edged towards the door, feeling the need to get back.

She nodded and gave him a dimpled smile, one hand on a dirty-apron covered hip, the other raised in farewell.

"Come back some time when you don't have to rush off, we'll compare notes..."

He smiled as if he agreed but thought, oops! too far! and was out on the street, his mind catching onto Lark. Where was he? *Why* was the bakery closed?

Pausing, he took a long slow sip of his tea, breathing deeply in appreciation, holding fear for Lark at bay as he purposefully guided his thoughts, sending strong positive energy instead towards his friend and lover, and hurried back to work.

It was almost getting too dark to see but Flem the unflagging faerie was close to being done. The leak was essentially fixed. The dirt had been dug out completely from around the piece of pipe and the pipe itself wiped off as meticulously as he could get it. Carefully, he slipped the band around the cracked pipe, feeling satisfied that they'd guessed correctly in selecting the ten inch wide one. The crack itself was probably about five or six inches in length, counting the weak areas and he positioned the repair coupling so it hung over a couple of inches on either side of the compromised area. Deliberately and delicately he threaded the bands together, tightening each of the six screws a little bit, one after the other so the pressure would be even.

A flush of accomplishment started creeping over him, satisfaction filling each Sylph cell. He couldn't believe how good he felt! All that remained was to fill in the hole he'd enlarged and turn the water back on so the automatic drip system could go to work once again.

Of all nights for Bud to call in too. It was so unlike him.

Oh well, he spared no more time on absent Bud, *he* still had a register to balance. And he planned on writing a long note to Mrs. Fletcherman regarding the day's events, capturing and explaining highlights along the way. *Bed* loomed a long ways away yet.

As he set the shovel aside, he looked down at himsylph and gasped. Mud and dirt stained his shirt and the front of this pants, both knees were wrinkly and stiff with engrained mud and his shoes had streaks along both sides. Cha! He wondered belatedly how long he'd looked like this, thinking of all the people he'd come in contact with the last few hours...

Whimsey C. Nimble

Reaching for his almost empty tea cup, he drained it and started towards the front, grinning to himsylph about being the *only* one here. And in charge, at that! Heh.

In his mind he was about to make the rounds, checking that all was locked for the night.

Feeling quite pleased with himsylph, he pulled out the remains of his dinner, which was most of it since he'd only taken a few hasty bites before dashing back to the water problem. Which he'd fixed, he thought for the umpteenth time, a deep satisfaction glowing in his chest.

Turning off all of the lights but the one over the front counter, the serious Sylph settled in, not sure what he was doing but giving it a go anyway. It was a day of firsts.

Nibbling on a marinated bean, he worked his way through the last column of numbers, trying to match it with the supposed total from the amount of inventory he'd sold today, but, what a surprise, no matter how many times he tried to balance it, it was off. Not much, under twenty dollars. But still, he made a note about that too and into the special orders book it went. Then he started on the note to Iris, a bit of nasturtium stuck to his upper lip by a spackle of pineapple cream cheese.

Deep in thought, his left hand stuck in his hair holding it straight up, he was almost to the end of the story of the long day when something prickled his awareness.

A cold sliver of fear crawled up his throat and he became utterly motionless, listening.

Soft footsteps could be heard coming his way and Flem's heart raced at being here *alone*! Oh Pan. All the money was just sitting here next to him in a pile. It was all suppose to go in Mrs. Fletcherman's office in just a few more minutes.

He dropped his letter and looked wildly around for something to defend himsylph with, grabbing the telephone to throw at the last minute, when *Lark* walked out of the shadows. "Who you calling?" he deadpanned, a twinkle in his eye.

"Oh great Pan, what are *you* doing here?"

"Sorry, I can leave," and the fabulous looking green-eyed *man* in black turned, as if to go but Flem came to his senses and yelled "No! No no," glee bouncing through his veins like spit on a hot griddle.

"Long story," Lark continued, "I heard you might be here alone and -"

Flem interrupted him, " Who'd you talk to?" wondering aloud if he knew Bud was out too.

"Too? Why, who else is sick?" asked Lark.

"Well, Mayapple. Lily. And Iris has hives and won't be in tomorrow, either!"

Lark laughed, "Careful there, you almost sound happy at her hives. That wouldn't do."

Flem was absurdly glad to have someone to share his day with, and that that someone was Lark.

As his guest took over the stool Flem had vacated getting ready to defend Fletcherman's and himsylph with the phone, they had a good laugh and Flem remarked, "You must have talked to Bud, I take it. Is he sick?"

"Nooo, not really. Cha, where to begin."

Flem jumped in again with, "Hey, what happened today? I came by and the bakery was *closed*. Everything okay? What's going on?" His eyes were big as saucers, his almost finished tasks forgotten, as curiosity seized him up one side and down the other, prickling his wings, making them quiver with need to know.

One long black clad leg stretched out as the other hooked onto the rung of the stool and Lark, that pretty boy, slouched. He undid a top bottom of his black linen shirt, and rolled up his shirt sleeves.

"Oh, it's been quite the day, I found out after I made two whole batches of, what-was-suppose-to-be, today's baking, that those damn little bugs had gotten into my flour again. I had to close. Can't bake without flour, well, for the most part anyway. I'm sure it's from my distributor, and since they agreed rather too quickly to credit my account, I suspect they've had this problem before. So I went looking for flour but I'm picky and couldn't find what I wanted here so figured what-the-heck, and headed for the Canyon, where I knew I could get what I needed, at a lower price, too! But, it *is* several hours away, so" but before he could finish, was interrupted.

"Wait! What? Are you telling me you just drove to the Canyon, *Thimbleberry* Canyon, today, *today*?" The temporary boss of Fletcherman's Nursery, a Sylph, was having a hard time computing this. He hadn't been back in six years, *six years*, since his life had been tuned upside down and Lark just casually and easily drove there and back in one day?

347

Whimsey C. Nimble

"You get your flour there? Where?" he asked feebly, in disbelief.

"Oh, it's a place Pootys Koons turned me on to, she gets hers there for the Café. You know Pootsy, don't you? Windfall Café?"

"Yeah! And Whimsey Nimble. You know her too?" he asked this rhetorically, as *everyone* knew Whimsey C. Nimble and her good friend Pootsy Koons, owner of the legendary Windfall Café.

"Oh, of course. In fact, she was there today when I stopped in for a mead. And that's when I ran into, believe it or not, *Buddleia*. HA!" he ejaculated, "Surprised *him!*"

"*BUD* was at Windfall Cafe? He's *not sick?*"

Flem was ready to fall over with shock. This day had already surpassed any he'd ever had before but he'd assumed it was on the downhill slide at this point. No so.

He waited for Lark to continue. Obviously *that* faerie was enjoying the drama he was creating.

"Well?" he asked a bit impatiently, wanting the rest of the story. "What was he *doing* there?"

"That jack-in-the-pulpit was sitting between Catalpah and Chinaberry, that's what he was doing! Drinking mead! It was a regular party." He grinned in remembrance.

Flem's eyes were rolling in their sockets so, that Lark was concerned he would end up with eyestrain.

Lark continued, "Evidently China and Cat came back after we left Saturday night and, um, the three have been together ever since, sort of like a bender, I guess you'd say. It appeared that nobody had had much sleep, and everybody had *too* much mead.

"You know, I've known Bud a long time and every now and then something like this happens. He goes off. I think it's kind of an antidote to keeping it all together, here, in this life, in San Francoa Ramosa. Anyway, the story he's telling is he got 'kidnapped.' Pffft. So, I don't know when he'll be back, and let's not give him away to the boss, or, the boss's daughter, for that matter. I'm sure he'll be back within a day or two. He's too responsible not to be." He smiled at the other. "So, how was *your* day?"

After that it didn't take long for the tale to be told and Lark showed Flem the trick of looking for an item that exactly equaled the amount of the difference between what was sold and what inventory said had been sold and lo and behold, Flem remembered a large-flowered, red climbing rose ('Blaze?') he'd rung up but hadn't marked off, which with the tax, was exactly the amount he needed to balance perfectly. Obviously, Lark was simply brilliant. Sigh.

Making short work of his final chores, he quickly finished his note, Lark oohing and ahhing over his shoulder, making him laugh, deposited it in Iris's office, locked the door behind him and took off to show Lark the scene of the leak.

To his dismay, while the water system seemed to be on, the irrigation line hadn't come on like it was suppose to. Before he could fall into despair though, Lark saved the day.

"Did you reset the timer after you had the water off?"

Flem looked blank. "What timer?"

"I'm just guessing, but I'll bet there's a water timer to control everything, probably near a main valve somewhere."

"Here, is this it?" Flem led the way and sure enough a little box was seen near the red shut-off valve and within mere seconds, Lark showed him how to reprogram it, its little features lighting up and gurgling noises being heard as the system sprang to life.

"Anything else you need?" asked the taller Sylph, his fingers coming to massage the back of Flem's neck.

Their eyes met and suddenly the air was fraught with electricity, the night inviting them in.

Flem swallowed, unable to look away, their steps bringing them closer to the old greenhouse.

"Do you want to see my new hammock?" he offered inanely.

"What do you think?" responded Lark, and crawled through the window door behind his favorite faerie.

Chapter 50

Much to Flem's amazement, he saw a pale rose blush
creep up Bud's neck above his dapper little scarf.

FLEM'S HEAD WAS aswirl. First the nonstop day and now Lark, here, seeing first hand his funny stolen home. Sylphconsciousness stuck out all over him and he got really nervous. His wings started to clatter and Lark's head swiveled around, eyes narrowing in concern.

"Hey," he said, but "Meow!" sounded at the same time, drawing him over to Flem's contraband cat collection, easing Flem's apprehension, taking his mind off implications.

Rustling around, Flem busied himsylph filling mama cat's bowl and talking about the different personalities he was seeing emerge from the little devils.

Rogue cat came over and hissed at the intruder, then flounced smartly by to say hello to his faerie, nose and butt in air.

Laughing at such antics, the baker Sylph slid down among the pile, letting them cavort upon hissylph.

Flem's fears melted away at this elegant Sylph's naturalness with life, and how casually he put Flem and the cats at ease.

Inspiration struck and for once he felt like it was the right thing to do.

"Would you like a glass of mead?" he asked.

"I would," Lark responded formally and they both grinned and Flem disappeared around the makeshift bamboo wall.

Lark looked around at the decrepit building, broken and missing panes everywhere, gravel-embedded uneven humps of ground grown over where potting soil had been dumped askew, cobwebs everywhere. Whew. What a job this intrepid Sylph had set for himsylph, he thought. Flem was quite the enigma, seeming so naïve on one hand but exhibiting such aplomb with his actions on another. It just went to show he had good instincts, and how could he not, being a Sylph!

Lark smiled to himsylph and fell a little more under the other faerie's spell.

He could see why Flem felt compelled to stay here - there was a charm, an old look that still hung with the tatters, imbuing the atmosphere.

A small brown hen made of glass was handed to him filled to her two and a half inch brim with that succulent savory nectar of the Gods and Goddesses, mead. Their eyes met and both sipped sensuously, tongue tips teasing the sweet droplets away from sensitive corners.

Night was falling but neither made a move to turn on a light.

"Is everything locked up, are we actually alone here?" questioned the visitor hesitantly.

Flem nodded, his heart beating rapidly, licking his lips a little too often.

"And the big gate out front?" Lark had to know.

Flem nodded, and then said, "Yes, I closed it all up. I am off duty until tomorrow. Nobody knows I actually stay here, well, except Mayapple of course."

"Mmm," was Lark's reply to that but he thought to himsylph, yeah right, darling fae boy, we ALL know you're here but for some reason, everyone is indulging you. Must be that old Sylph charm once again. And I can't resist either.

"Do you let your wings out here?" he murmured. "You must."

Shyly, Flem nodded.

A look of intense longing broke over Lark and he huskily asked, "Can we...?"

A quick little movement by the other and before long, there they stood, shirts and scarves tossed negligently aside, wings quickly untied and unfurled, trembling upright, finally free.

Senses overwhelmed once again by the nearness of Lark's unfettered natural state, Flem dropped to his knees and started in licking. Soon his tongue was eliciting tiny clicks from where the scales started snapping together on Lark's back at the base of his wings, causing him to groan in pleasure and he asked half jokingly if Flem had all night...

Flem stopped long enough to utter one word. "Yes."

Whimsey C. Nimble

Two days later Mayapple slipped up the driveway all bundled up even though the day was forecast to get warm later. She was up extra early to catch her mom at work, before Flem rolled in. He was such a silly Sylph, who did he think he was kidding, as far as she knew, everyone, well, probably not Lily, knew Flem was living in her dad's old greenhouse out back.

Which was precisely the topic she wanted to broach with her mother. She had her sales pitch all ready to go, with many solid reasons why her mother should go along.

Unlocking the front door with her own key, she shut it again behind her, hurrying towards her mother's office where a bit of light spilled out.

Clearing her throat to make some noise, she paused just outside the door frame, "Hey mom!"

"Mayapple! Are you well?"

"Yes, I was here yesterday, wasn't I? Oh that's right, *you* weren't here were you?"

Iris sighed in silent frustration at her daughter's tone, and wondered if other people heard it.

"Sorry mom. Just don't treat me like a kid, okay? Do you really think I'd come to work if I was still *sick*?" She coughed

"Sorry, sorry! I spoke without thinking," Iris apologized, irked to high heaven that *she* was apologizing to Mayapple when it really felt like it should be the other way around. Motherhood, bah.

"Well anyway, you're here early today, what's up?" asked Iris as neutrally as she could manage, her finger holding open the Special Orders book, which she had been just about to peruse, the note from Flem laying unopened behind her. This was her first day back and she still itched but overall she was much better.

"It's about Flem, mom. I think he needs a place to live," but before she was finished, Iris was shaking her head in a negative manner.

"*What*?" burst from the girl. "How could you possibly know what I was going to say to *already* shake your *head* at!"

"Don't go where I think you're going, Mayapple, I can't do that. I've been trying to figure out a solution for quite some time now, and I just don't think it's a good idea to have *someone*, Mayapple, he's a *faerie*, for God's sakes, living *here*. Don't you understand? People will talk." She shut the Special Orders book with snap, tossing it back on the counter and stood up. "Besides, that old greenhouse is too far gone; it's dangerous."

"Oh." It was a groan. "You are so unfair, mother. He *needs* us. Can't you see that?"

"Mayapple, really. Drop it, okay? I just got back. Let's get our work done without arguing." Transferring into professional mode, she continued, "We're hanging baskets today, remember?"

"Yes mom. I mean *Boss*. You say you have an open mind but I don't think so. *I'll* help him clean it up!"

"*Mayapple*. I will think about it, okay? Now, about today. Bud will be in. He must have really been sick too, his voice was really hoarse. Seems like the lot of you got sick together. And me with hives. I kept Santolina busy rubbing lotion on my back," and she gave a quick smile to herself.

Mayapple objected with "Mom! Gross."

Biting her lower lip, Iris looked at her daughter, the perennial champion of the underdog. It was a good thing overall, just inconvenient at times. Actually, she *was* grateful to Flem but until she saw the books and talked to him about possible problems that might have come up, she wasn't about to commit herself.

Mayapple gave up and slumped into work mode. "Where's the list?" she asked resignedly, referring to the Bridge Project and the lay-out they were to follow, although she knew where everything went. There were three bridges so that meant six sides, each a different color and her mother's theme this year was rainbow. So, it was planned for scarlet, orange, yellow, lime green, blue and purple.

Mayapple was planning on taking pictures from the tallest building around sometime late summer or early fall, when all the petunias would be at their lushest. She was sure glad her mother had this contract. It was a big deal and was fun to work on, when she had the chance.

Her mom was really good at this, how could she not see the logic of having Flem live out back? It was so obvious to Mayapple and she wasn't about to give up yet.

Rolling her eyes at her mother, she made to leave and Iris handed her a folder with all the pertinent information in it. "You and Flem get everything ready to go and when Bud comes in, and he's coming in early today, by ten, ya'll can load up and get them hung. Are you up to this?" she mostly asked to get Mayapple's goat and her daughter leaped up, taking the bait, hook, line, and sinker. Mouth open and eyes wide she gave a snort of protest, but a moment later laughed at her own self, not bothering to go on.

"I'll be here in my office, if you need me. Is Lily here yet?" Iris questioned.

Mayapple stuck her head out the door and looked up front, and there was Lily, putting her stuff away behind the front counter.

"Yep," she confirmed and slipped out the door with a nod.

Turning back, Iris picked up the Special Orders book but set it down again in favor of Flem's note, and started reading.

That same morning, Flem was feeling rather anxious as he had seen Iris Fletcherman arrive really early, when he wasn't expecting her for two more hours.

And then a flash of someone's coat, it looked like Mayapple but she tended to be *tardy* not an hour early, so it was probably Lily.

Yesterday had gone pretty well, Mayapple had come in, so there were two of them to answer the phone and wait on customers.

He told her about the leak, and she was flabbergasted that HE had taken the responsibility to actually fix it himsylph. He had not divulged that *Lark* had shown up and spent the night... It was too new.

From the way he'd caught Mayapple looking at him occasionally he'd gotten the clear impression she was full of avid speculation about the two of them. He wondered when the interrogation would begin, she couldn't hold it forever. They were pretty busy yesterday so she'd been distracted and he'd hied it out of there as soon as possible last night, after such a late night the night before...

Unsticking cats' claws from around his Sylph, he set the little furry bodies down upon the ground and thought about the day to come.

But not for long. Footsteps were heard and they didn't vie off the path which meant it probably *was* Mayapple he'd seen earlier.

Stepping around the bamboo wall he took a few mincing steps to be better able to see through a less-alged window pane at the right height.

It was indeed Mayapple and she had a piece of paper clutched in her hand.

"Flem!" she called softly and he cringed at her voice in the cool morning air.

"Shhhh! SHH! Yes, I'm here! Come in. Why are you here so *early?*" he demanded, meeting her at the window-door.

"Oh, grrrr!" she expostulated, before continuing on with, "I came in early to talk to my mother about something and she wouldn't even *listen* to me." Her face wore a disgusted look as she climbed through the splintery rotten wood casing, paper crinkling in her hand.

Flem her faerie friend stood before her and she peered closely over his shoulder, trying to casually discern whether he was alone or not.

Flem cleared his throat to get her attention and her eyes snapped guiltily back to his.

"Looking for someone?" Flem asked, all too innocently.

"No!" she blurted and decided to change the subject.

"Bud's coming in early and we're hanging baskets today." She waved her mom's list at him.

"Today? I didn't realize it was today." He fumbled with the shirt in his hands but Mayapple was quick.

"How's your wings, Flem, do you need some, ah, preening? I think we've got time."

She hadn't planned this but seeing Flem furled loosely behind him spurred her on to impulsiveness. And awe.

Belying the truth of the matter and Lark's loving touch he replied, "Yes. That would be just the thing. C'mon back." He turned and tip-toed over the uneven ground area, rounding the partition where his hammock hung and promptly unfurled, presenting his back to her in invitation.

Rather flustered by the immediacy of it all, the young woman swallowed and said "Great! Hold on." Folding her mother's Bridge instructions several times, she shoved it down into her pocket and set to work.

It didn't take long to realize it was too easy. Hmm.

"Flem?" she asked, her turn for innocence.

"Okay, okay, Lark was here Monday night, is *that* what you wanted to know, Miss Nosey?"

He tried to say it rather dauntingly but it came out smiley instead and he gave in, grinning at Mayapple, so glad he could say it outright.

Spinning around, his wings waffled behind him and he caught her hands to his chest holding them captive.

"Oh Mayapple, he is SO divine -" but before he could really spill the beans, Bud's voice was heard hailing Iris. Obviously *he* was early too, even though her mom said he wasn't coming in 'til ten.

Whimsey C. Nimble

"Oh crap! Flem, I would love to hear about Lark, but I've got to get back and you do too! What time is it? Yikes! It's five after nine, we've got to go! I'll go first. Get ready!"

As if he needed to be told.

She scrambled over the ledge. "Ouch! Darn it Flem, this has to get fixed," referring to the uneven wood that was apt to give away splinters unbiased.

He wasn't listening, he was tying down his wings, throwing on a shirt, flinging a scarf around his throat, running to catch up with her.

"Hey Mayapple. Oh, hi Flem. Nice to see you in the daytime," Bud joked, referring to his evening hours as they lined up front and center, full of breathless but rather guilty enthusiasm.

Iris stood there eyeballing the late-comers with skepticism and narrowed gaze.

"Where've you been?" she asked and two hearts flew simultaneously to two throats, stomachs dropping along the way.,

"You're six minutes late," she continued sternly, before snorting and saying, "Oh relax the two of you, good Lord, I was only teasing. God. Go ahead Bud, get the van and we'll all meet down at number three. Are you two ready to go? Did you have enough *time*?" she ended sweetly with an evil little laugh.

"*Mom*." Mayapple was so embarrassed by her mother's attempt at humor. How did she ever get along in life, Mayapple wondered once again. But, she reflected, she must be doing something right, business was booming.

The three of them walked down the path with Iris leading just a bit. The flower-splashed van was seen inching along behind the three greenhouses and by the time they were at the front, Bud was backing the van into place, glad once again Iris had talked him into getting his license, even if he didn't use it outside of work.

Flem was losing his sylphconsciousness in his enthusiasm for the project and Mayapple was over the snit, her bossy good nature back in place.

Iris had a twinkle in her eye. She loved having those baskets on the Bridges. It was her own personal victory and in her mind, a symbol of how good a business woman she'd become since Brodiaea had died and she's taken over. It was her idea and she'd approached the city with it and after a month of pins and needles, they'd given her a contract. The Parks and Rec handled it. Santolina.

"Be careful!" she admonished, the words popping out of her as she came out of her moment's reverie.

All three gave her a look but continued on with the loading of the full, blooming baskets of Grandiflora Petunia, scarlet going up first. Flem stood by, ready to assist.

The back doors of the van were opened and Bud helped Mayapple as she maneuvered the heavily laden cart with two baskets swaying from its cross arm into place. She looked very determined and Bud wondered if it wasn't a bit much for her.

"Hey Mayapple. Perfect. Here, let me get that," he said as he easily transferred one of the big hooks to its place on the automated line set from the reinforced ceiling of the van.

"Whew, thanks." She laughed, rather embarrassed.

"Say, would you be interested in working the button here on this panel and maybe I could go get the rest of them?" he asked diplomatically.

"Sounds good to me," replied Mayapple, relieved. She wanted to be professional and competent before her mother but really, Bud had the muscles for this. He lifted heavy stuff all the time. She gave him a grateful smile as they switched places.

Iris was glad to see this. The business policy was to *always* use whatever muscle was around if an item was very heavy. It made no sense to risk possibly harming one's body simply to prove you could do something.

"Okay, push the button," Bud called and the clank of rotating metal could be heard as they all watched the first basket in the van sway slightly as it advanced deeper into the back, out of the way.

Flem's eyes were wide and admiring as he took it all in, comprehension dawning on him. But questions started to form and he foresaw problems. "Don't they all swing madly once you're going?" he asked.

"Bungees," stated Bud succinctly, before turning to the van and shouting, "Go ahead!"

"I'm right here, Bud, you don't have to yell," spoke up Mayapple, giggling.

Much to Flem's amazement, he saw a pale rose blush creep up Bud's neck above his dapper little scarf. Luckily the conveyor belt jumped to life once again with a clank and now these two baskets also rode deeper into the van.

Foreseeing the next question, Bud hurriedly went on, getting past his blunder as fast as possible. So many years here, so much polish but still he made mistakes. Ah well, he was just Sylph, he couldn't be perfect all the time. He looked askance at Flem as he deftly moved the next basket into place on the cross bar for transfer. That faerie was coming along nicely, from what little Lark had said. It was getting near time to unleash him at the *S* Club. And that Lark; Bud had never seen him so goofy over a new Sylph in town, but then again, Flem sure did have a way about him.

"Six trips," he said, stealing the words from the tip of Flem's tongue, before turning to load the next.

They had to move slowly as the baskets were ponderous but it went smoothly and soon they were ready for two more.

Flem went with him this time and stepped in with a hand, doing a little jig on their way back.

Mayapple was peering around the inside edge of the van again, making eyes at them but was quick to jump down and lend a stabilizing hand before scrambling back in and pushing the button, causing the first basket to turn the corner and start back their way, bringing more empty hooks within reach, that handsome Sylph Bud nodding his approval at their team work.

While their attention was occupied, Flem backed the cart out of the way and made it down to number three greenhouse and had just managed to transfer the second to last basket which was still swaying crazily when Buddleia slid around the corner, apprehension clear upon his face.

"Thanks Flem!" was all he said but was quick to add, "I got it," as he deftly maneuvered the last one into place and in no time at all they were back.

As soon as they too were shifted, Flem watched in delight as Bud and Mayapple started bungeeing plants to the wall, to hooks on the ceiling, to hooks on the floor and some even to each other. Soon it was an intricate mass of flexible webbing, each basket securely held in motion.

"That's it. We're ready." Mayapple turned and waited as Iris hesitated before giving her the go-ahead nod.

"Relax Mrs. Fletcherman, we both know exactly where we're going and how to get there, don't we Mayapple?" Bud stepped in supportively, bless his soul.

"Mayapple, have you got my list? Do you know where you are going and how to get there?" nervously queried Iris Fletcherman, regretting the way she sounded.

Mayapple looked at her seriously for as long as she could hold it, and finally said with only a touch of the sarcasm she was feeling leaking out, "Yes Mrs. Fletcherman, I *do know* where we are going and how to get there. We'll see you late this afternoon."

"Let's go!" she commanded, hopping to the front, sliding behind the wheel.

With a questioning look at Bud who inclined his head to indicate Flem should slide in next, he did just that, swallowing a bit nervously at being hemmed in on each side by Mayapple and Buddleia.

Iris bit her bottom lip, shaking her head at the three of them but let it go and her thoughts returned to the note Flem had left and the Special Orders book. She decided to go see Lily and then read the note again. And think. She walked off.

"So, here we are on the Bridge Run again, hey Mayapple?" Bud said conversationally as he leaned out across Flem, giving the seed of sylphdoubt a push in Flem's psyche and suddenly the Sylph in the middle got really warm, trying to act natural but starting to sweat. He tried valiantly to recapture the glue, and it was there, but now it had an edge and he hoped it wouldn't be too long a ride.

Mayapple, even in brash-driver mode, immediately picked up on Flem's twitching of shoulders, and gave him a reassuring smile.

"Remember last year and those pink and blue ones? Cha, they were pretty, weren't they?" Bud asked and kept talking. "That Baby's Breath sure gave them a nice touch, filled in really well."

"Gypsophilia Paniculata," murmured Flem, almost to himsylph.

"What? Flem, what did you say?" quickly caught Bud and rebounded, Mayapple listening intently to them.

"Baby's Breath. Gypsophilia Paniculata," he repeated, and they all grinned at the same time.

"Ah Flem, where would we be without you?" mused Mayapple with affection, pulling into the parking lot on the north side of the Ceanothus river.

Bud jumped out and walked briskly beside the slow moving van, easing the way for Mayapple to actually drive onto the long rolling hump of the first bridge, dropping caution cones along the way like giant pink breadcrumbs marking the trail home.

There weren't many people about yet, so they had no problems.

Whimsey C. Nimble

Sliding in as close as possible, Mayapple killed the engine when the back of the van was flush with the first steel arch extended out from the bridge over the water below. It was from the tip of these arches that one of the famous Fletcherman's Baskets would hang and the moment of truth was coming up fast. The heavily laden planters were big and unwieldy.

She and Flem hopped down and Mayapple joined Bud as they started removing the oversized rubber bands that had kept everyone happy on the drive over. Flem crawled into the front of the van again, hanging backwards over the seat to help unhook the few he could reach.

This close up it was a magical cavern of vibrant scarlet petunias with fragrant alyssum spilling down the sides, and broad green ivy (Hedara, thought Flem, remembering all those gardening magazines he used to pore over.) curling sinuously from the bottom and hiding in with the alyssum.

The rounded leaves of the moneywort trailed downward, lending itself to the illusion of a living waterfall.

Unsnapping the last one, Flem hurried around to help Bud and Mayapple guide it to the end of the steel arch.

With Bud doing most of the lifting and leading, Mayapple and Flem gripped it carefully, and within minutes it was poised in place, waiting to slide the last six inches to where it would hang sweetly in place, a good four feet out over the river.

"Done!" crowed Mayapple as they watched it swing a bit before settling down with barely any movement. "One down, only thirty-five to go…"

Chapter 51

Guilt rose up like a no-good sinner on judgment
day, although *why* she couldn't say. Call it nerves.

BY FIVE-FIFTY-FOUR THAT same day, the last basket was in place and
three smiles rode back to the Nursery in unison.

Bud was driving, the bill on his cap turned to the back, almost touching
his rather high collar.

Flem sat near the window and Mayapple purred in pleasure between her
two Sylph bookends.

"Hey, let's go for a mead after work, how about it? First round's on me,"
the driver offered suggestively, a questioning glance at his co-workers.

"I can't," said Mayapple immediately. "I've got to talk to my mom about
something. Again." She was not about to be so easily dismissed from her mission.

"But Flem, hey you should go," she urged, eyes squinting at him directly.

He saw her lick her lips as she did so and he knew what she was thinking. She
was being nosy as usual and wanting to know what *his* plans were for the
evening.

Well privately, Flem was really hoping to see Lark maybe tonight,
somehow.

But still, he'd be back in plenty of time. He wasn't even going to go lurk-
ing 'til it got dark, a good three hours from now. And who knew, perhaps
Lark would just materialize again. Flem could practically feel it in his bones.
He would see Lark tonight, sometime.

Feeling confident, he looked past Mayapple's gaze and over at Bud and
said, "Sure! Just one. I've got things to do tonight."

Smiling happily to himsylph, he turned and looked out the window a minute, allowing Mayapple and Bud to trade speculative glances with each other.

Whimsey C. Nimble

"Oh, what's on your agenda, Flem?" Mayapple's voice was smooth as butter and as casual as the beach. "I need to catch mom before she leaves," she continued. "Maybe I'll see you around...?" she questioned hopefully.

Flem looked at her with a blank look and Mayapple jumped in with, "Well, you'll probably get back about the time I'm done with mom, so..." she trailed off again, hoping for an invite but grew impatient and gave up. "Need any *help* cleaning or anything, Flem?" she resorted to bluntly wheedling and it worked.

By this time Flem had done some quick mental calculations of the most reasonable hour he could go find Lark but he was not adverse to Mayapple for an hour or so first. This *friend* business was so satisfying.

"Yeah sure," he nodded finally. "I'll be back in about an hour - I'll see you there. Make yourself at home." He laughed at his own joke.

Mayapple shook her head but grinned as she did so, happy she'd gotten what she'd wanted.

Bud parked the van and they all climbed out, flower troopers, home at last.

Iris had seen the van pull in and was waiting for them, eager to hear if they'd had any problems but they hadn't and each had places they wanted to be, so Flem and Bud disappeared quite quickly, leaving Mayapple and her mom.

They each searched the other's eyes, wanting peace, only one of them sure of it.

Iris spoke up. "We need to talk. Can you stay?"

"Absolutely," her daughter said, not letting on she'd planned on cornering her mom and forcing her to listen until she gave in.

They walked down to the office and Iris just looked at Mayapple, her mind churning with all of Flem's accomplishments and how he'd held up under duress.

"Mayapple, did Flem tell you about his day here by himsylph?" she asked tentatively.

Always cautious lest she unwittingly got caught in some kind of mother-trap, Mayapple held her breath and noncommittally replied, "Sort-of. Why? Did something happen? Is it bad?" A moment of panic washed over her as she traitorously questioned what Flem *hadn't* told her.

"*No*, no Mayapple, he handled things beautifully. Listen to this." She reached out and picked up a list she'd made earlier, after verifying Flem's note, but then equivocated with, "Well, wait. First let me tell you this.

"There was a message on my office phone from a customer Flem talked to on Monday and she's ordered fifty fruit trees for some acreage she's got up north. Said something about starting an orchard. And she said quite specifically it was because of Flem's help regarding her question about cherry and apricot trees."

"What about 'em?" Mayapple, always curious, even when it wasn't her business.

Knowing her daughter's penchant, she indulged her with the short version so they could move on.

With barely a hint of impatience, Iris quickly summarized, "Some trees, like cherry and apricot, need another variety for true pollination to take place, in order to produce fruit. Most apple, pear, peach and plum don't. Okay?"

Mayapple nodded.

"Anyway, there's *more*," continued Iris. "Listen. Do you remember Calypso Bulbosa?"

"Yeah, she's a friend of yours, isn't she?"

"Well, we've known each other a long time. Does that qualify us as friends? Not really, in my book. Although, I guess we *are*, just not the glass-of-wine, and a good belly-laugh sort."

"*Whatever* mom. What about her?"

Iris ignored her daughter's tone and said, "Not only did Flem get her precious pots safely loaded, and very ingeniously, I might add," interrupting herself again to inject, "Mayapple, he got the boys from the Green Thumb to use their forklift, after they got done with the delivery. I think that's great. He was thinking on his feet," she gushed before continuing, "And there was a discrepancy when he balanced but by God, he even figured that out for me.

"Not only did that boy -" but she stopped abruptly for a moment at that word, and Mayapple took her look and raised her one-of-her-own, making '*so-what*' eyes at her, motioning her to get on with it.

Squinting a don't-give-me-any-sass look right back at her, Iris continued: "Whatever he did, he must have charmed Calypso because her original order came to around two thousand, not a sum to sneeze at, but *he* rang up an order for closer to three!" She nodded in satisfaction at her daughter.

Continuing her recitation, she went on. "According to the book here," she held up the green Special Orders book, "we have four people who want to attend a class given by *Flem* - apparently he knows his way around a hydrangea bush.

"Not to be confused with the group someone wants him to lead, on a hike in the woods somewhere, to look for horehound of all things.

"He also noted in here that if he makes a hanging basket of Black-eyed Susan vines, we have a customer who will buy it. That's a great idea. I love Thunbergia, and I know you do too. I'm putting you in charge of making six baskets with him, we'll hang the rest for sale in the shop. After all these others are hung, of course. Did you finish the Bridgers?" she added as today's business caught up with her.

Mayapple nodded and was about to say more when Iris spoke up sharply. "Mayapple!"

Mayapple jumped. "Mom, don't DO that. What? What's next? The broken pipe, right?" She just couldn't help it, the sarcasm leaked out, much like the water had.

"He told you?" Iris was shocked that Mayapple knew before she did. "Why didn't you say something?" she asked rather accusingly without thinking.

For once, Mayapple held herself in supreme indifference to her mother's ineptitude.

"And when would that be, mom? You just got back this morning, didn't you? And I tried to talk to you, re-mem-ber?" Oh, it was so good to be perfect and in the right.

Feeling rather chastened, the best Iris could come up with was "Well, you should have called last night," but it was feeble and they both knew it.

Irritation with Mayapple's pompousness buzzed around Iris Fletcherman's head like a blue-bottle fly on a hot summer's day but she swallowed reasonably and let it go. "Okay enough," she ordered, "Let's talk. Did he tell you *what* he did?"

"You mean about the leak? Yeah, he said he fixed it," responded Mayapple.

"Oh, he fixed it. Read this." She thrust his note at Mayapple and pointed out the particulars.

Mayapple read, her eyebrows going up as she did so. Finally, she looked up, a smile, an acknowledgement lighting her eye.

"You're going to give him Dad's old greenhouse, aren't you?" she guessed, unable to stop grinning in her presumptuousness.

Iris took a minute and did not respond. After a pause where Mayapple's eyes never left hers, she finally said, "Yes."

Mayapple's feet came up off the floor as she pulled up her knees in her mother's office chair and spun in a circle as fast as she could.

"Yippee!" she sang as she twirled, then dragging her toes to a stop.

"But not yet, Mayapple, *not a word* to him, or anyone, do you understand? I want to do this *my* way, so do NOT tell him, got it?"

"Oh mom!" groaned the young woman. "When?"

"Soon, I promise. You can help me plan it."

At this Mayapple perked right up.

Iris nodded to the door and said, "Go ahead. We're done here, unless there's something else?"

At the shake of her daughter's head, she added, "Oh, go look at our new lily display on your way out. Another thing of Flem's daring. I was rather skeptical when I first saw it but I must say, I *like* it! I probably wouldn't have given Lilium Superbum the time of day but she took advantage of Flem being here alone, and I've already sold three from that display today!"

After dutifully circling the pyramid of lilies and looking with disbelief at the life-size cardboard cut-out of Lilium Superbum in living color pointing the way, she wasn't sure what she felt. It was garish but effective, it seemed.

Completing her inspection she moved on, laughing a little to herself at this new display. Normally, her mother tried her utmost to portray a subtle elegance in all things she did, even when talking dirt with Bud. She must have really flipped when she first saw this. Skeptical indeed. Mayapple giggled at the image of her mom coming face to face with the Lilium person in all her colorful glory. Flem must have really gotten to her, for her to so easily accept this unauthorized display.

Trying to be as discreet as possible, Mayapple escaped out the back and quickly slipped between the last two greenhouses to cut over to Flem's. Flem's! How was she *ever* going to keep this a secret until her mother decreed the '*right*' time?

Whimsey C. Nimble

Nearing the greenhouse, she started ha-loooo-ing in a soft inquisitive voice, trying to rout the faerie out but there was no response.

With a quick look behind her, she scrambled through the window.

Taking two steps, she stopped and looked around, remembering the old days when her dad was still alive and this was the main greenhouse. The light was the same but that was about it. Taking it all in, she could see where somebody had been straightening.

"Flem?" she called louder.

"Meow" sounded faintly in the distance and Mayapple's head swiveled towards the end of the old bamboo wall that used to be part of a counter.

Obviously, Flem wasn't back yet and she relaxed, picking her way towards the back to feed the cats. Satisfying her nosy itch, she called, "Flem, are you home?" really loudly, sure she would get no answer, and could look over his 'nest' to her heart's content. He *had* said to make herself at home...

"Here kitty kitty," she called, looking avidly around at his meager possessions and her heart went out to him, but was also thrilled to the marrow at her good fortune of having a faerie living right in her own back yard. She stopped in midmotion, her heart swelling in gratitude until it spilled over and she sent rippling waves out into the ethers of joy.

Wiping cat food from her fingers, Mayapple watched mama cat pounce on the dish of wet food as if there were no tomorrow, her purr loud and rumbling, her kittens doing their best to imitate her.

She wondered how long Flem would be gone. He should be back any time now she thought, and walked out to the main body of the greenhouse, an idea forming as she waited for him to show up, rather nervous at being in here with out him, it almost seemed like trespassing. How ironic was *that*! She smiled.

Without further ado she started stacking old and moldy boards into a pile. A couple were attached to others and she had nothing with which to pry them apart, so left them in place, promising herself she would bring a hammer and a crow bar the next time.

A half an hour later she was beginning to wonder if coming here was a mistake. Her plan was to help Flem, not do it *for* him. How come he wasn't home yet? He wasn't suppose to have more than one drink, it was hard to imagine someone could be gone so long, almost two hours, at least an hour and a half, and just have *one* drink.

Not really wanting to give up and go home, she firmly resolved to wait just a little while longer, he was bound to be home soon.

It was eight-twenty when she heard footsteps nearing. The sun was low in the sky and dusk was fast approaching.

Finally.

Guilt rose up like a no-good sinner on judgment day, although *why* she couldn't say. Call it nerves.

"Flem?" she called, feeling ridiculous, here, in her own greenhouse, for Pete's sake, a bit unreasonably peeved he had taken too long, by her standards.

Nothing happened. No more footsteps.

Coming out from around the small partition, she called again, "Flem?"

"Hi Mayapple!" Lark finally said, a tad too late, so she knew he'd thought about it and probably hadn't wanted to be discovered but too late.

Hmmph, not surprising, she reflected to herself, recognizing the sharp irritation of jealousy, as it tried to get a rise out of her.

"Lark! How nice to see you," she responded, also a shade too late so he'd know she knew, but gave up the silly game with, "He's not here. Him and Bud are out having a drink. They've been gone since six, when we got back from hanging baskets."

What a snitch she was, she thought disgustedly to herself, it sounded like she was tattling on him.

Lark ignored her tone and instead commented on how much better the place was looking.

Mayapple brightened and proceeded to regale him with what she'd been doing the past hour, ending with "and I can't get them apart, so I left them laying where they were." She pointed.

Deciding to outwait Mayapple for Flem's arrival, Lark handsomely offered to get some tools from his car and give her a hand.

Twenty minutes later, it was an astonished Sylph who crawled through the window-door to behold Mayapple and *Lark*, working side by side, cleaning up. A whole uneven hill of whatnot had been *flattened*, there were no longer any moldy *boards* on the ground anywhere and the remaining dead, black rotten hoses had been pulled down and laid in a big pile.

Both Mayapple and Lark stopped in their tracks, rather guiltily, thought Flem, the mead he'd imbibed slowing his actions.

"Well, took you long enough!" Mayapple liked the offensive, especially if there was any guilt poking around.

Flem gave her kind of a dirty look, his eyes narrowing just a little before sparkling at the fae young man/Sylph next to her.

A little fire burned in the bottom of his belly and he felt his cheeks go warm before it hit his shoulders and ran like lava through his wing muscles. The scarf around his neck suddenly seemed to strangle him, it was much too hot and he ripped it away from his throat with fervor.

Mayapple's eyes bugged out at this show of temper and she flashed them at Flem like railroad beacons, telling him to put on the brakes.

"Pffft!" was all he said to that, his opinion of her bossiness but he smiled slowly as he did it, disarming any offense.

Looking at Lark, he said, "Wow, you guys have been busy!" his eyes never leaving the other's face.

He hesitated but then went on, "It looks great, but, well, what if Mrs. Fletcherman sees it like this? Won't she get suspicious?" His eyes traveled back to Mayapple, a questioning look upon his face.

"Oh crap!" said Mayapple, a bit flustered. "I'll distract her. Bud will help, I'm sure. And Lark, when you're here, always ask her questions about something near the cash register, okay? That's the opposite end from here."

"Sure," acquiesced Lark easy enough.

Flem's pulse fluttered more erratically by the moment being in such close proximity to him.

Mayapple knew a losing battle when she saw one and resigned herself to leaving, as much as she did *not* want to go.

Sighing, she shook her head and lied, "Flem. Lark. I've got to go. Oh, I fed your cats, by the way." She turned slightly accusing eyes on her friend and added, "An HOUR and A HALF, ago, ahem. No problem. Glad I could help."

The tone was not lost on Flem but he just grinned in relief and said innocently, "Thanks!" and made no move to stop her from leaving, so she knew she had to go.

"Well," delayed the young woman and Flem tossed a line to Lark, saying, "Hey, I need to talk to Mayapple, I'll be right back."

Taking his cue, Lark spoke up with, "I'll just carry these out back for you," pointing to the pile of holey old hoses. "And then I better go too…"

An alarmed look crossed Flem's face and Mayapple threw in, "*What,* Flem? I need to go," giving him an easy out. "Can't it wait 'til tomorrow?" She winked at him, scuttling towards the window door, moving through it but then stopped in mid-flight by the splinter which caught viciously on her sweater.

Lark spied it immediately, and was there before Flem moved, carefully untangling the snag.

As soon as the girl moved away, he inserted a long piece of metal under the dangerous splinter and gave it a sharp jerk upwards, breaking it off roughly,

The metal he had in his hand turned out to be a heavy file and within no time the dastardly obstruction was a relatively smooth hump.

He whacked the sawdust from the grooves of the tool and stuck it in his back pocket.

"There!" he said with satisfaction.

"Bravo!" sang out Mayapple. "Wow! Thank you. Bye." She moved off down the path, cutting through between numbers two and three greenhouses and disappeared.

"See you tomorrow" floated back to the boys. Er, Sylphs.

Chapter 52

───────── ⚜ ─────────

Rolling stiffly off the bed, he stood like a block of ice,
frozen in mortification, wings held out to a fine, pinched
point, reminding Lark of cold bare branches in winter.

"*D*o you really have to go already?" blurted Flem.
"Out drinking with Bud, huh?" asked Lark simultaneously, in a
rather stern voice.

Flem's eyes widened and he blanched at the mere thought that his friendship with Bud could be in anyway misconstrued.

Lark's eyes crinkled and he said, mouth twitching, "I'm just kidding
Flem. Bud's got a handful of his own going on right now. I'm pretty sure
Catalpah and Chinaberry are temporarily staying with him. Ah, at least I'm
assuming it's temporary. Who knows." He went on, "And I trust *our* mutual
attraction is just that, *mutual*, right?"

Flem nodded quickly, a lump starting to form in his throat, and he
cleared it, saying, "How long have you been here?" a rather coward's way
out for not going in any deeper to those pesky all-consuming feelings. His
were much too erratic, like lightening bolts, to look at objectively, yet. He
had come a long way since Thimbleberry Canyon but he wasn't there yet.
Perhaps when he'd been here as long as Lark and Bud, he too would be as sophisticated as they. The idea of staying male for that long of time was rather
daunting but the presence of Lark counteracted it. (Catalpah and Chinaberry
came to mind at that word, sophisticated, and he scowled. They were certainly sophisticated also but in a different manner and he hadn't quite figured
them out yet.)

"Well, I don't know how long I'm staying. You got anything to feed me?"
the tall green-eyed Sylph joked, although he really *was* hungry.

At this, Flem's heart slowed down and he relaxed again.

"Yeah, c'mon," and he led the way to the back room where his hammock was hung.

Night was quickly encasing them and for the first time it was easy to move about in the semi-darkness and not trip on anything.

Amazement danced upon his soul that *he* had such wonderful people in his life, Mayapple and Lark. *Cleaning his place.* Now *that* was something that would never have happened back home in the canyon. 'Course, he never would have had a residence such as this back in the canyon either. He *didn't* really have it now, either, come to think of it...

Before that worm intruded any further, he put it out of his mind, swinging his backpack onto the floor and squatting down beside it.

"Well, you're in luck," he offered gleefully, deeply satisfied he'd had the foresight to swing by the market on the way home.

Delicately he delved in, bringing up items one by one in rapid succession, like a crane with treasure scavenged from the bottom of the sea until there sat a little pile of goodies: two red apples, a wee bag of raisins, another of walnuts, a small container of vanilla yogurt and a lemon.

Popping up, he asked, "Do you happen to have a little knife on you?" a mysterious air about him.

"Yes. Always. Of course. Don't you?" There was a second communication going on, an intangible silent acknowledgement of their shared sylph-hood. Every Sylph carried a small sharp knife used expressly for cutting greens, flower stems or what-not.

Grinning at Flem, Lark bowed gallantly and asked, "How may I be of service? Your wish is my command." It was said with a light air but Flem's eyes darkened as desire crept up his spine.

Lark held his gaze and returned the compliment before moving on to, "Knife?"

Flem pointed past Lark's shoulder and explained, "There's a fennel plant just outside the back door and if you would be so kind, I need about a cup's worth of the smaller stems. I would think probably one or two would do it."

"As you wish," bowed Lark in acquiescence. "What are you making?" he asked, intrigued.

"Well, I found a recipe the other day in my book on edible plants by Charlotte B. Clark. It's called Fennel and Fruit Salad. You mix a cup of sliced fennel stems –that's why I want the new shoots- with a couple of chopped apples, some raisins, and a handful of chopped nuts in with some yogurt and a big squirt of lemon. Voila!"

Lark laughed at Flem's light hearted description and headed out back, returning in five minutes with two stems which he efficiently skinned and diced, dumping them onto one of two plates he found in a niche with some clothes.

Wiping his knife off, he folded it up and stuck it back in his pocket.

Flem was waiting, having mixed all the rest of the ingredients together in a brown ceramic bowl he'd recently found at Blossom's Attic. He held it out and Lark dumped his booty in. Flem stirred and then deftly glopped a couple of big spoonfuls into each of two smaller bowls he'd set out. Sticking a spoon in each, he handed one to Lark then reached over and picked up a small paper sack. Unfolding the top, he offered it first to his guest.

Glancing at Flem in question, Lark reached in and scooped up a handful of crystallized rose petals, sugared violets, some green pumpkin seeds, and fat golden sultans.

Flem immediately did the same but instead of popping them into his mouth wholesale, he first sprinkled most of them onto his creamy salad and then tossing the rest into his mouth.

"Great combination! Where'd you get these?" Lark asked, savoring the delicate flavors and itty bitty crunches one small spoonful at a time.

"Oh," shrugged Flem nonchalantly, it's just a little mix I like to keep on hand," feeling anything but casual at Lark's closeness and compliments.

"Oh, did you make these yoursylph?" responded Lark with an approving nod.

Blushing charmingly, Flem nodded.

They ate in silence for a few awkward moments and then momma cat came strolling in from somewhere, meowing piteously that she was so hungry, one lone kitty trailing behind, ambushing objects that looked deceptively hostile as she passed by.

Putting his bowl down, Lark asked, "Where should I put this? Is there water back here?"

"There's a faucet out back that works. I noticed it was wet beneath it the other day and finally realized it must be controlled from that main valve area I turned on and off trying to get a handle on that darn leak. So, I played around til I got the right lever turned, and now, *I* have running water!"

He was obviously so proud of this accomplishment that Lark laughed, thinking about *having running water* and how he'd taken it for granted for years and years.

A new thought occurred to him and he asked, "Where'd you live before?"

Flem's heart froze in his chest and his breath caught, unable to freely slide in and out.

He thought he might choke.

Lark casually caught up the other Sylph's bowl and spoon and headed for the broken back door, giving it a kick to help it along when it stuck at the bottom. He was rather shocked at the transformation that had locked up his friend. It was obviously a troubled subject and he was determined to help, his curiosity and compassion aflame.

Splashing cold water into the bowls, he gave them each the cursory swipes and came back in, saying "Hey, great salad. Thank you," hoping he'd given him enough time to recover.

By now dusk had dissipated into full night and Flem scrambled around nervously, praying Lark wouldn't continue with his questions, turning on a few small lights scattered about.

Lark was amazed and stood, hands on hips. The place had a long way to go but at least you could see where you were going. And the path was *clear*, thanks to him and Mayapple.

Flem spoke up. "Well, I'd offer you some tea but I don't have any way to heat it. I've been buying mine down the street before I go to work." He jerked his thumb to point out 'down-the-street.'

"Say, I've got just the thing and you can have it! It's a small electric pot, a tea-kettle that'll plug right in over there. Let's go get it. C'mon. My car's down the block. We'll be back in no time," he urged, dangling his keys.

Unable to resist a ride in that intriguing little black car and totally entranced by the other Sylph, Flem the fae creature from Thimbleberry Canyon, nodded, going on to explain, "I usually fly over the wall behind here, into the alley -" but sputtered to a stop when he saw Lark shake his head and scowl slightly.

"Chancy. C'mon, I want to show you something that Bud told me about."

Even though the night was upon them, there was plenty of ambient light among the darkened buildings to show their way. "Follow me," he said, and instead of walking towards the parking lot he went out the sticky back door and towards the fence.

373

Whimsey C. Nimble

Flem was nonplussed.

Underbrush and weedy clutter hugged the fence all the way down to the front of the lot and Lark walked right into it and disappeared.

"Coming?" his disembodied voice wanted to know.

Pulling branches aside, the slighter Sylph slid sinuously through the camouflaged tunnel to follow his partner in crime out to the sidewalk, ending up at the left front corner on the sidewalk in front of Fletcherman's Nursery.

It was a secret way in, and it led almost directly to 'his' house!

He stared at Lark in awe.

Straightening his scarf, Lark gave Flem a look of such sober superiority, the Flem actually snorted at the act.

"Okay, okay, you're brilliant," he admitted, wondering if Mayapple knew about this. "How'd you know about this? Who showed you? Does Bud know? Oh that's right, you said he showed it to you, didn't you? Do ya suppose Mayapple knows about this? She must. Do you suppose she showed *him*?" Flem sounded a bit perturbed that she hadn't told him about it.

Lark laughed and said, "Relax, ma petite fleur, Mayapple and Bud go back a long ways. She probably just forgot, since she *is* the boss's daughter and always has a key."

"Oh," was all Flem said, totally sidetracked by Lark's use of an endearment.

The car was just down the street and Flem looked back to where they had just exited and if hadn't known it was there, he wouldn't have seen it. He liked that but could also easily imagine a little arbor right there with some kind of gate. Hmm. Perhaps he was really getting carried away here, but still, the image was there.

The close quarters of the low black car easily lent itself to intimacy and Flem swallowed nervously as he settled himsylph onto the cushiony seat, wondering if he would ever get over being so sylphconscious in Lark's presence.

Surreptitiously, the passenger watched the enigmatic driver, marveling how the ability to shift gears seemed so flawless and innate, sexy almost.

Cha, I've got it bad, thought Flem to himsylph as the neighborhoods changed the closer they got to the water until Lark was shutting the engine off in front of his houseboat.

Flem's stomach roiled right along with the undulation of the current, as memories of his previous visit here flashed across his mind. He got out and followed Lark to where he stood momentarily still, fitting his key to the lock.

A wave lifted them up and Flem inadvertently had to take a step to keep his balance and he bumped into Lark's side, putting out a hand to steady himsylph and grabbing Lark's arm.

The next thing he knew, Lark was pressed full body up against him, one hand on the open door jamb and the other on the back of Flem's head, holding him close for a long soul-searing kiss.

The sea seemed to respond and rocked the two of them together, over and over, caressing vicariously.

Scarves flew, shirts fell, the door banged shut behind them and all thought of electric tea kettles was forgotten, as wing ties were ripped off, and raspy tongue found raspy tongue.

Two hours later, a satiated Sylph raised his head languorously and said, "Lark. I really should go home. "

Lark being satiated also, and sleepy, said without thinking, "Which one?" not really meaning anything by it, just not thinking clearly.

All of Flem's old life came crashing back, the other side of the coin landing face-up, so-to-speak.

His visceral reaction was one of a great clenching, his new found confidence too new, too thin, too fragile, it had not yet replaced the old programs of inadequacy that he'd carried for so long, exacerbated as they were by the fact that he had been living as a *male* Sylph for six years after being female for the first one hundred and eighteen.

Rolling stiffly off the bed, he stood like a block of ice, frozen in mortification, wings held out to a fine, pinched point, reminding Lark of cold bare branches in winter.

In a flash, Lark was beside him, running his warm big hands over the other's shoulders, his own wings in a loose furl.

"It's okay. Everything's okay. You're doing great Flem, what is it?" he asked with anguish, seeing his friend in such distress. He continued, "*Flem.* I care not about your past. Do you understand? We *all* have a story of our own. Me. You. Bud. But the important thing is who we are now. *Now.* I think you're really wonderful. Are you accusing me of bad taste?"

Flem's hazel eyes flew to Lark's green ones and he remembered the container that held those pretty green lenses in this very houseboat. (Or is that, *faerie* houseboat?)

The essential caring, the sincere concern, felt like love to Flem and all his insecurities went up in flames, a cleansing that once again brought him to a higher level of consciousness and confidence. He stepped gladly back into the role, straightening his spine and furling his wings, as was befitting.

"Thank you," he murmured. "I'm sorry."

"Oh great Pan, don't apologize. We're new at this."

At that, Flem's eyes narrowed slightly and he said "*We?*" a heavy question on Lark's background. He certainly knew he was new at this but *Lark?* He just didn't think so. Lark had been in this City how long?

"How long have you been here, anyway?" he voiced the question in his mind, hoping Lark wouldn't take offense at his nosiness. The only way to get to know somebody was to talk about things.

Before Lark could answer though, Flem went on, "I've been living in Sycamore Park. I've got a, a, well, a place I stay at. *Stayed* at." Embarrassed, he stopped, not wanting to go on.

Lark spoke. "I'm a hundred and eighty-nine. I grew up in Cow Valley. Bud and I hail from around the same parts but didn't meet 'til we both got here. I *changed* when I was ninety-five, so half my life I've been a male Sylph. I'm used to it, for the most part. You'll see. I've been out ninety-four years. The first few I spent on the road, as they say, trying to fit in. But *you* know how well *that* works, now don't you?"

Flem stood, his eyes wide in wonder and awe, the enormity of this whole world overwhelmingly him. He was so *grateful* his path had led him here.

"Now, are you a little more at ease with me, ma petite fleur?" Lark asked, as if it were *he* begging apology.

Love for this green eyed human imposter spilled from every pore the Sylph owned and Flem reached over and hugged his very good friend.

"How did I ever get so lucky?" he marveled out loud.

Stepping into some black velvet pants, Lark paused and rhetorically replied, "I don't know. Just good karma, huh?"

Flem laughed and Lark said, "Now, about that electric pot - I've thought of a couple more things you might like. I don't use them. C'mon. Here, I'll help you with those ties, turn around."

Obediently the smaller Sylph turned and furled as tightly as he could while Lark did the dirty deed of folding and tying. The favor was returned, shirts were donned and they were off, Lark leading the way.

Flem eyeballed the hammock in the corner and wondered if Lark slept in it anymore or just used the human bed. That question was answered when Lark snaked out a hand, unhooked it and draped it over one arm.

Not the least embarrassed, Lark cheerfully imparted: "Two in a hammock is fun if you're still young, but, well, I *sleep* better in my own." He smiled rather shyly at Flem.

Flem was struck by the thundering realization that he had a lover. Him! Flem Green. If Flumaria had only known, she would have felt so much better during those long Canyon days. Oh well, better late than never.

Chapter 53

———— ❦ ————

Chinaberry laughed, and said, "I've got twenty pair
at home and each a different shade of purple!"

Following Lark down the hall to the kitchen, Flem stood diffidently
by, not sure how to act. Meanwhile Lark unfolded a stepstool and
climbed up on it, rummaging in the back of a high cupboard.

"Aha! I thought so. Here," he exclaimed in victory, extricating a small
radio from other top shelf inhabitants, rejectees all.

Flem held up his hands and Lark let it slide down into them, the cupboard
door silently closing behind him as he hurried back down the small steps.
Slapping the handy stepstool back into its folded position, he roughly set it aside.

"Come along, ma petite, I have more brilliant ideas where this one came
from."

A smile of pleasure broke over Flem as this delightful escapade kept going. Dazedly, he trailed along in Lark's footsteps, following him down into
the living room where he'd stopped at a low window seat that sported a pleth-
ora of pillows. After a moment's perusal with a finger to his lips, the baker
chose five, handing them all to Flem.

"Not done yet!" sang that Sylph. "Come along!" He picked up his hammock from where it lay folded on the back of a kitchen chair and slung it over
his shoulder, heading out the door. "Go on over to the car, I've got one more
thing I want to pick up," and he disappeared around the corner, past a big tub
of red geraniums.

Flem stood on the spot, bemused by Lark's actions.

Clanking noises were heard and then a few crashes, such as someone
repeatedly banging something down deliberately, and Flem hurried around
the corner.

Lark was emptying a round metal brazier that hadn't been used in some time, the ashy remains for the most part being corralled into a big waste receptacle.

Flem wondered what Lark planned.

"Let's go!" grinned the man in black, shifting his hold to get a better grip

A short ride through the night time city, and Lark was parking in the same spot he'd vacated earlier. Flem looked pretty impressed and Lark grinned and said "I planned it that way."

"Yeah right," grinned the love struck fae faerie boy in blatant denial and full adoration.

Locking up, Lark followed Flem back through the hedge, Flem thinking it felt like coming home. Instead of struggling with the back door, Flem hustled around the end and up along the side of the decrepit old building 'til he got to the window door. He climbed through first, cords and pillows doing their best to hamper him every step of the way. Lark then proceeded to squeeze through with hammock and brazier.

Flem led the way automatically towards the back but stopped awkwardly, wondering what Lark had in mind with the pillows.

Lark let the hammock fall to the ground and suggested, "Hey, why don't you drop the pillows there for right now and plug in that radio. I'm going to go find a spot for this," he lifted the brazier. "You got a shovel anywhere nearby?" he asked, continuing on and out the back, kicking the door with his toe, before adding, "Bring it out back, okay?"

"Yeah! Yeah sure, I can get one. I'll be right back," and the slightly smaller Sylph jumped-to, carefully setting the electric pot down on the ground and letting pillows free fall from his body onto the pile of hammock before dashing outside. He remembered seeing a shovel of sorts across the way in number three, and quickly returned with a small odd shaped transplanting spade. Stopping for a second, he plugged in the radio as requested earlier and then pushed his way out the stiff old door to the back yard of sorts.

Lark took the shovel from Flem and looked around once again but he had already decided on the ideal location, a flat spot between the back fence and the back of the old greenhouse just this side of the catalpah, a tree known for the poetry in its soul. There was even a slight depression already in the ground there. Like a contractor breaking ground on a new project, the taller

Whimsey C. Nimble

Sylph in men's clothing dug in, shaping the shallow area to meet his own specifications.

Soon a dark cavity appeared in the hard packed earth and it wasn't long before he deemed it the right size. Throwing the spade to the side momentarily, he reached over and picked up the metal brazier he'd brought from his own back yard and dropped it right down into it. It slid in easily but crookedly. Two more adjustments soon had it flush with the hard pebbly ground.

Grinning in satisfaction, Lark wiped his hands off and said, "Surely there must be a little bit of something around here we could burn, don't you think?"

Flem finally believed what he was seeing: this Sylph was going to build a piece of the canyon, right here in Flem's own backyard.

Oh, that's right, it wasn't *really* HIS now was it? What was he *doing*, for Pan's sake, digging himsylph in deeper and deeper with every breath he took?

But it was an emotion that had become blunted, these stark, run-a-way train bullets of fear, dampened by his inner knowing, his sense that everything was as it should be. It felt *right*.

He felt loved. And he was starting to really understand what it meant to love himsylph, who he, *she*, really was, that inner core of goodness and light. He was Flem *and* Flumaria, it was just the outer shell, which of course had its own little set of anomalies, but still, the soul was the same. It made no difference what anyone looked like on the outside, male, female, green, black or pink, it was the inside that counted.

Lark was such a *lovely* addition to his new life. Imagine, a party in his own back yard.

"Hello?" laughed Lark.

"Great idea. I'll be right back." He quickly thought of a pile he'd been assembling in his constant clearing of debris and went to pick through it for some burnable tidbits of rubbish.

Lark went into the house and fiddled with the radio 'til he found some kind of soft classical music.

Grabbing up all the pillows, he took them out back and distributed them in a big circle around Flem's new fire pit, rubbing his hands together in delight at the completion of this impromptu brilliant piece of inspiration. He practically patted himsylph on the back in satisfaction.

Turning decisively, he headed back to find an obscure place for his hammock and was just in time to get the door for Flem who had quite an armful of ragtag fire fodder. Each nodded politely to the other, grinning as their bodies pressed against the other in passing.

Within minutes they were ensconced around a cheery miniscule fire, lounging on Lark's fine contribution, soft music in the background and each sipping a henfull which didn't really amount to much more than a big thimble. But such was the magic of the liquor, that just a taste was like a glass-full in the old days. Flem couldn't believe people poured out half a tumbler at a time. It was so crass, such overkill. Laughing silently at his new found snobbery, he took a deep breath and relaxed where he sat, half leaning on a fat pillow, staring into the small fire.

Neither said a word for several minutes, enjoying the glow of the magical ambiance, a hint of idealized memories.

"Oh Flem. Listen," invited Lark, a finger to hip lips, straining to hear the music.

Flem didn't recognize it but it certainly was beautiful.

"Come," Lark commanded as he suddenly stood up and held out a hand.

Flem looked at him, heart in mouth, wondering what adventure they were off on now.

Pulling the other faerie up, Lark captured him and asked, "Do you know how to dance, Flem?" while looking deep into his limpid hazel eyes.

Swallowing, the slighter Sylph managed to shake his head.

"Oh, you're going to do well, you have great rhythm," replied the other with lascivious inflection and a dirty smile, and Flem felt his ears burn as he remembered their shared passion.

By now they were back inside the old greenhouse which was dimly lit by a few well placed candles and moonlight through algaed panes.

"Don't move," ordered Lark as he dashed to one side to turn up the volume, then grabbing Flem's hand and pulling him into his arms, the magic of the waltz lifting them into swaying dance as nothing else could.

His feet flying into the right steps, Flem marveled at how easy it was to follow this Sylph and two butterflies spiraling in joy came to mind. Their clothes came off (again) and wing ties were rabidly undone. Wings swooshed into big loose furls, aquiver with purpose, the faint sheen of different patterns and muted colors on each set of appendages barely discernable.

Whimsey C. Nimble

Swirling and twirling, they hardly touched except for the fingertips of Lark's right hand where they rested lightly on Flem's waist. Flem's left hand caught just at the top of Lark's right shoulder's since he wasn't quite sure what else to do with it while his right one was caught up in his partner's outstretched left hand.

Not since the early days of flying uninhibitedly had Flem felt so weightless, so free.

As it became apparent that they were meant to dance together, both relaxed and stared into one another's eyes, wearing rather besotted looks.

Wings tightened and pointed, their toes lifting and soon Lark, who was an accomplished waltzer, was leading the two of them through long graceful strides, soaring with the music, feet not touching the ground.

Surely the most magical night of Flem's life.

A woman's deep and lyrical voice came on as the music ended, saying, "And that was the Dream Waltz, played by two violins, a viola, and a cello, a Scott Shumaker composition. Next, we've got Vivaldi, Concerto in A Major for strings."

The two faeries made their way back to the fire and sat down. Lark pulled his pillow close to Flem, and they both retied their wings, throwing on loose shirts and pants for propriety's sake.

After a bit, Lark spoke up and what he said was most unexpected. "Remember that day when Bud and I ran into you and Mayapple, and we all had that drink together? Well, we were just coming from the *S* Club."

Flem's ears pinged, starting in his eardrums and moving out and up, pulling things tight as it relentlessly moved on, 'til it leaped off the back of his head with a shove.

"What's the *S* Club?" he asked with bated breath, as he was suppose to.

"Ooh yes, tell us about the *S* Club, Uncle Lark!" Bud's mocking, laugh-filled voice came shooting out of the dark as he materialized from the brushy, almost invisible tunnel near the fence, Catalpah and Chinaberry right behind him, like the multi-colored tail of a comet.

Flem and Lark both shot to their feet in startlement, Flem's eyes wide in amazement at the *gathering* here. At *his* house. He never had one party back at the Canyon. Oh, he'd tried to but there seemed to be a knack for it, and *she* just didn't have it.

Everybody sank down next to a pillow, lounging, falling back to old instinctive habits of drinking and talking and staying awake for hours as they yakked the night away.

Flem looked at Catalpah and Chinaberry with questioning eyes, wondering who they were. Bud was Bud and could do no wrong and he knew Mayapple seemed to feel the same way. But Chinaberry and Catalpah. He couldn't figure them out.

Both were watching him and Flem remembered he was the host and blurted out, "Something to drink? I've got a little nectar, let me just go get it," and he forced himsylph to slow down and smile, welcoming each woman? Male, pretending to be woman? Sylph? Meeting their eyes directly, he was surprised to see that they each bore colored eyes to match their clothing, Catalpah's once again emerald green and China's a brilliant purple.

Rather unnerved by their direct looks, he slid toward the back door, pulling extra hard to get the darn bottom to let go and of course it did with a pop, grabbing his nerves. Once inside he stopped for a breath, looking out through the dim, greenish glass at the wavy images beyond, the dancing fire making magic of the air.

Unearthing the little box he kept the hens in, his own little chicken coop, he thought for the eight-hundredth time never failing to be amused by his old joke, he quickly unwrapped three, grabbed the opened bottle of mead plus his one spare and headed back out, wishing this moment would stretch out for days, perhaps even weeks.

As he gave the sticky door a helpful shove with his toe, mama cat came racing through as if the hounds of hell were after her and was out the door before another moment passed.

Flem saw the others talking about it as they were laughing and pointing at a particular tall clump of grass than now hid a feline inhabitant.

Holding the door open for himsylph as he emerged with a small tray and two bottles of faerie hootch, he was surprised into waiting as six kittens came ambling, trotting, and moseying after their parent, intent on following.

As they tumbled out past their doorman, there were oohs and ahhs heard and instantly Cat and Chinaberry were on their feet, scooping up kittens and dropping one each on Lark and Bud's laps. Two disappeared towards the back fence, one spotted his mother in the wiggling weeds and ran towards her, leaving one, the little rogue who liked to boss Flem around.

Flem helped him along with his foot so he could close the door and the little bratty catty took exception to such undignified treatment and hissed at Flem before raking a claw into his flapping pant leg and hoisting himself up, climbing like a sailor in cross-rigging, until he reached his goal. Rooting around at the nape of Flem's neck, burrowing below his scarf, the rascal soon made an opening and struck out cross-scapula for a certain well-remembered hollow.

"Well!" exclaimed Lark, "I see you two have met before!"

Everyone snickered as Flem squirmed and that faerie didn't even realize that here was a situation that in the past would have made him acutely uncomfortable, being the center of attention and others laughing.

Joining in their laughter, he reached behind him and tried to adjust the little bugger but his fingers were easily evaded. Giving up, he ignored his passenger and instead tilted the bottle all around, using the moment to really get a good look at each of his guests.

Bud got up, handed a kitten back, and said, "I'm going to go get a little something more to burn. I'll be right back," and he disappeared into the night.

Everyone continued to chatter and drink, playing with the kittens, unconsciously bonding and not realizing it.

China and Cat were deep in conversation with Lark and Flem tried to blend inconspicuously in with his pillow and the ground.

Catalpah, with her high cheekbones and broad shoulders, laughed throatily, throwing her long green glitzy scarf back out of her way, a studied grace to her movements.

Flem wasn't entirely sure she wasn't a man, a human male but cha, she *had* to be a Sylph!

With a quick look at Lark who looked up in time to throw him a fast and discreet wink, Flem focused on Chinaberry, an overwhelming picture when close-up. He never flinched but smiled into her electric purple pupils that matched her purple sequined jacket and for just a moment, Flem wished he'd never heard of vampires but then he got himsylph under control, and said, "Here, let me pour you some," very suavely and debonair, even though he was much overcome by having such big personalities here, *HERE*, in his own,

(*Not* his own, Oh Pan, Oh Pan) backyard. Was this folly of the worst kind? Was the universe setting him up to fail again?

His newly awakened sylphesteem pricked him.

Or rather, was *he* doing it again, sabotaging himsylph? His heart leaped, but he rose to the occasion as he willingly acknowledged that, yes, there was a fine little thread of fear that screamed those questions. And they were valid. But he decided to flow with the moment, and only let himsylph be in touch with the goodness that was bursting into his life like firecrackers. He trusted, as hard as it was to let go, and decided to think about it another time. Maybe tomorrow.

Feeling more in control of himsylph by the moment, after all, Lark chose him, he *must* be okay, he was able to say with hardly any nervousness at all, "What beautiful eyes you have!" swallowing leftover bits of anxiety.

Chinaberry laughed, and said, "I've got twenty pair at home, each a different shade of purple!"

Flem looked at her in amazement, Lark's arm easily going around his shoulders.

"So, Uncle Lark, I thought you were going to tell us about the *S* Club…" Bud whined, bringing up the subject that Flem was so curious about.

"Well, Bud old boy, how long have we been going there?' Lark returned Bud's banter.

Flem sat straighter, listening raptly. He couldn't wait to get the whole story on them both. Until he did, every piece was tantalizing. He waited but they took too long in their deliberations and finally he burst out with "Well, what *is* it?" impatience thrusting like a knife point as he looked from one to the other. "What do you do there?" he asked guilessly. "Is it just a place to have a drink?"

"No, it's more than that. Oh, you'll like it, ma petite fleur," promised Lark.

Flem turned to Chinaberry and Catalpah and enquired, "Have you been there?"

They both nodded, a secret little strange smile on their lips as Cat affirmed, "Oh, they know us there, don't they China?"

"Let's all go this weekend, what do you say?" asked Bud. "I think it's time, don't you Lark?"

The conversation ambled on, enough *S* talk to keep Flem on edge but as the five sat around the little glowing reminder from home and drank that elixir of the Goddess, they covered a million other subjects, fueled by curiosity, memories, and mead.

Mayapple was up way too late, but instead of going home like she planned on, she found herself heading for the Nursery, as if that wasn't where she had to be in not very many hours. But Sylphs didn't hold the patent on curiosity and she was compelled onward. She chided herself for being too controlling, too nosy, told herself to stay out of Flem's business but she paid that part of herself no attention and turned into the alley that ran behind Fletcherman's at the back of the lot, behind the old greenhouse.

She was just going to peek a little, disturb no one.

Probably wouldn't see a thing, she guessed.

But she wouldn't know unless she looked.

Walking softly, she hugged her coat tighter around her and determinedly started to cross to the old board fence when suddenly she smelled smoke.

Alarm shot through her and she flew to the knothole to see into their backyard and what she saw made her jaw drop.

There for all you please sat Flem and Lark and Bud AND Chinaberry and Catalpah! Laughing and talking and carrying on, and of course, drinking.

And from this angle they all looked suspiciously alike.

Chapter 54

My services? *My* services? Really. Like what?

ER LEFT EYE squeezed shut, Mayapple peered avidly with her right through the knothole in the old weathered pine fence that ran the length of their property along this part of the alley, her hands splayed flat on each side of her head.

She couldn't believe Chinaberry and Catalpah were here too! Where did they fit in this whole picture she wondered.

At that moment, the green one, Catalpah, stood up and dropped a kitten into Bud's lap, letting her hand trail over Bud's hair as she turned towards the brush further up along the fence from where Mayapple stood on the other side, shamelessly eavesdropping.

"'Scuse me a moment, nature calls," she laughed in her deep voice, disentangling herself from the group. "What a quaint place you've got here Flem," she added ambiguously over her shoulder as she walked away.

Both Mayapple's eyes popped open at this remark and her mind prepared to take offense at *all* the things that were wrong with that remark.

She found it hard to be quiet but contented herself with a disdainful sniff as she settled her fists back upon her hips, and reclosed her left eye. Purposefully, she repositioned herself to see if she could deliberately *spy* Ms. Fancypants answering nature's call.

Catalpah obliged her by staying within Mayapple's limited line of sight. It was dark, it was dim, it was late, but that didn't stop Mayapple from observing that that woman never squatted down but stood, with her back to the fire, quite some distance away, looking as if for all the world that *she* was a *he*.

The eye in the fence narrowed, the lips behind the wood pursing at what she was seeing. In her own backyard! It was too much, *hard* to keep quiet.

Whimsey C. Nimble

But she managed.

Cat returned, flipping her scarf and taking precise little mincing steps to settle herself back in, closer to Bud.

Fog was beginning to insinuate itself, little tendrils searching out every corner.

Mayapple shivered, wondering if maybe she shouldn't go home.

Chinaberry too snuggled in on the other side of Buddleia and together they all three slouched a little closer to the fire, Bud in the middle, arms outstretched around his two best gals.

Bestirring herself from where she sat in Bud's protective circle, Chinaberry brought a small dark purple knapsack around to sit on the ground in front of her, widening the top 'til she could reach in.

"Not sure," she half mumbled, everyone's eyes upon her, placidly observing from seats of inertia.

"I brought these along, it's probably not at all the thing to do, but, well, want some?" She held out a plastic container with a wide screw top.

No one moved, lethargy motivating that inertia.

"What is it?" finally inquired Lark from where he sat, his arm comfortably draped around Flem's lumpy shoulders.

"They're, well, they're, ah, *sweet ants.*"

"YUK!" was heard from *behind the fence.*

Everyone bolted upright and five heads swiveled in unison, instantly alert to being found out.

Only Flem was pretty darn sure he *knew* who was behind the fence.

"*Mayapple*, is that you?" he called, making his way toward the spy hole, the others right behind him.

"No," she said in Mayapple's voice.

"What are you doing? What are you doing?" his voice rose as he tried to figure this out.

"Well, well, I was on my way home and well, I didn't *want* to go home yet, so anyway, I just figured I'd take a quick look and see if you were still up." All this said in a little girl voice from the hidden alleyway.

"And you were. Are," she added quietly, a hidden beseeching note never noticed by any but Flem heard it. He knew it was there.

"Oh great Pan. Come on in. Or over. Or whatever." He sighed and went back towards the fire.

Not being one to hesitate in the face of good fortune, Mayapple ran to the old garage down the alley but instead of climbing to the roof she ducked inside, and with a few grunts and taps pushed out a couple of loose boards, allowing her to slide through sideways, all smiles, adjusting her clothing as she walked towards the group. This was not the first time she'd used that route but it had been a few years.

Dropping down around the glowing embers of the fire pit, she couldn't help herself from commenting, "*Quaint* place, Flem," rolling her eyes dramatically as she threw a stare into his eyes but quickly turning away as she continued with, "Let me tell you about the strangest thing *I* ever ate," to the rest of the nonplussed gathering who gamely went along with her.

The night wore on and the subject of being seen in the Canyon by Lark came up and Bud finally inquired as to *why* he'd been at Pootsy's place, Windfall Café.

Bud was easily brazening it out but underneath he was rather horrified at being busted like that. He'd planned on keeping his China and Cat secret to himsylph and sticking with the story he'd given Mrs. Fletcherman, that he was sick that day.

But good old Lark had to show up at the *unlikeliest* of places, for Pan's sake, on the unlikeliest of days. Talk about timing. Ah well, the jig was up, Lark knew him too well and he would have ended up telling him anyway. But still. Now Lark would give him that *look* he liked to use when he was feeling *righteous* in some way over him. They both laughed about it, Lark denying it whole heartedly but Bud knew. He saw it. Ooh, it got under his skin, way down there where there wasn't much light but he firmly tamped it into place, and came back to listen with two ears instead of only the one he'd been using.

"Bugs! Those god-awful weevils. I noticed the first one in my prune kolaches. We came eye to eye as I was loading the shelves below it with the second batch of the morning. I could have just cried. I saw my whole day flash before my eyes and it *wasn't* what I'd planned on!"

He paused and Chinaberry asked, "What did you do with them all? Just throw them away?"

"Oh, I took them down to the homeless shelter on Meadow Sweet street. You know that one that has a soup kitchen at five every night? They were *very* happy to get such a donation," but before he could go any further, cries of outrage and shocked disbelief came from all mouths there.

"Oh my God, Lark. *Really?*" Mayapple was beyond appalled. Every good thing she'd thought about this guy blown to pieces by this revelation of such thoughtlessness. How *could* he?

Flem had pulled back and was looking at Lark in fae disbelief, his world on hold.

Chinaberry and Catalpah were watching with quite disenchanted expressions, hands over lips in revulsion. Sweet ants were one thing, but *weevils?*

Only Bud didn't react.

They caught each other's eyes.

Giving his friend his moment of gory glory, he finally played the straight guy and asked, "Okay, what did you *really* do with them?"

Never missing a beat, Lark continued on, "Took 'em to the beach and fed the gulls..."

In ungagged relief, the five made nasty remarks about Lark's honor and pelted him with any kind of small objects that were nearby as he laughed and laughed.

It was close to four a.m. before a long lull transmorphed into a stupor. More mead had been consumed, the ants eaten, ("I just let it sit out with a little honey in the bottom and wait," explained Chinaberry) and all of Flem's tidbits and stashes long gone. Cha, it could be expensive to always be the one hosting the party, reflected Flem, not caring in the least.

Mayapple left, yawning.

Bud, Chinaberry and Cat slipped away and Flem wondered belatedly if all three rode on Bud's bike and giggled aloud at the absurd image.

"I've got to get to the Bakery, Flem. I gotta go too."

"The Bakery?" Flem burst out, sure he'd misunderstood.

"Yeah, I start work between four and four-thirty every day. I've got to see about getting some help," he trailed off.

With a quick hard hug that turned into a long heartfelt one, the two lovers parted and Lark slipped away too, handing Flem a sleeping, boneless kitty.

The fire was out and Flem stooped to pick up some remnants and straighten the cushions before he finally stumbled to his hammock, falling in sideways to accommodate the furry knot in the middle of his back. The one in his hands was more easily tucked into the hollow of his belly and soon all were snoring softly together.

It was a tired Sylph with grainy eyelids that stood dispiritedly at the time clock just a few hours later. It all came back to him *why* he had quit drinking. *This* was why! Only now he had a job, and couldn't afford to sleep the day away.

For the first time, he thought fondly of his hole under the rock in Sycamore Park, how *dark* it was, how *secluded* it was, how *easy* it was to sleep there.

Shaking himsylph, he determined to get through the day. Vaguely, he noted Mayapple wasn't here yet.

Stepping through the door, all bright eyed and bushy tailed, was Iris.

Instantly he did his best to belie his real condition, smiling hugely while straightening his, thankfully passenger-free, spine.

"Good morning Mrs. Fletcherman!" he got out between stiff cheeks, his smile feeling forced. One eyelid started to twitch, a little spasm he couldn't stop.

Nervously he ground at it with the knuckles of one hand but within two seconds it was back.

Eye twitching, slightly smelly, he stepped back, trying for a bit more distance between him and the boss.

"Good morning Flem! You're looking good this morning."

This took him aback and he looked at her rather askance but she was paying no attention, oh thank Pan.

Instead she was bustling about, obviously brimming with good cheer.

Hmmph. Perhaps he could escape with no injuries, he marveled, declaring to himsylph that he would NEVER put himsylph in this position again! Would he *never* learn?

"Oh, Mayapple called. She'll be in a bit late, something about a wrong bus, I don't know. That girl." Iris shook her head at her daughter's strange habits.

"In the meantime, Flem," she drew out his name as if savoring it and Flem stared at her. She appeared to be overflowing with good cheer and for that, he was grateful. Skeptical, but grateful.

Whimsey C. Nimble

Harboring her great secret, her planned act of altruism for this, this, *faerie*, yes, a FAERIE, she was helping a faerie, she giggled like her daughter and pinched his cheek.

He stared at her in amazement, wondering what this was all about.

But Mrs. Fletcherman did not let the cat out of the bag.

"Flem!"

He jumped, it sounded so like an accusation.

"*What?*" it came out rather panicked and Iris caught it but merely patted his head, having the audacity to tuck a lock of his hair back into place, and Flem's heart raced with adrenalin.

What the Pan was *wrong* with her?

Unable to contain herself, Iris smiled and winked at him before going on with, "You've got your work cut out for you mister! I've got fifty fruit trees being delivered today, thanks to you!"

Flem's head spun around. "*Me?* Why? What?"

But Iris was on a roll. "I had no idea you were such a wealth of information! Why, Flem, I've got, rather, *we've* got, a whole list of customers clamoring for your services!"

Slowly, a smile formed as Flem warmed to the understanding of what she was saying.

"My services? *My* services? Really. Like what?"

"Well, apparently you know a little something about hydrangeas and fruit trees? Among other things?"

Shyly, he nodded.

Iris continued, "How would you like to teach a class sometime? I'll let you pick the night. Well, don't pick Sunday, of course. And Friday and Saturday are no good, obviously. I don't think Monday, so I guess Tuesday, Wednesday or Thursday, your choice, like I said."

Flem followed all this, his eyes starting to freeze in his face. And then he laughed, in spite of himsylph.

"Can I get back to you on that?" he asked with no apparent hint of sarcasm visible just a pleased expression on his face, laughing inside. Wow. A *class*.

But Iris wasn't through. "So, you met my, err, friend, Calypso Bulbosa she goes by now, I believe." She gave Flem an unreadable look and said mildly, "Interesting person, isn't she?"

Flem's head nodded like a schoolboy's. "Wow," was all he said.

"And horehound of all things. Maybe you and Mayapple could put your heads together and overhaul that herb section, what do you say? You'd have to run all your ideas by me first, though, just write them all down and give them to me, when you get time. Do you know any places in the wild for plants and herbs, Flem?" she segued neatly into the next item.

He grinned in reply, nodding happily but said, "We'd need the van and I can't drive." He paused a half a second and then asked, needlessly, "Got my note, huh?"

"Yes Flem," she replied drolly, smiling into his eyes. "I didn't get a chance to tell you, but Flem, I am so impressed with the way you handled everything while I was gone! That leak could have been disastrous, but not only did you fix it, you really took care of it and saved me a huge plumbing bill!"

"Aw, thanks," he mumble. "Bud could've done it, couldn't he?"

"Bud wasn't here, was he? He was out sick too," Iris countered.

Lark flashed into Flem's mind telling him about seeing Bud and China and Catalpah at Windfall Café and the 'bender' he'd been on.

He didn't say a word and Iris never noticed.

"Now," she resumed briskly, "the boys'll be here from The Green Thumb sometime today. I'd like you to help unload, okay? I'll let you know when the delivery gets here, if you don't see it first. And when you're done, give our customer a call, would you? Autumn Royal is her name, but she said everybody calls her Bing. Whatever. Here's her number." She handed him a slip of paper.

Footsteps were heard.

"Well, Mayapple, you decided to grace us with your presence. Did you get your busses all figured out? I would have thought you would have had their schedule down by now." Her manner was light but Mayapple knew her mother and knew there was a reproach in there, no matter how well disguised.

Guilt flared up, making May even more defensive but as she was about to loudly defend herself, she was stopped by a big yawn, which immediately caught Flem unaware and he too yawned hugely, defenseless against the sneaky contagion.

"Well!" said Iris, looking from one to the other, a speculative look growing on her face.

"Am I keeping you two awake?" This was said in a joking manner but both Mayapple and Flem straightened, trying to appear wide awake. Flem did better than Mayapple who kept sniffing, trying to ward off another one but apparently they just kept coming. Arching her back, she stretched her elbows up and out before reaching as far out on each side of her as she could, pandiculating.

"Mayapple!" admonished her mother. "Good grief, girl."

Flem watched in sympathetic amusement, chewing any impulse to yawn into oblivion.

"I really need a cup of tea, how about you Flem? Mom, do you need me or can I go to work now?" she asked as if she wasn't late and as if *Iris* was the one holding *her* up!

Iris stood and just looked at her errant daughter with disbelief, the daughter who was fifteen minutes late and now stood yawning, from staying up all night, no doubt, a *work night*, and was smoothly trying to skate by.

A million sarcastic retorts of how she really felt slammed through Iris's thoughts like an expensive subliminal message but she calmly licked her lips and pushed them all away, thinking twice about engaging Mayapple in verbal duel. Best to be mature about it, she was the mom. But she was *also* the boss.

Sighing, she dismissed her, making sure Mayapple knew who was dismissing whom.

"Be sure you write nine-fifteen on your time card, Mayapple, and yes, thank you for asking, I would *love* a cup of tea too. Vanilla Chai, *decaff*. One of us doesn't need caffeine today…. I think I saw that in your drawer. Don't leave the teabag in too long and make *sure* the water is boiling completely, first, okay? Then add a squirt of agave and a splash of coconut milk. There should be some in the refrigerator back there."

Mayapple looked as if she couldn't believe her ears.

"Well? Go. I need to finish my conversation here with Flem." And Iris the boss turned away.

Ignoring her disgruntled daughter, she focused once again on Flem who was looking rather nervous by now, his eyes darting back and forth between them, clenching his jaw to stifle any yawns.

"Oh, did you want tea?" Iris asked Flem innocently.

Before he could stick his neck out, Mayapple snapped, "Oh, don't worry Flem, I'll make you some too." She turned to go. "I'll see you back there."

She looked at her mom. "Shall I bring yours to you, your majesty, or are you coming to the back?"

"Mayapple..." This was stated rather long and drawn out, an innocuous warning and for once Mayapple took heed.

"No problem boss." She yawned. "I'll find you."

Chapter 55

"No!" the faerie fairly barked, making
Iris Fletcherman swallow a laugh.

THE WATER HAD boiled and the tea made although not delivered. Mayapple procrastinated, taking greedy little sips of her own, blowing on it in between slurps.

Hearing Flem's footsteps, she looked over his shoulder and saw her mother in the distance walking through a doorway, heading up front.

Flem was now standing in front of her, trying to look awake but it wasn't working and Mayapple shoved a mug of tea in his direction.

He mouthed *thank you* at her gratefully and leaned back, inhaling deeply of the promise inherent.

Meanwhile, Mayapple further fixed her mother's, then brushed a "I'll be right back" towards him and left.

Returning five minutes later, Mayapple took in Flem, still leaning against the counter where she'd left him, his eyes unfocused as he appeared to drift in dreamtime.

Hearing her approach, he reanimated and took a sip of tea, yawning as he did so.

"Suck it down, Flemmy-boy, we've got work - " but here she sucked in air as yet another yawn racked her body.

"As I was saying, work to do," she finished lamely with watery eyes and a laugh.

"I made ours pretty strong," she added. "I figured we needed it."

Flem was looking at her and nodding, but his look was vacuous.

Mayapple took a healthy swig of her drink and said, "I can't do that again. I sure didn't get much sleep. You either apparently. Flem!"

He jumped. "*What*? Why do you do that?"

Mayapple was beginning to perk up as caffeine went from room to room, turning on the lights. "Bad habit I picked up from my mother," she said mischievously and then sighed. "Well, c'mon, you got the list?"

Flem nodded and padded his front pocket.

He paused then said, "Your mom was in such a strange mood. She had lots of good things to say, though. Wants me to teach a class and us to redo the herb section. And I'm helping with a delivery later, she's expecting a pretty big order of fruit trees. "

He smiled tentatively, the tea warming his soul along with everything else.

Mayapple had stopped, and with eyes like saucers she said, "Whoa! A *class*?"

Flem hadn't been nervous about it until he got the full effect of the Mayapple Treatment. She was a force unto herself, when she wanted to be.

She's *jealous*!

Realization dawned and just like that the cold shiver that had threatened to rattle his wings, disappeared.

Warmth flooded him for this human who was unknowingly giving him what he considered high praise.

"I have no idea how to teach a class Mayapple. I mean, wow, I'm flattered, but what should I do? Will you help me?" he asked desperately.

"Oh, quit hamming it up, drama queen. Are all faeries such drama queens? Of course I'll help you. We'll organize the whole thing. So, what's for today?"

"Here," he said, pulling the piece of paper from his pocket and handing it to her.

"She talked about quite a few things, I'm not exactly sure what we're working on."

"Oh no!" Mayapple cried, skimming down it. "She wants us to hang the City Center baskets today! Flem, I can't do that, I'm too tired," she wailed. "Not today!"

The Sylph pulled the paper from her hand, frowning at it.

"No, look here. That's not today. That's tomorrow. Gee," he mimicked, "Are all human women such, *drama queens*?"

"Flem! Okay, good. What's today's? Drink your tea!" she added, attempting to restore the balance of just who was in charge here.

He grinned, a rather irritating sylphsatisfied smirk really, and took a big drink. It was so good, he did it again and soon tipped it back, draining it. "Thank you. That hit the spot."

"Oh Flem, look what she did – we *were* going to hang City Center baskets today but she took pity on us and crossed it off until tomorrow."

"Yeah, either that or she didn't trust us today…"

Mayapple frowned at him, realizing he was quite probably right. Oh well.

"Today, we're collaborating on a new herb section, she wants a whole new idea. Boy, that sounds like fun to me. And look, what's this? Oh, I see, she'd detailed that you are going to be needed at delivery time, for the unloading of fifty fruit trees. Holy cow, is this one of the ladies from Monday, Flem, when you were here alone?"

He nodded.

"Good job!" She stuck out a hand to shake and patted him on the back with the other.

Further perusing the list, she exclaimed, "Oh, and we've got an order for some Thunbergia baskets." She cast a speculative look at her cohort and asked, "*This* doesn't have anything to do with Monday too, does it?"

Flem grinned happily and replied, "We probably better write up a note to go with it regarding its extreme sensitivity to frost."

"Oh, I didn't know that," exclaimed his companion. "They're so delicate though, I'm not surprised. Mom said to make several. Well, c'mon, let's go look at the herbs. She just wants ideas right now. I guess maybe Friday we'll plant Thunbergia baskets after hanging City Center tomorrow…guess we better get a good night's sleep."

Flem tried to look insulted but couldn't so instead smiled sheepishly.

"So," hedged his girl friend, "Are *you* going to the S Club this weekend, Flem?"

His heart leaped at the idea but he kept his words noncommittal, "I don't know. Why?"

"Oh, *why*, '" she said sarcastically. "I wanna go too!"

"Well, you know, if it was just me, of course you could go. But I guess Lark would be the one to ask. I'll talk to him tonight. Er, well, maybe not," he back-tracked thinking about their lack of sleep the night before. "We'll see. I'll talk to him soon," he temporized, "and let you know. Now what about these herbs?" he asked as they came to a halt. They both stood and appraised the few shelves in front of them.

"Let's make a list of what's here," suggested Mayapple and Flem willing took dictation as she called them off.

"Hmmph, well, I know some I'd like to see here that aren't, how about you?" he asked.

She slanted him a look. "Yeah." She paused. "What do you have in mind? Mint?"

"Oh, there must be mint here, we must have just missed it. Surely she has mint." Flem thrust his tablet and pen at Mayapple and went foraging himsylph and was rewarded with a label below an empty row that proved his point.

Satisfied, he rejoined Mayapple and they stood mirroring each other with crossed arms as they contemplated the display.

"Well, what about this, Mayapple?" Flem asked. "We'll remove the display behind it to make more room and we'll build a hut where people can go in and find everything they need *for* herbs plus a great selection, and maybe sell some books and cards or something with advice on it, you know, brochures, and hey, lots of things, how about that idea?" he finished rather abashedly, suddenly feeling sylphconscious for speaking up like that.

She thought about it for a moment and then said, "I like it. I've got a great book at home called the Herbal Drugstore and maybe we could order more and pair them with some of the herbs mentioned?"

Now it was Flem's turn to stare at Mayapple and she did a "aw gee whiz" look, toe-in-the-dirt act.

"Looks like between the two of us, we'll come up with a way to boost the herb sales, partner." She smiled when she said it. "Let's go sit in the break room and we'll swing by mom's office to pick up some of her catalogs that she orders stuff from." Mayapple led the way and Flem was content to follow the leader.

"I wonder what our budget is?" Flem heard ahead of him, and wondered if he was suppose to answer but apparently not, as Mayapple rapped hard on her mother's office door and rattled the locked door, calling, "Mom. Mother! Are you in there?"

Flem watched with a skeptical eye at such theatrical dramatics and was about to speak up when Mayapple took him by surprise, tilting her head and mouthing, "C'mon!" as if they weren't supposed to be going in.

She had the door unlocked and was inside, beckoning to him as if *they* were in cahoots!

His heart raced at this seemingly innocent action and he was caught – until she ordered him to "Come *in*!" and so he did.

"I thought we were just stopping to get some catalogs, Mayapple. *What is the matter with you?*"

"Shhhh!" she hushed at him. "Look." She opened a drawer in a back cabinet and there was a stash of chocolate the likes of which Flem had never seen.

"Her private collection," Mayapple whispered. "She thinks I don't know about it. HA! Help yourself. I always do," rapidly lifting the lid on a white box to eye the remains.

"Ah, *Mayapple*. What about the catalogs?"

Mayapple shifted the wad in her mouth to one cheek and pointed to a stack under a paper weight on the boss's desk, swallowing as she did so.

"Don't you want a piece?" she asked, lifting another lid, this one to a fat red box.

"Well...maybe one," said the faerie with a sweet tooth and helped himsylph, feeling like a thief.

He popped it into his mouth and garbled, "Let's GO."

"Okay, grab some of those, would you?" she nodded towards the catalogs before she looked regretfully down into the drawer, hating to say goodbye to such abundance.

It was at that moment the office door swung open and Iris's eyes caught Mayapple's and didn't waver, even though Flem was there too.

"Well," she said coolly, "I guess when you haven't had enough sleep, you must also get an overwhelming urge for chocolate too, hmm? Yes Mayapple, I knew you knew about my cache, quit looking so guilty. I don't care if you and Flem have some candy. I have to presume you *do* have another reason for being in here though. I hope." A question in her eyes, followed immediately with an "Oh, *relax* Flem. Following Mayapple and getting into my candy stash is not a big crime. Now, *why* are you two in my office?"

"Catalogs, Ma'am," said Flem succinctly.

Mayapple looked rather flushed but immediately pulled herself together. "Flem and I have a great plan, mom, for the herb section. I suggested we come get some catalogs so we could tentatively estimate how much it'll all cost. And Flem had a great idea for the outside," but Iris cut her off.

"Good. Good. Write it all down. Take the catalogs. Do you want another piece of chocolate?"

Oh, her mother knew how to tighten the screws of guilt and Mayapple had to laugh at her one-uppedness.

"No. Thanks for asking, though," she replied sweetly. "Flem?"

"No!" the faerie fairly barked, making Iris Fletcherman swallow a laugh.

Mayapple started towards the door and Flem nervously picked up the catalogs from his boss's desk, wishing he was anywhere but here.

"How many?" he managed to say.

"Oh, take them all," Iris spoke up. "I'm so glad you kids are on it so quickly. Good job! I'll look for your plan and estimate some time today. Mayapple, when the delivery comes in, I want you to go to number three and double check that we're all ready to go to City Center tomorrow, okay? And Flem, don't forget to call the customer after you price the trees." She handed him a sheaf of papers, saying, "The elastic-attached tags to use are in here. I think it's better if each one has its own tag. Oh, and be sure to find the other ones in there too, with care instructions on them. I printed them up earlier."

She stopped and it was clear they were done here. In case there was even a question remaining, she smiled, a predatory look, and Flem couldn't escape fast enough, even though there was nothing to fear from her.

Mayapple practically snatched his arm out the door, making him trip a little over his own feet, his eyes never leaving Iris's and he cursed himsylph for such faint-heartedness.

Mayapple reached across him to throw in a "Thanks for the chocolate, we'll get the herb plan back to you before we go home. Bye mom!" and she slammed the door, not too hard though.

"Get some *sleep* tonight, both of you. That's an *order*," was heard from the other side of the closed door.

Adrenalin and tea were taking ahold now, and Mayapple shouted back, "Yeah right, mom, no problem!" She had actually meant it seriously but it came out rather sarcastic.

Each syllable of "Mayapple," was drawn out in a growl and they dashed away before it was too late.

It was with perfect timing two hours later, after lunch, that they heard the delivery truck pull in.

Whimsey C. Nimble

"Go ahead Flem, I'll finish this up. I think we've got a good start on it. I'll go deliver it to the boss, and then head back to number three, to get the order ready for tomorrow. Come find me if you get done before I do."

Chapter 56

———— ❈ ————

Was that, Oh My God! Flem! *What* are you doing?

$\mathcal{T}$HE DELIVERY DOOR was up and Acaulais and his brother Schafta came
to a stop near the open entry, watching Flem approach, trying to look
like they weren't watching him as they kept moving, working, but of course
Schafta being the nice guy he was, called out "Hello! Good to see you! *Flem*,
right? How ya doing?" hand out in greeting, even though he too was nervous.

The brothers had an on-going conversation about this new guy at
Fletcherman's, whether he was a faerie or not. Acaulais, the shorter and more
conservative of the two with the curly mat of red hair thought Flem was one
of the faeries they'd heard about but Schafta wasn't quite so sure. (Actually,
he secretly *did* think there was a good chance Flem was a faerie but being
sensitive to other people's needs, he never agreed with his brother as he was
concerned Acualais might say something to their dad, Moss, and it might
come back to Mrs. Fletcherman's ears, and he didn't want to be the one responsible if Flem was found out and fired. So, he disagree on principle, with
Acaulis.) "No, he's *not*," he would say whenever Acaulis would bring it up.

But now today, here he came in person (so-to-speak) and both brothers
were agog with intensive curiosity, trying hard to be casual, and not succeed-
ing very well.

The tall thin man approaching definitely had a rather strange build but
it only enhanced his innate charm, no matter how nervous he got. You had to
like the guy, especially because he had some kind of strange shoulder thing
going on, yee-ick, that he actually bore with good grace.

His clothes somehow didn't seem to fit him right. Oh, he looked normal
but he was often seen pulling on the waist band of his pants.

Whimsey C. Nimble

And that scarf. He wasn't fooling any body with that scarf. Schafta knew he was hiding one of two things, but he was betting it was the latter.

First of all, it *could* be wings. He'd heard stories, but didn't discount that the poor sod had some kind of deformity going on. He never let on what he suspected though and wondered if it hampered Flem's social life. He was an odd duck, he was.

Flem glanced from one to the other, instantly aware of something else in the air but it was elusive and he wasn't sure if he was imagining it or not.

Acaulis immediately jumped down from the ledge, sort of like Humpty Dumpty taking a step, and walked over to the driver's side, climbing up and back in, getting the papers he'd left there.

Flem grabbed Schafta's long thin hand and shook it, looking at the lanky man with those little tufts of soft purplish hair that grew all over his pate.

They both appeared so odd to Flem but he always treated them with the utmost respect, as they did him. Mrs. Fletcherman had told him they worked for their dad, and he bet just by looking at them they didn't have much of a social life. Poor guys.

The back of the truck was opened and both Campion brothers quickly and efficiently unloaded fifty fruit trees, Flem standing sylphconsciously by. To his surprise, they unloaded four extra as a bonus for the order and that little dilly right there made Flem's day. He couldn't wait to tell Iris. Imagine, the Nursery was getting *free* trees, and it was because of him.

The paperwork took no time at all and soon The Green Thumb truck was on its way.

Flem watched them pull out and Schafta gave a salute goodbye just before they disappeared around the corner.

For the moment he was alone and he took a deep breath of relief, hoping he didn't wear out before the tea did.

He walked over to utilize a nearby desk and rifled through his papers, then proceeded to systematically tag the trees.

A good hour later he was finally able to say he was finished and looked for the customer's number in with the stuff Iris gave him.

Here it was, 'Autumn Royal' or *Bing* for short. He chuckled and wondered if she had apricots for eyes and cherries for a mouth. Or possibly the other way around.

Laughing, he dialed the number and when he told her who he was, she took the opportunity to express her gratitude once again for his knowledge.

She went on to tell him that as soon as these started bearing fruit, he would get one of the first jars of jam.

"Aw, that's really nice of you, Autumn," he started but she interrupted him.

"Please, call me Bing, everybody does."

"It was very kind of you to give Fletcherman's this big order. Thank you."

"Oh, you're welcome. Will you be there this afternoon when I come get them?" Bing asked matter-of-factly.

"Well, yesss." It came out in sibilant slowness.

"Good! Maybe you can help me load them up? I'm probably going to have to make at least a couple of trips, even though my pickup is pretty good size. Shall I just ask for Flem? I can't wait to meet you Flem, you sound like a big guy. Well, I'll see you this afternoon. Are you married?" She tacked it on so casually, Flem almost didn't hear it, but he did.

With reluctance, he answered, "No," wondering about this strange human race that seemed so frantic to get into one's personal space.

Just before they hung up, a Zing from Flem's past showed up, trapping his mind in amazement and he involuntarily cried out "Zing!"

"What? No, no, *Bing*," said the voice in the receiver, confused.

Zing buzzed around the faerie's head, a crazed bumble bee of energy, darting in and ringing in Flem's left ear - Zing! Zing! Zing! and then around his head again 'til Flem cried out "Zing! Stop!"

"I'm not doing anything! Don't call me *Zing*. It's *Bing*."

"I gotta go!" gasped Flem at the riot he was involved in.

"Yeah…yeah. Hey, I'll ask for you by name when I get there. Bye." She hung up, thankfully.

Zing did not let up and Flem saw this crazy hot spot was darting to and fro towards the back door. He followed. Out the door and back towards the old greenhouse he was led.

Totally bewildered and concerned, he crawled through the window door in broad daylight during work hours. His heart raced, his wings surged in place, Sylph adrenalin starting to race with faerie apprehension.

Whimsey C. Nimble

Everything looked normal and he was not seeing any cause for alarm. Nothing looked out of place from this morning and then he heard it, a tiny, piteous mewling.

Looking around he listened attentively, his ears picking up and tightening with the focus.

There it was again, faintly. Zing exploded in his face momentarily before reappearing high in a far corner, buzzing loudly to get Flem's attention.

A small kitty was seen clinging to some old scaffolding. It was easy to see the path he'd climbed to get there and Flem didn't blame him for not wanting to descend in the same manner, it was quite steep and convoluted.

A chunk of dried moss fell with a dusty thud, as of course it was the rogue, readjusting his hold, again complaining it was life or death and he really needed some help here.

Meanwhile Mayapple was adrift in scentsations, the sweet dusky presence of alyssum making her heady with joy, as usual. Forcing herself to straighten up, she backed away from the basket she had her nose buried in. Smiling, she looked around. This was definitely a version of *her* heaven, surrounded by the lushness of vibrant colorful flowers on all sides, with bees humming in the background, intent on the bounty call, oblivious to all else.

Carefully, she started at the end of the first row of baskets and with an expert eye, checked it on all sides for one final inspection before tomorrow, delivery day downtown.

Letting go of the big rounded swaying container, she noted with satisfaction that the Johnny-jump-ups they'd planted near the bottom were reaching up even as the main stem had lowered to accommodate gravity.

Further up, fat pansy faces dotted the sides, all interspersed within the spreading arms of alyssum.

Moving on, she inhaled the musky heady scent deeply once again of the small white flowers in the next one too. This would take her all day if she stopped to smell each basket... but was unable to stop. Breathing in, her eyes closed and she was startled to hear footsteps cross the yard towards the old greenhouse.

Releasing the basket, Mayapple whirled around and dashed to the back door just in time to see movement disappear through the so-called door.

Flem?

With a quick eye to her task, she hesitated briefly before she turned her back on it and dashed across the yard too, never even seeing her mother standing in the shadow just inside the back door of greenhouse number one.

Poking through the makeshift door, she called, "Flem?" as she looked around. "Was that, Oh My God! Flem! *What* are you doing?"

There he was, perched, sort-of, in a very awkward place, up near the peak of the roof, a small kitten clutched closed to his chest. His wings were out, hanging at an accommodating droop behind him.

He was planning on jumping!

Mayapple couldn't believe her eyes.

But before he made a move, the kitten wriggled free and raced pell-mell over the faerie's chest, not beyond a little toe nail dig every so of often and disappeared over a shoulder, as if he knew what he was about.

Flem froze in place, his eyes never moving a muscle.

Mrs. Fletcherman coughed slightly to let them know she was there also before saying, "Do be careful Flem. Is there anything we can do to help?"

Mayapple knew no bounds of love for her mother.

Flem was frozen stiff but upon hearing those words, icy panic started to thaw.

"Thank you," he said nervously.

After he got himsylph under control he shrugged his shoulders, trying to adjust his passenger and then leaned out, his wings stretching taut as they geared up and he eased into the air, fluttering. He could have jumped but he didn't need more needle picking toes in his bare skin. So, he opted for long and slow.

As if he'd been doing it his whole life, (he had) he gently glided down at an angle, furling the minute his feet touched the ground.

For just a moment there was silence, then both the boss and her daughter erupted into applause, well peppered with praise.

Iris was grinning broadly, which Flem thought was a good sign, wondering how in Pan to proceed from here. This changed everything. He fervently hoped it was for the better.

Chapter 57

Come and see me before you leave, okay Flem?

TRYING TO BE nonchalant, it was still hard for Iris not to stare around her.

It was obvious he was spending a lot of time here. There was a homier feel about it and the whole place was much tidier, no old planters in sight.

She was itching, well, okay, NOT itching, considering her recent ailment…rather, just extremely curious to see what lay behind that old bamboo wall Brody'd built, back when this was the main building.

Impromptu, she let her feelings go and impulsively gave in to what she wanted to do.

Mayapple was by this time helping Flem get his wing ties on and Iris noted she seemed rather *familiar* with the process…

Hmm.

Mayapple caught her mother's eyes and then blinked at what she saw there. Her mother was making a face at her and nodding her head purposefully as if Mayapple would know what she meant and suddenly, she did.

Her mother was saying she was going to give Flem the old greenhouse, right *now*! *His* place!

Mayapple couldn't say a word. She was too overcome, a delayed reaction to the drama of moments ago, her emotions at the flood gate.

Her mother stepped forward and put a hand on her arm, but never took her eyes from their, ah, *unusual* employee…

"Flem," she said almost hesitantly but gaining force with her remembered purpose, and why.

"Flem!" she said again clearing her throat decisively.

"I was going to wait, but I've made a decision and what the heck, now seems like as good a time as ever."

The Sylph was all ears, (well, and wings too) a nervous sense of apprehension trying to clamp on to him but he kept it at bay, only allowing positive scenarios to flow through his mind versus always picturing the worst. But it was hard, giving his predisposition.

"First off, let me tell you how impressed I am with your abilities."

He relaxed fractionally but still his heart raced at being so, well, *naked* before her.

He really hoped this wasn't the goodbye speech.

She went on, "You've helped me out so much, it was all so unexpected. I even got a call just a little while ago from my friend Calypso Bulbosa and man, she was crowing over you!" Her eyebrows rose and she gave him an all-knowing smile that made Flem feel all secrets were bared. And that it was okay, he didn't have to be ashamed to just be who he was. A *faerie*, mostly disguised as human, currently with a *kitten* on his back, between his *wing* blades...

"And I'm very happy over the herb proposal you two have put together." She included a quick glance at Mayapple, who was sniffing and biting her lip in anticipation nearby, before she went on. "We'll work on it before you go off adventuring for *horehound...*"

He nodded, wondering where this was going when Iris reached out and caught him by the shoulders, uncomfortably aware she was near to touching his *wings*, for God's sakes, and recoiled just a hair.

Like a rabbit caught in a high beam, he stared into her eyes and hardly heard the words, "Flem, the greenhouse is *yours*. Live here as long as you like."

Getting choked up herself, Iris was rudely pushed aside by her brash daughter who threw her arms around Flem while jumping up and down at the same time, pinching the stow-a-way who reacted with a haughty "Mrrr!" and a flexing of foot to remind this ride just *who* was in charge here.

Unable to comprehend the enormity of this magnanimous moment, Flem stared dumbly at his boss over Mayapple's rising and falling shoulder.

"Mayapple!" ordered her mother sharply. "For God's sakes, get *off* of him. Leave the poor man...oh," she trailed off awkwardly for a moment. "Get back to work," she finished, not knowing what else to say and feeling rather awkward with the whole deal, but happy too, to be the benefactor. Change was in the air. She turned to go.

"Wait! Wait, Mrs. Fletcherman -"

"Oh for goodness sakes, call me Iris, would you?"

"Oh! Oh yeah. Of course. Iris? *Thank you*, oh great Pan, *thank you*." He kept looking at her, trying to come up with words to convey the enormity of his gratitude to her, when he flashed on the bonus given them from The Green Thumb and proceeded to fill her in on their good fortune of four free trees.

Iris smiled at the bonus and made a mental note to call Moss Campion, the old pirate she thought fondly, and thank him. He'd certainly settled down since the old days.

Flem still had a haunted look about him, rather hunched over, with a stray twitch overtaking him a couple of times.

Iris realized the best thing she could do right now was leave and quickly turned to do so, saying over her shoulder, "All right, as soon as you can, get back to work. Mayapple, I would bet he probably *doesn't* need your help, so YOU can get back to work right now I bet, hmm?"

Heading back the same way she'd come in following Mayapple following Flem, she paused with one denim-clad leg over the sill and surprised them all, including herself with, "Just how many kittens are there, anyway? I presume there are others, right?"

Mayapple and Flem looked at each other and then at her and Flem said, "Ah, there's six altogether," a worrisome frown appearing against his wishes.

Mayapple looked askance at her mother, wondering what was coming next, but she needn't have worried.

"I'd like to see them sometime. I think I'd like one." And off she went, down the path.

"Hurry up and get back to work you two," her yell was heard as she walked away.

"I better go," said Mayapple "You better too! Want some help with your shirt? What about your friend there?"

Now that the moment was returning back to normal, Iris Fletcherman's good-will bomb was finally seeping in, and he turned big eyes on Mayapple.

Mayapple grinned into his face, carrying on with, "Flem, Flem, Flem! Oh my God! This is so great! I'm so happy for you. For us! For *me*."

"I *know*. I can't believe it." And he couldn't.

Never had he known such great good fortune.

A wave of panic assailed him. Always before, in his *old* life, something would happen to prevent the fulfillment of such promise.

Did he really *deserve* such bounty?

Well, of course he did! There was a part of him that didn't see it as a reward, per se, but just the natural order of things. It felt *right*, on an intrinsic level. The more he lived in the present, focusing on what was next, and did his best, then his path went easy.

Everyone here seemed so accepting of who he was that he blossomed. He had no contention with other Sylphs who were still female. (He laughed at the word, 'still.')

Perhaps it had always been *her* own fault, well, more like *perception*, that the others didn't like him/her, back in Thimbleberry.

Perhaps it had been her own sylphconscious behavior, her own low sylphesteem, that erected an imaginary barrier.

Perhaps if *she* had been less prickly, they would have come to her parties, and invited her to theirs. Oh, she'd gone to a few, but it wasn't nearly as many as she would have liked.

But couple that with *staying male*, when there were no other males other than those rare ones that were sequestered during a brief mating, and it was too much, too over- powering, too raw.

He fled.

And here he was.

Mayapple was waiting, hoping to embarrass him being so obviously caught daydreaming.

"Hell-looo," she drawled, crossing her eyes at him, bring him back to earth. "I'm leaving. I'll be in number three. Are you done with the delivery?" she questioned.

He shook his head. "Not quite," he said while tugging his shirt into place but holding it up around his shoulders as he turned and presented his back to her, a mute appeal to remove the fuzzy tick. If possible.

It was not to be and Flem finally said in frustration, "Oh, just leave the little bugger. *Pan.* Help me with my scarf, would you? We've *got* to get back to work."

Mayapple rolled her eyes as it seemed he just now realized the importance of that statement.

"Yeah," she agreed. "You ready?"

Whimsey C. Nimble

The faerie followed her out the window-door, his eyes searching for the invisible Zing. Not seeing anything, it was with surprise when his eyes landed on a spot of seemingly sunlight that brightened for a moment before blending once again.

Flem paused and looked harder but Mayapple urged him to shake-a-leg, buddy, and they hurried back to work.

The day was dragging on and the tea was wearing off. Flem couldn't remember being this tired in a long time and was thoroughly ready to lose his irritating hitchhiker.

He was close to being finished and looked forward to joining Mayapple down in number three. He *had* to get the small demon *off* his back, he was way too hot and itchy.

Not quite done cleaning up, it was with dismay that he saw Mrs. Fletcherman pointing him out to a rather large woman, up front.

Mrs. Fletcherman waved behind the woman's back and gave Flem the thumbs up signal, mouthing '*Fruit Trees!*' at him, and making a big deal about the approaching customer.

He nodded wearily, the shine he usually saw around the boss hitting him the wrong way at the moment. Cha, sometimes her perennial good cheer was a little hard to take.

He knew it was no doubt because his late night was really starting to catch up with him, but it did little to assuage his growing impatience.

"Hi. *You're* Flem?" The customer came striding up like she was in charge and that in itself annoyed him.

"Yeah! Hi. And who might you be?" he asked brusquely, trying to swallow his feelings and smother his unwarranted irritation.

Instead of replying, the woman had the audacity to remark, "I thought you said you were big," in an accusatory tone.

The faerie just looked at her in mute astonishment.

After an uncomfortable pause that neither hurried to fill, the woman capitulated and said, formally, "Autumn Royale, how do you do?" holding out a large chapped hand to shake.

Flem took it and it was all he could do to not cry out as she bore down, obviously intent on proving something.

"My trees?" she added, as if he'd stolen them and was waiting for the ransom.

Shaking his hand quietly as he led the way back, he grasped internally for the professional control he so badly felt the lack-of.

Leading her to the delivery area where her order sat waiting patiently, Flem realized with regret that he'd forgotten to completely finish the job and clean-up. Dirt littered the area where they'd been unloaded, his paperwork scattered where he'd left it after Zing had shown up, one sheet upside down on the floor.

The guilt at not being one hundred percent prepared when he'd thought he was, elbowed him and stepped in front. For some reason it seemed like this uncouth woman was in the wrong.

He was tired, too tired, and she was an unwelcome thorn in his day. He knew he was being unreasonable but she bugged him.

"Well, you sure look different than you sounded, you know, that day, Monday."

Flem's eyes twisted and he scowled. Pfft! As if he should apologize for his body size!

"Yeah, well, you're not exactly what I pictured either." He laughed. Actually it was a sideways snicker, as he went on with, "Is everyone in your family a fruit?" thinking he had been close in one of his summations – except it was her *eyes* that looked like over ripe apricots and her mouth a small withered cherry.

He laughed again and she gave him a dirty look. "What's so funny, bub? I haven't paid for these yet, and I don't *have* to buy them from this nursery, ya know."

The effect of her words was like a glass of cold water thrown into his face. Flem was brought back instantly, Sylph adrenalin riding the same wave as sylphconsciousness at his position here. The customer was always right.

Giving her a sickly smile, he pulled a "Sorry," from his soul and set about tidying the place quickly, issuing curt instructions as to where she should back her truck up into the bay here, avoiding eye contact. He was still feeling owly, but was doing his utmost to be respectful.

It didn't take long before the first batch was squeezed in rim to rim. She took off, after telling him she'd be back in about half an hour.

He was standing there dissolutely, at odds with himsylph in this small lull, when Iris showed up.

"Where'd she go?" she demanded like the boss she was.

"Oh. Well, she went to take the first half home. Said she'd be back (yawn...) in half an hour."

"Flem." She made it a short, abrupt sound. "Did she pay you yet? I didn't see her up front."

"No! But she said she'd be right back..." he let it trail off.

"Exactly... No doubt she will be." Iris looked at him sternly.

After the message was drilled in, she continued, "I *always* collect the money first and then load up the vehicle."

Flem flinched. Duh. It was obvious now.

"Sorry," he muttered, embarrassment flaming his cheeks, mortified that he'd never thought of her paying for her order! Never, ever again would he do this, stay up to the wee hours on a work night.

Iris didn't say much but nodded seriously at him, a half sympathetic smile on her lips.

"Won't happen again," he added, feeling like a fool, his sylphesteem continuing to crumple.

"Good. Don't worry about it. I know you're generally quite conscientious." She smiled, meaning it. "She'll be back, I'm sure. But *next* time..." she let it hang.

"Oh yes ma'am! I won't forget," swore Flem fervently.

"All right, go ahead and wait for her," ordered Iris, as if Flem had any other plan. "I'll be around," she concluded and then left, walking towards the front.

Flem breathed a big sigh, feeling like something under the rug, thinking longingly of his hammock and when he might crawl into it again. It seemed eons away. How was he going to get through the day?

But, Mrs. Fletcherman had *given him the greenhouse*!

He was so tired he was almost numb to this wonderful news. But he knew tomorrow would be a great day – the day *after* he got a good night's sleep was always a good one.

The close sound of a vehicle backing in again brought Flem around and Autumn Royale opened her door as he watched.

Startling him over his shoulder Mrs. Fletcherman said, "Oh good, she's back," making him jump and his nerves took off, his stomach involuntarily clenching.

He looked around, prepared to smile and nod, but Mrs. Fletcherman was contemplating *him*, one finger on her lips as she pressed down on them, then biting her thumb, shaking her head, her eyes on his.

Oh great Pan, now what? His wings clattered in their shroud-like bindings, causing one small kitten who had been able to sleep through all this annoyance, to wake up.

Flem felt it but before he could think 'Oh not now!' the little devil first stretched completely, itty bitty toe nails barely hanging on to tender flesh but hanging on, nonetheless.

The kitten's ride straightened right up, his back arching, a distracted look upon his face as he tried to keep Mrs. Fletcherman in mind.

She was watching all this with an incredulous look upon her face and Flem was just sure things were going down the drain rapidly, his heart tightening more so every minute.

By this time the small menace managed to tunnel his way out the bottom of the binding shirt and to came up for air, so-to-speak, inside Flem's pants, specifically right over his butt.

"*Ooob!*" The high pitched cry played counter point to his body twitching as the stow-a-way slithered head first down to his ankle, smelled freedom and bounded away, heading deeper into the shop, much to Flem's dismay. He reached down and rubbed at the cat marks left behind.

Autumn Royale walked through the entry just then and up to the two of them, not being witness to anything amiss.

"Hi," greeted the boss, taking over the moment, "You must be Autumn, right?"

The heavy set blond nodded and Iris continued, "I'm Iris Fletcherman, nice to meet you."

"Likewise," said cherry mouth. "Call me Bing, all my friends do." She threw a distrustful stare at Flem, as if they'd just see who had the upper hand now.

Flem half-way expected her to stick her tongue out at him.

"You got that invoice Flem? I'll just take Bing here up front right now since I'm here, while you load the rest of her trees."

Whimsey C. Nimble

Feeling like a schmuck and a loser, Flem wondered if Iris really thought he was incompetent of finishing this sale. That's what it felt like. A small, dim part of him said 'Hey, you're being too sensitive, overreacting,' just like back in the canyon but it was too easy to fall into poor-me. Cha, he was not ever going to stay up drinking again! The day had taken a dive and he didn't know what to do to pull it up. Poor me.

Much too soon Iris and Bing were returning and unfortunately, he wasn't done loading so he had to bear the extra scrutiny he felt they were aiming at him as he worked. It had been much easier alone.

Actually, they weren't talking of him at all, extra sylphconscious that he was, they were discussing orchard planting up north. Concluding their conversation, Iris shook the customer's hand, perfunctorily thanking her repeatedly, then smoothly turned and uttered those fateful words no employee wants to hear, especially near the end of a long day.

"Come and see me before you leave, okay Flem?" She gave a patent little smile and waited for his acknowledgment, then left.

"Here, I'll hand you these last two," said Autumn Royale late in the game.

Hopping in the back with Flem and the budding tree farm she quickly and efficiently helped him secure her load and was gone in a flash. She felt a little guilty complaining about this guy to Mrs. Fletcherman, after all, she *was* the owner, but appeased her conscious with the promise she'd made to her to come back for fertilizer next week.

Deciding to get it over with, Flem took himsylph directly up front before searching Mayapple out.

Cha, he felt like crap.

"Yes, Mrs. Fletcherman?" he asked hollowly, a damning yawn clawing its way out.

"Oh Flem. You and Mayapple. I don't know what you kids were doing last night, but you're not in very good shape today, are you? Either one of you." She sighed and then went on.

"My new best friend, Autumn Royal, known to her *friends* as *Bing*," she stated but it was with a facetious accent that she wanted Flem, really, one of her favorite employees, to hear before going on.

"Bing was not happy with you Flem. She said you yawned a lot and something about a disparaging remark regarding her family."

The Sylph sagged, this was far worse than he'd anticipated. Oh dam the mead, the party, Bud, Lark. This was all their fault!

"Now don't look so woebegone, it's not that bad. She struck me as a real butt kisser but still, *she is the customer.* That can't happen again, okay?"

He shuffled his feet, wishing the floor would just open up and swallow him.

"Sorry," he mumbled around a yawn, mortified to feel tears building in his eyes.

"Alright, go ahead. Is it cleaned up in the delivery area? Okay then, go find Mayapple, she should be back down in number three, preparing for to-morrow. Big day, tomorrow. Send her up here, would ya? I've got a few things I'd like to discuss with *her* too."

Flem's belly flip flopped at this order. Apparently they were both in trouble. For some reason it didn't make him feel any better, although he kind of thought it should.

With relief, he quickly nodded his head and hurried away, faster than was seemly, to spread the bad word.

Chapter 58

Oh Santolina, *why* did I give it to him?

$\mathscr{H}$E FOUND MAYAPPLE with dirt all over her hands, some on her cheek, and a stain on her chest.

"What are you doing?" the faerie asked in surprise, since these all had been finished quite some time ago.

"Oh, there was one, there always seems to be at least *one*, who doesn't get watered properly or something, and some of the plants shrivel right up. Bah, so I'm throwing some fillers in."

"Whose was it?" asked the Sylph even though it was *such* a moot point. Who cared?

Mayapple yawned tiredly and retorted, "Who cares?"

"Wait a minute, that was mine, wasn't it?"

"I'm not sure," hedged his companion, poking some purple verbena down next to some double pink wave petunias. "God, I'm so ready to go home. I'm so tired," she finished in a whine.

"Oh Mayapple, look what you're doing. There's a big gap right down there. You can't have air pockets, you know it promotes root rot. Take those out and, here, let me do it," his hands came out to take it from her and her eyes snapped.

Pushing him away, she growled, "*I* will finish what *I* started. *IF* there hadn't been an air hole in here in the first place, *these* wouldn't have wilted!"

"Oh, are you saying it's *my* fault? If you didn't talk so darn much all the time, I probably wouldn't have been distracted!"

She threw mud at him she was so mad.

Flem gaped at her. Appalled and eyes bright, he said, "I'm done. I'm going to check out. See you tomorrow, *Mayapple*." He said her name as if it were a curse before remembering Iris's request. "Oh, before I forget, your *mother* wants to see you before you go home," and stomped off, back to the employee area, checked out and guiltily hurried rather stiff legged back to *his* greenhouse.

Oh Pan. What a strange day.

Surely it called for a mead. It wasn't everyday someone gave him a place to live!

What if Iris changed her mind? His performance had certainly been less than stellar today of all days.

Sliding in the window door he was soon rummaging in one of the cubbies where he'd stashed some supplies, and pulled out the bottle from last night. It had about two swallows left in the bottom.

Cold dread that she would change her mind formed a posse in the pit of his stomach and rode out.

Sinking into his hammock, he uncorked the bottle and swallowed, his eyes closing almost instantly.

Mayapple caught up with her mother in the office and before Iris uttered a word, said "What?" rather belligerently, or so Iris felt.

"Why are you so dirty?" first questioned the boss. "I thought we were ready for tomorrow, which was suppose to be today, originally. What have you been doing?"

"Oh my God. Not you too," snapped the girl with an attitude. "What do you want?" she said petulantly. "I want to go home." Scowl.

Taking a big breath in the face of the current atmosphere, Iris rode it out and said, "Tell me they're all ready for tomorrow and I'll be happy."

Mayapple's shoulders sagged and she agreed, "Yes, they are. *Now.*"

A scant moment's pause and then she said in a much more reasonable voice, "What do you want mom? I'm sorry I'm so tired today. Is that it? Don't give me the speech, I know what you'll say, and no, I won't do it again," she lied straight to her mother's face because she was already planning on it, first chance she got.

Sighing and shaking her head, Iris the boss carefully informed her, "The hose in number one wasn't shut off all the way and I found it leaking all over the counter. I believe it was you who used it last?" rather rhetorically but not completely.

"Yes," sighed her daughter back at her, defeated by this day, giving up.

"Oh, go home. Be ready to go to work tomorrow morning, would ya?" This was an order.

Mayapple yawned and thankfully escaped.

Bud showed up soon after, late for work.

Pulling his cap low, this time with the bill in the front shading his hung-over eyes, he slouched in hoping to avoid Mrs. Fletcherman completely. Damn, he was tired.

He wondered if the kids (what he privately called Mayapple and Flem) were around, the place seemed pretty quiet. He also wondered if they were as tired as he was. China and Cat were at this very moment sleeping back at the treehouse where he wholeheartedly wished he could be.

They'd never gone to bed. Foolish, foolish, all of them.

"Hi Bud!" Mrs. Fletcherman sang out, walking towards him. Cha, she was still here!

He was bitterly disappointed, he'd so hoped she would have left by now. A yawn never escaped his lips but man it sure stretched his muscles inside as he swallowed it. And of course she'd have to catch him coming in late.

"How are you Bud? I sure hope you weren't up all night too!" she laughed gaily at her own joke, never dreaming their darling Buddleia was anything but perfect. There were no problems with *Bud*.

"That Mayapple and Flem, man! Kids, that's what they act like. I wonder just how old Flem is anyway, I'll look on his application, just out of curiosity."

"Mmmmm" murmured her caught companion, trying not to encourage her.

But she stood there, yammering about this and that, and that and this and Bud's over-tired mind began to close down in boredom, a tsunami yawn building and building until he erupted, hand over his mouth as if to hide it, ha ha ha.

Mrs. Fletcherman abruptly shut up, a dawning realization giving her a new perspective.

"Bud?" she questioned.

"Mmm?" Again, he tried to deflect.

"Let me see your eyes…" she suggested, as she snatched his cap and he erupted like a vampire caught in daylight, embarrassed to be found out by his employer, and friend.

His hair was askew from the cap and it was pretty obvious he hadn't taken a shower today. With bloodshot eyes he implored Iris, "Don't get too close. I'm afraid my breath isn't too good right now."

She held out his red cap gingerly and he jammed it back on his head. "Happy?"

Rather nonplussed to find seemingly all her employees had apparently partied together all night, including her daughter, she just shook her head and tsked at him, "Good Lord, you too?"

Bud just shrugged in defeat.

Shaking her head, she had to laugh. "Get to work." Smiling, she turned and headed back to her office.

"Don't worry, all will be ready to go tomorrow," Bud called, reassuringly.

"It better be," came the disappearing answer.

Flem woke up, groggy and disoriented. He couldn't figure out if it was morning or night. Had he slept the night through? He was so tired yet. It must be evening.

His head moved and came in contact with the hard surface of the empty bottle, thunk. Oh yeah, that's right. He ran a hand through his hair, grimacing at the foul taste in his mouth, wondering why it was he felt he had had to drink the dregs, when he was already exhausted and hung over.

Getting up, he stumbled around, wishing he felt better but with a new nugget under his belt: *he* had an actual place to live, legitimately, and a fire pit for gatherings. *Him*. Flumaria Greenwood! Well, Flem Green now-a-days.

Reaching for his pack, he discovered it wasn't in its place.

Looking around, his eyes searched for the familiar shape but never found it. Thinking back, he recalled the incident with Mayapple in number three, and the huff he'd left in. Oh cha. He'd even clocked out a few minutes *early*, something he *never did!*

His pack must still be where he dumped it this morning, back inside. Surely the coast was clear by now, probably seven-thirty or so.

Whimsey C. Nimble

Mama cat came strolling by, followed by five kids and all were vocal over his lack of standards regarding the feeding of the cat family. He wondered where the little bratty catty was. He wasn't here. Could he still be inside? Not good.

Dumping cat food into their bowl, he then made his way over and out, to meander back to the employee area to look for his knapsack wishing he had something to eat. All his supplies had pretty much disappeared last night…

Passing Iris's closed door, he realized with a start she was still here, because he could hear her talking! Oh Cha.

A shot of Sylph adrenalin spurted into his system, jangling his nerves, but it was nothing to what he felt when he heard her say, "Oh Santolina, *why* did I give it to him?"

There was a silence as he pressed himsylph closer to the wall, straining to hear anything more but her next reply was muffled, although he thought he heard something about getting it back.

Oh great Pan, no, it couldn't be.

He'd jeopardized everything by his foolish foolish behavior.

Despair tore through him, shredding his life.

Gasping as if a giant fist had landed in his gut, he found his pack and stumbled out the door and down the driveway, blind to everything.

Santolina asked Iris from where he sat in his office if she couldn't just call up the salesman she'd given the order to and cancel it, but she wailed, "No, he told me on the phone it was going in today at five. Oh Santolina, why'd I give it to him?"

She paused, then replied, "Yeah, I know it's not that much more. I just like the Green Thumb's better. If only I had checked with them *first* and not gotten suckered in. Oh well. Live and learn. Next time I'll call Moss first. And they deliver. I wouldn't have to pay shipping too. *Bah*."

Flem reeled down the sidewalk, aghast at his predicament. He'd done it again. He was going to lose everything, he could see it so clearly.

No doubt he would be fired in the morning. No job. No greenhouse. Mayapple would no doubt shun him after this. And *Lark*.

Ha. Lark wasn't going to want to hang out with him if he was penniless and homeless. It was back to under the rock for him.

Almost paralyzed with horror at how quickly life had turned upside down, he could think of nothing but numbing the pain.

How had it come to this? If only he wasn't so tired, but he fatalistically knew that had nothing to do with how desperate everything had become. Obviously, he'd been kidding himsylph all along to think he could have a better life. It was hopeless.

Catching himsylph in time to stifle the sob that was next, he clumsily entered a liquor store. As luck would have it, it was the same one he'd been in before.

Cringing, he hurried past the same overweight fellow that was in residence behind the counter, who never looked up from the small TV screen turned on behind the large gum and gun display, and hurried straight to the mead.

Idly, he wondered if Bud ever bought any bottles of mead or only drank his own. A fresh pain of loss ripped through him. He'd never have the chance to ask him now.

Two tears of sylphpity rolled down his cheeks as he doggedly fulfilled his own prophecy.

Standing at the counter, little piggy eyes squinted at him and unfortunately, recognition dawned.

The man with the big beer belly slicked back his hair and gave Flem a come-hither look.

Flem's stomach heaved.

Once again, he was not in a good frame of mind for this ghastly fellow's shenanigans.

At least he'd gained a little back-bone in the interim, even as sad as his life was right now. A small flame that had been almost smothered, fanned into being.

Tears running down his cheeks, he nonetheless threw his hand palm up in the other guy's face and said "STOP! Just stop right there, you hear me? I am in *NO* mood. Here, here's the money. Take it. Put the change anywhere you want."

The man stood looking at him in awe, hurrying to do exactly as this god among men told him.

"Thank you," the distressed faerie said with quiet dignity, a calm fatalism now taking over.

His new servant nimbly danced out from behind the counter, catching the door, with an adoring look in his eye.

Flem began to feel marginally better and was disgusted with himsylph for allowing this man to assuage his poor battered Sylph ego.

"Come again!" pleaded the clerk, but there was no reply.

Now what, thought the displaced Sylph. Should I just catch a bus back to the Park? His stomach dived at this old path he was about to reenact. He actually staggered but uprighted himsylph immediately so as not to break his precious bottles of Egret's Beak and Marshland Melody mead. They were all out of Manzanita, of course.

There was actually a rather grim joy in this downfall he was having. Why try? It was so much easier to just let go, kiss it all goodbye. He knew he was no good, cha, this went back to way *before* she decided to go through the change.

Turning into Flem had just been the frosting on the cake.

The fact that he was actually starting to lead a somewhat *happy* existence after all this made the separation that much sharper.

More tears started up and he couldn't get them stopped.

Only drinking into oblivion seemed the answer, what other choice was there?

A shop had closed, one with a deep recess and he hunkered down, pulling a bottle from its bag, as his pack cushioned his back.

He was just going to have one, he told himsylph. And then he'd go get something to eat before heading, sob, home.

Taking a drink from the Marshland Melody, he savored the hint of a redwing black bird's song, and wondered how they got it in there.

He took another drink, this time tasting sunshine from little glossy yellow flowers.

His rear sunk a little as his back rest slipped and within moments he was actually sitting on the dirty sidewalk that went right up to the Busy Bee's shuttered door.

Taking another little swallow, the bottle blocked his view at first but as he put it down, movement across the street caught his eye.

He stared. A human woman accompanied by a slighter, shorter human male were walking down the sidewalk across the way. The woman, on this side of the man, looked so familiar. She *looked* like Lark. In a dress. A short BLACK dress with a puffy throw around her shoulders.

Flem set the bottle down, swiping his nose with his finger and clumsily chasing away accumulating tears, blinking in dumb wonder.

She *walked* like Lark.

Flem's gaze latched onto the familiar profile and never let it go. It couldn't be. He knew that. But the façade was such that it drew him in and without his own volition, he was corking the melodious mead, and thrusting it into its bag.

Lurching upright, he shrugged his backpack into place, the bottles held too close together and dully clinking as they rolled towards the other and hit, separated only by thin paper.

The faerie flinched but didn't slow down, following the bright lure of ridiculousness, fingers clenched tight between his twin solutions to keep them still.

Slowly, he trailed behind, intent on seeing this doppelganger, but with his few remaining brain cells, remembering enough to stay hidden.

He strained to hear any conversation but even though he saw them talking, he couldn't hear anything but a random giggle.

With red rimmed eyes and a sniffly, dripping nose, he darted to the next cove, continuously keeping his eyes on the two. He wondered briefly if he was crazed, what was he *doing*? That couldn't possibly be Lark, this was madness but his gaze never left the subject as she stood reading a menu with her friend.

Pan, it *looked* like Lark. Her *male* friend pointed to something in front of them and they both guffawed before agreeing to go inside, this was the place.

Flem the fatalistic faerie crept closer, sneaking up to the window and peering in, down low, trying to see where they were being seated.

Hmm. He saw them following a waiter to a far booth, the 'other' Lark sitting with her back to the room.

The booth on this side of them was empty.

Whimsey C. Nimble

Flem went into action like a skilled soldier, Sylph craftiness coming into play. Without saying a give-a-way word, he managed to get himsylph ensconced in the booth that backed up to theirs, and sat right behind *her* head, waiting for his tea. Holding perfectly still, he leaned back as far as he dared, and listened.

OH MY GOD, Oh Great Pan, it WAS Lark's voice!

Flem almost fainted from the actual truth that he didn't want to believe.

Lark was out with someone else. Lark, who claimed to be enamored of Flem. Why, they'd only said goodbye in the wee hours of this very morning.

Flem had heard all he cared to hear. Throwing some money on the table, he fled before his tea even arrived.

"I'm so glad you came to the city, Linaria! We don't do this often enough," Lark was saying, dressed similar to how he used to dress before the *change*. Of course, the major difference being that he was now a city dweller and wings were not part of the landscape, at least out in public. But when one of his sisters from his birthtree came to town, they liked to cross dress, the females taking great delight in the whole masquerade and deception and any male Sylphs they kept in contact with dressing like their old Sylves.

Sylph humor being what is was, they all found it quite titillating, amusing themselves to no end.

Chapter 59

―――――――― ❦ ――――――――

It was still early when he looked up to see *Mayapple* and
Bud coming through the door and they didn't look happy.

*I*T WAS TEN after nine the next morning and Mayapple was beginning
to fret. Flem didn't seem to be here yet and he had never been late
before that she knew of. Today of all days - today was City Center day and
her mother was all nervous about it. Mayapple knew they both had to be in
top form and with-it today. She hoped he'd just overslept and would be along
any moment. The pit in her stomach said she was dreaming. Something was
wrong.

Nervously, she started to pace, cutting over to number one and randomly digging through her drawer near the planting station, trying to cover
for Flem's absence.

Bud swung in and off his bicycle, nodding to her graciously as he hurried
to check in before returning to her side.

"Hey Mayapple. We all set to go? Should I go back the truck down?
Where's Flem? Is Iris here yet?"

"I don't know where Flem is!" Mayapple said in a controlled panicky
voice, wringing her hands at the same time.

Bud looked at her, rather taken aback by this unexpected development.

"Did you check back there?" He jerked a thumb in the obvious direction
of the old greenhouse.

"No! I should do that, you're right. Will you cover for me, well, us, Flem
too?" she asked, feeling like it was such a huge favor she was asking of him
but he poo-pahed her with look.

"Of course. Go," he said, heading for the furtherest corner so Iris would
have to work at finding him.

427

Whimsey C. Nimble

Unfortunately, he just knew Flem wasn't going to be found here, the greenhouse felt 'empty' to him when he placed his attention on it. He was already figuring out a way to forestall Iris even longer if need be.

Momma cat complained vociferously to the young woman who was not paying any attention to her.

Actually, Mayapple *was* paying attention; she was telling the cat family as she strode through calling the faerie's name, that she *would* feed them before she left, because it was obvious Flem hadn't been here all night.

Could he be with Lark?

Mayapple was scared and after dumping way too much food out and scattering it all over the place, she ran for the windowdoor.

About the time she came thundering up the path, she saw Bud re-emerging into sight, whistling loudly, way back in the far corner, along with her mother who was hurrying out the back door calling both their names, and Flem's too, with a wave of her wrist.

Heart in mouth, Mayapple forced herself to slow down, not sure how to cover this one for Flem, when Iris spoke up, "City Center is off today. I just got a call from Santolina and there's some kind of gas problem with the city. There's emergency crews at practically every intersection downtown – barricades everywhere. Lucky for me, I'm going the other way! Ha Ha! Santolina wants Fletcherman's official opinion on a park they're thinking about redoing, so, since *I'm* Fletcherman's, I must go." She smiled sweetly.

Mayapple stared at her in astonishment.

"Bud, I'm so sorry you came in early for no reason. Nothing I can do! Oh well. If you want to stay and work, that's okay with me. Or, you can go home, since we're not hanging baskets. Mayapple, you and Flem work on that list, okay? Where is he anyway?"

Mayapple flapped an arm and nonchalantly said, "Over there. He'll be right back."

Iris paid no attention. She was off to play hooky once again. It was irritating because it was actually legit.

"I expect a full day's work from the two of you Mayapple, and I'll talk to you and Flem when I get back. I should be back, oh, no later than five." Her eyes twinkled.

"Bye mom." Mayapple leaned in and gave her a peck on the cheek, shaking her head at her mother.

"Gee mommy, when I grow up I want to be *just like you.*"

Iris pinched her and said, "No more sass, missy. You could never be just like me." She gave the moment a brief pause before continuing with, "You'll be a whole lot better. You'll be just like *you.*"

Mayapple grinned. "Have fun. Don't worry. We'll take care of business." Her smile was perfectly controlled, hiding the cascading relief that was dancing right below the surface.

Bud stood mutely in the background, thumbs hooked in back pockets, as he witnessed the byplay with fascination. The two of them always held his attention.

Iris left and Bud stuck his hands into his armpits, rocking back on his heels.

"Okay, boss's daughter, what do we do? What's the plan?"

Mayapple smiled tentatively, glad Bud knew her well enough to assume she had a plan. She always did.

"I'm going to wait a bit 'til I know she's good and gone, then I'm going to go talk to Lily, tell her what's going on and give her a cover story if anyone, like my mom for instance, calls.

"What do you mean? Where are you going?"

"Well, I plan on doing an 'unexpected' delivery, and I will have to take the van. I'm going to the Blackberry Bakery first, of course. Maybe Lark will know. I would guess that he would. I hope. Maybe Flem's even there," she trailed off.

"Good. I'll go with you. But let me check out first." He smiled and said, "She said I didn't have to stay, so, hey, I'm free to go with you."

Flem had unfortunately gotten through a good part of one bottle and he woke up with it still almost-clutched in one hand, tipping but not over.

Whimsey C. Nimble

There was a drool pool from one corner of his wide open mouth that occasionally rode the elevator down to the next floor.

He did not awaken gracefully. Consciousness came creeping in and he tried hard to ignore it but it came marching forward, pulling strings of thoughts as it did so.

His hand caught at the bottle in his fingers and he looked at it with bleary eyes and decided he'd had enough, so set it on the floor next to the other, unopened, bottle.

A glaring memory of Lark, Lark! danced through his vision, making his belly shrivel and then he remembered Mrs. Fletcherman's words, *why did I give it to him?*

Instead of getting up he curled deeper into a bug-like ball, wings in a messy half-furl, rough and prickly.

The pit in his stomach spasmed and he shut his eyes tighter.

Good thing he left his old hammock here, he thought miserably, trying not to start the day crying.

His breath caught and then he gave in, giving himsylph up to his misfortune, sylph-inflicted torture that was all in his own mind.

He thought about work. He didn't know how to face them. So he wouldn't. It was all too humiliating. How could he have been such a fool's cap to think someone like *Lark*, for Pan's sake, would actually want to be with someone like *him*? (Oh, poor me, poor me) But still, what a *secret* to have kept from him! It reminded him painfully of how all Sylphs dressed, back in Thimbleberry, *before* the change... Loose, free, wings out at all times except when inside, unlike *here*.

Mayapple. Oh, how he would miss here. His heart ached for this premature loss.

Sniffing, feeling sorry for his sad Sylph, he fell back asleep.

Lark was behind the cash register at work this time of day, which was busy. Mornings were always busy. How he'd hated to close the other day but his regulars were back in force the next day as soon as he flipped over the 'open' sign.

It was still early when he looked up to see *Mayapple* and *Bud* coming through the door and they didn't look happy. He was sure Flem would be walking in right behind them but waited in vain, a small hole opening instantly with his absence.

This visit was most peculiar, Mayapple and Bud never came here, together, on a work day, in the morning.

His heart lurched. It must be *about* Flem.

Hiding his apprehension he waited on Mrs. Pemberton, who was a very tall woman dressed all in dark blue and as he handed her a crisp white folded-over bag, she remarked, "Rubel was just saying the other day how he loves your blueberry tarts, Lark, he was very firm about it. They make a luscious desert, if we can hold off long enough!" She grinned at Lark and thanked him, then strode vigorously toward the door.

Unable to take the suspense, Lark asked the next customer if she could wait just a moment?

When she nodded acquiescence, he stepped over to where the two Fletcherman employees huddled, eyes on his face in a question.

"What?" he demanded. "What's wrong? Where's Flem? Why are you guys here?" panic building in his throat.

Mayapple darted a quick knowing look at Bud before she asked the question that had already been answered. "He's not here?"

"No! You mean he's not at work? Are you sure? Did you check out back?" He was grasping at straws, ridiculous words.

Mayapple sighed. She knew where she had to go next but had never envisioned it would be with Bud and Lark in tow. She wasn't sure if that was what she should do.

If Flem *was* there, she was guessing he would probably *not* want Lark and Bud to see him. If he was there, she wasn't so sure *she* wanted to see him, for that matter. But that wasn't true. She *did* want to see him, no matter what. Something must be terribly wrong and she wanted to help.

Thinking fast, she came up with a plan. "Lark, don't panic, I think I might know where he is."

Lark's eyes caught with hers and she said hesitantly, "I know where his old place is," feeling like a traitor when all she wanted was the best for Flem.

"Is that where you two are headed?" asked Lark.

"Yes," said the girl decisively.

"I'm coming too! Can you wait a minute?"

Whimsey C. Nimble

At their nod, he swiftly stepped back to wait on the next customer. To appease any ruffled feelings, he wrapped a cheese Danish up and handed it to her. "On the house," he announced. "Thanks for your patience." Ah, Sylph charm.

The customer nodded, completely mollified and a bit enchanted. Dazedly, she headed out the door.

Bud rolled his eyes, saying, "They're dropping like flies, old friend; better be careful or you'll have quite the fan club and will have to beat them off from your front stoop."

"What? And turn away business? Never," promised the Bakery owner. "Back in a minute."

He took off into the back room, untying his apron as he went, calling out to his assistant, "Kahili, you're in charge. Just start the dishwasher and then come out front, to the cash register. I'll clean up when I get back. Hopefully soon. I'll definitely be back by the time you need to leave."

A beautiful woman of indeterminate middle age with heavy, shoulder-length black hair that was pulled back in a low queue slipped through the door and stood shyly behind the front counter, ready to take over for her boss.

"Very good," she reported in a slight accent. "You go. I will be so careful. No worries."

"Thank you," stated Lark simply to his new part-time assistant.

"Let's go!" he ordered and the three made haste, the importance of their mission asserting itself.

Chapter 60

———— ❧ ————

"Oh no! No no. *Lark?*" he shrieked.

HE SECOND TIME Flem awoke, he felt a bit more like his old Sylph.
Rubbing a hand over his eyes, he sighed deeply at all his troubles, rolling a bit in his hammock to accommodate a bent wing edge.

What was he going to do?

Cha, he felt like such a loser. Back under his *rock*, on a work day! Pan, he'd really blown it this time.

Without warning, tears again welled up in his eyes and he angrily swiped at them with a grimy sleeve.

Gripping the hammock, he pulled himsylph upright, bringing his wings into a proper furl, as rough and scratchy as they were.

Indecisively, he yawned, and wondered what to do. How could he go back to work *now?* Half the day was gone and here he was, sleeping off too much mead once again, something he'd sworn never to do again. He'd had just cause, he felt, but still.

Overcome with hopelessness, he sat back down, smelly and hiccupping, wishing he could just dive into the bottle again, but it held no appeal. That was no answer. Look where he'd come to from making brash and rash decisions!

A faint call was hear, somewhere outside, but in the near vicinity.

"Flem?"

He could barely make it out, but that's what it sounded like.

"Flem, are you in here somewhere?"

Mayapple!

Her voice came closer, and still he froze, trapped by relief on one hand but horror at her seeing him like this on the other.

The voice teetered off, as if it was going away from him and without thinking he shot to his feet and had the door open, listening.

There it was again.

"Oh *drat*, Flem, which in the *hell* bush is yours?" she ground out in frustration, talking more to herself than to him, as she blundered about in some nearby shrubbery.

"Mayapple," he called softly.

Abruptly, all noise ceased.

"Oh thank God!" was heard fervently. "Where *are* you?" she demanded.

This was it. Time to face the music. Say goodbye. Might as well get on with it.

"Here," he said resignedly, "over here. "

Bushes snapped, crackled, and popped, and it sounded more like an elephant coming through but no, it was just a slight human woman.

And did she look cross. He took a step back when her narrowed gaze finally beheld him and her eyes became even beadier. There was no softness there now.

Flem gulped and he started to sweat, as if he didn't smell bad enough already.

"What the *HELL* do you think you're doing, Flem?" Oh, she was working up a steam now. "Are you *hurt* in some way?"

Before he could reply, she added, "You better be, buddy, to pull a stunt like this! You have a job now, mister, none of this back-in-the-canyon hoopla, this *isn't* the old days, you hear me?" Obviously rhetorical as she certainly didn't wait for an answer.

"But, but," he blubbered, trying to convey the despair in his heart at the great misfortune that had befallen him.

"Your mom," he sniffed, "she said, I mean, I *heard* her say, she wished she'd never given me the greenhouse, Mayapple." He looked at her like a sick puppy hoping for a miracle.

"What? Ach, I don't believe that. She wouldn't *do* that. Nope. I don't believe it. I think you heard wrong, that's what I think. Now, don't worry, we'll ask her tonight, when she gets back."

"Back?" repeated Flem blankly. "Where'd she go? What about the City Center baskets that were 'spouse to be hung today?" he asked in anguish.

"Oh *you*. You are one lucky sucker, Flemmy boy."

At the endearment his heart lurched, his bottom lip quivered and two crocodile tears appeared in his eyes before rolling right down his cheeks.

"Oh come here you silly Sylph, good Lord." She caught him in a big Mayapple hug, rubbing his wingulacture with her thumbs as she squeezed him tight.

"Oh Mayapple, what have I done?" he wailed as the tears kept coming.

"*Nothing.* That's what I keep trying to tell you, you big gooseberry. She's *gone for the day!* Some kind of problem downtown and we can't hang the baskets today. Flem, *she doesn't have a clue you aren't at work!*"

Flem looked at her in wonder.

"What?"

About that time an impatient voice, Lark's voice! called through to them, "*Mayapple.* Where are you? Did you find him?"

"Oh no! No no. *Lark?*" Flem shrieked. "No no, oh Mayapple, you don't *know.* He's in love with somebody else, and he's not who you think he is!"

Like a wraith, he slipped from her arms and stumbled through his doorway under the rock and it closed behind him.

Mayapple groaned.

"*Flem*, let me in!"

"I can't. Go away!"

"What is the matter with you?" she cried in exasperation.

A sob was heard inside and Mayapple tried to pound on the door, but since it was rock, it did no good.

"Grrr," she growled. "We don't have all day, we've got *work* to do, demit, Flem. Come out now. Come with me, mom will *never know the difference.* Just think, we're getting paid to *stand here and talk*! That ought to feel good on your guilty conscience," she threw out deliberately.

A thrashing of brush was heard and the next minute Lark and Bud were both standing beside her.

"Whoa, I had forgotten about this place!" exclaimed Buddleia to Lark. "Cha, do you remember that time -" but he got no further because Lark slapped a hand over his mouth and said, "Not now!"

A high pitched "No! Oh no! Eeeek!" was heard hysterically from behind the rock.

"*What* is the matter with him, is he hurt Mayapple? What's going on?" demanded Lark, reaching to slide the rock out of his way.

Whimsey C. Nimble

Mayapple's hand flew out and she stopped him in time.

"I don't know. First of all, he said something about mom taking *back* the old greenhouse…"

"Oh Pan, she gave it to him! Bud -"

"Yeah, I heard."

"But that's just it. She wouldn't retract something like that. I don't know what the hell he's talking about. And there's more. Something to do with *you*, Lark."

"*Me?*" he asked in disbelief. "I can't imagine," but he broke off at the sudden recollection of *last night* and being out with Linaria, in his short dress, Linaria dressed like a *human male*.

"Ohhhhhhh," the word came out long and hurtful, a little painful song.

"Oh no, I bet he saw me last night," he muttered. "One of my, ah, *sisters* came in to the City and of course, for some unknown reason, Flem must have seen us, and recognized me," he explained on a rather under-breath to Mayapple and Bud, all of it confusing to Mayapple but none of it to Bud.

"Cha, what a mess," said Lark rubbing his forehead between his dark brows. "Listen, I would really like the chance to talk to him alone for a few minutes." He looked enquiringly at his two friends.

Mayapple didn't like it but what could she do? Flem was her friend first, but she swallowed such childish nonsense and graciously stepped back, looking up at Bud and he took his cue and said, "Sure, you bet. C'mon Mayapple, let's walk back to the van for a moment."

Scowling, Mayapple followed him but not without the last word which she shouted, to be heard through a rock door: "We need to get back to work Flem. I'm not kidding."

Giving a huff of frustration, she too disappeared through the greenery.

Lark turned back to the hidden-in-plain-sight door, the entrance to a hole under a rock, for Pan's sake. He wondered if there was a Sylph in the City who didn't know about this Sycamore Park place. Cha, practically everyone he knew had passed through this hide-a-way at some low point in their lives, usually right after their arrival in San Francoa Ramosa.

In the meantime… "Flem, it's me. Let me in, we need to talk."

Flem had never felt worse in his life. And we was sure he'd never *looked* worse, for that matter. How could he possibly *face* Lark?

Much to his panic, the rock moved and in walked the green eyed man, well, Sylphvestite, a bit of flour clinging in unexpected places.

To his credit, Lark's eyes never left Flem's face but his peripheral vision filled in plenty. Overturned bowls, a stray bottle or two, old food containers, and a musty dank smell, soured by old mead. Whew.

Flem looked a sight, eyes red-rimmed, wings furled but with a pathetic droop to go along with the sag of his hunched shoulders.

"How *could* you?" flung the disheveled Sylph in accusation, deciding to take the offensive, guilt sticking out all over him like bumps on a bee-stung person.

"*Flem*," Lark said emphatically. "Look, there's a lot you don't know yet."

"No kidding!" interrupted the other. "Like, how is it you can go out with another after, after," but he broke down and instead picked up a handy dirty cup and flung it in the general direction of his lover, who easily evaded it, but took a step back nonetheless.

"Flem! *She*'s from my birthtree, for Pan sake. Auntie *Oxalis* is her mother. Didn't *you* have sister Sylphettes from *your* tree?"

"But, I saw *you* dressed like a human woman with, with, ooooh, I see, *he* wasn't, was he?" The light dawned. A glimmer of survival showed up.

Could he really be so misinformed, he wondered once again, a complete lack of understanding as he went off half-cocked, prematurely, presupposing the worst scenario without checking the facts? Apparently, yes.

Lack of sleep hadn't helped either.

Groaning in sylphloathing, Flem sat down heavily in his hammock as the enormity of his false conclusions came crashing in on him. He'd done it again. Sylph sabotage.

Lark watched with compassion.

Transitioning took a long time. Flem wasn't the first he and Bud had helped but usually *he* didn't get so enmeshed.

He loved Flem.

Coughing discreetly, the tall, sophisticated sylphmade baker crossed the dirty little cave to kneel beside his friend and lay his hand upon the other's.

"It's not too late Flem! Come back to work with Mayapple. Cha, you've got a 'free' card, Mrs. Fletcherman isn't there! You can still save the day. Do it."

"What about us?" the question barely audible. "Why were you dressed like a woman?" he mumbled further.

Whimsey C. Nimble

"Boy, lack of sleep and alcohol must have really scrambled your brains, ma petit fleur."

The faerie's head swiveled sharply at Lark's use of the pet nickname. His heart lurched with emotion.

"Why?" he asked plaintively, befuddled, cobwebs for brains, missing something here.

"Cha Flem, *who else* dresses in short tunics, anybody WE know?"

The realization crashed over the bedraggled faerie and he sat up straighter, feeling even more foolish, only this time it was laced with heaping amounts of chagrin.

Back when *he* himsylph was *she*, there'd been many such dresses, tunics, call them what you will, in *her* trunk back in her *own* tree. Cha. How could he have forgotten such an integral part of himsylph, err, *her*sylph. Whatever.

Relief was starting to rise in him that *maybe*, just *maybe*, all was not lost.

"You still want me?" he asked in a small, pathetic voice that grated on his own nerves but he had to ask.

"Oh Flem!" Lark raised his chin with one finger. "You don't have to ask. You can just *assume* it's me and you."

Flem couldn't believe his ears. Anything was possible if this sexy Sylph still believed in him.

Lark stood up, holding out his hand. "C'mon. Let's go. Grab your pack, I'll come back with you another time and I'll tell you a story about *this* very cave."

Sylphesteem began to rise, like mist off a pond at dawn.

Life flowed back into the faire, and the world righted itself.

Within moments, they were out of the rock cave, Lark easily closing it behind them as if he'd done it before. Flem was agog with curiosity.

"Flem!" stated Mayapple gladly, pleased as punch he was coming back and everything seemed in order again, not hesitating a minute to take charge.

"Bud, you drive. Lark, we'll drop you off. Thanks for coming with us." She gave him a look and climbed in the front passenger side of the van, leaving the two of them in the back.

They sat loosely side by side, shoulders and thighs pressed together.

"How 'bout I come over later tonight, you know, like around eight or so?" Lark looked directly into Flem's eyes and Flem nodded, wishing he were a little cleaner and his breath didn't smell so bad.

"Blackberry Bakery!" called out Bud like an old fashioned bus driver.

Giving Flem's shoulder a squeeze, Lark immediately hopped out. "See you tonight," he said softly, and then quickly made eye contact with Bud and a nod to Mayapple. "*Thank you*," he mouthed and disappeared through his own front door.

Minutes later they were pulling into Fletcherman's and Bud slid the van into place.

Meeting Flem's eyes, he said, "Hey, this city can be hard on a guy. I'll tell you a story sometime about your 'house' back there in the Park. It's got quite a history. Anyway, I'm glad you're one of us, Flem," he finished ambiguously, leaving Flem wondering exactly what he meant; one of 'us' – the Fletcherman crew? The 'boys' - him and Lark? Or 'us' - male Sylphs? Or perhaps 'us'- as in San Francoa Ramosa residents?

"Yeah! Thanks. Me too," he responded brightly, feeling like a sore thumb what with the way he looked and the conditions they'd found him in.

And here he was, being gracious.

It just went to prove that the Sylph soul was so resilient, it always came bubbling right back, given half a chance and a good attitude.

"Anyway, as I was saying," finished Bud, twisting has cap in his hands, "Don't be too hard on yoursylph. Everybody goes through a hard time, trying to land on their feet. We've all been there."

"Oh God, me too!" chimed in Mayapple. "Are you staying or going, Bud?" in a hurry to get this faerie friend of hers cleaned up and back to work. Her mother was going to want something done off that list today. They needed to hustle.

Chapter 61

❧

His panting became louder and the restrictions
holding him captive felt like they were
burning through his very Sylph skin.

*A*BOUT TO PUT on a clean shirt after he'd cleaned up from his night of exhausting, emotional debauchery, the faerie's hand was stayed when the filmy material snagged on an exposed rough spot near his wing blades, where his wings were bent over.

Ready to get back to his old Sylph, he jerked impatiently which Mayapple caught and she immediately put down the kitten she'd been holding and came over to assist, the feline following like a fraidy-cat, tail up and fluffed.

"Oh, you must be more careful, Flem! Look at all these uneven spots. Here, hold on," she ordered. She was soon back with a glass of water and immediately started smoothing and popping scales into place, a mama bird misplaced. Or perhaps, just from a different lifetime.

In no time at all, the preening was successfully done and he was gliding smoothly once again.

He felt like he'd been to the underworld and back. Would he ever get over his tendencies toward drama, he wondered. Closing his eyes he thanked the powers-that-be for friends like this, ones that *liked him* and wanted the best for *him*, and, were willing to help. They were truly a blessing.

He looked around the greenhouse, heart in throat, and hoped against hope that he'd been wrong about what he was sure Iris Fletcherman had said but he couldn't even imagine what else she could have been referring to, for Pan's sake. There was just no scenario that fit, in his mind.

Mayapple assured him that he was wrong, she knew her mother and she *knew* she would not renege on something this big. She trusted her mother when it came to important matters. Maybe not her fashion sense or even her taste in men, although she liked Santolina well enough, he was just so, so *conventional*, so mainstream. But unless Flem had royally screwed up, and from what he'd told her, he hadn't, just stayed up too late and went to work tired. So what? They'd *all* done that!

She grinned a little at the thought, her mother was actually peeved at *all* of them, not just Flem. Which was why they had to prove themselves this afternoon! *Today*, or what was left of it.

Abruptly, she slapped his shoulder and said, "We need to go, we've got to get a *lot* done before she gets back and remember, not a word. No guilty confessions, do you understand?"

As they hurried along the path back to work, it occurred to Mayapple for the first time to wonder exactly *what* her mother had said, and when.

Flem explained and Mayapple's brows beetled together at what she *wasn't* hearing.

"You didn't hear anything else? You're sure?"

At the shake of his head, she said, "She wasn't even talking to *you*, was she? Oh man, Flem, you're a great speculator, aren't you? Have you always filled in the blanks with worst-case-scenario?" She shook her head.

He flinched. "I don't see it as worse-case scenario, what do you mean? I see it as logical. Best to be prepared."

Mayapple looked at him with compassion in her eyes and said gently, "I believe trust is the issue here."

"What's to trust, Mayapple? She wasn't happy with my work yesterday. I was way too tired, and a customer complained about me, for Pan's sake. And, she was telling someone, I'm sure it was Santolina, about her regrets. Hey, I understand. I'm different. And I messed up."

Mayapple bit her lip in skeptical consternation, muttered, "Yeah, we were all tired," but still, it didn't feel right.

"Well, we won't *know* 'til she gets back, will we? So we need to show her *today* how great we are, now that we've only got *half a day* left to do it." A little aggravation slipped out and guilt laced through the Sylph's veins like poison.

"You're right, you're right! Let's go. Got any coffee, boss?" He so easily slipped into servile that Mayapple smiled at his antics, aware he was feeling guiltier by the moment. "Now that's more like it," she laughed, snapping her fingers.

"I've got an idea to help us shine. Remember that outline we gave mom about the herb hut? Well, let's fill it in and be one hundred percent prepared for it, and we can also use it for the herb class. It'll be the perfect forerunner to introduce people to our new and improved herb section! They'll already be familiar with everything from our class. Hey, maybe we shouldn't advertise it as a class, maybe it should be like, I don't know, the Herb Event? Herb Night? Whattaya think?"

"That's a great idea Mayapple!" responded Flem. "I think I like Herb Night. Um, isn't it in her office?" he asked skeptically, nervous about Mayapple's sometimes hidden agendas that he found out about too late...

She gave him a devilish, sly look and tweaked her imaginary mustache, as if she were a villain, and said, "Precisely! Coming?" just as they arrived at the Nursery's back door.

One look at his face and she said, "Oh, never mind, I'll dash and go retrieve it. Wanna chocolate?" she added with mock innocence, and a syrupy, big-eyed smile.

"No! Just get the outline. I thought we were in a *hurry?* Ahem?"

Without another word she was there and back in less than five minutes, no candy visible.

"By any chance did you bring that book you mentioned, you know, the one about herbal antibiotics?" queried the faerie.

"As a matter of fact, I did indeed; I stuck it in my bag this morning, meaning to leave it here at work so we'd have it when we needed it, and here we are. I must be psychic, huh? I'll go get it. Do you have any reference materials, or do we need to make a list?"

"I do have quite a bit, back there." He nodded back the way they'd just come from and a fresh wave of terror that Iris would take it back swept over him, although, it didn't feel like that would happen, he realized suddenly, even though the fear ran like wild fire through his brain. He had the sudden insight that if he simply controlled his mental cogitations and let life go with the flow, perhaps it wouldn't be so stressful. Pan knew, he had been his own worst enemy more than once.

Inhaling deeply through his nose, he held his breath for several seconds, before exhaling sharply. His heart chakra opened and his sensitive, fae-blood pressure dropped.

"I'll meet you back here right away, okay?" Mayapple confirmed.

At his nod, she went one way and he another.

Slipping through his window entry he hurried to the quasi room behind the bamboo where his, (and Lark's!) hammocks hung. Kneeling down in a corner near a stack of books and papers he lugged around, he pulled out his resources for various herbs and such, and laid them to one side. As he got to the bottom, he was satisfied with his pile and straightened them neatly on a nearby counter.

Before he could slip out unnoticed, mama cat came out to help, investigating what he was up to. She looked like she was escaping her kids, as her underbelly was arranged perfectly, five little milky nipples showing, standing up and out from her flattened fur, as if five little mouths had just been popped off.

Flem smiled at the endearing picture she made and grabbed a bag of cat treats to hold her over 'til dinner. As he spilled some into his hand, it occurred to him that little snotty cat, the hitch-hiking rogue must not have found his way back, since only five mouths had found dinner.

Dropping crunchies in front of her he went looking for the babies and was rewarded with a snoring, twitching pile back in with some fallen clothes of his. Counting bodies, he confirmed his conclusion: yes, only five.

Clutching his herb information, he met Mayapple back where they'd parted. She was licking chocolate off her fingers and acted as if she'd been waiting a long time.

"Well, I see you did find your mother's stash again, didn't you?" he asked with a snide little shift of the eyes, laughing.

She deigned not to answer the obvious, but instead replied, "Let's see what you've got," thrusting out a stolen chocolate-covered pecan caramel at him, one with only a little piece of fuzz attached from her pocket. "I couldn't resist. C'mon, let's get busy," she ordered as means for recompense towards her thievery, which included the handing out of stolen goods to flakey faeries who drank too much, and didn't show up for work on time.

They were soon seated side by side in the break room at the table, papers, magazines and books piled around them.

Picking up a sheet, Flem started with, "Well, let's define an herb, first of all. It says here," waving an old red dictionary held together with grey tape, that 'it's a flowering plant, whose stem above ground doesn't become woody.'"

Whimsey C. Nimble

"Doesn't become *woody*, huh? You mean, like a tree? Hmmph, I wouldn't have thought *that* would be the defining element, I would have thought it had more to do with, well, its properties, for instance."

Flem nodded at her reasoning, as he continued. "According to this," he shook another paper at her, "there are four basic categories: culinary, aromatic, ornamental, and medicinal. They've got a note here that says the culinary ones are the most useful, but I would disagree. I would think it would be more a matter of personal taste. I do use some in my food, but I'm more apt to drink gallons of chamomile, which I would think would be considered medicinal. Let's see what it says here," he let it hang for a moment while he shuffled and then said, "Aha! Listen to this. There are two varieties, German and Roman. It's the German one that's usually used in teas and herbal medicines and it's an annual versus the Roman one, which is a perennial."

"Flem, can you cut to the chase, we've got a lot of herbs to cover and if we, meaning *you*, cover the entire history of each one, we'll be here for two weeks, not just the few hours before mom gets back. We want to be *finished* by six, you know?"

"Well, 'scuse me." He managed to drag the whole thing out and look insulted.

"Oh, c'mon, don't take offense. Can't you capsulize it though?" she asked beseechingly.

"Yup," he bit out succinctly before immediately bawling out a list: "Acne, anxiety, blisters, canker sores, cardiac arrhythmia, endometriosis, eyestrain, flatulence, hives, indigestion, irritable bowel syndrome, morning sickness, nausea, stress, toothache and ulcers. How's that, boss, is that what you wanted? Just the facts, ma'am?"

"'*Flatulence*?" she picked out with mock horror, an evil gleam in her eye, but then overrode her own distraction with, "Hives? Geez, too bad we didn't know about this earlier, huh? Do you just drink it?"

"No, you make compresses that can be used hot or cold in addition to drinking several cups a day, it says here," replied her coworker. "Oh look," he added, reading further. " Here's an actual list *for* hives. Did she ever say what it was that caused them, anyway?"

Mayapple raised her brows and said, "She acted rather embarrassed and mumbled stuff like "it was the chocolate, or maybe the crab," but there was something rather fishy about it. I wonder just *how much* chocolate a person would have to imbibe to break out in hives? Hmm." She tapped a long finger over her lips a moment but quickly reverted to form: "Okay, good, chamomile is definitely on the list. Let's move on."

"Well, what do you have? Shall we look there next?" Flem enquired with politely asking eyes.

"No, you're on a good roll. Keep going. Plus, mine is a little more complicated than I first thought but I have a plan."

Well, of *course* you have a plan, thought Flem. You *always* have a plan. I should be half as together as you, to always have the wherewithal to see the next step – *the plan*! If I'd ever had *a plan*, I would not have gotten into all the trouble I have, cha, the hole under the rock in Sycamore Park certainly wouldn't have been part of *the plan*.

Hmmm.

But if he *hadn't* gone that route, life by default, so-to-speak, he *probably* wouldn't be *here*, Fletcherman's.

"Flem, hello?" Mayapple snapped her fingers in front of his face, and he scowled at her but let it go, picking through several sheets, pulling ones here and there together into a new pile.

Scanning them briefly, he stated, "There appears to be a few schools of thought as to what comprises 'must-haves' for an herb garden. I like the approach this one uses, though. It asks what type of food you're most likely to prepare, things like pizza, herb breads, pastas? It then suggests a kitchen herb garden, with things like oregano, sage, thyme and basil. Perhaps you're more of an herbal tea drinker? Try *chamomile*, any of the mints, perhaps lemon balm. Or maybe you're more into medicinals? In that case perhaps some calendula, borage, with a bit of comfrey around the edges. But be careful with the comfrey, it's roots tend to spread underground and you might have a heck of a time getting rid of it. And let's not forget the Echinacea of course, in the sunniest spot you've got. Shall I continue?"

"Sure! Keep going. I like this. I think it's great material," affirmed Mayapple.

Scanning, he started paraphrasing: "It seems the first thing to do is take stock of the different locals one has. Then you can go from there and figure out which herbs where. Questions to be considered are, how much sun or shade, wet or dry, how tall, who needs what? And here's a list of the most popular ones: basil, cilantro, dill, mint, oregano, parsley, rosemary, thyme, garlic, fennel, chamomile, lavender and sage." He looked up to get her reaction.

She pulled at her lower lip, rolling it between her fingers, looking thoughtful, before nodding, "Yep. Great start. Those are easy, familiar names. In fact, there may still be a couple in the old herb display. The rest we'll talk to Moss Campion – you know – the Green Thumb? Geez, I've known him forever. He was a friend of my dad's, too. So yeah, that's what we'll do," she trailed off, reminiscing.

"Uh, I've got more, Mayapple, from these other pages, see?" Papers crinkled.

Mayapple gave him a wide-eyed stare of appreciation, then quick as a whistle, licked her forefinger and stuck in on her thigh, making a crackling, sizzling noise as she did so, captioning it with "Ooh, you're *hot* baby, you're HOT."

Flem laughed, rather embarrassed but pleased too.

He continued. "What do you know about sesame?"

"Sesame? I would not consider it an herb," replied Mayapple.

"It says here that sesame is the oldest oilseed crop known to humanity, dating back to something like five thousand years ago. It's very drought tolerant once it's well established. Hmm." He read silently for a moment.

"Wow, listen to this. Sesame oil is used almost exclusively for human consumption," (That's true, thought Flem, I've never known one Sylph who used sesame, or even knew what it was, for that matter) and due to its high antioxidants, it's more stable than most other vegetable oils AND twenty five percent of it is protein! Wow! That's exciting, isn't it Mayapple?" His eyes danced with love of new information.

"You're *too* funny, Flem!" exclaimed Mayapple. "Okay, we'll include sesame too, I guess. It's an *herb*, huh? It's not green, though," she complained, as if all herbs were suppose to be green. "What's it say about growing it, anything?"

"Yes, here -" jumping around, he read spurts: "Most commercial crops are grown in hot climates like China, Mexico, and Central America. But, it's an annual and can be grown in your garden. Plant after all frost is past, in well drained, fertile soil, plant shallowly. Hmm. Make sure soil is moist when planted. Hmm. Usually grows two to four feet but can get much taller under optimum conditions."

"Sure, put sesame on the list, why not. But it doesn't seem like an herb to me. Can we move on? What else you got?"

"Oh hey hey, listen to this, I like this," he giggled and Mayapple couldn't help smiling, but said, "*What?* We need to move on, Flem. We can't keep spending so much time on each one, we'll be here 'til next week!" her voice ended rather high and sharp and the smile disappeared as she worked her way slowly towards a righteous frenzy; at least, given enough time she would end there.

In other words, Flem was on thin ice at the moment in Mayapple's mind, and that, along with that little squirrelly feeling that came from being gone all morning looking for HIM, and trying to perfect her project before her mother showed up, in too short of time! And Flem was talking, talking, talking. The simmer range was fast coming to a boil.

Her eyes flashed with impatience as her temper soared and Flem actually leaped back from the sparks suddenly shooting out. He knew trouble when he saw it. "Oh, never mind. Let's move on."

"Good idea! Can I see that list, the one you mentioned earlier, of the most popular ones?"

He handed it to her with another that had more 'must- have' herbs on it.

"Let's combine these two," she said after looking them over a minute. "So, here, you want to write these down?" she asked, thinly veiling the command as she handed him some paper, a pencil, and a smile.

"Anise," she read. "But wait, you mentioned fennel, didn't you? Aren't they the same thing?"

Flem animated right up. "No!" he said excitedly. "They do tend to be used interchangedly and often one is referred to when meaning the other, but they're two different plants. Fennel," he went on in his best lecture voice, "is a perennial herb which is often grown as an annual. *Anise* on the other hand, A.K.A. Pimpinella Asisum, IS an annual. They both like full sun in light, well-drained soil. Full grown *Fennel* is drought toler-ant, Anise is not. *Fennel* can often be seen growing wild, alongside the road. That's what's behind my greenhouse," and he stopped, looking at Mayapple with woeful big eyes, the mention of 'his' greenhouse crashing about his ears.

Rolling her eyes but not without sympathy, she put her hands on his shoulders and looked squarely into his eyes.

Whimsey C. Nimble

"Don't go there! I mean it. It's all going to be fine, you'll see. Now, where were we? Keep going," she ordered.

Searching her eyes as if there were an actual confirmation to be found there when they both knew it must come from Iris, he nodded and resumed, "Not much else, Anise gets to be about two feet tall and has little *white* flowers in umbrella-like clusters whereas Foeniculum Vulgare, common Fennel, can grow to five feet and has wide clusters of *yellow* flowers. Both are good in salads, (the young, tender shoots) and the seeds can flavor bread or sweeten your breath," he petered out and stopped.

They both looked distracted until Mayapple decisively said, "Okay, let's continue. Let's just write them down and we'll embellish *later*, no matter how interesting the plant is, okay?" She gave him a hard stare as if *he* had asked about the difference between anise and fennel. Cha!

"Shoot, boss. I'm ready. I've got chamomile, sesame, anise and fennel so far."

"Here's the list. Perhaps we'll edit some out later but we'll include them all for now." She cleared her throat and then recited the list Flem had already ran through once: "Basil, oregano, parsley, rosemary, thyme, garlic, lavender, sage, cilantro." To this she added "Chervil, horehound, chives, hyssop, borage, coriander, peppermint, spearmint, caraway, dill, catnip, marjoram. Hmm." And then tacked on, "I don't see many of *my* herbs in here."

"Did you get the book?" inquired Flem.

She picked up a slim volume from beside her and paged through it.

Flem read the cover with a sideways tilt of his head: Herbal Antibiotics, by Stephen H. Brunner.

"Here's a list he's labeled 'The Top Fifteen Antibiotic Herbs." She read off: "Acacia, aloe, cryptolepsis, Echinacea, eucalyptus, garlic, ginger, goldenseal, grapefruit seed extract, honey, juniper, licorice, sage, usnea, and wormwood."

Flem looked at her, and then said carefully, "Geez, some seem kind of exotic, don't they?"

"Yeah, but I've been thinking. I'll talk about this book and mention the herbs in it on our herb night and then, take orders! I'll set it up with Moss to offer a package deal and we'll stock the book. We'll do a couple of alternative ways, if they want. That way, *we* won't have to order herbs nobody's heard of and then have them sit on the shelf. 'Course I guess it wouldn't hurt to carry some, regardless, would it?"

Flem was keeping up and was right along with her. "Yeah, great idea, Mayapple. We could stock honey, garlic, Echinacea, and aloe vera for sure. What about that, what was it? Crypto Lopsis?"

Mayapple laughed but corrected him with "Cryp-to-LEP-sis, not Cryp-to-LOP-sis. Yeah, I'm sure everybody has heard of that!" She perused further and then said, "Oh perfect. It's mostly used just for *malaria*." She grinned over at her cohort. "Guess that's *one* we probably won't need to include!"

It didn't take long and the Herbal Antibiotic project was efficiently wrapped up, Mayapple directing Flem on how to make an outline for her mother and the packaging idea with which to approach Moss Campion regarding orders they would receive.

"So, we'll let the boss decide if we should stock all these on our list, or not." Mayapple's eyes crinkled as she added, rather snidely, "Gotta make her feel like she's the boss, right?"

Flem nodded, admiration for Mayapple blooming in his eyes as they continued to talk herbs.

"I've got something else too that I thought it would be fun to incorporate. How do you feel about edible flowers?" Flem cocked his head at her, pretty sure he knew how she would feel.

"Ooh, very intriguing, Flemmy." Mayapple arched an eyebrow at him. "How would we market it? What are you thinking? Are they herbs? Would we carry the actual plants, or what?"

"I have a list," he replied, "and I thought between the two of us, well your mom too, no doubt, we could showcase each one that makes the cut, with its own narrative of how to use it in whatever dish it's for. Like this one: 'Basil. Flowers of the basil plant are milder than leaves, an attractive addition to pasta, salad, or in a glass of ice water."

Mayapple jumped in with, "Another section in our hut! What are some of the others they list?"

"Marigolds, of course – calendula variety only. Actually, calendula should be over with the medicinals, *and* here with the edibles. The fresh flowers are a great addition to a salad and dried, can be made into a tea for inflammations, particularly in the mouth along with a gargle for sore throats. Oh, look here. It says there is an oil that can be made with it that's good for skin irritations and helping wounds heal faster. And they give the recipe! Oh, I'm going to make this for me!" And he read: "Take equal parts of calendula, comfrey, and marshmallow root and put them in a glass container 'til it's two thirds full. Fill with a light olive oil. Cap tightly and set in warm place for two weeks. Strain and reserve the oil. Then add an ounce of beeswax for every seven ounces of oil. Heat 'til the wax is melted and pour into ointment jar. Voila!"

Flem continued, "We could probably list several, if not most, as having medicinal benefits as well." He read thoughtfully for a moment and then muttered, "Yep. Look here. Angelica, garlic, anise, hyssop. Forget the separate section in the Herb Hut for the edibles, Mayapple, we'll just have to overlap them with the others."

Mayapple was silent, watching him process, wondering if he knew what he was talking about.

"So," she clarified. "No on the edibles section? Gee, it seemed like such a good idea."

"Well, yeah, it *IS* a good idea still. I'm just saying we'll have to have a special note by those herbs whose *flowers* are edible too, in addition to their *other* qualities."

"Oh, I see. Sure. We'll make a cute little placard, I can see it now," dreamed Mayapple.

Flem dryly cleared his throat and said, "I knew I could count on you."

Her moth snapped shut as her eyes narrowed. Was he being sarcastic?

Deciding to be the bigger person, ah, faerie, *whatever*, she changed the subject. "What do you think about *this* idea?" she said as she pulled a folded piece of paper from the inside cover of the book. "Gardening by the Phases of the Moon," she read. "I know it's not about herbs, per se, but I think people will like it. What do you think?"

Flem was struck and stopped with his hand over his mouth, a look upon his face. "Of *course*," he said, his eyes recalling bits and pieces from his 'other' life that never fit and here it was, a mystery explained.

"I always wondered why Whimsey and Pootsy and now that I think about it, WilloB too, always talked about sewing their wild oats under a full moon... I was never sure what they meant, you know? But now that I think of it, there was always lots of jars of seeds on Pootsy's shelves, behind the bar, at Windfall Café. They were planting, for Pan's sakes." He paused. "At least, I *think* that's what they meant..."

Mayapple was skeptical about that and gave herself a quick inward smile to warm up later and went on with, "Do you know how it works, Flem?"

"No," he said, thinking about sewing seeds under a full moon back in at the canyon.

"First of all, the Earth is in a large gravitational field that's influenced by both the sun and the moon. They all line up at the time of the new moon and the full moon, when the gravitation pull is at its strongest, affecting *all* things water-based everywhere. The *tides* are at their highest at these points. And just as the moon pulls the tides of the ocean, it also affects all the more subtle *bodies* of water, and one affect is to cause moisture to rise in the Earth. This in turn encourages growth and seeds will absorb the most water at these times. So what this means is, your best planting times, by the phases of the moon anyway, are the first quarter, known as the new moon, and second quarter which 'waxes' into full. According to this," she waggled her information in his general direction, "certain types of plants do better at different stages of the moon. For instance it says to plant cruciferous vegetables such as broccoli, cabbage, cauliflower, and interestingly enough, grain crops – any above ground annual that produces its seeds *outside* its fruit, during a new moon. This time of increased water and increased moonlight promotes balanced root and leaf growth.

"Now in the second quarter, the gravitational pull has decreased but the moonlight is still strong. This creates strong leaf growth. This is considered the best time to plant *above*-ground annuals, whose seeds form *inside their fruit.*"

"*Really?* Like what, you mean like peas? Um, melons? What else...? Tomatoes?" His whole demeanor was one of rapt attention, her unwitting but willing slave in any endeavor she suggested. (Except rifling the boss's office. Nope. Not going to do *that* again.)

"Yes!" she confirmed, well satisfied with her pupil. "Beans, peppers, and squash are some others."

"What about when it's full? I thought that was the time to, ah, sew your seeds, so-to-speak?"

She grinned at him and he knew his suspicions were right.

She continued, "Actually, it sounds to me like the optimum time is essentially before the full moon. Here, let me see what it says – oh okay. Listen. Full moon. Hmmm. Well, technically I guess it immediately passes from full to starts-to-wane but it appears full for a couple of days after it reaches its peak. Anyway, it says the gravitational pull is still high, creating more moisture in the soil but the moonlight is decreasing, putting energy into the roots. So this period is good for planting root crops, like carrots, potatoes, beets, onions, peanuts. Oh, and look here, it says this is a good time for transplanting biennials, perennials, and bulbs because of the active root growth. That makes sense."

Flem was nodding, his mind formulating the next question, when Iris's voice came booming out from behind them causing them both to jump, papers even hitting the floor to their mutual chagrin.

"Is this what you call *working hard*? Gee, anything I can get you so you don't have to get up?" Iris's tone was sweetly sarcastic and Flem's heart dropped to his toes. He started to lurch to his feet but Mayapple twisted her fingers in his sleeve and yanked him back down, hissing "SSSST" at him under her breath.

Carefully, she extricated herself.

"Hi mom! You're back early. How was your day?" she put forth to test the waters.

Knowing it was bait, Iris took it regardless, wanting to talk about her boyfriend to *somebody*, and these two were perfect, she could even probably work in a bunch of *work guilt* before she was done. The inward smile never reached her lips though, and she managed to look stern.

"My day was *very* fruitful," she said with a twinkle that Mayapple caught but not Flem.

"Remember the park out in Maple Grove?"

"You went all the way to *Maple Grove*?"

Ignoring her daughter, Iris continued as Flem contrived to stealthily stand up unnoticed but Mayapple SSSSTed him again imperceptibly, her hand waving behind her back, signaling no! No! She did NOT want him facing her mother right now, she was afraid he would unintentionally blab his guilt all over the place.

Swallowing nervously, he reached out and officiously gathered papers, trying to look like he had a clue what he was about.

Iris's eyes flicked his direction and she wondered what escapade these two *now* had going, seeing as how Mayapple was practically shielding him with her body.

"Maple Grove!" again exclaimed Mayapple. "*Why?*" Maple Grove was *not* known for its, ah, outstanding citizens…

"Do you remember Acer Park?"

"You meant that pathetic square of land on the outskirts, near that thrift store we used to go to when dad was alive? *That's* where you went? *Yuck.*"

Iris focused on Mayapple with a squint and the beginning of a scowl.

Mayapple immediately realized her mistake and hurried to rectify it. "What's happening with that gas leak downtown you told us about? And how come *Acer Park*, for God's sakes?"

Knowing her daughter's diversionary tactics well, Iris didn't let her off this time and turned it around. "What are you guys working on?" she asked, a little too neutrally, with an emphasis on *working*.

Mayapple knew when to retreat and brightly placated the boss with "Mom, guess what! We've got the herb section, well, the Herb Hut, all figured out!" Crossing her fingers behind her back, she stretched the truth a little. They were way behind with her plan and now here was her mother, *early*, and that didn't help. She figured she'd better talk to Flem and maybe both of them could stay an extra hour to get it finished.

Giving her daughter an unreadable look, Iris changed her mind about saying anything regarding Santolina and her day and smiled blandly as she glanced at Flem's back and then back to Mayapple again, wondering what was really going on. As usual, she felt like Mayapple hid things from her, right in plain sight, but of course, there was no proof.

Mayapple watched her with a sweet, trusting smile of complete innocence, getting more loving by the minute and Iris shook her head, signaling defeat. "Okay, get back to work. I'll be in my office. Flem, come see me sometime before you leave, would you? I need to talk to you about something," she sighed in surrender and turned to go.

Flem froze in place at her words.

Mayapple hesitated a moment then finally called after her mother, "Would you mind if we stayed a little later, mom?"

"Yeah, that's fine. I'll be here for at least a couple more hours. Take your time. Flem- I'll see you later," and with a flick of the wrist she disappeared around the corner.

Mayapple breathed a sigh of relief that *tha*t was over and turned to Flem.

Whimsey C. Nimble

He was breathing hard through his mouth and rather fast, with an occasional deep sniff thrown in as he tried to bring strength into his backbone but who the Pan could do that when his *WINGS* were tied down!

His panting became louder and the restrictions holding him captive felt like they were burning right through his very Sylph skin.

The goddess Mayapple knew just what to do. She laid firm hands onto his upper back and started pressing downward with her thumbs and he sagged, wings limp once again as she worked her way over knobby wingulacture through his soft old shirt. "Oh Flem, *relax*. I'm sure, I really am, she would *NOT* rescind an offer like that."

Her only answer was a small groan as he slumped beneath her hands.

"Now c'mon!" She gave him a little shake. "Pull yoursylph out of this. We *need* to finish this and it has to be *good*."

"Oh why bother. You think you can buy her favor back, Mayapple? She changed her mind, that's all. Cha, I've been taking such a chance all along, I knew that, but it always *felt* right, so I foolishly put blinders on and ignored obvious implications." He sighed deeply.

"What am I going to do?" he wailed to himsylph and Mayapple wanted to slap him. Instead, she channeled it to a not-so-soft pinch, in frustration. "Quit being so negative!" she ordered through gritted teeth.

"Listen," she continued, "I'll go with you, if you want me to. I'd like to get to the bottom of this myself. In the meantime, snap out of it, buddy! Where were we before the boss had the nerve to so rudely interrupt?..."

Chapter 62

Now don't go all twitchy on me here,
Flem! Pull yoursylph together, man.

*P*ULLING HIMSYLPH TOGETHER with an effort, Flem flatly said,
"Gardening by the phases of the moon, remember? You'd just mentioned *root crops* and transplanting that was recommended for that week right
after it was full. So what's for the last week, then, anything?" It was obvious
he no longer cared and while Mayapple was ready to go home and quit too,
they couldn't, and so she opted to talk her faerie friend back to the Light.

"Yeah, there's one more phase and I think we should at least give it a nod
before we figure out what else to include. *Flem.* We are good at this. *You* are
good at this."

Flem's eyes flickered to her before they slid to the last spot Iris
Fletcherman had been seen and he sighed deeply at all the trouble he seemed
to be in. *Again.* He resolved that *IF* things worked out, by Pan, he would be
extra careful to stay on his very best behavior. He would take time to think
about what he was doing and he would train himsylph to consider *consequences*
for once. No more flying into drama fueled by his own lack of confidence.
No matter *how dire* a situation seemed at face value, he would investigate
what the *truth* really was and would guide himsylph to follow the path that
resonated the most with what he felt in his heart to be the true essence.

"Flem?" questioned Mayapple, watching the progression on his face,
waiting for him to return, as she knew he would.

He smiled, peace starting to soften the worry lines etched in his face.
Whatever came next, he was determined to be okay with it.

"Hey Mayapple?" he asked.

"Yes?" she replied.

"What do you say we finish with planting by the phases of the moon, and then, because I can't stand it any longer, go see your mom. You said you'd go with me, right? I have to know, one way or another, where I stand."

"Yes! Yes, let's do that. And then we'll come back and finish up. I have one more thing I'd like to see covered."

"Yeah, I've got a couple too," he tacked on dispiritedly.

She paused.

"Listen Flem. I can't imagine for a moment she's going to take back her offer, BUT, if by some one hundred million to one chance she *does*, well, I *insist* you come live at my house. I mean it, okay? That'll be Plan B."

Flem looked at her with big round eyes, overcome by this unexpected generous offer, and felt so much better.

"Oh, Mayapple." He could hardly speak.

"I mean it. You are not going back under that rock, d'ya understand? Now let's get to work so we can get out of here, okay? What else have you got? Did we finish phases of the moon?"

Flem looked at her from a budding flower of warmth in his chest.

"Thank you," he said very softly, looking at her directly, sending the message from his heart and out his eyes, before jumping back to his business voice. "No, no we didn't. We were at the fourth quarter when 'mom' walked in-" He left it hanging and then continued, "So, what do we plant in the last quarter? This is what leads up to the *new moon*, right?"

"Actually, they don't recommend planting anything during this time. It's considered a resting period as both gravitational pull *and* moonlight is decreasing. They do say, however, that this is a good time to cultivate, harvest, transplant and prune."

"That's it," she added.

"I wonder what your mom will say," Flem said suddenly, actually forgetting his woes briefly. "It's not about *herbs*."

Mayapple considered him and apparently what he'd just said with a dazed look in her eye, drawing the moment out as her mind leaped to the unknowns still present in the moment.

"C'mon," she ordered, "let's go. Let's go find out once and for all what the heck she meant. As for the phases of the moon, let's not mention it just now, okay? I think she's more likely to go for it if she sees the details on paper and can get the whole picture versus us just giving her bits and pieces in a nervous moment."

Flem's eyes were starting to glaze over with the immediate ordeal looming before him so all he was able to do was nod mutely. There was no backbone to straighten, there was only jello. He could barely walk.

Rolling her eyes at such fae theatrics, nonetheless Mayapple's compassion enveloped him like a thick rug and he let her propel his feet to the boss's closed door.

Before he could faint, Mayapple yelled, "Hey mom, can we come in?" in a rude, loud fashion that made the faerie cringe.

The door opened quickly and Iris waved them in as she continued to give her attention to the phone in her hand.

"Sit," she mouthed, and smiled.

Mayapple caught Flem's eye and gave him a 'See? Nothing wrong' look to which the nerveless Sylph just shrugged. He'd believe it when he heard it from Iris Fletcherman's own lips and not before.

Iris kept on talking and Flem tried not to fidget.

Mayapple snooped around, impatient with her mother. The longer she talked, the sicker Flem looked.

It was hard not to hear every word Iris was saying, she wasn't attempting to lower her voice at all.

"I've got to go, but I just want to mention one more thing," she said into the phone. "You'll never guess what! Remember yesterday when I was bemoaning giving that salesman, Juglans I believe is his name, that order and how much I *regretted* giving it to him? Well, he called this afternoon and it seems he was wrong! Ha ha! His company can't fill it! Oh Santolina, isn't that *great*! I was so sorry I'd given him that order before I checked with Moss! What? Yes. Okay, I'll see you later." Her voice dropped to a whisper and she said, "I love you too. Okay. Bye," and turned around to intercept a wild-eyed stare going on between her two employees.

"What's the matter with you two?" she asked with mild annoyance. "And what are you doing here too Mayapple? I asked Flem to stop by, I don't remember saying I needed to see you. I thought you guys were staying late. If that's so, I would presume you've got a lot of work to do. Hmmm?" She waited.

Mayapple was obviously communicating with the faerie but for the life of her, Iris couldn't figure out *what* was going on with these two.

Whimsey C. Nimble

Deciding to keep the upper hand, feeling rather piqued by her exclusion, she raised her eyebrows at her daughter, who was STILL looking at Flem with big wide eyes.

Flem was acting rather peculiar himsylph, nodding back at her rapidly, excitement growing in his face with every passing second.

"Oh, *WHAT IS GOING ON*?" thundered Iris, at the end of her patience.

With an apologetic look at her friend, Mayapple came clean.

Without naming names, she came right out and said, "Oh for some silly reason, we thought perhaps you'd changed your mind about letting Flem have the old decrepit greenhouse, but you haven't, have you?" It was more of a statement than a question and Flem about peed his pants.

Iris scowled at such an unexpected turn but lights started coming on and she looked speculatively from one to the other, as she put two and two together.

Instantly all other emotions stepped aside and she slumped a little in her posture, biting her lip in sympathy and kindness. "Oh dear," she stated.

Flem's heart constricted, fear only one track away.

"No Flem, I am *not* sorry I gave the greenhouse to you." She smiled in support and then continued. "I'm *sorry* I gave that walnut-headed salesman an order before I checked with Moss, at the Green Thumb. We go way back. You've met his sons, remember? Acaulais and Schafta?"

"Yeah. I know," was all he could manage, his eyes embarrassingly betraying him, filling with unshed tears of relief, gratitude and love.

Iris was beside herself with curiosity as to who had overheard her but she bet it was Flem. Casting a look at Mayapple as if *she* should have known better, Iris turned back and said, "A *kitten*, Flem, *that's* what I want to talk to you about. A kitten. I want one, that's all." She sat back and smiled reassuringly.

Mayapple was affronted by the correctly interpreted look she'd received and shot her mother a glare before she jumped up and threw her arms around Flem.

"*See?*" she drew out.

Flem hiccupped in relief, his nose and his eyes flowing. Now that the dam had broken, the stress was melting like an ice sculpture in hundred degree weather and his relief knew no bounds.

Constricted wings beat against their cloth captors uselessly, and it sure made his shirt look funny. Iris took a deep breath and averted her eyes, afraid they'd bug out of her head if she gave in, and the poor guy, ah *faerie*, that is, was already discomforted enough by his uncontrollable body parts.

Mayapple took charge as only she could. "Oh Flem, *relax*. I *told* you it was okay," as if *that* was the whole point of contention here and *she* should get the glory.

By this time he was merely blinking rapidly, *very* rapidly, but he'd been able to relax his back.

"*Sorry!*" he exclaimed in an undertone, aiming it towards Mrs. Fletcherman, eyes shooting back to the floor in embarrassment.

Before it could get any more awkward, they were *all* saved by a small rogue kitten standing in the doorway, looking in, mewing questioningly.

When he spotted his ride he roared his happiness and then came charging in but just as quickly veered off on a sharp angle to instead take cover under Iris's desk rather than make it all the way to his faerie. Shyness can overtake *anyone*, it seemed.

All three burst into laughter and Iris continued with "Is this one spoken for yet?"

"Well, ah, yes, it's ah, hmm, I think he's *mine*," Flem tried to explain what he himsylph wasn't sure of.

"Yes, they do kind of pick us, don't they?" she mused. "I remember."

At Mayapple's questioning stare, she elaborated briefly: "I had a cat before I married your dad. Actually, the cat had *me*. He just presented himself to me one day, and would not leave! Thank God. He was a real friend and was pretty old by the time I met your father."

"*You're* getting a kitten mom?" Mayapple was skeptical. Her mother liked her independence.

"Yeah, we thought we might," Iris offered rather hesitantly, wishing Mayapple hadn't been with Flem. She was always *so* nosy, and so bossy. And so opinionated! Iris tried to think back if she had been like that at Mayapple's age. Surely *not*.

"*WE?*" the young woman pounced on the word like a cop at the scene of a crime.

Iris could have bitten her tongue in remorse. Trust Mayapple.

"Why are you still here, Mayapple?" she countered.

Making a sound of disgust deep in her throat at her mother's unfair tactics, Mayapple theatrically said, "*Whatever*," and flounced out the door.

Whimsey C. Nimble

Flem was nailed to the floor, his heart in his throat, wondering if he would *ever* get used to working around volatile people. *Women* specifically. Was *he* this bad, he wondered? Mayapple seemed to think so.

Oh, he *was*, wasn't he... The realization hit him like a ton of acorns. Everybody's drama was different and *everybody* seemed to have something in their life that made them crazy.

This new concept was very freeing. He felt much more his own Sylph, more of an *equal*, in a very basic, life-affirming way, to Iris. And Mayapple. And no doubt Bud. And *Lark*. Sigh. He drifted off in his mind's eye, smiling inwardly at how *urbane* his boyfriend was! Well, Sylph; sylphfriend.

Snapping out of it, he found his boss with her eyes on his face.

"When do you think would be a good time for me to come over to YOUR house, Flem, and take a look at those kitties?"

If nothing else, Iris Fletcherman knew how to stay on task.

"Now *don't* go all twitchy on me here, Flem! Pull yoursylph together man!" She made a strangled sound. "*Oops*! Faerie. You *are* a faerie, right?" Iris could feel the hot water she was in by this time, rising over her nose as she floundered.

"Yes," he said, admitting it. "Yes, I am" He paused. "Thank you Mrs. Fletcherman, for hiring me. I am so happy with this job. You have no idea what a boon this has been to my life. I don't know what I would have done without it. Not nearly as well, that's for sure! Someday, well, someday I may tell you how I got here..." He smiled his best enigmatic smile, practicing from the old days as *misfit* Flumaria Greenwood back at the canyon.

Mrs. Fletcherman tilted her head and said, "I really do mean it, Flem. The greenhouse is yours." She paused to take a breath before going on, "I've never known a person, a faerie, -?"

Flem interrupted, "A Sylph. I'm a Sylph, that's the kind of faerie I am."

Iris crossed her legs and sat back, steepling her fingers, reveling in this conversation, awkwardness and all.

"A *Sylph*. No, you're my first, although this City is rife with rumors but I guess I move in the wrong circles. I don't know any others. And neither does Santolina. I wonder if Mayapple..."

"No, I think not. I'm pretty sure I'm her first."

At this, Iris raised her eyebrows at his wording.

Flem hastily assured her they were merely friends, *very good* friends. He *loved* Mayapple, he professed, and he proceeded to list her many *favorable* qualities which was rather ironic as they were essentially the same traits the irritated the hell out of her mother.

She waited 'til he was done espousing and then reminded him of *why* she'd asked him to come by in the first place.

"How long does Mayapple have you talked into staying?"

"Oh, I don't know. An hour maybe? What time is it?"

"Oh look at that, it's six-thirty. I've got an idea, Flem." She smiled sweet-ly to let him know she was the boss and said, "Let's go look at those kittens right now, whattaya say, okay? We'll swing by Mayapple on the way out and I'll make sure *she* keeps working, heh heh heh, and you and I'll be back short-ly, you don't even have to check out."

"Okay," he replied hesitantly, thinking Mayapple was going to be mad and short-handed without him. And *Lark* was due to show up tonight too! He really didn't want *his boss* back there right now.

Scowling, he tried to come up with some valid reason why *now* wouldn't work but Iris took pity on him, from the look on his face.

"Oh never mind. I won't spring this on you right now. Another time. Just give me first pick, okay? Other than *yours*, of course," she joked. "Go ahead. Get back to work. The '*boss*' will be waiting for you, I'm sure." She paused. "Welcome to Fletcherman's, Flem. Let me know if you need anything and I'll see what I can do about helping you out."

Flem wanted to kiss her hand, that's what he wanted to do but instead he inched towards the door, Iris Fletcherman, like her daughter, forever en-shrined in the hall of great humans in his opinion. But he didn't really want to spend any more time with her, he wanted out. He was fast disintegrating towards overload. Or something. And maybe he *wasn't* disintegrating, maybe this sizzle was what unmitigated joy felt like! His body had that same electric buzz but this time it seemed he was in control of it and he channeled it into love and not fear.

His hand was on the doorknob and he was almost free when that love overtook him and he abruptly turned around and resolutely marched back to where Iris now stood, throwing his arms around her shoulders and pulling her close, far closer than she was comfortable with, actually. Squeezing her again, he said "Thank you!" so emphatically that Iris got tears in her eyes at his gratitude. Sometimes it didn't take much to drastically alter someone else's life for the better. She liked Flem. He'd certainly looked a little rough around the edges there at first but she'd come to trust him.

She hugged him back and murmured, "As I said, welcome to the family, Flem."

Chapter 63

⸺ ❧ ⸺

What are you doing this weekend?

*W*ALKING UP TO the doorway of the break room, Flem saw Mayapple's back where she sat amidst all their papers.

"Well?" she said without turning around, "Are you two best friends again?"

"Tsk, Mayapple, don't be like that. She's your mother, for Pan's sake. She's a wonderful person."

"Yeah, she is *now*, isn't she?" Mayapple replied with a touch of asperity, which she felt entitled to, given her opinion all along.

"Let's finish this up so we can get out no later than seven," she continued, "Sit down."

"What's the matter with you, did you suck on a lemon after your mom chased you away?" He couldn't resist teasing her, they both knew he'd been a basket case just minutes before and obviously his life would probably be in tatters if not for *her*.

"Here, this'll sweeten your mood," and he deposited a pristine, still-in-its-paper, shiny, orange-striped chocolate in front of her.

"Ooooh," she uttered, "Sit down, all is forgiven."

"It's an orange cream from that shop downtown, Candytufts, do you know it? That's what your mom told me when she offered one to me. I stole one for you but I think she figured I would, anyway. Orange creams," he repeated. "Aren't they divine? That hard dark, bittersweet chocolate shell around that soft, creamy, *heavenly* orange flavor. I'm *hooked*. Between *your* chai soy lattes, and *her* orange creams…I don't know. We didn't have stuff like this back in Thimbleberry Canyon. They're so good, I'll bet neither one is *good* for you."

Whimsey C. Nimble

Mayapple laughed, licking off her fingers.

"You're probably right! Guess we better not make a habit of them. So, where were we before out trip to Oz?"

At Flem's look, she waived aside her silliness with, "Never mind. Here. Listen to this, I've got an article here on ten mistakes people make when they're new to herb gardening. Perhaps we could use it on our flyer, what do you think?"

"Oh, we're going to do a flyer too? I hadn't thought about that."

"I hadn't either but I just saw it so clearly, I figured it must be a good idea. So, okay, here they are. One, look your plant over properly first and be sure to pick the healthiest one you can find. Don't start with an unhealthy specimen. Two, don't put it in the wrong environment! Read about it before hand or immediately upon purchasing. Three, be sure to cut back and don't let them get spindly. Four, overcrowding. Tempting when planting, but you'll be sorry later if you give in. Five, allowing flowers to go to seed. Pinch! It's good for the plant. Six, spraying CHEMICALS when none are needed! Ach! Seven, don't over water or let things get too dry. Pay attention. Eight, are they protected from adverse elements? Watch out for hot and sunny, all shade, or wind corridors. Nine, have a fertilizing calendar somewhere and feed them properly. And ten, it's all in the details, just like life. Pay attention to the little stuff."

"Actually, it sounds like a list for all gardeners, one that could be applied to just about any plant, wouldn't you say? But I think it's a great idea, Mayapple. What else would we have in the flyer? Is there an example for each of those things you mentioned, or is it just the way you read it to me?"

"Yes, there's a further explanation below each one, I just didn't read it. And yeah, I agree we could use this list as a guide in other areas too. Regarding the flyer, I don't know what else to put in it. Any thoughts?"

"Are you sure it should be a flyer? Perhaps a newsletter would be more the thing. You know, a once-a-month publication, one sheet, front and back, and maybe we could highlight a different herb every month. And still keep your *Ten Mistakes* in each one. It's a good reminder to reread for all those busy gardeners out there – which is everybody!" he said happily.

Mayapple's eyes gleamed with pleasure and she stuck out a hand towards Flem and said, "We're good, aren't we?"

The faerie took it and she shook it, pumping enthusiastically.

"Are we done?" he asked hopefully.

"*No*. Didn't you have something else?"

"Oh that's right. Let me find it," his voice trailed off as he sorted through his stack.

Mayapple waited patiently, ready to be done so she could go home and this project completed, at least for the day, which was wearing thin by now. She was tired.

"Flem," she said idly, "What are you doing this weekend?"

At that, the faire looked up at her, his mouth agape and she saw something flash behind his eyes, which he quickly veiled.

"I'm not sure," he hedged, Bud's voice echoing in his mind - 'Let's all go this weekend, what do you say? I think it's about time, don't you Lark?'

It was the *S* Club he'd been referring to and Flem's heart picked up speed at the mere thought of it. There was *something* going on, he sensed it, something that didn't quite fit, but for the life of him, he couldn't figure it out. Going there was the only option and while it was immensely appealing, it scared the lightening bugs right out of him. He'd been such a social misfit for so long *before* he'd turned male, that he couldn't imagine that *that* life-altering experience would have *enhanced* his social skills, at least, those that went past the immediate circle here at work. He felt relatively safe here, even in the throes of the greenhouse debacle he'd recently engaged in; well, actually, invented. There had been this little worm of knowledge that knew Mrs. Fletcherman wouldn't fire him, for all his hysterics, and *if* she had actually taken back the greenhouse, he still felt relatively sure his job would have been safe, no matter what kind of drama he fed Mayapple. Cha, sometimes it was so embarrassing just being *him*.

"Got plans, huh?" Mayapple managed to sum it up in those three little words.

He looked at her in surprise.

"I guess so. At least, I think so."

"Well, woo woo," she countered, bringing him back to earth with her derisive tone. "Aren't you lucky. What are you doing, are you going to that *S* Club" she asked artlessly. She was nosy, always had been, always would be. Flem knew this by now.

Seeing his hesitation, she leaped in, in full cajoling mode.

"Aw c'mon. What have you two got cooked up? You can tell *me*, for God's sakes, it's not like I'm coming along, now is it?" This was asked rhetorically but Flem knew there was a concealed inquiry built right in.

"No, not this time," he answered the unspoken question first, to make sure she understood, which of course, inflamed her curiosity.

"What is the *S* Club, do you know? Is it just a club? What do you suppose they do there? Will you take me sometime?" this last said so sincerely.

"Mayapple! I haven't even been there once, how would I know?" never giving away all his secret suspicions, which had to do with more Sylphs, somehow, but he didn't want Mayapple to know. Yet. He loved her, she was his best friend but Lark's identity was *his* to reveal, not Flem's. Cha. He would probably tell her *after* the weekend. An edited version...

"Listen, I can't talk about it, not yet, okay?" Then he tossed out the bait to get her to comply, "But I promise to tell you all about it Monday at work, how about that?"

Her bottom lip came out and she mock scowled at him. "BAH! I want details, Flem, lots and lots of details. You *will* give me that, right?"

He nodded.

"Okay, in that case I won't *grill* you, darling." It was said forcefully but it was accompanied by a rather wistful look though.

It worked.

"Aw Mayapple. I promise, if at all possible, *you* will go with us sometime." He should have stopped there but no, he added, "I don't know if they let girls in. I mean, women. You know. *You*. Oh Pan. Can't we just get back to work?" he ended plaintively.

With that speech, Mayapple's curiosity billowed like smoke from a burn pile on a windy day and she resolved to find out as much as possible about the *S* Club immediately, but all she did was say meekly, "Sure," with a small twitch of her head.

It was obvious to the Sylph Mayapple was devious, crafty, loving, harmless and would lie through her teeth, if it suited her purpose. Him and his big mouth. Nonetheless, he deliberately turned his back on the subject he wished hadn't been brought up and doggedly resumed their work project.

"Silybum," he presented, as if it were a box with a big red bow on it.

Mayapple stared at him as if he had lost his mind. "Silybum?" she repeated inanely.

"Produces Silymarin." Flem stopped with an irritating smirk that Mayapple itched to slap off his face. It didn't help that he had plans for the weekend and she didn't.

Luckily for him, Flem decided not to press his luck and henceforth, expounded: "*Milk* thistle. Silybum Marianum. A plant, nay, a noxious weed considered by most. But oh, it has incredible properties – listen to this. The main ingredient that is so important is Silymarin." He grinned. "Silymarin comes from Silybum. Are you with me? Or am I being too silly?"

She cracked a smile. "Go ahead. "

"The Silymarin is what makes it so medicinally beneficial. It improves and protects your liver AND it's a powerful antioxidant that can protect your body from free radicals that destroy cells. It reduces inflammations and can block toxins, even removing those that might already exist within the liver! Isn't this amazing, Mayapple?" His eyes sparkled with his love of learning.

"And listen to this," he continued with gleeful zeal, "The most commonly used part is the seed, (which incidentally, according to some, is not a seed AT ALL, but rather, an *achene*, a FRUIT with a hard coating!) which you can easily get in a health food store but, BUT," he held up one finger as if to forestall any questions coming from his audience, and continued with, "There's more! The use of milk thistle as food has long gone out of style and is overlooked even though *all parts of the plant* have healing benefits!" He looked as if he'd just delivered the winning lottery to Mayapple and stood with shining eyes awaiting her profuse astonishment and gratitude.

Mayapple wanted to snort and even snicker a little at his botanical frenzy but she opted for asking a civil question instead: "Are we talking *thistle* here, like the kind one sees along a road somewhere? Flem, I seriously doubt anybody's going to want to grow *thistles* in their back yard."

He looked at her blankly before sputtering, "Didn't you hear what I said about its properties though?" his mind unable to believe her less than ardent response.

"Yeah. I did. It does sound fantastic, I admit. But a *thistle*, Flem? I am *real* skeptical of, one, mom okay-ing it, and two, people *buying* it. But go on. Do you have anything else on it?"

Well, that dampened his parade. He shuffled his papers, a small lump in his throat that he gamely swallowed and tried to regain his focus. Luckily he had more information on it right near the top, but he hadn't read it yet, only skimmed it.

Whimsey C. Nimble

He glanced up at her unsurely and she stifled an impatient impulse, merely nodding at him. "Go on. But Flem, we've got to watch our time, we need to be wrapping this up pretty soon, agreed?"

Quickly he scanned.

"Uh-oh." The more he read the more he knew this was *not* an herb they would stock.

"*What?*" snapped Mayapple, starting to inhale forcefully when he didn't speak up fast enough.

"Hmm. Apparently it is definitely a wonderful plant, but, oh well, you can't just snip off a piece like you can with say, *stevia*, that will sweeten your tea," he mumbled, lost in Silybum Marianum world.

"Well, what do you do?" Mayapple asked against her better judgment, curiosity winning out, before adding as an aside, "Stevia? We'll be sure to include *that* one Flem. Good one!"

He cocked an eyebrow at her and half smiled before going on with "Cha. Well, I bet not many customers would be willing to grow it, wait for it to bloom and then harvest the seeds in late summer. The whole plant *is* edible, like all thistles, but it's the *seeds* that contain the Silymarin, and they're not water soluble. So that leaves drinking it as a tea out. You can take capsules but you have to have high concentrations for it to be effective. Hmm. It tells here how to make a tincture: a fourth of a cup of crushed milk thistle seeds to one and a fourth cup alcohol, perhaps vodka. Put it in a glass jar with a tight lid, shake it and let it stand for a few weeks, four to six it says here, and then strain out the seeds and bottle your Silymarin Marianum tincture. Apparently twenty drops four times a day is a good maintenance, but that seems like a lot to me. I'd double check it. " He paused. "I'm not sure how long you're suppose to take it though. Oh, look at this! Mayapple, Silymarin is the *only known* antidote for the usually *lethal* ingestion of the Death Cap mushroom, Amanita Phalloides! The best delivery system is intravenously and it has to be within a very short amount of time. Isn't that interesting, Mayapple?" Not giving her time to answer he continued, "Another way to utilize the effect of Silymarin, which is in fact, composed of several polyphenolic flavonoligans," but he was interrupted.

"Flem! Good lord, stop. You've gone over the deep end. It's great. It's fantastic, it's fascinating but I do *not* see it in our Herb Hut! Mom is not going to want to carry *thistles*."

This time he interrupted her, "I know, I know. Just one more thing," he begged. "Apparently to just support good liver function they suggest grinding a teaspoon of the seeds daily in a coffee grinder and then adding it to whatever you're making. But that doesn't make sense – it still wouldn't be water soluble unless it was really, really fine. And even then I'm not sure. There. I'm done. You're right. I don't think it's appropriate for us here. But perhaps we could do an article on it in our, ah, newsletter/flyer and perhaps point people to where they could find it, either capsule or as a tincture?"

Once again Mayapple's eyes were sparkling at her friend here who kept coming up with new and bright ideas, but didn't say anything for a moment until, "I like it, Flemmy, I like it. Actually, I love it. Get the article written, okay? And do some looking into where people would be able to get it, you know, health food stores in the City, especially any here in our neighborhood. And that way, it'll hopefully be a done deal by the time we present it to Mother Dearest." She looked at him for assent which he bashfully gave, not sure how he felt about the work laid out for him that she'd handed right back at him.

"I think we're just about done here and look, it's almost seven. I'm starved. Let's get this laid out and take it to the boss, okay? So we can go home. It's been quite a day." She raised her eyebrows at him in a superior way just to remind him WHO had bailed out *his butt* again and he took the hint and flew into action, gathering everything up and straightening as he did so.

Mayapple giggled at her power over him. "You're going to stay in and be good tonight, right Flem?" She was only needling him as she was sure he was going to do just that.

Thinking of going *home*, Flem's spirits rose accordingly. It was *really his* and he was going home! It occurred to him for the first time that he could completely vacate that hole under a rock in Sycamore Park.

It was a reverent moment. Probably the holiest and happiest he'd had since his change. Perhaps in his, well, *her*, whole entire one hundred and twenty-four years. He felt healthy, which was rather ironic since just the night before he'd imbibed a rather large quantity of mead…

Never again, he resolved.

And then it hit him.

He was *happy* about *his* life, about who *he* was and *where* he was. *HE*. He was the happiest he'd even been and it automatically included *him*sylph.

Whimsey C. Nimble

The revelation astounded him. Deep down hidden away in a buried recess was the unconscious assumption that life would always be better as his old female Sylph. It had always been about going *back*, back to the canyon and back to what it was before.

But now, now his life as a male Sylph was *full*, he had better friends than he'd ever had before. He had a *lover*! And now, he had a secure place to live.

A deep sense of intrinsic Sylph-value welled up.

He looked at Mayapple who had been caught by his face during this momentous Sylph revelation, her impatience curbed and held in check by compassion, afloat atop forbearance.

"Congratulations," she said quietly, guessing it would be appropriate, hoping he would *hurry up*, but giving the moment its due.

He had to speak.

"*Mayapple*. This means I can move out of the Park!" His eyes shone brilliantly, getting wider by the moment.

"Great! I'll be glad to help you. What are you doing this weekend?" and she snickered at the full circle they'd come.

Chapter 64

—— ✤ ——

"Hey, looks like your own private thrift shop, *boys*"

"*A*CTUALLY, ARE YOU really going to be busy *all* weekend? Let's do something Sunday. Hey, I know!" she snapped her fingers and pointed at
him. "Let's clear out that *dive* you were living in, what do you say? A trip to
the park? I promise I'll be quiet."

That'll be the day, thought Flem, contemplating the idea.

"No," he said after a minute. "Too many people."

"Okay, Sunday *night*." The reply was instantaneous as Mayapple was
now firmly attached to this brand new but already formulated plan, being a
woman of action.

As he didn't say no, she assumed command.

"You can't have that much stuff, can you?" she wheedled, her curiosity
popping like fireworks about his background but holding herself back from
actually intruding.

"Are you sure we should do this on a *Sunday* night, before we have to go
to work on Monday?" Not that the faerie wasn't up for it, but recent escapes
involving Mayapple had started a hesitancy to just blindly jump on whatever
bandwagon she was pulling.

"Yeah, I think it'd be really deserted, you know, maybe around ten-thirty
or eleven? Especially if the fog rolls in. Brr. How about I just pop over to *your
house* Sunday afternoon for a few minutes, and we'll see what's going on for
both of us, okay?" she worked her wiley way in.

Flem wasn't fooled. He knew Mayapple had insatiable curiosity just like
he did. Nosy, plain and simple. No doubt she couldn't wait to squeeze every
detail of his life from him. He smiled. He didn't really mind it. It was fun
having a friend.

Whimsey C. Nimble

"Okay," he gave in gracefully, stacking his herb information neatly.

Happy to get her way, Mayapple grinned at the floor as she too pulled various papers into a semblance of order.

"C'mon, let's get this project to the boss and get out of here!"

In no time at all they were clocking out and Mayapple was telling Flem what *she* thought he should do with the rest of his evening!

He marveled at her blatant self assurance and nodded at everything she said, letting it drift in one ear and out the other.

Finally she was gone, braids swinging behind her as she disappeared down the driveway to catch her bus.

At last he was off work, Magpie Mayapple GONE, a house to go home to AND company coming over. Lark!

Turning, he happened to catch a glimpse of Bud as he went about his nightly duties, perched on the planting counter in greenhouse number one.

Arrested by the sight, Flem looked on. Bud's long lean arms easily manipulated the bulbous bag of moss as he fiddled with the top, pulling it down so he could refill it. His movements were graceful, an economy of motion and Flem gazed at him with admiration.

He looked so natural up on the counter and Flem was beset with the mystery of their upcoming night out at the *S* Club. Would it have anything to do with his suspicions? A deep pounding excitement in his very veins said *yes*. Now that he knew, it was so obvious that Bud was a Sylph too. His treehouse screamed it and to clinch it, he *made mead*, a Sylph's favorite, nay, *only*, drink.

He looked on, unobserved, almost expecting to see his coworker *fly* down from the counter where he was standing. But of course, no *wings* were in sight.

Just then Bud looked up and hailed him. "Hey, you're here kinda late, aren't you?"

Flem nodded and found his feet carrying him towards Bud, wondering how he kept *his* wings down...

"Good news!" Flem informed him and proceeded to regale him with Mrs. Fletcherman's confirmation and what he'd misconstrued with the overheard conversation, the, ah, *fragment* of overheard conversation, that had thrown him into such a tizzy. One with almost disastrous consequences, as Bud himsylph already knew.

Bud kept his attention on the other Sylph's face, admiring those hazel eyes so many sought to conceal, and nodded in empathy.

He didn't say much and Flem felt sylphdoubt flash its little face again and began to question inwardly, instantly reverting to sylphconsciousness. Him and his babbling.

Bud dispelled this though when he enigmatically said, "*S* Club. We're all going this weekend. Believe me, you're ready."

Flem's adrenalin jumped around like a high-strung horse at the starting gate but no matter how much he cajoled, Bud would say no more than, "Talk to lover-boy Lark."

Knowing Bud was busy, Flem moved on, a small part of him actually rather peeved at the perfect Bud for not telling him *anything*. Cha. What was the big deal?

Bidding Buddleia goodbye, he remembered Mr. Rogue and decided it would be prudent to find the rascal and return him *home*.

A warm glow suffused him at the mere mention of the word, *home*. Ahh. A never-ending satisfaction.

He stood for a moment looking longingly back towards the old greenhouse but knew he'd better take kitten-cat with him, he did not want anything to upset the applecart of Mrs. Fletcherman, no siree-Pan.

He'd only taken one step when wouldn't you know it, there was Iris herself, rogue in hand. Beady little eyes were sending messages to his faerie: get her off of me! A rather strangled meow came out and Flem stepped lively to avert disaster, hands outstretched.

"Iris! Thank you! I was just coming back to see if I could round him up."

Iris deposited the deceiving bundle of fluff into his arms but the snotty independent one managed to hook his toes right into Flem's shirt and hauled himself up and over, nose diving down beneath the faerie's collar.

Mrs. Fletcherman looked on in amusement, fingers shutting out any words she thought, eyes wide.

Flem's back heaved and then settled down with a strange extra lump right in the middle of his back. Teeth on edge, Flem flailed an arm over his back, but was so ineffectual as to be laughable.

Iris did not laugh but her jaw clenched to keep it in check.

"So, doing anything over the weekend, Flem? I'd sure like to see those kittens and stake my claim." She looked at him hopefully.

Whimsey C. Nimble

Flem twitched, wanting to run away, but how to do so tactfully from the *boss?*

A tiny, needle-thin toenail, just one, attached itself to a particularly tender spot and the Sylph jumped, one shoulder arching higher in a spasm.

He swatted backward, hitting air.

Iris's eyes grew rounder and her mouth worked as she swallowed bubbles of gaiety.

"Flem, we'll talk later. It appears you're busy now..." and she quickly turned her back and walked briskly into the depths of the arbor, but her shoulders were shaking and muted sound was leaking out.

"Grrrr!" The Sylph danced, shaking, arms like wild things of their own, and ran to the back, ready, oh so ready, to be *away* from all responsibilities.

For nothing other than perversity's sake, he eschewed the window door and tramped around the side, making a path through the fennel. The volatile oil released, sending a pungent greeting through the air.

He stopped and looked at *his* backyard. With *his own* fire pit.

Remembering the impromptu Sylph gathering of just the other night, his eyes glistened with gratitude for his great good fortune.

The place wasn't much yet, but he had visions of what could be. He'd always been able to imagine it in full splendor. *Now* he actually could settle in and give it his whole heart's attention without that nagging fear of discovery and consequent eviction.

Grinning inanely, he shrugged his hitchhiker into a better spot and softly kicked the door frame with his toe, pushing on the top.

Stepping through the joke of a door he entered the back room, his bedroom, and who should be waiting, swinging nonchalantly as if he didn't have a care in the world but that dashingly good looking fae creature, Lark Spurastic.

A deep sigh of appreciation escaped Flem's mouth as he stopped short.

That fae faerie fellow cut a fine figure as he sprawled elegantly, one long black-clad leg hung over one side of the hammock, toes touching the floor just enough to keep himsylph barely rocking, arms crossed behind his head.

Flem's eyes took in the small overnight bag that sat nearby and his pulse leaped in anticipation.

Without even thinking, he was drawn over, a hapless moth to the bright sylphlight and touched his fingers to Lark's hair, all of his good fortune and karma coalescing in this magic moment. He had never been so happy, or healthy, in his entire life.

Lark's hand came up and caught Flem's, which he brought up to his lips and kissed, his eyes dancing wickedly, never leaving Flem's face.

Flem's own Sylph started to melt right there, his folded up wings relaxing and drooping across his shoulders, loosening in their usual innate tautness, causing a knobby bone to rudely move into cat hollow.

About that same time, mama cat came to investigate, hoping this faerie who'd come to share her residence was going to be able to keep up.

"Meow?" she asked, hoping he'd get the clear message she was sending.

Unable to pull himsylph away from those gorgeous green eyes, Flem didn't respond immediately.

Cranky cat on back helped speed up the slow faerie's understanding: he shoved off with unnecessary force, his teeny tiny toes spread wide, using mostly the pads to climb up and out but not adverse to using sharp climbing tools if it suited the purpose.

The faerie ride danced but it in no way hindered the rider's escape.

"*Meow*" demanded mama more forcefully, butting her head aggressively against Flem's shin.

Laughing, Lark held the hammock still and lifted himsylph free. "Where's the cat food?" he inquired. "We're going to have a mutiny if we don't follow orders."

Resigned to the inevitable, Fled led the way to the food and together they accomplished the homey task of feeding the cat, catkins appearing from different directions at the sound of dry food hitting the bowl.

Lark's green eyes took stock of the six babies and then he pointed to a butterscotch and vanilla one with dabs of chocolate here and there and said, "That one. That one's mine. It's not spoken for yet, is it?"

Pleasantly surprised and secretly very gratified, Flem shook his head, no, but as he started to speak, *Iris* was heard somewhere outside, close-by. "Yoo-hoo! Yoo-hoo! Flem? Yoo-hoo."

Giving in to the inevitable, he yelled, "We're back here, Mrs. Fletcherman."

No doubt she came for the kitten, and now seemed as good as time as ever to get it over with, seeing as how they were all congregated in one spot, making a mess.

Whimsey C. Nimble

Iris picked her way towards the back, her eyes carefully focused on her path, trying to be as unobtrusive as possible but obsessed with picking out a kitten now that the idea had taken hold. There were still a few lingering doubts in her soul about relinquishing Brody's old greenhouse to a *faerie*, for God's sakes, but she firmly squashed them aside.

"Oh! Lark. Hi," she greeted, wondering why exactly *he* was here and slanting a quick look at Flem.

He smiled warmly if a bit blandly, not about to give anything away.

Eyes upon her, he waited for the explanation of why she was there, and on another level trying to second guess which kitten she would choose.

Ignoring him altogether, she turned her attention on the kittens, who were now straying from the spilled cat food and nuzzling their mother, who was still eating. A rather muted growl arose from her as she warned them away but it did no good and she gave in, flopped down and let them finish. Ah, motherhood, one long interrupted meal.

Iris was charmed, her fingers laced together as she looked on, a doting feline grandmother.

"Oh," she breathed, "aren't they adorable?"

Flem nodded at her, giving her a laconic "Yup" in acquiescence but thinking about their wicked little toenails and bossy manners, wondering how long this was going to take.

"Mrs. Fletcherman?" he asked hesitantly, but Iris ignored him, her eyes roaming incessantly, trying to decide *which* one she wanted.

Meanwhile, Mayapple was taking the long way home and instead of heading for the bus stop, she had gone down and over to the next street, and was now making a beeline right to a very specific shop, one she'd never been in before but had passed many times.

And there it was, an opening the led right down a neat concrete spiraling set of stairs.

The young woman's heart picked up speed at her own forthrightness but she didn't let that stop her. Life was all about stepping out and taking

chances, doing something new, being first and not always waiting for someone *else* to take the lead.

Taking a deep breath, she picked her way down the stairs, pausing to
sharpen her focus as she studied the rippling neon words set in the small
window at about sidewalk height:

RAINBOW MERKIVA
INTUITIVE & CARD READER

It was time to really talk turkey with this other woman. And, most impor-
tantly, to find out if Rainbow Merkiva, diva from Revelry with Cybele who
hung out with Chinaberry and Catalpah, knew anything at all about the
mysterious *S* Club.

It hadn't been easy but Iris Fletcherman made a decision. Really, there was
one that just seemed to stand out from the rest and her heart was given to the
snowy, all white kitten that sat and tried to groom herself like a proper cat
but was too sleepy and full to do more than hunch over a little round fat belly
and keep a suspicious eye on everybody, rather overwhelmed. She looked
entreatingly at the woman who just moments ago, had scratched her belly.
"Meow?" she asked in her little cat voice.

"Oh!" exclaimed Iris, a dramatic hand to her heart. "Look! She knows
me, Flem!" Within a flash, woman and cat were nuzzling.

A courteous Sylph by nature, Flem agreed whole heartedly, watching the
two of them.

"Okay, looks like we've only got four to go. If Mayapple and Bud each
take one, that'll only leave two!" Flem was happy about this but felt rather
bereft nonetheless, ahead of time…

Now that the decision was made, Iris was loathe to leave but regretfully unstuck the small cat from the front of her and chucked her under the
chin, promising to be back as soon as possible, making Flem cringe.

Just what he needed, a new, exciting place, a new exciting friend and *lover*,
and a *boss* who was promising to drop in unexpectedly and frequently.

Whimsey C. Nimble

Starting for the usual exit, Iris stopped herself and turned back towards the misshapen, falling-apart door.

Giving it a slam with the flat of her hand, she simultaneously kicked it with her toe, making it pop right out like it too was aware *SHE* was the boss.

"You know Flem, get Bud to unlock the old shed, I don't know if you've seen it yet, and take a look in there for stuff you can use here. I'm presuming you *do* have plans to fix this old place up, right?" she asked needlessly but thought it better to be very clear. Without waiting for an answer she went on, a mere raising of one eyebrow cocked in his direction briefly to mark her enquiry. "I'm pretty sure we've still got some greenhouse doors that might fit here and I wouldn't be surprised if there were boxes left over of glass panes."

All irritation with his sure-to-be-frequent visitor, at least for the next few weeks 'til the kittens could leave, vanished at this piece of news.

"Really?" he breathed, feeling like a pampered Sylphette on their first trip out to another birthing tree.

Overcome, he forgot everything else, including Lark.

"Can I go see it right now?" he demanded, imagination running rampant with possibilities.

Pleased by his eagerness, Iris grinned as she replied, "Well, sure, if you want to. I've got to get back to my office and get out of here. Go see Bud, tell him I told you to have him unlock it. Don't forget which kitty is mine, okay?" She was backing through the fennel by this time and Flem came to the backdoor to see her off, holding the decrepit appendage open wide, his fingers where an inset window had been.

"I won't. I won't. The black one, right?" he teased.

Mrs. Fletcherman started to protest, realized he was kidding and settled for a half serious scowl.

"The *white* one, buster, if you know what's good for you."

He raised a hand in protest. "Just teasing. Miss Snowball has your name written all over her. I promise."

"And I'll help," chimed in Lark, glad she hadn't settled upon *his* kitten.

Wondering exactly how Lark fit into all this, (she had her suspicions) Iris waved and nodded, then tuned and left. *Finally.*

She disappeared from sight, although a blurry motion was faintly detected outside as she walked past the far end of their sanctuary.

Flem decided right then and there to plant a mess of vines along that far outside wall, perhaps Pasa Flora or Wisteria. Trumpet vines would be pretty too. He didn't need anyone spying on him.

Turning back, he was torn between just staying here with the lovely Lark or hot footing it to Bud and getting into that treasure filled shed.

"C'mon," Lark spoke up immediately. "Let's go see what goodies you can score. Wow, this could be a real windfall."

Warm happiness washed over Flem at how *easy* it was to be with Lark.

Minutes later they were in front of an old tool shed and Bud was inserting a key into the old sliding metal doors that were locked together.

"Hey, looks like your own private thrift shop, *boys*." Bud waved them in as if it were his place, looking around with interest.

Moving over to a brace of shelves that were thick with dust and cobwebs, he tilted his head to read obscure words, while talking to his friends at the same time. "So, are we all *on* for Saturday night?"

This was said so casually, at first Flem didn't even realize it was the *S* Club Bud was referring to.

Lark cast a quick glance at his partner who was on the other side of the stack of old doors that had accumulated over the years.

"Flem, what do you think? Ready to go to the *S* Club tomorrow night?"

Chapter 65

—⟨≫⟩—

Both locked up Sylphs ceased their caterwauling
immediately, relief and embarrassment
dancing around their heads like fireflies.

NOT ONLY DID his breath catch in his throat, it felt like every function in his body was in stasis from the cellular level up.

His ears prickled and his eyes tingled. Nothing intelligible came out of his mouth, until he was finally released from his paralysis and then he said, showing his sophistication, "Huh?"

Shaking his head in mock despair, Lark exchanged a look with Bud, and said, "Oh yes. We'll be there."

"Good," confirmed Buddleia, then repeated it, saying "Good. I'll be there. Look for me. What time do you expect to arrive?" His gaze held steady and it almost looked to Flem like there was more being exchanged than a few words and he wondered what secrets lay in store for him.

"Oh, don't want to be too early. It *is* a Saturday night after all. I'm guessing tenish. Is that good?" he asked guilelessly, fake green eyes wide but with the merest hint of deceit and humor tugging at the corners of his mouth to give the lie to his demeanor.

"Flem?" Bud turned to his motionless co-worker. "This okay with you? I've got to get back to work, I've still got soil to mix. I don't want Iris to call me over the weekend, you know?"

Heart beating rapidly, Flem gave a vigorous nod and said "Yes!" but threw a questioning look to Lark for reassurance.

"We'll be there. Go on, get back to work. Your job here is done." Lark smilingly looked over at Bud, dismissing him, while also winking at Flem.

480

Throwing a "Pffft!" back at such condescension from one who didn't even work here, Bud ignored this ridiculousness and continued with, "Lock up when you've gotten what you need, just push the lock together 'til it snaps in place. I'll talk to Iris about getting another key made for you, *Flem*."

Tit for tat, Lark and Bud exchanged grins, both enjoying the game. Bud stepped out, carrying an extra hose he had found and a new nozzle, delighted with his finds.

Lark adroitly slipped his fingers over Flem's hand where it was stilled on forgotten greenhouse artifacts and said, "This is going to be fun, I promise you. And you know the most important thing, don't you?"

Flem drew a blank, totally flummoxed by the whole encounter.

"*What?*" he finally said.

Lark milked the moment before at last he said, with a flourish, "*What* are we going to *wear*? Rather, what are *you* going to wear, I'm pretty sure I know what I'm going to wear, it's a little something I picked up recently. Hey, it was at Bud's fair, the one at Sycamore Park, in the Lonicera Grove to be precise. Oh, that's right, *you* surely remember *that* fair, now don't you, my darling little mead drinker. Or should I say, mead guzzler?"

Flem wanted to drop through the floor and disappear, he was so mortified at this blatant ribbing to an awful memory, a humiliating experience. He knew Lark was just teasing him and really, it should be counted as a good thing, that *Lark* liked him well enough *to* tease him, but cha, it sure didn't feel good.

"Oh Flem, don't take offense, for Pan's sake! Cha, I'm just kidding around with you! And besides, I think it's more common than you think, dropping into a bottle after a traumatic experience. I've drank more than my share of mead in the years past. I still drink, just not like the old days. You're doing fine, trust me."

He continued, changing tact. "How many boxes of window panes are there? I see two over there," he pointed.

Flem gratefully refocused, glad to escape from too much personal emotion and instead let it flow out to fill his housing niche. Turning, he saw the boxes and joy filled his heart at Mrs. Fletcherman's largesse.

Lark was going through the stack of old screen doors, when he stopped. "Ooh, look at this one, ma petit fleur." Tugging, he carefully extricated an actual door, one with an attached screen-door of its very own. It was a narrow, delicate combination and there was scroll work involving dusty vines and roses. "Look, Flem."

His partner was already there, helping him pull it free. Both Sylphs quickly examined it and Flem's heart gave an extra little beat he was so inspired by this.

Lark looked on, not able to keep a silly grin from twisting his mouth into funny shapes.

"We'll get Bud to help us, he's good at these things. Or do *you* know how to put a proper door in?" Lark asked.

Flem was struck dumb at such a question. Of course he did. He'd taken over another's tree when they'd vacated, way back *when* in the Canyon and made many improvements. To think for even a minute that *Lark* wasn't good at *every*thing was mind blowing to the faerie.

But what he said was "Yeah, let's definitely get Bud involved," and smiled happily into Lark's eyes.

The moment sparked into ignition and Lark's hand came up to cradle Flem's jaw line from across the old forgotten doors. Bud could be heard in the far distance, whistling.

Hazel eyes bore deep into green ones, hidden wings surging in protest. Faerie blood ran *hot*.

"I've got an idea," brazenly bespoke the taller of the two, Mr. Spurastic.

"If we just pull the doors almost shut, it would look like it was locked, *we* could still get out, and nobody would be the wiser..." Passion made his voice husky as he proposed the idea, a meaningful look in his eye as he spoke earnestly to Flem.

Alas, Flem was a foolish faerie who'd let his emotions override him on more than one occasion and so he covertly looked outside the shed and then pulled the doors shut until there was just a large crack of light between them.

It was not long before human clothes were flung away, wing ties ripped off and a great clattering was heard, which was instantly muffled, but then resumed unheeded almost immediately.

Mrs. Fletcherman had gone home and Bud was on his last chores before he and Lily locked up for the night.

After hanging out with her for the last twenty minute, Bud said goodnight and walked back to put his part of the business to bed. There hadn't been any customers for quite some time and it was a quiet night. As he passed the arbor over to greenhouse number one, he thought he heard a noise and turned his head to the right.

Nothing looked out of place.

He figured it was a cat and kept on walking. Thinking of Flem's feline family, he decided he'd better get his order in quick before there weren't any left. Preoccupied, he missed the thump to the door from the inside of the shed and the consequent click of the doors coming together.

Passing into the greenhouse, he put items away, straightening areas he'd been working on, thinking about stopping at Oleander's for ten minutes before he biked home. He wondered what Cat and China were doing, if they'd gone out.

Again, a muffled sound reached his ears. Taking his red baseball cap from his back pocket, he stuck it on his head and went to investigate.

It sounded like it came from the back corner, near the shed.

He stopped to listen and obligingly, another thwump was heard. It sounded suspiciously close.

Baffled, he inched along and sure enough, he could *hear* something, it sounded like perhaps an animal was caught inside the old shed.

Then he heard a groan and a voice and he froze, realization flooding into him, bringing an almost embarrassed flush to his cheeks. He wondered why the doors were locked and *how* they'd accomplished *that*!

Hilarity started at his toes and shot like a geyser up his body and he turned and ran back to the greenhouse doubled over with spasms of uncontrollable mirth. The question was, go home or wait?

He was tempted but couldn't be that mean, so he went on with his chores, wondering how long he'd have to wait and wishing he could go to Oleander's and just stop by on his way home but, well, heh heh heh, he *would* do that. Pan, he could be back in twenty minutes.

Chuckling at this new development, and the rich joke he was in on, he thought fast. Hurrying up front he saw Lily was about ready to leave.

"Hey, I'll close up. Go ahead," wondering if he was overstepping his authority with this plan to leave a light on and the gates open briefly, making it look like someone was still there…　.

"Okay. See you tomorrow," she replied.

Hardly able to contain himsylph, Bud raised a hand in response to her "G'night Bud," as she headed out.

Whimsey C. Nimble

Wild snickers erupted randomly as he made his way to his favorite watering hole for a night cap, savoring the future reference and blackmail that was now tucked away forever in his brain. Ah, life was sweet, he gloated, rubbing his hands together as he arrived at his destination.

Meanwhile, back at the shed, two spent Sylphs lay draped among the dirt like fallen angels, wings now unfurled and with distinct limp tips.

But still their gaze had lost none of its warmth and the toes of Lark's right foot meandered up and down the other's calf, kneading along the way.

Neither realized yet that the lock was performing its true duty with admiralty.

Bud had left ten minutes ago but neither had realized that either.

S Club thoughts lazily reinserted themselves and Flem bestirred himsylph. Going back to something Lark had said with that humiliating reference to *that night*, his brow furrowed and he questioned, "What did you buy at that fair? You said something about knowing what you were going to wear?" He let it dangle in innocence and confusion but there was a sneaky image that kept showing itself, parading by his mind's eye.

"Oh, you'll see, ma petit, you'll see. Wouldn't want to spoil the surprise, now would we?" his lover replied rhetorically with a secret smile as he sat up.

It was then Lark noticed the door had been shut completely. His first thought was Bud and his idea of a joke. Not too worried, he shook himsylph, which included a rolling wave that ended in ripples out to his very wing tips, which snapped smartly, like a pirate's flag in the wind. Without further ado, he furled, wincing in pain as debris spoiled the glide.

Instantly Flem was on his knees, saying "Spread 'em." And feeling cocky enough to scold, "I can't believe you didn't wait for me!" before attacked Lark's, now unfurled, wings, right at the base, with his raspy tongue.

Soft popping noises ensued, with the taller Sylph groaning (once again...) in enjoyment at the mere feel of another's tongue setting one to rights.

Preoccupied, the recipient of such glorious personal attention said, "Flem, I think Bud locked us in," in a dreamy voice.

Flem's head snapped up, "What?!" he exclaimed, horrified at the thought that someone, *Bud*! was close by and had been witness to the interlude with Lark! Oh no! Cha, I guess I should have thought about it first, he chastised himsylph with regret and a whiny attitude, panic eroding his mellow mood.

"Here, hold still. I'll do you now," said Lark as he attempted to put his hands on the other faerie's waist to hold him still while he performed the age old ritual of cleaning another's wing scales but Flem was moving.

"Do you think he heard us??" Flem asked in a stressed voice. "Do you think he *saw* us?"

"No, no I doubt it," Lark lied. "I imagine he just saw it unlocked and locked it before he, oh no, went home for the night." This struck him as an awful real possibility all of a sudden.

Whirling around, his Sylph adrenalin traveled at the speed of light and he joined the other at the crack in the door, a crack so slim it let no light in, in and of itself. Whereas the previous dimness had held only promise and enhanced the atmosphere, it now sat mutely and refused to help at all.

Trying to furl, Flem couldn't help but flinch at his dirty wings and the hindrance that proved.

"Oh stop," an exasperated Lark exclaimed. "You, wiggle the door, see if it's as tight as it seems, but don't move any more than you have to. I'll see to your wing base. Maybe he's still here, you know?" he added without much hope. He had a bakery to run and could not spend the night locked up with Flem, no matter how great an appeal that idea held.

Flem stiffly leaned forward, both hands flat, pushing to see if there was any *give* to the door.

Ha. The door itself creaked but did not move.

"Do you think he might still be here, somewhere else?" whispered Flem with a touch of despair, feeling more like crying with every passing moment much to his chagrin.

"Well, *call* him," urged the busy faerie at his back, wondering how they were going to get out of this predicament.

He stood abruptly and pushed Flem aside, laid his mouth sideways along the crack and proceeded to call "Bud" in a loud whisper, himsylph.

There was no response and it was getting darker by the minute.

"Cha Lark, if you're going to *call* him, then *call* him!" And Flem looked condescendingly at Lark in a mute appeal to step aside and let *him* do it right.

Whimsey C. Nimble

Holding out both hands as if to present the opportunity to one better suited to it than himsylph, Lark gave the other Sylph a have-at-it look and took a step back.

Wasting no time, Flem, hesitantly at first, swatted the inside of the small building with his open hand and hollered into the night, "BUD!"

When there was no immediate response he didn't wait but hit the metal door with a lot more force, sending reverberations throughout and yelled at the top of his lungs again, "BUD!!"

Lark stood back, shaking his head in soulful resignation. What would this do to his business to again close randomly?

Flem did not give up but kept calling, pounding out a beat lightly as background to his voice, making an awful racket, truth be told.

Cringing, the taller faerie laid an appeasing hand on the other's arm, but Flem shook it off and called again, desperation making him giddy. He had an official home to go to and he couldn't get there! So close, so close.

Oh Pan Portulaca, the usual calm, cool, and collected Lark threw away his carefully nurtured sophistication. Now *both* of them were making way too much noise and Bud could hear them from a goodly distance as he hurried back, his personal joke beginning to sour in his mouth, his own adrenalin shooting about in his guilt and nervousness.

Slipping up the driveway, he mentally excused himsylph to Mrs. Fletcherman for not locking the gate before he actually *left* the grounds but he was sure glad as he broke into an all-out run that he hadn't.

"Okay, okay, I'm here! Calm down, both of you," he was yelling as he skidded to a stop and frantically searched his pockets for the key.

Both locked up Sylphs ceased their caterwauling immediately, relief and embarrassment dancing around their heads like fireflies. Flem's feelings dived from one to the other and back again while Mr. Cool merely brazened it out with aplomb, returning to his usual sangfroid manner.

"Where've you been?" he asked their savior as the door mercifully opened, hoping to deflect the flack he knew was coming. Oh, this was an infamy that would go down in the books, and well he knew it in his soul. Still, a Sylph could hope, now couldn't he?

"Ah, Oleander's," replied Bud, has face averted, doing his best to remain expressionless.

Lark nodded but stared at Bud 'til he finally stared back, laugher not far away.

"I can't believe you *locked us in*, Bud," accused Flem, hurt by this cruel prank.

"Whoa! *I* didn't touch this lock, now see here! I had no idea you two were still in the *tool shed* for Pan's sake. *Cha*. The *tool* shed. Don't either of you have a home to go to? Flem?" He drew Flem's name out in paternalistic, guilt inducing manner.

The faerie looked properly chagrined, but puzzled too, as he turned to his partner.

Clearly, Lark still harbored suspicions from the way he gazed at his long time friend.

"Yeah, that's right Larko, I did *NOT* lock you in, although I would have if I could have, but I didn't, you see, so how *DID* the two of you come to be locked in together like that, hmmm?"

A hazy memory floated over Lark and a remembered thwump rang in his ears.

Cha, they'd done it to themsylves.

Recognition wrote itself on his features and was picked up immediately by the other twos' radar.

Bud waited for his golden admission, while Flem just stood there, head hung in embarrassment, not caring.

"Oh cha, okay, okay. Surely you can understand, Mr.-Call-in-sick-and-I-later-find-you-at-Windfall-Café-with-China-and-Cat..."

Lark was still trying to brazen it out but it was so uncomfortable being in the hot seat so once again he was trying hard to shift attention but all he got for his efforts was Bud's "I'm all ears."

"Oh, alright then. So what. Yes, our blood ran hot, didn't it ma petite fleur? Can you blame us? And it seemed like such a good plan, we'd be *hidden* from all." He went on to explain the almost locked lock that wasn't locked, until, apparently *they'd* locked it themsylves, in the throes of passion.

Bud started to laugh and it wasn't long before the other two joined him, Lark because he saw the humor, Flem because now *he* was trying to brazen it out.

When Bud got done wiping his eyes, he explained *how* he'd come to discover the two illicit lovers, and yes, his deliberate decision to go to the bar.

Flem stood open mouthed at this admission but Lark took it in stride, merely giving his bud a whack on the back and saying, "Yeah, I'd have probably done the same."

Flem thought of all his faux-pas back at Thimbleberry, and with new insight, saw the light. *IF* he'd laughed and gone along with all those perceived insults, if he'd *laughed* instead of gotten mad, he probably would have made more friends. Cha. Not *more* friends. *Friends.*

Camaraderie. How he'd envied it, longed for it, *yearned* for it. Shaking his head at missed opportunities, he let them go. *Now* was the important moment. He could start over. He already had.

Coming to a decision, he too grinned, much more lightheartedly this time and wise-cracked, "Good one, Bud. Better keep your eyes open, we'll be watching for our turn."

All three laughed at this quip. Flem and Lark automatically turned and started back towards the old greenhouse,

"Ah, aren't you forgetting something?" reminded Bud, nodding at the wide-open door of the shed.

With a shared sheepish Sylph smile, the two jumped back inside, Lark loading Flem's arms with the two boxes of replacement glass rectangles before he dragged out the door prize.

"Here," quickly offered Bud, stepping in to take one end. "I'll give you a hand."

The awkward group moved off, nighttime hindering their steps but high greenish lights illuminating their path just enough to see.

They made their way bumping along over rough ground until Lark ordered, "Set it down," and they leaned it up against the side of Flem's new old house.

Debating, Flem decided to take the precious glass inside with him and walked around to set it on an old table just through the window-door.

He looked up to see Bud's shadowy form wave goodbye and heard him say, "See you tomorrow night."

Flem's heart lurched to his ears. With all the recent excitement, he'd *forgotten* the *S* Club.

Chapter 66

"Pretty much *everything* in this store is made
from bamboo," Lark said quietly.

SLEEPILY, FLEM RETURNED Lark's kiss goodbye as the bakery owner untangled himsylph from where they had both crawled, Flem's new hammock. Lark's hung nearby but so far neither seemed inclined to climb back over to his own and so slept like a faerie pretzel in the other's, taking their chances with stiff necks and painful wingulacture. Ah, young love.

"See you tonight," whispered the disheveled faerie in human black clothing, popping his green lenses back onto his deep hazel eyes, trying to wake up. It was four in the morning and he was staying up later now-a-days than had been his norm in the recent past. But, the bakery couldn't wait. Maybe it was time to start teaching Kahili the morning routine. He wondered if she knew much about actual baking. That day wasn't today unfortunately, he reflected as he crept through the night to keep a date with magic that melted in your mouth, and that people lined up for, at seven a.m.

Opportunist to the core, a small furry feline came to investigate the noises and within minutes had ensconced himself near his curled Sylph's rounded belly, still warm from where it had lain against Lark's derriere.

Flem's hand stole down to scratch a soft chest and the answering rumble soon put them both right back to sleep.

Close to four hours later.

The soft tinkling of wind chimes drifted on the air and gently woke the backyard faerie in his very own greenhouse.

Whimsey C. Nimble

Faintly he could hear Iris's voice with muted morning traffic in the distance.

As his mind started working, so too did his cat counterpart who stretched and pointed sharp toes randomly.

"Ach, *when* are you going to learn NOT to do that?" Flem demanded of his companion, unhooking a toe from his skin.

Sleepy-eyed adoration blinked at him, butter would not have melted in that kitten's mouth, he was so sweet and complacent.

"Aw, you little sprite. I guess you should have a name, shouldn't you?" Flem lay back in the hammock and got comfortable, contentment taking him down a different path, blanketing him, easing so many pressures that had only recently taken a much lesser role in the forefront of his life.

He was understanding what it meant to really *relax*. It had been a long time.

Idly, he scratched behind the rogue's ears and miraculously no one was hurt.

Squirming around, Flem mused on what the day would bring. Lark was picking him up at twelve-thirty and they were going shopping for an hour before Lark had to return to work. Then he wasn't coming back 'til they left for the *S* Club.

A deep thrill took hold of Flem's very soul and stayed even when his thoughts strayed back to the present.

No work had been accomplished last night other than they'd built imaginary walls around the door prize, and tried to envision which panes to replace first. It was prudently decided to start above Flem's head, back here, where his meager stuff resided. Looking up, the faire calculated that he would probably have almost enough to do this entire back section. There were still lots of unbroken windows in place and he intended to talk to Bud or Mrs. Fletcherman about a hose he could use to start with the cleaning of those remaining green panes.

But not today. Today he had off. He hadn't had a day off from his constant to-do list, his life actually, for as long as he could remember. One that he felt truly entitled too, one he'd earned.

Lazily, he scratched under a very small chin and in return, a miniature claw wrapped around a knuckle, leaving tiny itchy streaks that welted immediately, like those won from a bramble bush. Speaking of brambles, he thought of the most famous two, both known for their edible berries, blackberry and raspberry. Flem laughed as it became obvious what his kitten's name was to be: Rubus, for bramble, the two sharing an ability to draw both fae and human blood.

"Okay Rubus, unhand me fiend," said the Sylph trying it out, helping the rascal to the floor and off of his tender Sylph body.

Mama cat came prancing around a corner to get a lazy faerie out of bed and to remember his duties: ALWAYS feed the CAT first. He would do well to remember it. She wondered just how long it would take.

The morning was advancing and the faerie-at-home putzed and lollygagged and did nothing but straighten here and there, raking around the fire pit out back, totally delighting in the small homey task.

Lark had clucked over his choice of clothing the night before when he'd asked Flem what he was wearing. It seemed he was looking for something special but it remained a mystery as to *what* was required. Flem shook his head at that little piece of bafflement. Cha. Sometimes it seemed these (meaning Lark) City Sylphs were awfully particular about things and while part of Flem scoffed at it, another part craved the inside understanding, the aplomb they all seemed to effortlessly exude.

He wondered about Yushania's, the store Lark was taking him to.

Not able to get much done no matter how he tried, the faerie finally gave up and set about cleaning and preening his own Sylph, able to feed the cats and push Rubus, Ruby for short, towards his litter mates and mama without too much trouble.

Wishing he had a door to lock, Flem laughed at himsylph for such nonsense and took himsylph out to the sidewalk to wait for the baker. He wanted every moment of this lunch hour to be properly utilized.

It wasn't long before the sleek black car was spotted and Flem's heart picked up speed.

Maneuvering through town, Lark didn't say much and Flem stole a little look at his lover. Flour dotted his pants and collar and there was dried dough under his nails.

Turning back, Flem smiled to himsylph at the ordinariness that so belied the incredible, unfathomable *man* beside him.

Whimsey C. Nimble

After only a few minutes the suave Sylph was easing the car into place, paused briefly and then slipped into the parallel parking space against the curb like a greased peg.

Leaning over, he placed one finger beneath Flem's chin and said, "For you, my little flower, this will be my treat," and he kissed his own finger and then placed it on the other faerie's lips.

Flem blushed a becoming fae pinkish all the way to his ears, which tightened around the tips.

Moments later they were walking up to an exotic looking store with a green forest of bamboo depicted over the large plate glass window to their left. Distant dark mountains were the backdrop to a green and lush rice paddy with a man and his water buffalo right in the middle of it. Gold foreign letters spoke something of importance below it but they made no sense to Flem.

Lark held the door, so Flem ducked in under the wooden sign announcing *Yushania's*, intricately carved bundles of bamboo cradling the word.

"Pretty much *everything* in this store is made from bamboo," Lark said quietly.

Flem looked around in wonder, his mind boggled in disbelief. How could that be?

Down one whole side hung clothes, with more in folded stacks running with them. Hats, sunglasses, scarves, socks, purses, jackets, sweaters, even underwear spoke for themselves.

Directly down from where the two Sylphs paused lay displays with the well stocked kitchen in mind: every kind of tray imaginable was displayed along with cutting boards, plates, plate holders, and dozens of unique bowls of all shapes and sizes. There were bamboo chairs around a bamboo table which was laid out with a complete setting for four on a bamboo tablecloth, with bamboo napkins and to include bamboo cutlery.

Flem could hardly believe his eyes.

Lark was enjoying watching *him*.

Slowly they made their way deeper into the store. A bicycle stood beneath three skateboards hooked to a wall.

In a dark far corner stood a roll of bamboo fencing tightly bound, along with at least two score of poles. Bamboo shades hung on the wall behind them.

Near the front again they were obviously catering to gardeners and Flem gravitated in that direction. Screens, umbrellas, trellises, benches of three sizes, several fountains and an actual gazebo stood, with several oblong boxes being stacked nearby with the small, airy structures pictured on the outside, a happy family enjoying a picnic on the inside.

Flem snickered and wondered if *they* were made of bamboo too.

"Pssst," came the call from the wall. "C'mere."

Flem's eyes were bright as he followed Lark's command and strolled over.

Lark held up an arm from which dangled a soft pair of black pants and with the other he held up a collared, olive-green black and brown patterned shirt. Both flowed with a soft wave of their own, obviously a material to hug one's body, a comforting, sensual personality.

"These are a blend, actually, of *cotton* and bamboo," Lark informed him. "There are others of course, but I see you in these forest colors and not so much the indigos or the crimson," but before he could say another word, Flem jumped in to assure him he was right, and without another word, took them and headed for the dressing room.

Shedding one set of human clothes for another, the Sylph wondered wryly if that day would ever come when he wore Sylph clothes again, the way a true faerie was *suppose* to dress... Ah well, one day at a time.

The pants accentuated his lithe and nubile body. He noticed they didn't seem too tight and was happy about that. The shirt was odd. Long sleeved, it hung lower than he was used to plus there seemed to be a heaviness around the back. If he didn't know better, he's almost think there was extra room around the shoulders, it didn't bind the way most others did.

"Flem?" Lark wanted to know.

"Yes," he answered, opening the door, stepping back.

"Mmm mmm mmm, quite the cat's meow. I'll have to keep an eye on you, won't I?" drooled his partner.

Flem had just enough time to give the other a strange look before he was twirled around, Lark's long baker fingers pulling, twitching and massaging the shirt the way *he* wanted it.

"*What* are you doing?" asked Flem when he felt Lark pat along the upper part of his back.

"Nothing. Nothing. Just making sure it hangs right, that's all. Well, ma petit, do you like it? Do you want to try on others?"

Whimsey C. Nimble

Deftly diverted, Flem shook his head. "No, this is perfect. Very comfortable. I didn't know they made clothing from bamboo," he added, fingering a cuff. "It sure is soft."

"Bamboo hasn't come into its own yet, globally," prophesized the more urbane of the two. "I did some research and here's what I found out. To get this marvelous texture, this divine drape," he let the folds of Flem's shirt spill through his fingers like liquid, and continued, "it has to go through a process that basically turns it into a rayon first. The *cellulous*, which is the chief component of *all* walls of plants in general, you know -wood, cotton, hemp, bamboo, et cetera, is broken down by *caustic* chemicals, (usually) and then processed through spinnerets, which result in a *regenerated* (textile) filament, something capable of being woven into cloth. The solution is known as *viscose* and the fabric it produces, *rayon*. So, *rayon* can originate from many different sources. For some reason bamboo produces this incredible material that when woven, absolutely delights the body, including the eye. Luckily bamboo cellulose is suitable for what's called, a 'closed-loop viscose process,' which purports to capture and recycle all the solvent involved, and as such, the finished product is suppose to contain no trace chemicals that pose any kind of health threat to the consumer. Now I have read that there are other ways to process cellulose involving water and not harsh chemicals but I couldn't find any facts to support it." Lark stopped and said, "There's more. Should I go on or not?" worried he was boring his audience of one.

"Yes! Most interesting, please do," confirmed his rapt partner, amazed at this wealth of information. That Lark, he was pretty much perfect AND brilliant. Sigh.

"Bamboo clothing is costly because at his point, most of it comes from China and that means there are shipping costs, of course. And I've seen a little from Viet Nam. The bad news is, it's pretty likely these were produced in a 'sweat shop' - cheap labor, long hours, deplorable conditions."

Flem looked aghast at this latest admission, wanting to rip the clothes from his back.

"I've never been overseas to see where these actually come from and I don't know that last for a fact. So, because I really like these and Snow Gum assures me they are all from very legitimate sources, we have an agreement. She also does alterations, so if anything doesn't, ah, *fit right*, we can have it fixed." He smiled blandly, like a man, a *faerie*, with something to hide, a secret in plain sight under the guise of guilelessness.

Flem listened and of course he heard the unspoken but couldn't figure it out so opted for face value.

"So you must have a shirt or two at home, is that what you're saying?"

Wondering if his delightful fae companion actually indulged in the art of sarcasm, Lark ignored him and continued, handing Flem a small furled flyer that was strategically placed in many locations around the interior. It extolled the virtues of bamboo.

As Flem looked down at it, Lark recited from memory: "Unlike trees, bamboo never needs to be replanted after it's harvested, so it's only a one time planting. It *regenerates* after being cut, just like a lawn *because* it too is a grass, the largest one in fact. It grows really densely, doesn't require irrigation and it's biodegradable. When it's harvested it can yield up to twenty-four tons per acre versus something like eight tons for most trees, and only about eight-tenths of a ton for cotton. That's what you'll find on this delightful flyer. What they don't say is that are inherent problems that involve unscrupulous companies, as I mentioned my suspicions regarding *who* is actually doing the weaving and under what kind of conditions. In addition, some forests have actually been clear-cut so bamboo can be planted instead and there goes our biodiversity. Fertilizer has been used when it's not needed, with no thought to how polluting the run-off is. And of course, there is no actual proof they are using the closed-loop system and recycling the harsh chemicals that are used on the softening of the bamboo's cellulose. I'm not an expert in these matters, just someone who likes nice things. I try to educate mysylph but unless you follow the trail back for everything you purchase, it's all second hand information, and what they choose to tell you. Companies will make false and insubstantial 'green' claims that their products are made from environmentally friendly processes and that they retain the natural antimicrobial properties of the bamboo itself. Which is true to a degree. *Rayon*, regardless of whether it's from wood, bamboo or whatever, doesn't mildew as easily as some other *natural* fabrics. It's not just bamboo, although it is often show cased as one of its magical features. They also claim bamboo is thermal regulating, anti-fungal, anti-static and will keep you cooler, drier, warmer, and odor-free. And while it's true, like I said, it's true of *all* rayons, not just bamboo." He sighed and continued, "Like so many fabulous things in this world, it's potential hasn't been properly managed, of course. Greed propelled by a few has ruled the world for far too long, but, eternal optimist that I am, I believe that's changing and people, and others," here he shot a quick conspiratorial glance at Flem with a wink, "are evolving, opening up to simply working for what's best and most natural, for all involved, including our dear and precious planet, Earth."

A bedazzled, betwitched, adoring look adorned the slighter Sylph's face as he marveled at this evidence of the other's shining character.

With downcast eyes fluttering shyly to downplay Flem's attitude, Lark rubbed his hands briskly together and said, "I gotta get back to work."

Flem jumped in response, ducked back into the dressing room and minutes later, they were out the door, assurances to the pretty, dark-haired woman who waited on them, that they would certainly be back if anything needed adjustments.

Pulling up outside the nursery, the two faeries exchanged a brief touch of the lips, even though it was broad daylight and then Flem hopped out and slammed the door.

"See you tonight," was left on the air as Lark hastened away.

Iris happened to glance up at the right time to witness the exchange and the mystery cleared up as to how Lark figured in to all this.

Ah ha.

Chapter 67

This City has been attracting faeries for a long time.

*A*N INTANGIBLE, INVISIBLE weight settled on Flem and he wondered if he really *was* feeling it. Something was in the air and he suspected his life was about to turn some kind of corner. Every cell in his body was on alert.

It was a little after nine Saturday night and the faerie was ready to go, cats were fed, place cleaned up and he was dressed in his new clothing, feeling *very* fae and wishing briefly he could be back home in the canyon, and show off who *he* was now. Maybe someday, he thought, but he couldn't imagine it anytime soon.

Black pants molded his slim, lithe body and his woodsy shirt fell to mid thigh. He loved the feeling of them and did a couple of slinky moves around the old greenhouse just to have a laugh with himsylph.

His back was to the window-door when Lark materialized through it and coughed lightly to alert him of his presence.

Flem whirled around, eyes as bright as lighthouse beacons, fixated on the love of his life.

"Ready?" questioned Lark, the lone word coming out a bit huskily.

Numbly, the slighter Sylph nodded, and Lark pulled him into his arms, running his hands carefully over Flem's shoulders and disguised wings, a sly Sylph smile slipping through.

Flem's heart couldn't beat any faster but all the devastatingly handsome, tall man in black, Sylph in disguise, did was step back and with a mock bow, say "After you, ma petit fleur, it's almost ten."

It seemed odd to be leaving so late but Lark just poo-pahed any concerns and replied, "No, no really, things barely are getting going by ten. We are right on schedule."

Whimsey C. Nimble

In no time at all that seemed to take forever, they were stepping out of the car onto the sidewalk and walking toward, yes, the *S* Club, about a block away.

Flem swallowed in nervousness as Lark reached out and grabbed the handle of one of the black quilted double doors, allowing him to see up close and personal a stylish large dark pink *S*.

They walked into a dimly lit foyer, elegant blue sconces on the walls giving nothing away in their subtlety.

Two more doors stood silently before them, nondescript sentinels, guarding who knows how many secrets, sharing none.

With a knowing smile, Lark reached to open the door to the magic kingdom but was abruptly checked when back they flew, wham! in total surrender to the force coming out, pushing each Sylph-in-disguise back.

"Whoa! Sorry. Say, is that you Lark? I was just leaving for awhile, thought I'd hit Gazania's for a bit and come back when B...oh, hel-lo, who are you? Lark, you sly devil, who's this?" Without waiting for a reply or even taking a breath, the brightly colored personage zeroed in on Flem, practically salivating, a hand snaking out to caress Flem's hesitant hello and reluctant greeting. In fact, he was electrified, captured by the sheer magnitude of personality projecting at him.

Swiftly, Lark slipped right around the pink and white creature, deftly extricating Flem's clammy hand from the other's, neatly making introductions as he claimed *his* property.

"Vinca Pink." It was a statement, not an introduction but there was a world of information in the two words.

Flem heard acknowledgment, resignation and something else. Familiarity? Yesss, there was definitely an unspoken hidden history here. He found himsylph inappropriately wondering if he would ever hear the story behind *this* acquaintance.

Meanwhile, his tall, dark, and handsome faerie-in-disguise was making introductions although for some reason Flem kept hearing a note of mockery in his tone. Tsk tsk tsk.

"Flem, ma petit, let me introduce you to the one and only, Vinca Pink."

Seeming to cooperate, Vinca Pink stepped back and executed a delightful bow with a curtsey ending with a kiss blown to Flem, long flirtatious eyelashes fluttering.

Puzzled as to what gender the person was, Flem stumbled out with "Nice to meet you," but could say no more and only gaped like the green faerie he was. Vinca Pink was startling to a mere fae from the country.

A bold fuchsia streak dominated a thick head of white hair that hung heavily to the jaw line, a bit longer in the back, a few long tendrils passing the chin.

High cheekbones were the playground for slashes of color with pink, lavender and red streaks that blended nicely over taut skin. Interestingly, these did not clash with the weird vermilion eyes that had tiny green flickering pupils or the lightly patterned pink flowered skin. In fact, the whole ensemble worked, including the tunic-like dress of brightest white dotted with pink starbursts of flowers and dark pink edging along every hem.

Vinca Pink's pink diamond-studded tongue came out and traced the generous outline of the crimson mouth while sharp, knowing eyes took in Flem's assessment and reaction.

Blinking deliberately, Vinca Pink gave the slight Sylph a sultry look that somehow came across as cynical in Flem's eyes, and said, "I must be going. I'll probably see you later though, especially you, pussy willow. Save me a seat," before disappearing out the double doors.

"Shall we?" suavely motioned Lark, sweeping an arm towards the door he held open.

Expectations high now that he had met such a wild patron of the *S* Club, Flem was prepared for just about anything except what he saw: a normal club scene, nothing unusual at all. *People* sat at the many tables and lined the length of the polished wooden bar three deep, jazz filtering out from a nearby alcove.

As far as Flem could tell, the place was *filled* with men and women. *Human* men and women.

Surely not. He squinted.

It was a sophisticated scene to be sure but the *S* Club was just another club?

"Come my sweet, let me get you a drink," the green eyed Sylph man led him astray up to the crowd and with a squeeze on the back of Flem's neck, he let go and bellied up to the bar, money held out in a flag as he leaned in for a view.

Whimsey C. Nimble

Flem let out a sigh and relaxed a moment, looking around. A knowing glance, a fleeting meeting of the eyes, an awareness came to the faerie as if he too was part of a great well-kept but oh-so-obvious secret.

A furtive smile of welcome was given casually, like it didn't matter at all and eye contact was *not* held, more like a gotcha! sliding by.

The faerie quit looking out and starting looking in. A spark in his soul danced. Could it be true?

A glass of Egret's Beak mead was thrust under his nose and he laughed as he took it from Lark's outstretched hand then sipped to lower its sloshing content.

Green eyes met hazel and they stood, surrounded by a pregnant bubble. The cacophony of sound transformed to melody, background to their magical world as the seductive notes of a deep saxophone kissed their ears, lulling the senses.

Breaking free first, (someone had to be in charge) Lark twined his fingers with Flem's and pulled him through the cocktail party scene.

Flem saw no one he knew and yet there was a sense of familiarity. Following in his lover's wake, he stopped trying to analyze it and just let it flow over him.

Before long Lark stopped and Flem saw a dark entrance to something, its only explanation a neon outline of a pink palm tree on a small green neon island.

Lark motioned 'careful' and started up a covered set of stairs. They climbed in near darkness, people clamboring down as they made their way by, feet thumping, jazz and tinkling ice cubes, cool chatter fading behind them, another noise overtaking them the higher they went.

A fast repetitive beat assailed their ears, grabbing their blood, pounding to be let in to their Sylph adrenalin.

And it worked. By the time they were upstairs and onto the landing, both were twitching with the need to jump and dance.

Taking Flem's drink from his unsuspecting fingers, Lark set it and his own down on a nearby table and led him into the maze on the dance floor.

Loud music throbbed as Flem let himsylph go, a little sylphconscious at first. Looking around he saw lots of writhing bodies, faces set in various degrees of bliss. The dance floor was reflected back to the dancers as a bar with a full mirror behind it framed the dance floor from two sides.

The novice faerie was so caught up in the enchantment, the novel situation of actually being out in public with Lark he forgot he was at the *S* Club and danced hard, danced away all cares, all worries, all concerns and let it go at the euphoria of being alive.

Twenty minutes later his blood had taken up permanent residence with the consistent beat that didn't change much no matter what song came on but his body was crying for a break.

Two patrons moved off as Flem and his partner came back and they snagged their drinks and settled in at a high table.

Neither said a word but sipped their remaining mead gratefully.

Flem looked around at the crowd which was definitely more exotic than the one downstairs.

Bright, vivid colors and unusual hairstyles were the norm and Flem realized Vinca Pink had most probably come down from up here.

To be honest, he still couldn't see what all the fuss, their secretness, was all about. There was a part of him really disappointed that this was it. Still, he was having a good time.

"Where's Bud?" he asked suddenly as he recalled the conversation. "I thought he was going to meet us here, wasn't he?"

"Oh, we'll see him shortly, I'm sure," placated Lark as he finished his drink. "Finish up." He nodded at the other faerie's swallow that was left. "Want another?"

Flem was mightily tempted but decided to wait a while. Mead seemed to slow him down and he wanted to dance some more. He opted for water instead.

As Flem waited for Lark to return, he watched the people around him and a feeling of déjà vu swept over him and he wondered where that came from. For some reason he felt really comfortable here. Everyone was happy, involved and living with enthusiasm. A flash of a Sylph party he'd been to many many year ago flickered into his mind's eye. The same sense of camaraderie surrounded these people here in the City just like a gathering he'd been to at Penlei's, or was it WilloB's?

Looking around he wondered if everybody knew everybody, because it sure looked like it from where he sat.

'Course maybe that was because he was an outsider and didn't know anybody but Lark.

Whimsey C. Nimble

The music kicked up a notch, a rapid pounding of the airwaves and people scurried onto the dance floor. Pinpoints of light flashed in time with the throbbing beat, while outside the dance floor it grew dimmer.

He stared at the bar on one side, registering the many bottles filling every available spot for the entire length of both bars.

Blue and green neon snaked in and out and around the word, "Oasis," which was connected to a pink palm tree on a small green island.

Hmm. Then the bottles lined up captured his attention.

He got up just as Lark set two glasses of water down in front of them and blindly made his way to the bar to get a better look.

Standing close but trying to be unobtrusive, Flem's eyes strained past people to see that it was *all* mead, as far as the eye could travel. Egret's Beak, Cranberry Bog, Manzanita, and Dancing Crane were just some of the names and there was even a bottle of Bud's mead with the double capital Bs entwined!

Leaning between two pretty girls, he tripped and found his hand clutching the one on the right's upper arm which he let go of like it was on fire, he was so mortified by his gaucheness.

She merely shrugged it off and responded "No worries, you're fine, really," looking him in the eye intensely for a moment before turning back to her friend. Now they both looked him over, and he kinda felt like he was on the menu.

Rapidly he backed up, grateful for the hand that caressed his shoulder from behind, and relaxed against the tall strong body he mistakenly thought was Lark. It wasn't until an overly-minty mouth breathed heavily in his ear, the sickeningly sweet smell falling like mist over a cliff to his nose, and a rough voice whispered, in between licks to his earlobe, *raspy* licks, asking if he was new here, that he realized his wrong assumption.

His wings surged in blind panic, his heart raced and he rudely shoved away, his eyes wide with alarm, and excitement.

Lark had stopped after half-rising, on alert, but Flem extricated himsylph quickly.

As he slid into his seat, his eyes lifted to Lark's for confirmation but all that Sylph did was say, "Let's dance a little more, what do you say? Good for the nerves," and smiled entreatingly, a soft supplication in his gaze, a silent avowal that all would be well, to *trust* him.

Another fifteen minutes and muscles were relaxed, cares were flung aside and Flem would have been giddy if he wasn't now well grounded from all that exercise.

Taking a breather they made their way towards their table but only Flem flopped into his seat, Lark remained standing and threw down the rest of his water.

"I think it's time, my petit fleur. Yes, it's here. Are you ready?" he asked enigmatically.

Everything in Flem's life went blank as he could make no sense of his friend's words. But it didn't stop a deep feeling from brewing, a tempest in a Sylph teapot.

"Cha," was all Flem could sputter, eyes limp with intense expectation, but he wasn't sure of *what*.

"Drink you water my dear. You need to be hydrated. We have a very big evening ahead of us."

Again, Flem was steeped in wonder. He'd thought they were *having* a big evening. It was still to come??

He threw back his water so hard he choked, making Lark laugh against his will but for once Flem felt no fire at the burn.

Scraping his chair back, Flem was front and center in no time, feeling better by the minute.

"Lead on!" he commanded fiercely.

Threading his way through the constantly moving thicket of bodies, Lark kept glancing over his shoulder to make sure Flem was right behind him and of course he was closer than a shadow.

Around the dance floor and behind the bar was another dark doorway but this had a golden rope across it with a 'PRIVATE, NO TRESSPASSING, NO ADMITTANCE' sign to go with it.

Two very discreet words said it all: *'Members Only'* in small italicized script, black with a pink outline.

With total disregard, Lark easily unhooked the symbolic barrier and handed the end to his partner, saying, "Here. Hook this behind you and watch your step. We're going up," at which point he disappeared.

At the top another door barred the way again and this time, the cacophony from the dance floor was still audible. *Quite* audible, in fact. Also a *guard* of some kind actually sat at the door, checking IDs.

Flem gulped and nervousness shot a thrill through him; surely Lark had this handled, for Pan's sake. He had no ID!

Much to his relief Lark turned to him and the words came out, "Come, ma petit, meet Bignonia. No, his name is not because of his height!" He laughed at his own joke, as if poor Bignonia hadn't heard it for years and years.

Dressed in glossy green with splashy highlights of purple, he gave the impression of vigorous health but with an overgrown lankiness that lent an appealing impression.

"Hi," he greeted. "Actually my given name is Dick Rivers, I go by Rivers and you can forget Bignonia, thank you Lark for that." He smiled a smile with a little too much white showing, as if all he really wanted to do was clasp someone and hang on, that someone being Lark but Flem wasn't taking any chances and oozed charm, pretending he was an old hand at being in places like this, whatever *that* meant.

"Glad to meet you," he purred, eyes wide and beguiling, flutter flutter.

Rivers relaxed under the planned spell and expounded, unasked, "Distictus Rivers, I shortened it to Dick, you can see why." His grasp curled around Flem's like a grasping young tendril. A small, trumpet-shaped purple hat of sorts clung to his curly brown hair.

Holding Flem's sweating hand a little too long, he dived into that one's hazel eyes and remarked off handedly, "Hmm, hazel eyes; beautiful. First time here?"

"Uh huh," Flem nodded, uncomfortably aware that his hand was still caught.

"Busy tonight?" asked Lark, his gaze boring down on Rivers, who apparently read between the lines and unhanded the newcomer, but not fast enough because Lark took a step closer, smiling himsylph, but he meant business and the warning was there in his look.

"Please, be my guest. Go see for yoursylph." This was said with a long flourish and the doors opened in invitation, as if by magic but really, from a button on the floor that Distictus pushed with a slight of foot.

Flem's head was aswirl and he felt like he was floating on air.

The door whooshed shut behind, a whispered finality.

Lark was still walking and Flem hurried to catch up, his senses confused by what he was seeing.

Rows of *lockers* surrounded them and a funny little tickle starting waving in Flem's stomach, like the leader of the parade was marching around down there, but instead of a baton, he waved feathers, making Flem's belly quiver and jump.

Pulling out two small gold keys, Lark handed one to Flem and said, "Here. Yours is next to mine. It's good for a year before we have to renew it."

With that said, he halted and inserted his own into the small hole, pulling his locker open.

Flem's eyes were like saucers as he tried not to be overwhelmed by the implications.

Taking his hand, the tall dark Sylph pulled his love over to a nearby bench and they sat down.

"*Here*, we can be who we really are, Flem. There's a lot of us. This City has been attracting faeries for a long time. But as you know not everyone is so accepting. Humans are everywhere and far outnumber us.

"Mrs. Fletcherman is cool. And Mayapple. I don't know about Santolina, I think he's okay but old school, you know? I think we *bother* him," he ended with a chuckle.

Flem was swallowing convulsively and he felt his emotions sky rocket, but he was able to easily control it, thanks to all the dancing they'd done.

"You mean, I can let my *wings* out, Lark? And you? And *others*?" this was said in an incredulous voice. "*Really*?"

Pulling the other faerie close, Lark hugged him tightly before holding him at arm's length and declaring, "Yes, ma petit fleur, yes. Welcome to the *S* Club. Let's fly!"

Chapter 68

Crawl into bed with a faerie? He
didn't have to ask her twice!

S HYLY, FLEM TUGGED at his waist band, not quite able to just so matter-of-factly *strip* in a strange place, even if it *was* the S Club.

In the distance, metal locker doors were heard slamming open and closed, voices chattering, coming their way.

Flem looked at Lark in panic but Lark merely shook his head and shrugged his shoulders, while continuing to unbutton his black silk shirt and kick off his shoes.

Two Sylphs came into view, down at the end of their row and Flem stared.

If he didn't know better, he'd think he knew those two Sylphs!

At least, he knew their faces.

They weren't *women*, that was for sure. But he knew that, of course.

A flash of the *faeries* from Revelry with Cybele flashed through his mind. Surely *Rainbow* wasn't...? Nah.

Heh heh, he laughed nervously to himsylph. But no matter how delightfully intriguing this all was, being confident was still new to him, at least in this Sylph social scene. What that meant was, fear still had a small fist wrapped around his entrails and liked to fire up his nerves with little lightening bolts of adrenalin. Without warning of course. Like right now.

Cha.

China and Cat strolled up, arm in arm.

As they stopped, Flem was overcome. It was one thing to sit around a fire pit in one's own back yard but the top floor of the famous S Club was a whole 'nother matter.

Chinaberry took the lead. "Flem! Ooh, you are looking *fine* tonight. Are you ready?"

He nodded distractedly, eyes glued on their wings. All he could think of to say was, "Don't you furl?" meaning inside a building. Oh, but he had so *many* questions.

"Yep. Sure do. Watch." With a snap Chinaberry's lavender wings with deep purple wingulacture snapped into a tight furl.

Cat's green ones gleamed as she did the same but they immediately stepped apart and unfurled, showing off, furling and unfurling, snap! Furl. Snap! Furl.

Flem and Lark burst into laughter at such silliness and the colorful pair went on, calling back, "Hurry up Lark, get him in there, for Pan's sake. You remember your first time, don't you?" and a trail of laugher, like bubbles, floated in their wake.

Lark came up behind him, his shirt gone, his wings still tied down, and turned him around, steering him back to their lockers.

Flem was almost embarrassed to be seen like this in such a public place.

"Here, let me help you," commanded Lark, running his hand up the back of Flem's shirt.

"What are you do-?" but to Flem's astonishment, a big piece of his shirt came away in Lark's hands!

"What-?" was all he could say as next, his sleeves were deftly unsnapped from within the hidden seams and before he knew it, his wings were untied, first one side, then the other.

Barely controlled nerves kept them furled even though at home his wont was to untie and unfurl simultaneously.

"You can unfurl Flem. This is what it's for. You can be yoursylph here. You don't have to furl inside. Be polite of course. Good manners are never remiss. Now, untie me, would you?" He arched his shoulder towards the other Sylph and Flem quickly complied, letting the wave of the moment carry him with it.

"Go ahead; and then, Flem, we'll go for a fly. What do you say?"

Mutely, Flem stuck out his hands and Lark grasped them, and together they unfurled.

Still not used to his enormous good fortune, Flem felt a wave of deep gratitude swell within his chest as he once again took in this mighty Sylph, one with great translucent wings that wore a light coating of black over their natural coloring of golden brown and dusty green. Who, against all odds, had taken such a liking to him.

The Canyon and the 'old' days shifted around Flem's ears as not-quite-déjà-vu drifted over him.

Lark had chosen well with the clothing he'd helped Flem pick out. The forest colors blended with his own natural coloring, and the faint leafy pattern that was Flem's own was just barely discernable throughout his opaque wing scales.

Quick as a wink, Lark dropped to his knees and threw a few licks at Flem's now-exposed wing base, but only one little click was out of place.

Not to be outdone, Flem pulled Lark up and returned the favor, eliciting three from him but they'd done so much, well, preening lately, that neither's wings were very rough.

"About your pants, Flem, you can keep them on, but you won't need them. I'd say get rid of them."

Into the locker they went and as Flem ran approving eyes over Lark's lithe fae figure he saw what that faerie was wearing. The little black dress he'd watched him buy, the very one he'd worn just the other day when Flem had followed, lost in his own pathos and sylphpity. Hmm. Maybe he wouldn't 'fess up quite yet to watching him *buy* the altered-dress-now-tunic. Not yet. Not always good to admit you were *spying* on someone…

It's cut was very similar to what Flem himsylph was wearing, and now he saw *why* his shirt had been so long. It wasn't a shirt, it was a tunic! (He made a note to ask Lark about this miracle some other time.)

Dark green wingulacture stretched and pulled wing tips taut but Flem furled before he could stop himsylph. So many years of furling inside was an ingrained habit hard to break.

Lockers were locked and off they went, Lark with his glistening evening wear of black-boned wingulacture held behind so Flem could walk right beside, furled and jumpy with anticipation.

The exit loomed just ahead.

Giving Flem's hand an encouraging squeeze, Lark looked at him and said, "Ready?"

Taking a deep breath, Flem nodded just as the automatic doors pulled apart taking them back in time to canyon days. *Sylphs* everywhere! The room was enormous, a giant fly-way in a seeming forest, walkways cling-ing discreetly within the outer edges, lights twinkling throughout, small tables, chairs, and landing pads scattered about. Inside, outside, at the bar, *Sylphs* flying from one spot to the other, spurts of gaiety crackling on the airwaves.

"C'mon, let's go check out *this* dance floor!" And just like that, Lark leaped, the launching pad twanging behind him in reverberation.

With an ecstatic laugh, Flem's wings snapped to attention and his heart soared as he too was finally flying! Flying! *Flying* to catch up with Lark.

An uninhibited thrill took hold of Flem's soul and before he could stop himsylph he was tumbling through the air, circling Lark's head, skidding by with scant inches between their wings, rolling through the air in a curled up ball before snapping out to stretch toe and fingertip as far as they would go, glee shooting from his mouth.

Lark Spurastic caught the whigmaleerie and turned in the air, chasing after Flem, two faeries frolicking through the large bower, one with branch-es spreading near the ceiling, all with wide inviting places to sit.

With a suddenness that caught Flem by surprise, he saw Lark fly off ahead and zip to a large landing, where he gently lowered himsylph feet first and then walked into the shadows, a flash of his face turned back just before he disappeared.

Flem followed and soon saw Lark's profile leaning gracefully on the rail-ing of a small bridge over a gurgling forest stream, all part of this wonderful fantasy land that reminded virtually each and every one of them of back home.

Flem wasn't sure how all these Sylphs came to be in this City and he wondered mightily if they were *all Sylphs* who had stayed male? Or, were there actually female Sylphs? Who would leave in the first place, if there wasn't a dire need to do so?

As he reached his lover's side, strains of music could be heard from some-where off to the left, and Flem realized with a start that it was a waltz.

Lark ran his fingers through his hair before holding open his arms to Flem in mute appeal.

Moving into them, Flem's feet moved of their own accord, his wings half furled. Little eddies of energy guided the pair in grand sweeping circles as the strains of enchantment lilted through the air. Dreamily Flem fell in with Lark's masterful lead, head thrown back as they moved as one within the swirling magic, toes barely touching the floor letting the puff of wings keep them afloat.

Flem's gaze was unfocused somewhere near the ceiling when with a jolt he realized *eyes* were watching him, watching them. *Sylphs* were lounging in those high 'trees,' *Sylphs* laying upon branches, sitting, congregated, drinking mead, *Sylphs* laughing, talking, chattering. Oh glorious day, it was a shot straight out of Thimbleberry. The best day, that is. Not necessarily one *he* had experienced on a regular basis, unless of course they were laughing at him from where they sat...

Lark's arms kept the other faerie on track when his feet missed a couple of steps and Lark observed wryly, "You'd never know this City had so many closet faeries 'til you came here, would you?"

Flem didn't know how to answer that but Lark went on without noticing.

"No doubt you're wondering, as most of us do when we first arrive, *who* these Sylphs are. They're *US*, Flem. Or should I say Flumaria?" He grinned impishly down at his partner, fingers tightening where they held on to Flem's waist.

He went on. "Yes, most everybody here *is* male. We still age very well, no matter that we're no longer our old Sylves," he chuckled sylphdeprecatingly, then continued. "But I do know a couple of regular Sylphs. At least, I'm pretty sure they're female. I heard their stories a long time ago but I can't remember exactly how they came to emigrate from Thimbleberry Canyon or Cow Valley. Pretty much everyone's from there, by the way. Of course, we get visitors from all over the planet, but when it comes right down to it, we're all kin, we're social, we're mead drinkers."

Flem's head was reeling with this information, this alternative camaraderie that was available, flaunted almost.

As the music faded away, Lark came to a stop and asked, "Want to go get something to eat? We should do it now, before Bud, oh, I mean, *Fanwort's*, show begins."

"*Bud?*" repeated Flem. "*Fanwort?*"

"Yes, ma petit, you'll see." That was all he would say, just led Flem to the outer edged and coaxed, "C'mon. I want you to try the sherbet here, it's pineapple peppermint. It's really good with a hazelnut crumb cookie they serve. I've never been quite able to duplicate it."

Always a ready sweet tooth, Flem gladly jumped into the air and flew, more sedately this time, behind Lark to a giant saucer-like landing pad big enough for a crowd. Flem was reminded of a lily-pad he'd seen once at Koot Loon Lake.

The café was in the background and looked to be part of two big 'trees' that overshadowed it, one on each side with steps cut into the trunks allowing those who were inclined, to climb up. It was too dense for flying, although pads indicated one could drop in from a higher level.

There was also outside seating and Flem grinned. Tables resembling moss stumps were surrounded by various 'mushroom' chairs.

A hedgehog was shown reading a scroll, where the menu was posted for Gloxinia's: Sunflower Muffins or Barley Bread, with a choice of Carnation or Concord Jelly; Creamed Wild Onions; Blossom Fritters; Marigold-Orange Pudding; Pineapple Peppermint Sherbet; Hazelnut Crumb Cookies; Candied Violets; Dried Raspberries; Mixed Nuts.

Bowing, Lark gestured 'after you' and Flem led them through the tables and up to the open window.

Cha, but it sure looked like a human woman waiting for their order and bemusement washed over Flem. He glanced uncertainly at Lark.

Immediately, the faerie suavely performed introductions as if that would clear up Flem's question.

"Popcorn, this is my friend Flem. Flem, meet Popcorn."

"Nice to meet you." Her eyebrows flew up and down repeatedly, like twitchy hot kernels of corn. "What can I get you?"

"One order of sherbet and two cookies, please." Lark turned to Flem and asked, "What else looks good, ma petit?"

Flem studied the menu but declined anything else. Tonight was not about eating.

Choosing a spot on the edge of the dining area, the two faeries sat and delicately nibbled using their cookies as spoons. Flem was pleasantly surprised at how *well* pineapple and peppermint went together.

A commotion of color, a flurry of wings was seen through the trees over at the landing.

"Well, it's almost time. Let's finish up here," said Lark standing, one wing twitching for a moment and he shrugged at it with practiced irritation, an eye on the purple and emerald disturbance.

Whimsey C. Nimble

His partner obediently stood up, wondering what was going to happen. Wings straightening but then hesitantly starting to furl as he flew into fluster so easily. Years of training, unfortunately.

"Where to?" he said, his voice a little too high, blinking a bit fast.

He loved this but still, it *was* his first time here. These City Sylphs seemed so sophisticated, so sylphassured. It was hard to imagine himsylph ever reaching that level of sylphconfidence but perhaps if he stayed on center from now on he too might reach that aspiration.

By now, Catalpah and Chinaberry walked with them, one on each side, China talking nonstop to Lark and green-eyed Cat bouncing alongside Flem, giggling and making faces and eye contact with camouflaged kin, cozy hidden parties everywhere.

"Incidentally, what's Bud do, anyway?" Flem asked with feigned indifference, striving for that elusive cool that he never seemed to actually *feel*.

Smiling wickedly, the green Sylph had the audacity to pinch his cheek and shake it, as if he were a small *Sylphette*! Oh the indignity, he couldn't believe it but before his ire got too high, she laughed in his face and said, "Relax Cupressus, you remind me of a little Johnny-jump-up, you're so fiercely independent. As for Bud, well, you'll have to wait and see!" and she stepped into the air off the landing, wings vibrating like a jar full of mad bees, toes pointed down, hands on hips, and rattled at him, a Sylph dare in the flesh.

The spirit of joy and irreverence radiated out infectiously and Flem felt his wings clatter in response to her show of adrenalin.

"You still know how to fly, you poor old thing?" she taunted, sticking her tongue out and giving him a sneer.

Flem's eyes bugged out at her loud and obnoxious manner but he leaped to the challenge and dove into the air after her, reveling in a good old Sylph chase, his hot fae blood revving him on.

She led him a merry chase around the outer perimeter of the cavernous room before climbing to the top of the ceiling and darting away in a straight line.

He hovered, uncertain as to what to do, his breath coming in fast little pants, then heard his name called.

"Flem! Wait up, gooseberry. Cha!" Lark complained as he caught up with him.

Cat had disappeared but Chinaberry flew sedately by them heading in the same direction and called "Coming?" back over her shoulder.

Lark looked expectantly at Flem as if there was a question and Flem rolled his eyes at such overplay. "Of course!" he answered a bit snippily before he remembered his manners. "Lead on." This was commanded with a preemptive swipe of an arm, manners barely in place.

Lark laughed at Flem's show of impatience, taking it as a healthy sign and turned away, following the purple splash in the distance.

They soon angled down to a seating area before a giant screen that 'grew' between two heavily vined areas.

An arm that sparkled emerald in the light waved them over and soon four faeries in a row sat on a big wooden swing built to hold at least another four, but before you could say freesia, those spots were filled too, Vinca Pink winking and waving from one of them.

The swing creaked and moved as they all squirmed together, wiggling. Flem had furled but it was awkward. A look behind and he saw the answer: a multiplicity of brilliant wings poked *through* the back and within seconds he too had shimmied into place. A strange voice came eerily from down at the end: "And ONE and TWO," accompanied with a grunting sound and then he felt it. They were *synchronizing* their wing power to move the swing!

Flem found the experience deeply gratifying as they all had to work together and fine-tune to get the most lift and push for their efforts. As they orchestrated their rhythm, he found he could keep part of his mind on the job and still be able to converse with the two of either side of him. This was like the best of old times that he'd never had. This was *better*, as usual!

A flask and then another made their way around and Flem happily indulged in the ritual, taking mere sips then licking the taste of honey off his lips.

His ears sharpened as the muted roar of babbling voices engulfed them and he glanced about to see a full house of chattering social fae, wings furled or not as was their wont.

He was struck with deep wonder at what in the Pandora *Bud's* involvement in all this could be.

He didn't have to wait long as the lights dimmed and soft multi-colored spots of light drifted through the air, sifting down like rainbow snowflakes to sit on everything and everybody. Magic was astir.

Whimsey C. Nimble

The darkened screen transformed to a muted glow surrounded by lacy scrollwork, trees and jungle but stark silhouettes to each side.

The crowd quieted right down except for laugher in a couple of places, easily heard in the pre-show atmosphere, then they too paid reverence and all held their collective breath as the screen grew much brighter and a dim green glow now backlit the woodland jumble to each side.

Both flared up as if in agitation but then were doused completely.

It was only for a long moment, but when they once again sprang to life, it was instantly obvious what the difference was: an elaborate shadow was held in place on the screen as if pinned to it.

But it was no ordinary shadow.

It was almost as big as the screen itself and when the staccato hand clapping started that created a calculated but frenzied beat, it moved.

Minute twitches in the fingers, the head, and a shoulder were beheld first, connected to the same wave length as the clapping, and uncontrollable.

A fast and sassy violin along with a flamenco guitar joined the ruckus, demanding attention, and the giant Shadow Sylph leaped to life, each and every movement precise with passion, wingulacture dramatically outlined against the light.

Arms and wings spread out as if commanding thousands and there were no soft movements, all was rapid, tense and rigid, little sharp lines thrown out like invisible ether knives, accompanied by music that hounded the dancer, taunting, loving, pushing, sometimes almost sneering at the boundaries between them, flaunting its ability to grab the soul, as if the feast for the eyes wasn't just as valid in the whole.

Flem sat open mouthed, agog with the overwhelming display.

As the last strains of music faded, the dancer struck a corresponding pose, a striking, fierce abrupt cessation of all movement that looked frozen in place on a slowly darkening screen.

The crowd went wild, whistling, stomping, cat calling.

The screen lit up again, but only the words "Fanwort Cabomba will be right back" were seen on them.

Mouthing the name, Flem bequeathed a quizzical look upon Lark but Lark was ready for him and he mouthed the word "Bud" right back at him, making Flem's eyebrows burrow towards his nose in consternation.

Shaking his head in denial, Flem bit his bottom lip then repeated after Lark, "Bud?" with disbelief dripping from the word.

Lark nodded his sincere affirmation.

Flem had a hard time absorbing this fact and sat quietly fanning his wings in time with everyone else again. They'd lost all thought of synchronization while held in thrall by Fanwort's electric performance but sporadically resumed when she'd stopped.

It wasn't long before music was heard calling them all back in and Flem sat glued in place, wings forgotten, eyes riveted on the again darkened screen.

Softly the sweet enticement of shore birds mingled with the growing fervor of a violin, as the rhythmic slapping against a guitar coerced the senses, exhibiting with non-words the verve of life, content to let the smaller stringed instrument have center stage.

The screen was still dark but with a hint of life around the edges, the musicians invisible.

As the light awoke like the dawn of a new day, silhouettes again became visible.

Delineated crisply in the top right corner were miniatures of the fevered music makers coupled with swooping gulls and prancing sandpipers on the left.

Fanwort spread her wings, becoming the sylphification of the compelling melody.

The audience sat spellbound, compelled to take the journey, each Sylph spirit riding the notes right along with the dancer, hardly able to sit still, uncontrollable wing twitches jumping to match the beat.

Flem found his mouth open more than once during the next dance, closing it only when the dancer once again froze and the screen darkened.

Licking his lips, Flem turned to look at Lark with such innocence and wonder that tears came to Lark's eyes at the joy of sharing his rich life with this special Sylph. He smiled gently into Flem's gaze but the light of the screen pulled them back.

A Sylph ablaze stood there behind that screen, a screaming out of life, of controlled energy pouring from her cells, radiating in time to the stomping of her feet, a constant crisp clacking accompaniment.

Wings held down like a matador's cape, the passion drove her faster and faster, her wings now moving up and down to match jerky arm movements, as if they were attached to her hands, which they were not.

Whimsey C. Nimble

Her chin rose and regally pointed first one direction and then another, her feet expressing the heart of the matter.

Not a breath of movement existed outside of that stage as everyone's love for Fanwort Cabomba escalated to unknown depths, each one envisioning her as their own personal muse.

Head thrown back, it was obvious that the love affair was mutual as the socially acceptable coupling of music and dancer continued. A front row of Sylph hands broke into rhythm with her, raising her intangibly to the top of their shoulders in exultation.

Accepting it merely as her due, she urged everyone on, leading and chasing the demanding music by turns, the clappers now an integral part of the show.

After several frenzied minutes, the violin sought refuge, slowing the pace, 'thinking' about its partner who now bowed her head as if in acquiescence and the two stepped down together, slowing in time simultaneously, until their movement ended with a blackened screen.

Moments later the words 'FANWORT CABOMBA' lit up the screen in flashing techno color as the audience thundered to its feet, applause deafening.

'Thank you Willie and Lobo' came on to the screen and as the audience kept applauding and whistling the two miniature silhouettes in the top right corner took bows and flung kisses.

Fanwort did not reappear.

Lights came on and rustlings were heard as Sylphs blinked back to reality, but oh thank Pan it was *S* Club reality.

Flem's wings began to come alive, subconsciously keeping rhythm with the unknown leader who diligently worked to get the swing moving and soon all fanned together, peaceful now in the aftermath of such tumultuous power, happy to share the afterglow with others.

Lark's hand stole down between them and gently caressed Flem's thumb as they rocked.

Chinaberry and Catalpah were chirping like birds on caffeine, oohing and ahhing over Fanwort Cabomba's electrifying performance, practically salivating.

The swing jounced as one Sylph and then another extricated their delicate appendages and flitted away, leaving the rhythm disturbed but not unpleasant.

Feeling no inclination to move, Flem felt himsylph go lax, enjoying the interlude where time hung suspended. His head found a cushion on Lark's shoulder, eyes closing for a moment as he savored the *first time* of anything. Rudibeckia Gregg's voice from back in the canyon came to mind and he smiled in remembrance at how she used to emphasize that particular delight and urge her class of Sylphettes to savor it when it was upon them.

"Over here!" came a sharp gleeful command and a shudder ran through the lot of them, uneven cadence bouncing randomly.

A little spurt of adrenalin touched Flem's core and his wings started to furl right where he sat until he caught himsylph, smiling widely at Bud, A.K.A. *Fanwort*, to hide his blunder, his newness.

Bud almost looked like Bud but Flem had never seen his *wings* before. And now that he had seen him/her dance, well, it was hard not to be tongue-tied and in awe.

Buddleia was soon tucked between his two favorite 'girls,' as he called them, Cat and China, a blissful and adoring look upon each of their faces as they combed their fingers through the Sylph star's golden locks, made glittery for tonight's show.

Fidgeting, Bud popped his wings through and soon all joined whole-heartedly in recovering a singular common beat.

Dreamily everyone settled down again, waiting for words of wisdom from the golden one's mouth, petting and stroking whatever part they could of the famous (in some circles) Fanwort Cabomba.

Silence reigned for about thirty seconds while Bud laughingly plucked fingers from intimate places and returned them to owners, shaking his head, trying to not be strangled by green and purple arms that claimed ownership.

Flem peeked from under his lashes down the row at the star and found himsylph asking, "Is there a name for what you do?"

China and Cat swooped in, making great sport with the statement and repeating it with a mocking edge that Flem had not intended, a sexual twist rampant in their innuendo to match their groping hands and suggestive wiggles.

Laughing at their audaciousness, the multi-talented faerie swatted playfully to try and get them to behave, saying, "Later! Later!" before clearing his throat and expounding on one of his loves.

Whimsey C. Nimble

Leaning forward, he looked down the line to catch Flem's eye and replied seriously, "Yes, it's called Flamenco, Flem, literally meaning flamingo in Spanish. It originated from the oldest known form of song, before musical instruments were invented, where rhythmic stomping, beating, and clapping accompanied the call of chanting, like you heard earlier. I personally find it exhilarating, satisfying a deep primitive part of mysylph that demands expression."

He stopped a moment to pull out someone's hand from under his tunic in the back and then said "Oooh!" and sat up straight in surprise as a tongue found a rough scale in back but just as quickly ignored it and leaned out again to enlighten his audience a bit further.

"There are three principal parts to today's Flamenco," he instructed. "There is the *cante*, which is the voice – the singing; the *toque*, which is the music, and of course the *palmas* – the clapping. All of which is Sylphified by one's demeanor – a proud carriage, regal expression or bearing and how well one is able to portray passion, emotion."

At this, several deep heartfelt sighs were heard up and down the swing as every Sylph there fell more in love with the charismatic faerie, each envisioning the passion *Fanwort* so eloquently portrayed...

Chinaberry and Catalpah draped themsylves nonchalantly over every piece of him available, a casual display of ownership that did not go unnoticed, though many still tried to cop a feel.

Bud leaned back into their embrace, immediately ensnared by a tangle of arms and he wondered momentarily if this was what a trapped fly felt when caught by a deceptive but carnivorous plant. Looking into adoring lustful eyes on each side of him, he merely smiled and resigned himsylph to his fate.

Dreamily the swing lifted and fell back but it was apparent that everyone was losing attention and soon it was almost still, only a few reverberations trickling through.

"Well, ma petit, shall we go home?"

Flem breathed deep, inhaling the moment. Could it really be over already? But there was barely any regret in the reflection, as he was replete with his evening and sylphsatisfaction.

Sunday, the next afternoon.

"Flem, are you here?" inquired Mayapple's voice as she hesitated.

And even though the question seemed innocuous enough, Flem knew there was a world of interrogation behind it.

He groaned. Last night he and Lark had ended up at the houseboat but Flem had opted to be dropped off at Fletcherman's, or *Greenwood's*, a name he was trying on for *his* abode, when Lark went off to open the bakery at a god-awful time this morning. It was Sunday, and while the Blackberry Bakery opened later than usual, it was still pretty damn early by Sylph standards. Cha! Especially after a Saturday night out.

He groaned again.

"Yeah," he called feebly, unwillingly. "I'm here. Come back." Such a gracious invitation and Mayapple heard the reticence in his voice but opted to flat out ignore it.

Daintily she picked her way back to the bamboo wall, peeking around it with a, "I can't believe you're still in bed!" exclamation as she did so, slightly embarrassed but nonetheless determined.

"I'm not. I'm up," said Flem from his hammock, trying to look awake.

"Flem! Well? Tell me all about it!" she commanded as only queen Mayapple could. "Are we still on for tonight?" she asked before he could even think where to start and beside which, he really wasn't up for it right now anyway. He was exhausted and Mayapple in and of herself was exhausting and he didn't see how he could combine the two but as usual, Mayapple was way ahead of him.

"Here. How did I know you might need this? Gee, I wonder..." A tall paper cup with *Canterbury's* embossed on the outside, colorful bell-like blue and pink flowers gracing the name, was set upon a nearby shelf.

"Careful, it's hot," she cautioned.

Swinging his feet around and onto the floor, Flem ran his hands through his disheveled hair and blearily cocked an eye towards the boss's daughter.

"Whaddayawannaknow?" he asked.

"Oh My God! *You*. Oh my God."

Flem wondered if that was suppose to make sense but Mayapple huffed and handed him the hot cup rather rudely.

"*Here*. Drink this. God."

Whimsey C. Nimble

The faerie flinched but obediently took the container and sipped, a blissful look transforming his expression.

He kept sipping, blowing occasionally into the hole in the attempt to cool it off faster.

Maybe it was a good thing she was here, his attitude started to soften as sweet chai soy latte trickled in.

"Finally," erupted Mayapple, watching him revive, as if it was a personal affront that he'd been having a lazy day following an eventful night.

Impatient, Mayapple pushed her luck even though she knew better and prodded rather tactlessly "Well, are we still on for tonight?"

Not nearly enough caffeine had seeped into his Sylph system, he didn't think there was enough in the city truthfully, and he did NOT want to go to Sycamore Park and check out his old hole under that rock tonight. Not even a little bit.

"No. No I *can't*, Mayapple. Not tonight. We will soon. But not tonight, cha, no way. I'm sorry."

She didn't say anything which really made him feel bad as he knew she was disappointed but Pan, sometimes you just had to let people BE disappointed, you had to do what was right for *you*.

Mayapple's whole demeanor drooped but she rallied and said, "You're *sure*? Maybe you'll feel like it after you're done with that. Drink up!" But she knew.

"I'm *way* too tired for that job today. I can't," he said with finality, amazing himsylph with his own conviction and strength.

But a new thought was occurring and he easily decided to be flexible, yes, that's what it was called, flexibility.

"I've got a good idea Mayapple. Here, c'mon into my hammock with me, and we'll sit here and drink our delightful drinks, thank you very much," he kissed her hand then tugged her closer, "and I will tell you all about my night at the *S* Club, how's that?"

Crawl into bed with a faerie? He didn't have to ask her twice!

Chapter 69

As I was saying, FLATULANCE, colds, flu, morning
sickness, motion sickness, and gallstones.

"WHEN? C'MON FLEM, when? You need my help and you know it."
Mayapple was exasperated with the Sylph and wanted to boss him
around in her frustration, but the faerie was intractable in his resistance to
actually setting a date and making the trek to Sycamore Park. He was in no
hurry to clean out that dive under a rock he used to call home. Mayapple on
the other hand wanted badly to come over and make a plan and then go do
it. (Privately, she wanted no escape routes open to him so he would always be
her backyard faerie.)

No, he didn't stay there anymore and most of his stuff *was* here, that was
true. But, the luxury (who was he kidding) of having *two* places was rather
enjoyable. And a first for him. Oh, he'd heard of Sylphs who had a tree in
Thimbleberry Canyon AND one in Cow Valley. In fact, it almost seemed
like *WilloB* had mentioned a second place, a long time ago. And Whimsey
Nimble didn't even live in a tree, she lived way up Moonlight Creek behind
that big mossy boulder but her place was so cool, especially with that rock
throne in the middle of the water, that she didn't *need* two places. He wondered about Pootsy Koons and where she'd lived before inheriting Windfall
Café in that old bus. 'Course her and Whimsey were pretty tight, perhaps
both just spent time at the other's seeing as how they were in the same neck
of the woods, way up Thimbleberry Canyon.

He chuckled to himsylph at his reminiscence as if *he*, A.K.A. Flumaria
Greenwood, had actually been *friends* with them. They were always friendly,
he would give them that, but no, *she*, Flumaria, had been the odd one. He
could see that now, and why. Back then, *she* knew she was odd and now *he*

realized it stemmed from such a lack of true sylphconfidence. It was hard to see, though, what to do to *change* that when one was living it.

But now just by being himsylph and stumbling in the right direction thanks to Iris's hiring him and his own determination, he understood so much more. Sylphconfidence wasn't just something you decided to increase one day, it instead tended to blossom with accomplishments, and time. He saw that now. And they didn't have to be big accomplishments, they could be anything he decided to take charge of, do it right, and then let himsylph *feel good* at his talents, for that's what they were, talents, strengths. Everyone had them, whether they acknowledged them or not.

He thought of Lark's fabulous skill with food and how effortless he made it seem. He, Flem, couldn't produce a blackberry tart if his life depended on it. But he did know how to hang a door and had always assumed that that was something *everyone* knew. Pan, they *were* Sylphs, after all.

But Lark didn't. It never failed to amaze him. Perfect Lark wasn't perfect.

"Oh my God. Hello? Where'd you go this time?" Mayapple asked rather caustically. "Good grief, how do you ever get any work done?" This was accompanied by a dire shake of her head and a rolling of eyes as she continued loading plants onto her low wagon.

Flem ignored her, checklist in hand, a faraway look in his dazed eyes, a sea of green surrounding them.

The rolling door was up and the Green Thumb's truck had rolled out of sight not five minutes before, delivery accomplished.

"Soon Mayapple, I promise."

He was being so silly and he knew it. It's not like he was going back there. Yuck. And he did need to get the last few things he'd left there and clean it out. Wouldn't take much. Cha, just a good sweeping would improve it ninety-five percent.

"Oh, I give up. Did you have your tea this morning?" she rattled on, fast becoming irritated with her preoccupied fae friend.

Heaving a martyred sigh, the girl sniffed in aggravation as she filled the remaining empty spots before her with an array of newly arrived herbs.

Giving it one last try, she asked "Did those fronds show up yet for the Herb Hut's roof or do I need to call the company to see where they are? I can't believe they didn't come in when the walls were delivered!"

Flem blinked, his eyes focused on her and he came back to reality.

"Yep," he replied. "They're wrapped in plastic, they came in the other day when you were at lunch and I set them back in our planting areas over in number one. And, we got a delivery, or rather, you did. It said, "Attention Mayapple" on it, so I haven't opened it. I put it with the fronds. Shall I bring them too?" he inquired as he made one last note on their invoice and then shoved it in his back pocket.

Before she answered he went on, "I'll get the rest of these. I'll make two trips if I have to. Why don't you stay there and start organizing everything, okay? As soon as I get the fronds, we'll put the roof on, how's that?" He looked at her with a steady gaze as if saying so much more but she wasn't so easily placated and they both knew it. He hadn't really answered her question and she wasn't happy.

Biting her lip, she growled deep in her throat, abruptly deciding to change tactics. "Of course," she agreed sweetly through her teeth, moving on, plotting. "Good idea."

Instantly he was on guard and laughed at her, although a little warily. "*Mayapple*," he addressed her, and the issue, with a big sigh, a plaintive note in his voice. Flem did feel a little guilty in that regards, seeing as how much time he and Lark had been spending together, but luckily Iris chose that moment to show up, striding right towards them, vanquishing any reply he was to make. Saving him, in Mayapple's opinion.

A little flushed and breathless, Iris Fletcherman came to a halt, her eyes switching from one to the other and back again. "Good Lord, you two look like an old married couple who've been squabbling. Whatever it is, get over it Mayapple."

At that Mayapple's eyes flashed and she turned on her mother only to find her laughing as she shushed her and said, "Oh for goodness sakes, I was just teasing. I'm sure it's all Flem's fault, whatever is going on." She said this in a joking manner looking over at Flem but the words themselves struck fear into the faerie's veins and started to shrivel his fae blood; he was *such* a woos.

"Oh for Pete's sake will you two quit acting like children and listen to me? I have some very exciting news that I'm dying to share, but hey, don't let *me* interrupt you, you just go on with whatever you're doing, working on your Herb Hut, I assume. I'll tell you later, bye," and she turned her well trimmed self right around and walked away.

"*Mother*. Get *back* here. We're sorry, aren't we, Flem?"

"Oh yes!" he piped in immediately, wondering what the Pan *he* was sorry for. These humans were so baffling at times.

Smiling, the boss turned around and hurried back. "Guess what!" she began, which irritated Mayapple to no end. Her mother could be so childish herself at times in her opinion.

"*What*? Just tell us." Mayapple stood by her wagon full of plants, glancing over at her partner for a moment, an automatic truce in times like this.

Flem nodded bashfully, feeling funny about *him* encouraging the boss.

Sure, *now* she got nervous, thought Iris about herself.

Flem and Mayapple waited expectantly.

Iris swallowed, wondering how Mayapple would take the news.

Santolina's voice suddenly rang out from up front, "Okay, okay, I'll find her, thanks," he called to the cashier.

"Hey, there you are!" he continued, spying the three of them and clip clopping his way back, a definite spring to his step.

"Hi honey!" greeted Iris, rather flustered by his unexpected appearance!

"Hey baby," said the short dark man, his hands deep in the pockets of his Parks and Rec jacket, leaning in to exchange a peck of a kiss.

"Well, did you tell them?" he asked, just as Iris was afraid he would. She giggled a little.

"No. Almost." Squeezing his arm, she held him in place right next to her, grinning and licking her lips.

"We're getting married!" she finally blurted out.

Whatever Mayapple had been expecting, it wasn't *that* life-altering bomb. In fact, her life flashed before her eyes. *Fletcherman's* was *their* place, her *dad*, Brody Fletcherman, her *mom*, Iris Fletcherman and *her*, Mayapple Fletcherman. Santolina was no doubt a nice man but he didn't belong *here*.

"Wow, that's great!" boomed out Flem at her side, freaking out inside, wondering if *his place* was still secure, as his future crashed about his ears.

"Iris, you got a minute? Could you step outside for a moment? There's something I want to show you." Santolina was gazing at Iris with love-struck eyes.

She returned the besotted look, completely oblivious to her shell-shocked victims, and with a little wave off she went, arm in arm with her new fiancé.

Neither Flem nor Mayapple moved, both caught in the what-ifs until both started talking at the same time.

"Oh Pan, do you think this is gonna affect my greenhouse?" wailed the faerie while Mayapple said despondently, "Oh man. Oh my God. I wonder if she'd going to let him ruin our business?"

Flem dispiritedly started pulling their delivery into a smaller area and Mayapple heaved a sigh. "Yeah, bring the fronds up when you come. You think you can get all these in a couple more trips?" Who cared about their wonderful Herb Hut idea now? Obviously not her mother if she was going to *marry* Santolina. He'd probably change everything. Probably wouldn't even be called Fletcherman's Nursery anymore.

Grunting, she tugged on the wagon handle and moved off at a snail's pace. Why bother if it was all going to change anyway? Before she turned the corner twenty feet away, Iris came skipping back in, sunshine her middle name. Flem watched as she bounced down the aisle then stopped and held out her hand for her daughter to admire. Mayapple nodded, words were exchanged, then a big hug, followed by a loud whoop from Mayapple. Iris kept going towards the cash register and Mayapple came at a run back to Flem.

"Okay, quit your crying Flemmy-boy and don't let your wings get twitchy. Ha! All is well. I have saved the day! Well, actually I had nothing to do with it, I just asked her straight up if *he* was going to run our business and what about *your* greenhouse. She said he's not going to have anything to do with our nursery! 'And for Pete's sake, she *gave* you the greenhouse Flem, not to worry.' *Her* words. Whew. You should probably invite me over for a drink to celebrate, what do you say?" she laughed. "I could pick out my kitty and she better not be spoken for either!"

The Sylph looked at her with brows beetled in astonishment as she landed on yet another topic, in fact two and he was reminded of a bug skeetering around, dancing on the surface of water. His mouth actually hung open a little at the facileness of her mind. Human women were a species unto themselves, he decided. A vague recollection came back to him, one he decided not to expound on with Mayapple, at least not at the moment. It almost seemed, well, as if *Sylphs* had that same trait, but not *male* Sylphs. This recognition was from the old days when he was surrounded by female Sylphs, and virtually everyone was female, for Pan's sake. Male Sylphs just didn't come into the picture unless two were mating and you sure didn't see them then. No, these were female traits in his opinion. He decided he was going to discuss this with Bud and Lark and see what their male Sylph take on it was, or if it was just his imagination.

Mayapple's voice broke into his lingering reverie and with great disgust she reiterated, "Oh. My. God. You are so hopeless today. Here's the deal Mr. Dreamer. I AM going to go organize our new project. Do you think you can stay on task long enough to remember to get all these plants and my box AND the fronds and bring them up?"

Flem winced a little at her sarcastic tone even though he knew she wasn't being unkind, merely her version of funny. At least, he thought so. He hoped so.

Pulling himsylph together he called after her, "Hey, I'll get on it right now. So...you want to come over after work *today?*" Her retreating figure stopped and she turned around, a big giddy grin plastered on her face. "Yes I do," she said, deep satisfaction lighting up her eyes. Thank you. I thought you'd never ask." She paused, then said, "But I can't. How about tomorrow after work?"

"You *can't?* Why not?" Flem spluttered, feeling indignant that he'd finally acceded to her wishes and her she was, declining. More emotion than thought carried him along even though he'd been only lukewarm to the idea two minutes ago.

Mayapple stopped what she was doing and gave him the eye. Very demurely, she recited, "It just so happens I, ah, have *plans* for once after work. Dicksonia didn't really work out and unlike you, my fine faerie friend, *I* don't have that magic of love in my life right now other than my friends, you know, *you*, and so it's a sad state of affairs when your friends don't even want you to come over," here she heaved a giant, dramatic sigh before continuing. "*Tomorrow* would be so much better. Shall we call it a date?"

Not realizing she hadn't answered him and feeling rather hoodwinked though he wasn't sure why, he agreed, "Yes, yes okay."

"Well perfect," she said. "I'll see you later partner. I'll be waiting for that roof." She turned and walked out of sight, pulling the green cart behind her.

Feeling puzzled as usual by Mayapple but renewed by the assured patronage of Iris Fletcherman, Flem wondered if Mayapple was going to hound him about Sycamore Park. He was starting to feel a twinge of pre-irritation but stopped it in its tracks with a change of attitude and decided instead to be grateful for all his blessings, including a friend who had different opinions than his own.

Forty minutes later all the herbs sat in a mishmash around them, some on shelves, some within the roofless Herb Hut frame, a lot on the floor and several still on the wagons.

The frond roof was still rolled up in its shipping plastic but close enough to trip over which they both did. All in all it looked to be quite chaotic but Mayapple had the plan in her head. Flem did too, sort of. He had a general sense of what they had written down in the outline but hers was seemingly crisp knowledge. Not wanting to rock the boat, he simply waited for directions and let Mayapple take the lead.

She never gave it a second thought and started organizing while throwing orders to the Sylph: "We'll get the culinaries first. Bring me all the pots of parsley, rosemary, basil, thyme, and, well, you know." She started looking at tags and all the small green plants on her wagon, lifting one off and saying over her shoulder, "I figure all the cooking herbs will go here," and she indicated the inner wall on the right. "And the medicinals along the back, along with the 'Herbal Drugstore' book display and we'll put the mints between the two as they seem to go either way."

"Mom ordered a bunch of stuff too and that's what those are," she said, nodding her head towards some nearby boxes. "We'll wait 'til we get our plants mostly situated, then we'll dig out the other stuff we ordered and open hers."

Flem grunted "Okay, sounds good," as he continued checking tags on the myriads of greenery, setting aside all those he associated with food.

"When do you want to put the roof on?" queried the faerie, knee deep in his job.

Mayapple looked at him and then over at the log-like package.

"Well actually, let's do it now, since the walls are up and the framework is in place to hold it. That way we won't be stumbling over the plants inside when we adjust the roof."

They both stepped towards the obstacle, Mayapple plopping down to sit astride it as she pulled a little orange tool from her belt and deftly slit the plastic from one end to the other.

Flem watched with great admiration. That Mayapple was *so* talented.

"Let's unroll it," she invited and together they unfolded two green mesh panels with several layers of 'palm fronds' sewn right on. Awkward, but effective.

Within minutes the Herb Hut had officially come together, the thatched roof securely tied in place.

"When I was researching structures like this, I found this company offered a free sign if you bought their product so here it is." Mayapple unrolled a long piece of paper that had The Herb Hut in fancy letters, each themselves made from various herbs. A transparent slot above the door and just below the roof soon held the announcement.

"Wow. Good job Mayapple! This looks great. Well, let's get it finished. What else goes where?"

They worked steadily, Flem following Mayapple's orders the rest of the afternoon and by the time Iris came back around five, they were just about done, the only things remaining were the boxes which as yet, remained unopened.

"Oh, this is so cute! Good idea kids. Oops, sorry, not kids. Well, hey! Where's the stuff I ordered? Didn't you even open these yet? Why not? God, am I going to have to rearrange everything?" and she whipped out her own little tool and instantly all three boxes sprang open.

Mayapple stood aghast. Had her mother just said she was going to *rearrange* all their hard work? She looked over at Flem for support but that bubble-head was on his knees helping unpack.

"Oh, these are cool," he exclaimed as he unwrapped several clay plaques imprinted with natural plant indentations and the delicate words: 'O Great Spirit whose voice I hear in the wind and whose breath gives life to all the worlds, let me learn all the lessons you have hidden in every leaf and rock.'

Well, there was always room for sayings Mayapple granted, drawn over to help, holding onto her skepticism with both hands as she leaned in. "What else you got?" she asked reluctantly.

Iris smiled but didn't look up, her hands busily pulling paper away from objects and small boxes.

"Oh, just a little of this and that. You know." She passed her daughter a small wooden crate with six miniature soaps embedded in straw. Each had a distinctive piece of herbery affixed to it. "I ordered two rose, two lemon-balm and two almond. Think there might be a spot for them too?" she asked innocently.

Mayapple smiled. Bested again. Of course.

Meanwhile Flem was oohing and ahhing at his excavated find. "Look at this Mayapple! These are for cats!" He laughed in delight, reading "*Cat Grass. What is it?* Oh, look, it's just oats, and you plant the seeds in this little container they include. Oh Mayapple, look."

Iris spoke up. "I bought catnip too. It should be here with these, I would think."

Flem held one up, smiling in agreement with that darling boss of his, Iris Fletcherman.

"You are *such a peach*," he said to her without thinking and then realized he's just called his *boss*, the owner for Pan's sake, a *peach*.

Color flooded his cheeks and his heart lurched, wings tremored briefly at his burst of candor but then the new Flem, the one who *imagined* he was totally sylphconfident, stepped in and took over. Swallowing fear, he smiled shyly at Iris.

Helplessly charmed, Iris smiled back before fishing out the last pieces from the box, turning to Mayapple and saying rather abruptly, "Here. "

Her daughter took the package from her mother but before she turned away Iris felt the quick poke in the shoulder, as if to say, 'See? I was right all along.'

Iris was captivated and realized they both shared the delight in the novelty of having a faerie in their life, a humorous, joyful, quirky but enriching experience.

Mayapple opened the last of her mom's purchases and to her surprise there were three different packaged items in the one box – ceramic coasters with a separate wildflower on each; twelve small vials of essential oils, and a compressed dozen Irish linen tea towels, words and herbs hinted at beneath their transparent wrapping.

Mayapple was dazzled and thrilled at her mother's contributions.

"Okay, it seems you two have everything under control. I'll leave you to it. Do you think you'll get it finished before quitting time?" Iris queried, ever the boss, standing up and making ready to leave. The hand with the diamond flashed and twinkled and there went her mind. Stretching her arm out, her gaze locked on the ring. Barely listening to them, she nodded but it was clear she had changed gears and left them and their Herb Hut, behind.

"Bye mom," prompted Mayapple, a bit condescending which was really rather rude considering how Iris had just enriched their project.

The edge caught Iris's ear and she threw Mayapple a hard stare with narrowed eyes but just as rapidly turned her back on them and walked away, holding her hand out to admire the whole way.

"Ha ha!" laughed Flem. "She's something, isn't she? Well, let's get your box unpacked, whattaya say?"

Mayapple stared balefully after her mother for a moment but then put her out of her mind. "Right-O."

"Shall we?" politely inquired the Sylph, gesturing towards the one remaining carton.

A slow smile warmed her eyes and Mayapple said "Yes!"

Together they dived in like it was Christmas.

"Wha-at?" questioned Flem as he pulled out a bundle of something with lots of pointed ends but couldn't figure out exactly *what* they were.

"A-ho!" crowed Mayapple. "Do you deign to dabble with my dibber? Don't dribble on my dibble!" and started guffawing at her own wit.

Flem stood frozen in skeptical bewilderment. Just when things were flowing along smoothly, she went off half-cocked.

He stood looking at her waiting for more of an explanation, a flash of impatience flitting across his features. "*Mayapple.*"

"Okay okay, they're for planting seeds, you see. A dibble OR a dibber."

"Oh! Of course. Basically just little sticks with pointed ends, aren't they?"

"Tsk. Well. Hmmph. *More* than sticks, geez, here, give 'em to me. Let's go on." She reached in and brought out a five by six inch package of heavy plastic cards, saying, "Oh look, I forgot about these!" and quickly ripped them open, handing one to the faerie to read.

His eyes widened and he read "Planting By The Phases Of The Moon," turning the card over to see the illustrations that went along with the quick advice.

"See, each one hangs up by this little chain right here, through this hole. An easy handy reference, wouldn't you say?" and handed the pack to Flem before starting on another.

"Ah, my books," she said pulling out several different sizes including a package of six with that crisp new look to them. "I'll have to double check and see what herbs to pull to go with these. I ordered some specifically but I can't remember off-hand which ones they are, I'll have to check my notes. Anyway, these will be the main display in the middle of medicinals along the back wall." Digging among the packing paper she uncovered a small metal stand, the perfect display for the books and took herself off to arrange it.

Wondering what else she'd ordered, the Sylph dug in and brought up six pair of stretchy gloves reinforced along each finger with matching leather pads, all different colors. Flem eagerly thrust his hands into a bright aqua pair, stretching his fingers in adjustment.

Mayapple appeared at his side, watching. "Yeah, I like 'em too. I bet they'll sell."

Flem nodded and wondered if he could buy a pair right now or if he had to wait until another order went in someday.

He asked Mayapple and she said normally employees should order the things they really wanted but what the heck, this time it would be okay. In fact, to go tell Lily up front and she would put it in the Special Orders book. On payday, her mother would look there first and would subtract such items from their paychecks, minus their twenty- percent wholesale discount!

Gleefully, Flem skipped off and Mayapple turned, pushing packing paper out of the way as she searched through the rest of the order, her fingers coming in contact with a large package. Using two hands she pulled out a thick, bubble-wrapped, twine-tied bundle, trying to remember what she ordered.

Ah, she looked on in delight as it finally came free. Much lighter than the clay plaques Iris had ordered, these were of a different, lighter material, eight inches by twelve and each sported a hand painted scene: a garden shelf with three potted herbs upon it, plants growing lushly throughout and spilling over. Mayapple was already planning on buying at least one. A decorative border ran along the top, along with a heavy satin cord from which it hung.

Flem came hurrying back, slapping his turquoise gloves together over and over, a smile tugging at his lips.

"So what's left, Mayapple-snapple-dapple-doo?" he asked, laughing at his own wit. "What do you want me to do?" (Always a sure-fire perfect line to use, he'd finally figured out.)

Whimsey C. Nimble

Mayapple stood and gave him the eye. "Let's get this finished, we're almost done," and not being able to resist, she added, "And *I've* got plans this evening."

Flem's head whipped around and his eyes narrowed. "Yeah. You never *did* tell me what they were, either."

Smiling her best secretive smile the young woman agreed, "No, I didn't, did I?" a superior sort of look coming into her eyes and for some reason Flem was reminded of mama cat.

"Just *plans*, that's all. How 'bout you Flem, Lark coming over?" she asked guilelessly, attempting to steer the conversation back to before her bravado, wishing she'd kept her mouth shut. Her plans weren't a hot date, as she was implying. Rainbow Merkiva and her had merely decided to have a drink together at Oleander's right after work. It was no big deal. Still, it was fun to egg Flem on.

Ignoring that faerie's quizzical look, she reached in and brought out two more items, a box of plastic bottles filled with scented shampoos and a flat box.

"Oh Flem, I forgot to tell you, here what do you think of this idea?" she asked in a roundabout way, all pretensions brushed aside in her excitement.

"Look," she ordered.

Opening the box, she laughed and held up a cardboard pair of big red smiling lips fastened to the top of a long dowel with a pointed end.

"I'm going to stick these in all the pots with edible flowers. There will be a list of which ones those are on the wall, and listen to this. How do you like my name for it? 'Garden EATiquette.'" She was literally bubbling with delight.

Flem took the box from her and poked around in it, stirring lips.

"Brilliant Mayapple, you're the best. So who's your hot date tonight?" He slipped it in unobtrusively as a tag but Mayapple ignored him and rushed about, pulling all into one cohesive layout.

Her way of answering was to sharply say, "Here. Help me," and thrust several items into his hands. "Follow me. We need to get this finished."

Abruptly she stopped in her tracks facing the Hut, cocked her head to one side and put her hand on her hip as she compared their work thus far with the picture in her head.

"This is really coming together nicely, isn't it Flemmy boy? We're a good team," she said over her shoulder to him, but her eyes were roaming as she took it all in.

"Yeah!" was all the Sylph could muster as he too pictured it full. It went so much further than their outline and planning.

To their left was a seeming forest of lavender, sitting on a simulated mound, looking for all the world as if it grew there.

Snuggled in right behind it several feet down was a display Flem had suggested, the 'pest away' section. A neat little type-written explanation was given below the big proclaiming title with rows of garlic, chives, mint, rosemary, sage, and thyme with some marigolds to keep the mosquitoes away.

Delighted, Flem looked from the overall picture back to Mayapple and she nodded in happy acknowledgement.

Next came a combination from Iris's and Mayapple's boxes; first a display of various herb-related books such as The Green Pharmacy by J. Duke, the new Garden Book by Sunset, Herbal Antibiotics by Buher, and of course Anna Pavord's beautiful big The New Kitchen Garden with luscious photographs, plus a couple of pamphlets related to herbs and the growing and cooking of them.

Next, cheek and jowl were the hard goods – coasters, linen tea towels, shampoos, moisturizers, herbal soaps and essential oils with *five* pair of gardening gloves lapping over the edge.

Flem felt a deep thrill of satisfaction at those gloves, planning on ordering every color eventually.

Next was the cat corner. Little plastic-wrapped holey bowls vied with one another for space, a large close up of a feline with bright eyes featured over and over on half of them advertising cat grass, with a different bright-eyed pussy on the other half for the catnip, a distinct section for the discerning gardener and cat owner before easing into the medicinals along the back wall.

Officially starting the back wall of medicinals was a gathering of that goddess in succulent form, aloe barbadensis, known to all as aloe vera, a plant that promoted healing and was the go-to plant for soothing sunburns, bites, and inflammation.

Moving further into the little room, Flem came to a halt in front of the herbal drugstore display, amazed at the abundance of small pots, most whose greenery was indistinguishable from its neighbor yet.

Checking tags, his coworker couldn't resist continuing to rearrange, commenting, "So many seem to overlap, like the mints and fennel, lemon balm and lavender. Peppermint has been around a long time soothing upset stomachs and easing tension. Not only does it smell good, it tastes good *and* it's effective for about twenty more ailments that I can think of right off the bat. It's a really versatile, all around tonic and easy to grow too, all those moist, kind of shady areas are right up its alley."

Well, any Sylph worth his salt certainly understood *mint*, for Pan's sake. It was everywhere back in the canyon.

"Fennel," he spoke up suddenly. "I cut up fennel shoots for my fruit salad."

Mayapple looked at him kind of strangely. "Really?" she said, curiously.

He nodded, wondering if this was another strange, non-human trait he was unintentionally revealing but couldn't imagine *fennel* being anything but innocuous.

But she didn't say anything more, just added that the seeds were known as a digestive aid, keeping the breath fresh and also useful as an antispasmodic.

He had forgotten it but now that she mentioned it, he had an old vague memory of someone back in the canyon, a long time ago, pressing a cup of fennel tea on him. It was years ago.

He laughed. Maybe if he'd drank it then, he wouldn't have been quite so spastic now!

"What are you laughing at? Let me in on the joke, Flemmy boy."

"No, let's keep moving. It's not a big deal," he assured her, chuckling, marveling at how good it felt to be able to laugh at himsylph. "So, what were you saying? Tell me about lemon balm and lavender."

"Lemon balm, Flem, is a perennial herb, officially called Melissa officinalis, easy to grow. Spreads rapidly, very hardy. And like so many others, we'll place it in two categories. We have some over in the culinary section too, since it's great in lots of things, like drinks, mixed in with fruit or in regular salads. But listen to these *medicinal* properties – it can be used for herpes, insomnia, ear infections, sore throats, colds and stress! And, it smells good. Wow, what an herb!" she enthused.

Flem rolled his eyes a bit at her but did nothing except agree.

"And lavender?" he prompted, hoping for the short version, casting an eye at the wall full of culinaries to their immediate right.

"Have you ever stood near a lavender bush right after it rained, Flem, or on a hot summer day?"

He shook his head.

"Oh, it's heavenly," she breathed. "Just the smell of it is suppose to help relieve depression and anxiety. It's also used to treat acne, blisters, burns, bug bites and stings, nausea and of course, stress. And, it's beautiful!" she rhapsodized, closing her eyes in reverence briefly. "I couldn't get all the herbs mentioned in the Herbal Drugstore of course, but I think we have a nice selection."

Flem agreed with her but evidently she recognized the fact the he didn't comprehend the *scope* of what she'd envisioned, plants from their own growing greenhouses and what they'd unloaded from the Green Thumb, and, it's placement. "Look here," she said, sweeping her arm out. "Echinacea purpurea, A.K.A. purple coneflower. Flem, this perennial *herb* is used for *everything*, practically every kind of infection heard of, plus things like Lyme disease and even skin problems. Whether you ingest it or apply it topically, it's got to be a staple in any medicinal herb garden.

"And this itty bitty guy is chamomile. I believe we've, ahem, covered *that* previously, right?"

He deigned to answer but his lips quirked.

Pointing, she enumerated, "Hops, ie: humulus. Perennial. The obvious culinary connection being that it's a main constituent of beer but you can also eat the young shoots. In and of itself as a tea it's noted for relaxing the central nervous system and helps insomnia and headaches. It grows fast and is good for trellises and arbors."

Continuing, she shortened it, spilling out just the names in a burst of verbal dehiscence. "Hyssop, lobelia, yarrow, red clover, um, that's, yes," she looked at the log, "saw palmetto, let's see, that's mullein, what's its proper name ?" She turned the tag around and read "verbascum," before continuing nonstop with "valerian, St. John's wort, ooh! Comfrey! External use only, anymore, and of course, pot marigold - Calendula officinalis."

Flem recognized the gleam in her eye and manner as that of the mad gardener and forestalled hearing the name of every single plant in the hut with a sharp *"Mayapple!"*

"Wha?" her head came up, sanity returning to her gaze.

"It's getting late. Is this side finished?" He cocked his head towards the wall of culinaries. "And are you going to stick these lips around today?"

A slight irritation at Flem for no good reason pulled at the girl's attitude, but she merely squinted and swallowed before wetting her lips and going on with her info cast, as if she hadn't just been rudely interrupted.

Whimsey C. Nimble

Bending over she lightly brushed all the greenery that seemed to come down in a line, kitty-corner, between the back medicinals and those along the right wall of popular culinaries.

A minty smell wafted around them and Mayapple inhaled deeply of her empty cupped hands, as if they were full of scooped up aroma.

"Oh *mints*. Aren't they just your favorites, Flem?"

He knew better than to answer, it was obvious they were ALL her favorites.

"Did you know peppermint is the favorite between the two, spearmint and peppermint, but spearmint is almost as good for a lot of the same ailments, from bronchitis to flatulence."

Here Flem guffawed loudly, sylphettishly overcome again at the mere word but, while Mayapple's mouth did twitch at the corners, she calmly kept on. "As I was saying, FLATULENCE, colds, flu, morning sickness, motion sickness, and gallstones. In fact, spearmint is almost better known for its help in treating gallstones although any and all mints can be used for a gallstone tea."

"Fascinating, Mayapple, fascinating," he said dryly, reaching down to finger the tops of some chives that were snug up against the garlic. His hand moved on to idly pinch the next leaf but Mayapple jumped him and batted his hand away.

"Flem! Don't bruise the basil!"

The smell of basil filled the air and panic caught hold of the faerie's heart at his thoughtlessness, his eyes flashing to Mayapple in contrition.

"Oh, it's fine, relax my faerie friend, here, let's space these out a little more." She started moving pots around and urged him on with a quick look.

Dutifully, he surveyed the whole right side and its cooking herbs all the way to the end, murmuring their names as he moved down the display. "Rosemary, fennel, lemon balm, dill, cilantro, parsley, garlic, thyme, what is this?" He bent over to flip a tag, "Oh, coriander. Coriandrum sativum – Chinese parsley/cilantro. What?" He moved back to the cilantro he'd already passed and bent over to read the tag: Coriander Sativum.

"Hmmph," he muttered. "Interesting."

Almost to the end, he nonetheless kept track of everybody he was passing, bending over to read the ID on some soft bristly new leaves and was surprised to read 'Borago officinalis. Borage.' He went on to read, 'Edible.

Tastes like cucumber. Young leaves can be cooked as vegetable or in salads. Graceful blue flower.'

It sounded delightful and he looked over at Mayapple with pride. She had gone above and beyond his expectations when the idea first came to him.

The long, gray-green leaves of Sage were easily recognizable and he passed it right by without realizing it's other name, Salvia. More Rosemary, then a round of garlic, ah, what was that? Hmm. Chervil. Anthriscus Cerefolium. Tastes like mild parsley. Easy to grow.

There was only a couple more rows to go and while he recognized the little leaves, he couldn't place a name on this one. Ah yes, Origanum Majorana. Sweet Marjoram. And the one next to it Origanum Vulgare. Oregano, wild marjoram. Tarragon slipped in next and last was more rosemary.

"Here, hang these on the end with the others, I'll stick my lips around, and we can go *home*. Whattaya say?"

Gratefully, Flem nodded, accepting an awkward transfer. Stepping around to the end, he carefully set his armload down.

Empty hooks hung invitingly and he reached for the stack of *Gardening by the Phases of the Moon* and hung each one neatly by its little silver chain.

Next he found a great pamphlet on Edibles and Non-Edibles and hung those up.

Mayapple had just finished poking her dowel into the last pot and Flem looked over her shoulder to see red smiles mixed in everywhere, indicating that plant had edible flowers.

"Did you have enough lips?" he asked in disbelief.

"Oh yes!" started Mayapple enthusiastically.

Oh no, she's going to recite them all to me, thought Flem in a panic and without thinking he put his dirty fingers right over her mouth.

Which fell open in astonishment.

Knowing why he was doing it didn't stop Mayapple. At least for very long. Her tongue came out and she started licking all over the faerie's sweaty Sylph hand where he had it clamped, and he moved his hand so fast she burst into laughter and then pleaded, "Oh come on. Let me tell you. You know I'm dying to." She paused imperceptibly and added, "And then we'll go home! You'll be a free man! Err, Faerie. A free faerie, okay? So you can go and smootchy-smootch with Larky Sparky, oooh la la. But *first*, you will listen. Okay?"

Whimsey C. Nimble

He nodded as fast as he could, laughing at her great silliness. Folding his arms, he appeared as waiting royalty and then stated, "The minute that last word is out of your mouth, I'm outta here, got it? Cha, I'm late already."

"No, you're not! It's only five of. We're here for five more minutes and I intend to make full use of them so *listen up!*"

Bested, Flem struck a pose with both hands cupped behind his ears, his hip stuck out at a jaunty angle. Raising his eyebrows in disdain at her delay, he then tapped his arm as if he were wearing a watch, pantomiming hurry hurry! Time time!

The dam broke and the words flowed out, it was like she was trying to win some kind of contest and had memorized them alphabetically so she knew just where to go and who was who.

"Anise, basil, borage, chamomile, chives, clover, coriander, dill, fennel, garlic, marjoram, mint, rosemary, sage and thyme. Bye Flem. I'll let you know tomorrow, about my hot date tonight, when I come to your house for that drink, remember? Give Lark a kissee kissee for me too, wont'cha Mr. Faerie-in-love. Gawd. It must be nice. Anyway, BYE." And off she went, never looking back.

He stood for a moment and then made his way to the time clock, hearing Mayapple calling to Lily as she ran out the door in the distance.

Ah, home. He was a free faerie.

Chapter 70

Hello there Mr. Faerie. How are you, sir?

"**W**HOOPS!" EXCLAIMED MAYAPPLE and Flem wondered why she acted surprised every time she stumbled through the window-door. It seemed to him to be a frequent occurrence. He turned and watched, waiting to see if he'd need to catch her, nerves at the ready.

She avoided falling face first by floundering for five or so foot steps before she transmorphed back to an upright position confirming his suspicions, giving him a cheeky grin as she stepped past him calling, "Kitty kitty! Kitty kitty kitty. Where are you? Where are they, Flem?"

"C'mon, follow me," he said, trying to catch up with her as she marched towards the back, guessing at their whereabouts.

"Alright my darling fae boy, you may serve me that promised drink now," she lavishly allowed, scooping up a small butterscotch and white kitten from the floor as she took liberties with Flem's hammock.

"Ooh, I think that might be Lark's," Flem's voice rose in dire warning but Mayapple was having none of it.

"Well, he's not here, now is he? This is my kitty, *the* one. I knew earlier, I just had to make sure." She nuzzled the kitten under her chin, her eyes daring the faerie to contradict her. "I've already told Blakeana about her and he said bring her home!"

Flem had learned it was easier in the long run to simply acquiesce if at all possible to Mayapple but this was Lark's choice and he didn't know how to resolve it, his loyalty torn between two friends.

To stall his obvious dismay, Mayapple stared at him and reminded him innocently, "Mead?"

Hating this quandary, Flem scowled but stepped towards a small cabinet, squatted and pulled a bottle from its depths. He was just straightened and was wondering if he had any clean *hens* to pour into, when the rest of the cat family padded into view, mama meowing vociferously, chastising, him, them, everybody in general for *not* feeding the cat first! Could they not see she was starving? It took a lot of energy to keep up with this bunch. Purring loudly, mama cat was rather irritated that she couldn't control herself and batted at Flem's pant leg several times, hoping *something* would get his attention.

Something did.

A small butterscotch and vanilla cat sat looking up at him, darn near a twin to Mayapple's. Flem scooped it up, all prickly tiny feet and a big rumble, a bit of sauciness in its bright, bright eyes. His hand came in contact with its little privates and Flem discovered the cat he held was definitely male. And, there were dibs and dabs of chocolate interspersed with the vanilla and butterscotch. Relief flooded through him and he said, "You're right, Mayapple, *this* is the one Lark wanted."

Camaraderie restored, Mayapple melted back, her world righted as should be.

"Exactly. And mine's a girl, I'd know her anywhere," she went on to claim, eyes on the still-empty hens Flem had produced. "Here, give him to me and you pour," she ordered, reaching up imperiously, motioning rapidly with her free hand when he didn't respond quick enough.

To even the matter, he thrust a very full henfull at her a moment later and she had to release her hold on both kittens to steady the too-full glass to her lips.

He snatched both of, what-he-considered, *his* kittens, out of the hammock and with a rather sharp reprimand, "Do not spill that in my hammock, I *sleep* there, you know," he stalked off, flinging back over his shoulder, "I need to feed the cats, I'll be right back."

"Well, woo woo," came back his guest's unrespectful taunt. To further the insult, she added, "You better hurry grumpy, it sounds like you need this more than I do."

Shaking his head, Flem had to laugh. Nobody ever topped Mayapple. And she was right, a henfull did sound good.

An hour and a half later they were stretched out together sideways in his hammock, toes through the holes, socks off. Both had had a wee bit more and discussed everything under the sun, except Sycamore Park, much to Flem's relief. Both had reassured the other that the status quo of their daily lives was not going to be affected by the marriage of Iris and Santolina.

It was all a ploy and somewhere in Flem's mind he knew it. Mayapple was persistent and Flem knew in his faerie marrow that she had NOT forgotten or given in to his request to cease and desist with her yattering on about helping him clean out that hole under a rock he used to call home. (And still did in odd, frightening, unguarded moments.)

He waited.

He knew.

Here it came, finally.

"Flem," said Mayapple enticingly, as if he were her best friend in all the world.

His heart responded, and it washed over him like love juice, dousing his very neurons.

His pulse kicked up a notch in protest. Cha! He was such a sucker!

"Yes Mayapple, what?" he sighed, knowing he was already beaten, he could feel its inevitability. "*What?*" he repeated, the mead and small talk doing their jobs, softening boundaries.

"I've got a *good* idea."

He resigned himsylph.

"Want to hear it? And could I just have a teensy bit more of your mead? Mm, it is *so* good." She held up her glass without moving any other part of her body. "Gee, I feel so relaxed," she sighed. "You're *such* a good host."

Never sure if he should completely relax his guard, he slanted his eyes at her with an almost-scowl as he untangled himsylph to reach the Egret's Beak bottle.

"Oh RELAX. Geez, I was paying you a compliment, you big gooseberry. And what I was going to say was this -" here her tone quickly turned wheedling. "We could just go *look* and see how everything's doing, no need to clean it out yet. Heck, you may *need* it someday if this," she cocked her eyebrows towards the ceiling, "doesn't work out."

Flem's eyes turned saucer-like at her insinuation. After all this time, that she would even *think* that that was an option, even as a *joke*. His heart in his throat, his blood started to pound in his ears but Mayapple started laughing and chuckling, spilling mead down the front of her and he bit his lip, trying to lighten up but the mead seemed to slow him down.

Whimsey C. Nimble

"OH MY GOD, Flem! A JOKE. Mother *gave* you this place. It's a done deal. Geez, I just want to go look at your old place again, that's all. Don't be so serious."

Reckless relief coursed through him plus he felt a little ashamed at being so gullible. Him and his knee-jerk reactions. He should know better by now, what with Mayapple's smart mouth and that never-fail attitude she carried like a shield.

Topping off his own glass he wondered briefly if that was a good idea but when he looked at his half empty glass and then the uncorked bottle in his other hand he couldn't imagine why it wouldn't be and filled it to the brim.

Mayapple slurped most unbecomingly and managed to knock his arm a little before he recorked it, letting him know he could pour just a teensy more.

He complied then actually forgot himsylph and took a slug right from the bottle itself before recorking it efficiently and stowing it underneath the swaying bed.

Mayapple's gaze widened and she coughed at him in protest, never mind her own bad manners.

He blanched at his mishap as the girl went back to prattling about her cat, but it was all show. "I think I'll call her Lucy. You won't give her away now, will you?" glaring at him as if he was on the street corner already, box of free kittens in hand.

The change of subject was duly noted but Flem was feeling more expansive by the moment, life's sharp edges blurred by golden overtones. The words popped out of his mouth, taking both of them by surprise, "Oh c'mon. We'll go right now. Just to *look*, mind you. I'm missing a scarf anyway and I wanted to see if I left it behind."

Not expecting this even though it was precisely what she'd wanted, the young woman's eyes opened in shock but Mayapple had her merde together. As usual.

Her eyes narrowed in gleeful abandon, corralled by manipulation, fed by adrenalin. With extremely precise movements she disengaged her body, shrugging her clothes and self back to order immediately. Plunk went the empty hen onto Flem's makeshift table. "Okay, I'm ready." A couple of deep sniffs as she pumped herself back into shape.

Flem's heart swelled with admiration at her eagerness to just go with the flow, forgetting momentarily she was actually getting *her* way and, unknown to him, had in fact envisioned this entire scenario earlier in the day, with precisely this outcome. Oh, she was good.

Picking her way towards the window door, Mayapple said without thinking, "Guess Lark's not coming by later, is he?" wishing immediately she'd kept her big mouth shut.

"Oh! Maybe. I hope so," remembered Flem but much to Mayapple's relief just continued with, "I'll just ask him to wait, we won't be gone long."

He cast a questioning look at her for confirmation and she waved a hand and said "Of course not."

The faerie hurried to the back and scribbled a note which he placed on Lark's interwoven hanging bed, where he'd be sure to see it. Unbeknownst to him, his toe came in contact with the much diminished bottle of mead, the cork slipped out noiselessly, rolling aside for nectar to find its new path, pooling on the floor near a discarded sweater.

Mayapple and Flem disappeared down the driveway towards the bus stop.

That last shot of Egret's Beak was definitely having an effect. He felt very magnanimous towards everyone, the gallantry of Sylph charm rising from his DNA, unrestricted.

"C'mon lover boy, sit down." Mayapple tugged him to the seat beside her on the idling bus that was like a warm mechanical womb.

"Oh the *bus*, Mayapple. I *miss* taking the buss to work." He sighed in fond reminiscence, but Mayapple barked out a laugh of derision at his maudlin demeanor.

"Oh *please*. What's to miss? I think you've had too much to drink." She paused and then added, "I have." She smiled dreamily, then laughed at her own joke, poking him in the side.

Fifteen minutes later they disembarked, then stood and watched as the next bus pulled in that would take them out to Sycamore Park. A breeze filled with exhaust wafted over them and into the indifferent cavernous vehicle, the two of them following in its wake.

"You miss this, huh?" needled Mayapple briefly as they boarded the gaping mouth of the kneeling bus.

Swinging onto a bench seat together, Mayapple tucked her arm through Flem's and mocked him with a look.

He shook his head severely at her childish antics but she merely stuck out her tongue as if bedeviled.

He ignored her, anxious to get to his old place and see it, wondering if that errant scarf was indeed there and what else he'd left behind. He hadn't actually been back for a while…

Not paying close attention to anything except his intent to pull the bell so the bus would stop he didn't realize his shirt had caught on a sharp edge of the old seat in front of them and when he went to reach up, his arm was stayed. He was already in an awkward, hunched over position melding with the inside wall of the bus.

"Mayap-" he gasped in panic as theirs was the very next stop but Mayapple, the girl with eagle eyes, had already comprehended the situation. She bounced out of her seat, pulled the cord and came down with her arms around the faire, deftly unhooking him, *once again.*

Chagrinned, he looked at her, his heart in his mouth but plainly on his sleeve also.

Clenching her teeth together to keep the laughter from exploding out, she brusquely commanded, "Let's go!" as the bus eased in to the curb, back doors flapping open to disgorge them.

Reigning himsylph in, Flem hurried down the steps behind his cohort, bracing for her derision, the fun gone from the adventure.

Instead she actually gave him a sympathetic look and merely pretended to straighten his sweatshirt, adjusting his scarf and then surprised him even more by stepping back and nodding for him to take over, lead the way. That wild gleam was still there but it appeared she had it under control, and her manner spoke of compassion.

Flem felt his true Sylph swell with confidence and stepped into the moment completely, relaxing his wariness and meeting it head on. "Thank you," he said, meeting her eyes briefly, hoping to Pan the contact wouldn't ignite her, before they moved off down the deserted sidewalk bordering Sycamore Park.

Darkness and fog were hand in hand in the shadows, appearing to wait but like wolves with prey in sight, you knew it wouldn't be long. Flem quickened his pace, Sylph adrenalin kicking on in key places to spark up his blood.

Mayapple hurried along with him, adventure giving her rosy cheeks. "How'd you find this place anyway?" she asked as they veered into the park, the fae leading unsylphconsciously.

Giving her an odd look, he replied, "I just stumbled upon it accidentally, there's berry bushes not too far away, you see, and there's violets, and actually, it's a *park*, you know?"

She nodded, trying to figure out where he was going with this. "Yeah? So?" she responded.

"Well, *Sylphs* eat lots of berries, and flowers, and stuff, stuff they have in parks. This is a *big* park. Plus, I didn't really have, um, a place to live at first, so I ah, lived here, in the Park, and well, you know I drank a lot back then." He petered off, rather embarrassed but also knew it was okay to say these things to Mayapple. By now they were in a deserted area and after looking around, Flem took off cross-country, keeping to large bushes and big shadows as much as possible.

Mayapple huffed along, enjoying the clandestine posturing she'd adopted, assuming the male Sylph would not even notice. He did, but just thought she was acting weird and ignored her.

After a careful minute of listening, they were through a hedge and stood before the big stone boulder. Looking around one last time, Flem fingered the hidden lever and the boulder glided back but it wasn't a smooth sound. The faerie bent down and picked the track clean, muttering, "I didn't think it'd been that long," before ducking through, the human girl right behind him. A rather musty smell met their noses, not really pleasant as there was also a bit of sourness tainting it.

It was too dark for Mayapple and she stopped right in the doorway and waited as Flem hurried to get some light on, cursing and swearing under his breath as he stumbled about. "Come in, don't just stand there, cha. Here, sit down." Host manners never were forgotten, apparently.

Mayapple looked askance, wondered *why* she'd wanted to come here but then spied his old hammock hanging in the nook. Picking her way across the floor as if it were strewn with litter when in fact there wasn't that much, she arrived at the forlorn hanging bed. Giving it a shake to dislodge any spiders, she gingerly opened it enough to sit down within it and watched her fae faerie friend Flem carouse the interior. He did so with a possessive air and she hoped he wasn't going to pee in the corners to mark his territory, even though he was leaving. It seemed a male trait that easily crossed species barriers.

There wasn't much here, she could see that and laid back to look around while Flem paced and pawed.

"So, ah, Mayapple, do you want a, well, a *drink?*"

Her head flew around and she said "What?"

"I just found a half full bottle in the back of the cupboard over there," he nodded. Feeling guilty, he went on, "I used to always keep a stash here, no matter what and looks like I forgot about this." He held up a half full bottle of Manzanita Melody and said, "We probably shouldn't," but he looked at her hopefully as if she was the boss of him.

"You're not going to start drinking again, are you? I mean, you know, too much?" She was very stern, adding, " We've had quite a bit already. We probably shouldn't."

"No! Oh no. You're right, we better not." He looked so crestfallen so of course, she relented, with only a little twinge of guilt over whether she was actually being helpful or not...

"Well, I guess a little one wouldn't hurt though, would it? But no more Flem! I mean it," as if he was begging for it! Cha! But, being easily susceptible to temptation, Flem smiled and ran to the same cubby hole and reached in up to his arm pits hoping to come in contact with more glass hens, and he did! Two, in fact.

"Move over," he ordered, scootching in beside her. The hammock jumped and bounced, countering every move they made until, like low tide at sunset, they all fell into rhythm together.

Mayapple was having the time of her life. They both had to work tomorrow but it wasn't *too* late yet. They'd still make it home at a decent hour. No problem. As more mead trickled into their bloodstreams, human and fae, Mayapple naturally offered to rub the poor faerie's shoulders and Flem willingly discarded his shirt, sighing in relief as her nimble fingers untied the bondage that held his wings down.

"Wait. Don't collapse. Go get me a little water, remember? I don't have all that Sylph saliva you guys have."

Blood was surging through those unrestricted wing veins and he let himsylph go, wings rising on their own, pulsing with relief, almost gasping for breath. Handing her a small cup of water, he draped himsylph face forward over the hammock, head lolling, kneeling in abandon.

"Oh please Flem, *DO* try to relax," Mayapple commented dryly.

Flem muttered something unintelligible.

"What? Speak up faerie." She took a drink and giggled, rubbing her hands together.

"I said, sarcasm is *so* unbecoming." He flopped back into place, groaning in anticipation, twitching his naked wing blades at her to get her to hurry up.

Elsewhere:

Lark finally locked the back door of the bakery behind him, sighing. It was even later than usual. He was looking forward to snuggling with his other Sylph.

It wasn't too long before he was creeping through the underbrush along the back of Fletcherman's Nursery. Something just didn't feel right. He hoped he was wrong but it felt *empty*.

Moving steadily on he slipped into the old greenhouse, calling "Flem? Hey, I'm here," but to no avail. Disappointment dropped through his body like little heavy darts as he verified what he already knew.

Where *was* he?

Should he wait? Well of course he would wait. But he didn't like it. He'd thought it was perfectly clear about tonight. They spent pretty much every night together. Walking dejectedly around, he noticed mama cat and kids hadn't come running so that meant they were still full. Hmm.

Eyes randomly circling the room for a clue, by Pan if one didn't appear. He snatched up the note Flem had scrawled and decided to follow. Better than waiting here for who knew how long.

The human girl straddled the limp Sylph's back, his wings gloriously unfolded right in front of her face. Eyes dazzled, she snapped and rubbed and well, *preened* him like the mother bird she was.

Someone, (Lark) was *obviously* filling this niche on a frequent basis, as it wasn't too long before she remarked, "God Flem, your wings are actually in really good shape."

She moved off of him as he squirmed upright, furling as he did so. Not replying to her observation he instead stretched and said "Oh, I *so* want to go for a fly!"

Mayapple looked at him but didn't say a word. That obviously wasn't going to happen. Her heart went out to him. Oh, to have *wings* and not be able to *fly* when ever you wanted. The pain, *his* pain, brought tears to her eyes. "Oh Flem. You poor dear. How dreadful."

Actually, it hadn't been *that* bad. She looked like *she* felt worse than he did. Without warning an earlier flight he'd taken from not too far away flashed into memory.

Did he dare?

"Shush Mayapple. C'mon – I've got an idea." He was furling and unfurling in soft agitation and then uncharacteristically commanded, "Help me tie these. Loosely. Yeah. Good. Hand me my shirt."

"*What* are you *doing*? Where are we going?" Flummoxed, she looked around. Work was the furtherest thing from their minds.

"Well," he slowly revealed, "I've actually done this once before and I think it should be okay. It's dark enough. Would you be okay with being my lookout and I could *go* for a quick spin?" He couldn't believe he was saying the words *and* planning on carrying through with it.

With saucer-like eyes, she nodded, awe etched on her facial features.

"*Really*? Right *now*? Where? Here?"

"*No*, not here! C'mon, I'll show ya." He took a quick look around and decided he didn't need another thing, just a good quick fly before heading *home* and to bed. And Lark. Oh yes, Lark. A good incentive to hurry and do it and leave.

Mayapple stood motionless, mouth shut tight for once and watched him like he was going to disappear before her very eyes.

Humans, thought Flem, following the energy pulling him forth, moving towards the door.

"*Mayapple*. Snap out of it. I know a place nearby -" he let it trail off as her eyes turned shiny bright and she came to life, rising to the occasion like a bubble from a mermaid's mouth.

"Let's go!" Jamming her fists into her long outer pockets, she hurried on by and out the gaping door.

Fog danced around distant street lamps that dotted the park like quiet guardians, myopically embracing only their own little circle of yellowish light. Ambient illumination from the City itself lit up the underbelly of the low hanging clouds and somewhere, moonlight shone.

Mayapple ran her hands back through her hair, waking up more by the minute, mead fumes dissolving with every breath she took, her eyes sparkling at this unexpected adventure.

Flem was ahead of her now and she stepped sprightly along, once again mimicking his furtive manner. Within minutes they had come to a clearing deeper within the Park, one encircled by various lumbering eucalyptus giants, a stateliness permeating the air.

Heart pounding, Flem didn't falter, his need to be in the air racing through his body, not *confined* by any kind of walls.

Staring at Mayapple, she stared back for a moment before saying, "Well?"

Quickly divested of human strictures the faerie let his sylphcontrol go and ripped the shirt and loose bindings off, his wings chattering and clattering in his clumsy excitement, thrusting the clothes blindly in Mayapple's general direction.

She clasped them without seeing what she held, her eyes never leaving the powerful image of that slim Sylph's back sporting his great vibrating wings. Wasn't quite the same as when she clicked rough scales together, all limp and polite. It was a crime to keep them tied down and hidden.

Unable to stop, Flem bolted into the clearing with great bounding steps, *running* into the air, it seemed to Mayapple.

"Oh," she gasped, her eyes unbelieving as he climbed higher and higher and higher, an ever-expanding spiral with loop 't loops thrown in out of sheer exuberance.

"Oh," she breathed again, "be careful!"

But Flem had no ears for her. Pure unfettered freedom burst within his heart. There was no caffeine that could match this.

Like an ethereal Ferris-wheel, the crazy faerie spun circles, dancing and darting, laughter trickling down to where Mayapple stood, mouth agape in wonder.

"Wow. He's something, ain't he?" A voice spoke from just behind Mayapple, a rough and raspy male voice and she jumped about a foot in the air, emitting a shriek, spinning around and stumbling two steps back, Flem's clothes clutched tight across her abdomen.

"Hey, hey! Easy lady, I ain't gonna hurtcha, I'm in bed, for Chrise's sake."

Whimsey C. Nimble

Mayapple stared, the sky-rocketing faerie forgotten momentarily. He *was* in bed.

A rough, unshaven older man was sitting up from where his sleeping bag and pillow lay on the ground. General housekeeping implements were lined up to one side, all in a row: small dishpan with cloth folded neatly over the rim, cup with toothbrush, razor, (if by chance he ever needed it) and of course, two bottles of wine, each sporting an upended glass over the top.

Not quite sure what to say, Mayapple felt her eyes get bigger and the skin on the back of her head behind her ears seemed to tighten as she became more and more stressed at this unexpected turn of events.

"Actually," the man said, "I think I know that faerie, by golly. Ain't that Flem Green? Ah, lessee, what was it? Oh yeah, Flumaria Greenwood, hey?"

Mayapple's jaw hit the ground and you could have easily poured a gallon of milk right in, her mouth was hanging open so wide.

"How do, ma'am? My name's Weed. Us fellows met the other time when he was in my neck of the woods, that there's my living room," he nodded towards the clearing.

Both looked over and then up, watching the frolicking faerie gamboling about.

Lark had only been gone from the old greenhouse for twenty minutes when Bud and entourage sidled in along the back fence and found no one home. It was Chinaberry who found the dropped note and the three of them were in immediate accord as to their next step.

Leaving noisily, they hurried out the way they'd come in and were soon trailing Mr. Spurastic, although not as elegantly. *He* had a car. *They* rode the bus. Bud felt it was cheating not to arrive by bike, but China and Cat had assured him that wasn't so. Any discomfort he experienced was quickly assuaged by their charming presence. It was so nice to have one on each side.

The pent up emotion was gone, leaving a beautiful balanced joy behind. Flem knew they should leave here soon but he couldn't tear himsylph away.

His mind cleared, his eyes looked outward focusing down on the ground, on Mayapple.

Riding a lazy loop, he stayed up high, sharpening his gaze. Something didn't look right.

Was she *talking* to somebody?

His lazy loop became edged with a bit of panic and he immediately put more distance between them, darting up really high and hovering, as he squinted at the scene below.

Suddenly his encounter with the homeless guy, Weed was his name, popped into mind.

Weed would be okay, he had *seen* him fly before.

That's when the vision overcame him. He, Flem, could do a good deed. He would *give* his old digs to *Weed*.

Ready to flitter back down to see if it really was him, the Sylph was unprepared for what happened next.

A shout was heard from an entirely different part of the small round meadow and Flem's whole being became electrified when another faerie came barreling out from the upper regions of a massive tree across the way.

Lark! It was Lark! The two Sylphs spiraled around each other at manic speed.

Mayapple felt like she might faint.

Weed chortled and said, "Time for a drink now, don't ya think? C'mon girlie, wanna a little nip here with old Weed whilst we watch them there airy faeries? Whoooeeee!"

Clank clank and Mayapple found a glass of red wine in her hand, her bottom lip still dragging in astonishment.

Like a robot, she saluted the man, *Weed?* and tossed it back.

"Whoa, you're a healthy drinker, now ain't ya?" Weed praised, wiping his mouth on his sleeve before tucking his shirt into the pants he'd just pulled up.

"Oh c'mon, smile gal, this ain't no ordinary sight, now is it? I ain't telling nobody. Ain't nobody going to believe me, anyway. Ain't that right? Relax."

Mayapple eyed him at this little speech and when he motioned with his bottle she let him fill her glass again.

Both looked skyward, watching the two Sylphs caper in abandon.

That first rush of adrenalin was tapering off and Flem and Lark were now starting to play air tag when the whole kit and caboodle of Buddleia, Chinaberry and Catalpah came running into the air from still another part of the circle, maniacal glee shooting out their mouths.

Mayapple dropped her glass from sheer shock but luckily it was empty when it hit the grass and rolled.

Weed was more respectful although not any less enthralled. He looked at the glass in his hand and wondered if he'd drank too much again but no, there *was* a woman beside him and he thought she was real. Slowly his hand dropped lower and lower and there they stood like twins, eyes wide following the air show, mouths hanging open, tonsils exposed to the wind, all else forgotten.

Twirling in a colorful pulsating circle together, Mayapple thought the gaggle of faeries looked like a living halo for Mother Earth and smiled, relaxing.

Weed recovered enough to remember to take another drink, delight shining in his rheumy red-rimmed eyes.

Flem had never had so much fun and couldn't believe he was participating in an actual Sylph Circle.

It felt balanced and normal.

Slowing down, the faeries pealed off in their own signature style but Flem called them back and told them of his plan to bequeath the hole-under-the-rock to the human vagabond, Weed, who was even now down there with Mayapple, watching their every move.

All five looked down, hovering in mid-air, heels digging in, so-to-speak, arms akimbo or on hips, creating invisible air waves from the great fan they made together.

After a moment Bud nodded, agreeing. "Yeah! Good idea, Flem. The greenhouse is, well, *yours* for sure?" he asked tentatively although he thought it so.

"Yes. Yes it really is," Flem said with deep satisfaction, a knowing that his intuition had been right all along.

"When?" asked Catalpah, emerald eyes practically glowing in the dark like a cat's, her wings shimmering in a translucent explosion of green, vibrating so fast they were hardly visible.

"Well, right *now* I guess," responded Flem.

Lark gave him a proud look of approval. All Sylphs were intrinsically altruistic, it just didn't show up right away, one had to get past the Sylphette stage. And besides, Lark was besotted. Flem was almost perfect in his eyes.

"Ah, should we *ALL* go down? I mean that guy down there IS a human, correct?" Chinaberry with the neon purple eyelashes and sparkly iridescent wings of deep lilac was concerned, more for the human than them.

"And for that matter, what about Mayapple? You don't think seeing us *out* like this might be too much?" she continued, caution and reason always one of her fortes, albeit at times hidden quite well...

Flem tapped a finger to his mouth, considering this good point.

"I'll tell you what. I'll go down alone and see how it feels." He took off.

"What are they *doing*, do you think?" Mayapple asked in exasperation to her new drinking buddy, Weed, homeless man of Sycamore Park.

He leaned back, thumbs hooked in his pockets and craned his neck back at an awkward angle.

"Beats me. You don't think they poop like birds, do you?" He took a step back, laughing uproariously at this joke.

Flem chose that moment to drop gracefully down, fluttering to plant himsylph in front of the two humans. "What's so funny?" he asked, looking from one to the other.

"Oh never mind, for goodness sakes. Everything okay up there?" Mayapple gave the air a couple of sharp little jabs, pointing to the crew. "How come they didn't come down? What are they doing here anyway?"

Weed had recovered his aplomb and seconded the invitation, "Where's your friends, bud?"

Whimsey C. Nimble

"Bud? You know Bud?" repeated Flem, staring at Weed. "How do you know Bud?"

"Oh for Pete's sake Flem, he doesn't know Bud, bird-brain, he called *you* bud. *Duh.*"

Flem glared at Mayapple. He'd forgotten how irritating she could be. Cha.

With a roll of her eyes to let him know how obtuse he could be, she stuck two fingers in her mouth and blew, hard. A shrill whistle split the air and Flem flinched.

Grabbing her arm, he yanked her hand down. "Mayapple, stop. Sssh! Remember where we are?" He put on his best worried look although it was more for show. It was too late and nobody was around. Still, simple precautions were basic.

"Hello there Mr. Faerie. How are you, sir? You know, you kin bring your friends down, it's okay. I only got two glasses but if you don't mind sharing, I'd be delighted to offer your esteemed group a drink. Please. Really." Weed stood humbly, his manner hinging on beseeching, hope and quick skyward glances alight on his bewhiskered face.

By that time Mayapple was throwing her arms around like a propeller, trying to pull the others from the air, her regular bossy nature surfacing easily.

The four who were now hovering just above tree top level on the far side of the clearing must have come to a decision and directly bee-lined it right to where the sylph-appointed air traffic controller was suggesting.

Moments later soft shushing with a bit of clicking was heard as wings were quickly furled, although it was certainly too late to be discreet at this point.

Mayapple stared. No matter what she had suspected, the reality of standing here so nonchalantly in the middle of the night in the middle of Sycamore Park with five faeries was almost too much to bear. Calling up every bit of self discipline she'd ever owned, she kept her emotions under tight wrap and looked upon the whole escapade as intellectually as she could. No use letting her sense of the absurd get the better of her. But it didn't stop her from staring, no matter how hard she tried to look somewhere else.

Eyeballing Catalpah and Chinaberry, she wondered if they *were* female Sylphs since they sure looked like women, sort-of, to her. But her intuition told her no, they acted too much like Flem and Lark. And Bud, for that matter.

Male. Sylphs, yes, but still *male.* Boy, what a story this would make, she thought, hoping to do a little information picking when she had the chance. Intrigue was so irresistible.

Weed was aglow with good fortune and was hurrying to get the other bottle and glass. Excited by such regal unexpected company, high flyers, all of 'em he thought, then stopped and guffawed at his own wit. Still chuckling, he stepped back into place by Mayapple's side and almost didn't hear what Flem said.

"I've got an idea, Weed."

Busy unscrewing the cap of the second bottle of wine, he didn't look up, just said, "Whaz that?"

"Well," Flem dragged the word out, considering how to deliver his decision. Wondering how it would be received.

"Uh," he ran a hand up his forehead, pulling several loose curls straight out between his fingers.

Everyone looked on, waiting for this proclamation.

"I used to live near here," he blurted, "and I'm moving. "I, I have a new place. It's a great place," he reached over and squeezed Mayapple's hand, feeling Lark's fingers come to life and massage his neck in support.

Bud looped an arm around the Sylph to each side of him and they both leaned in to give him a quick nuzzle on the cheek, their arms encircling his waist.

Weed was standing ramrod straight, wondering where this was going, his attention completely garnered since for some reason this Flem fellow, one of them there fae guys, seemed to be talking directly to *him,* Weed.

"Yeah?" he prompted, too ensnared to even take the time for a drink. "What's that got to do with me?" he asked, curiosity sticking out all over him like porcupine quills.

"Well, ah, I thought, you know, if you *wanted,* that is, you could move in there. You know, my old place. Near here." There, he'd *said* it. Great Pan. And it was the right thing to do. He knew it in his soul.

Weed's mouth opened and quivered before he licked his lips and swallowed, staring at Flem. "Is this a joke?"

"No! No! No joke. It's hidden. You'll see, And it's free rent. And it's dry. Well, mostly. Ha ha. What do you say, want to see it?"

Numbly, Weed looked from one to the other to see any disbelief but no, all were smiling and nodding.

Mayapple was standing with her hands crossed over her heart, a beatific smile of hopeless admiration transforming her once again to a sappy girl, awe of Flem and his Sylphlessness raining down upon her. Love flooded her being and she threw her arms around that faerie's neck. "Oh Flem," she gushed, tears leaking from her eyes.

At this display of emotion, all four of the other fae teared up, sniffing into their sleeves.

Even Weed swallowed a lump.

Catalpah was the first to recover and brusquely came up with a new plan. "Okay," she sniffed, "Let's not stand around here, caterwauling. Whattaya say we make this a *work* party? Look at all the free help you guys are getting to *move*! Cha, there's seven of us. We can do this all right now! What do you think Flem? Ready to cha-poop-a-doop-boop, clean out that dump for good?"

Flem bristled silently at her use of the word *dump*, even if it was, but China stepped in with "*Cat*," and a reproachful look at her partner. Turning to Flem, after a quick glance at Bud and Lark, she explained: "Well, the fact of the matter is, Flem, we've *all*," she did a quick backwards thumb movement to include her three other cohorts, "been in your house before, before you lived there. In fact, didn't you live there briefly too, Bud?"

"Yep." Bud's eyes never left Flem's face.

Lark spoke up, "Actually, ma petit, me too. A *long* time ago. I think I had just met you, hadn't I Bud?"

"Yep."

"And we found it not too long after we arrived in San Francoa Ramosa. But no doubt it's not a dump anymore. I bet you fixed it right up, didn't you?" Chinaberry smiled at the faerie who was coming up in the world.

"Nope. Still a dump." Flem laughed, as did they all. He then turned to Weed who was standing mutely, taking this all in. "Now it's *your* dump!" and they all laughed again.

It didn't take long after that but nonetheless it was still three in the morning before Mayapple got to bed after helping five faeries move Weed out, move Flem out, move Weed in, move Flem in.

All in all a very eventful night.

Chapter 71

———— ❧ ————

Well, one healthy plant averages fifty thousand little tiny
seeds, which are high in protein, about sixteen percent.

*H*AVING LIVED IN the foothills roughly a hundred miles away from San Francoa Ramosa for months and months before getting brave enough to actually set foot in the City, Flem was fairly cognizant of which plants were good to eat, and which weren't.

Before actually leading a group out, Iris had quizzed him thoroughly, taken notes, and then verified everything he'd told her. She had to admit, he knew his stuff.

"Now please be sure to have everyone sign this before you leave today, okay?" The boss handed him a clip board with a bunch of release-of-liability forms on it that made sure everyone knew that Flem was just a knowledge-able employee and not a licensed herbalist.

He adjusted his scarf once again over his shoulder and held out the other hand for the packet.

"And Mayapple knows where you're going?" Iris asked for the third time this week.

Flem slanted her an intense look and thought you can't be serious, you're asking this *again*. Smiling, he pursed his lips and nodded, a series of quick little movements, eyebrows held rigid in suppressed exasperation.

"So, you'll try to be back by five, right Mr. Green?" Iris asked, silently chastising herself for making it appear a question, thinking she should have *told* them what time to be back, but opting to *show* them she trusted them as responsible employees.

Why, she didn't know. Force of cultivated optimism and the need to be polite, evidently. It wasn't like they hadn't once again pulled some kind of all-nighter and came to work dead tired but that had been a couple of weeks ago now, and they'd been on their best behavior every since. Even Lark seemed more chipper and polite. That man was so polite, sometimes she felt like his mother.

Briefly a picture of those two girlfriends of Bud's flashed through her mind and she wondered how they fit in the picture but dismissed it immediately and tossed the faerie in her office the keys to the company van.

"You driving?" Iris deadpanned.

"Yeah," Flem replied dryly, giving tit for tat.

Mayapple swooped in from behind, grabbed the keys from his hand and drolly inserted, "Maybe later my fine fae friend, but *today*, today *I'm* driving. Sorry. Hey Mom, can I, ah, *we* have a little chocolate for our busy day?" She smiled hopefully, her tongue coming out to lick her top lip in suggestive anticipation.

Pausing a moment to give Mayapple a blank look just long enough to make her squirm, Iris tossed her thumb in the general direction and finally said "Yesss, then get going! How many people signed up for the nature walk, anyway? At last count I saw four names on the sign-up sheet. Did you get any more?"

"Six altogether," answered Mayapple. "If we'd gotten any more, we wouldn't have been able to fit everyone in the van. Speaking of which, did you pull all the seats back into place?" This last was directed at Flem and he nodded.

"I did. And I swept it out too."

"Mayapple, do you know where you're going?" Iris questioned, and Flem spun around towards the door, his eyes wild and his teeth clenched in exasperation. Mayapple saw and bit back a laugh as she calmly reassured her mother, "Yes mother. Geez." She then recited, "We head out of town on I-Eighty-One, then we cut over on Eight-Eighty-One, then Ninety-Eight is next and then Seventy-One and finally Twenty-One. The rest I'll have to have my copilot read when we get close. We're starting out at horehound, fig and Osage orange, isn't that right Flem? *You* know where you're going, right?"

As they'd already talked, plotted and mapped, the faerie knew this was for Iris's benefit and he replied smartly, "Yes, I certainly do," but didn't turn around, his fae blood getting gassier by the moment with bubbles of impatience rising like the champagne bends through his body and the capillaries surging with hot fae blood tightened, making his wing musculature feel like ants were crawling around on his back.

Screwing her face up at his retreating form, the owner made her daughter laugh and Mayapple took the opportunity to kiss her on the cheek and say, "*Bye* mom. We'll see you tonight. We'll definitely *try* for five, but…" She let it hang but when Iris didn't take the bait, finished with, "Don't worry. We'll be back *by five*." She heaved a sigh as her mother said "Get!" and pointed towards the door, laughing at their shenanigans.

Catching up with the Sylph, Mayapple matched his step and together they strode into the parking lot, dispersing the knot of women waiting for them.

Greetings and introductions were made, forms signed, and soon they were all tucked in, nice and proper. Mayapple sprightly assumed control, her right-hand fae man doing his utmost to be his charming Sylph and acting gracious co-captain, even though it was *him* with the knowledge…

It was surely sweet, this sylphsatisfaction with his own success.

Smugly, he smiled at the group in the back, glancing at Mayapple in between chit chatting with the three ladies on the seat behind them.

Mayapple drove silently, wondering how long she could keep quiet about her main objective of the day: to talk Flem into taking her to the *S* Club.

Catching his glance, she held it and smiled hugely at him, full wattage turned on.

Flem felt its warm benediction wash over him and his whole body tingled, a literal cell-reaction, no doubt about it. Unguarded, he returned her joy amp for amp and a tiny sliver of guilt traced up Mayapple's spine and over to her gut.

She quickly squelched it and almost said something then but held her tongue a little longer.

Eventually the faerie who couldn't stop talking, did, and turned fully around in his seat much to Mayapple's relief.

Finally, she had him to herself.

Taking a deep breath, she kept her eyes on the road and hummed a little under her breath, waiting to see if Mr. Chatty here would have anything to say to her, but now the fae fellow clammed right up.

"So, this is fun, huh?" making a 'all-this' motion with her head.

Eyes flashing, Flem nodded, cheek bones high as he grinned, his jaw muscles aching a little from actually smiling *so* much.

Not quite able to open the can of potential worms yet, Mayapple concentrated on her driving and Flem sank back and relaxed for the ride, the longest he'd ever experienced in his life.

Time passed and he dreamily watched the country side go by until he thought to ask, "How much further?"

"Well, we're on Highway Twenty-One now and when we come to a specific intersection, we'll be turning left. I'm not sure how far that is, probably within thirty miles. Then we'll check the map and directions," she petered out but a moment later, gave in. "Um, Flem?" she broached. "So ah, are you and Lark going anywhere special again this weekend?"

Unable to believe his ears that she was even bringing up the subject, Flem just looked at her, aghast for a split second before rapidly shaking his head, trying to negate her probing.

"*Mayapple*," he hissed, as if in warning.

"Oh, tch, nobody's listening, you paranoid putz. What, we have no social life?" she asked with a touch of sarcasm.

Peeking into the rearview mirror Flem saw the passengers apparently talking to their seat mates or over their shoulders to someone behind.

Nobody was paying any attention to the two up front.

"I wanna go," whispered for his ears alone.

Flem thought he had heard the words but wondered if he really did.

Mayapple shot him proof with an appealing look to punctuate her plea. "Please? *Flem*," she added, knowing he knew what she was referring to.

He did. She wanted *him* to finagle a way to get her in to the *S* club.

He couldn't imagine it. "*Stop*," he ordered, as brusquely as he could manage.

Mayapple kept quiet, forced to focus on her driving and their safety but she was not about to give up.

An intersection was seen in the distance. Flem spotted it about the same time Mayapple did and he smoothed out the directions they'd written.

Whimsey C. Nimble

"If this is Polygonatum Valley Drive, and I think it is, we turn left here," he said, rereading the directions for the umpteenth time, excited to be back in familiar territory, under much, much, *much* better circumstances.

It was and they did.

"What's next?" asked Mayapple.

"We just stay on this for about ten miles. It'll get really curvy and narrow as we descend into a canyon but we're going to the Yucca River, and that's at the bottom. I think there's a place to park there. I remember seeing lots of cars."

"Flem, you know you can trust me, right? I would be so good if I went with you to the *S* Club. Really, I would. I promise not to drink too much. C'mon, just think about it, okay?" This was delivered rapidly, sotto voce, just prior to oohing and ahhing loudly over some goats standing on some rocks in a nearby field.

Before Flem could snort his annoyance however, a question was interjected loudly from the back.

"Hey, do you suppose we'll see any Blue Dicks today? I hear they're good to eat." The old lady in the black hat with the red rose cackled, apologized for her 'blue' humor, cackled again, sniffed and shriveled back down to respectable sweet old lady out on an herbal outing.

No one said a word until Mayapple gasped loudly, unable to stop herself from spluttering and hee hawing, honking and gasping, which eventually made everyone else laugh all the harder in their embarrassed hilarity until the van was rocking and rolling.

"Ookow," the lady spoke up again.

Wait.

What?

"Ookow?" questioned Flem back at her.

"Ookow?" Mayapple had to get in on the act.

"Ookow," the lady repeated firmly.

By now 'ookow' was reverberating in the air as *everyone* started repeating it. Someone started a song, ookow being the only word in a very melodic verse. And then another sang 'ookow' to the tune of Shoo Fly Don't Bother Me, replacing the Shoo Fly.

"Brodiaea," clarified the old lady, before elucidating further: "You know. Blue Dick. Good to eat. Brodiaea. Also known as *ookow*."

Well, this little speech set everyone off again, already tinder-ready, and Flem knew deep in his bones today was going to be a *good* day, a special day. He hadn't laughed this hard in years.

Mayapple was laughing just as hard as they all were but Brodiaea had been her dad's, Brody's, full name. *Now* she understood *why* her mom used to call him Mr. Dick occasionally when Mayapple was growing up, usually when she seemed to be rather *peeved* at him for something.

She filed it away to mention to her mother later, slowing down as the road narrowed, becoming snake-like as they writhed their way down into the canyon.

A mile later, two deer suddenly sprang off the uphill side from the underbrush and thank God Mayapple's sixth sense activated and she was braking before they even hit the bottom, right in front of them. She didn't have to stop completely but it was her quick reflexes that blessed them. And the deer.

That shut everybody up for a minute, but being all women and one fae man, a good looking one at that with those soft curls and broad, if a bit lumpy, shoulders, they all picked right up where the last word had been cut off.

Chatter arose from the back but Flem was quiet and Mayapple jumped right in again.

"Flem!"

He slanted his eyes at her briefly but went back to helping her watch the road, hoping she wouldn't but of course, she did.

"C'mon Flem. I wanna go. Ask Lark. Talk to him. Tell him *why* it's a good idea. Okay?"

Flem could not think of even one good reason at the moment. This was too new in his life. He loved Mayapple, but really.

"*No*, NOT a good idea," he said as firmly as he could, wondering how long he could hold out and hoping Mayapple didn't sense any weakness in his voice as he said it but feeling a curl of resignation, way down deep.

The last curve stayed behind them, buildings and a large parking lot came into view and Flem directed Mayapple to go past them and over the Yucca. Everyone got excited at the covered bridge, seen down river.

"Park over here, I think," Flem directed tentatively, so happy for the diversion from Mayapple's pestering and to be back on track. "Yeah," he confirmed. "This is it."

Whimsey C. Nimble

Rustling was heard as everyone started gathering up lunch bags, purses, hats, and paraphernalia.

In no time at all, the nature brigade was under way.

Flem was grinning ear to ear, for all his nervousness. He had his notes but once he had figured out the spots he wanted to check out, he really didn't need them.

Everyone had a pack and he shifted his, rubbing as it was now on a hidden wing knob.

"Wow! What kind of tree is *that*?" came the question before they even got to where Flem was headed, which was that tree.

"That, ladies, is an Osage Orange tree. Totally inedible. Big thorns. Big fruit; they look like brains, don't they?"

Everyone was off, delighting in this minefield of coconut-sized pebbly 'fruit.' Mayapple made a bee line right back to him, her own green specimen in her hand.

Eyes sparkling, she tossed it to Flem, who was standing and watching. He'd already had his first time with Osage Oranges and didn't need any rotting outside his greenhouse over the next several weeks, possibly months.

He smoothed his hand over its rounded surface, feeling like he was petting an alien brain. He handed it back, his eyes not meeting Mayapple's, hoping to dissuade her from her chosen path, which was becoming clearer by the moment, judging from the too-bright, fevered look about her.

He braced himsylph.

Dampening down her enthusiasm, Mayapple surprised him by not saying a word. Warmly smiling, she blinked at Flem with her 'cat' look, a blink that said 'I love you, you're fabulous.' Flem in fact, saw it on mama cat's face right after she'd had her dinner and wanted her belly scratched.

Practically purring herself, Mayapple deftly stepped behind Flem and started massaging his shoulders, saying, "Flem," in a soft, wheedling sort-of-way.

Flem hated to do it, her fingers felt so good, but he stepped right away, giving his coworker a speaking look.

Assorted women were making their way back across the hillocks to them, each with their own devilish-looking fruit.

"Okay boss, what's next?" asked Gladiola of the red rose black hat.

Flem didn't respond right away, and Mayapple of course grew impatient and jabbed him in the ribs with her elbow to wake him up.

He glared and shushed her, telling her in an aside that he knew what he was doing, smiling at the group who were assembling around them.

Chatter died down and Flem held the moment, amused by his own importance, feeling powerful for once in his own Sylph.

"Now let's see, what was that original plant that started the whole thing?" he mused out loud, distractedly drumming his fingers repetitively across his mouth in a big show.

"Okay, show-off. *What*?" this of course from Mayapple, the woman who lacked respect. She should be showing reverence to his Sylphness but as usual she was treating him like a close friend who knew you well enough to rib you and egg you on.

He smiled fondly at her a moment before taking a little jump sideways and making a "Ta-Da!" movement with both arms, highlighting the greenish grey, overgrown plant low on the ground he'd been standing in front of. "Horehound," he announced proudly.

Oohs and ahhs were heard as everyone crowded around, trying to touch and feel, but the faerie didn't move out of the way, rather he pointed out certain facts: "See these small, grayish, kind of oval leaves? How crinkly they are? That's horehound. And here," he turned one over, "here's these little white hairs underneath. And see how its flowers come in directly on the stem here – the upper part, and see where they are? Right here at the leaf junctures. They circle around."

Mayapple stepped in then with her own two cents, and referring to her notes, segued neatly with "Marrubium Vulgare. The whole plant is useable. It seems everyone is familiar with its association with coughs, but it's also known as a gastric tonic, in fact, a tonic in general, treating bronchitis and asthma, in addition to being an expectorant and cough suppressant."

Smiling she confirmed silently with Flem that this was exactly how they'd practiced it and both grinned at their co-brilliance.

"How does it do in a garden setting?" someone inquired.

"I've never seen it domesticated, personally, although I have seen it around town, but I know it can get rather weedy looking with its long branching stems. It does well in the wild because it grows easily in poor, sandy dry soil, in full sun. If you're looking to grow some at home, I would suggest sowing the seeds in flats in the spring and then transplanting later," advised Flem.

There were no more questions so they moved on, the group falling in easily behind Flem and Mayapple.

"How far to the fig, Flem?" asked Mayapple immediately cracking up, adding in the same breath but quieter, "How far to the *S* Club, Flem? C'mon, think about it at least, won't you? *Ask Lark*. Please?" She paused and dared a quick look at her fae faerie friend's face and saw that little jaw muscle in front of his ears jump three times and wondered if she'd gone too far too fast with her campaign. She decided to shut up and looked around. Where was he headed?

There was a little creek that ran perpendicular to their path which was following the river. Flem turned left and started climbing. About thirty feet up the hill he disappeared into the darkness beneath a tree. Mayapple was right behind him by this time and the troop not too far behind her.

One by one they materialized inside the interior of a gigantic canopy, a natural woodsy room. All were enchanted, especially when they saw the trunk and rounded ceiling of laced limbs.

"What is this wondrous tree?" came the reverent, inevitable question.

For answer, Flem reached up and broke off a thick stemmed dark fruit. "This is a fig, wild, direct from the tree and not packaged. Check for bugs, and you can eat it right here, right now, the original fast food. But watch out for the sap where it's been broken off." He showed them the thick milky end and said "The white goo is really sticky and too much on your hands, or face, can become an irritant in no time at all. If it gets on you, wash your hands and you'll have to use this," he held up a small rough looking bar of soap then popped it back into its case.

Hitching a colorful woven-bag's handle higher onto her shoulder, a woman with long hair and sandals asked, "Do you happen to know how much sugar is in a fig?"

"Well, yes I do," injected Mayapple, and took off with, "A fig weighs approximately two ounces, has about ten grams of fiber, about forty-five calories and twenty-three grams of sugar."

"Twenty three grams of sugar *per fig*? Guess I'll be able to have a small bite every now and then. That's a lot for me, I have to watch my sugar intake. In *all* forms." This came from a thirty something, husky tall woman, one with many visible tattoos, and many that were just peeking out from beneath clothing's frayed edges, standing the furtherest away, her legs braced and her arms crossed over her chest. She caught the woman's eye and they nodded at each other in agreement.

"Beautiful tree though," added the amazon.

Flem watched her reverently running her hands down the tree's solid middle, petting branches as if greeting a revered great aunt. He nodded and smiled sympathetic-ally over her probably fig-less existence but secretly glad *he* could eat figs. And Lark. Lark loved figs. He said they reminded him of sensuous delights…

Mayapple gave him a poke and brought him back, his ears hearing the echo of the question can we pick 'em?

"Yes," he declared. "Just don't go sprite crazy!"

No one paid any attention to this last except Mayapple. "Sprite-crazy? Huh?"

Flem realized he'd slipped and tried to ignore it by being as matter-of-fact as possible. "You know, *too* much, pushing the limits, out of control."

"Oh, you mean hog-wild," she grinned. "Sooo, *sprites*? Get crazy?" A speculative look had come over her as she drifted into this whole new concept.

Slapping his forehead at what he'd done, he called the group together. It seemed all of them had sprawled like Greek goddesses, the magic of the old fig canopy transforming their very psyche.

"Onward! We'll be turning left again when we hit the path at the bottom of the hill." He waited behind until all were scrambling down before him.

Mayapple caught his eye on the way by and fluttered her eyelashes at him as she blew him a kiss.

He just shook his head.

The others were seen in the distance, stopped and clustered around something at the edge of the meadow that bordered the path.

Someone shouted back, "Blue dicks!" but before Flem took off to catch up, Mayapple snagged his sleeve and mouthed the words "Talk to Lark!" at him.

He rolled his eyes, shook her off and beat a hasty retreat.

Mayapple quickly thumbed through her notebook 'til she found the right page, stuck a finger in it and moved off after the others.

Whimsey C. Nimble

"Actually, the whole thing is good to eat. I read about a Native American tribe that use to dig the bulbs, actually corms, in large quantities and hold feasts. They ate them raw, fried, boiled, and baked," Flem was saying.

"But," he emphasized, "BUT," he repeated, holding up a cautionary finger, "Mayapple? Anything to add?"

Cued in, she opened up her notebook to read: "Never dig up any blue dicks, Brodiaea, ie: Ookow, that isn't flowering."

They all looked at the compact cluster of purple, funnel shaped flowers atop a long stiff stem with no leaves.

"Because," she went on, "the white flowered death camas bulbs grow in the same habitat, and they're called *death* camas for a reason!"

Here Flem interrupted with, "Usually, the camas is found higher in the mountains in wet meadows but I've seen plenty of blue dicks intermingled..."

Everyone was nodding in serious agreement, and Mayapple continued, "Actually, it's best not to pick Brodiaea at all, but they are edible."

"Speaking of *not picking*, did you know this was edible also?" Flem pointed to a delicate personality that stood about six or seven inches high, its white cup-like flower almost hidden in some tall damp grass.

"That's a Mariposa Lily, isn't it?" A voice asked, then went on to question, "Edible?"

Everyone gathered in a circle, hunching over or squatting down to examine the swaying beauty. Spots of dark purplish red were visible near the base of the creamy white petals.

"Again, the Native Americans were reputed to eat these. The buds are good raw, and the flowers are tasty too." He tried to look as noncommittal as possible while he said this, firmly keeping his own memories of popping off heads and eating them locked in place, coupled as it was with not such a good time in his life - too much mead, no sylphcontrol and low sylphesteem.

Looking up he caught Mayapple watching him with a much too knowing look on her face and he knew exactly what she was thinking. She was feeling sorry for him, for his imagined life before Fletcherman's...

He turned his back on her innocently, thinking how it was all a ploy to soften him up, so she could get him to say yes about her insane idea on making them a threesome at the *S* Club.

"Alright, let's move on," he commanded. At least he was in control of *something*, he thought, wishing his life itsylph was as organized as work was, with specific tasks to be accomplished on a daily basis.

Mayapple skipped up beside him, linking her arm through his, notebook tucked securely under the other arm.

"What's next, boss?" She gave him her best deferential smile, holding it as long as possible before grinning irrepresively. "Do you need my notes?" she asked, unable to *not* tease him.

He ignored her.

They picked their way across a rocky, tree-shaded, dry gully. Flem merely replied, "Watch and learn, little girl," making Mayapple laugh and bow him on.

The path climbed once they were out in the open again and the troop followed Flem and Mayapple obediently like good little sheep, one behind the other on the narrow hillside, the path winding up and up and over, leveling off again once a higher parallel path was reached. Distant pieces of it could be seen interspersed between trees and hills as it wandered off into the distance.

"Have I told you how nice you're looking today, Flem?" Mayapple smiled charmingly at her companion.

Flem looked over at her warily, feeling gauche in his skepticism of her sincerity. Cha, but she put him in an awkward position.

"Thank you," he said blandly and sure enough, before he could return the compliment, she leaped.

With a quick glance behind them, she poked at him again. "Flem," drawing it out as if in anguish.

"Sssst! Not *now* Mayapple, what is the matter with you?"

"Oh come on. Why not? *Please*? I'll bet there are *humans* there."

Flem considered for a moment, seeing all those 'people' on the first and second floor of the *S* Club, wondering deeply if they were all human. He didn't think so, but didn't know.

Sensing she had her foot in the door, she whispered urgently, "Just think about it, would you?" then turned and greeted Black Hat and the others.

Waiting 'til all had assemble around him Flem led off with, "Another common face in the foothills is this right here," he pointed to a large overgrown evergreen shrub, one that looked like it could be a scraggly tree but technically wasn't. Beautiful exfoliating reddish bark could be seen on its many trunks and limbs.

"Manzanita. See the little clusters of bell-like flowers?" He held up a bunch with his fingers. "Cider. Flour from the dried berries. Poultices. Utensils, you name it."

Most of them had seen it before but not realized its many properties.

They kept going, everyone now looking at the Manzanita that dotted the hillside so heavily with new respect.

That Flem sure knew his stuff.

"Look, horehound!" pointed out Ms. Sandals excitedly as they walked by. Everyone exclaimed with her, feeling mightily smart.

"And there's a blue dick, several in fact," threw in tattooed figless amazon.

Flem nodded proudly at them, his students.

Mayapple rolled her eyes with her back turned to them all, then groaned just loud enough for Flem to hear her, thinking she would use all at her disposal to get him to give in, even stooping to cheap shots and low dramatics.

Flem groaned back at her, they both broke into laughter and old black hat right behind them said "Hey, what's so funny?"

Flem shushed right away and said "Oh nothing. Do you ever use bay leaves in your spaghetti sauce?"

Taken aback at this non sequitur, there was a pause before she nodded and said, "Yeah?"

"Where do you get them?" quickly filled in the faerie, diverting.

"I have a little bottle full, I got it at the market of course."

Flem stopped and everybody eyeballed the entire area, trying to guess what he was going to show them next.

Pulling a branch down from a nearby tree, the Sylph plucked several long dark green leaves until he had enough for everybody and passed them around.

"Bay laurel, also known as Myrtle in Oregon. Our bay is quite a bit stronger than the European version, which is what used to be widely used in cooking, so you don't need as much with this." He broke his leaf in half and inhaled deeply, a little too deeply, and the fresh pungent scent hit his nostrils like a kerosene fire, searing a minute path straight to his brain. He staggered. He gasped once and then again, breath coming rapidly, the scarf around his neck twitching in an unseemly way as his wings were taken by surprise, a bomb out of the blue. His entire world evaporated, replaced by one fiery, all encompassing moment.

Everyone looked warily at the leaf they held, a few brave souls daring a tentative sniff but none breaking it in half as their leader had so foolishly done, not sure what to do, stealing looks at his flushed face and watering eyes, sympathy and awkwardness heavy in the air.

Mayapple of course took charge. Forcing a tight smile, she said brightly, "Be right back!" before grabbing Flem by the shoulder and marching him off a little distance.

Flem's shoulders were randomly spasming and Mayapple got her bottle out and gave him a drink of water.

"Flem?" she questioned gently.

"I'll be okay. I just shouldn't have inhaled so deeply," he hoarsely gasped.

Unable to hold it back, Mayapple-the-always-tactful responded with "Well, no shit, Sherlock. Are you going to be okay?"

He inhaled deeply in annoyance at her manner, unfortunately fanning the burn, sending screaming nerve endings onward.

"Owwww," he cried in pain against his will, wincing.

"Listen, what's next on your list, your plan? I have my notes on just about everything we talked about back at work, so maybe I could fill in for a bit? You want me to?"

He nodded, a headache forming in his frontal lobes, sinuses alight, a worry line etched between his eyes.

"*Cha*," he said with heartfelt frustration. "I'll be okay in a few minutes." He sounded pinched. "Violets. There should be violets down that way." He pointed.

Mayapple took charge. "You go ahead of us and I'll just ignore you and keep talking, that way you can have a few minutes to yoursylph, how's that?"

He nodded, grateful for her capabilities, and took off with a rather wobbly gait.

Gathering everyone together Mayapple fended off questions about Flem with assurances he was fine, just taking a break and that meanwhile *she* would be their leader.

Keeping the faerie in sight ahead of her, she kept her companions busy with questions and stories, letting her feet mindlessly carry her along in Flem's wake.

Whimsey C. Nimble

He was walking pretty fast, fingers to his temples on each side, massaging as he went.

She glanced away and when she glanced back, he was pointing to the ground in many places – then he kept going, not stopping until he was several yards away, not close, and sat by himsylph on a nearby log, his head in his hands, fingers still working the sides of his head.

Mayapple stepped in competently, paging through her notes 'til she came to 'violets'.

"I know people eat violets, I've even had cake with candied violets on top, but somehow it just seems wrong to me eating something as beautiful as that," put in long-haired hippie sandals.

Everyone was oohing and ahhing over the hearty clumps scattered about, some purple, some white and several voices agreed with her sentiments.

Tattoo arms got down on the ground a little ways away and laid her whole face down amongst the welcoming flower heads, sprawling uninhibitedly on the earth, breathing loudly, making them all laugh at her antics.

Mayapple kept her eye on Flem in the distance, wishing he was up and moving.

As if reading her mind, he rose and pantomimed he was going on, not too far.

She nodded and turned back to her violet-drunk set.

"Ready?"

Well, they didn't all agree with the sentiment that violets were too pretty to eat, obviously. Three different people had violet petals clinging to their mouths or chin.

Figless amazon actually swallowed and Mayapple wondered if she'd been *eating* the whole time she'd been face first in the flowers?

'Grandma,' Mayapple's private name for the older woman with tightly curled grey hair, big shoes, and a big black bag was one of them and Mayapple could hardly believe her eyes.

The third was not so surprising. The woman was young, after all. Adventuresome. Long blond hair. Very pretty. Probably only around thirty or so.

Before Mayapple could say anymore, a soft squawking shout was heard and Flem was urging her on, waving 'this way.'

Mayapple smiled tightly and hurried to catch up with him.

"Can you do elderberry?" he asked hoarsely. "After elderberry there's just two more and then we'll be back to the van."

Mayapple understood immediately; they had another stop to make and he could take it easy while they drove there.

"Sure," she nodded. "What about the next two, what are they? Want me to do these too?" Concern was real in her voice.

"Maybe," he reluctantly replied, "although I'm feeling better by the moment. Do you have notes on elderberry?"

"I do."

Their eyes met and Flem's heart sank its lowest, quietly, as he knew he was going to be saying yes to her outlandish *S* Club petition by the end of the day.

Mayapple swallowed a smile, squelching the victorious triumphant taste in her mouth. No good ever came of crowing too early and many a game lost by arrogance.

Concentrating on the task at hand, ignoring Flem as he wandered down the path away from them, she refocused on the gangly bush sporting a myriad of umbels, both flowering and of tiny round, bluish-black clusters of fruit.

Glancing at her notes, she started her spiel, telling her audience about the reputed joys of elderberry blossom tea, which was supposedly good in reducing fevers as it was high in vitamin C. The flowers were also known to be a delightful addition to pancakes, muffins or a cake but it was advisable to not actually eat the fresh *fruit*, as it was known to make some people sick. Instead the berries lent themselves more readily to being cooked, ending up in wine, jellies, syrup and sauces, the cooking apparently negating any nauseating effects. In addition, musical instruments were made from the hollowed out stems, and dye was obtained from the twigs and fruit.

A professional middle aged woman dressed perfectly for a woodsy outing in crisp khaki walking shorts, a matching tan blouse and a jaunty neck kerchief around her throat, took a step forward, raising a purple-colored umbel to her nose, and asked, "Can we take any of these home?" breaking off a piece as she did so.

Mayapple thought it was okay but the woman's blatant assumption irked her, so she smiled sweetly and said, "Well, a few would probably be allowed but be careful, the twigs and leaves themselves have a pretty rank smell."

Whimsey C. Nimble

Ms. olive-green cotton socks in the impressive new hiking boots irreverently dropped the picked posy on the ground and then accidentally stepped on it as she backed up, all of which grated on Mayapple's sensibilities. "Let's move on," she said with a bit of an irk.

Flem was nowhere in sight and he hadn't told her which two were next. A little nervous, she quickened the pace, avidly searching the ground and hillsides for any plants she might recognize from her notes. The group had dwindled into almost silence and they all scuffed along, raising occasional puffs of dirt on this particular stretch of trail.

Coming to the top of the rise of a small hill, they crested it and Mayapple spied her faerie sitting on a bench in the shadows down the road apiece. He waved.

The girl guide made a bee-line right for him. "How're you feeling?" was the first thing she wanted to know.

"I'm better. I still feel a new track where I used to have flesh, but it'll go away." He smiled a little tiredly.

"So, what's next then? Are you doing them or am I?" She waited. Oh, she wanted to get in a new zinger, it was such an opportune moment but the poor guy wasn't quite himsylph and besides, she knew she was racking up golden points just by fulfilling her duty as co-guide. He knew it too, she knew. No, best to wait. The perfect moment would come. He would say *yes*.

Watching Mayapple, Flem was surprised she wasn't badgering him right now, but she was smart. He knew she knew he would no doubt say yes after her saving his fae butt today.

"Look around," he suggested. "What do you see?"

"I see the parking lot right over there."

Making a sound of disgust at her literal response, he waited.

"Ooh, those are wild roses, aren't they?" she exclaimed happily, getting up to inspect the bushes that clustered a tiny stream rivulet, a seepage of sorts.

Flem moved to stand beside her and soon the entire fauna clan was nose deep in a little aroma therapy spot all of their own.

Groans of pure bliss could be heard along with the occasional "Ouch!" as they, like giant human bugs, moved from one wild rose to another, running into prickers with a hand out, trying to impede their progress.

Red Rose Hat was the first to pull away, eyes dilated from so much pure love. "Oh," she said, putting a hand to her forehead, "that was lovely," as if she were done but then succumbed right back to inhaling the next one, like an infatuated bee.

Flem got ahold of himsylph and cleared his throat loudly, then whistled a little tune and sure enough, heads popped up and eyes blinked themselves back to reality.

"Rose hips," he said, his voice still rusty from the bay leaf burn, "are high in vitamin C, calcium, phosphorous, and iron." He stopped and coughed and Mayapple looked at him for a minute before deciding to step in.

"These little pods, or *hips*, are good raw and like Flem said, really high in vitamin C. Be sure to remove the zillion inner seeds first. I've also read of the flowers being used in lots of things, like butter, perfume, candy, jelly, and of course tea. In fact, rose *leaf* tea makes a great drink." She paused and Flem made a walking gesture with his two fingers and pointed towards the van, coughing intermittently.

She nodded okay.

He pointed to some big brambles to the side of the parking lot and mouthed the word "Blackberries" at her, smiled, then waved 'goodbye' and walked away.

"Okay ladies, look what we have here," Mayapple said as she watched Flem bend down towards some greenery first then disappear into the vehicle.

Pulling her attention back to the berry lovers, she said "Here, I have a small bag for each of you. That's our limit. I don't think anybody needs me to tell them the benefits of blackberries…"

Forty-five minutes later, they were winding up a sharply curved country road, climbing to a lake Flem had been to that should be perfect on a day like this.

Mayapple had only made one impassioned plea right at the beginning when it was still noisy, about how important it was to her and how she'd really like to go to the *S* Club, making it short, sweet and emphatic before saying, "Okay, I'll let you rest in peace the rest of the way," her eyes dancing at him, both aware she was going to get her way, and now it was only a little game they were playing, just a matter of time.

Flem merely nodded, said "I'll think about it," then leaned back and closed his eyes, shutting her out, sipping from a water bottle that now held a little chamomile and horehound with a pinch of some mint, all of which had been right beside their vehicle.

Three miles up the miniature mountain brought them around a bend and there before them was a small round lake, one with a parking lot and easy access.

"Now, which lake is this again? I know you mentioned it but I forgot," a voice in the back asked.

"Koot Loon," answered Flem, mostly recovered, thank Pan. "It's actually a reservoir but it's far enough off the beaten path that it's never lost its wildness. Great for birds too. You're apt to see osprey, loon, cranes, egrets, herons, and there's coots on the lake a lot, plus ducks of course. Beautiful, isn't it?"

Mayapple's eyes were shining with a whole new level of awe at this hidden jewel Flem had just magically produced for them. A priceless gift of nature herself. How could she ever have been irritated by this charming faerie, her favorite fae friend, she wondered, hero worship swooping from her like returning spring swallows.

Flem was embarrassed by everyone's reaction, it was like suddenly he was a rock star, famous, and they all *loved* him.

He rose to the occasion by suavely deflecting them with orders, directing them to cast their eyes out on the water: "Look out there. Too deep for us, but those are *all* culinary delights."

Shading their eyes, they looked out across the glittering body of water, the picturesque scene almost too much to bear. Cattails, bulrushes, and acres of lily pads hugged the entire circular shore. Geese laughed in the far distance, across on the other side. The fresh water marsh that surrounded this Shangri-La was evident in many places while forest filled in every other spot, the exception being where they had just parked. A humble path of sorts skirted the edge.

Feeling smug, Flem cleared his throat, (which was still a little sore but nothing like it'd been) and began with a little joke. "If you've ever had anyone who wanted to take you out to the tulles, well, no doubt it's none of *my* business, but tulles are another name for bulrushes, and are pretty good at hiding anyone, IF they're in a canoe, because they're always going to be standing in water!" He laughed at his own joke and everyone sort of laughed with him, but Mayapple could tell most of them didn't think it was that funny.

The pause was such that he knew he was stretching it and immediately went on, "Like any new greens, the fresh new shoots of the bulrushes are the tastiest, but a sweet flour can also be made from the roots, which are actually tuber-forming rhizomes, and I've heard of the *pollen* being added to cakes. Cattails share these same traits and they frequently grow side by side, but are different in that one can cook the green cattail spikes still wrapped in their leaves, add butter, and voila! A different version of corn-on the-cob, I guess we'd have to call them cattail kabobs then, wouldn't we?"

"Are we collecting any today?" asked the young blond woman licking her lips, looking about near the shore, hoping to spot some closer-in, and sure enough, there were *plenty* everywhere.

All moved forward, drawn by the water and the spell of nature that was its cloak. Red-wing black birds chortled and called and hung sideways in their favorite playground- bulrushes and cattails all surrounded by water, some only a few inches deep, others seen far away, accessible only by boat.

Utterly charmed, everyone spread out, the atmosphere catching them in its soft loving embrace.

Like the rest of them, Mayapple had been pulled to the waterline, laughing in delight as unseen presences plopped into hiding spaces around her feet, a frog head occasionally seen coming up a few feet away.

Flem was feeling better by the moment, bay leaf fast becoming a memory, a VIVID memory, but his sinuses no longer hurt. And they sure were clear, that was for sure!

Trailing behind Mayapple, he walked past, out to the nearest cattail clump, reaching out to gently bend the first brown spike towards him, admiring the golden spire that rose out of the top half.

"Hellooo," he sang out to get everyone's attention, calling them to him.

Hopping and splish-splashing like frog hunting fowl, the women gathered on his piece of the shoreline, Mayapple smiling from the side as if she knew what was going on. Unfortunately, she'd forgotten her notebook in the van.

When everyone was waiting expectantly, he once again bent a cattail head over and explained, "The male half produces pollen at the top," he paused to point to the golden stringy material, then continued "while the lower half is what we so easily recognize as a cattail – this big brown tufted thick sprig, which is made up of millions of dense feathery seeds."

"And yes," he looked around to make eye contact with the young blond woman and then nodded as he answered her question. "We are collecting today. They said we could take what we like but not to strip the place." This last was said as a joke as there were hundreds and hundreds of clumps encircling the entire lake which was a rather large, small lake - they could have filled the entire van and it wouldn't have made a dent.

The blond addressed him again and Flem winced as he tried to remember her name; Macadamia Mackenzie? He thought that was it. They called her Mac or maybe Mick, he wasn't sure.

"Mr. Green?"

"Oh, call me Flem."

"Ah, Mr. Flem? Oh, ha ha, I mean, Flem? Do you think we'll find any green spikes today? My brother Riley Ribes, our family calls him gooseberry just for fun, well, he loves young steamed cattails and the way you were describing them made them sound really mouth watering."

She was so cute, Flem felt his smile become a little warmer than he meant to and his eyes seemed to send little flashing signals all by themsylves and he thought "Eek! Lark! Lark!" before he finally was able to tear his gaze away.

Now she was looking at him in that adoring way they all seemed to get to, what *was it* about his charming Sylph that they all seemed to respond to? How come nobody back home in Thimbleberry Canyon ever responded like this when *he* was *she*, Flumaria Greenwood?

He *knew* why, of course.

He was responsible now, whereas before *she* was too intent on appearing something she wasn't. Now, *he* didn't worry about who he was or how he looked, he was happy, life's challenges were satisfying to solve, not something to be avoided. He was much more just himsylph. (Hidden wings not withstanding, he laughed ironically to himsylph, his own joke.)

But still, the most important people *did* know and loved him anyway.

If he had not *stayed male* and had returned to female, what would have changed? It was hard to imagine what his life would have been like, still in the canyon. Probably still at her old tree…

If the *change* hadn't stuck, he wouldn't have moved out of the canyon, eventually ending up here, in San Fran, and needing a job. Where would he be without Fletcherman's?

He'd grown, become sophisticated simply by living, paying attention to what those intuitive nudges from the universe were telling him. Follow your heart even when you think it's broken and things seem black and irrevocable. *Pay attention to the details.* And, it was so much easier being healthy, body and soul, than being unhappy.

He realized his attitude was what had changed the most. He was more accepting of himsylph, and others, and in return they easily accepted him. He was less anxious, less stressed.

"Flem?" Even her voice tickled him. Cha. He'd never been in a real relationship for any length of time before and he couldn't believe he was attracted to a human woman! He loved Lark, how could this be?

He decided to just bluff his way through, be very professional, *chatty*, and just not act on his feelings, to *pretend* everything was fine.

It worked like a charm. "No. I don't believe there are any green spikes right now. There's more in the spring, now you see everything in bloom, both male tips and female bottoms in full splendor."

She smiled a wide smile directly at him and he nodded acknowledgement before letting his attention be pulled away by another question, re-engaging himsylph with the rest of the group.

"Yes I do," he answered. "I have several recipes for cattails. I'll hand them out at the end of the trip."

For the next hour, they waded and pulled up roots of bull rushes and cattails, not too many and not all from one clump.

Mayapple went back to the vehicle and returned with a box of big garbage bags to wrap their booty in, coming to stand next to Flem as they watched the excitement, joy, and contentment on their companions' faces.

Flem chanced a look at Mayapple and she gave him her most beguiling gaze, willing him silently to love her more than anybody, AND, feel *compelled* to bring her along with him and Lark to the *S* Club. Surely he trusted her implicitly, after all theses times, including *today*, of saving his behind.

She gazed back at him a little too long and too hard and the faerie sighed. It wasn't over yet, now was it?

Whimsey C. Nimble

"I will *think*, about it, okay?" he said in a very clipped voice, his public smile hardly wavering, almost like a ventriloquist, each sound rolling around his teeth and up, over his lips, instead of flying out his mouth together.

Wisely, Mayapple didn't say a word, just walked to the water's edge to start handing out bags and help everybody stuff them. She decided she better just button her lip. She would wait the entire day if need be but promised herself she would get in one more little plea as they parted at the end of the day if it hadn't been decided by then.

She glanced back at Flem and he was standing with his back to them, studying the gentle sloping hillside across the road.

"Hey," she called, "Are we leaving or what?"

"Almost," he replied. "Have everyone put their shoes on and put their *dinner* in the van, then come over here. I have something to show everyone."

Fifteen minutes later, the damp-kneed but happy group gathered, waiting expectantly for the next pearls of wisdom that would drop from that great nature guide, Flem's, mouth. All were completely enamored of him by this time.

Straightening his scarf, he cleared his throat (and it didn't hurt!) and launched into, "We have practically a garden, right here, all within twenty feet of each other." He illustrated with a sweeping motion of his arm, indicating a variety of natural inhabitants before them.

"First of all, here's one probably no one thinks of as *dinner*. Thistle. But the young flowers, stalks, and the roots are delicious when boiled. All thistles are edible, just clean and boil 'til tender. There are certain medicinal properties also, associated with the liver but it's quite involved. If you're interested, remind me after we get back and I'll fill you in."

"Moving on, see what's hidden here? More violets." He cast a questioning look towards Mayapple and she confirmed with a quick nod that yes, *she'd* covered *violets* already, and then gave him a *See?*- I- *deserve*- to-go-to-the-S-Club look which he blatantly ignore, although he *did* see it.

Reaching into the shade he ran his hand through some gangly mint, saying "*Mint.* Ah, we all love mint, now don't we?"

"Back here," he went down the path and beamed like he'd planted everything there himsylph, "are two more of my favorites. These things, I always called them pop-reeds when I was a Syl-ah,-kid. When I was a kid."

Obviously a low spot and well watered, the field of scaly reeds stood stately, spreading out 'til the hill became too high, easily obscuring their feet.

He hurried to rush on. "Horse Tail. Their property is more medicinal than as a staple for food, I believe it's used as a general membrane tonic, especially for deep areas, like lungs or urinary tract."

He pointed to a different patch of plants, ones that looked like skinny succulent straws but with a one-leaf wrap-a-round bonnet. Some had an itty bitty white flower in the middle. He reached down and gently pinched a stem down low, then popped the whole thing into his mouth. "Miner's lettuce," he stated. "Loves water, doesn't like it hot and dry and is great in a salad. Or, can BE the salad, if you've got enough," he smiled.

They followed him in a circle as he started back towards the van, stopping once to point out the chamomile that grew down low, a ground cover that seemed to thrive being walked on.

"Is this the same kind I'd buy in a store?" said the other old lady, the one of clumpy shoes, stooping to the ground to roll some of the abundant greenish-yellow heads between her fingers. "It looks the same."

"I don't think it is, right Flem?" Mayapple didn't wait for an answer. "I think this is the German, the other is the better quality for tea, right Flem? What's its name?"

"The other kind is the Roman, that's what is mainly used for tea. This stuff, I'm pretty sure it's the German, although I'm not positive, is more likely to be used topically for rashes and such, and not drinking."

"Well, let's go," he said after a moment. "We've got a schedule to keep and I want to get back in time to walk around the block."

Mayapple gave him a look and he went on, "There's an empty lot over behind us?" he questioned to see if she knew where he was referring to and she nodded, pleased at his resourcefulness.

"Urban herbs?" she grinned as she said it.

"Yep," he agreed with a proud but bashful smile

"What's there?" she asked.

But he wouldn't tell her, just said, "You'll see," but then went on and gave it away with, "You should know. I would imagine most if not all are in your notebook."

"Hmm. Of course. Let's see, what *haven't* we seen today? Oh, I don't care," she suddenly burst out. "I'm sure you have it all figured out, Mr.

Green." She almost sounded jealous of his knowledge but then went on generously, "This day has been such a success, Flem. You really know your stuff out here." She nodded, indicating the great outdoors. "So far you've been right on about what you thought we'd see today."

"I was a little worried that some things might have changed, it's been years since I've been to Koot Loon Lake, or the Yucca River trail, but so far, so good."

He turned the compliment around. "Thanks for trusting me enough to go with this. And for doing extra research on my suggestions."

He waited for the *S* Club plea at this point, but it didn't make an appearance.

That felt good. He was more inclined to consider it if she'd just quit yammering about it and give him a chance to *think*.

Their conversation halted as the van quieted down after everyone got settled, the sound of seat belts snapping like a bale of eight hungry turtles.

Mayapple drove.

It had been a busy day and the group was no longer quite so rambunctious.

Mayapple turned on some quiet jazz and everyone drifted into their own thoughts, a soft murmur of words occasionally breaking the surface.

By late afternoon, they were pulling into the Nursery parking lot and Flem was again metamorphosing into group leader.

"Come now ladies, don't poop out yet, we're going for a walk. Yes, another one. Just around the block. We'll be back in time for tea and cookies before five." Five was the official end time for the nature walk.

There were groans as everyone by this time was sleepy and stiff from the long van-ride home but all gamely pulled themselves together.

Heading down the street in a pack, it soon sorted itself out to twos, Mayapple and Flem in the lead of course.

Flem's plan had been to just hot foot it to the big empty lot he knew of, but how could he, when they were passing windowsills, lawns, and flower boxes filled with delectable edibles? He couldn't stand it and they came to a conspicuous halt in front of a business set back in a ways from the sidewalk.

By now, everyone was fairly savvy and all were conjecturing upon what here was useful.

Carnations grew profusely bordering the small manicured lawn, with vibrant nasturtiums sprawling away from them onto the sidewalk. Violets could be seen scattered throughout and Mayapple glanced at Flem who was observing quietly.

"Yes," he agreed with his almost graduates as they knowingly discussed various methods of preparing flowers for consumption, lingering over jellied carnations. "That's right. And look there, there's a dandelion they should eat before it gets any bigger and goes to seed and spoils their pretty green grass."

They all giggled at that and then spooked a little when someone came bursting out the front of the building, unknowingly chasing them away.

Laughing, they straggled on, Macadamia Mackenzie talking animatedly with Tattoo-Figless, right behind Mayapple and Flem, followed by Gladiola of the black hat to carry on in the middle with Hippeastrum, Hippie for short, of the long hair. Ms. Khaki took the arm of Old Clumpy Shoes and brought up the rear.

Coming around the corner, the vacant lot lay just ahead when Mayapple was arrested by several pots alongside a passing stoop.

"Ooh look, Flem, pelargoniums, and I think they're the scented ones! I wonder if they have more than one kind here?" She was excited and stealthy rubbed leaves, urging them to release their scent and introduce themselves.

"Oh!" and she gushed on and on, about the lemon! The rose! The apple! The peppermint! And the delightful herb sauces or sachets one could make with the leaf of the scented geranium.

Several people took notes, two were on their hands and knees, feeling leaves, sniffing, sniffing, sniffing, letting out cries of ecstasy.

Mayapple succumbed finally and trying to maintain decorum, held her hair back out of the way in a civilized manner but soon let it flop down, a waterfall that effectively shielded her face and a rose geranium together and she closed her eyes in delight.

After a moment Flem coughed and they all came to, looking around a bit sheepishly.

Two minutes later they were lifting their feet high as they stepped into the vacant, weed encrusted lot, Ms. Sandals complaining she should have worn socks.

Mayapple was skeptical, waited for the show. Flem was full of surprises today. She eyed him, wondering if she'd go to bed this night with the answer she so desperately wanted, or not.

Whimsey C. Nimble

Keeping his business persona in place, Flem was not fooled that Mayapple had given up. He also knew he was only delaying the inevitable but planned on keeping it just so, for as long as Sylphly possible.

Spreading out like treasure hunters on a land-fill site, the faerie watched them all continuously walk by several hidden-in-plain-sight delights.

Chortling, he gave them another minute before reeling them back in, asking, "Who here has eaten oatmeal? Or perhaps had an oatmeal cookie?" His tongue came out between his lips and he held it there, a shy pink showing of cuteness, his eyes dancing. He'd never had such fun, it was so gratifying to be able to use his knowledge, to share what every Sylph automatically accumulated growing up in the canyon as a Sylphette.

Sharp eyes landed on the plant nearest his knees and "Oats?" was tossed around like a big rubber ball from one to the other.

Flem nodded, putting his hand behind the tall spindly grass to highlight the awns, – the bristly appendages hanging from the end of the branchlets.

"Oats," he reaffirmed, "found in waste fields and disturbed areas everywhere. If there's enough to collect, just be sure to look carefully and not gather any with a black fuzzy mold on it. Only pick the greenish or golden ones. The mold could be the poisonous ergot. Oh and by the way, oat straw tea is one of my favorites."

He walked away, moving in the direction of the old brick building that bordered one side of the lot.

In the distance some purple pebbly spikes stood out and Flem looked forward to introducing amaranth to them but meanwhile he stopped and pulled up some of the ground cover, two different species dangling from his hand.

"Whattaya got there sonny? I mean Mr. Green." Clumpy shoes looked like she should have a cane to poke him with, but she didn't. She kind of cackled and looked slanty-eyed at New Shoes like she was being cute and New Shoes nodded sweetly to her, although in actuality gritting her teeth a little at being stuck with the old woman who smelled like she needed a bath when you got right up next to her. At that moment the old dear stuck her arm through hers, looked up at her and smiled demurely, happy to have a date once again.

Ah well, can't win 'em all, thought New Shoes, A.K.A Penstemon, Penny to her friends, and smiled back, manners overriding personal feelings once again. It would never do to hurt someone's feelings.

"This thing right here," Flem held up one of his finds, one with long skinny arms, and rather rounded leaves. "Malva, or chickweed, also known as mallow. It has ancient associations particularly with Greece, and, oh yeah, it's better cooked or you can eat the little tiny cheesy looking fruits raw in a salad, minus their husks of course. It's a common weed and can be very invasive. And this," he showed them a long reddish-stemmed plant of what looked like miniature birds' heads with long bills on one branch, with lacy leaves. "Officially called red stemmed filaree, I've always called it crane's bill or stork beak or even cork bill. When it dries out it curls in a precise spiral. One that LOVES to get tangled in a dog's coat, as mayhaps some of you may have noticed. It tastes sort of like spinach when it's cooked but it's good raw too," he raised his eyebrows and looked around. "*Weeds*. Delicious weeds. Now you know what to do with your back yards. Eat them!"

Everyone laughed and Mayapple sank deeper by the moment into faerie enchantment. This was the same Sylph who used to quake and twitch in fear, so much so that his wings clutched and her mother thought he was an epileptic. Well, today he was in his element.

"Alright, let's head over here." Flem steered them towards the big spiky shapes dominating a corner.

"This right here?" he pointed out, making it sound more like a question, "this beauty is something called amaranth." Lovingly, he stroked the lumpy flowering head, which mimicked a full armed Christmas tree, with lots of heavy branches all coming from one trunk. "This conglomeration of branches is the 'flower' of each plant. These will all be seeds when this baby dries out." He went on, "Someone had to have planted this. These gorgeous colors," he pointed to the various shades of crimson, purple and gold, " are usually associated with cultivation. In the wild, feral amaranth is barely two feet tall, and mostly green, sometimes with red veins and stems. My guess is this stuff was somebody's pet project here at one time and now reseeds itself every year."

"What do you do with it, anyway?" asked Stevia, folding her tattooed arms in front of her. "What part do you eat?"

Flem was secretly glad they were meeting under these conditions, she could intimidate the wing scales right off of him with out too much effort, all unknowingly.

Whimsey C. Nimble

"Ahhh, *amaranth*," sighed the faerie in his best heartfelt manner, a bit dramatically, fluttering his eyes as if in love. "What *can't* you do with it?" He looked coyly up.

On cue, everyone grinned.

"Well, one healthy plant averages fifty thousand little tiny seeds, which are high in protein, about sixteen percent. They're also high in fiber and contain calcium, iron, potassium, phosphorous, and vitamins A, C, and E, plus a couple of amino acids not found in regular grains. *Amaranth* is called a pseudo-grain because it's from a different plant family than the true grains, like wheat. Also, I've read that its protein is a 'complete' protein, meaning it's more akin to, *yuk*, animal protein because of one of the amino acids, lysine. You'll definitely want to soak the seeds overnight to reduce the saponin content, which is the stuff in certain plants, like soapwort, that *foams* up. Are you with me?" he interrupted himsylph to seek their agreement and several voices complied with yes, yes, do go on, urging him to continue, they were rapt with attention.

"So okay, we'll pretend it's later in the year and these flower heads are heavy and dried out. You take a bag and carefully bend the heavy head into the bag and shake carefully. Voila! Seeds to dry out and turn into *flour*. That's one thing you can do with it!" He looked Stevia in the eye as he presented his answer to her earlier question. "Or, after you've winnowed it, instead of roasting for flour perhaps you'll cook it in water and then lay it out to dry and sprinkle it on your salad, or, *pop* it like popcorn! But make sure you have a big pot and some oil. An air popper won't work. OR, turn it into flakes and perhaps do some baking with it. If you don't want to go to that trouble, even though it's a high quality food, perhaps snipping off the young leaves and cooking like mustard greens by boiling a few minutes would be more to your liking. If this aspect appeals to you the most, you'll probably have to go foraging-" he stopped as a light bulb went on behind his eyes and he made a serious joke: "Remind me to give you our number in case you need someone to help you with that!" He laughed and so did everyone else, politely waiting for him to go on but you could tell it stuck in many a mind.

"Yes, foraging - or, grow it yourself, like you would any other crop. It's not something you're going to see readily at your local grocery store." He paused and then commenced with, "Well, we're going to start back and I'll point out a few things en route but if we want to make time for tea..." he let it hang and adjusted his slight pack, nodding to Mayapple to come along, they were leaving.

She scurried into place, hero worship plain upon her face and in her eyes and the faerie wondered how long it would last. He doubted if he'd get home safely from work today without her bringing up the *S* Club at least once more.

Ah well, a faerie could hope.

The group fell in behind him as they cut across the lot to finish going around the block.

Enthusiasm was starting to wane the closer they got to Fletcherman's.

Half way up the block Flem stopped a moment on the upper edge of two very uneven pieces of sidewalk and briefly gestured towards the plants growing between. "You'll never look at weeds the same again, will you? Just imagine, you could be collecting salad or dinner ingredients everywhere you go on your daily errands!" He laughed.

Various exclamations of disgust were made and everyone peered then scowled at it as they passed by, shaking their heads as if the thistle were at fault somehow, and a muttered, "Not a chance. I'd have to be pretty darn hungry to eat thistles!" was heard. Laughing agreements were echoed about.

By now they were coming around the corner that was just down the street from Fletcherman's and Flem pointed to one side saying, "More nasturtiums. And look, here's a 'weed' that everybody walks by." There was no stem to speak of and the broad elliptic leaves seemed to come right from the ground, distinctive with its tall shiny flowering spikes.

"*This* is something *useful?*" came the incredulous question. "I have these all around my backyard!"

Flem asked, "Do you water a lot? They like damp places," and went on to elaborate with, "See where he's growing? It's damp right here from the sprinklers. Plantain can be eaten, just pull the heavy strings off and then parboil with a little salt until tender but it's also an extremely useful herb, good for treating wounds, sore throats and coughs." He paused. "Right here in plain sight. As so many are."

They walked up the driveway, past carefully cultivated spots by the nursery's owner, of thyme and savory and even a small rosemary bush.

Whimsey C. Nimble

Holding the side door open for his diligent troops, Mayapple passed by last, giving him a direct stare, a 'look' as he well knew and he gave in. It was going to happen sooner or later today anyway, he might as well capitulate.

"Okay ladies, you've been a fabulous group. Why don't you look around inside for a moment, while I get the tea and cookies ready. Then come back in about ten minutes, okay?"

Relaxed, everyone veered off in the direction of the main show room and Flem said for Mayapple's ears only, "Come. Help me get this ready, please? And yes, yes Mayapple, I've thought about it today and you've been such a help, I'll talk to Lark."

He glanced at her after this momentous announcement and wasn't disappointed. Her hand was clapped over her mouth and her eyes were like saucers in her disbelief at finally, FINALLY, getting what she wanted.

"You won't be sorry, I promise you!" and threw her arms around his neck, knocking several unopened packages of tea to the floor.

Chapter 72

———— ❧ ————

She promised to not drink too much and
get carried away. She did. Really.

AYAPPLE AND FLEM were wrapping it up at the end of a long day,
the faerie sweeping, Mayapple wiping off dirty counters when Iris
came bursting back, half glasses stuck in her hair like small and determined
head lights.

Mayapple noticed she sure waved her beringed hand around a lot and
wondered if she was doing it on purpose. Probably. Her mother leaned towards subtle dramatics herself even though she claimed that was Mayapple's
trait.

"Hey mom, what's up?" inquired the girl

Flem kept sweeping even though he had just finished. He was happy
to have something to occupy his hands as he too looked inquisitively in the
boss's direction.

"Oh Flem, put that away. It's clean. I can see it from here," ordered his
employer, stopping by the time clock.

Both employees quickly finished and came to stand by Iris.

"Here. I have something for the two of you. You did a really good job on
that nature walk, I've had nothing but positive comments and several sales
from that venture." She held out a small box to each of them.

"Ooh, are these *business* cards with our *name* on them?" excitedly exclaimed Mayapple.

Flem was nonplussed.

He pried the lid off and sure enough, it was a box packed tight with small
greenish-grey cards. On one side was *his name*, 'Flem Green, Associate,'

right in the middle under the Fletcherman's Nursery logo. He could hardly believe it.

Mayapple was squealing and dancing around, handing them out to imaginary people with "My *card*," uttered in a very low and sultry voice.

"Your welcome," drawled Iris, since no one had actually thanked her but cut off their belated acknowledgments with, "Turn them over."

On the back of each one was some planting advice. *When to Harvest* was written in big, bold letters at the top with a succinct paragraph below: 'When to harvest depends on what part of the plant you plan to use. Flowers - when they blossom and are only half open. Stems and leaves - before they flower, as essential oils are strongest at that time. Seeds - should be slightly hardened.'

Flem looked at Iris with gratitude shining from his eyes, a wonderful present, she had no idea.

He got really nervous at times, thinking about the enormity of her giving him the greenhouse, in his panic blotting out the mesmerizing pull that had drawn him to it in the first place.

This lasted until he finally relaxed and let his trust in the natural flow of the universe come back into play.

Now she had given him an acceptable alternative identity, one he liked. He was Flem Green, associated with *this*, Fletcherman's Nursery. He was proud, gratified, and honored to be here.

She *liked* him.

"Thank you." He strode over and grasped her hand. "Thank you, these are great."

A bit embarrassed at his fervent response, Iris looked at Mayapple, who was eyeballing Flem but who immediately gave her mother a one armed hugged and thanked her profusely.

The boss didn't stick around but headed back up front after a last wink and a "Good job. See you tomorrow. Oh, actually, do you mind if I stop by out back for just a minute Flem? You going to be home?"

His heart lurched a little at this, oh cha, but of course he smiled and nodded his head, saying "Oh! Sure. Great!"

Iris left with a laugh, assuring him "Not to worry. Just want to see that cat of mine, I won't stay long."

They watched her out of sight and then Mayapple turned to Flem. "Sooo, any news, Flem?" This was said in a very casual manner but Flem knew exactly what she was referring to.

Before he could defend himsylph, Mayapple came in with, "Have you talked to Lark or not?"

Actually he had meant to but it had just never been the right time and had planned on doing so tonight.

"Um, I was planning on asking him tonight." It sounded kind of lame and he knew it.

Mayapple set her box down and came around to his shoulders, pressing her thumbs through his scarf layers to rub some thick cartilage.

"Really?" she wheedled, oochng her magic fingers down the line.

"Yesss," he breathed, much more relaxed and sensible.

"Promise?" Oh that human knew her stuff, rubbing deep circles with her fingers, a melting Sylph practically puddling on the floor in front of her.

"I will, I will, I promise I'll bring it up tonight." It was kind of pathetic really, just how easy it was to manipulate him, thought Mayapple, but loved him dearly just the same.

They parted shortly there after, Mayapple overtly staring at Flem with beady eyes until he said "Stop that! I *will* ask him tonight, I said I would."

She merely said, "G'night. See you tomorrow," but just couldn't resist one last little squint before she turned and was out the door.

Oh thank Pan, it'd felt like she was *never* going to leave. He immediately gathered his things, threw his pack over one shoulder, then had to pull the scarf ends out from under its straps where they were pulled tight, choking him. Ah, impatience.

His free time here was just heavenly and he never grew tired of living this close, well, *inside*, Fletcherman's Nursery.

He made his way around to the back of *his* greenhouse where he and Lark had put together a beautiful frame and entry way for the door they'd absconded with from the treasure room, the *fondly* remembered treasure room...

Renovation was slow but Flem continuously plodded on, working in large circles, going as far as he could in one area and then moving on to do the same in another, always taking each project one step further towards completion. For instance, the glass in the ceiling was slowly being replaced and all the gaping holes had been covered so that at least there were no more leaks. But it was far from finished. The trim was old, moldy, and peeling and needed to be completely redone.

The new door was great but it was rather an anomaly as no other actual remodeling had been done yet, other than a bit of sanding at the window door.

He had just flung off his pack and scarf and was spooning out cat food when he heard Iris you-hooing and making deliberate noise to announce her arrival.

"Here kitty kitty," she called theatrically and basically ineffectually as his first off-duty duty was to feed the cats. Hey, he finally had his priorities straight, thanks to mama cat's continuous training. It seemed she was finally getting him into the correct habit. Consequently, no one paid Iris any attention. At least, those of the feline persuasion. They were busy waiting.

By now Mrs. Fletcherman and her live-in employee, that faerie, Flem Green, were standing shoulder to shoulder watching the domestic scene, laughing fondly at the mess that was happening.

"Rats, looks like I picked the wrong time. Drat. Oh well." Iris was conceding but it was with obvious reluctance that she turned to go. "I've got an appointment, so I can't stay. You know which one is mine, right Flem?"

"Yes, of course," Flem replied with a hint of amused exasperation, but then went on to tease her. "It's that one right there," he said, pointed to the right cat but deliberately saying "Fluffy, right?"

"*Snowball*. And you know it." She flicked a glance at him and decided to play a 'boss's' card and lever just a wee bit of pressure with, "Found a home for them all yet?" so innocently.

Flem blanched at the implied power play and momentarily succumbed to old ways but quickly tightened his gut firmly and replied, "I think so, although they look pretty young yet."

"Oh, six weeks and they can be separated from their mother. And I'll pay for getting her fixed somewhere down the line after all the kids have found new homes. But you're keeping one, aren't you? That *wild* one? Got him named yet?" She smiled, a peace offering.

He smiled back, glad to take it, and said, "Yeah. He's Rubus, he's got sharp little claws just like a bramble bush and draws blood easily."

"Be it fae or human, huh?" Iris laughed and Flem laughed with her, slightly taken aback by her thorny comment.

She turned to go, calling a goodbye. "Bye Snowball, mommy'll be back soon. Bye Ruby, try to be good."

Flem started to protest her take on his rogue's moniker, but on second thought let it go, smilingly escorting his guest to the back and out. Good*bye* Iris, he thought, goodbye, pulling the door closed behind her retreating form, replying in short monosyllables to her exclamations of delight about the in-progress work of the entry way.

She was actually very considerate Flem knew, just as he knew it was *him* being too prickly but the joys of his new found respectability and freedom were such that they blotted out some of his previous socialness, which he now saw as more needy than as a hundred percent healthy. *Now* he was healthier, much more balanced. And sometimes that even meant wanting to be alone and even keeping his friends out, amazingly enough.

Grinning, he moved from one task to another, a faerie bumblebee happy amidst his own 'flowers,' straightening his backroom first, then a cup of tea and some marigold pudding he'd picked up the other day. He only sat for a few minutes though, anxious for the time to pass and Lark to arrive.

Since that was at least two hours away, he took his cup with him and started on the far end, replacing more glass from the box he had, and working on a flower bed – the first of several indoor areas he'd planned. Big ones were going here and outside to afford him some privacy. He wasn't sure what he was going to use for scaffolding to hold the jungle he envisioned but one step at a time.

The tea was long gone and so was the amaranth muffin he'd had for dinner when that Sylph with such good fae manners showed up, his black form stealthily slipping in the window door.

"Cha, Mr. Spurastic, how many times have I told you to use the *door*. We're *civilized* now."

Both were grinning at Flem's jest and met in the middle to kiss and hug. Lark snuggled his nose into Flem's collarbone, sighing, saying "Ah, I've come home," and giving that neck a raspy little taste.

Whimsey C. Nimble

Smiling besottingly, Flem led his fae lover to the back, easing his burdens, pushing him into his hammock, feeding him almonds and cherries and a little shot of mead to revive him after his long day.

After a sufficient amount of time had passed and they had efficiently said hello, Flem twined his fingers through his partner's hair pulling one half curl out over and over, wondering how to broach Lark about Mayapple's insane idea. Was he being way too presumptuous? It certainly felt that way but how would he know if he didn't ask?

"So *Mayapple* had this crazy scheme, Lark, and I, ah, oh Pan, I said I would ask you what you thought. She really *is* very trustworthy, actually, but, oh cha, I don't know, I probably shouldn't have brought it up, but, well."

"Well *out* with it ma petite fleur, what?"

"She wants to go to the *S* Club with us! Are they, well, is everybody? I mean, those first two floors… They sure looked human. Were they?"

There, he'd said it. He wanted to know too.

"Mayapple? *There*? Hmm. I mean, she *is* really nice, I do like her but as you know from Cybele, she can get a little wild."

Flem felt an unfamiliar surge and realized he was rather *irritated* with Lark for not instantly agreeing. For some reason, he felt he had to *defend* his friend and the funny thing was, he couldn't imagine her there either.

"She promised to not drink too much and get carried away. She did. Really."

"Hmm. Well, I don't know. I've never had an actual *human* guest there before, although I know it IS done."

"Well, I'd say it's already BEEN done, by the look of you two!" Bud threw out lasciviously, materializing right inside the back door. Green and purple wraiths shimmered right behind him, his colorful entourage.

"Aren't you Sylphettes in bed kind of early?" Buddleia taunted. "And here I thought you'd be up for company."

A traitorous little spurt of annoyance ran up Flem's backbone and his wings chattered momentarily and everyone looked at him in surprise. *Flem?*

Even that faerie was rather surprised at himsylph, he must be growing more confident than he'd realized, or perhaps it was just his day to feel snappish with everyone, from Iris Fletcherman to Lark (!) and now Bud and his gang. What was wrong with him? Too much of a good thing?

"So come, my little twin flower buds, tell Uncle Bud all about it. And cha, my throat is sure dry…"

Snorting at Bud's obviousness, Flem extricated himsylph but got a toe tangled in the open weave, lurching like a drunken bird towards his stash of mead.

"Oh don't get up, we'll help oursylves!" Bud said after the fact, tongue in cheek, asking Flem with his eyes to forgive his audacity. "So what were *we* talking about before being so rudely interrupted?" Bud accepted the henfull of golden liquid from his host with an innocent, inquisitive look.

"*Mayapple* wants to come to the *S* Club with us," Flem stated baldly, feeling more confident by the minute. Imagine, they were *all* congregated at *his place, again*!

"*Mayapple*! Hmmph. I don't know. What's that?" he asked, as Chinaberry and Catalpah looked at each other and then at him with a request in their eyes.

"What?" he said.

"*Rainbow* has been hinting ever since we met at Cybele that she'd really like to do the same," spoke up the green-eyed Cat, Chinaberry nodding her accord.

As one, they all looked at Lark, to see what he thought.

"Rainbow and Mayapple? Well, I guess that'd probably be okay. They could keep each other amused when we weren't right there."

Lark looked seriously at all, than asked Flem directly, "Do you think she can keep a secret?"

Hoping to Pan she could, he nodded.

Lark turned his stare on Bud, China, and Cat. "Well? Can we trust Rainbow Merkiva?"

Looking at each other, they nodded.

Chinaberry gleefully called out, "To the Muse!" and all lifted their hens in a toast.

Raising his eyebrows at Lark, Bud asked, "Do you want to talk to Bignonia about the passes or should I? And don't forget to get their names on The List. What night shall we go?"

Chapter 73

Flem raised his eyebrows at her, like, that's it?

"They're almost three months old Flem, you really should send these guys home, I mean *their* home. Which one is mom's, anyway? Are they all spoken for?"

Mayapple and Flem were sitting on a rickety table in the middle of the old greenhouse, discussing Flem's plans for renovation. He and Lark had long conversations about it and of course Mr. Green-eyed Spurastic's advice had been invaluable. They made a good team.

"They're going! They're going tonight as a matter of fact," exclaimed the faerie. "And yes," he stumbled over what he didn't want to say explicitly, a gathering at his house, and he hadn't planned on inviting Mayapple. Could he still save face?

Like a cat on a cornered lizard, Mayapple pounced.

"Tonight? Why, whatever do you mean? Is everyone coming over?" demanded his nosy and pushy best friend.

Giving in, Flem came clean. "Mayapple, they're just coming by later to pick up their cats, that's all."

She scowled at him, sure there was a party brewing and she was left out but after searching his eyes soulfully and he couldn't be pricked into saying anymore she gave in sort of gracefully.

"So tell me again, who gets who?"

They were watching kitten antics as the siblings raced around the greenhouse, in and out of everything.

Two grey striped frantic-eyed kittens chased each other, tales slung low to prove how *serious* the game was.

"Those, both of them, thank Pan, are going home with the Trio." The Trio was what he and Lark had started calling Bud, China and Cat.

"Okay, whose is that one?" she pointed to a pure white ball of fluff grooming its wide spread toes.

"The Snowball? Oh, that's your mom's. She just didn't want to take her 'til all the others left. *Tomorrow*, I'm sending her home with her new owner," he promised, then continued, "And we know who that one belongs to, right?" They both watched a wild butterscotch and white kitten climb a nearby splintery grey post that was buried too deep for easy removal, claws wide and eyes crazed.

"Yes, of course. She's mine. I hope Blackie likes her..." said Mayapple demurely. "When I go, she goes. I sure hope she's not this wild at home." She looked at Flem for reassurance and while he *knew* kittens were *trouble*, he also knew they were so cute that everyone laughed instead of getting mad and simply sighed as they bought new curtains, screens, tablecloths, leggings, and etc...

"Lots of toys, that's my suggestion. You'll be okay." He hoped.

Mama cat came strolling, zigzagging around objects on the floor, another butterscotch and white kitten traveling with her, but this one had dabs of chocolate here and there. He batted occasionally at her tail, once jumping in mock ambush but missing his mark.

"That's Lark's, isn't it?" Mayapple ascertained, even though she was pretty sure it was. "What's happening with him? Staying here with you and mama and Ruby? Where is that nasty little rogue cat, anyway?" She looked around.

"Hey, don't call Rubus *nasty*," defended Flem just before something landed with a thud on his back and the next thing he knew, a cold nose was worming its way through an armhole and arrogantly making for the hollow that could be had in Flem's wingulacture. 'Course, it often took a certain amount of prodding from him to make sure his faerie paid attention and kept his wing blades in the right position, but *that's* what claws were for.

"Rubus, settle down!" snapped the recipient of the pin pricks of pain.

"You're right! He's not nasty at all, is he? Ha!" laughed Mayapple irritatingly.

Flem wiggled and tried to throw an arm backward to adjust the hitchhiker but it did no good. He wondered if he'd ever break the little rogue of this pattern. Warning bells went off in his head that he was letting it become a habit but he ignored them because it was just easier. Tsk.

"Well, I better go -" Mayapple let it hang, hoping for an invitation to stay, it sure sounded like a party to her.

Sighing deeply, hoping to sway Flem, she dragged out her departure until the Sylph thought she'd *never* leave.

Finally, a last goodbye and she actually picked up her kitten, gently stuffing her way down in the bottom of her big cloth purse, poured in a large handful of cat crunchies mixed with catnip from her pocket and drew the bag loosely closed.

Flem raised his eyebrows at her, like, that's it?

Mayapple spoke up rather defensively, "Well, I gotta get her home, somehow, don't I? How else? She should be okay for half an hour I think."

"WHO should be okay for half an hour?" Lark's voice came from the window door. Both Flem and Mayapple started towards him with Mayapple's lumpy purse swinging and meowing indignantly.

Lark burst into laughter and took pity on her, but also making sure she was leaving.

"C'mon, I'll give you a ride home and you won't have to chase that rascal all over the bus and we won't have to bail you out of jail an hour from now."

Everyone laughed and Mayapple gratefully followed the sophisticated but rather rumpled looking Sylph in black out the door.

"See you tomorrow at work. Bye Flemmy." Mayapple blew him a kiss just before she disappeared.

Flem waved and then went out back to sweep the patio area once again. The Trio was coming over and this time they weren't leaving empty handed.

Chapter 74

Trillium, one ledge over, poked Babiana and whispered,
"Wake Robin, the show's about to begin."

FLEM STARED AT Mayapple. He was *sure* it was Mayapple. But this person was a vision, a picture of elegance. His mouth hung open and the person in question laughed gleefully at his discombobulation.

Without a doubt, Mayapple.

Lark stood motionless on the other side of the car, one foot inside, one hand resting on the top, caught in the same spell.

Between now and the last time they had seen her, Mayapple had cut her hair. It was now *short*. Her thick, long dark braid, gone. Gone! She looked like a different person, a thousand times lighter, all sexy innocence with the way the bouncy electric curls framed her face to the three-quarter length sleeves of the short black cashmere sweater she wore over a little black dress of her own. Not quite Sylphish but pretty dem close.

She pirouetted for the 'boys' and then looked in expectation towards her waiting chariot.

Flem gallantly swept open his door again, bowing officiously to his queen.

Mayapple regally seated herself, Flem hopped in the back, Lark woke up, and they sped off to meet their cohorts.

Some girls who weren't technically girls nonetheless called themselves girls and Rainbow Merkiva, who was driving at the moment, was thinking about that, wondering *who*, and *what*, they'd see tonight. Girls? Sylphs? Men?

Whimsey C. Nimble

Women? Who was what? It was all terribly mysterious and her blood pulsed. She was looking forward to that dance floor China and Cat had talked up.

They'd intimated so much but put off real answers with double talk. Still, they were fun and she knew they knew she knew they were faeries. They didn't flaunt it but they didn't hide it around her either. Apparently they trusted her after working together on the Revelry with Cybele production and they had to know *Mayapple* would surely tell *her* after that escapade in the Park with that old guy, Weed. It would be so interesting to see them naked, she thought but quickly moved away from that image.

Would she see their wings she wondered, remembering how huge the ones were they'd all 'worn' for Cybele. Their real wings couldn't possibly be that big, could they? Or, she was so curious about tonight.

And Bud. *Yum*. Buddleia. She glanced in the rear view mirror at the colorful Trio in the back seat, Bud in the middle, as usual.

One hand on the steering wheel, with the other she adjusted the spaghetti straps on *her* little black dress, then gave a quick tug to the silky-fringed bust-hugger. Lacy stockings came down to mid-calf, below which were red spiky heels.

"Hey," she said. "I don't mind being the chauffer but somebody has to sit up front on the way home." She paused, then continued, "We're there!" Easily she backed the car into a parking space, dropped the keys into her little bag, and slid out of the car to wait for the fae bundle to sort themsylves out and make it to the sidewalk.

Chinaberry sidled right over to her and stuck a soft purple-clad filmy arm through hers, saying "Thank you my dear Rainbow for driving. So much more *convenient* than on a bicycle..."

"Oh, I heard that!" defended Bud immediately. "But yes, there certainly are times when a car *is* appreciated, just not most of the time. Who needs that headache?"

"Oh, there they are, Flem and Lark and Mayapple! Woo hoo! Woo hoo! Here we are!" Catalpah waved a slinky green arm and the two groups quickly merged, Rainbow and Mayapple kissing the other's cheek in their excitement, standing right in front of the double quilted doors with the famous pink *S*.

"Here you are, one for each of you," announced Bud, handing them each what looked to be a design on a small piece of paper.

"These must be shown when we go upstairs." He momentarily looked taken aback at what that meant – humans in *their* environment...

"Upstairs? You mean to *dance*?" immediately piped up Rainbow, tucking it away safely as Mayapple studied hers. Two interlocking hearts composed of miniature leaves and flowers were printed on the small card.

"Come ladies, after you," Lark held open one of the big double-quilted doors, waving them in to the blue sconced foyer, laughing Catalpah scooting in right behind the girls, and Bud hurrying to make it too.

"Can't stop now. C'mon!" Dashing to the second set of doors, Chinaberry took her turn as doorman, ah doorperson? Doorfaire? Doorsylph? Doorbelle?

Catalpah linked her arms with their guests, pulling them close in on each side of her, and stepped through to the sacred inner sanctum, nodding her thanks to the doorbelle as they strutted by.

Sinuses cleared, senses vivified and Mayapple's eyes gleamed, trying her utmost to see *everything*.

Rainbow's heart was pounding pretty hard too but the small calculating part of her brain that never stopped cataloging or analyzing immediately started a new tally card, one to be relived and scrutinized in great detail for years to come. First impressions were so unique.

Bud and Chinaberry were close behind her but then Lark grabbed his love and bestowed a passionate blood raising kiss upon his fae lips, stalling in the entryway a moment, letting the inner doors shut them out, away from all eyes briefly.

No one noticed.

The place was crowded, a regular crush.

China and Cat wanted to dance. No one seemed to have a plan, so Cat headed around the tables, skirting the bar and heading towards the back but was continuously intercepted along the way. Obviously, she was well known here.

Watching Catalpah get waylaid ahead of her at a nearby table, Chinaberry got distracted and excused hersylph from their two human guests, hurrying to catch up with her friend.

By this time, Mayapple's brain was coming alive, an automatic coffee pot whose timer had dinged. Foolishly, she had expected to see Sylphs, *Sylphs* everywhere. But these were all people. Colorful, yes, but not a Sylph to be seen in the sea. Hmm.

Whimsey C. Nimble

She glanced at Rainbow to gauge her reaction but all she got in return was a quizzical smile and a faint look of *'Where are they?'*

A look of suspicion was passed between them but was interrupted when Cat called, "Over here – Mayapple, Rainbow, we want you to meet someone."

A creature stood up and Rainbow and Mayapple came to a halt, mid-step, each thinking well, *here* was one, no matter she had no wings in sight.

With a helpful air, Chinaberry introduced them, "Rainbow, Mayapple, this is Vinca Pink. Vinca Pink – Rainbow and Mayapple, friends of ours, first time here." This was stated with a sweet and innocent smile, her eyes holding Catalpah's for a mere second, an invisible shared anticipation.

They were not disappointed.

Mayapple actually swallowed and took a step back, mortified she was doing so.

Vinca seemed to be eating them up with her eyes, the pale pink diamond stud in her tongue flashing in the light as she wet her lips and looked from one to the other of the humans.

Rainbow thought of a snake confronted with two plump mice simultaneously. She froze, fascinated by the almost reptilian gaze of this *person's* strange vermillion eyes, watching the little green pupils dilate and shrink repeatedly as that gaze lobbed back and forth between the two of them. Human? Yeah, right.

"Ooh, *hello*. New here, huh?"

Mayapple tried to hold her own and gamely stuck out a hand, almost pulling it back when Vinca snatched it between hers and hung on, fingers playing underneath with the soft valley of her palm.

Rainbow stood motionless, entranced by what looked like lightly patterned, flowered *skin*. Squinting at it, she then looked around at the others but it was too dim.

Reluctantly Mayapple's hand was released and that red intense gaze swung around and landed on Rainbow's, who immediately found herself swallowing in nervousness and wishing that prickle of caution wasn't running amok up her back.

China and Cat tittered in naughty delight and Bud didn't notice because his back was turned as he yakked with someone at the bar.

About that time Flem and lover boy Lark were weaving through the crowd, Flem feeling like an old hand now but still plenty nervous or maybe it was just full-on titillation.

He stopped so abruptly that Mr. Spurastic almost bumped into him, putting his hands out to catch the other's lumpy shoulders, saying "What are you doing? Why'd you stop... Oh, lookee here, I see our guests have met Vinca Pink."

After a moment's pause as they both looked on to study the scene ahead, Lark stepped around his love and decided to help out.

"Vinca!" he called. "Hey, nice outfit."

Slowly she released Rainbow's gaze and smiled her crimson smile that matched her vermillion eyes, green pupils rippling at that tall good looking Sylph in black, Flem right behind him, smiling timidly. What a delicious duo.

Her eyes narrowed and her pupils tightened in anticipation but the wide mouth never lost a beat, diamond stud winking out as the tongue sent messages of its own.

Ah yes, Lark could remember how fascinated *he'd* been, a fresh green Sylph in the City. And she *did* look good, he would grant her that. It was rather daring of her to expose so much natural skin but trust Vinca to highlight what others downplayed.

Those high cheek bones were never without neon color that he knew of but the bright streaks always matched some shade of pink, and there were *many*, elsewhere.

With sultry affectation, the tall Sylph-in-disguise motioned for Lark and Flem to come closer, hard oval long nails beckoning, come, come.

With a hand thrust behind his back, Lark caught Flem's and gave a squeeze of reassurance before stepping to the circle, Rainbow and Mayapple all eyes.

Mayapple edged closer to Rainbow and discretely dug her elbow into her side, asking with her eyes if Vinca Pink was, 'one of them?'.

Rainbow deftly nodded, looking at Mayapple than back to Vinca before nodding again at Mayapple, yes, had to be. Both grinned and turned fully towards the three-some where Vinca was dripping like a water-fed jungle vine doing her best to pull Flem closer, closer, ignoring the look of panic in his eyes.

Whimsey C. Nimble

Bud finally turned around and took it all in at a glance, threw back his mead, swiped his lips, set the tiny glass down with a thunk on the bar and came forward, thrusting out a hand to Vinca Pink, saying " Vinca! You're looking good. You've met our friends Mayapple and Rainbow? And *obviously*, you know Lark and Flem…"

Releasing the duo, Vinca clasped Bud's warm hand and exerted just a tiny bit of pressure, trying to pull *him* in but he was prepared and quickly dropped her hand, rubbed his palms briskly and stepped back between his twins. "How about a drink?"

Flem nimbly stepped beyond Vinca's grasp, dancing on his toes a little as he dashed to the other side of Lark and then beyond, behind the Trio.

He'd been planning for just such a moment and here it was already. "I'm buying," he announced, getting his money out. The group materialized behind him, all smiles. He was relieved to see Vinca Pink stay at her table.

Minutes later, Egret's Beak, Cranberry Bog, and Honeymoon mead were being passed around.

Mayapple took a drink noisily. Flem was rather embarrassed and hoped she'd live up to her many promises to 'be good and not drink too much.' It wasn't looking good the way she was going at it.

A tall empty table was spotted off in the distance and soon the seven friends were staked out around it, transforming to a part of the club and not just observers.

The golden nectar of the gods seeped into their respective fae and human bloodstreams easing tensions they hadn't even know they were holding.

Mayapple's glass emptied rapidly and Rainbow's wasn't far behind. Of one accord, the two slid away from the table like fog off a cliff, disappearing while the others were talking and headed straight for the bar.

Minutes later they leaned in like old familiar barflies who'd been here a hundred times before. Relaxed. Poised. Confident.

Clinking their glasses together at their success, both turned and cast a fascinated enquiring eye back out, over the crowd. At first glance it looked like any normal, upscale club scene. Well, except for Vinca Pink, of course, who really stood out. Mayapple idly wondered if they'd get to see any wings tonight and what *hers* would look like.

They caught more than one look cast their direction that went on past but oddly, often returned full blast a moment later, along with a bemused smile from its owner, who frequently winked an acknowledgment, as if they were all in cahoots together.

Blatant suspicions danced in the air but no answers were forthcoming.

Mayapple was shifting and studying, her mind alive with curiosity. "Well?" she said, easing her elbows back on the bar, "Who's what here?"

Before Rainbow could answer a voice from a small distance away lilted into their ears. "Ethcuse me, any chance you beautiful ladies know if that'ths Flumaria Greenwood?" He pointed to Flem.

Mayapple's mouth dropped open.

Rainbow was shaking her head no, but stopped when she saw Mayapple's reaction.

Her head whipped around to stare at Flem, then the newcomer, and back to Mayapple. Mayapple who wasn't saying anything, just babbling, "How? Who? *Flumaria?* How do you…?"

But he wasn't listening, he was looking at Flem who hadn't noticed him yet.

Tearing his eyes away like they were flies stuck in sap, he got his attention back on Mayapple and said with great excitement, "It *ith* him ithn't it? Oh, my great Pan, I never would have expected *her* to end up here." His eyes gleamed and he smiled at the young woman but it was the funniest smile because his long thin lips pulled straight back and it almost looked like there were two parts to his head, the top part and the bottom. A fine spray accompanied this opening of his mouth and Mayapple ducked a little, pretending the flinch was a normal thing she often did.

"I thaw you were at hith table," he said and they all looked over.

Flem caught the movement and sort of smiled, wondering why they were all staring at him.

He turned back to listen to what Bud and Catalpah were talking about and when he glanced up again, he was able to study their profiles at his leisure.

For some reason his gaze never left the strange person Mayapple and Rainbow were talking to. His eye roved almost distractedly over every detail, safe and objective from a distance.

The more he looked, the more he couldn't look away. With a thundering flash of insight, he realized he knew that person! That *Sylph!* It couldn't be.

"Sissy?" he spoke out loud, blatant disbelief, taking a step away from the table, his mind on fire, so distracted he never heard Lark ask him what he was about?

Stumbling only once, he was carried forward until there he was. One hand came out and he tapped the tall, long headed man on the sleeve. It just could not be. "*Sissy?*"

"*Flem,*" was said with all deliberateness, and then, "Your friendth here told me your *name* now. *Not* Flumaria, right?"

Flem could barely nod. Of all the Sylphs he'd ever encountered, this was one he'd never thought about again except for a couple of minutes, after they'd parted company, way, *way* back in the Canyon days. Probably because *she*, Circumscissle – Sissy- was just as pathetic as *Flumaria* was back then. Seeing Sissy brought his own stark past into sharp contrast with *now*. True, he still had issues but cha! Compared to who he used to be, they were nothing.

Unexpectedly, Circumscissle's arms were around him and they were hugging.

Rainbow and Mayapple were eating it up. The night just kept getting better and better and it had hardly begun.

"So, I take it you two are old friends...?" Rainbow couldn't stand it anymore and let it hang, hoping for the story.

Circumscissle nodded, seeming to cling to Flem a little longer than necessary and Flem's heart dropped and he shot a mute appeal back towards his friends where all four were watching avidly. He felt the flush as it flamed up his fae face not stopping 'til his cheeks burned and his hidden wings trembled with the fire.

Smiling, China, Cat, Bud and Lark came sauntering over, curiosity so bright it lighted the way. Lark's green eyes held a bit more than idle curiosity as he watched this stranger's hand on *his* fleur.

Awkwardly, Sissy backed up 'til he was against the bar, his long thin lips opening and closing as he took little gasps of air, much like a newly landed fish, a subtle mist of spittle spraying the Sylphs.

Lark immediately softened his demeanor as he realized how intimidating it must be for all four of them to show up and surround the little group.

Nonetheless, he laid an arm over Flem's shoulders, smiling but with a lot of teeth showing. Those pesky male hormones. They seemed to transcend fae or human. It made him kind of want to pee around Flem, marking his territory.

Gathering his wits, Flem the faerie suavely made the introductions and was barely done when Bud leaped in with the question on *everyone's* mind. "*How* do you know each other?"

Everybody hung in suspense for a moment with bated breath, waiting.

Embarrassed, as was Circumscissle, (Pleath, call me Thithy, he'd said right from the beginning,) *Sissy*, and Flem looked at each other and Flem flashed on how uncomfortable the other Sylph looked. His eyes were twitching and his thin bloodless lips were compressed even more. The shades of grey that comprised his color scheme did nothing for him. At least, nothing flattering.

Before Sissy could answer, Flem had a question of his own. "How long have you been out?" inquired the new and improved faerie, meaning, out from the Canyon.

Sissy misunderstood and thought Flem meant he'd told everyone that he was a faerie, a Sylph, not really the human man he portrayed. Or thought he portrayed.

"I'm not," replied Circumscissle, with a rather haunted air.

Flem gave him a blank stare and repeated his question: "When did *you* leave the Canyon?"

"OH, I thee. Well, I wathn't in Thimbleberry, if you'll recall, I lived down in Cow Valley, actually not too far from the gym." He cast an eye at Flem, who nodded.

"Okay you two. Spill the beans. What are you talking about?" this from Mayapple, three drinks under her svelte belt.

China and Cat jumped in immediately, "Yeah, tell us more!" they demanded.

Bud and Lark moved closer, shoulder to shoulder, arms tucked akimbo across their Sylphish-mannish chests. Bud adjusted his scarf.

Rainbow pulled all her charm in and then let it float out, beautiful light particles that drifted like golden pixie dust, surrounding Circumscissle with love.

Instantly he relaxed and looked at Rainbow intuitively although not really grasping what she'd done. She gave him a warm smile and asked, "What gym?"

"Oh, that would be Jingle Jane Geranium'th Gymnathium. That'th where we met. Flumaria, *OOPTH*, I mean, *Flem* and me uthed to climb the ropths together."

"Ah, you know," said Bud, snapping his fingers. "I remember now, there *was* a gym named Jingle Jane's way back up in an arm off the back of Cow Valley."

Whimsey C. Nimble

Everyone now turned to *him* and gaped.

He good naturedly shrugged but clammed up. "Go on," he entreated.

Lark was still staring at him with a 'Do tell!' look upon his face.

"Never been there, I take it?" innocently queried Bud.

Lark shook his head, no.

Bud grinned in his face then turned back around to the others.

Ah friendship. It encompassed so many aspects. Lark shook his head in laughter and resignation. He and Bud often played one-up, the best riposte being of course when the other was completely not expecting it.

Chinaberry and Cat were ready to boogie and pantomimed over heads that they wanted to go upstairs and pointed towards the back.

They looked especially fetching tonight, soft and squeezable. Long tight cotton leggings wrapped their respective sylves in soft dark purples and muted emeralds. Clingy skimpy cotton shirts rode haphazardly over their hips, hanging in disarray but matching the energy of the leggings. Gauzy scarves wrapped around their collarbones, trailing over their shoulders. Curls the same color as her amethyst eyes adorned Chinaberry while Catalpah's hair was layer upon layer of bright and dark greens, short, sassy, and stacked, her eyes a sunlit green for the evening. Not all male Sylphs chose to cover their hazel eyes but it was pretty common.

Bud jumped ahead to catch up with his two best gals and Lark thought about how well matched the three of them were. The same body hugging cotton rode his slight Sylph self but whereas theirs was rather obvious, Bud's was an understatement of dark brown accented with amber piping, a hint of gold here and there. His hair fell to his shoulders, much more conservative than the others. The scarf was almost nondescript except it was of heavy silk.

When Lark looked over, Circumscissle was facing away, trying to flag the bartender's attention. Flem stood looking at Lark, ready to follow him anywhere.

"Ladies!" a voice called.

Mayapple and Rainbow straightened right up, adjusting themselves, and stepped sprightly to catch up with the Trio ahead, Flem and Lark lagging behind.

"Dancing?" Rainbow asked, eyes sparkling.

Cat answered with a grin and a nod to follow her, looking over Mayapple's shoulder to see if the two love birds were keeping up, wondering if Sissy would be coming too but he looked up just then and waved them on.

Following behind Rainbow as they threaded their gangly way through the crowded club, Mayapple couldn't resist and reached out to poke her friend with one finger.

Rainbow's head whipped around and they locked eyes momentarily.

Mayapple leaned in, whispering, "Well, see any *humans*? Biological ones, that is."

"Ha!" laughed Rainbow back at her. "They're all 'humans,' you know that. Look- nary a wing to be seen."

"Guess we'll see -" Mayapple let it hang and Rainbow nodded, turning around and hurrying to catch up with the others.

Eyes slid over them, winking, squinting, following, occasionally smirking.

It was all very mysterious, but outwardly looked so familiar. If both women didn't know what they knew, neither would be looking for what was hidden.

Chinaberry and Catalpah stood poised at a dark doorway, beside which glowed a pink palm tree on a green neon island.

Several people clattered down invisible stairs and then emerged, thundering past.

"Hey Bud, where you been? I haven't seen you lately." A short petite woman with suspicious shoulders pulled up, her entourage flowing on without her. Delicate blue curls framed her wide eyes, which she batted shamelessly towards Buddleia.

Sparks were kindled in two sets of eyes, one violet and one green with golden flecks.

"Hey! Floxie! How's it going?" bit out Chinaberry with a bit of an attitude.

Catalpah moved in from the other side. "Better move along, don't want to keep your friends waiting!"

Scowling at the two of them, Bud motioned Mayapple and Rainbow closer. "I'd like to introduce you to someone. "

Cat and China rolled their eyes and groaned, but mostly to themsylves.

Whimsey C. Nimble

Mayapple and Rainbow were front and center, each with a hand out to shake.

Bud laughed and formally presented "Floxie Diva Ricata –THE Diva of our little club here."

"Oh Buddleia, *that's* not true and you know it. Fanwort Cabomba is *the* Diva."

Mayapple and Rainbow looked lost as they had no idea about this other piece of Bud's personality.

"Ah. Ha ha, yes, well, nice to see you Floxie. Come along girls, let's go dance." Bud hurried them all on.

Rainbow and Mayapple exchanged looks, their eyes following the blue-haired Diva before turning back and heading into the unknown – up the stairs.

An insistent beat was felt more than heard, firing their imagination, beckoning louder and louder as they climbed until their blood was popping like chili peppers over an open grill.

Faeries and humans alike burst through the door together, natural de-hiscence but with no seedpod other than excitement coupled with a dark stairwell.

Bright lights flashed and ran past, circling the entire room but concentrated over the dance floor where bodies kept the beat, everyone moving passionately.

Rainbow grabbed China and Cat's hands, pulling them to the dance floor, motioning Mayapple and Flem to hurry, telling Bud to *dance* first, get a drink later and urging Lark to loosen up and step lively.

Throwing herself into the rhythm, Mayapple let the music carry her away, feeling the cleansing of her soul as she did so. After ten minutes of joyous abandon, she suddenly remembered *where* she was and her head whipped up and her eyes shot around the room. No wings in sight but a look about the place as if an understanding was passed from one to the next, giving an understated, exhileratory look to all.

Her gaze found Flem's. He smiled at her and she smiled back but then gave him a questioning look, a narrowing of the eyes, a 'This is it, no Sylphs?' kind of look.

He mouthed one word at her, "Patience," and turned back to that man in black who wasn't a man and *wasn't* wearing black, he suddenly realized.

Under the spinning spotlights, Lark's impeccable attire took on a whole new look. The deepest darkest red, so dark it looked black shone forth as they cavorted beneath the spinning lights, the music never letting go of its hypnotizing power, a vibration that connected them as one.

Mayapple saw Rainbow break away and head towards the bar, which out-did itself, wrapping around two whole sides of the room, mirrors backing it up, reflecting myriads and myriads of bottles, faces, and lights. And, a small pink neon palm tree on a miniature neon green island with *Oasis* below it.

"'Scuse me," Mayapple was lightly touching people to open a path for herself as she followed the back of Rainbow's colorful head. Compared to so many people here, her own brown hair was pretty tame. Still, she knew she looked *good* and was very pleased with the whole hair-cut thing. It felt like a whole new person had emerged, and with this new image it was much easier to let her have her way, her 'head,' so-to-speak, she grinned to herself.

She liked this place, Sylphs or not. Well, of course there *were* Sylphs, look who they were with for God's sakes... Flem was one thing. He was her best buddy, her friend and she loved him dearly. And he'd told her not to expect anything special 'til the third floor, but *still*. Could *all* these people really be faeries? Surely not.

It was hard to imagine.

She was two steps away from Rainbow's side when she and another collided.

Startled, Mayapple looked up to meet limpid green eyes with a silvery sheen.

The Sylph was tall and spiky and dressed like a woman but Mayapple knew instantly, this was a Sylph. She forcefully, through an act of sheer de-termination and will, kept her eyes from even flickering once to the other's awkward shoulders.

"Sorry!" offered Mayapple and the soft green woman who had a silvery shine over her whole body, not just her eyes, quickly put a hand up to her bosom and said in a velvety voice, "Oh, it was all *my* fault, I should have been watching where I was going."

Small yellow flowers encircled her neck, matching more circlets around her wrists and even one around an ankle.

Penetrating eyes bore into hers from under thick blond hair and Mayapple stared back. Never had she seen such a creature before.

Whimsey C. Nimble

"Come here often?" asked the newcomer to the young woman in the short black dress with the little black sweater. "Say, is that cashmere? Beautiful. May I?"

Mayapple inclined her head and held out an arm for stroking.

They grinned at each other, bonding over the sensuousness of the material.

"I'm Mayapple Fletcherman. How do you do?" Mayapple stuck out a hand and a hopeful smile.

"Vervacity Verbascum. Just fine, thank you. And you?" They shook on it.

Taking note of the other's small delicate form, including shoulders, Vervacity asked again, "Come here often?"

Mayapple artlessly responded with "No, tonight's my first time. Ha! And I've lived in this City my whole life!"

Vervacity was tickled with the answer. A new human in the Club, up close and personal. She wondered who she was with. You had to have a pass and be on the List to get any further than the second floor. And it was rare for humans to come here at all. A few always managed to infiltrate but it was only those with close fae friendships that went *up*.

"Verbascum. Hmm. That sounds familiar. Are you related to..." but she got no further for the other interrupted, actually rather impatiently, for such a new acquaintance.

"Yes! The Mulleins. Cha, I don't know why people always ask me that!" but then remembered her manners and smiled irresistibly at the girl, who appeared to be a very sweet and beguiling young woman.

Their eyes held and Mayapple wondered what the hell she was doing! It was almost like she was flirting with a woman but she knew Vervacity was *not* what she seemed, no matter her first name.

Rainbow turned around and saw Mayapple engaged, taking in the tall, slender woman she was talking to and had her doubts.

More chit chat and eye contact was made, Mayapple eating it up. Rainbow showed up, nudged her and handed her a glass.

"Oh, thank you." She paused imperceptively before making the introduction, "Rainbow – Vervacity Verbascum."

Mustering her charm, Rainbow smiled deeply into Vervacity's eyes and noticed they had little yellow pupils in amidst all that greenish silver.

About that time China and Cat barreled up, eyes snapping with glee. Bud snaked in behind Rainbow and waited for the bartender's attention.

"Pan-A-Miga, we can't leave you two alone for a minute, can we?" chortled China. "Who's your friend?"

Introductions were made but Vervacity's gaze kept returning to Mayapple.

By now Lark and Flem were part of the crowd, Lark standing protectively right behind Flem as close as he could, the two of them swaying slightly together.

Taking in the ring of on-lookers, Vervacity decided to move on but made sure she slipped that cute human woman her card before she did, in case she didn't have enough fae friends already.

Mayapple was flattered and intrigued, carefully slipping it into her bag, bestowing the sage-eyed beauty with a shy smile.

"Call me!" mouthed the mullein look-a-like as she melted into the crowd, turning and calling "Vanda, wait up!" to an exotic airy-looking beauty.

Rainbow nudged Mayapple, unable to resist taunting, just a little, "Ooh, looks like *you've* got a girlfriend, girlfriend!"

"Oh stop," Mayapple said reflexively, her senses lulled but her mind dallying with what her instincts told her. That woman was *not* a woman, she was sure of it. New horizons opened up like delicious possibilities.

Buddleia was standing with a patient look upon his face, waiting for the hubbub to die down, his sidekicks flanking him like complementary bookends. Lark and Flem had taken up a waiting position also, Lark now hanging over Flem's back like an old towel.

Looking up, Mayapple realized they were all apparently waiting for *her*.

"Well? Why are you all standing here? Are we done dancing?" She smiled guilelessly, putting Vervacity Verbascum behind her.

Chuckles were heard and there was not a serious mien to be seen as the group encircled Mayapple and Rainbow.

Mayapple's stomach fluttered and she cast a coup d'oeil at Rainbow. Had the time come?

Rainbow met her eyes but then turned to look beseechingly at China and Cat, moving on to search Bud's countenance, and finally asking Lark and Flem with her expression if it was true? Her heart raced.

Mayapple's hand crept into hers and squeezed, which was fervently returned.

Whimsey C. Nimble

Linking arms, they faced their fae friends with determination, excitement radiating from their eyes like beams from a lighthouse, there for all to see.

"Are we going, *upstairs*?" reverently questioned Mayapple. Her eyes flew to Flem's and his flew to Lark's.

Lark massaged Flem's back while confirming over his shoulder with the rest of the group that yes, this was why they were here, with two humans, and it had been agreed. It was time.

"Oh for Pan's sake, could you all quit being so serious?" tittered Catalpah. "Come on!"

Transforming to gracious hostess, she led the way around the bar to the dark doorway with the golden rope.

Flem kept stealing glances at Mayapple. Now that the moment was here, misgivings rose like a swarm of newly hatched moths and his stomach tied it-sylph in knots. Was this a mistake? What if those two gabby girls told everyone they knew and Lark left him? Would he lose his job? Would he lose *the greenhouse*? No, no, he told himsylph, Iris knew. At that moment, Mayapple turned and caught his eye, smiling her wonderment and gratitude, mouthing "Thank you, I love you," and giving him the cat blink.

Suddenly he couldn't wait to show them this divine new dimension of his life. Stolen flights in the middle of the night in the middle of the park would probably still be in his future but this, *this* was the *real* night life he craved. He was free to be himsylph, to do what *all* Sylphs were born to do, fly, drink mead, and talk.

Giddy with expectation, Flem slipped from Lark's hold and nodding at Cat, asked "May I?" his hand ready to unhook the symbolic barrier.

At her agreement, he held the rope back ignoring the 'Members Only' sign that dangled impotently upside down, waving everyone through before him.

"Watch your step," was heard through the thumping and clumping as they all climbed towards Nirvana.

Flem wondered who would be at the door, Bignonia? His shoulders twitched convulsively with nervous anticipation.

Bringing up the rear, Flem peeked around the girls to see someone who bore a marked resemblance to Distictus Rivers but was not he.

A big hearty fellow sat there, his arms twined around both Catalpah and Chinaberry and was even seen reaching for Bud. Lark had prudently stepped back but wasn't quite fast enough to pull the girls away in time and before you knew it, both were being embraced by the handsome doorman sporting a beautiful, purplish-brown-spotted, pinkish-white scarf around his throat.

Flem was scowling and beginning to wonder if there was sap on the guy's hands the way they were clinging to Mayapple.

Irritation at the fellow's presumptuousness brought him forward, clearing his throat repeatedly, louder and louder until Lark grabbed his arm and pulled him back.

Giving him a little jab with his elbow, Lark scowled at him, then sang out in a loud and over-bright voice, "Pandorea! Hello, so nice to see you again. How's things Down Under?"

It had the desired affect and Pandorea Pandorana loosened his hold on the party, eyeballing Lark like he wanted to climb him next but Bud stepped in with "Rainbow, Mayapple, show Wonga here your passes."

"Wonga?" repeated Mayapple.

Sighing loudly, Pandorea spoke up, "Pandorea Pandorana, how do you do?" He paused briefly with this rhetorical salutation but then went right on. "As Buddleia here knows, my friends call me Wonga Wonga, so please, do the same."

Flem watched in horror as Mayapple's face contorted and he realized with icy comprehension that she was about to go off like a maniacal hyena.

Babbling in desperation to thwart her hysteria, he flung himsylph to the forefront, "The list, the list, they're on your list!"

Eyes wide at Flem's frenzied outbreak, Lark looked at him like he was crazy before suavely turning back to the doorman and smoothly interjecting "Where's Rivers tonight?"

"Bignonia?" ascertained Wonga Wonga and they both guffawed at the funny name until he said, "We're cousins, you know. Bignonia is my family name too, it's just that I don't use it much here in the States." As he spoke, he was removing a clipboard from the wall. This action caused both women to dig deep and pull out the cherished passes Bud had procured for them.

Making a big ta-do, Wonga Wonga scrutinized each, verifying information with that on the list, before finally proclaiming, "Welcome!" and handing them back.

Exhaling noisily with pent up relief coupled with a razor's edge of anticipation, Mayapple and Rainbow quickly returned them to their evening bags, missing the tongue-in-cheek joke passed around silently between all the others, except Flem, with the flick of an eye.

Unbeknownst to the humans and one Sylph, the words Human Companion that were carefully interwoven in with the small leaves and whatknot that comprised the two hearts was an inside joke amidst all Sylphs.

Bowing low with mock obeisance, Wonga Wonga unfurled his arm to grant entry and the doorway to heaven opened.

Heart in mouth, the girls followed the fae boys, a bit of trepidation stealing into their veins now that *the* moment had arrived.

Hardly able to breathe, Mayapple looked wildly around, stunned at the mundanity of a, a *locker room?*

But just as quickly recovered as she realized the import of what that meant.

Feeling suddenly like an interloper, Mayapple's rush of belated conscience took her by surprise as she watched Rainbow grow quiet with realization also.

Awkwardly, they shuffled in, feeling very out of place, looking around wide-eyed.

China and Cat stopped and pulled Flem aside, whispering and pointing before disappearing towards the back, in the direction Bud had gone. A locker door slammed in the distance.

Shyly, Flem stood in front of Mayapple looking at her. This was it. Was she ready? *This* was taking everything up to a whole new level.

Rainbow wandered down a row, surreptitiously watching Lark, where he was sitting on a bench rummaging through his pockets, his shirt half unbuttoned, a small gold key dangling from his lips.

"Okay," Mayapple was replying to Flem. She turned, "C'mon Rainbow, we're going down to that lounge area to await our charming escorts." She nodded towards some chairs in the distant open room, next to a wide closed door.

But it was too late. Like glimpses of a towering mast seen moving behind a maze of buildings as a ship stately moved through a harbor and out to sea, an emerald wing tip bobbed above the last row of lockers, and Rainbow couldn't have moved if she'd tried, her eyes glued to it. Laughter floated on the air. "Look!" she whispered urgently, "Look!"

Mayapple turned. "Oh!" She may have seen them that night in the Park with Flem and Lark but to be here, in *their* world, was overwhelming.

Eyes like saucers, they stood transfixed and the joining of its jostling purple twin moments later was electrifying.

"Oh my God! Are we ready for this Mayapple?"

"Well, you better be!" came Lark's voice behind them. "You're here and we're certainly not leaving now, are we, ma petite fleur?"

Both humans spun around, heart in mouth, to stare at the two people they knew so well, who obviously, were *not human*.

Magnificent golden-tan and dusty-green translucent wings rose from Lark's back, the ribs within his wingulacture easily discernible under the bright lights.

Flem stood a little apart, a rather apprehensive look upon his face, but coupled inexplicably with unabashed glee. It was too late to turn back now, so he decided to just let go and succumbed to the exhilaration, a maniacal gleam growing in his eyes.

His color scheme had been more of a frothy layered sea-green but now that he was stripped down to practically naked - his lithesome supple little Sylph - the tunic that hugged his body shone more forest green, thus blending naturally with those big beautiful, *furled* wings of his.

Rainbow was agog but Mayapple was recovering nicely, per usual.

"Oh Flemmy, let's see! Turn around," she directed, without a thought for lover-boy Lark standing proprietarily not five feet away.

She twirled him like an impatient French modiste, clucking and pulling as if he were her creation.

"*Do* unfurl, can't you?" she stepped back, urging him with both hands to do as she instructed.

Wondering how *she* had come to be in charge all of a sudden, Flem took one step and let his wings down. Ah, up. Well, *out* anyway.

"Ahhh," both young women sighed in unison as they watched the unfurling.

Mayapple heard it at the same time Lark did and Flem felt the fleeting tiny snag but opted to ignore it.

Lark made a mental note but *that* was rendered obsolete immediately by *Mayapple's* mind-blowing reaction. "Uh oh," she acknowledged, giving them forewarning but little good it did. Before you could say jacaranda that girl was on her knees, spitting on her fingers, running them up and down the blood warm skin that covered, what on a bird would be the calamus - the part that went into the skin - but since this was not a bird, but rather, a fae creature, a faerie, a *Sylph*, for heaven's sake, the calamus was simply an extension of his body, the outer, apparent, beginning of the wingulacture, the part hardest to reach for recalcitrant scales...

Lark gasped. It was *obvious* this had happened before. She knew exactly what she was doing!

Rainbow gasped, deliciously shocked. Mayapple had experience with this, this *faerie*. Oh my God, the implications...

The unnatural quiet brought Mayapple's senses back 'round and she gulped with dismay to spot Chinaberry, Catalpah, and Bud at a complete standstill, halted completely by her unconventional behavior. Would she *never* learn?

"Well, you sure don't need me, do you *Flem*?" spit Lark curtly and took off at a stiff legged gait, wings jerking as they rode the air behind him. Out the far door he went, nary a glare back. Bang.

Realizing how she'd stepped in it now, Mayapple rose slowly from her knees, looking aghast at those frozen around her, the enormity of her now exposed secret blatant.

Staring at the door through which Lark had disappeared, Mayapple shot an apologetic look to her dearest friend and abjectly said, "Oh, what have I done? I'm so sorry, Flem."

"It's okay," soothed the faerie, himsylph staring at the closed door, petting Mayapple's soft black-clad arm like a stray kitten.

The funny thing was, it *was* okay. He knew it wasn't serious. Lark loved him. Mayapple had *preened* him, big deal. Perhaps it wasn't done here in the city, but how was he to know? But look where they were, for Pan's sake, and just WHO was with them! If it wasn't appropriate here...

A little spark of righteous indignation ignited. Who was *Lark* to get mad at *him*, and, make Mayapple, his dearest friend, feel bad in the bargain? Cha!

Sylphworth and confidence, there all along but never accepted unreservedly, now burst into being, claiming their rightful territory.

Suddenly all those misbegotten months, nay, *years*, of wasted 'poor me's,' of sylphpity, of nervousness and regret seemed such a waste of time. But of course, he knew it wasn't. Everyone lived their own life at their own pace, learning their lessons in *their* time, no one else's. *Nothing* was a waste of time, it was simply the next step carrying you towards your own awakening.

Mayapple was still looking rather abashed whilst Rainbow simply watched respectfully from her side, ready to lend support but avidly curious, her eyes searching out the other three spectators for confirmation.

China and Cat were about to surge ahead but Bud caught them by an elbow and pulled them back, motioning to give it a minute, watching Flem process.

An ethereal shaft of steel rolled up that faerie's backbone and he seemed to grow inches taller even as they watched, a look of determination clarifying in his eyes.

"Step back a little, would you girls?" he commanded.

In the space now afforded him he let himsylph out, *himsylph* filling himsylph fully, wings taut and firm, held proudly, his fae body pulsing with sylphawareness and his own potency.

Ah, sylphconfidence, a sight to behold, one that couldn't help but inspire.

"Shall we?" he asked, offering an arm chivalrously to each woman, wings adjusting automatically behind them, as if this were an everyday occurrence and he'd had lots of practice in portraying Sylph Royalty.

Spontaneous applause broke out from the audience, along with shouts of encouragement and glee but then they too followed suit, Chinaberry and Cat dramatically slipping their hands through Bud's proffered elbows, the Royal Sylph Entourage at their finest.

"Lead on, Flem, we're right behind you," called Bud, vivid sparkly fae *jewelry* adorning each side.

Mayapple couldn't stand it and clenched her teeth briefly, letting out a small choked squeal while simultaneously squeezing poor Flem's upper arm in anticipation, her eyes going wild, her whole body overcome momentarily from this buildup of monumental curiosity as The Moment was finally upon them.

"Ha!" laughed her escort. "Take it easy, I'm not as young as I used to be."

"Oh puh-lease. It's not exactly like you're the old faerie, now is it?" drolly returned Mayapple.

The door opened, Nirvana breached.

"Oooh," breathed Mayapple in astonishment, a sentiment echoed by Rainbow Merkiva on the other side.

Releasing his arm, the two humans drifted immediately to the edge of the adjacent balcony.

It wasn't quite the Grand Canyon but it felt like it.

Whimsey C. Nimble

Space hung before them, a huge bower-like room, filled with *Sylphs*, faeries! flying in and out, cavorting daringly, laughter pealing out in streaks, bubbles of mirth bouncing off the walls.

Gripping the edge, neither woman moved, eyes dazzled, mouths open, fingers clenched.

"I'm off to find Lark. Let's meet at Gloxinias' in a little bit, okay? Just follow the path that way," he pointed, "and you'll come to it."

Humanized automatons, they could do no more than nod mutely.

"The walkway goes all the way around!" yelled Cat as she ran by them, right out into thin air, tightening into a fae cannonball for a split second before righting hersylph and shooting up, into a large loop t' loop.

Chinaberry was hot on her heals and within seconds the two were holding hands at arm's length, twirling and giggling in space, wings working mightily, emerald and amethyst blurs.

Flem groaned, "I gotta *GO*," and leaped off the ledge, nose diving because he thought it would scare his audience the most and secretly showing off.

Mayapple gasped.

Rainbow said, "He's fine."

Bud chuckled. "Ladies, will you be okay here alone?"

Instantly they reassured him, urging him to *go*, FLY! They'd be fine.

Smiling, he reiterated, "Gloxinia's – it's a great little café about half way down, on the right side. Your passes entitle you to one free item, and one free drink from the bar up here. There are lots of scenic viewpoints all along the path. Enjoy yourselves. We'll catch up with you at the café. Bye!" And that handsome fae Buddleia, the darling of the *S* Club set and all those faeries, laughed manically, throwing himsylph into a dramatic pose and flinging himsylph off the cliff, wings beating furiously above his still-as-stone Sylph until he could hold it no more and broke, himsylph joining Cat and China in frenzied loop t' loops, freedom erupting from his blood.

Meanwhile Sylph Spurastic wrapped his wings around his shoulders and waited.

While the three behind him shouted and let off steam, Flem flew reconnaissance, trying to locate that Sylph of his.

Cruising the perimeter, it wasn't long 'til the errant Lark was spotted, looking rather medieval what with his wings shrouding him like a deformed giant bat.

Feeling like the older, wiser one for once, Flem softly fluttered down onto the nearest lily-pad shaped landing pad and determinedly walked the last ten steps, thinking how attractive that fae-man looked, even sulking as he was.

"Where's your *girl*-friend?" The question was sharp, the tone hurt, but Flem suddenly knew it was all an act.

Hmmph, he thought, this must be what it feels like to grow up. To see, or rather to feel, to *know*, the bigger picture. One just had to *decide* to not get sucked into another Sylph's drama, to keep to the image of your own truth, but also be ready and able to bend a little, to flow.

Standing before him, Flem reached out and brought his thumb softly down over Lark's cheekbone and then down further still, to softly caress that beautiful mouth, puckered as it was in feigned displeasure.

Scootching in closer, Flem's hands were soon inside the other's Sylph-made cloak and one thing led to another.

Lark's lips found his as his wings, forgotten, fell back on ingrained muscle memory and slowly made their way back to their most natural position: out, pointed and with the deepening kiss, becoming more taut by the moment.

Of the three paths, Rainbow and Mayapple immediately found two, one in the middle and one that hugged the railing, creating a woodsy balcony. Not able to tear themselves away from the edge, they inched along, trying to follow the flights of their fae friends.

Bud and his entourage were rather easy to continuously spot as they were loud, whooping it up with many others, darting hither and yon, aerial acrobatics, all for free.

Squinting, Mayapple wished she had brought her *opera* glasses with her, la ti da. Not that she used them at the opera, but rather that they were small, although not tiny enough for *this* bag, she thought wryly. She resolved then and there to indeed bring them *next* time, heh heh heh, and simply use a different purse.

"Ooh Mayapple, *look*. Isn't that whatshername? Periwinkle Pink?"

"Periwinkle? No, that's not right." She made a sound of disgust. "It was Myrtle. Or something like that," she tapped one fingernail against her front teeth, thinking, watching these hidden faeries caper about, revealing their true Sylves.

Awe stole over them as they stared, humans in faerieland, drinking-in the rarified atmosphere.

"Come, let's move on a little," suggested Rainbow, tugging on Mayapple's arm.

Unbeknownst to them, anytime humans were in the *S* Club, (on the third floor anyway) it was known immediately to everyone in there and *all* kept an eye on *them*. Sylph eyes looked down, and around, through tree limbs and from behind leaves, settling on them like pollen from blooming trees.

It wasn't long and what had to be Gloxinia's was seen in the distance on the other side of the middle path.

Mayapple looked hard at the seating area, not really believing what she was seeing. It looked like something that should be at a park, for God's sake. Mossy stump tables and mushroom chairs?

"Look! *Look*. What a hoot, Rainbow!"

Mayapple was starting to snort at the hilarious fact that obviously, Sylph sophistication was only a front! Here, *at* the *S* Club, on the exclusive third floor, was where they really let their hair down, er, wings out, as it were.

And *look* at them! Playing and giggling like school girls. She would never see them the same way again.

As the two made their way towards the small café set between two big trees, a movement caught Mayapple's eye and she stared, her head coming out a little like a turtle's and held stiffly in her intentness to make it out.

Two Sylphs were passionately embracing, their wings trembling with tautness, electrified, under a tree up ahead near the crowd-size landing pad.

It almost looked like Lark. It *was* Lark. And so that had to be Flem.

Oh my, it was almost embarrassing to watch but she could not tear her eyes away.

"Rainbow, isn't that Lark? I guess he's not mad anymore. Wow." Mayapple turned around finally, as did Rainbow and they decided to go look at the menu and leave the two by themsylves, although Mayapple wasn't about to leave this alone for too long. Opportunities like this didn't come around very often. I mean, *faeries*, for God's sake, *kissing*. She made a mental note to bring her camera next time, along with those sweet little binoculars. She'd better just plan on a backpack and be done with it.

Forcing herself to ignore them, she concentrated on standing beside her friend and reading the menu held by Mr. Hedgehog.

The more she read the more she got excited. Oh my God, faerie food! You had to admit, it wasn't the usual deli fare.

"What are you getting?" she asked Rainbow, licking her lips, Flem and Lark completely forgotten for the moment.

"Ooh, the sunflower muffin with carnation marmalade sounds pretty good. What about you?"

"Oh, I've got to have some blossom fritters, but oh dear, I can't eat *flowers*, can I? Oh sure I can, just this once," she grinned. "Want to share some pineapple peppermint sherbet?" she added, digging out her pass.

Rainbow nodded, pulling out her own pass and they stepped up to the window.

A strange, rather closed smile lit the thin small face of the woman? behind the counter.

Rather condescendingly she said, "Bet you gals got passes, don't you?" She smiled knowingly and waited, making both Rainbow and Mayapple feel kind of funny, like there was more here than met the eye, but of course, there always was, wasn't there?

"Are we that obvious, Rainbow?" whispered Mayapple in sudden concern, looking around with a new, nervous awareness, like they were lost in the woods on the way to grandma's house but Rainbow clucked her tongue at her and said, "Darling. Are we special or what? Who *cares* if we're *obvious*, I think *that's* a good thing!" and she gave her short, beaded, bust-hugger a shake, accompanied by a come-hither look cast to the entire area, causing Mayapple to break into laughter, restored to balance.

Smiling at the counter person, Mayapple tried to figure out if the woman who looked like a woman was Sylph or not. So far, everyone they'd seen up here *was* a Sylph.

Shoulders were covered by a shawl and Mayapple couldn't see behind her, darn it.

Examining first Mayapple's and then Rainbow's pass, the woman's eyebrows twitched and ran up and down and she peered at the two of them from underneath these two bone-white wild bronc caterpillars, not able to contain her impatience in dealing with the newbie public, be it Sylph or human.

623

Whimsey C. Nimble

Seemed like they all showed up here sooner or later, and always had since she'd opened this place, years ago.

Her wings gave a twitch in the back, the green silk shawl doing a pretty good job of camouflage, so long as she didn't turn sideways. She liked to keep 'em guessing, although nobody else was fooled.

Smiling a practiced smile, she encouraged the two skittish humans to place their orders, it was hard for her to see those two young fae bloods going at it over across the tables at the edge of the woods, while these two stood in her way.

Unable to take anymore, Lark grasped Flem's shoulders and whispered passionately, "Let's go. Back there. Or *up*." He nodded briefly to two general areas he knew where they could be alone.

Panting, Flem gasped, "Good," and followed Lark to disappear into the trees.

"Here you go ladies," said the café owner, as she handed them back their passes, which now had *three* interlocking hearts on them, but it was obvious that the letters of 'Gloxinia's' now comprised the new one.

Giving their order, they then sat down to wait.

Remembering Flem, Mayapple jerked around but that hot love affair was nowhere to be seen.

Perched delicately on a sturdy amanitas, Rainbow swung out a sexily clad lacy leg, rhinestones on her bright red heels bestowing bits of light to anyone lucky enough to be in its path.

Neither said anything, just waited, looking around, taking it all in, listening.

Mayapple heard it first, as it happened. Her gaze swung out and you could tell she was hearing something, as her eyes looked inquiringly around, trying to find it, whatever *it* was. Some odd little noise.

Then Rainbow heard it, and she too grimaced and kind of looked around.

Then it was gone.

"Did you hear that?" asked Mayapple after a moment. "Whattaya think that was?"

There it was again.

"I think it's behind us, behind there-" she said, pointing at the little establishment.

Both women got up cautiously and were about to go investigate when their threesome slid in like it was home base, apparently having just landed, laughing and panting, still exuberant from their acrobatics.

Into the noise came the announcement: "Your order's up!"

All of which served to admirably distract any further investigations of strange noises.

Bud bounced up. "Allow me, just stay put. China? Catalpah? Want anything?" he asked as he walked to the open window.

"Candied violets!" affirmed Chinaberry.

"Ask Popcorn if she's ordered those green-apple crisps yet, would you? The ones coated in cinnamon and sugar?" Cat instructed.

"'*Popcorn?*'" mouthed Rainbow to Mayapple and they both laughed, picturing those hoary caterpillars that rode upon Popcorn's face that did indeed jump around like popping corn.

Bud returned laden with goodies and was handing everything out, explaining to Cat he'd gotten dried raspberries for her since Popcorn no longer carried the crisp apple slices when who should come sauntering nonchalantly out of the woods behind Gloxinia's but Lark and Flem.

China and Cat's eyes flew to the other's but neither said a word, dried raspberries and candied violets effectively soaking up their wisecracks.

Bud gave the two newcomers a droll look, his chin quivering with suppressed words, but contented himsylph with "Oh, there you are, we've missed you. Where you been? What have you been doing?" in a very innocent tone, because he knew Pan well *where* they'd been and *what* they'd been doing.

Glaring at Bud, smiling reassuredly at their guests, ignoring Chinaberry and Catalpah, Lark explained, "Flem had never been *up* before, above Gloxinia's and I was just showing him."

"I'll just bet you were," muttered Bud under his breath.

Flem just stood and blushed becomingly, trying not to look as embarrassed as he felt.

Rainbow and Mayapple got it about the same time, suddenly realizing where those strange noises had come from and what had caused them.

Whimsey C. Nimble

Hmm.

No wonder they'd disappeared. Apparently fae libido was similar to human.

With no resistance, Mayapple, Rainbow, Chinaberry and Cat gravitated together, munching and freely sharing food, eyes all on Bud, Lark and Flem.

Flem looked about awkwardly for a moment but soon shook it off and headed towards Mayapple and the rest, leaving Bud and Lark to trade smart remarks.

Deciding their friendship would be better served by tact and not derision, Mayapple offered some blossom fritters to the slightly disheveled Sylph but then smiled and said, "Well, how far '*up*' did he take you?"

Not only Flem's but Rainbow's head swirled at that blatant innuendo, and Flem choked on a piece of muffin and marmalade Rainbow had just handed him.

Of course China and Cat had to overhear which was immediately evinced by a bout of Sylph insanity.

Clucking and whooping, food forgotten, off they went, wings clattering, vibrating uncontrollably, disturbing the containers left behind, sending them dancing down the table and to the ground.

Mayapple was round-eyed at this reaction to her question, mortification burning her cheeks as she realized how it'd sounded.

"We went to the top, did we not, ma petite fleur?" Lark's voice brooked no more questions.

Mayapple had frozen, much like the pineapple peppermint confection she now held.

Lark continued, "Shall we move on?" He smiled warmly at the girls before continuing, aiming his words towards Buddleia, "Walking with, or catching up with your fly girls?"

Bud's jaw muscle clenched a little but other than that there was no sign of the irritation that occasionally flared up at the Sylph he'd been friends with for close to seventy years, meeting him shortly after he himsylph had arrived here. "I'll join you, thank you. Surely you're not walking all the way, are you?" He said this as if there was an obvious destination and both Mayapple and Rainbow heard it and wondered.

"No, no, I figured we'd jump off down-a-ways. Our seating is reserved, so there's no hurry," replied Lark.

"WOO HOO! Flumaria! Whoopth, I mean Flem. Helloo. Up here." Movement caught their eye and Lark let go of Flem's arm as they all turned and peered towards the voice, ensconced with another on a big 'tree' limb thirty feet away and above their heads.

"Sissy? Hi! Great to see you up there. Hello," Flem nodded politely to Circumscissle's companion, a rather heavyset Sylph with her legs hanging down, which had the unfortunate effect of making her look like a brown treehopper attached to a branch.

"Oh, where are my mannerth? Everyone, thith ith Thathafrath. We jutht met but I think we're going to be good friendth." His great grey mouth sprang spittle and Mayapple for one was quite happy to NOT be right below them.

"Are you going to the thow?" asked Sissy, pulling himsylph together, preparing to flutter down to their vicinity. This caused Sassafras to grunt and pull her legs up, readying hersylph to follow.

They were such an ungainly pair it almost hurt to watch them and Flem flinched as the two of them jumped into the air.

Thank Pan they were much more graceful in their element than they were sitting around and came to an easy landing beside the little group.

Immediately the collective nose caught the difference; *somebody* smelled really good.

"Mmm," breathed Mayapple, "that's so nice. What is it?"

Looking at her friend Sissy, Sassy mumbled, "It's me."

"Oh!" said Mayapple brightly. "Very unusual. Where'd you get it?" she inquired further, digging the unknown hole a little deeper.

"It's, it's…" and fumbled but luckily Circumscissle was her new ally and took a step towards his own emancipation by noticing acutely that Sassy was uncomfortable and deciding to take the pressure off.

"It'th her own thmell, that's what it ith," he declared emphatically.

Mayapple was taken aback with the realization it *wasn't* a perfume and felt her cheeks grow warm, gritting her back teeth at her own tendency to blunder into things when all she was doing was talking, and resolved to THINK before each and everything she said from now on - no more spontaneity.

Yeah, right! Like that's really going to happen! She snorted out loud to herself just as the talk turned to the upcoming show and how everyone wanted to fly there, looking at her and Rainbow as if for permission to leave.

Whimsey C. Nimble

As the two humans looked at each other quizzically in confusion, Lark rushed in, "Just stay on this path, we'll be down there; here, come over to the railing, I'll point it out."

Shading her eyes even though there was no glare, Mayapple peered into the giant hollow, absently noting the twinkly lights that were interwoven everywhere. Sylphs glided along, some merely flying from one landing pad to another while others lazily stirred the air in circles. It was hard to concentrate but finally Mayapple spotted the shadowed area on the ground floor that she thought Lark was showing her.

"Yes, yes, okay, we'll meet you there. We'll come to it by just following this path, right?"

Lark nodded, smiling at her and Rainbow. Flem ootched closer, wings rattling faintly in impatience but Lark heard them and hurried.

Grabbing Flem's hand he pulled him to the landing but before they could leap those dastardly but gay fae faeries Chinaberry and Catalpah materialized like wraiths in a graveyard, blocking their way.

Two sets of wings, huge opalescent purple ones and the other emerald green, rattled and clacked, whirred and snapped, taunting their sneering contempt for the two in front of them and of course, any Sylph worth her, ah, his salt must respond to such a blatant dare.

Eyes flashing, Lark let go of Flem's hand and leaped at the rude pair before they knew what he was about and the three of them whumped, bumped and buzzed, like chest pounding, wing bashing, shin-kicking hummingbirds defending their territory.

Rainbow and Mayapple stood open-mouthed, wondering if it was for real when Flem freaked and flew into the fray.

A buzz rose until it grew higher in pitch and then broke into masses of giggles and laughter, antics still high-jinxing about.

Flem pulled away and bee-lined to Mayapple, hovering in the air, his look still quite imputent and excited, hair rumpled.

"Meet you at the swing, bye!" It came out jerky and breathless, there was no denying the maniacal look in his eye and Mayapple scowled and wondered what he meant, Lark hadn't mentioned any swing.

Flem turned and pointed to where he was going, and said, "Don't worry, it's hard to miss, I'll watch for you. Bye!" He peeled off.

She watched him go until Rainbow pulled her attention back with, "Amazing, isn't it? Where we are, what we're watching. So," she paused. "I've got a question and I want your opinion. What do you think China and Cat are? Are they really female Sylphs? Or male? I mean, do you think these are ALL male Sylphs, Mayapple? Even the ones you'd swear are female? And what about *Popcorn*? What is she? And, oh yeah, that woman, what was her name? Your, ahem, *friend* you met downstairs. Vervacity? She sure looks like a female, doesn't she? What a bosom. What do *you* think?"

Mayapple didn't know the answer but said, "We'll ask them. C'mon let's go," but practically bumped into Circumscissle and Sassafras as she turned.

Perversely hoping they weren't going to join them on their walk, Mayapple smiled and said brightly, "Well, where are you two off to, are you going to the show too?" forgetting to step back and thusly getting sprayed with waterworks.

"Thorry!" said Sissy sincerely and used his loose cuff to wipe spittle off of Mayapple's cheek.

She sighed. Turning to Sassafras, she said, "Nice to meet you Sassy, you do thmell good, oh! Thorry! Oh! I mean, you do SMELL good. We gotta go." Embarrassed, she wiped her cheek where Sissy had missed a wet spot, gave the two a quick fake smile and grabbed Rainbow's arm to glide forcefully down the path.

"Did they jump yet ?" whispered Rainbow. They both cautiously peered back in time to see the two disappear into the air.

Trying not to get overcome with funny business and odd Sylphs, Mayapple pinched her own arm to stave off the hysterics lurking closely right behind her eyeballs.

"Do you really like the way I smell, Sissy?" asked Sassafras wistfully as they flew towards the show.

His tall skinny head thrown back, Circumscissle's spray drifted harmlessly to the floor as he replied, "Come on over tonight and I'll thow you just how *much* I like your thweet thmell, thweetie," he invited.

Whimsey C. Nimble

They came to a stop on a landing pad that was still some distance away from the stage, near a thicket of tall nandina.

Looking enquiringly at Sassy, Sissy's eyes beckoned and Sassy finally nodded, sealing a match made in heaven or at least, heavenly bamboo.

The atmosphere quickened the closer they got to the stage area and there were tables and nooks scattered everywhere, a few still empty.

"Leth not get too clooth, and then we can leave early if we want to," suggested Sissy with a meaningful look at Sassy.

Shyly, she nodded as they settled in.

Rainbow and Mayapple strolled on, arms hooked together, enchanted with the glamour of the fae world they found themselves in.

Keeping to the path closest to the flyway, Rainbow pointed out a strange little sign. It only had one word on it, Helianthus, with a crooked arrow.

"Wonder what that's all about?" remarked Mayapple idly before they moved on.

Music and laughter could be heard in the distance and they hastened their step.

A figure could be seen hurrying towards them from the opposite direction and the closer he got, the older and more weather beaten he looked.

Tall and thin, his face was very round, and he had yellow blond hair that stuck out all around from under the edge of his head-hugging dark brown cap.

He looked rather harried.

Tilting his head in greeting, he barely acknowledged them with a grimace that passed for a smile, hurrying by only to turn around and belatedly ask, "You didn't happen to see a large group did you, gathered in one place? I mean, they all would have been blond like me. We were suppose to meet here and I can't find them." He looked around in a rather irritated manner.

"Would that by any chance be the 'Helianthus' group?" Mayapple took a stab in the dark.

"Yes!" He lit up like a sunflower.

The ladies grinned at this tall lanky Sylph, delighting in his color combination of yellow and muted green.

One could definitely see the fae in all these 'boys,' if nothing else it was often obvious by their choice of colors.

It was then that Mayapple saw the faint pattern in pale iridescent yellow that sparkled on this guy's arms below his elbow-length green sleeves. Trying not to stare, she wondered suddenly if ALL Sylphs sported such patterns. Did *Flem* have one? She bet he did and made a mental note to really look closely at the next bare appendage she came across. Maybe she'd just never seen him in the right lighting. Hmm.

Quickly she spoke out, "Yeah, right back there. It was sort of a funny arrow, it pointed back that way," she motioned towards the inner wall, "but it also pointed up, if that helps at all," she finished.

Bobbing his head, it almost looked too large for the thin stalk of his neck but Mayapple saw cords of sinew that ran straight up and down and surmised he was stronger than he looked.

"Thanks!" and he disappeared behind them and was seen looking at the sign they'd just passed. Glancing up, he caught them watching and waved then veered off from the main walkway and went on, looking around him.

Mayapple and Rainbow turned back around, the sound of the swelling Sylph soiree pulling them down the path, which dropped lower and lower until the balcony railing stopped and took a sharp left, curving back in a long slow bend to partner the top seating tier which ran down the inner face of the small amphitheater-like room that comprised the floor here on the third level of the famous *S* Club.

Movement was discernable everywhere, Sylphs of all shades and color landing from up above, flying, walking, waving, drinking, swinging. It was like a well ordered airport only instead of planes and helicopters it was an urban faerie land, the next best thing to Thimbleberry Canyon or Cow Valley.

Mayapple looked hard at what appeared to be a giant swing, nudging Rainbow with an elbow but that girl was too busy gawking.

The air swooshed right out from between them and Buddleia settled in, furling his wings for the moment.

Grinning devilishly, he offered each an arm, saying, "Ladies, may I be your escort from here? We're headed for that swing, yonder," he nodded, "but we'll take the long way around and I'll introduce you. Okay?"

Charmed silly, Rainbow and Mayapple were swept on, easily riding the Buddleia wave.

Whimsey C. Nimble

The place was definitely crowded and there were Sylphs everywhere down here, not like the path they'd taken to get here, where they'd only seen a few.

And they all knew Bud. And he them. Must be a small world here in the land of City Sylphs.

Smiling ear to ear in his role as informal *S* Club host, he graciously slowed way down, making introductions, albeit short, as they kept moving their way down to the others.

Mayapple realized her cheekbones were starting to ache from ginning so much, she was having so much fun.

The hour was getting later, Sylphs were relaxing now and they draped themsylves over every conceivable surface, they didn't just sit at a table, they blended, becoming part of the furniture. Some might even call it possessive slouching.

Their host slowed down again and both bright and sassy ladies looked avidly at the two in front of them, and Mayapple suddenly flashed on how *Vinca* had seemed to want to eat them up and now *she*, Mayapple, felt the same way. She loved this place!

"Poppy. Puschkinia. Mayapple. Rainbow," came the amused introduction.

Everyone nodded, sizing all the others up.

With a lift of the brows, Bud said see-you-later, and they moved off, regret plain on everyone's face that they couldn't stay longer.

Three steps later Bud slowed again.

"Veronica. Laurel. Sophoria. Mayapple. Rainbow."

Again they moved off, Mayapple really wishing she had time to stop and talk to every single one. They MUST come back some time, she decided, when she could mingle more.

About to start down to the next tier, Bud looked twice at a far corner, then, laughing to himsylph, he tugged and said, "C'mon."

As they threaded their way through the throng, Mayapple and Rainbow recognized Circumscissle and Sassafras at a table with three others, one who's back was to them but had a familiar air, and two others, unfamiliar.

Bud actually stopped, meeting the first set of eyes, "Bunya Bunya," he introduced. The next Sylph turned around at that and Bud went on, "Wonga Wonga," with both humans smiling in recognition but feeling much more secure this time. Then acknowledging Sassafras and Circumscissle, "Sissy,

Sassy," and finally introducing the last one, the one dressed in all white and with a large panama hat on his head, "Jipijapa."

Rainbow was struck by Jipajapa's style, feeling a magnetism towards him, while his eyes never left hers.

And then Mayapple keeled over, peeling away from her sophisticated stance and sniffed deeply, head down by her knees, hands on hips, trying to inhale enough oxygen to her poor starved brain, because she was about to overload.

Her eyes watered and her ears tingled, riding a trail of goosebumps running rampant over her skull.

Whoops of laughter started in her chest and made her boobies tingle, and she rubbed furiously at them to get them to lay down but alas, the twins were on alert.

Skyrocketing gales of gaiety shot out of her until she was wheezing, wheezing and mumbling over and over, "Bunya Bunya, Wonga Wonga, Sissy, Sassy, Jipijapa," at which point she'd go off again, repeating it, "Bunya Bunya, Wonga Wonga, Sissy, Sassy, Jipijapa." Her countenance took on the cadence of the melodic refrain and there was wild look in her eyes.

Starting to draw undue attention, Bud shot a look at Rainbow and then back to out of control Mayapple.

Linking his arm roughly through hers, he pulled her away without a backward glance.

Mayapple hung tight but kept repeating the litany of names, like it was some kind of song under her breath.

Humans in a fae environment didn't always behave with the decorum expected but by and large, nobody cared. In fact, they kind of admired it.

Word of the incident spread like flaming Sylph gossip and within minutes all eyes were traveling with them and wouldn't you know it, Mayapple began to hear it repeated in whispers all around them. She grinned.

Bud pointedly ignored her, instead gamely pointing out Distictus Rivers, A.K.A. Bignonia where he lounged several tiers away, with Vinca Pink. They watched as the pair twined around each other. When they finally caught their breath and looked up, Bud called, "Vinca - Dick, hey, next time-" before hurrying his party on.

The swing was in sight and Mayapple wondered how many it'd hold, it looked like it was full already when Bud slowed again to make more introductions.

Whimsey C. Nimble

"Spurge, Spekboom, Statice, Stoneface. Mayapple, Rainbow. Where's Sydney?"

"Sydney Blue Gum?" Spurge clarified.

"Yeah."

"Oh, you know him, loves to shoot pool, wants to hang onto his title, 'Fastest Gum In The West.' He'll probably be around later."

Spekboom spoke up, "Hey, have you seen Trip in your travelings?"

"Trip O'Gandra? Yeah, he's here someplace and he's with Deutz."

"Deutzia?"

"Yeah."

As usual, Stoneface didn't say a word, keeping up with Statice on his right. Statice didn't change much and the two of them made a good pair.

Inclining his head in a graceful farewell, Bud strolled on, subtly guiding his armfuls to where he wanted them to be.

"Mayapple, over here!" rang out over the din, and all three jerked as one, six eyes searching.

It didn't sound like Flem's voice and Mayapple couldn't imagine who else it would be.

"Oooh, look who's on the swing. C'mon girls." Bud stepped lively and both women had the thought at the same time. Releasing his arms, they hesitated long enough and were left behind, like flotsam from a motor boat, bobbing in his wake.

They came together naturally, Rainbow leading, Mayapple right behind her and made for the swing, spying Flem and Lark then China and Cat close after them.

Bud zeroed in and made for the far end. Who was on this end, it was so confusing, it looked like two but then became clearer. Vervacity Verbascum was planted on the very end, the closest one to them and while there was still plenty of room for others, her friend Vanda perched on her lap, like a hothouse orchid.

"Come, sit by us," implored the sturdier of the two.

Mayapple hesitated, looking over at Flem who immediately detached himsylph from Lark's side and hastened over.

He plopped down on the swing, patting the opening between him and the double V's, and Mayapple slipped right in. Lark lightly dropped into place right on the other side of Flem at the same time. Rainbow grabbed the seat next to Lark, Catalpah followed her, Bud landed next and Chinaberry squeezed in last. A full complement of Sylphs. And humans.

The noise level in the big acoustic room escalated the closer it got to show time. Everyone squirmed and wiggled trying to get comfortable, including Mayapple and Rainbow, but they settled down after a couple of minutes. Yet there was still movement going on and with a gasp Mayapple realized the giant wooden swing was ponderously moving and that there were *wings* synchronizing up and down the line, out the back.

Eyes wide, she leaned forward, putting a hand on a knee directly on each side of her, and looked down the line for Rainbow, thrusting out her legs automatically and straining with the momentum, doing her best to move the swing too.

Rainbow was staring all around her, Catalpah just past her talking animatedly to someone outside the swing. On the end, Bud and Chinaberry huddled and whispered.

Mayapple felt the giant porch swing sway backwards and leaning back, looked down the line behind everyone's heads, catching sight of all those wings resting but ready for the other side of the wave and sure enough, back they went the other way, and all the wings beat mightily, synchronizing almost instantaneously, harder and faster 'til poof! Done. Repose.

Mayapple was so enchanted by the sight she merely pointed her toes at the right time but didn't pull at all, savoring the sweet sight of so many Sylphs swinging.

They didn't have long to play before the lights started dimming and brightening a couple of times, telling everyone the show was about to begin.

Wings slowed in synchronicity. A hand snaked into a pocket and out came the first flask. With a sip and a nudge it was passed on.

The swing gently rocked, holding seven faeries and two faerie wan-a-bees in its palm, and the chatter in the background became less obvious as the collective attention was drawn to the stage.

Flem recognized it as the same one that had held the giant screen behind which Fanwort Cabomba had worked her magic.

Instruments were set up, waiting to be brought alive and Flem wiggled in anticipation as did they all, his hand finding Mayapple's and their fingers laced. Anticipation was always the best condiment for life, thought Flem. It was but a bubble of strange contentment, usually brief, but very full.

Whimsey C. Nimble

Lark's arm draped heavily over Flem's shoulders just at the top of his wing blades and he let his fingers hang down to tweak Mayapple's hair, like a little sister.

The tall green spiky woman gilded with silver grasped Mayapple's other hand and gave it a squeeze, smiling into Mayapple's eyes, looking past stick-thin pretty Vanda on her lap.

All this camaraderie was interrupted by the arrival of a small engraved flask.

It got to Mayapple's hand and as she took a drink, she looked down the line for Rainbow, wishing they were closer together. Of course, Rainbow was waiting for her.

Nodding at Mayapple, she toasted her and the flask in her hand with the flask in *her* hand, then grinned and pantomimed 'Meet me *behind* all these faeries.'

Mayapple thrust the flask into Vanda's tenuous grip and then leaned back to catch sight of Rainbow two Sylphs down, Flem's and Lark's wings separating them. Rainbow was grinning at her when all of a sudden her focus shifted as she caught sight of something behind Mayapple and her expression changed to one of rampant speculation.

Mayapple turned, trying to follow her gaze.

Seeing nothing unusual at first, just a whole room full of furled, half-furled and full-out Sylphs, Mayapple was about to turn back around when a bright spot caught her eye, way back in the upper levels from whence they'd come.

Rich simulated sunlight bathed a small leafy platform upon which stood several members of the Helianthus clan, for there was the blondie that had been lost, right in the midst of them. Like a field of sunflowers, they stood shoulder to shoulder, their faces all at the same angle, like they were basking in afternoon sun, yellow and green wings mostly furled. Almost all had short blond hair. Occasionally an arm lifted to imbibe a sip of mead.

Taking it all in, Mayapple then flopped back into place before trying to catch Rainbow's eye again but just as they finally connected, someone walked out onto the stage and everyone straightened right up.

Trillium, one ledge over, poked Babiana and whispered, "Wake Robin, the show's starting."

"How do you do?" boomed a deep male voice with a sexy accent, zeroing in to every ear in the place. "My name is Sauro Matum, perhaps you've heard of my humble band before, Voo Doo Lily?"

At this the place erupted, cat calls, whistles, wings furling and unfurling zip, zip, zip.

"Okay, settle down. I don't blame you one bit for being anxious. We've got a great show lined up for you."

By this time his band members had filed onstage and taken their places.

"We're going to start off with an old favorite, *Swamp Mellee!*"

Those Sylphs, and you could tell they were fae no matter how soberly they were dressed, started off with a bang, throwing themsylves fully into it.

Pan, they had every Sylph in the place jumping to the jive, toes were tapping, fingers were snapping and wings were rocking.

The number came to an end and Sylphs everywhere surged to their feet, furling their wings tight, clapping hard, whistling loud and shrill.

Mayapple sat back and grinned.

"Okay, I want to introduce our band members here. That's Datura on bass." A conservative looking female Sylph who actually tended to be mannish, gave a small wave from beside the big instrument and Flem thought, why *bother* with a female appearance, why not just give in and be male, since we all are.

Ah well, different path in life, different lessons to learn.

Sauro went on. "Next we've got Draco on conga drums." The dark haired faerie gave a brief nod, then beat out a quick staccato as a hello, furled wings coming undone a little as his whole body portrayed the beat.

Nodding and smiling, Sauro Matum went on, "Our piano man is Woodruff." The Sylph had long curly brown hair and Mayapple felt a pang go all the way to her marrow when she saw it. His wings were furled but hung close to his body.

He lifted the bill on his cap to say hello, half standing up for a minute.

"Our two saxophone players, Nelly Moser and Mrs. Chumley." Two very hip looking older female Sylphs nodded, wings furled tight and almost invisible.

"That's Dudleya back there on drums." Bangety bang bang and a quick nod with a wave.

Whimsey C. Nimble

"Prins Hendrick, guitar." A gangly fellow wearing a beautiful azure shirt gave a salute.

"And two special guests tonight, one you'll meet right now! May I present Dizzy Gotheca!"

Both Mayapple and Rainbow looked twice at this, as they'd both heard of him, but not as a Sylph!

Drat, but Mayapple wished again she'd thought to bring her camera. She couldn't wait to see if the famous trumpet virtuoso's legendary cheeks puffed out, like she'd heard they did.

Dizzy grabbed the microphone from the band leader's hand, and spoke to the crowd: "And this guy, one of the finest clarinet players you'll ever hear. Let's give it up for your band leader, Sauro Matum and Voo Doo Lily! Sauro Matum IS Voo Doo Lily!"

The fae crowd thundered their approval.

Dizzy handed the mic back and clapped a little before the band leader went on.

"Last but by no means least, let me introduce our other special guest tonight – Floxie, come on out here!"

As she walked onstage, he continued, "Floxie Diva Ricata! Our very own *Floxie* Blues!" at which point she broke into Swan River Daisy, drawing each word out and telling you why she *had* been so unhappy but had found her way to the sunshine, something to do with DNA and a sign of the times.

Everyone was electrified and roared their appreciation.

Thanking them modestly, she waited for the house to settle back down, then launched into two more fritillaries, and a ballad about a Brambling Rose, ending with a knee slapper called The Dancing Lady.

By now the crowd was in love with her and it was easy to see why she was the apple of the S Club's eye: dressed in a vibrant shade of violet, she had a vivid yellow sash around her tiny waist. Flem thought she looked like a living pansy from this angle.

Smiling at the adoration thrown her way, Floxie announced they would be taking a short intermission, and bowed out, the band disassembling as everyone took five.

The swing bounced and rocked like a giant swipple at harvest time as itchy butts came off of it and moved around.

Vonda and Vervacity gently eased away, the silver sage gaze lingering over Mayapple's, promises of bedevilment in her look as she watched Mayapple's eyes.

"Let's get together sometime…" she invited. "Too bad I have to leave so soon."

Oh thank God, thought Mayapple silently. This 'woman' Sylph scared her and excited her and confused her and she needed distance.

"Yes," she agreed, wondering what to do and why she carried it forward but couldn't stop herself. All these Sylphs, these *faeries*, were all so intriguing.

"You still got my card?" asked Vervacity as Vonda kept tugging.

"Oh yeah!" assured Mayapple, trying to find some words.

Flem said something to her, Vervacity saw it and finally took hersylph off.

Chinaberry moved down to their end and plopped hersylph down heavily, purple stylish wings furled for the moment.

It rather made Mayapple breathless to be so up close and personal like this. Rainbow slipped into place on the other side of her, which she was very glad of so they could talk, when green-eyed Catalpah followed her and they were hemmed in by those two jokesters, China and Cat, not that it mattered, right? She had questions and so did Rainbow.

Stealthily a small flask of an unusual design was pressed to her hand and Mayapple looked up quickly into amethyst irises and an encouraging nod.

"Dutchman's Pipe," explained China, finger tracing the outline of the flower shaped container.

Mayapple thought of Flem and his tendencies to imbibe too much and held it to her lips but didn't actually drink, then passed it on.

Chinaberry seemed so big next to her and Mayapple swallowed, almost wanting to pinch the faerie, to see how real she was. Thank God Rainbow sat tucked in snug right beside her for confidence, and she reached over and kicked her surreptitiously with one foot to get her attention.

All they did was give each other a starburst look and blink hard a couple of times, then, like scouts on a mission, snuggled back towards their colorful companions.

Mayapple's heart tripped a little bit when she realized Bud sat between these beauties all the time, in fact, she was pretty sure the Trio lived on a permanent basis at Bud's treehouse now. God, who wouldn't, she laughed to herself, admitting her total fascination with anything fae and in love with them all.

Chinaberry's wings could be felt pushing out the back, getting in position to push again and her purple sleeves were pushed up as her arm twitched, helping wing musculature adapt.

Mayapple stared. One of the myriad of tiny spotlights that dotted the ceiling traveled brightly, illuminating Chinaberry's arm and there was a pattern discernable. A leafy lilac colored vine rode her skin like it had grown there and Mayapple had to ask, "Is that *real*?" It came out in a rather strangulated voice, which she immediately tried to disclaim by choking, like that would help, making the Sylph laugh.

"Oh come on, Mayapple, I won't *bite*," China said with a serious twist to her mouth, before adding, "Yet," a smirk hiding in one cheek.

She went on, "Yes, my patterns are my patterns. We all have them, see?" She pulled up the long, slightly baggy purple cotton leggings and stuck her leg out in front, toes pointed and sure enough, Mayapple could see the faint viney outlines than twisted around the shapely, firm leg.

"But your *hands*...?" pointed out the human at Chinaberry's pale long fingers.

"Well, cha, you see, *Sylphettes* are born with the vine gene, but it doesn't come out right away, it varies. Usually between thirty-five and seventy-five. When it appears, you know you will have the opportunity to change now, to become male and mate. It's our coming-of-age symbol, so to speak. Wings on the other hand, tend to show up much earlier."

Mayapple couldn't make sense of this and asked, "Seventy-five? Did you include that in this coming-of-age thingy, the vines, you know? What? Just how old do Sylphs get, anyway?" she stared into the amethyst eyes, trying not to be disconcerted but, she was. These people, ha! these *faeries*, were a different race all together. Nobody was playing, it was all real, and they *weren't human*.

Chinaberry easily replied "Seven, eight hundred. I think there might even be somebody back in the canyon who's like, the oldest Sylph."

"How old are you?" Mayapple couldn't stop herself.

"Two hundred and sixteen," she relied matter-of-factly. "And like I was saying, things don't show up right away. I think it's a hormone thing, you know?"

Mayapple nodded mutely like she knew what she was talking about, her eyes resting again on China's pale, pattern-less hands.

"But wait, what's this have to do with your hands?" she brought Chinaberry back to the original point.

"Oh, well, when the pattern appears it's really really faint at first but comes out on almost our whole body you see, everywhere except our hands, feet, and faces although some do get a few up their cheeks but most don't. And each one is different, so we are all unique unto oursylves, all different colors, each their own." With a lascivious swipe of her tongue over her sparkling, purple-tinted lips, China looked directly at Mayapple and issued an invitation: "You should come over to the Treehouse sometime, I'd love to show you my vines."

Mayapple gulped.

China went on, "I'm sure Cat and Bud would be *happy* to show you theirs too, we could make it a party..."

Meanwhile Rainbow was working up enough nerve to ask Catalpah the question that had burned in her mind since they'd met, right before Revelry with Cybele. What *was* she? What *were* they? Female, like she thought at first? And even now, both looked like female Sylphs. Were they? Or were they males like Flem, Lark and Bud. And practically everyone else here, but who chose to portray themsylves as females? *Were* there female Sylphs that lived in the City?

Catalpah sat on the other side of her, one arm draped around the back of the swing above Rainbow's shoulders, and the other emerald clad arm twined around Bud's neck in ownership. Bud was paying no attention and was talking to Flem on the other side of him.

She looked down at the small human woman with the colorful hair beside her and said, "Enjoying yourself?"

Eyes sparkling, Rainbow looked up into a gaze that held the depths of the deep green ocean and nodded, rather intimidated herself to be in such close quarters with the larger than life green Sylph. When they'd worked together at Revelry, she'd had her own dressing room and had never gotten this close before. Even her eyelashes were a deep forest green, she noted.

Whimsey C. Nimble

Chinaberry's Dutchman's Pipe-shaped flask came down the line and after taking a quick sip, Rainbow passed it on to Catalpah who got Bud's attention and then proceeded to let the golden mead dribble from her mouth into his, laughing and gurgling the whole time 'til it ended with a short but passionate kiss between the two of them, while Rainbow looked on in blatant voyeurism. Two faeries kissing.

She sighed.

Finally they broke apart, Bud laughed and resumed his interrupted chat with Flem.

Cat turned around with a suspiciously smug look upon her face and Rainbow almost expected to see canary feathers around her mouth, she looked so satisfied.

Breaking into a mischievous grin at the sight of Rainbow's open admiration, she swung both arms around and squeezed the human tight in an impromptu hug, spontaneously sticking her incongruously pink and raspy tongue into the woman's ear for a rude second.

Pulling back, Rainbow scrubbed at her ear furiously, trying to rid herself of that wet, intrusive feeling. "EEEW!" she sputtered, grimacing and sort of smiling against her will.

"God, what *are* you, anyway?" she blurted out. "Are you *really* a female? What about China? What's she?"

"Aho! The real Rainbow speaks out! Well, okay, if you must know, I'm a male. Technically. Wanna see?"

Rainbow screamed, "No! Go on!"

Laughing, Catalpah confirmed, "Chinaberry too. But neither of us ever resonated with being male, I mean, even when I *changed*, I still felt like my oldsylph. I didn't really feel any different even though others said they did. So, I just kept dressing as me, you know? But for most of us who never changed back, everybody *knows* back home in the canyon and it's just too hard to stay where it's *all* female when you're the only male, we had to get out, go somewhere else, no matter *how* we decided to dress... I mean really, who cares? So here I am. I've been male for fifty-two years. And in San Francoa just about the whole time. I met Chinaberry right at the beginning and we just sort of hit it off."

"So how *old* are you?" asked Rainbow with bated breath.

"A hundred and seventy-five. But we Sylphs age well, as you've no doubt noted..."

"No kidding! Oh my God. *Really?* One hundred and seventy five years old?"

Catalpah just smiled and blinked.

Rainbow had to keep asking as her mind computed, "So, the female Sylphs here, they're all male too?" Her voice held avid speculation.

"Well, yes, most of them anyway, or some variation thereof," she muttered but then her voice picked up and she went on with, "Look, they're coming back onstage!"

Sauro Matum lifted that clarinet and the tune that sprang from his lips danced up and over the air waves, climbing onto everyone's backs, running amuck over the tops of their ears, shooting down to their elbows, then leaping off in a wild jump to their feet and *everybody* starting moving, dancing in the aisles, and making that swing rock.

By this time you can be sure all the band members were one with that red hot bug that couldn't be stopped.

The top floor of the *S* Club was alive, rafters shaking, Sylphs beating a rhythm on every available surface, wild gyrating dancing going on as a few had succumbed and jumped on top of the tables. Wings clattered and chattered almost out of control.

Mayapple was dancing so hard in place on the swing she made it jerk from side to side and Sylph wings beat erratically, out of control, as all kept time in their own way.

Man, the place was HOT.

On a wild ending note, the music suddenly stopped and several Sylphs actually lifted straight up into the air, clapping and shouting, unable to control themsylves.

"Thank you...thank you...thank you. Okay, good." Mr. Voo Doo Lily himsylph tried to be heard over the crowd.

"That was a little number called Chokecherry Stomp. And now, Dizzy, step on up here." He turned to the band behind them as the trumpeter stepped forward. "Busy Lizzie!" he instructed and handed the mic to Dizzy.

Not only did the famous Sylph blow a mean horn, he kept removing it to sing unintelligible words that sounded like Dit Dat Dot Bebop with a bunch of other sliding notes placed along on the scale, and it should have sounded like mish mash but it *worked*, and they all sang their own rendition right along with him.

Whimsey C. Nimble

As the last crazy non-words came to an end, Floxie came striding out from the wings, singing her own version counter-point to his, and they both ended with a laugh.

Well rehearsed, the famous musician asked the Diva what she had planned for them and she replied, "I've got a little something from the Rhododendron Songbook. You remember the three Azaleas, don't you? They're the ones that made these songs the ones we all know and love. Hit it!"

The small orchestra leaped right into the familiar Madam Pericat and then segued nicely into Sweetheart Supreme before ending up with Floxie's favorite and her signature song, Twenty Grand.

Dizzy backed her up every step of the way, cheeks filling with so much air they looked like miniature balloons, bringing them to the last number of the night, Squirrel Foot Fern, a toe-tapping, double jig of Irish descent.

Unwilling to let the entertainers go without an encore, which clearly everyone including the band expected, they were easily wooed back for one more number.

Chiming Bells melted into the atmosphere, soothing jumping nerves and wild hairs.

Sylphs slid down from crazy spots and once again became civilized company.

This time the musicians were allowed to depart, albeit amid a cacophony of thundering approval until the stage was empty.

The swing gently swayed and Mayapple wondered, what next? She was *not* ready to go home.

Without warning, Chinaberry, Cat and Bud flounced from the swing, leaving the remaining four to jounce wildly behind them.

"Gotta fly," announced Bud, "C'mon you two. Let's do it while we can." He was talking to Flem and Lark who were still lolling about in the post-show ripple as Cat and China had already run off. Turning to their guests, he politely asked permission to take these two off, saying "Listen, instead of going back the way you came, go up there," he pointed towards the back, "and find the path that runs along the outer edge, the one that will have come out from behind Gloxinia's. You'll see it. Follow it to you *left*, don't go right, and it'll end up over *there*," he pointed to the other side of the giant bower, straight across the 'canyon' as the crow, ah Sylph, flies, "and you'll run into a woodsy secluded area but it's got lots of seating. We'll meet you there, how's that?"

Oh goodie, thought Mayapple, relieved the night was not over and nodded vigorously. The adventure would continue but it did seem to be winding down.

Catching Mayapple's eye, Rainbow nodded *her* agreement happily, neither were ready to go home and this suited them perfectly.

"How will we know when we get there?" Rainbow asked.

Bud's wings were chattering in his anxiousness to fly and Flem and Lark were up and about, wings warming up like propellers, as they pumped blood to their appendages.

Lark answered for Bud, and Bud took off, Flem trailing behind him.

"Look for a 'Y' in the path and stay to the right. There'll be lots of big trees around you. There's also a big log that's a planter, it's on its side and it's filled with impatience. As am I! You can't miss it. We'll see you somewhere close in there. Bye!" And he ran and jumped into the air, circling higher and higher to catch up with Flem, who was trying to go slow so he could wait but was having a hard time with impatience also.

Laughter pealed out and they disappeared.

"Well, let's carry on, shall we?" said Mayapple, offering her arm to Rainbow.

"We always do!" wisecracked Rainbow in return, grinning.

The place was still crowded but you could tell it was thinning out.

They wandered arm in arm, watching Distictus Rivers and Vinca Pink take off from a landing pad, slowly spiraling up, like sun-seeking wild vines.

Rainbow found herself looking for the table where Bunya Bunya, Wonga Wonga, Sassy, Sissy, and Jipijapa had sat and lo, the only one left *was* Jipijapa, and he was watching *her.*

Her heart jumped a little and she waved back when he twiddled his fingers at her, but Mayapple tugged her on.

They climbed back up the incline until they could go no further, it was either right or left. Pointing to the right was a little sign that said 'Gloxinia's.'

To the left just looked like a walk in the park so away they went, chattering like magpies.

"Mayapple, guess how old Catalpah is, you won't believe it."

"I might, Chinaberry's two hundred and sixteen."

"WHAT?"

"So how old is she and *is she* a she?" Mayapple's eyebrows went so far up, Rainbow wondered if they were going to fly right off her face.

"Catalpah is a hundred and seventy-five. *And*, they're both male. Boy, you'd never know, would you? I think pretty much most Sylphs here in the city ARE male, because of that change thing they went through."

Then she added the piece the Sylph had added just before being interrupted, "Well, *most* are, she said. I think there actually are some who *are* still female, but she didn't actually say; looks like we *still* don't know who's who," lamented Rainbow.

"Yeah we do. China and Cat are both male, oh my God! Bud's a male, obviously, I mean, I guess. Lark's a male. Right? And Flem, Flem's a male," asserted Mayapple.

"Oh, that's right, *you* would know." Rainbow gave Mayapple an appraising look, one that fairly screamed at her to divulge all, and continued with "How long have you been, ah, *straightening* his feathers, so-to-speak?" she bluntly asked, remembering clearly that little incident back in the changing room.

Mayapple turned a becoming shade of pink and corrected her: "*Preening*. I was helping him with a couple of rough spots, that's all."

"And what else have you *seen* while you two were *preening*?" Rainbow asked in a sweet voice.

"Oh stop," Mayapple commanded. "Flem and I are friends, good friends, but that's all. Now, do you want me to tell you about their vines or not?"

Snapping at the bait like a hungry trout, Mayapple chuckled at Rainbow's instant affirmation, "Yes, yes, yes!"

"Don't bite the hook," laughed Mayapple.

"What?"

"Never mind," she said, quickly launching into Chinaberry's tale of gene programs and hormones that could kick on anytime from thirty-five to seventy-five. And the different colors each Sylph sported. It was all told in fits and starts with rampant speculation on both humans' parts every step of the way until they suddenly found themselves at a Y intersection, complete with large log planter bursting with color.

"I guess we beat them here, I don't see anybody, do you?" said Mayapple, looking around.

"Well, Bud did say we'd be on the other side of this crazy place, and we are," answered Rainbow. "I'd imagine that little café is straight across from us."

"Let's go out to the railing and look," Mayapple urged. "C'mon, they're not here yet," but as she said this, something thunked onto her, bouncing off her head.

Her hand flew back to smooth over the spot and she looked around to see nothing.

Rainbow was watching her quizzically and said "What?" just as another unseen missal ricocheted off of *her*.

Spinning around, she too scanned the park-like setting seeing no one.

Both immediately looked up and studied the sturdy so-called limbs stretching above their heads amongst the many stately 'trees.'

All was silent but a wisp of movement caught Mayapple's attention and her eyes never left the spot as she deliberately walked closer, seamlessly maneuvering around obstacles until she stood below a fat limb.

"F-l-e-m?" she asked the air and the tree. "Are you-?" but she got no further because a myriad of hushed giggles drifted down and covered her.

Within seconds leaves quivered and branches shook as faeries wiggled and became more comfortable, laughing and talking.

By now, both women were standing with heads thrown back, hands on hips, searching for who was saying what, squinting to get a better look.

Finally, Flem's voice rang out, "For Pan's sake, get up here."

Four other opinions hopped on board and the humans finally understood that there was a stairway carved around back that Sylphs never used, it was for the *humans* who were lucky enough to be friends with a faerie, (or two) and whom had gotten an invitation to the exclusive *top floor* of the *S* Club. Or as in Mayapple's case, had harangued certain of the fae involved until they had said *yes*.

As they stepped around back, Mayapple kicked off her shoes, flexing her toes, salivating with anticipation. Rainbow's sparkling red heels soon clattered right behind them, and, hitching up their elegant but inappropriate tree-climbing finery, the two human guests at a fae club, started to climb. Toes curled over warm wood edges getting the hang of this new element, although really, there was no danger. The steps might have been small but there was an unassuming adjacent handrail for those with*out* wings, poor dears. So thoughtful of Sylphs. As usual.

Mayapple's head came higher and higher, along with the rest of her and Flem's eyes met hers, waiting.

She grinned in delight, it was really such a joy.

"Come over here, you can sit by us," invited Flem. Lark immediately moved farther out on the limb they were holed up on and Flem followed, creating a big space for Mayapple right at the beginning, near the large crotch.

Thank goodness she had lacy leggings on because she couldn't resist putting a leg over each side so that she was facing out, towards Flem, her dress practically to her waist.

That silly Flem faerie was now hanging from his elbows down into the air, his wings held out loosely behind him, ready to pop into action if need be, toes curling up and knees locked straight down.

It made Mayapple nervous.

Lark was astride the great branch also, just like Mayapple only they both faced in, towards Flem.

Rainbow thought they looked pretty cozy and kept on going, wondering what she'd find, when she came to a little landing and got off to walk around.

Voices were calling her name, three voices, calling her like a kitty, cajoling, enticing, promising, begging.

Quick laughter bubbled up her throat and she giggled in nervousness and anticipation.

On the other end of the platform, on the other side of the tree, where two thick long limbs stuck out at different angles from beneath the walkway, sat the Trio, Bud on one of the limbs, with China and Cat on each side but their legs dangled from the platform where they sat. Small, hollowed out areas dotted the entire area, seating for a crowd.

China and Cat each moved out a little, indicating Rainbow should plop herself down right between them, with Bud right in front of her. He smiled warmly and Rainbow smiled back, gulping a little at what'd she'd gotten herself into. China and Cat both massaged a shoulder very softly and it felt so good, she didn't worry too long. Bud patted her knee briefly, handing her his own engraved flask with the signature rose bud in one corner.

Gratefully, she tippled it back, delighting in the mellow soothing flavor of the mead. "What is this?" she asked, licking her lips which all three faeries noticed.

"Mmm. It's buttercup and honey. It's new," Bud answered languidly, twitching one shoulder. "Very smooth, isn't it?"

"Umm," agreed Rainbow, relaxing under the skillful massage her shoulders were getting and that wee softening sip of Bud's homemade elixir.

"Do you *all*, always bring your own flasks?" she asked as she melted inch by inch into their grasp.

Heads nodded as Bud replied, "It's pretty much a given although that Egret's Beak they carry *is* awfully good." He slumped a little and Rainbow thought he looked kind of tired.

"Here, lean back, and I'll rub your shoulders," she impulsively offered, goodwill expanding exponentially at this late hour of the evening.

Bud fluttered and hastened to comply, his wings and back now in front of Rainbow as they both faced the same direction, out from the tree.

Catalpah and Chinaberry scootched a little closer to Rainbow and leaned in until they were a knot of four.

Wings came up on either side of the human but it was a sad state of affairs, as those two silly Sylphs had drank quite a lot.

Bud was pretty relaxed himsylph and Rainbow had the opportunity to study the wings so close to her nose and noticed a rough patch, right near the base. She could *see* it. There were translucent *scales* of some kind and they snapped together in most places but she could *tell* these were unzipped. It was plain.

Without even thinking she reached out and tried to finger the edges together but they didn't close as easily as she thought they should have.

"Spit," offered Catalpah.

"Saliva," corrected Chinaberry.

"Works better with a little, ah, *water*," clarified Bud.

"Here," sang out China and leaned in over the human to throw hersylph face forward at Bud's wingulacture, slightly pushing Rainbow to one side.

A slurping sound was heard as Chinaberry mouthed the entire area unsylphconsciously then leaned back again and said, "Have at it," with a flick of the wrist, offering up Bud's back like it was a tasty morsel on a serving platter and she the hostess.

A high giggle escaped but Rainbow leaped in with both hands and Buddleia's wings crackled into place.

"Ooh!" she cried, "I'll do you guys next!!"

Obligingly, both Sylph female impersonators half turned a wing towards her. Their scales were dry and Rainbow sat perplexed for the moment, trying to work up the nerve to put her *mouth* down there, when Cat heaved a deep dramatic sigh and said, "Here. Lean forward, closer to Bud, and I'll do the honors."

Rainbow did and Catalpah zoomed in, practically laying on her belly across the floor behind Rainbow to hurriedly wet the scales at the base of Chinaberry's wingulacture.

"Well," Catalpah harrumphed as she sat up again, "just be sure to save some of those magic fingers for me too," but Bud came to the rescue and soon all four were being petted and preened and stroked together.

Meanwhile, things were moving kinda slow down below...

Mayapple leaned back and watched Flem fiddle around and wished he would not hang like that, with his heels in thin air, even if they were in a contrived tree. There was still a pretty good drop to the ground.

And Lark just sat there with a silly Sylph smile on his face, watching Flem do nothing and Mayapple wondered just how much he'd had to drink.

Nobody said anything and Mayapple was rather disappointed that suddenly it was dull. Maybe it was time to go home. I mean, it was no fun just sitting here like a lump on a log.

A groan of pleasure drifted to her ears and she stilled, listening to see if that's what it was.

Hmm. The giggles and laughter she'd been hearing were noticeably absent.

She wondered strongly just what was going on up the tree further. What were they doing?

A startling burst of wings beating furiously, panicking, erupted in front of her as Flem must have fallen asleep and slipped.

Seat first, he plummeted from his perch, catching himsylph rather awkwardly, nose close to but not touching the ground, wings doing their job and keeping him afloat. But it was embarrassing, no doubt about it.

Lark was beside him instantly checking to see if he was alright and although he didn't laugh there was a suspicious twitch to his mouth, which Flem ignored and Lark fought to keep under control.

But Mayapple sat there, riveted by the incident, her fist against her tight lips until she finally relaxed and let go of the adrenalin that had accompanied the rush of fear.

Oooh, that *faerie*! And then the reactionary giggles started, erupting up from her belly, on through her chest, and out her mouth like rats running from a burning ship. Traitorous wretches.

Peals of gaiety rang through the air and Flem flew right on by her, cha, and kept on going 'til he reached the landing where he slipped in, nice as could be, furling, and feeling much better. That Mayapple. He was just not going to talk to her, Pan, she was so *rude*. She wasn't coming here again! At lease, not with him. Hmmmph.

"Flem, everything okay?" came Bud's voice from behind the trunk, on the other side of the tree. "What's got Mayapple going?" he added as China and Cat both started to giggle. It started out as sympathetic giggling but they each had a funny bone easily roused and soon they too were rollicking where they sat, Mayapple was so contagious.

Lark flew in and distracted all of them by walking past Flem and around to where the other three sat, not so gently nudging all three with a foot and saying, "Move over, would you?" before continuing with a "Ma petit, come over here," directed at Flem and then, " Mayapple," he called loudly to catch her still tittering self, "climb up here. Come on. We'll all sit together. And QUIT your laughing! Cha! You too China and Cat."

He actually sounded so cross even Flem cracked a smile and then they all chuckled, just in time for Mayapple to arrive.

"What are *you* laughing at?" she asked dubiously, suddenly self conscious about her behavior.

Flem's smile slipped easily back into place as his heart opened and he took a step back to see the bond they all shared, one of love and acceptance. "Come on. Find a seat. There's plenty."

Sure enough, like a giant wooden fruit patiently waiting for its seeds, empty concave spots abounded, beckoning to be filled, both limbs sporting their share up and out of sight.

Eyes lighting up, she picked her way through the crowd and found her own little niche.

Everybody settled back down, all within close proximity to one another and audible sighs were heard as everyone relaxed, the high energy of the evening finally waning.

On the outskirts between Catalpah and Flem, but within easy reach of Bud and Rainbow, Mayapple stretched her legs out but them pulled them back under her and leaned out to pat Flem's shoulder, sort of a gratitude and apology all wrapped into one.

He clasped her hand over his shoulder and glanced up.

Whimsey C. Nimble

"Thank you," she whispered, squeezing wingulacture disguised as a shoulder blade.

He nodded, and then as her fingers kept going, rubbing and prodding, his face changed to one of pure pleasure and she smiled to herself watching him. Ah, wing rub.

Everyone was furled except for Cat and China on the outside, but even their wings hung rather dispiritedly after such a night.

Lark was just on the other side of Flem so it wasn't long before wandering fingers came questing his way, as Flem carried forward the love.

Catalpah suggested that perhaps Rainbow would like to further her acquaintance with *her* back once again which make Chinaberry roll her eyes and turn to Bud with a possessive touch, pulling him towards her.

Bud went willingly but just couldn't stand it anymore and wormed his way between Chinaberry and Rainbow, so he could unfurl.

Flem and Lark lost the last bit of tension that had been holding their furl in place and both unrolled about the same time.

"Oops! Sorry Mayapple. Are you okay? I didn't get you, did I?" asked Flem with real concern as his wings sprang from his back to the outside of the circle.

She uttered a short bark and replied, "No!" but thinking it was good she had such quick reflexes even after such a long night and God knows how much mead...

Everyone settled back down, each Sylph turned just right to accommodate wing spread as they all sat around, high off the ground in the big old *tree*.

Bud reached over and put a hand on both Catalpah and Mayapple, while Chinaberry took one hand off of Bud and repositioned it on Rainbow.

Everyone was connected, reassuring and being reassured they were a part of all.

Flem fell into a sort of daze, one where his mind took in the awe of the moment but he was too tired to be properly overcome, thus affording him the luxury of contemplation from a very safe and secure point.

These, these *Sylphs*, these *women*, were so wonderful, so *important* in his life. Suddenly he had family and was not the outsider. He was new, yes, but he belonged.

He snuggled deeper into the moment, his energy easily encompassed by Mayapple's presence close by and Lark's just ahead.

Tonight definitely was a turning point, he realized, feeling much closer to these kindred spirits. And they *were* ALL kin, of that there was no doubt. He'd never experienced such bonding as this, even as a Sylphette. *Then*, everyone was trying to prove themsylves, *now* it was about recognizing the best, or worst, of yoursylph in others, and not judging but simply accepting everyone for who they were. Really, each just wanted the best for everyone. So simple.

At least, with his circle! Here he was, one hundred and twenty four years old which wasn't very old by fae standards, six years an unhappy male, five months happy faerie, yes, who was still male, but he found he liked himsylph and that's all that mattered.

Yes, he could say for sure, he had tuned a corner. And, it was all new yet.

He looked over to see Bud, China, Cat and Rainbow all collapsed in a half stack, Rainbow having no problem licking a scale on Chinaberry's back. Bud was leaning towards them, but his chin was propped up in his hands where he sat with his elbows on his knees, wings rather droopy as he watched the love fest, admiring Rainbow's choice of hair.

Flem loved them all. This camaraderie was what was important. Too many didn't understand that *all* are equal, no matter what you looked like, male or female, faerie or human, wings or no wings. Who cared? Love and a sense of humor were all that was required.

Being honest, he also knew he'd had to take a step up and admit he had good instincts, to acknowledge to himsylph that he had worth. His track record proved it. (These last few months, anyway.) Sylphconfidence had grown with every step along the way as he had proven himsylph to himsylph, realizing he was not a loser if he didn't *act* like one.

Again, made a mental note to not drink so much but considering where he'd been and where he was now, he knew he was doing pretty good. He really didn't drink at all like he used to. Yes, he still drank to excess occasionally and he was working on that but overall, he was a new Sylph.

He was the one who had taken the steps to better himsylph. He'd gotten healthy. Healthi*er*, anyway. Even without these friends of his, Pan forbid such a thing should ever happen, he would be okay.

Had he turned a corner? Ha! Absolutely! A definite yes. Actually, more a *divine* yes.

Whimsey C. Nimble

It was all about trust. Trusting your own instincts, trusting goodness, trusting in the Universe to support you as it would if you relaxed and paid attention to the signs posted, subtle as they may be. It was just a matter of having enough confidence to do your best at whatever was on your plate, so-to-speak.

Plates, hmph. That gave him an idea.

"Hey!" he said, but it came out rather quiet, so he cleared his throat and tried again, "Hey!"

Acknowledgement sounded around him in various small voices.

"Hey," he said a third time. "I've got a *great idea*. Let's all have a party! Well, I mean," he stumbled, "*I'm* having a party! Next year, a year from to-night. What do you think? Want to come?"

Chapter 75

Fine Chocolate was not something to be truffled about.

*L*ARK PADDED BAREFOOT around the houseboat wearing nothing but a little turquoise and silver number that sparkled whenever he walked through a patch of direct sunlight.

Tonight was Flem's party.

Lark had helped of course, but...... his mind went blank and he stopped in mid-thought as the strangest feeling came over him, almost a nauseousness.

His hand came out to steady himsylph, palm against the sky-blue cupboard.

What was going on?

It was like a great intake of air was swooshing into his lungs except that, his *breathing* was not in sync with it...

There was a small electrical charge, a live spark it seemed, that skated down his backbone just once, a zip line of fire leaving havoc in its wake. Sympathetic nerve endings lighted up in response laterally across his chest, jumping from nipple to nipple, meeting around back again before winking out simultaneously.

But that was not all.

Other areas were having *their* reactions.

His groin tightened spasmodically several times and he had the oddest feeling, like things were, well, *changing*, somehow.

It didn't make any sense and it left him feeling very unsettled.

Whimsey C. Nimble

Back in Thimbleberry Canyon, Whimsey C. Nimble had finally been able to tear hersylph away from Nimblenook and was now climbing the small stairs that led up into Windfall Café, a long, rounded, bus-like affair that housed her best friend's business.

The bells announcing her weren't loud enough to suit her so she whacked them soundly on the way by.

"Whimsey! Do you mind? Cha!" complained the smaller of the two Sylphs, the one with a penchant for dark dramatic colors- reds, blacks, chocolate browns, rich golds, and a bit of forest green to compliment them.

"Sorry," Whimsey automatically responded, but they both knew she was unrepentant and would more than likely do it again.

"Ready?" asked Pootsy, a bit of disproval evident still in her tone.

"I'm here, aren't I? Yeah, let's go." She paused before adding, "I'm sure glad the grapevine still works. This party of Flumaria Greenwood's ought to be really, *ahem*, interesting. You remember what she was like, don't you?"

They looked at one another. Neither had seen Flumaria, *Flem* as he was now called, for years.

"Oh yes," replied the café owner as she turned out the lights, checked the stove and made sure all the windows were locked. No sense *inviting* Sprites in, if you could help it.

Bud had assured them there was no sweeter faerie than Flem, that he'd *changed* quite a bit and that they could trust *Lark's* word, couldn't they?

Which was true. Lark and Bud went way back and although neither spent much time in the canyon anymore they still played hooky every now and then and showed up for a drink, usually when things got overwhelming in the outside world.

Still, it was hard to imagine. I mean, *really*, Flumaria had always been so pathetic. It was sad.

Unfurling, they took off, buzzing straight up to above tree top level and continued at a decent rate down canyon. The plan was to fly to Cow Valley straight ahead several miles and then on to the southern edge, where they would tie wings down, change clothes, and walk or hitchhike the rest of the way to San Francoa Ramosa.

The two faeries sitting on the top step up to Bud's treehouse looked like sisters waiting to go to a party.

Someone had gotten out of control with glitter and it looked it.

Bud was rather taken aback at just how, well, *sparkly* these two looked tonight. He wondered if they had gotten into his mead this afternoon while we was gone. Even their eyelids had gotten the treatment and he resolved to be on his toes tonight because he did *not* want a lot of glitter all over his good charcoal-grey tunic. Or his little red silk scarf.

"I take it you two are completely ready?," he asked tentatively, before walking back towards their sleeping quarters where he had left Flem's house-warming gift.

"Oh, oh we've got to get Flem's presents, where are they, do you know?" Catalpah was very agitated to have forgotten them but Chinaberry shook her head at her sister Sylph and partner and said, "They're right there, *we* didn't forget them, *I* knew where they were all along. Oh Buddleia, do be a dear and grab that bag as you go by the counter. Yes. Good. Thanks. Well, *we're* ready. Are you?"

There were times when Bud wondered what he was doing, living with these two wild and bossy creatures, but it was just so hard *not* to.

He himsylph had had a custom-made hammock woven just for him, or rather, them. It was a triple and he'd never seen any for sale so he'd contacted someone from the canyon and ordered it.

He knew others wondered about their three way relationship but he was Sylph enough to not care. It was his life. Being a master mead maker didn't hurt either. Most didn't pry but of course, there *were* the Vinca Pinks of the world who not only had slippery hands but slippery tongues too, and not just in the way of scale licking either. Those that wanted to know everything about you, who seduced anyway they could. He'd found it best to simply smile through her and back away as unobtrusively as he could, any time they met.

He took a deep breath and returned to the present. "Let's go, *ladies*." He stepped out the open door, turned and locked it, then stuck out an elbow on each side in invitation.

"Pan!" he continued. "I should have told Lark yes we needed a ride. Now we'll have to take the bus."

"What?" squawked Chinaberry.

Cat pulled sharply on the other arm in a reprimand at such thoughtlessness.

"Oh don't sweat it, I've got enough for all our fares."

Whimsey C. Nimble

"Bud!" A plaintive cry from one side.

By this time they were down the lane and out to the sidewalk. A car was seen approaching in the distant and within a minute a green and white taxi had pulled right to the curb.

Unable to keep from smiling in sylphsatisfaction, Bud hardly reacted to the sly pinches and pokes he was getting in return for his teasing, merely opening a door and ushering the purple and green splashes into the back seat.

Mayapple checked her image in the mirror, then tuned her back to see what she looked like from the side and behind, chin over shoulder.

Liking what she saw, she slipped on a long necklace of silver beads with small round amethysts in between each one.

The transparent and sleeveless purple silk top was on the order of a vest but hung to her knees. It matched the color of her thin cotton leggings exactly, hanging nicely over the form fitting top of indigo blue with swirls of black, purple, and soft pink. She wore no shoes other than the flip flops she'd found at a discount store.

She had liked her new haircut she'd gotten for her first trip to the *S* Club so well that she'd never looked back and did not miss all that heavy long hair. In fact, she'd gone even shorter in what the stylist had called a '*pixie*,' wispy curls sticking out impishly and unruly.

Mayapple still snorted and giggled over that one, wondering for the umpteenth time if pixies were related to faeries. Ha!

Blowing a kiss to her reflection, her eyes as always were drawn to the small sparkling diamond that sparkled from the side of her nose. Painful, but *so* worth it.

Satisfied, she picked up her purse and a skinny, gaily wrapped, five-foot-long package.

It was time to leave.

Rainbow Merkiva seemed to spring from the middle of soft and short velvet petals, her body-hugging top a dark greenish black with impossible short sleeves that emerged stiffly, like epaulets, above the pastel pinks, blues, golden greens and the occasional soft metallic brown of her flower-like skirt.

A charming package, especially with bare legs and slippers of the same material as her top.

Only one thing left to do and she deftly laid out a quick reading for the evening ahead to see what she could expect. Turning over the card that represented the *past*, she laughed at what she saw: an ant, representing patience. Ha ha, she didn't have to wait any longer, the party was now! Flipping over the *present*, a sleek otter looked out at her and she smiled at the compliment, otter signifying balanced female energy, the kind that creates a space for others unconditionally, joyful in all's accomplishments.

Switching back, she turned over the next one, *future*, and there was the raven, her favorite. *Magic.* A good portend for the evening ahead.

She had to laugh as beaver appeared next in *just completed* and so true as she had been busy, busy, busy all day. Wondering what else was happening at this moment, she flipped over *going through your life right now*, and of course it was antelope. Action!

Holding her breath she reached out and overturned the second to last card, *what is working against you*, and mouse sat there. Scrutiny. Well, that made sense. Tonight was a time to *party*, not sit and analyze everything. Quickly she turned over the last one which represented *what is working for you*, and it was none other than eagle. Eagle, which represented *Spirit*. Grateful for the overt reminder, she reverently closed her eyes and offered up a brief prayer of gratitude and love before picking up the cards and setting them aside. Grabbing her purse, she picked up a package about the same size as the cards she'd just put down but one wrapped in holographic silver paper, and was out the door.

Seven fifteen, that evening.

Flem was home alone and his stomach was in knots. It was exactly one year ago tonight he'd invited everyone back for a party, here, and that party was now only fifteen minutes from commencing.

Everything was perfect. That helped. If ever there was a good time to sit down and relax, this was surely it. He stepped around the heavily laden counter that separated the kitchen from the rest of the place, situated to the

Whimsey C. Nimble

immediate left of the front door. The two-part blue and yellow door was in the same location the window door had been but that was its only similarity. The top half was a giant setting sun. Its extended rays were painted yellow with great overtures of orange that held just a hint of red, along the 'horizon.' Three unidentifiable bumps marred the otherwise smooth line and it wasn't until the door was closed that one saw the 'bumps' for what they were, for the bottom half was the big blue sea, all waves, with a pod of dolphins playing amongst them near the 'horizon,' three whose backs extended just a bit above, backlit into the sinking sun.

This masterpiece now stood open, in invitation.

Deciding he'd earned it, he headed for the table with the mead and poured himsylph half a hen, fondly smiling at this little chicken-shaped glass. Before he brought it to his lips, he held it up and toasted the greenhouse, once again mentally blessing Iris Fletcherman.

A lot had been accomplished in this past year. He had invested all his extra money into remodeling and it showed. And while Lark was here constantly, it was still Flem's abode. He in turn spent a lot of time on the houseboat, which was definitely Lark's domain.

Slowly he took a sip and contemplated the changes he'd seen come into his life.

The first change of course had been extremely unwanted, throwing *her* life into complete disarray. Actually, Flem realized that that wasn't true. It was the non-turning- *back*-change that he'd *thought* had ruined his life.

It had taken him over five years of senseless drinking and moaning and groaning and bewailing his fate before he got sick of himsylph and decided to try and get a job. Not sure how to proceed, fate had stepped in with an opportunistic find – stacks of old gardening magazines someone had left out by the curb for trash collection. He'd carried each and every one back to his cave, that hole under a rock he'd found, and read them from cover to cover, fascinated by how much thought humans actually put into gardening. He had known quite a bit already but by the time he was done, he knew a *lot*.

Again, not sure how to go about finding a job in a city of humans, it had to be pure synchronicity that took his feet through Fletcherman's Nursery that one day, lost in admiration.

Iris was watering and they'd started talking, one thing led to another and he was very gratified that he'd been able to keep right up with her for the most part, as she talked plants, until out of the blue she'd asked him if by any chance he was looking for work?

He had dumbly nodded his head and the next thing he knew, he had a full time job!

In retrospect, it appeared that the golden road to happiness was built one little step at a time. First, there must be a desire to change but the important thing was to be able to lay aside the need to know exactly *how* to go about it. It seemed to him that just holding the desire for freedom in his heart had opened a doorway in his consciousness and opportunities were thusly magnetized to him.

First the desire. Second, following his own interests, the magazines, and third, saying *yes* when an opportunity presented itself! Now it all seemed divinely guided; then it had seemed like just dumb luck.

Glancing at the time, his heart jumped when he saw it was now seven twenty-five and he could not believe Mr. Spurastic was *not* here yet.

Just as he was reaching for a sunflower crisp, footsteps were heard practically running to his front door and who should pop through but that very Sylph, one stylish foot first followed by a black, loosely woven pant leg.

Relieved but now having the luxury of aggravation since he was *here*, Flem started to make a remark but one look at Lark and he stopped.

"What's the matter?" he asked, as Lark smiled tremulously at him and then to Flem's horror he saw tears fill his beloved's eyes. "*Lark*, what *is* it?"

The faerie looked wildly around and to his relief saw no one.

"The place looks *great*," he blurted but Flem was having none of it. Taking Lark's arm, he led him through the kitchen, past the table and out the back door, fennel wafting faintly on the evening breeze.

Heading over to the fire pit he pulled his lover down in a more intimate setting, putting an arm around him and handing him his own hen which he had kept in one hand.

"*Tell me*," he ordered, as Lark took an obligatory sip.

Under a discrete arch of greenery stood a charming wooden gate, long slim slats so close together it was impossible to see between them.

It fit nicely into its niche when closed, which was most of the time. At the moment though, it stood open.

Whimsey C. Nimble

Pootsy and Whimsey C. Nimble picked their way daintily down the long hidden walkway that Bud had told them about. It had helped that there was a bouquet of flowers right at the edge of the hedge. Also, an elegant little sign had pointed down the secret garden path, just through the wooden gate. It had an elegant scripted 'F' on it, plus one gaily painted balloon, both done in a bold fuchsia with a slim black arrow below to point the way.

Giggling in nervousness the two Sylphs from Thimbleberry Canyon crept along, fingers trailing in the shiny green foliage.

"What is this?" asked Whimsey curiously and was about to add, honey-suckle or jasmine, when Pootsy spoke up.

"Poison oak."

Whimsey jerked her hand away as if she'd just discovered a reptile, even though she KNEW it wasn't poison oak.

"It is not. Cha!"

"Gotcha!" shouted Pootsy, laughing. "Hey, hold up." She went on, "Here, let's have a nip for nervousness." She reached into a pocket and extracted her small flask.

"Now that we're here we can start the evening," and she unscrewed the top and handed it to her bosom pal, Whimsey.

Nodding at her cohort in agreement, Whimsey shifted, slinging her backpack around and off her shoulder to carry. It had her gift in it for Flem and it made a bulky lump.

After sharing a tipple, they continued on through the little hidden path, following a decided bend to the left. Lights could be seen through the woodsy tangle and soft voices murmuring in the not-too-distance were heard.

It certainly hadn't been the plan to eavesdrop, I mean, they hadn't been espe-cially quiet, just their normal stealthy Sylphs sylves.

They had come to the end of the so-called tunnel and paused, more to just catch their breath and get their bearings than to *listen*, for Pan's sakes.

Whomever was sitting over by the fire pit, not too far past the catalpah tree which was right in front of them, had clearly just revealed an amazing secret, one that obviously was not meant for anyone else's ears.

The two hidden guests looked wildly at one another and Pootsy Koon's hidden wings clattered in response, irritatingly tied down.

They both backed up. Eyes wide, they looked helplessly at each other.

"Let's go back!" pantomimed Pootsy frantically, pointed and pulling Whimsey with her.

"SSST! Get ahold of yoursylph," hissed Whimsey, shaking the other's grip off of her. "Let's *think* a minute."

Pootsy spoke up and said, "I bet *that* wasn't part of the party plan."

Whimsey darted a look at her and ruefully nodded, "Yeah. I'll bet you're right. Cha!"

"C'mon, let's creep back the way we came. I think I saw a thin spot back before the corner. Let's see if we can find a different way in. Surely there's more than this one."

Within two minutes they were cutting across a yard of some kind and heading for what had to be the party place, a brightly illuminated old fashioned greenhouse but one that was obviously now a residence.

"Look," commanded Whimsey, stopping Pootsy so she could point out something. "That's vintage glass. I wonder what it looks like inside?"

"Well, Bud said the owner Iris Fletcherman, *gave* Flem this place and that he's been fixing it up ever since. Suppose to be pretty fae."

They turned right just past the end of the greenhouse which was now smothered in a cacophony of growing vines, but unlike music, this cacophony didn't hurt the ears.

Both stopped to stare.

Heavy exotic-looking blooms that almost didn't look real dotted a large swath all the way up and over.

"Beautiful," breathed Whimsey.

Pootsy nodded. "Passion flower, right?"

"Yeah, I don't know which Passiflora, but probably the alatocaerrulea variety, it's the best known. I only remember it because I know someone named Kay Rully, and I think of this as her plant – 'All to Cae Rulea.' Ha ha."

Pootsy rolled her eyes at such foolishness, further studying the heavy foliage. Bright orange trumpet flowers could be seen in amongst it all, along with a myriad of others – wisteria, ivy, jasmine, sweet sweet honeysuckle, and of course beautiful white climbing roses that reminded Whimsey of dogwood blooms. (She actually *knew* someone back in the canyon named Dogwood Blooms but she meant the botanical kind.)

"Well, he's certainly created a privacy curtain, hasn't he? Just imagine this thicket when it turns into a jungle within a few years."

"Hey, I planted some of those vines, be careful what you say!" thundered a voice from behind them

Both country faeries spun around and Buddleia laughed, flanked as he was by his two bright sparkly friends. Pootsy gracefully inclined her head at seeing Bud's sidekicks again and introduced Whimsey. The flask passed and all babbled at once in true Sylph fashion, gradually making it inside the door, where they stopped, briefly.

It was pretty quiet.

China and Cat immediately drifted into the kitchen and started looking over the food, two Christmas lights who'd run away from home.

Bud, who was obviously no stranger here, called out, "Hoo hoo? Hoo hoo? Flem?"

Whimsey and Pootsy looked at each other rather nervously, both wondering if the news they'd overheard would have an effect on the party but at that moment the back door opened and in walked that handsome fae guy, Lark Spurastic and it had to be Flumaria Greenwood with him, but it wasn't the same Flumaria Greenwood that *they* had known!

Lark rushed over to embrace them, pulling Flem along, one hand tightly clasped in his. They had just had an extremely emotional moment and he wasn't about to let go yet.

Flem's eyes were bright but at least his wings were not chattering and he pulled forth that inner faerie, the Sylph of steel within us all.

Gripping Lark's hand extra tight, he exhaled rather breathlessly as this was a sweet, *sweet* moment and he wanted to give it his full attention.

These were two Sylphs he'd known back in Thimbleberry. Most of his Canyon memories were not that pleasant and *most* Sylphs from back in those days didn't hold a lot of pleasant memories for him. These two on the other hand, had *always* treated him with respect. He was most gratified and honored that someone or someon*es*, namely Bud and Lark, had invited them. His fabulous renovated old greenhouse, his relationship with Lark, and his easy camaraderie with *other* Sylphs, not to mention his recent promotion at work to being manager of his own section, all sat about his shoulders like a royal cape of sylphconfidence.

More voices were heard talking and laughing, some coming from out back while others traipsed around the outside and within minutes, more and more guests started arriving.

Flem stepped back from the door while Lark and Bud moved off together, Lark casting a questioning look at Flem.

Smiling brightly, Flem shooed them away and turned to meet and greet his guests.

Whimsey C. Nimble and Pootsy Koons moved around to the other side of the counter, sampling as they went.

"Hey look, isn't that your dish?" Whimsey held up a small nasturtium wrap filled with pineapple cream cheese.

"I don't have an exclusive on that. Cha, I've eaten them at practically every party I've ever gone to!" retorted her friend.

Whimsey wasn't paying attention but was focused on the food. "Oh, look here, *cherries*. Yum." She bit into one to reveal a deep, blood-red interior, crisp but juicy, as evidenced by the red trickle down her chin.

Mayapple then burst through the entryway keyed up as usual, the long brightly wrapped package sort of behind her back. A little too giddy, she thrust out an arm and squeezed her faerie tight, rather awkwardly, bumping his lumpy wings that were hidden under layers of greens, a long slinky green and black velveteen scarf dangling from his neck.

"Ooh, sorry!" she apologized. "I'm just a wee bit excited! Ooh ooh ooh, who's *that*?" She was staring at Whimsey and Pootsy, who had by now made their way to the table where Flem had set out a variety of meads, along with small glasses he'd gleaned from thrift shops over the past year.

"Did we meet them at the *S* Club? I don't remember them, if we did..." she whispered emphatically in an aside just for his ears.

"No, no, they're friends of mine, well, ah, ours, from back in the canyon."

"*No*. Really?"

"I'll introduce you in a minute. I'm sure you've heard me mention them," Flem said. "In the meantime, you got your haircut again, Mayapple!" as if she didn't know.

Whimsey C. Nimble

"Yeah, guess what it's called, Flemmy! It's a *pixie*. Hah!"

Flem cringed but before either could continue Bignonia, Vinca Pink and Wonga Wonga stepped through, looking around and Whimsey and Pootsy came right back to help look at the newcomers.

Vinca's Pink shown especially well, set off as it was between her two vigorous and colorful companions bedecked in vibrant greens, purples and oranges.

"*Pixies*? Here? I don't see any," deadpanned Pootsy to Whimsey who went right along with it of course. The more nonsense these two could stir up and laugh about, the better they liked it.

"*Where* are the pixies? You didn't invite *sprites* too, did you *Flemmy*?" asked Whimsey with a straight face and a batting of eyelashes, making sport of Mayapple's pet name for him.

Ah yes, Sylph parties. You better be able to take it, because once that group got going, nothing and no one was safe from Sylph wit, or what passed for it in the presence of that golden nectar of the Gods and Goddesses – mead.

Bright eyed, Mayapple's lips pressed into a thin line as these two unknowns raked their fingers through Flemmy's hair, pinching his cheek, tweaking his well hung scarf, and patting him like they were old friends… *Her* faerie.

She just stood there, taking it all in, two red spots highlighting her cheekbones, set off so nicely by her new, short hair cut. A *pixie*. "*Are* there pixies?" she blurted out to the group in general but by now Vinca Pink had come unwound from her buff escorts and rippled her way to Mayapple, eyeballing Whimsey and Pootsy on her way by, eyes overly eager with invitation.

"Beautiful, human honey-child, beautiful," whispered Vinca as she slithered her hands over Mayapple's newly shorn head.

Eyes snapping, Mayapple turned, pulled those hands *off* her head and moved away with a glare and a snort.

A quick little high laugh slipped out as Whimsey tittered in glee at this show of spirit, and she nodded in approval. She liked this human woman who was so *young* by Sylph standards.

When Mayapple shot her a quick look to see whose side she was on, anyway, Whimsey quickly gave her a sympathetic smile and stuck out her hand with an introduction and then said, "Can I pour you a mead?"

Mayapple knew these two had to be faeries too but no-one had their wings out. It must be de rigueur to cover up in Sylph society. At least, in the City. She wondered, not for the first time, what Thimbleberry Canyon was like.

"Yes, I would love a drink," she said, moving around the counter and falling in with Whimsey and Pootsy quite naturally, laying the silent present on the counter, back away from the food.

Vinca wandered off with Bignonia, ("Please, call me Rivers") and Wonga Wonga, both ostensibly two human males with a flamingly vivid human female but nobody was deceived by *that* act for even a minute.

Not only Flem but Whimsey and Pootsy surreptitiously watched the three of them head to the far end of the greenhouse and flop down together on the large inviting wrap-a-round sofa which graced that end of the room. A long, low wooden coffee table sat on the rug in front of it and the three immediately plopped down then propped their feet up and pulled out the inevitable flask, prepared to watch the unfolding.

Flem glanced around to see where Lark was and saw him and Bud still deep in conversation. They were standing on the other side of the room between the seedling bleachers and the *planter* - what Flem called the low, brick-enclosed area three feet out from the wall that ran down one side of the greenhouse, across the back and half-way up the other side. He had peppered it with a garden variety of small citrus such as orange, lemon and lime trees and the ground area was a jumble of romance: calla lilies, ferns, wild strawberries, oxalis, moss, and anything that volunteered, like the asylum, morning glories and wandering Jew. Flem loved it, and had gotten the idea from one of his 'new' gardening magazines. He had not lost his penchant for midnight garbage-run treasure hunts. He had discovered much to his delight that City folk threw away a lot more than garbage. His good fortune.

His bedroom was in the same back corner where he'd originally hung his hammock but it had acquired a big bathroom and sturdy walls, no longer separated by only a flimsy bamboo partition. Lark's hammock still hung right beside his.

There were two doors in his bedroom, one that opened towards the kitchen, across from him in the other back corner, and the other leading out to the main room.

Lark and Bud both had helped him tremendously with the remodel but the design was pretty much his. Lark of course had been extremely insightful.

Whimsey C. Nimble

The back door, now hung properly in its handmade doorframe, had gone through a thorough renovation. Flem had tightened it, oiling rusty hinges and sanding the rough design, which proved to be interlocking vines and hidden flowers. When Lark came over in the evenings, they had enjoyed painting the delicate artwork together.

The screen latched right to it so it could stand together as it did now, leading to the flagstone back yard. Smooth sandstone covered a patio-sized area to the fence that shut out the alley, but didn't go up the side past the original stand of fennel. From that corner, a thyme-edged dirt path ran between the long side of the greenhouse and Flem's front yard.

For safety sake, the flat warm stone also encircled the fire pit out back, just outside Flem's bedroom. Around its perimeter sat low slung canvas seats, holding Lark's original pillows.

Rainbow's voice was heard hailing someone and Flem stepped out the door, an anticipatory smile on his lips.

"Oh, look at you!" exclaimed the woman who, like Mayapple could be fae but wasn't. "YOU look *divine*, darling."

She hugged him enthusiastically and let go just as suddenly when she spied Mayapple inside with two creatures whom she'd never seen before.

Grabbing his shoulders, she planted a quick kiss on his cheek and said, "We'll talk later," then hustled through the door.

Flem was standing with his back to the west side and didn't realize Iris and Santolina had obviously come in another way, alongside the main building, and were taking the long way around, past number one, the planting greenhouse, and then down past numbers two and three and around the outer edge of the lot in a big half circle.

Hearing murmuring voices behind him he turned and saw them strolling on the more deserted work path that eventually came right by the end of his greenhouse, or Greenwood's, as he had named it.

Iris twirled her fingers at him and Santolina nodded but they were strolling arm in arm and in no hurry. Not married yet, they obviously were deeply in love and while Santolina still looked at him, well, *all* of them actually, funny, he was a good guy and Flem was glad to know him.

"Ah ma petit fleur, how's it going?" Lark was beside him and while the voice sounded almost like his own, there was a small catch there, a new note, one of uncertainty.

Before Flem could respond Blossom came trotting towards them in tall black boots, a short black skirt, a black V neck t-shirt, and a black leather jacket. Her hair had been bleached on the ends and she wore it in two high pigtails, each tied with a little red bow which matched her lipstick. She carried a white, tissue-wrapped object that looked heavy, with a purple curly ribbon trailing from it.

"Here," she said shyly, and held it out, awkwardly, as it was heavy. "House-warming gift. Wow," she continued, looking around. "This is so sweet! This yours here?" she nodded at the brightly illuminated greenhouse.

"Yep," said Flem with deep satisfaction. "This is *mine*," never losing the awe he held for this fortune or failing to bless Iris.

Holding the heavy object, he wasn't quite sure what to do with it but the problem was taken out of his hands when Blossom snatched it back and said, "I'll put it inside for you. You look busy," nodding towards the swarm of people coming up the path. She disappeared inside.

Flem was happy to see The Green Thumb's representatives, Acaulis and Schafta Campion on the leading edge.

Surprising the faerie, Iris stepped past him and greeted the two business associates personally, asking after their dad, Moss Campion and their mom, Silene.

Flem kept silent, as did Lark right at his side.

Iris looked coolly elegant in knee length tan linen shorts with a sleeveless black knit top, dull gold slippers on her feet that matching the slim belt, a bright gold bangle on one arm.

Glancing over at the two Sylphs she nodded, eyes crinkling in a royal smile above sparkling half glasses worn only on special occasions and then caught Santolina Galvezia's arm and they stepped through the entry way, his dark brown Bermuda shorts, loafers and Hawaiian shirt blending well with Iris's outfit.

Flem thought Santolina's new thick, well-manicured mustache suited him very well.

The two Campion sons stood respectfully to one side, waiting 'til they had Flem's attention, elbows hardly able to keep from nudging the other over these two fae boys right here, front and center, before them. In fact, they were so stoked to be invited to Flem's greenhouse and party they were practically salivating. *Never* had they resolved the issue of *what* Flem was and speculation ran rampant at all times between them. Their father had told them it was none of their business but nonetheless it was a favorite topic of discussion. They figured tonight there was a good chance of the mystery being solved.

"Come in, come in!" invited the homeowner, reaching out to shake their hands which was rather awkward since Acaulis had his cap in his hands and kept turning it in circles while Schafta held a big round rather shallow planter that was completely grown over with soft springy moss, snuggled in and around little dark caverns and shadows made by strategically placed agates and pieces of drift wood, complete with tiny birds and frogs.

Flem was enchanted with it from the first moment he saw it and tried not to show his excitement but found his mouth saying "Oh, is this for me?" before he could stop himsylph.

Tall gangly Schafta with his dear little tufts of soft purplish hair colored all the way to his ears, saying "Yes! Yes, we thought you might like it. And besides, Dad said to give it to you. We've got another one for Iris too, we'll leave it by the back door of the shop, what-a-ya-think?"

Flem was charmed. "Thank you! Delightful!" and his tied down wings fluttered a moment under his scarf, a movement not missed by either of his guests.

"Come in!" Flem grinned and patted egg-shaped Acaulis on the arm as he pointed their way through the open door.

Music started up inside and Flem and Lark both laughed as they heard the beginning strains of Fairyboat Serenade by the Androsace sisters which was a most popular song at all fae parties. Somewhere along the line, out it would come and all the faerie in the place would sing along. And then no doubt drink more mead.

Flem wondered who had put it on and felt a flush of deep contentment when he heard it now, as it was almost like a stamp of approval in his mind. It was something so normal, that he'd craved back in the old days and here it was naturally, not forced. This party was a success not because of the amount of Sylphs he now knew, but the relationships he'd made.

Suddenly he knew those canyon Sylphs, Whimsey C. Nimble and Pootsy Koons had brought it. They always were so thoughtful.

Who would have thought *they* would have showed up here, that was a surprise!

Flem watched Lark as Lark's attention was riveted by someone coming up the path but blocked from view by a tall, large woman who was dressed in heavy, pale orange silk that just reached her knees and that seemed to swirl with her energy. A little yellow silk scarf with dark splotches of brown adorned her neck, the same color as her eyes.

Flem had forgotten Lilium Superbum's strange eyes 'til she got close and he looked *up* into her eyes.

A natural salesperson, she gave him a hearty smile. "Hi Flem! Thanks for inviting me, nice place you got here!" She nodded once at Lark and kept going, some kind of box in her hand.

Lark was stepping out, going to meet someone, two people Flem didn't recognize who were coming right towards him.

Whoever they were, Lark was hugging them and Flem was astonished to see a young human girl here with this other. Her *father*?

With a sparkle of amusement in his brilliant green eyes, Lark smiled in a rather cryptic manner, then casually said, "Flem, you remember my, ah, *brother*, don't you?" staring at him with great intensity. "*Linaria*." He spoke with great emphasis and this time did a quick wink.

"Ah, that's Uncle Lin tonight. Don't blow my cover, this is so much fun! And *this*," she who was in men's clothing said with a flourish, "is Gypsophilia, our *sister* Lewisia's daughter."

Flems stared at Linaria and thought back to how he'd been so insecure and jealous, highly emotional and prone to dramatics back in the beginning.

He had grown, no doubt about it. No longer so sylphconscious about every little thing he said and did, he had come to trust his instincts, realizing that *he* didn't steer himsylph wrong, that *he* took care of himsylph automatically if he let go and trusted his instincts and intuition and didn't react to everything with 'worst-case scenario-itis.'

"We call her our *Bristol Faerie*, since her dad's a Brit," Uncle Linaria informed.

About that time the name *Lewisia* rang a bell. Lark and Uncle Lin were waiting for Flem to catch up and both nodded at him simultaneously when the light in his eye finally came on and recognition dawned.

Gypsy thought they were *all* rather strange but all the Sylphs she knew were kind of quirky. Except her Sylph mother, who was married to her *human* dad. All her friends were *human*, as were her little sister and brother which was exactly *why* she was here. She was *only* around humans except for that rare visit back in the canyon or when one of her mom's sisters showed up, Linaria being the most regular.

It was hard on her mom at times to be without her sister Sylphs, so they accepted the fact that their mother had wings and their dad didn't and didn't make too much of a fuss about it, for now.

But *mom*, Lewisia, was concerned. Puberty was fast approaching, *human* puberty that is, and Lewisia knew of no one who had mated and born children with a *human* male. When would puberty hit, thirteen or thirty?

She needed her daughter to be around Sylphs, to get a feel for them so that IF those wings came out, or her vines showed up for Pan's sake, or *whatever* happened, she would at least have *some* experience around the fae. Since the canyon was out of the question at this early date, Linaria's idea of letting Gypsophilia come with her to a party where a lot of Sylphs were suppose to be present seemed like a good idea. *She* would be personally responsible, Linaria assured her, as *Uncle* Lin.

"So, are *you* my 'Uncle' too?" asked the girl in a suspicious voice to Lark, eyeballing his back. "What about *you*?" she turned to Flem.

"No, Flem's not," Lark spoke up. "But I guess, *I* am. Hmmph," he went on to reply to her question, a quizzical look upon his face. "Hmmmph," he said again. "Uncle Lark. Fancy that."

The young girl, for all her suspicions, one of which was now confirmed, was nonetheless terribly excited to be here.

A very neat and tidy person by nature, she announced rather archly "I'm hungry," her eyes going wide as she innocently played the group for fun.

Every one of them responded as she'd intended, tripping over themsylves to make her happy and it took both Lark and Flem to escort the girl and her *uncle* to the entryway not six feet away, Flem trying to tell Linaria where the food was.

Lark tugged on his arm and said, "I'll bet they can figure it out on their own. C'mon."

Flem was kind of getting antsy about missing his own party inside but there were more guests gaily tripping up his path, stumbling and la-la-ing, laughing and talking and Lark said in an undertone, "Looks like *someone's* been tipping the old flask already, now doesn't it? Hello!"

Bud, China and Cat chose that moment to fill the doorway behind him and when Bud saw who it was he called back over his shoulder to the threesome on the couch, "Hey Wonga Wonga, Bunya Bunya, Sissy, Sassy, and Jipijapa are here."

Wonga Wonga, Vinca Pink and Rivers came flying, well, not literally, towards the door, spilling out, greeting their fellow disguised Sylphs, everyone talking at once, as usual.

A thick set old human male with big bushy eyebrows, large hairy ears, and a purplish nose almost turned around right then and there but an attractive heavyset woman was standing in his way.

"Who're you? You know these, these *people* too?"

It was rather brusque but Calypso Balboa didn't take offense. Her dead husband's money had provided quite a nice cushion over the years, insulating her from anyone she chose not to interact with. Tonight she was feeling expansive and let his rudeness slide.

"Yes, 'I know' these people and I know Flem there," she clarified. "He really knows his business. I've known him a little over a year now and by God, if he doesn't know the answer to something, he doesn't stop 'til he's got it figured out! And, he's stronger than he looks," she added.

"Hmmmph," grunted the older man, looking at the woman grudgingly with respect. He liked a woman with fire.

"*You're* not, *ah*, well, that is to say, I mean, *you're* human, right?"

Oh, thought Calypso rolling her eyes mentally, you are so tactless. But she liked a challenge. Grumpy here looked like he might clean up well and it was a pretty safe bet that there was no woman in his life. He never would have gotten out of the house in *that* outfit if there was.

Deciding to take pity on the poor man, she linked her arm through his and pulled him along.

"*No*, I'm not one of *them*," she said with a dark, unspoken reprimand at his intimated bigotry. "And so what if I was? What's your problem?"

She did not release her hold on his upper arm and dragged him along with her, closer to the raucous group in front of the door.

"What are *you* doing here, anyway?" She could be just as rude as he was and thought it might be good for him to get a dose of his own medicine. "Sweet on Iris, are ya? Well, you're too late bub, she's engaged."

"Now see here, now see here, young lady, my reason for being here is none of your business. I knew her husband Brody for many years. Good fellow. Glad to see she jumped on it and made a go of this place after he died.

Whimsey C. Nimble

Yes sir, she's always been an attractive lady. Hmmmph. Engaged you say? Her note didn't mention *that*. Hmmmph. That *is* too bad. What's your name, anyway? Mine's Stinkweed, by the way, Jimson Stinkweed," and he held out a hand to shake in mute apology for his bad manners and Ms. Bulbosa thought, now that's more like it.

"Name's Calypso," she answered civilly.

The group at the door couldn't stop talking, everything seeming *vital* that it be said.

Calypso and Stinkweed skirted the group and Flem backed out of the crowd to squeeze Calypso Bulbosa's hand, one of the nursery's best customers, eyeballing Stinkweed at the same time over her shoulder, who eyeballed him right back.

"Hi, nice to see you again," said the polite faerie.

Stinkweed actually hemmed and hawed for a moment before nodding and saying "Yeah, you too," wondering if he should have come at all and hoping he'd find Iris soon. These people looked awfully light in their tights. And you could never tell if the girls were boys or the boys were girls. It made him so uncomfortable. Suddenly he was really glad of the lassie on his arm.

"C'mon Missy," he said to the woman fifteen years his junior and she laughed, because at forty-seven, she wasn't used to being called missy anymore.

They stepped through the open double door and the unruly party of ten followed on their heels, Flem and Lark hanging back, looking around to see if anyone else was arriving and by Pan, there was.

Music and laughter went up a notch inside and Flem looked longingly through the open door, trying not to be impatient, trying to enjoy every second of this evening but he was keyed up, wings throbbing where they lay, nerves jumpy and asking for release but there was nothing he could do but wing-it, so-to-speak. They certainly couldn't come out *now*.

Vervacity Verbascum was upon them, stick-like Vonda practically perched on her arm.

"Hi *Flem*. Hi *Lark*." She gave them both a sultry look which Vonda imitated the best she could but anything more than just looking beautiful was a bit much for her, being the delicate flower that she was.

"Mayapple here tonight?" questioned Vervacity in her deep velvety voice and Flem's stupid eyes went unbiddenly down into her darkly tanned, heaving bosom, where little yellow flowers nestled between the soft quivering mountains before he could get a hold of himsylph and pull his eyes *up*, back to her face.

"Yes!" he said brightly, wondering if he looked as foolish as he felt. "Please, come in. You'll probably find her by the mead! Ha ha," he laughed.

"*Flumaria*," called Mayapple in a high falsetto voice, "are you spreading *rumors* about me again? Hmm, Flumaria?" Obviously, Mayapple was *not* at the mead table although it was equally obvious she'd *been* there. Whimsey and Pootsy flanked her, suspicious smirks on each of their faces and Flem just *knew* they'd all been talking about him. Hmmph. *Flumaria* indeed.

Mayapple continued, "Hello Vervacity! Come in, come in Vonda. Meet my friends, Whimsey C. Nimble and Pootsy Koons. Just here for the party. Flem! Come in!" she commanded as if it were her place, her party! "Anybody else who shows up can just show up, they don't need you personally to greet them, *geeez*. Oh, wait, who's that? *Gary*! Hi, oh look, Garriya's here." She rushed off to meet her friend, the owner of The Silk Tassel, a more upscale clothing establishment.

"C'mon Flem, she's right. This party's *happening*." Lark spoke up as he motioned Vervacity and Vonda to precede him through the door.

Flem quickly capitulated. "I'm going to go take a quick cruise around. You okay?" he asked briefly, his eyes holding Lark's for a breathless second, a world of questions and meaning inherent.

"I'm okay. Go ahead," said the Sylph in his sophisticated black fae human clothing, kissing him lightly on the lips. "Ah ma petit, you are such a success! Go, spread your charming fae Sylph around, rub elbows with your adoring public. Oh, be sure to give Sissy a kiss for me too," and Flem grimaced at the thought.

"Lark. Not nice." He shook his finger at Lark's derogatory comment, mouth twitching. "Go on, I'll see you somewhere."

The first thing he did was look to the kitchen to see how the food was holding out.

Still beautiful, he laughed to himsylph, it must be early. He dropped a handful of blueberries mixed with bits of dark chocolate into his mouth, moving towards the table with the mead, ready for a refill.

Whimsey C. Nimble

"Did you make this?" inquired Blossom, holding up a piece of ginger-bread that was topped with a delicate orange frosting. "This is delicious. What is this?"

"No, *Lark* owns the Blackberry Bakery and he made that. Good, huh? That's gingerbread of course, and I think he uses orange zest and cream cheese somehow. And I think he said something about a teensy amount of orange oil. Yeah," he sighed, "I love licking his bowls."

He went on, "This sponge cake here?" He pointed. "He layers scented geraniums on the bottom first so the whole cake has the most delicate flavor - apple, peppermint, rose, whatever. He's *so* talented," Flem praised, loving to talk about his beloved, Lark Spurastic. And it didn't take much to get him going. Mayapple was eavesdropping behind them and was glad *she* hadn't started the conversation. She had enough of wonderful Lark on the three days a week she worked with Flem. Lark *was* wonderful but really, nobody wanted to hear about it all the time.

Standing at the end of the kitchen counter she looked over at Chinaberry and Catalpah, perched like jeweled twins on the high stools that faced out over the counter into the long open room.

They weren't saying much at the moment, just sat there glittering, keeping an eye on Bud who was hanging out near Gypsophilia, Uncle Lin, and Lark, down at the other end of the room. All four faced the sofa and were bantering with Wonga Wonga, Bignonia (Rivers) and Vinca Pink. Lilium Superbum stood nearby but wasn't saying too much other than adding a word here and there.

Across from her, on the other side of the rug, sat Sissy and Sassy, close enough to the group but not in the thick of it.

Vervacity Verbascum and Vonda stood nearby watching those two new-comers, Whimsey and Pootsy who were on the other side of the room.

Further back stood Acaulis and Schafta, a little removed from every-body and drinking in every detail. Nearby at a large table sat Santolina and Iris, Santolina looking slightly uncomfortable. On their right in a couple of overstuffed chairs sat Stinkweed and Calypso Bulbosa discussing plants and finding out they had a lot in common.

The wilder bunch, Mayapple, Blossom, Rainbow and Garriya hung to-gether in the kitchen, near the mead of course. You could always count on them to be in the thick of it, be it human or Sylph mayhem and in that vein all four of them were doing their best to charm their current companions: Bunya Bunya, Jipijapa and Flem, smiling and flirting.

Flem filled his glass then grabbed the bag of crystallized rose petals, sugar coated violets, blue borage and mint leaves, stuck an open bottle of Egret's Beak under his arm and moved on.

Circulating among all these people he knew, he reflected on how normal this all seemed, a natural progression in his life. More grounded now with the inherent stability that came from having a steady job and a secure place to live, he was able to approach life from a higher perspective, his very *thinking* patterns altered. He had seen it coming together a year ago but it was only as he worked at it every day and clung to his vision with diligence did he realize he was building a solid foundation for life. And the more he looked at the bigger picture, the more he understood that HE was in charge, not some random force that flung him around, and that he could plan from a bigger perspective that would only work if you believed in yoursylph first. Now his thinking patterns were healthy.

Topping off dainty dishes as he moved deeper into the renovated old greenhouse, now his living room, he made his way to where Iris and Santolina sat.

Standing behind Iris, he gave her shoulder a squeeze and said, "Refill?" showing her his bottle.

She looked up at him, eyes crinkling as she nodded.

Deciding now was as good a time as any, he said, "Iris, I, um, I have something for you, it's in my room. Stay here, I'll be right back," and he took off.

Santolina looked over at her and said, "What's that all about?"

Iris gave him a look and said, "Well now, you heard as much as I did, we don't really know yet, do we? We'll have to wait 'til, oh hi Flem. You're back. What's this? Really?"

Santolina was all ears and eyes. He didn't understand how Iris could be so casual with this group. He had of course met Flem and some others several times now over the past year but they definitely weren't part of *his* social set.

He caught Stinkweed's look and gave him a laughing 'grimace,' as if he had no choice about being here, that he was only here because of Iris.

Stinkweed responded very favorably with a grunt. Of course, he knew *exactly* what the man across from him meant. Here they were at some damn suspicious party given by women and fae boys. This was not his usual

Whimsey C. Nimble

hangout. Both him and Santolina gave each other a manly look. Stinkweed was only here because Iris had invited him and he was itching to see her again. He wondered if she really was engaged. But yes, she certainly was, and to Santolina no less. He nodded and the head of the Parks and Rec department nodded back in acknowledgement.

Sissy and Sassy looked back and forth to the animated fae group in front of them and then over to the main table where Flem stood, handing something to that human woman, and laughing.

Both scenes pulled at them and Sissy said, "Leth go see what Flemth doing, ya wanna?" Tall, grey, long-heading, wide-mouthed Circumscissle held out a hand to Sassafras, helping 'her' up.

Sassy was not used to being around so many humans at one time, coupled with the fae, and his wings twitched a little under the brown, nondescript top *she* wore.

Sissy felt the tremor and smiled encouragingly at his very good friend. "Leth go."

Grey gangly Circumscissle and squatty brown Sassafras wandered hand in hand towards the table, right past Stinkweed and Calypso Bulbosa. All nodded politely but Sissy and Sassy kept moving, much to the human's relief. (And bemusement.)

Stinkweed gave his new girlfriend a look and she nodded, then they both turned around and watched the two badly disguised fae boys in human clothing, one male, and one 'female,' saunter away, arriving in time to see Iris holding a box that Flem had put on her lap.

She removed the lid to reveal three more boxes inside it. Looking at Flem, she asked, "What's this?"

"Here, open this one first," Flem commanded as he tapped the largest.

As she lifted the lid, Flem started talking. "This is your official Hives Emergency Kit, ma'am. Here we have a host of herbal teas – steep two to three tablespoons with three cups of hot water and drink, or make it extra strong and use in the bath, or, cool it to use as a compress. Did you know that many plants actually have antihistamine compounds? I've read that chamomile and wild oregano each have seven different ones, rue has six, and believe it or not, basil, Echinacea, fennel, fig, ginkgo, grapefruit, passion flower, tarragon, thyme, *tea*, and yarrow ALL have five! You will find a sampling of a few of those here. Plus," he picked up a small bottle of capsules, "these contain stinging nettle. It's strange that something that *causes* hives can be taken internally when externally, it's anathema. I find it so odd that stinging nettles have an anti-allergy effect when ingested. If you're so inclined, you can even steam a couple of cups and eat the stuff. I think it might be the herb of the future!" He grinned.

Picking up a small bag of seeds, he said, "These are amaranth seeds. The ratio is about the same as the others, two to three tablespoons to three cups of water, let it steep twenty minutes and you can drink it, bathe in it, or compress it. Oops, I forgot something, be right back!" He dashed out the side door, the one between the end of the planter and his room, reappearing not two minutes later with a potted plant.

"Oh, what is this, Flem? It looks familiar but I can't place it," remarked the owner of the Nursery.

"This is Impatiens Capensis. Otherwise known as jewelweed. I consider it a jewel in your arsenal, ma'am." He laughed at his own joke while everyone around him smiled indulgently, waiting for him to carry on.

By now others were drifting closer, curious as to what was going on.

"Jewelweed contains a compound called lawsone that helps to immediately relieve itching. At the first sign of hives, just crush some of these leaves and rub it on." He held out the shiny yellow ceramic planter with the beautiful orange spotted, pendent-type flowering plant in it and said, "Here," and smiled, his eyes glowing hazel.

Unable to stop himsylph, he continued on with his dissertation: "Jewelweed, a wildflower, also goes by the name Touch Me Not," his face warming as he noticed the growing crowd of onlookers, but before he could say another word, Mayapple's voice rang out loud and clear.

"And why is that, Mr. Smarty Pants? God, you'd think he worked in a nursery or something," she commented, playing to the crowd who rewarded her with adjacent chuckles and twitters.

Giving her a dark look he nonetheless rose to her taunt with great fae aplomb.

"*Because*," he gave her a sniff to show his disdain of her rude manners. "Because," he reiterated, "when their seeds are ripe, they *explode*, hence the name, 'Touch Me Not'.

Whimsey C. Nimble

Mayapple rolled her eyes and mouthed the words woo woo at him. Flem suspected right then she'd been hitting the mead and was tipsy already.

Ignoring her, he pushed determinedly on, compelled to finish telling Iris and his audience what he knew of impatiens capensis and her aliases, jewel-weed and touch-me-not.

"They like moist wet soil, and seem to thrive along damp areas such as drainages, ditches, waterways and they can tolerate shade to full out sun. Their color ranges from yellows to spotted oranges with red and they're annuals - reproducing from their seeds." He threw a hard look at Mayapple as if that last word was some kind of dare but her nose was already poking into the box on Iris's lap.

"Mayapple!" exclaimed Iris, "Get back."

Ignoring her mother, the young woman with the pixie cut jabbed a finger at the remaining two boxes and said, "Ooh, more?"

Giving her daughter a dirty look, Iris carefully picked up Mayapple's hand and returned it back to its owner. "Do you mind, dear?" Her eyes flashed in muted annoyance and she glowered at her pushy child.

"Well, ex*cuse* me!" huffed the young woman and then accidentally hiccupped, which caused her to snort in embarrassment that unfortunately led to squirts of laughter.

Flem watched in breathless trepidation, wondering if she was about to go off half-cocked as she was wont to do but was immediately gratified to see those canyon Sylphs step in and take charge.

Sidling up one on each side, they nonchalantly each hooked an elbow and gently maneuvered her away from her mother.

Mayapple squawked but they pulled her discretely away, petting, cajoling, and admiring, whilst still endeavoring to be insouciant to the casual observer, Whimsey even going so far as to *wink* at Iris.

Iris may have appeared indifferent to the small comtionless commotion but that was far from the case, there wasn't much she missed. She made a note to find out more about these two guests of Flem's that she'd never seen or heard of before.

Preoccupied, she nonetheless did not miss a beat and smiled up at Flem as he announced, "Okay, now you can open the other two." His eye twinkled, and he was much more relaxed now that he was *doing* what he'd planned for so long, finding the whole thing very satisfying.

Intrigued, Iris first inhaled deeply of the overflowing hives kit, the mix of so many herbs a heady scent indeed.

Flem watched fondly and waited patiently for her to reveal the other two presents he'd given much thought to.

Plucking out the flatter of the two, the one with the wide white ribbon around it, Iris shook her head and chanced a look up, saying, "*Flem.* You didn't need to do this."

Embarrassed, the Sylph-in-disguise mumbled something but it went unheard as she lifted the lid and everyone around the table oohed and ahhed at what lay inside, with exclamations being heard in the background.

"Ooh, look!"

"What are they, are they all different?"

"Do they smell?"

"I'd like to get some of those. I wonder where he got them?"

"How delightful Flem!" Iris held up the colorful printed box wherein nine delicately molded soaps lay like a nest of exotics, each one different.

"I picked them out mysylph," Flem admitted shyly. "You'll notice they're a mixture of both butterflies and moths."

"Oh come on Flemmy, *spill*. We all know, hic! Oops. Sorry! Anyway, *tell us*. We've got your number boy, I mean," but Mayapple was cut off from saying another word right behind her mother's head, by a hand clapped tightly over her mouth and she was unceremoniously dragged off, eyes wide at such effrontery but nonetheless sticking her tongue between the fingers of her captor and hiccupping throughout, laughter squeezing out from behind the imprisoning hand like forbidden bubbles in a bathtub...

There was a lot of elbow poking, raised eyebrows and hilarity all around the perimeter at that scene. Even Sissy was spraying and people nearby were ducking and wiping off.

"Where was I?" asked Flem, wondering what had happened to cause the wave around him, knowing it must have had something to do with big mouthed Mayapple, since she was now conspicuously silent.

"California Dogface, although why it's called that I don't know," someone helpfully supplied.

Flem grinned and added an aside, "And they smell good too! This yellow Swallowtail smells like lemon grass, the Monarch here is essence of orange. This one is, let's see, yes," he pointed to one that was soft orange and grey with yellow spots, "this is the Regal moth, smells like pomegranate!" He laughed. "Here, this one is, ah, the Rosy Maple moth, rose geranium scented, of course." He held up a soft pink and pale green soap for everyone to see.

"What old Dogface smell like? I'm almost afraid to ask!" someone teased from the back.

Rolling his eyes in a reproachful way at Catalpah, (who else?) he retorted, "Lavender. Thank you very much."

"Is that a Luna Moth, Flem?" asked Iris, picking up a large pale green shape. "What's *it* smell like, moonbeams?"

Everyone chuckled as Iris sniffed. "Hmm, hard to place. What is it?" she finally gave up.

"Cucumber, with a hint of mint," answered the Sylph host, who owned his own greenhouse.

"Now this beauty is, hmm, I've forgotten…"

"Oh, right here Flem, there's a key here on this paper. That's a Green Swallowtail. Doesn't look very green though, does it?" Iris asked rhetorically, bringing the beauty to her nose.

"Rose," she stated unequivocally, "That's a surprise! With its black top wings and the turquoise bottom wings, it doesn't look green or even hint of red."

"I didn't make 'em, I only picked 'em out. Sure is pretty though," agreed the faerie.

"OH COME ON! Let's party! What a bunch of old poo -" but once again the voice was cut off followed by a gurgle of sorts as Pootsy shushed Mayapple by cramming a chunk of red pepper heavily laden with drippy chive dip into her open mouth, forcing her to swallow and not talk.

"Now these last two are both *moths*." Everyone leaned in to get a good look and Wonga Wonga expressed what they all felt.

"Cha, they look like they've got *eyes* on them, don't they?"

Indeed, the one had rather nondescript mottled brown on the upper wings but the surprise came with the two hind, or bottom wings, which sported two large yellow 'eyes,' complete with big black pupils.

"Io moth. Made with shea butter and a hint of amber. And this one," Flem pointed to the last soap, "is a polyphemus moth, cocoa butter and a hint of vanilla."

"Ooh, four eyes!" put in Bignonia right next to Wonga Wonga and it did look like a purple and yellow eye in each light brown wing, but with the two on the bottom appearing to peer out from dark, black-ringed circles, almost like a tree spirit from fire-charred holes.

"Well, I could use a refill!" announced Vinca Pink dryly. "Swinging party, Flem."

The faerie's head whipped around and all his old insecurities came crashing back to tighten his belly.

Cha! Here he was, the host of his own party, his own social coming out, so-to-speak, and what was he doing? Nattering on about soap for Pan's sake! He felt just like the ninny he'd always played back in the canyon.

Beneath his thinly disguised human male clothing, bent over wings clenched and he gasped in down right foolish insecurity.

Lark's hand came down upon his shoulder reassuringly, grounding him, at the same time that Iris stood up and pulled him into a hug.

"This is a great party, Flem, I love my soaps and my, ahem, *Hives Kit*. *Very* thoughtful, as usual. But I think…excuse me, what's your name sweetie?" She smiled most benignly at the Pink One, teeth hardly showing but with a fierce protective gleam in her eye.

Vinca's hand snaked out and she may have been shaking in her shoes but was determined not to be intimidated by this human woman.

Eyes flashing sensuously, almost desperately, the Sylph clasped Iris's hand with both of hers, up to her usual tricks.

"Friend of Flem's, are you?" Iris asked sweetly, such an innocent question, but the warning was there, implicitly. "Me too," she answered the unspoken assumption and continued, "He is a *dear*, isn't he? He's one of *my* best employees," letting this Pink *person* (ha!) know who owned the place…

Carefully disengaging from Vinca's predatory clasp Iris turned her back, saying, "I'm going to leave that third box alone for the moment, and go get something to nibble on. I'll be right back," and went off gaily to the kitchen, chattering about the food, the soap, the remodel, hailing her daughter who was standing between the two newcomers.

Whimsey C. Nimble

Soon everyone was jammed into the kitchen, filling plates with sweet-potato crackers and banana blossom salsa, current pie, (courtesy of the famed Blackberry Bakery), heaps of fresh green salad heavily laden with cranberries, walnuts, almonds, spouts and crunchy baked kale leaves.

"Yum, what a feast, Flemmy. What's that?" Mayapple, on good behavior now that she'd gotten a little food in her to go with the magic mead, pointed to a yellow dish.

"Those, my dear, are curried day lilies."

"No! *Lilies?*"

"Yes. *DAY* lilies. *Hemerocallis*. Not *Lillium*. Be sure they are either Hemerocallis Fulva, which I've heard are the original from Japan or Hemerocallis Aurantiaca, a smaller version. As the name implies, the flowers are present for only one day. You can eat them raw or cooked. Now, not all lilies are, oh! Hi, Lilium. Mayapple, let me introduce you to Lilium Superbum."

Mayapple looked up and up into eerie yellow irises with big brown spots and smiled, her eyes glazing in mild fear. But she needn't have worried. Lilium Superbum was merely an aggressive saleswoman and she didn't eat young women for breakfast. And she *knew* her lilies!

"Glad to meet you. Did I hear *Flem* here," and she licked her lips, "say something about *eating* my flower display??"

"No. No no. *Day* lilies. Hemerocallis," Flem quickly clarified.

"Ah. Exactly. Do you know how to tell the difference?"

Immediately Flem felt put on the spot and even though he DID know the difference, he couldn't think of one to save his life, what with this big tiger-lillyish imposing person interrogating him suddenly. And those spotted yellow eyes. Whooeee.

Mayapple laughed weakly, fascinated by the by-play between these two. This woman seemed to affect Flem like he was a leaf to her storm.

"It's quite simple, if you know what to look for, " she stated. "First, check the soil line. If there is a bunch of flat, strap-shaped leaves and they appear to be growing in a clump, it's probably Hemerocallis, the day lily. Each flower presents itself at the end of a long, *leafless* stalk, whereas *Lilium* have one central, unbranched stem that grows from a bulb (unlike the thick tuberous root of a day lily) with leaves growing *around the entire length of the stem* in whorls or spirals. A day lily only blooms *one* day. *Lilium*," (here she chuckled at her namesake) blooms usually last a week or more and can get up to ten feet tall!" She smiled proudly.

Flem just stood, hand over his mouth as the innate salesperson flowed out and over them all. There was no trying to stop her he knew from experience.

"So what else you want to know, dearie?" inquired Ms. Superbum, taking a drink from her glass, unnerving eyes above the rim, watching.

Mayapple schooled her expression to one of innocent admiration, careful not to look at Flem who was fidgeting with straightening bowls and non-existent tasks.

Feeling trapped momentarily by this big woman, she glanced up and found Rainbow watching her from over at the watering hole.

"Oops, there's Rainbow! I've got to go talk to her. Nice to meet you, eh, Lilium," and away she flew like purple dandelion fluff scattered by a strong wind.

A burst of laughter erupted not far away and before he knew it, Flem was surrounded by a wild and raucous group which meant essentially everyone there, Iris herself leading the way.

Preemptively removing a bowl from her host's fae hands, she set it down with a thump and said, "Come on lover-boy," her eyes flicking to Lark involuntarily for a moment. "I still have one more box to open, and rumor has it you have a few to open yoursylph; after all, it's *your* housewarming."

Giggling like a little girl, Flem the faerie stood up tall from where he'd been lounging against the counter with Ms. Superbum and let himsylph be led off, a silly Sylph smile adorning his sweet fae face.

"Me?" he tittered sylphconsciously, trying to act as if he hadn't seen all those not-so-hidden gaily wrapped packages that had come in surreptitiously, his eyes darting around the room, his raspy pink fae tongue coming out to nervously lick his lips in embarrassment and anticipation. He was to be the recipient of *presents*. Pan! Not that he hadn't received a few over this past year, including the biggest of all, his own greenhouse! But the novelty of having presents brought for him, to him, was unique. If someone brought you a present, well, it must mean they *liked* you. Deep inside he found that to be a miraculous gift but at the same time, not surprising. He now liked *himsylph*, the Sylph he was now, someone he'd been steadily growing so why *shouldn't* others like him?

Whimsey C. Nimble

His boss plopped down, pulling the remaining unopened box into her lap, laughing and shaking it, making guesses as to what it contained.

By now the party-goers were all relaxed, the food delightful, the mead - that magic elixir of Gods and Goddesses - flowing like the great mother Ganges herself, all partaking of her life giving attributes.

"Oh Flem, how did you know?" this being tongue-in-cheek of course because Iris *did* have all those chocolates 'hidden' in her office, of which he and Mayapple had succumbed to more than once. As Iris knew.

"Aw shucks, just a guess, ma'am.," replied the coy-boy with wings.

Iris laughed delightedly but made it a point to immediately wrap a ribbon tightly around the little gold matte box and stuff the whole thing down in her bag. Fine chocolate was not something to be truffled about.

"*Here.*" Mayapple had slipped away from Rainbow and retrieved an intriguing long skinny *something*.

Biting her lip she looked up at Flem from under thick lashes and gruffly thrust the surprisingly light package at him.

Not quite how she envisioned it but oh well.

"Open it, open it," she demanded, suddenly extremely impatient to see his reaction, her heart held tight for what she was absolutely convinced would be his extreme delight.

Looking at her with an amazed expression already on his face like he couldn't believe it, he started carefully peeling a small strip off one end but at Mayapple's large audible groan, said, "Oh, *all right!*" and tore all the pretty paper to shreds.

He had half expected it, I mean, what else could it be with this shape, but the reality was too too exciting.

Clasping it to his heart, he breathed in, in cherishment, big hazel eyes holding Mayapple's as he just looked at her in wonder.

"Oh *Pan*dorea!" ejaculated a bystander.

Wonga Wonga's head snapped around at this but Lark ignored him. He and Buddleia were acquainted with the didgeridoo from being at the art fair but neither had ever been this up front and personal with one.

"Cha, Flem!" he continued, "Your very own didgeridoo. I remember how fascinated you were with them at the fair."

Flem blinked and smiled at his lover, but he *hadn't been* with Lark when he got lost at the didgeridoo tent, he'd been alone. So how did he know? But that thought got lost by the clamoring around him as everyone had questions, peppered with demands for a demonstration.

Not knowing the first thing about the unique wind instrument, Flem gamely blew into it, no sound whatsoever coming out.

Laughter floated around him as everyone waited, offering suggestions. Flem kept blowing, his face getting red with the effort, becoming more giddy by the moment until suddenly a big fart-like noise blurted out the wide-lipped bottom of the highly decorated tube.

Everyone went into gales of laughter, even the sylphconscious but by now, light-headed host, giving in to the hilarity, slightly embarrassed that he was the center of attention but going with it.

"Can I try?" came a voice. Their fae host immediately relinquished his hold, handing his new toy over and before long, many throaty, groaning, drawn-out *blmmphs* were resounding throughout the crowd, interspersed with hysterical laughter as more than one guest started hyperventilating from lack of oxygen.

By now, everyone wanted to be part of the scene, retrieving the gifts that had come in with them and setting them on a table in Flem's vicinity.

Rainbow's arm appeared from right over his lumpy shoulder, a small wrapped box clutched in her hand, which she deposited right in front of him.

"Love you kiddo," she whispered in his ear.

He picked it up, a small bemused smile on his lips, hoping it was what he thought it was.

Having learned his lesson, he made no attempt to carefully unwrap it but stripped it quick. Ah, it was indeed his very own medicine card set. He felt rich.

Most of his thinly disguised fae guests were still captivated by his instrument, a raucous group whose noise level seemed to go up another notch with every passing minute.

Schafta and Acaulis stood attentively nearby, doing their best to be inconspicuous as they ostensibly examined Flem's planter and the greenery therein, but speaking realms to each other with avid looks as the din grew.

Unable to resist, Flem slit the thin cellophane encasing the new cards and thumbed through them briefly, pulling out a couple with instructions on them before Rainbow plopped down beside him, saying "Come on, let me do a quick reading for you, Flemmy boy, I'll make it quick, I promise."

Flem wasn't so sure but the chorus of fascinated onlookers drowned him out, everyone urging him on.

Seconds later seven cards lay face down in the pathway spread and the shop owner with the rainbow-hued hair was crisply directing him while taking sips of Egret's Beak with one hand, occasionally picking up a nut or a bit of ginger bread with the other from a small Limoges plate nearby.

Squirming a little at being subject to another, he nonetheless gave in graciously and prepared to start flipping cards over, one by one, as directed.

"Okay sweet pea, let's see what you've got." She tapped the first card, saying, "Past."

Flem flipped it over to reveal a moose.

Making it quick and to the point, the card reader merely said, "Ah, moose represents sylphesteem. A pat on the back. You're doing something right. Makes sense to me, this place is *great*. You should really be proud of yoursylph, Flem, that's what this card is affirming." She nodded, then tapped the middle card.

He turned it over. "Oh, look at this," she said with regards to the regal hawk. "You're about to get a message of some kind. Or possibly, have already gotten one. It will be very distinct, and will define a big piece of what is going on with you right now, presently. Hmm. Does that make sense to you? Only you know if that rings true or not."

Flem felt the blood drain from his face as his conversation with Lark came thundering back and he sort of gasped and managed to say "Uh huh, it does," as if it was no big deal, smiling what he knew to be a sickly smile. "Go on," he forced out trying to not give anything away. "What's next?"

"Future," she stated as she nodded and then tapped the last card in that line.

The sweetness of a hovering hummingbird hung there and Rainbow said, "Oh, look at this. Hummingbird is *joy*, Flem." Unable to resist, her arm came out and with the back of her fingers she stroked his cheek before catching his chin in her hand and looking at him seriously. "You're doing a good job Flem. This is a really positive message." She paused, then added, "They're all different, you know. Nonetheless, I believe the purpose of the messages is just to confirm what you already *intuitively* know."

"So, okay, where were we? Ah yes, 'something just completed.' Go ahead." She pointed.

A squirrel holding a nut stood there and even Flem laughed and got that one. Yes, he'd been running all day, many places, and yes, he was glad it was over and here they were, at the party, finally.

Silently, Rainbow pointed out the next card. Flem turned it over and Rainbow hooted "Oh perfect!" at the stately turkey, making even those dancing and drinking and didgeridoo-blowing Sylphs at the far end of the room look at her.

Flem's eyes got extra bright as he looked at Ms. Merkiva and waited for an explanation.

"*Give-a-way*, Flem," she deadpanned. "This indicates you are about to *receive* something. Could be a sunset, a beautiful moment, or money on the ground. Have you *received* anything, Flem?" she asked with a laugh in her eyes and he laughed with her.

He nodded for her to go on and she said, "Second last one; what's working *against* you, which is not really true, it's more of a revealing of how you sometimes work against your own Sylph. You know what I mean? I think we all do it, sometimes it's camouflaged by the little things we ignore."

He turned it over and the silent lynx looked back at them. "Ooh, secrets Flem. The universe's, your own, somebody else's. Maybe even stuff you're not acknowledging to yoursylph. Do you have any secrets, Flem? No, don't tell me. We ALL have secrets, now don't we?" She smiled broadly, and he thought *oh sister, if you only knew*, and returned her smile.

"Ready?" asked Rainbow, nodding to the last card. "This is what's going on in *your* favor, right now. Always my favorite of course, although it comes in many disguises..." she let it trail off, a distracted look in her eye.

He flipped it over, and looked into the face of the big black jungle cat that stared back.

"Hmm. Looks like the universe is telling you to keep going, you're obviously on the right path, this is what's working *for* you – embracing the unknown. When I get this card, it usually means I'm literally going somewhere. Got vacation plans, Flem? Are you planning a trip or anything?"

He shook his head, no.

"Well, you might be! Or it might just be a journey of the emotions. It always behooves one to be open, be kind, be loving, be responsible. You can go anywhere and do anything by following the path of the heart. And that's what embracing the unknown is all about."

Whimsey C. Nimble

Just then Blossom plunked her heavy something down on the table and proceeded to slide it noisily towards her host.

Rainbow got up and slid off, giving one of his shoulders an affectionate squeeze goodbye as she did so.

His hands caught the sliding present at the same time his eyes flashed at his departing friend and he mouthed the words "Thank you," before rapidly gathering the cards.

Cat and China sidled closer, glitter wafting in their wake, leaving little sparkles in a trail behind them.

Catalpah kept jiggling her package, making tinkly sounds that rattled against the inside of the paper until finally Chinaberry grabbed it and held it behind her back, giving China a glare to stop with the jangle.

Catalpah's eyes widened and she made to grab it back but tall darling Bud appeared between them and slung an arm over both their shoulders, a gleam in his eye. Glitter floated around him, some even landing on his sexy dark grey clothing but by now he didn't care.

China rubbed against him as did Cat on the other side and both noted the hard bulge outlined against his leg.

"What's this?" purred Cat, as her hand came down to explore.

"Something sweet in here, now isn't there?" she asked.

"Just leave it alone, it's for Flem."

"Where's ours?" China wanted to know, tracing the outline of the lump through Bud's pants, fingertips hungry.

"Right here." He bumped towards Catalpah and said, "Take it out."

Deftly, she slid the silver flask out of his tight back pocket.

"Did you give him *your* present yet, ladies?"

"No, he's occupied with the Gothic Milkmaid over there. Who is she, do you know?"

Flem turned, a quelling eyebrow raised in their direction.

It must have been that Gothic Milkmaid comment wryly decided Bud, deliberately moving forward, oozing charm, smiling and nodding squarely at Flem's other guest, his arms holding China and Cat right with him.

Flem relaxed and introduced them to Blossom.

Bud noticed for the first time what Flem was holding, now unwrapped – a small sculpture that incorporated two figures. His eyes widened in appreciation as he let loose a long appreciative whistle. "Is that *Pan?*" he asked incredulously.

Flem nodded. His smile couldn't have gotten much bigger. He was a changed faerie. The presents he was getting were overwhelming.

"Who's he talking to?"

A fae young woman, one with wings, looking very distraught, leaned back in front of the Pagan God almost into his lap, he behind her, one leg sprawled over the other, holding her close, obviously giving counsel, no doubt lascivious. He took his ease upon a large flat rock, which she didn't have room to sit on, thus pushing her to stay back close against him.

"I don't know," answered Flem, stroking the precious gift with a thumb. He went on to explain, "Blossom here is the owner of a thrift store and this came through her hallowed portals, just for me, she says."

"Hey, you're one of my best customers, Flem. Well, at least my favorite." She gave him an impish grin but Bud knew that look in her eye, she was hot for the faerie. He wondered if she knew he was fae.

Sizing her up underneath his facile charm, he was a pretty sharp Sylph himsylph and it appeared to him that the kooky human had intelligence in her manner even with cutesy braids, that pouty mouth, and the short black skirt. She was playing it cool but to Bud's experienced eye, he knew faerie lust when he saw it. Whether the object of her affections knew it or not, was another question.

"So," he continued, "do *you* know who the randy old goat," he nodded quickly towards Pan, "is talking to?"

"Oh, it was just here. I *should* know. Um, let's see, no doubt it's in my *psyche* somewhere-" responded Blossom. "No, sorry, I can't remember. Why, does she look like someone you know, was she a friend of yours?"

"Ha! No! Ha." Bud was startled by her droll perspicuousness, and felt rather foolish that he'd even wondered if she knew Flem was fae. After that comment, he figured she probably had every hidden Sylph in the room pegged.

He grinned as innocently and as *humanly* as he could, Mr. Nonchalant.

"Hey, let's have a toast! Here Flem, this is for you," and he reached into the other back pocket and brought out Flem's flask, the one he'd bought specifically for him that was filled with his best mead, which surprisingly turned out to be the Buttercup and Honey one. Delectable hot, sunshiny-meadow overtures. He hoped Flem liked it, but how could he not? He was a Sylph, after all. Clearing his throat, Bud then sang out, "A toast! Raise your glasses!"

Whimsey C. Nimble

The room quieted down, flasks and glasses clinking as all responded to the call, bottles being grasped and brought round.

The Campion boys shot a look at each other; things were heating up.

"To our wonderful friend Flem and his wonderful greenhouse. We are *all* so jealous!"

Yeah right, thought the recipient, picturing Bud's treehouse and Lark's houseboat. But it didn't matter. He wasn't jealous anymore, nor intimidated by their respective living quarters. Well, okay, he was *still* acutely aware of each's casual good taste and unique style of living but he had found that higher Sylph inside and managed to relate as if *he* too were an equal. The ironic part was how easy he slipped into that mode. So much so that he actually forgot himsylph (his poor, poor Sylph, that is) and didn't think twice about how much more 'together' Bud and even Lark for that matter, supposedly was. It was no big deal unless he made it a big deal. That was the old way of thinking, he knew. And for the most part, he let it go. Yes, he was acutely aware of where he'd been for most of his life the second he stepped onto that houseboat or into that treehouse but he firmly relinquished it each time also. These were his friends and this was simply where they lived. It was so much easier to just go with assumed confidence and put the old 'poor me's' behind him. It hadn't been easy, growth never was, but he was a new Sylph now.

"To The Muse, Flem, the one that brought you into our midst!"

Everyone echoed "To The Muse!" and clinking was heard all around.

Chinaberry and Catalpah moved closer but Stinkweed and Calypso stepped in front of them and Bud suspected they were making an early departure.

The old man had his hand delicately perched on the small of the woman's back, as if guiding her.

"Here you go, boy. I brought ya a little something from the garden. It smells really, hee hee, *good*, when it blooms, so be sure to plant it, hee hee, upwind from your fancy digs here." He laughed again, shoving a big, almost-clean planter with just a rough top sticking out of the dirt, towards the faerie.

Flem looked up in surprise. "Why, *thank you*. That's very kind of you." He was touched that the old man, who obviously had suspicions about him, would not only show up but bring him a specimen from his beloved stinky garden. And he knew without a doubt he would NOT plant it upwind. It was going in a far, downwind corner.

"Oh, say, I forgot. This here card's from this young thing right beside me. You know Calypso, don't you?"

Flem and Calypso grinned hugely at one another.

"No, don't open it right now, Flem," fluttered Ms. Bulbosa. "I'll just tell you what I did. Remember those big pots I got last year? Well, I bought one for you." She smiled. "Bud knows which one it is, it's in the back of the store with a sold ticket on it and your name. Anyway, open the card later, I got kind of gushy. Don't read it now, okay?"

Flem was oohing and ahhing at everything she said, his eyes moist with gratitude, feeling overwhelmed at her generosity, at *everyone's* generosity.

"Hey lover-boy, don't get all choked up yet. Cha. Here!" Chinaberry thrust a small tinkly package at him. "Open it."

Stinkweed and Calypso melted into the background, moving off towards the food, stopping to talk to Iris and Santolina.

Catalpah leaned onto Chinaberry's back, arms akimbo sticking out around China's face, watching with avid eyes.

Just as Flem started to open one end, Ms. Superbum nudged to the table and quietly set a yellow box down, trying to edge away unnoticed but Flem said, "Lillium!" and she looked up to see him wink and mouth the word "Thanks."

Gratified by his attention, she pointed and said "*Lily*. For you," and smiled as she continued edging out of the crowd.

"Oh thanks, Lillium, I would never have guessed…"

She ducked away and he returned his full attention to the small package in his hand.

Cat sighed loud and deep, as if they'd been waiting for hours instead of thirty seconds.

Pulling the paper off, Flem was star struck at the sparklies in his hand.

Four sets of wing bling winked up at him, disguised as human earring studs to the untrained eye.

He'd never owned wing bling before.

In fact, he'd rather scoffed at it when he'd seen it adorning others' tips at the club.

But my, it *was* pretty, wasn't it?

He was hooked.

He shot an adoring look to the two crazy fae boys who looked like girls until they let their wings out and then furtively looked around, calculating human to Sylph ratio, the idea of a *wingout* dancing through his mind again but it was way too early to even contemplate at this point. He'd just have to see how the evening progressed.

China and Cat watched intently, their eyes meeting Flem's with hidden messages.

Flem felt they were all thinking the same thing but deflected that line with this comment, "Pan, these are beautiful! I'll have to get my ears pierced, won't I?" Sylphs snickered into their drinks around him. He lifted two perfect emerald stars up, each outlined in gold and stared admiringly. Setting them down he picked up the silver leaf silhouette and laid them side by side with some ivy shaped gold ones. "Do you think it would be too heavy to wear all of them?" he asked as a joke but actually wanting to know.

"Tsk tsk tsk," China shook her head. "Greedy little thing, aren't you?" but was laughing kindly as she said it. 'The first time I would just go with one pair. Let's hope you get to try them sooner rather than later." Under her breath she asked, " Want us to help you get the pesky humans out of here?" She smiled but with a hungry look lurking in her eye.

"No!" laughed Flem. "No, don't chase anybody off!" He laughed again, pleased he was seeing the lighter side of it, flashing on how much more troubled he'd been a mere year ago.

He was growing, had grown and felt himsylph deepening, caring more about some things and less about the trivia. He liked himsylph and he liked most people and he liked his world.

He looked up to see Whimsey Nimble, Pootsy Koons, and that coy-boy Lark waiting to speak with him but at that moment an escalating whirlwind of noise catapulted, like a rampaging wind spirit, right through the back door into the kitchen and stopped, banging the doors shut behind her.

All conversation in the entire place came to a screeching halt.

Nobody knew her.

She looked wild.

Garish flamboyant harem-type pants of filmy gold with a matching buoyant blouse settled into place about her body, accented by dark, almost black hair. Stilettos were strapped to her feet, making her even taller.

As everyone waited, time stood still.

She finally spoke, sounding a little desperate in Bud's opinion.

A long, nasally accent twanged out, a fast and rather, well, *pinched*, quality to it. He thought it sounded like she was talking through her *nose*, for Pan's sakes.

"Hello! Listen, I know this is weird but, well, yoo see, I wuk next door and this creep was followin' me and well, I duckt 'n *here*. I hope yous don't mind. I was *scared*."

Bud and Lark exchanged a look. Did she come from *Sundrops*? Both fae looked harder. Sundrops was not the classiest of places, the women who made their pay checks there did so in a dubious manner.

Still, her shoulders were concealed by that gold blouse and Lark looked at Bud with one question.

Fae?

The Sylph shrugged, he didn't know.

Flem finally jumped up, solicitude at the ready, expansive in his heart, always ready to help everybody, assuming the best right away. (the new Flem)

"Of course! Come in. Meet my friends."

A sniff of delight and she was off the door and onto Flem's arm.

That was quick, thought Bud and Lark silently agreed.

"Who's the guy following you, do you know him?" called out Bud to the newly arrived guest, referring to her 'tail.'

Giving a shudder, she said, "Yeah. Yeah, he comes into the club, a big prickly guy. His name is Cynara Cardunculus. I just don' trust him. He's kind a thorny looking, yoo know? Like he'd *cut-cha.. Brrrr.*" She exaggerated a big shudder and everyone uneasily looked at the door she'd come in, wondering if *he* was now going to burst in like *she* did. Bud and Lark immediately came to a tacit agreement and turned into patrol faeries, ready to do reconnaissance and moved off with nary a nod to anyone, stealth their middle name.

Out the back door they slipped together, Lark heading to the left and eventually to the tunnel and Bud to the right, down past the three greenhouses, making a rapid circuit.

Outside all was quiet, except for the party going on at Flem's, which had quieted down a notch.

Bud slipped into the green tunnel behind the catalpah tree by the fire pit and lightly ran down to catch up with Lark.

Whimsey C. Nimble

Coming to the archway that opened onto the street, they both peered out and, seeing no one, Lark looked at Bud and said, "I think everybody's here, don't you?"

At Bud's agreement, he reached out and snatched Flem's sign from where it hung, returning the passageway to quiet anonymity once again.

Stepping back, Bud then swung the gate closed, the cold hard latch falling into place with finality. If you didn't know the party was here, it was too bad. Nothing gave it away anymore.

Anxious to see the newcomer and find out her story, the fae boys with wings hidden under human clothing hurried along, loping back to the party, slipping in the kitchen door themsylves, causing a momentary stir but everyone's attention was really focused on the interloper, who was cozening up with the host, drink in hand, batting eyelashes a little too much for Lark's taste. A scowl marring his delicate but strong profile, he started forward determinedly but Bud held him back with one hand. "Oh relax. Do you *really* think she's competition?"

Not appeased, Mr. Spurastic nonetheless hung back, thunderclouds riding his attractive brow like a storm on a distant horizon.

Slowing down, the two Sylph scouts walked toward the pair and Lark watched as her shoulders twitched briefly. His eyes flew to Bud's who nodded; he'd seen it too.

The newest guest handed something to Whimsey, who had just walked up. Whimsey nodded, then headed back down towards the couch areas where the music was set up.

Lark and Bud watched as she slipped something into the player and within minutes, loud suggestive music slapped into everybody like waves lapping a gravely beach, molding their thoughts as surely as hands in wet moist clay.

Well, that certainly answered one question. There was no doubt she *was* from Sundrops, *that* was stripper music if ever they'd heard any.

Everybody felt it and the lights grew dim.

Flem's head whipped around as he wondered wildly what was happening, almost afraid to know.

Lillium was dancing and undulating sexily by hersylph, eyes glazed. Chinaberry and Catalpah instantly sought out Bud and started towards him. Vinca Pink, Bignonia, Wonga Wonga, Jipijapa, Sissy, Sassy, Vervacity and Vonda all stood close together, dancing and twitching to the sexy beat.

Uncle Linaria took 'his' charge, who was taking it all in with saucer-like eyes and big ears, quickly out the side door and 'round back to the fire pit area, talking fast and furious to cover up and distract.

Gypsophilia let herself be swept along, shaking her head at her Aunt Linaria's conservative approach. Cha, she was almost *thirteen*, after all, not a baby, what was the big deal?

Stinkweed was hurrying Calypso out the door and Santolina was urging Iris to come along and leave at the same time. She was, but it was obvious she was doing so rather reluctantly.

Garriya wasn't sure what to do but finally succumbed to trepidation, grabbed her wrap and bid a quick farewell to Mayapple where she stood entranced and entrenched, snug between Rainbow and Blossom.

Schafta and Acaulais panted hard at the scene unfolding right before their very (human) eyes and deliberately stepped back even further, intent on being invisible.

The music got deeper and more suggestive and the woman at Flem's side flew into action, leaving Flem's mouth hanging open behind her as she started prancing and leaping about, shaking her hips, shimmying her chest and shoulders, jingling loudly beneath her flimsy gold clothing, legs long because of the extra four inch heels.

With great flirty eyes she looked at everybody, intense direct energy keeping them all spell bound, hands beckoning. Most moved hypnotically with her, all Sylphs sucker to a good party, the crazier the better.

Was she fae? they all wanted to know.

Her blouse was now unbuttoned and she was taking it off as if shedding a second skin, winding her way through the crowd, rubbing her shoulders and hips against all that she came in contact with. Mead was gulped quicker than usual as the gold blouse went sailing overhead to land harmlessly near Flem's bedroom door.

Encasing her upper body was a short tight top covered with shiny electric-blue sequins shaking for all their worth, made rattley by small coconut shell bits sewn in between them. Not missing a beat her hands came down to tug at her waist band.

About that point Bud wondered if she really had been followed or if that was just a ruse to cover her party crashing. He made a note to be alert for an act that no doubt would lead to a request for money when it was all over.

Or, maybe not, maybe it was true. He reserved judgment for the time being.

Pants were now almost off and a matching sequined bikini bottom was flashing at everyone, whistles and comments flowing just like the alcohol and everyone leaned in, trying to see if she had wings hidden but alas, it was hard to tell.

Flem was agog, speechless. Was she really going to *strip*, right here *in his house*, at his party?

But the music changed, segueing nicely into a catchy island beat as Whimsey took charge again. Everyone's feet and funny bones started to play with the air waves, dancing, laughing, having a good time, clothes staying *on*.

The music never stopped, the two Campion boys dancing right along but stayed out of the way, lurking in corners unnoticed, blending with background greenery. That Flem, fae or not, and they were pretty sure he *was*, sure knew how to throw a party. And his *friends*. Well, there was an interesting bunch. Both wondered mightily just who in this crowd *was* human.

Mayapple was a safe bet, plus those two girlfriends of hers looked pretty human. Acaulis wouldn't stake his life on it though, because man this crowd was as colorful as a hothouse full of zinnias.

Uncle Linaria and niece Gypsophilia slipped back inside, staying in the kitchen for the time being.

Flem took a break and headed back that way to check on supplies.

The newcomer pulled China and Cat aside and inquired, a little tactlessly as it turned out, "Hey, hey. Yoo two. Hey, how's it goin'? What can yoos tell me about this place? That Flem guy, he the ownah? Is he, yoo know," and here she made a fluttery, suggestive movement with her eyes, wiggling her fingers to indicate something, perhaps fae?

Catalpah guffawed outright at this rather crude social blunder but Chinaberry had hersylph under better control. Still, a scowl marred her features. One just did not ask questions such as this.

"Hey, hey! Take it easy! Sorry! My mistake, geeez," and with a hurt sniff, the party crasher and stripper backed up and turned the other way, heading towards her flung about clothes, eyeballing the crowd. She never seemed to get it right, no matter how hard she tried.

Flem furtively watched the exchange while outwardly making small talk with Gypsy and her 'uncle.'

The newcomer, whatever her name was, was decidedly odd and he realized with a start that it wasn't too long ago that that's what people had been saying about him!

A movement caught his eye and Flem looked out at the crowd and down to where Whimsey stood, hands on the controls of the music.

He waved a definite thumbs up at her which she returned with a nod and a grin.

Looking about for the party crasher, he found she'd come closer and was looking from one dish to another.

"Help yoursylph!" he invited, feeling a bit awkward as he still didn't even know her name.

"I'm Flem as I said earlier, and this is my place." He smiled with the pride of ownership, and nodded, waiting to hear her name.

Smiling a little more shyly at him now, she relaxed a bit.

These people were so nice, even if they didn't want to see her act. She wondered if they were all rich. What great friends they all seemed to be. How come *she* never got invited to parties like this?

"Nice place. Nice friends," she said with a bit of wistfulness showing and Flem detected something in her voice that he'd never expected to hear from another, directed towards *him*. She sounded *envious*. He was struck by how much she reminded him of *himsylph* a mere year and a half ago, when he first got to San Francoa Ramosa.

"Thanksss-?" He left a question mark there for her but she was pointing over his shoulder and said, "Hey, your friends over there want yoos to come back."

Flem looked around and grinned. He had more presents! Woo hoo!

Turning back, he said, "The mead's down there. The plates are right here. Why don't you get yoursylph a glass of the God's nectar and something to eat and join us, okay?"

"Awww, thanks Flem. Yoo're a good guy," and she took hersylph off, buttoning her blouse back up.

Whimsey C. Nimble

"Okay sit," commanded Pootsy, owner of Windfall Café back in Thimbleberry Canyon. She helped him along by placing both hands on his lumpy shoulders and pushing him down onto a chair. A package appeared in his lap and the colorful little Sylph commented, "I know you've always lusted after mine so I got you some of your own."

Raising his eyebrows at that cryptic statement, Flem's curiosity was whetted and he dug in, unwrapping and unpacking to finally reveal one large wind chime comprised of layers and layers of bells, tissue paper silencing their many tongues.

"Oh! Yes, how did you know? *Thank you*, Pootsy," and he gave her a big hug.

Whimsey grimaced comically, groaning "Oh Pan, more noise," but laughing as she said it. Pootsy Koons pinched her.

"Do *not* bat these around like you do mine. That's an order."

Whimsey rolled her eyes at this, then ignored her busy friend to hand their host a small wrapped box, not much bigger than five by six inches.

"Hmm. What's this?" asked Flem, looking up at the taller Sylph.

Whimsey smiled modestly.

"That, Ms. Greenwood," here she stopped and yukked at her old joke before continuing, "is *your* copy of my just published vignettes, signed by the author, yours truly." The modesty gave way to a big grin.

Flem reverently undid the taped ends and neatly extricated a small red matte box with embossed gold letters on two sides, chuckling as he read them aloud: "A *Gaggle* of Faeries. Oops! No, that's a *Giggle* of Faeries! Ha ha!" Gaggle was lightly crossed out and Giggle stenciled in gold right below it, so it actually read 'A Giggle of Faeries.'

Whimsey bowed her head in acknowledgment and hoped he wouldn't take offense at the story she'd inserted from one of 'his' many escapes long ago. Maybe she should have checked with him before the publisher said yes. But, in her defense, they'd only just found out where *she* was, recently. She better talk to him before he read them…

Flem looked up to the newcomer standing on the edge and motioned her closer, intending to introduce her but he still didn't know her name.

Before he could figure out what to do, Bud, China and Cat joined them and Bud stuck out his hand with a Sylph introduction of him and his two particulars.

Rather taken aback to be face to face with China and Cat again, the stripper covered it well with the quick response, "Lauryl. Lauryl Sulphate. How do yoo do?" and proceeded to hand every one of them within range her card.

Apparently her night job was just around the corner at yes, Sundrops, but during the day she worked on hair.

Lark spoke up, "So, what's the S stand for?" Her card read 'S. Lauryl Sulfate.'

"Oh, that's my first name, Sodium, I don't use it. Lauryl is so much nicer, don't yoo think so?"

Everyone nodded.

Flem thought privately she looked a little lost even though her smile was bright.

He glanced at the card again. She worked at *Sundrops?*

Lark was talking and everyone was listening but Flem who was taking stock of this, this, *stripper* who'd landed in their midst.

She must be human, if she was taking off her clothes for money, but something didn't click.

Then his eyes snagged on her shoulders, still disguised beneath that long scarf and what appeared was some kind of skin suit, now that he really looked at it.

Was she, could she be, *fae?*

Something wasn't right.

Looking closer, he noted that one of the long skinny heels on her stilettos looked pretty ratty, like it had been broken and was ill repaired.

Now that he looked, the gold pants looked like they'd seen better days too and Flem was suddenly struck with the insight *she* was probably *he*, probably fae, and not happy, despite appearances to the opposite. It was all too familiar, hauntingly familiar...

"Flem!"

His head jerked to Lark's voice.

"Yes?"

"Ah, ma petite, here, you have one more present to open." He pulled a big awkward bundle wrapped in cloth from down on the floor beside him and dropped it on the table. "Oh, and this," a small bronze-ish bag made it into Flem's hand.

Whimsey C. Nimble

Flem gave his lover an intimate look and Lark blew him a kiss.

Opening the small bag, the faerie removed a vial of his favorite scent, amber, almond, and patchouli with just the faintest whiff of rose.

"Oh!" cried Flem in delight, sending a savoring look at the other Sylph.

"Oh for God's sake, save it for the bedroom, you two coy boys. Geez. Open your present! I want to see what lover-boy here gotcha." Mayapple, giving orders again.

Making fluttering big eyes at Lark the whole time, Flem the faerie un-did the cord that held the material around the bundle together to reveal a tightly rolled hammock. Its special attribute wasn't immediately discernible and Flem felt a stab of disappointment. He *had* a very nice hammock.

"Unroll it. Here, I'll help you," put in Lark, watching his faerie's face and hoping he hadn't made a mistake.

As the bed was revealed, Flem got more and more tickled. It was a dou-ble! Finally, they would actually be able to *sleep* together, here. "Wanna help me hang it?" he asked and before the words were out of his mouth Lark was tucking it up and heading for the bedroom.

With the last present no longer a mystery, guests scattered and Whimsey C. Nimble, that faithful DJ, cranked up the dance music and Pootsy Koons stepped in as a Sylph-appointed hostess.

Bottle in one hand and a delectable tray filled with a variety of Flem's goodies, she made the rounds not even noticing Moss Campion's boys where they now stood, deep *in* the planter, blending with the cultivated indoor woodsy garden.

Lauryl Sulfate kind of trailed behind, not sure what to do with hersylph and feeling rather out of place and more disgruntled with her lot in life by the minute.

Cha! It was obvious these Sylphs, even thinly disguised as human as they were, were happier than she was. Two fat tears of sylphpity welled up in her eyes and she angrily swiped them away, hoping no one was paying attention.

No one was, she thought, her eyes skipping around the room.

And why should they? They didn't know her, they didn't care.

Again she sniffed, then headed back to the kitchen. Spying a rather large water glass by the sink, she dashed out the contents and quickly filled it with the free mead, immediately sucking in a big swallow.

Taking another gulp, she watched the crowd gather at the other end, dancing hard, laughing, having a good time.

Her irritation grew as her blood alcohol went up, along with her poor-me hopelessness.

She took another drink.

It was always like this.

Everyone always seemed so confident, so, so, *together.*

Except her. Except she wasn't a *her,* she was a *him.* Wings constantly tied down.

But nobody knew.

Topping off her freshly poured drink, she felt the tears gathering and slipped quietly out the back door, the way she'd come in.

Now that she wasn't so nervous, she noticed the Sylph-like fire pit and headed straight for it, maneuvering sideways to slip down to a comfy seat.

Wedged in, she sat there, tears leaking uncontrollably, plopping into her mead.

Drinking didn't help, although she always thought it would before she started. Did she never learn?

Nothing seemed to work right in her life and she wasn't sure how to turn it around.

She hadn't been a *he* for very long, and neither job she had was working out very well.

Truth be told, if that steady old customer, Weed, hadn't been in his cups that one night, babbling on about where he lived and moving out, something about a hole under a rock in some park, she wouldn't have a place to live right now. Seems a long lost brother discovered him and he was no longer homeless. She was very thankful but nonetheless…

She didn't know anybody and was worried sick that the club owners would discover 'she' wore a skin suit and had wings to boot! She didn't know how long she could put them off, they were already getting impatient for her to lose the blue sequined bikini.

This being male really sucked. Fresh tears blurred her vision as she slurped noisily at her tumbler.

The hair salon, Harebell's, at least had a higher caliber of customers than Sundrop's but she was constantly accused of drying people's hair out! It was so unfair, when all she did was lather them up in a preparation for the stylist. No doubt *that* job was going down the drain soon too!

"Are you okay, what's the matter?" The young human-looking girl was squeezing in beside her and tentatively put her hand on the other's shoulder. Realization struck. She may not know many Sylphs other than her mother, but Aunty Linaria was around sometimes and Gypsy was familiar enough with wings that she knew what wingulacture felt like.

Rapidly, she reassessed. Were they *all* fae, even that Mayapple person? As she wondered this, she felt impossibly grown up, a new awareness taking up residence with her old awareness. Why were they all so secretive? Who cared? If what her parents had always drilled into her was true, that it was *who* you were on the inside, not the color of your skin, or your eyes, or if you had wings or not, then why were there no wings visible? She made a pact right then and there with herself to not be so paranoid and secretive with her own kids someday. *Grownups*! Always making a big deal out of *something*.

"You know, you really shouldn't be drinking that much mead. It's not good for you. You're gonna not feel so good in the morning, I'll bet. Hey, how 'bout I get you a glass of water and some food, okay? I'll be right back." And with a deliberate rub to Lauryl's bent-over hidden wing muscle, she vanished back inside.

Ms. Sulfate, Sylph-in-disguise, temporary almost-stripper, ambivalent hair aid, was stunned with the child's simple acceptance and practical advice. Obviously *she* cared enough to try to help.

Linaria was talking to *uncle* Lark and Flem when all three noticed Gypsy materializing through the back door, her eyes searching for someone.

Looking determinedly grown up for such a slip of a slight Sylphish half-human, she made a bee-line right towards them. Rather precocious to those that didn't know her, her expression was troubled as she came forward.

Earnestly, she told them of the party crasher's sad state of being, ending with a plea for understanding and maybe they could come help too?

Flem was astounded at her maturity and an old wave of envy for that Sylph-held confidence washed over him. Oh, where did she get it? It had taken him one hundred and twenty five years to get here, and she was what, twelve? Thirteen? Perhaps it was just something one was born with. Perhaps having a human father helped, who knew.

Immediately, Linaria, Lark and Flem headed for the back door but the girl stopped them with "Wait, wait," and suggested that instead of bull-dozing out the door, they come out a little later, discretely, one by one or so, so as not to embarrass the poor *woman* any more.

They all heard the word and the slight emphasis the girl put on it but nobody commented.

Feeling rather embarrassed at such candid and simple advice from this human girl, they all stopped in their tracks and nodded.

Smiling her approval – her mother had taught her well – she went back to the kitchen and filled a plate for her new friend, grabbed a big glass of water, and left.

In the meantime, Lauryl had imbibed as much mead as she could possibly hold because she had a feeling it was going to be the last for the evening, once that child got back.

Consequently, she was pretty toasted when Gypsophilia put a plate of food into her hands, saying sharply, "Don't spill this!" and then put down the glass of water.

Laughing at the young one's impudence, she couldn't believe she was laughing because the tears of sylphpity kept tumbling down, like a dem leaky faucet.

Gypsy didn't say much, just a uh-huh here and a really? there, letting the distraught faerie unravel.

The on-dit traveled with lightening speed around the inside of the greenhouse as Lark and Flem told Bud, Chinaberry, Catalpah and Mayapple too, what was happening, which was overheard by half the others who quickly told the rest.

Everyone wanted to help but Flem and Lark made sure it was known to be mandatory that if you came outside, you were to be your most discreet Sylph. Here they eyeballed China, Cat and Vinca Pink rather pointedly.

All three looked as innocent as possible but nobody believed that for a minute.

Uncle Linaria made his way through the kitchen, piling a small plate high, refilling his goblet and then, sauntered nonchalantly straight across to the side door and disappeared.

Whimsey C. Nimble

Lark and Flem moved slowly but surely towards the back door, Flem grabbing a tall can of chocolate chip and coconut cookies on his way by, while Lark hurriedly refilled their glasses. Out the door they went, noisily casual, in a quiet sort of way.

Mayapple stood with Rainbow and Blossom, trying to decide on her course of action, as all the remaining guests continued to disappear every five minutes or so.

Shrugging as if the fates conspired against her, Mayapple could no longer ignore this drama unfolding than she could stop breathing.

Never a dull moment at this party.

"C'mon, let's go see what's happening," she suggested, eyes bright with anticipation.

Out the door they slipped.

Whimsey C. Nimble and Pootsy Koons were the last two left and ever-thoughtful, both canyon Sylphs had too much savvy from putting Windfall Café to bed to just ignore the little tasks that no one paid heed to, and before they left they turned lights down low and refrigerated perishables, whilst choosing some soft music that would play repeatedly 'til someone changed it.

Satisfied, neither noticed the extra shapes concealed within the indoor shrubbery where the Campion boys stood motionless, all eyes and ears.

Hardly daring to breath in case it made too much noise, Whimsey and Pootsy stood just outside the back door, taking it all in.

Shadow Sylphs were everywhere, negligently sprawled around the fire, others pulled up close in various chairs Flem had scattered about, pulling together, a studied air of indifference so palpable if you didn't know any better you'd think it was merely a Monday sewing circle come to meet.

S. Lauryl Sulfate was sitting hunched over, wings bulging, straining at the seams of her skin suit, useless scarf hanging limply. She had recovered her gold gauzy blouse but not the pants and so everyone was treated to long legs and sparkly blue sequins. Heels were still on, but now looking rather knock kneed what with the way her toes flopped and pointed in at each other.

The tumbler of mead had been replaced by the tumbler of water but still the sound was the same, sniff, plop, sniff, plop.

Everyone's eyes darted around, wondering just how to address this issue, all willing to help but not sure where to start.

Gypsophilia took matters into her own hands finally and assertively went and sat behind Ms. Sulphate, giving her a back rub like she often did her mom.

"What's the matter, anyway?" she asked nonchalantly as she traced a big muscle with a thumb.

A bit of awareness was able to get through finally to the party crasher as she relaxed and some sixth fae sense told her there were people about, many people.

Slowly she lifted her head, nose dripping, barely missing the glass of water, and hiccupped as she wiped both eyes.

No one was looking at her, all were talking softly to one another but she knew they knew she was crying. And they were showing support.

And just why was this child here?

"Hey sweetheart, yoo related to somebody here?" her accent so funny when you weren't expecting it. There was no answer as Gypsy just kept on rubbing her thick corded muscle and the next thing she knew, her wings were being untied!

Gasping, she made a grab to stop the process but the girl spoke up.

"Yeah, that's my, ah, *uncle*, over there, Linaria, and that guy," she pointed to Lark, "that guy is my *uncle* too, but *he* really is, if you know what I mean."

S. Lauryl Sulfate's eyes widened at this blatant statement and her mouth opened but no sound came out. The girl revealed so much and didn't appear to think twice about it!

Had she been brought up by the *fae*?

By now, wings were undone, and she somehow managed to furl politely, seeing as how crowded it was and all.

"Man, you're wings are really a mess, aren't they?" spoke the girl artlessly. She knew she was pushing it, acting audaciously even, but the situation just seemed to call for it.

"Ah, ah," stumbled the embarrassed would-be stripper, ashamed to be caught out so unexpected, who *were* these people?

But as she looked around, she knew who they were. They were kin, everyone here, and she was mighty suspicious about them all being human.

The child was another story.

Whimsey C. Nimble

"Hey kid, where yoo from, anyway?"

Gypsophilia looked back at her aunty who was watching and nodded.

Knowing the real question being asked, Gypsy replied, "My mom's a Sylph, there are you happy now? My dad's human, okay? God, are you always this nosy? Sorry, I didn't mean that. Are you okay?" She kept kneading the tight wingulacture but her touch was growing lighter by the minute and it was easy to see she wanted to be away and not do this anymore.

Bignonia slipped away from Bunya Bunya, Sissy, Sassy, Jipijapa, and Vinca Pink to slide in and take over the child's spot as soon as he could get her to vacate.

Gypsy wandered off.

After waiting an interminable long time, both Green thumb employees climbed out of the planter, Acaulis having a harder time than tall skinny Schafta getting over the short wall.

Leaves were stuck to the purplish tufts of hair on the taller one's pate but he never noticed.

Brushing off his pants, short egg-shaped Acaulis hurried to catch up with his brother and together they crept towards the back of the converted greenhouse to find the best spot to spy from.

Lauryl noticed the difference immediately. *Strong* hands, and oh! A raspy tongue to actually lick those irascible scales back into place! It had been forever since anyone had done him this kind service so easily exchanged by most Sylphs.

New tears started up at such easy acceptance.

"Oh Pan, a real watering pot, aren't you? Geez," this said in disgust by Mayapple but she turned to her two girlfriends and said, "C'mon, let's neutralize the playing field, ladies, and maybe he'll quit bawling for a while."

Laying a compassionate hand on S. Lauryl Sulfate's throbbing shoulders as she went by, Mayapple took herself over to Buddleia, Chinaberry, and Catalpah and gave Bud a beseeching look.

Pretty sure he understood her, nonetheless he had to ask, *"Me?* Now?" and darted his head around to see if anyone else had their wings out and they didn't but Pan, it wasn't going to be long.

"Okay," he gave in easily, and China and Cat set to, making quick work of divesting him of that pesky human clothing and up his wings came, never really coming out of their curled furl, just standing up straight now.

A collective sigh was felt at this sign from Bud, their beloved, and instantly, all was set in motion as the Wing Out commenced.

The girls were impressed with how fast these lackadaisical looking faeries could move. Truly, it had seemed that everyone had taken the admonition put out by Lark and the others to be nonchalant seriously and had succumbed to the mellow vibe. But as usual, appearances can be deceiving.

Every hue in the spectrum was revealed as Sylphs did what Sylphs did best, undress and let their wings out. (and drink mead) (and talk)

If you could undress and let your wings out, (at home didn't count) – well, it was a wonderful thing, a gift that happened but one never knew exactly when that would occur. The *S* Club was a sure thing, but *wing-outs* at a party were a real treat.

Various patterns were revealed but the light was too dim to see many details.

A deeper level of bonding occurred with all present and appendages moved into sight, like the first flowers after a rainstorm.

Flem was intensely gratified, wondering if he should feel so good, when obviously the uninvited guest was feeling so bad. Ah well, he'd *earned* this. Cha!

The best part was that it had all happened so natural, if you could call a stripper crashing his celebration, which catalyzed a deeper bond of love all the way around, natural.

Bignonia ("Please, call me Rivers") and their 'guest' were talking and Flem heard "No kidding! Actually, there have been *several of us* that have made stops there. Hey Flem, guess who lives at Sycamore Park now?" followed by a burst of laughter and they kept on talking, not waiting for a reply from their host.

"Hey," called out Rivers again, "anybody know of any jobs around, Lauryl's not happy with her present one."

Whimsey C. Nimble

Everybody muttered commiseratingly with not liking your job – it seemed many went through this when they first got to the city.

Unexpectedly, Lark spoke up, "I've got an opening but you have to be there early, five a.m. in the morning. I need a dishwasher, somebody who knows how to handle suds. Can you do that?" he asked Sodium Lauryl Sulfate.

Lauryl couldn't believe her ears. "Yoo're offerin' me a *job?*" she asked incredulously, her accent so thick Flem thought he might be able to walk on it.

"Yeah, and you leave your clothes on!"

Everyone laughed.

"Yah! Yes, I *doo*. Really?" and then she started to cry again.

Ah, those drinking binges just brings out the best in us, Sylph or human. The only way is up.

"Mayapple," whispered Flem to the woman behind him, who had left Bud and taken over Flem, telling Lark he had to share and to go see Bud. "I wasn't this bad, was I? Cha."

Mayapple laughed, "Well…there at first, Flemmy,…well, if the shoe fits…"

"What in the Pan is *that* suppose to mean?" he asked, bewildered and a touch irritated.

She explained and he had to pause.

There certainly was a pattern here, it seemed. Hmm.

He looked around and it occurred to him that everybody, well, *practically* everybody here had a story of moving to the city, a story of *changing*, and *staying male*. You couldn't tell it by most of them, they all seemed pretty well adjusted no matter which way they dressed.

China and Cat for instance looked more at home dressed as they were, like maybe this wasn't too far off from their old Sylph sylves. Just a little more citified and glamorized.

Bud and Lark on the other hand looked like the handsome males they were. Even putting Lark in his little black dress, he looked *good*.

Vinca Pink was going to be loud wherever or whomever she was.

Vervacity appeared calm, cool and sophisticated, like nothing much rattled her and Vanda looked vacuous no matter what.

Whimsey C. Nimble and Pootsy Koons carried themsylves with élan, no matter if they were in the canyon or here in the City. Obviously, those two had been around.

Sassy was now preening Sissy and Sissy was drooling, big wide mouth held at half attention, no spray at the moment but wet and drippy regardless.

"How about a toast?" rang out in Rainbow Merkiva's familiar voice. "To the Muse! No matter *how* we got here, we're all here *now*, thanks to her!"

Pootsy turned to look at Rainbow and asked curiously, "How do you know about the Muse? Do you *know* Penlei?"

Surprising them, the woman said *yes*, there was a *Penlei* that had often stopped in at her shop over the years, and that was *his* favorite toast. And then she said, "But I never knew he was fae 'til right now, although I suspected. Thanks for confirming it!"

Whimsey Nimble turned to Pootsy and said, "Are you sure its Penlei's?" at which Pootsy smartly replied, " Of course. She's *my* aunty, remember? She left me the café. Hel*lo*."

"You're *aunty*?" picked up Rainbow immediately. "Oh. Of course. Hmm. He doesn't come in very often, just when he's come to the *City* for a while…" She cast a speculative eye at the two canyon Sylphs as the wheels turned in her mind. "Friend of yours from, where you from again?"

"Thimbleberry Canyon."

"Yeah, Thimbleberry Canyon. He's a *she* and she's from there?" Rainbow knew she was being way too nosy but they'd brought it up, after all.

Giving the human a quick affirming nod first, Whimsey turned to her shorter, more hot-tempered friend and clarified, "What I meant was, had she gotten it *from* someone else, or did *she* come up with it?"

"Oh," said Pootsy in a small voice, realizing once again she'd jumped to conclusions and let her blood heat up for no good reason.

"I don't know." This was said almost as if a confession before she went on to say, "I've heard it my whole life and she's always saying it at her parties."

Both turned to look at the human woman with the fae toast who simply smiled and held out her glass.

"Alright, here's one then. Here's to Flem! Great party!"

A general roar of approval burst out, even Lauryl had been cajoled and preened and petted enough to transcend all the thorns of life. She was not alone, anymore.

Furls loosened as everybody fell into the magical spell created by unconditional love and acceptance, a place to be yoursylph.

Whimsey C. Nimble

By now the circle of Sylphs around the fire was jam packed, shoulder to shoulder, wings deliberately furled tight, preening, talking, eating, drinking – faerie babble at its best.

Bunya Bunya, Wonga Wonga, Sissy, Sassy, Jipijapa and Vinca Pink sat bunched together, hands on each other, rubbing wing muscles, licking scales, talking, sipping mead.

The humans, Mayapple, Blossom, and Rainbow sat on a small patch of grass with Gypsophilia.

"No," said the half-Sylph human girl, "I don't have wings. Mom doesn't know if I'll get them or not. I think it'd be pretty awesome if I do, but like she says, ha ha, I'm the eldest, I'm the guinea pig. My dad says it makes no difference to him if I have wings or not, so long as I do my homework. Geez, it would serve him right if they DO come out, big and beautiful and oh, I don't know, purple with orange stripes?"

The three women laughed at this droll observation and the girl continued, "My shoulder blades itch sometimes, do you think that means anything?"

Flem was sitting beneath the catalpah tree with Lark, feeling like all was well in the world, catching most of what the girls were talking about, feeling like there wasn't anything they couldn't handle so long as they did it together. His hand tightened on Lark's thigh where it rested.

A small spot high in a tree overhead brightened momentarily before dimming back down, catching the Sylph owner's eye briefly and a pleasant realization washed over him that even Zing was attending his party!

Linaria walked up and remarked, "Pretty savvy kid, huh? Her mom's done well. Wings don't faze her a bit, do they?"

Indeed, you could tell the human-looking girl was having a good time, and didn't appear flustered or intimidated by her surroundings.

Flem felt a furry head butt up against his arm and pulled Rubus onto his lap, happy the year-old cat was getting away from the habit of riding between his wing blades, it was much nicer to have him on his lap, no nails digging in. He fondled the soft stand-up ears, causing the rumble from the kitten's chest to grow louder and louder.

Leaning into Lark's embrace where he sat with his arm around him, wings furled loosely behind each of them, Flem thought about where he'd been and who he was now.

He was a different Sylph.

No, that wasn't entirely true. He was still Flem/Flumaria, but the *better* version of his old Sylph. His instincts had always been good, he'd just not followed them, he'd let himsylph be diverted by fear, afraid to follow his heart because he didn't want to change. So *change* was foisted on him and he had no recourse except to make peace with it, with himsylph.

The outside changes that everyone could see were merely a reflection of how he saw himsylph and as he gained sylphconfidence, his *life* reflected those changes. It took a year for things to flush-out, so-to-speak; he had *good* habits now, a rich life, and it was a happy positive circle. The more he trusted his own decisions, the greater the rewards. Mrs. Fletcherman had even made him an assistant manager in his own department. That was surely a boon!

Looking over at the transforming stripper, S. Lauryl Sulphate, he realized once again that life didn't have to be hard, but *we* made it hard. By the same token, *we* could make it much easier by simply trusting, trusting oursylves and the path in front of us.

He looked over at Gypsophilia, human and Sylph mixture, so at ease here with the fae and the human alike. He was glad Linaria had brought her. She was a lucky girl to be surrounded by such open minded people at home.

A laugh broke out over by the fire pit and Lauryl looked like she fit right in.

His heart warmed at how much easier her path would be now, with a group of friends to be counted on.

Imagine that, her living in his old place, that hole under a rock in Sycamore Park! It seemed the world wasn't as big as he'd always thought it was.

Eyes, human eyes never blinked from where they peeped out from behind a curtain in Flem's bedroom.

Acaulais and Schafta were beyond gleeful.

The amazement had turned to exhilaration at what they'd seen unfold here tonight.

As they eased cramped muscles from awkward positions, that exhilaration transmorphed into respect. These people, fae and human, *liked* each other. They *helped* each other!

Whimsey C. Nimble

That Flem guy was *Okay*.

"Shall we go?" whispered Acaulis to his taller brother.

Their eyes met and not a word needed to be said out loud.

Schafta nodded and reverently they backed up and silently crept back through the kitchen, picking out food to go with them for the ride home.

Moments later the old greenhouse was empty.

A faint voice was heard calling across the fire. It had a nasally twang to it. "Hey Mayapple, who cut yoor hair? You know what? That's a *pixie* cut! Ha ha!"

Laughter sparked and jumped and gurgled, and Flem laughed alongside everyone else.

He, and they, had come full circle.

THE END

Well, not quite.

Epilogue

Shaking their heads at such unbelievable news, they
toasted the moment with a ca-clink of glass.

*L*OOKING LIKE TWO nondescript human women, Whimsey C. Nimble and
Pootsy Koons stepped down from the small van they'd been riding in.

"Thanks for the ride!" they both reiterated to the nice human couple
who'd picked them up an hour ago.

Waving goodbye, they shouldered their packs and walked along 'til the
car disappeared.

Climbing over an old wooden split-rail fence, they headed into the woods
to let their wings out and fly home.

It was late in the day and the sun threw long rich shadows on everything
it touched.

Halting a moment, Pootsy dug into her bag for the two remaining pineapple cream-cheese nasturtium wraps and handed a bedraggled one to her
friend.

Smiling, Whimsey nodded her thanks at the gooey delight and as they
licked their fingers, brought up the subject that had never left her mind since
they'd overheard that private conversation not twenty-four hours previously.

"Well, what do you think is going on? Do you think it's possible for
someone to change *back*? I've never heard of that, have you?"

They looked at each other speculatively as they walked, adjusting their
packs and watching where they put their feet.

Pootsy didn't say much because she had never heard of such a thing but
was definitely ready to go on a mission and hunt down anybody else that
might have. She smiled at how easy this would be because as the sole owner
of Windfall Café, Sylphs came to *her*.

Whimsey C. Nimble

The sun was getting lower and they hurried their steps, anxious to get into the air and get to the café.

"Are you coming in or going home?" queried Pootsy to her friend. "It's early yet," she added. "Come in for a nightcap, at least."

Whimsey smiled and nodded, looking around for the opening to the meadow which they used as their landing field when flying back and forth but what she saw was a white blur, darting behind a tree, weeds waving it its wake.

"Ignore her," advised Pootsy, who saw it too. "It's Hasp again. You know she likes to come this far down sometimes."

Whimsey agreed, still looking around. "We should go see her more often, you know."

"Yeah."

Hasp was a Sylph that wasn't quite normal. She was someone they looked in on, in her strange abode up further in the canyon. Hasp didn't talk much, and had waist length white hair that she braided and unbraided constantly, more often than not incorporating whatever was at hand right into it.

Whimsey and Pootsy had taken it upon themsylves to be the ambassadors of the neighborhood and so kept an eye on her.

By this time, the meadow was in front of them and with a quick flick, wings were unveiled and the two climbed into the air rapidly, thankful the sun was still lighting their way.

Fifteen minutes later they were stepping down into Pootsy's front yard and soon the folding door of Windfall Café was opened, Pootsy leading the way, stopping to turn on little lamps along the way 'til she disappeared into her bedroom at the rear of the old converted bus.

Whimsey dropped her pack on a chair as she went by, heading behind the counter in front of the little kitchen area to pour them each a mead from the barrel-like glass container set right on the bar, identical to Bud's.

Moving back she came around and sat down at the nearest small booth. Pootsy slid in opposite and took the glass of nectar that Whimsey handed her, eyes locking on her friend's. Shaking their heads at such unbelievable news, they toasted the moment with a ca-clink of glass. "Imagine. Lark Spurastic a female Sylph again. I wonder how *that* will affect Flem. There certainly are *changes* ahead for them, now aren't there?"